THE YEAR'S 25 FINEST
CRIME AND MYSTERY STORIES
Third Annual Edition

THE YEAR'S 25 FINEST CRIME AND MYSTERY STORIES

Third Annual Edition

Edited by the Staff of *Mystery Scene*

With an Introduction by Jon L. Breen

Carroll & Graf Publishers, Inc.
New York

First Carroll & Graf edition 1994.

Carroll & Graf Publishers, Inc.
260 Fifth Avenue
New York, NY 10001

Library of Congress CIP Data is available

Manufactured in the United States of America

TABLE OF CONTENTS

Introduction
THE MYSTERY IN 1993

Call 1993 the Year of the Comeback. James Crumley's C. W. Sughrue, long among the most famous one-book sleuths in detective-fiction history for his 1978 appearance in *The Last Good Kiss,* finally had a second case in *The Mexican Tree Duck* (Mysterious), while Gregory Mcdonald's most famous character returned for the first time since 1986 in *Son of Fletch* (Warner). Ivan and Nan Lyons created a sequel in *Someone is Killing the Great Chefs of America* (Little, Brown) to their famous *Someone is Killing the Great Chefs of Europe* (1976), and Nicholas Meyer returned to Sherlockian pastiche with *The Canary Trainer* (Norton) for the first time since the same year's *The West End Horror.* And while publisher/bookdealer Otto Penzler was never really gone, the founder of Mysterious Press returned to the center of the action with a new Macmillan imprint, Otto Penzler Books.

Jack the Ripper, who has never left the public consciousness for long since his series of murders of prostitutes in London's East End over a hundred years ago, fueled one of the year's biggest fact/fiction controversies when *The Diary of Jack the Ripper* was published in Great Britain by Smith Gryphon and in the United States by Hyperion. The original American publisher, Warner, pulled out when a report by documents expert Kenneth Rendell convinced them the purported diary was a forgery. The supposed author of the diary, and thus the newest celebrity Ripper suspect, was James Maybrick, himself a probable murder victim in a notorious Victorian poisoning case. Whether the diary is authentic or not—and the question remains unresolved—the idea of combining two classic crimes into one narrative is a fiction writer's dream.

What about the numbers? They're still healthy. Using M. S. Cappadonna's stats in *The Armchair Detective* for the first three quarters of 1993, I count about 250 new hardcover crime novels, which would play out to a year-end total of 333. That suggests a slight drop-off from the last couple of years, but speaking as a reviewer whose mailbox contains at least one new mystery and often several almost every day, I don't believe the number is that small. Cappadonna lists few paperback originals. I catalogued about fifty new ones for my own collection, and I certainly don't get (or keep) them all.

It was another good year at the movies. Both *In the Line of Fire* and *The Fugitive* are superlative action films that may be regarded as classics in years to come, but the surprising Edgar winner was the Michael Douglas film *Falling Down.*

BEST NOVELS OF THE YEAR 1993

If my list of fifteen favorites this year has a theme, aside from the usual caveat that no one reader can cover the whole vast crime-fiction field, it's critical contrarianism. At least a third of the novels I've listed, including those by Burke, Hansen, James, McBain, and Picard, though getting few outright pans from the reviewers, drew occasional discouraging comments that suggested they were products of an authorial off day. I beg to disagree.

James Lee Burke, *In the Electric Mist with Confederate Dead* (Hyperion). Burke's introduction of a supernatural element, in the form of Louisiana cop Dave Robichaux's periodic meetings with the ghost of a Civil War general, was a risky move, and obviously it didn't quite work for some readers. To me, it made the novel one of the most richly textured and memorable of the year.

Colin Dexter, *The Way Through the Woods* (Crown). A Gold Dagger winner in Britain, this novel may be the very best of the distinguished Inspector Morse series. Certainly it's as close an approach to the combination of intricacy and literacy found in Golden Age writers like Dorothy L. Sayers and Michael Innes as you're likely to find in the 1990's.

Warwick Downing, *A Lingering Doubt* (Pocket Books). Lawyer Downing's series about the National Association of Special Prosecutors occupies a special niche among the current flood of legal thrillers: always enthralling, always unpredictable. This time, for once, the NASP representative is *not* on the side of the angels.

Susan Dunlap, *Time Expired* (Delacorte). Is there a more reliable pro around than Dunlap, whose Berkeley cop Jill Smith is one of the best series policewomen in the genre? Here, a radical lawyer's murder and some pranks against meter maids are among the elements in a typically complex puzzle with a typically vivid cast and setting.

Joseph Hansen, *Living Upstairs* (Dutton). You could argue that the latest novel from Dave Brandstetter's creator is more a mainstream novel of gay life in World War II Los Angeles than a crime novel. There is a whodunit at its core, though, and it has a satisfying surprise twist. Whatever you call it, it is compelling reading.

P. D. James, *The Children of Men* (Knopf). James's what-if novel about a near-future world where humankind no longer reproduces may be more science fiction than mystery, but it provides renewed evidence of what a fine and versatile novelist she is.

John Lutz, *Spark* (Holt). The cases of Florida-based private eye Fred Carver are always excellent reading, and this one, about the mysterious death of a retirement home resident, is one of the best.

Ed McBain, *Mary, Mary* (Warner). Some critics found the latest Matthew Hope novel, in which the Florida lawyer defends a retired schoolteacher accused of child murder, disappointing. I found it a fascinating example of authorial misdirection, as well as being riveting reading from beginning to end.

Margaret Maron, *Southern Discomfort* (Mysterious). The second novel about North Carolina judge Deborah Knott follows *Bootlegger's Daughter,* which managed the unprecedented feat of winning four best novel awards: the Edgar, the Agatha, the Anthony, and the Macavity. Since the voters usually like to spread these things around, that virtually ruled out any such sweep by this book, splendid though it is.

Steve Martini, *Prime Witness* (Putnam). Following up on 1992's equally excellent *Compelling Evidence,* the second novel about California lawyer Paul Madriani demonstrates that no one, including guys named Grisham and Turow, does better legal fiction than Steve Martini.

Ellis Peters, *The Holy Thief* (Mysterious). The nineteenth medieval mystery about Brother Cadfael is one of the best in the series, harking back to the first, *A Morbid Taste for Bones* (1977), when the relic of Saint Winifred disappears from the Abbey of Saint Peter and Saint Paul following a rainstorm.

Nancy Pickard, *But I Wouldn't Want to Die There* (Pocket). Maybe I just can't resist a good New York book, but I found Jenny Cain's adventures in the Big Apple totally captivating, though the critical consensus seems to have branded it lesser Pickard.

Steven Saylor, *Catalina's Riddle* (St. Martin's). This is the third novel about Gordianus the Finder, likely the best of the several Ancient Roman sleuths currently on the scene. Though this extraordinary novel was overlooked by the Edgar selectors, it was a finalist for the International Association of Crime Writers' Hammett Prize.

Julian Symons, *Something Like a Love Affair* (Mysterious). The three titles I chose to compare with this novel (*Lady Chatterley's Lover,* the film *Brief Encounter,* and Pat McGerr's tricky detective novel *Pick Your Victim*) should give you an idea of what an unusual book this is—and how good Symons remains in his ninth decade.

Barbara Vine (Ruth Rendell), *Anna's Book* (Harmony). This long and multi-layered novel combines mystery and family saga. For all her insights into character and milieu, Vine/Rendell can handle subtle clueing with the deftness of Ellery Queen. The book may be too leisurely for some tastes, but it will reward the careful reader.

SHORT STORIES

The best single-author short story collection I reviewed in 1993 was Jennifer Rowe's *Death in Store* (Doubleday/Crime Club), containing the title novella, a prime example of the Christmas department-store mystery somewhat in the *Miracle on 34th Street* vein, and seven short stories, all about amateur sleuth Verity Birdwood. Many writers are inaccurately likened to Agatha Christie, but with the Australian Rowe, a fluid writer and builder of tricky puzzle plots, the comparison is apt. In a time-honored tradition, the publisher tries to disguise the collection as a novel, not mentioning on the jacket that there is more than one story inside and furthering the illusion by not providing a table of contents listing the stories.

More up-front about offering a collection are the publishers of Antonia Fraser's *Jemima Shore at the Sunny Grave and Other Stories* (Bantam). Television reporter Jemima, a character I prefer at this shorter length, appears in four of the nine stories. Other collections of note include Joseph Hansen's *Bohannon's Country* (Viking), June Thomson's fine set of pastiches *The Secret Files of Sherlock Holmes* (Penzler), and the first collection of Leo Bruce's short stories, *Murder in Miniature* (Academy Chicago).

The most distinguished reprint anthology of the year was Mike Ashley's *The Mammoth Book of Historical Whodunnits* (Carroll & Graf), which combined a fine selection of stories with considerable reference value in its notes and appendices. Others included the star-studded first anthology of the International Association of Crime Writers, *The New Mystery* (Dutton), edited by Jerome Charyn; Ed Gorman's *Dark Crimes 2* (Carroll & Graf), and *Mystery Scene's* gathering of movieland mysteries, *Hollywood Kills* (Carroll & Graf). Some of the most interesting reprint anthologies were created for the "instant remainder" market, among them the pulp magazine compilation *Tough Guys and Dangerous Dames* (Barnes and Noble), edited by Robert E. Weinberg, Stefan Dziemianowicz, and Martin H. Greenberg; and Peter Haining's *Great Tales of*

Crime and Detection (Chartwell), published in Britain under the more informative title, *The Television Detectives' Omnibus*. The volumes gathered from the vast backfiles of *Ellery Queen's Mystery Magazine* and *Alfred Hitchcock Mystery Magazine* have been running to themes recently, examples being two edited by Cynthia Manson, *Grifters and Swindlers* (Carroll & Graf) and *Canine Crimes* (Jove), the latter somewhat balancing the mystery world's feline bias.

Among the year's original anthologies is the first in an annual series from the Crime Writers Association, *1st Culprit* (St. Martin's), edited by Liza Cody and Michael Z. Lewin. Slightly more than half the stories are new, including contributions by Catherine Aird, Robert Barnard, Simon Brett, Sara Paretsky, and both editors. A strong paperback anthology series continued with *Malice Domestic 2* (Pocket), introduced by Mary Higgins Clark. Other original anthologies had specialized themes: Christmas mysteries in Martin H. Greenberg and Carol-Lynn Rössel-Waugh's *Santa Clues* (Signet); Washington-based cat stories in Ed Gorman and Greenberg's *Danger in D.C.* (Fine).

REFERENCE BOOKS AND SECONDARY SOURCES

It was another good year for secondary sources. The deserving winner of the Edgar Award for best biographical or critical volume was Burl Barer's fascinating and thorough account of Simon Templar and his creator Leslie Charteris, *The Saint: A Complete History . . .* (McFarland). G. K. Hall's series of mystery guidebooks continued with two volumes from highly knowledgeable collector/critics: Marvin Lachman's *A Reader's Guide to the American Novel of Detection* and Gary Warren Niebuhr's *A Reader's Guide to the Private Eye Novel*. Editors Ed Gorman, Martin H. Greenberg, and Larry Segriff brought forth the large-format trade paperback *The Fine Art of Murder* (Carroll & Graf), with a distinguished line up of contributors and various section introductions by the present writer. The hundredth anniversary of the birth of Lord Peter Wimsey's chronicler was celebrated with *Dorothy L. Sayers: The Centenary Celebration* (Walker), edited by Alzina Stone Dale, and Barbara Reynolds's Edgar-nominated biography, *Dorothy L. Sayers: Her Life and Soul* (St. Martin's). The team of Hal Blythe, Charlie Sweet, and John Landreth produced *Private Eyes: A Writer's Guide to Private Investigators* (*Writer's Digest*), a valuable consideration of real-life versus fictional gumshoeing.

SUB-GENRES

I. Private Eyes. Parnall Hall's Stanley Hastings returns to his stage career in *Actor* (Mysterious), an atypical P.I. novel but a captivating theatrical mystery for fans of Ngaio Marsh, Simon Brett, and Jane Dentinger. Among other shamuses on the scene were A. E. Maxwell's Fiddler in *Murder Hurts* (Villard), Marcia Muller's Sharon McCone in the Edgar-nominated *Wolf in the Shadows* (Mysterious), Bill Pronzini's Nameless in *Demons* (Delacorte), Robert Irvine's Moroni Traveler in *The Great Reminder,* Al Sarrantonio's Jack Paine in *Summer Cool* (Walker), John Lutz's Nudger in *Thicker Than Blood* (St. Martin's), Harold Adams's Carl Wilcox in *A Perfectly Proper Murder* (Walker), Jerome Doolittle's Tom Bethany in *Head Lock* (Pocket), and Robert J. Randisi's Miles Jacoby in *Hard Luck* (Walker).

II. Formal Detection. Apart from Ellis Peters (Edith Pargeter), whose first pseudonymous mystery was published in 1938, E. X. Ferrars, known as Elizabeth in Britain, is probably the longest active author in classical detection, having first appeared with two novels in 1940. *Beware of the Dog* (Doubleday/ Perfect Crime), starring the unconventional husband-and-wife detecting team of Virginia and Felix Freer, finds her in top notch Golden Age form, turning some old chestnuts (the will, the nonbarking dog, the Australian claimant) on their heads. Classicists should also appreciate Emma Lathen's *Right on the Money* (Simon & Schuster), E. X. Giroux's *A Death for a Dodo* (St. Martin's), Will Harriss's *Noble Rot* (St. Martin's), Aaron Elkins's *Old Scores* (Scribners), Hazel Holt's *Mrs. Malory and the Festival Murder* (St. Martin's), Barbara D'Amato's *Hard Women* (Scribners), Barbara Michaels's *Houses of Stone* (Simon & Schuster), and Nancy Pickard's posthumous collaboration with the late Virginia Rich on a new Eugenia Potter mystery, *The 27*Ingredient Chili Con Carne Murders* (Delacorte).

III. Police procedurals. Besides Robichaux, Morse, and Smith (see the top fifteen), other procedural heroes were in impressive action, among them Seattle's J. P. Beaumont in J. A. Jance's *Without Due Process* (Morrow) and Tony Hillerman's Joe Leaphorn and Jim Chee in *Sacred Clowns* (HarperCollins). William D. Pease's *The Rage of Innocence* (Viking) is as compellingly written and trickily plotted a combination of procedural and Big Trial novel as you're likely to come across. Much as I love the novels of William Harrington and the TV exploits of Columbo, their mutual examination of the John F. Kennedy assassination in *Columbo: The Grassy Knoll* (TOR) does not rank with my highlights for the year.

IV. Historicals. Mysteries set in other times are more plentiful than ever. Anne Perry offered good new entries in both her Victorian series: *Farriers' Lane* about Thomas and Charlotte Pitt and *A Sudden Fearful Death* about William Monk and Hester Latterly (both Fawcett Columbine). The team of Annette and Martin Meyers, writing as Maan Meyers, brought forth the second in a promising series of American historicals, *The Kingsbridge Plot* (Doubleday/Perfect Crime). Robert Barnard, using the pseudonym Bernard Bastable, joined the historical writers with the brief and engaging *To Die Like a Gentleman* (St. Martin's). To go with the Saylor novel on my list of fifteen, Lindsey Davis returned to a Roman background in *The Iron Hand of Mars* (Crown). See also from that list the works of Joseph Hansen and Ellis Peters.

V. Thrillers. I'm the first to admit I don't review much international intrigue, but I'm a sucker for a really good example. Best I read in 1993 was Dev Stryker's *Deathright* (TOR), a wild ride indeed. The attentive reader will have no trouble guessing what husband-and-wife writing team is behind the Stryker pseudonym. Another pseudonym that is a poorly kept secret is Daniel Ransom, a.k.a. Ed Gorman, author of the semisupernatural thriller, *The Long Midnight* (Dell). For that rarest of hybrids, the espionage cozy, you can't go wrong with Dorothy Gilman's *Mrs. Pollifax and the Second Thief* (Doubleday).

VI. The Lawyers. The legal thriller continued to be one of the most active sub-genres. See the titles by Downing, McBain, Maron, and Martini that make up more than a quarter of my list of fifteen. Among others worth the trial buff's attention were Philip Friedman's *Inadmissible Evidence* (Fine), George V. Higgins's *Defending Billy Ryan* (Holt), Harold Mehling's *Assumption of Guilt* (Carroll & Graf), and Lisa Scottoline's Edgar-nominated *Everywhere That Mary Went* (HarperCollins). Among the lawyers staying out of court was Marisa Piesman's witty Nina Fischman in the under-plotted but charmingly written *Heading Uptown* (Delacorte).

OTHERS MENTIONED IN DISPATCHES

With all the stellar names mentioned above, did no one else of major reputation produce new work in 1993? How about this list? Steve Allen, Linda Barnes, Lilian Jackson Braun, Simon Brett, Liza Cody, Richard Condon, K. C. Constantine, Thomas H. Cook, Patricia Cornwell, Robert Crais, Jonathan Gash, Sue Grafton, Jeremiah Healy, Joan Hess, Stuart M. Kaminsky, H. R. F. Keating, Faye Kellerman, Jonathan Kellerman, Patricia Moyes, William Murray, Robert B. Parker, Lawrence Sanders, Julie Smith, Dorothy Uhnak, Phyllis A. Whitney, Donald E. Westlake, Colin Wilcox, and L. R. Wright.

A SENSE OF HISTORY

It's amazing that some books, even by American writers, are published only in Great Britain. A typically expert 1983 collaboration of Bill Pronzini and Jeffrey Wallman, *Day of the Moon* (Mystery Scene/Carroll & Graf), finally saw its first U.S. publication ten years later. Michael Crichton's Edgar-winning novel *A Case of Need,* published in 1968 as "by Jeffrey Hudson," was published in a new hardcover edition by Dutton on the coattails of his bestselling *Jurassic Park* and *Rising Sun.*

The new Penzler imprint may have been the best news for seekers of really vintage reprints. Along with new editions of some classic Sherlockiana and a facsimile of the first edition of Dashiell Hammett's *The Maltese Falcon* came a paperback of one of the scarcest of Golden Age collector's items, S. S. Van Dine's final Philo Vance novel, *The Winter Murder Case.*

A FINAL NOTE

As we all know, the mystery genre has developed and matured to a point where lists of rules, such as those propounded in the 1920's by S. S. Van Dine (Willard Huntington Wright) and Ronald A. Knox, no longer seem appropriate. However, writers entering the field need some guidance, so I'll offer the following ten tips for writing the contemporary mystery:

1) Include at least three pages of acknowledgments, citing every expert who answered a research question, every friend or relative who read the manuscript, and every person involved in the publication process from agent to copy editor—and you'd better not forget anybody.

2) Stock your story with plenty of food references, but if you are a male writer, remember that actually including recipes is unmanly.

3) Include some kind of religious angle. It's okay, but not mandatory, to ridicule evangelical Christianity.

4) Take familiar elements from successful books and use them in fresh combinations. Be creative but careful. As we all know, half the mysteries on the market have serial killers and at least half have cats—but the idea of a serial killer of cats would be commercial suicide.

5) Include in the plot some kind of social issue related to sex: on-the-job sexual harassment, poronography, and incest are always good ones, but you can probably think of others.

6) Draft your novel at the ideal length for the story you want to tell. Then double it with unnecessary background notes on minor characters and other extraneous details. Now it's ready for the market.

7) If you are male, either feminize your name (I'm thinking of Jonelle Breen) or use initials so that readers will assume you must be a woman.

8) Have a trial if possible. If you can't, act like you're going to. (If you have a law degree, flaunt it. Mystery writing is one endeavor in which lawyers are not pariahs.)

9) Cast a strong independent contemporary woman as your central character.

10) Set the whole thing in ancient Rome.

AWARD WINNERS FOR 1993

EDGAR ALLAN POE AWARDS
(Mystery Writers of America)

Best novel: Minette Walters, *The Sculptress* (St. Martin's)

Best first novel by an American author: Laurie King, *A Grave Talent* (St. Martin's)

Best original paperback: Steven Womack, *Dead Folks' Blues* (Ballantine)

Best fact crime book: Bella Stumbo, *Until the Twelfth of Never* (Pocket)

Best critical/biographical work: Burl Barer, *The Saint: A Complete History* (McFarland)

Best short story: Lawrence Block, "Keller's Therapy" (*Playboy,* May)

Best young adult mystery: Joan Lowery Nixon, *The Name of the Game Was Murder* (Delacorte)

Best juvenile mystery: Barbara Brooks Wallace, *The Twins in the Tavern* (Atheneum)

Best episode in a television series: David Milch, "4B or Not 4B" (*NYPD Blue,* ABC)

Best television feature or miniseries: Allan Cubitt, *Prime Suspect 2* (*Mystery,* PBS)

Best motion picture: Ebbe Rose Smith, *Falling Down* (Warner Brothers)

Grand master: Lawrence Block

Robert L. Fish award (best first story): D. A. McGuire, "Wicked Twist" (*Alfred Hitchcock's Mystery Magazine,* October)

Ellery Queen award: Otto Penzler

AGATHA AWARDS
(Malice Domestic Mystery Convention)

Best novel: Carolyn G. Hart, *Dead Man's Island* (Bantam)

Best first novel: Nevada Barr, *Track of the Cat* (Putnam)

Best short story: M. D. Lake, "Kim's Lake" (*Malice Domestic 2* [Pocket])

Best nonfiction: Barbara D'Amato, *The Doctor, the Murder, the Mystery* (Noble)

Lifetime Achievement Award: Mignon G. Eberhart

Hammett Prize (North American Branch, International Association of Crime Writers): James Crumley, *The Mexican Tree Duck* (Mysterious)

AWARD WINNERS FOR 1992

AMERICAN MYSTERY AWARDS
(*Mystery Scene* magazine)

Best traditional mystery: Anne Perry, *Defend and Betray* (Fawcett Columbine)

Best private eye novel: Sue Grafton, *"I" is for Innocent* (Holt)

Best romantic suspense: Mary Higgins Clark, *All Around the Town* (Simon & Schuster)

Best true crime: Harry Farrell, *Swift Justice* (St. Martin's)

Best crime novel: J. A. Jance, *Without Due Process* (Morrow)

Best espionage novel: David Hagberg, *Critical Mass* (TOR)

Best police procedural: Ed McBain, *Kiss* (Morrow)

Best paperback original: M. D. Lake, *Poisoned Ivy* (Avon)

Best scholarly work: John Loughery, *Alias S. S. Van Dine* (Scribners)

Best short story: Doug Allyn, "Candles in the Rain" (*Ellery Queen's Mystery Magazine* November)

ANTHONY AWARDS
(Bouchercon World Mystery Convention)

Best novel: Margaret Maron, *Bootlegger's Daughter* (Mysterious)

Best first novel: Barbara Neely, *Blanche on the Lam* (St. Martin's)

Best true crime: Barbara D'Amato, *The Doctor, the Murder, the Mystery* (Noble)

Best short story: Diane Mott Davidson, "Cold Turkey" (*Sisters in Crime 5* [Berkley])

Best critical work: Ellen Nehr, *Doubleday Crime Club Compendium* (Offspring)

Best motion picture: *The Crying Game*

SHAMUS AWARDS
(Private Eye Writers of America)

Best novel: Harold Adams, *The Man Who Was Taller Than God* (Walker)

Best first novel: John Straley, *The Woman Who Married a Bear* (Soho)

Best original paperback novel: Marele Day, *The Last Tango of Dolores Delgado* (Allen & Unwin)

Best short story: Benjamin Schutz, "Mary, Mary, Shut the Door" (*Deadly Allies* [Doubleday])

Lifetime achievement award: Marcia Muller

DAGGER AWARDS
(Crime Writer's Association, Great Britain)

Gold Dagger: Patricia Cornwell, *Cruel and Unusual* (Little, Brown)

Silver Dagger: Sarah Dunant, *Fatlands* (Hamish Hamilton)

Last Laugh Award (best humorous crime novel): Michael Pearce, *The Mamur Zapt & the Spoils of Egypt* (Crime Club)

Short story: Julian Rathbone, "Some Sunny Day" (*Constable New Crimes 2*)

Nonfiction: Alexandra Artley, *Murder on the Heart* (Hamish Hamilton)

Diamond Dagger (lifetime achievement): Edith Pargeter (Ellis Peters)

MACAVITY AWARDS
(Mystery Readers International)

Best novel: Margaret Maron, *Bootlegger's Daughter* (Mysterious)

Best first novel: Barbara Neely, *Blanche on the Lam* (St. Martin's)

Best nonfiction or critical work: Ellen Nehr, *Doubleday Crime Club Compendium* (Offspring)

Best short story: Carolyn G. Hart, "Henrie O's Holiday" (*Malice Domestic* [Pocket])

ARTHUR ELLIS AWARDS
(Crime Writers of Canada)

Best novel: Carston Stroud, *Lizardskin* (Bantam)

Best first novel: Sean Stewart, *Passion Play* (Beach Holme)

Best true crime: Kirk Makin, *Redrum the Innocent* (Viking Penguin)

Best short story: Nancy Kilpatrick, "Mantrap" (*Murder, Mayhem and Macabre* [Mississauga Arts Council])

HAMMETT PRIZE
(North American Branch, International Association of Crime Writers)
Alice Hoffman, *Turtle Moon* (Putnam)

THE YEAR'S 25 FINEST
CRIME AND MYSTERY STORIES
Third Annual Edition

F. Paul Wilson is not only one of the modern masters of horror, his crime fiction—from the stunning novel *Sibs* to his powerful short story "Faces"—is in the front rank of modern dark suspense. "Slasher" is fresh, frightening, and utterly unforgettable.

Slasher

F. PAUL WILSON

I saved the rage.

I let them bury my grief with Jessica. It cocooned her in her coffin, cushioned her, pillowed her head. There it would stay, doing what little it could to protect her from the cold, the damp, the conqueror worm.

But I saved the rage. I nurtured it. I honed it until its edge was fine and tough and sharp. Sharp enough to cut one day through the darkness encrusting my soul.

Martha was on the far side of the grave, supported by her mother and father and two brothers—Jessie's grandparents and uncles. I stood alone on my side. A few friends from the office were there, standing behind me, but they weren't really with me. I was alone, in every sense of the word.

I stared at the top of the tiny coffin that had remained closed during the wake and the funeral mass because of the mutilated state of the little body within. I watched it disappear by tiny increments beneath a growing tangle of color as sobbing mourners each took a turn at tossing a flower on it. Jessica, my Jessica. Only five years old, cut to ribbons by some filthy rotten stinking lousy—

"Bastard!"

The grating voice wrenched my gaze away from the coffin. I knew that voice. Oh, how I knew that voice. I looked up and met Martha's hate-filled eyes. Her face was pale and drawn, her cheeks were black with eyeliner that had flowed with her tears. Her blond hair was masked by her black hat and veil.

"It's your fault! She's dead because of you! You had her only every other weekend and you couldn't even pay attention to her! It should be *you* in there!"

"Easy, Martha," one of her brothers told her in a low voice. "You'll only upset yourself more."

But I could see it in his eyes, too—in everybody's eyes. They all agreed with her. Even I agreed with her.

"No!" she screamed, shaking off her brother's hand and pointing at me. "You were a lousy husband and a lousier father. And now Jessie's dead because of you! *You!"*

Then she broke down into uncontrollable sobbing and was led off by her parents and brothers. Embarrassed, the rest of the mourners began to drift away, leaving me alone with my dead Jessie. Alone with my rage. Alone with my guilt.

I hadn't been the best father in the world. But who could be? Either you don't give them enough love or you overindulge them. You can't seem to win. But I do admit that there were too many times when something else seemed more important than being with Jessie, some deal, some account that needed attention right away, so Jessie could wait. I'd make it up to her later—that was the promise. I'd play catch-up next week. But there wouldn't be any later. No more next weeks for Jessica Santos. No catching up on the hugs and the playing and the I-love-yous.

If only ...

If only I hadn't left her on the curb to go get her that goddam ice cream cone.

We'd been watching the Fourth of July fireworks down at the harborfront. Jessie was thrilled and fascinated by the bright flashes booming and booming in the sky. She'd wanted an ice cream, and being a divorced daddy who didn't get to see her very often, I couldn't say no. So I carried her back to the push-cart vendor near the entrance to Crosby's Marina. She couldn't see the fire-works from the end of the line so I let her stand back by the curb to watch while I queued up. While she kept her eyes on the sky, I kept an eye on her all the time I was on line. I wasn't worried about someone grabbing her—the thought never entered my mind. I just didn't want her wandering into the street for an even better view. The only time I looked away was when I placed the order and paid the guy.

When I turned around, a cone in each hand, Jessie was gone.

No one had seen anything. For two days the police and a horde of volunteers combed all of Monroe and most of northern Nassau County. They found her—what was left of her—on the edge of old man Haskin's marshes.

A manhunt was still on for the killer, but with each passing day the trail got colder.

So now I stood by my Jessica's grave under the obscenely bright sun, sweating in my dark suit as I fought my guilt and nurtured my hate, praying for the day they caught the scum who had slashed my Jessica to ribbons. I renewed the vow I had made before—the guy was never going to get to trial. I would find a way to get to him while he was out on bail, or even in jail, if it came to that, and I would do to him what he'd done to my Jessica. And then I would dare the courts to find a jury that would convict me.

When everyone was gone, I said my final good-bye to Jessie. I'd wanted to erect a huge angelic monument to her, but Tall Oaks didn't allow that sort of thing. A little plaque would have to suffice. It didn't seem right.

As I turned to go, I noticed a man leaning against a tree a hundred feet or so away. He was watching me. As I started down the grassy slope, he began walking too. Our paths intersected at my car.

"Mr. Santos?" he said.

I turned. He was a big man, six-two at least, mid-forties, maybe two-fifty, with most of it settled around his gut. He wore a white shirt under a rumpled gray suit. His thinning brown hair was slick with sweat. I looked at him but said nothing. If he was another reporter—

"I'm Gerald Caskie, FBI. Can we talk a minute?"

"You found him?" I said, my spirits readying for a leap. I stepped closer and grabbed two fistfuls of his suit jacket. "You've got him?"

He pulled his jacket free of my grasp.

"We can talk in my car. It's cooler."

I followed about fifty yards along the curving asphalt path to where a mono-tone Ford two-door sedan waited in the shade of one of the cemetery's eponymous trees. The motor was running. He indicated the passenger side. I joined him in the front seat of the Ford. The air conditioner was blasting. It was freezing inside.

"That's better," he said, adjusting one of the vents to blow directly on his face.

"All right," I said, unable to contain my impatience any longer. "We're here. Tell me: Do you have him?"

He looked at me with basset-hound brown eyes.

"What I'm about to tell you is off the record, agreed?"

"What are you—?"

"Agreed? You must never reveal what I'm about to tell you. Do I have your word as a man that what I tell you will never go beyond this car?"

"No. I have to know what it's about, first."

He shifted in his seat and put the Ford in gear.

"Forget it. I'll drive you back to your car."

"No. Wait. All right. I promise. But enough with the games, already."

He threw the gearshift back into park.

"This isn't a game, Mr. Santos. I could lose my job, even be brought up on criminal charges for what I'm going to tell you. And if you do try to spill it, I'll deny we've ever met."

"What is it, goddam it?"

"We know who killed your daughter."

The words hit me like a sledge to the gut. I felt almost sick with relief.

"Have you got him? Have you arrested him?"

"No. And we won't be. Not for some time to come."

It took a while for the words to sink in, probably because my mind didn't want to accept them. But when it did, I was ready to go for his throat. I reined in my fury, however. I didn't want to get hit with assault and battery on a federal officer. At least not yet.

"You'd better explain that," I said in a voice barely above a whisper.

"The killer is presently a protected witness in an immensely important federal trial. Can't be touched until all the testimony is in and we get our conviction."

"Why the hell not? My daughter's death has nothing to do with your trial!"

"The killer's a psycho—that's obvious. Think how a child-killing charge will taint the testimony. The jury will throw it out. We've got to wait."

"How long?"

"Less than a year if we lose the case. If we get a conviction, we'll have to wait out all the appeals. So we could be looking at five years, maybe more."

Cool as it was in the car, I felt a different kind of cold seep through me.

"Who is he?"

"Forget it, I can't tell you that."

I couldn't help it—I went for his throat.

"Tell me, goddam it!"

He pushed me off. He was a lot bigger than I—I'm just a bantam-weight accountant, one-fifty soaking wet.

"Back off, Santos! No way I'm going to give you a name. You'll have it in all the papers within hours."

I folded. I crumpled. I turned away and pressed my head against the cool of the side window. I thought I was going to cry, but I didn't. I'd left all my tears with Jessie.

"Why did you tell me any of this if you're not going to tell me his name?"

"Because I know you're hurting," he said in a soft voice. "I saw what you did to that reporter on TV."

Right. The reporter, Mel Padner. My claim to fame. As I walked out of the morgue after identifying Jessica's tattered body, I was greeted by an array of cameras and reporters. Most of them kept a respectful distance, but not Padner. He stuck a mike in my face and asked me how I felt about my daughter's death. I had the microphone halfway down his throat before they pulled me off him. His own station never ran the footage, but all the others did, including CNN. I was still getting cards and telegrams telling me how I should have shoved it up Padner's other end instead.

"And this is supposed to make me feel better?" I said to Caskie.

"I thought it would. Because otherwise the weeks and months would go on and on with no one finding the killer, and you'd sink deeper and deeper into depression. At least I know I would. I've got a daughter myself, and if anything ever happened to her like . . . well, if anything happened to her, that's the way I'd feel. I just thought I'd try to give you some peace of mind. I thought you'd be able to hang in there better knowing that we already have the killer in a custody of sorts, and that, as one father to another, justice will be done."

I turned and stared at him. It's a comment on our age, I suppose, that decency from a stranger is so shocking.

"Thanks," I said. "Maybe that will make a difference later when I think about it some. Right now all I'm thinking is how I want to take the biggest, sharpest carving knife I can find and chop this guy into hamburger."

He raised his right fist with the thumb stuck in the air.

"I hear you, Mr. Santos."

"Call me Pete."

"I'm Gerry. And if the government didn't need the testimony so desperately, I might be tempted to do it myself."

We shook hands, then I got out of the car and walked around to his side. He rolled the window down.

"Thanks again," I said. "You didn't have to do this."

"Yes, I did."

"Sure you won't tell me his name?"

He smiled. "These are some *bad* dudes we want to put away with this trial. But don't you worry. Once all the legal proceedings are over, justice will be done." Again, the thumbs-up sign. "We'll see to it that she gets what's coming to her."

And then he drove away, leaving me standing on the path, gaping.

Her?

It wasn't working.

The day after Jessica's body was found, I went back to my apartment—Martha got the house, so I've been living in a two-bedroom box at the Soundview condos—and trashed the place. All except Jessica's room. The second bedroom had been reserved exclusively for Jessie. I went in there and with a black magic marker drew the outline of a man on one of her walls. Then I took the biggest carving knife I could find and attacked that figure. I slashed at the wallboard, driving the blade through it again and again until I was exhausted. Only then was I able to get some sleep.

I'd done that every night since Jessica's death, but tonight it wasn't working.

Caskie's last words were driving me crazy.

My little Jessica had been slashed to ribbons by a woman? A *woman*? I couldn't believe it. It gnawed at my insides like some monstrous parasite. I couldn't work, couldn't eat, couldn't sleep. The FBI knew who'd killed my Jessica and they weren't telling. I had to know, too. I needed a name. A face. Somewhere to focus this rage that was coloring my blood and poisoning every cell in my body.

A woman! Caskie must have been mistaken. Jessica had been—I retched every time I thought of it—sodomized. A woman couldn't do that.

I lasted two days—and two nights—of heartlessly attacking the male figure outlined on her wall. Then I acted.

First thing in the morning, I took a trip to the nearest FBI office. It was on Queens Boulevard in Rego Park. I knew I'd given Agent Caskie my word, but ... my daughter ... her killer ... no one could expect me to hold to that promise. No one!

I was in the lobby of the FBI building, searching the directory, when I heard a voice to my left.

"What the hell are you doing here?"

I turned. It was Caskie. I stepped toward him with my hand extended.

"Just the man I was looking—"

"Don't talk to me!" he hissed, staring across the lobby. "Get out of here!"

"No way, Caskie. Your people know who killed my daughter and they're going to tell me, or I'm going to the papers."

"You trying to ruin me?"

"No. I don't want that. But if I have to, I will."

He was silent for a moment, then he made a noise like a cross between a sigh and a growl.

"Shit! Meet me outside. Around the corner in the alley. Ten minutes."

He walked away without waiting for my reply.

The alley was long and narrow, blocked at the far end by a ten-foot cyclone fence. I waited near its mouth, keeping to the shady side. Mid-morning and already it was getting hot. Caskie showed up a few minutes later. He walked by as if he hadn't noticed me, but he spoke out of the corner of his mouth.

"Follow me. I don't want to be seen with you."

I followed. He led me all the way back to the rear of the building. When we rounded a rancid-smelling dumpster, he turned, grabbed me by the front of my shirt, and threw me against the wall. I was caught by surprise. The impact knocked the wind out of me.

"What the fuck do you think you're doing here?" he said through clenched teeth.

I was ready to take a shot at his jaw but the fury in his eyes made me hesitate. He looked ready to kill.

"I told you," I said. "I want to know who killed my daughter. And I'm going to find out."

"No way, Santos."

I looked him in the eye.

"What're you going to do? Kill me?"

He seemed to be considering it, and that made me a little nervous. But then his shoulders slumped.

"I'm so fucking *stupid!*" he said. "I should have minded my own business and let you stew for a year or two. But no, I had to try to be Mr. Goodguy."

I felt for him. Actually, I felt like a shit, but I wasn't going to let that stop me.

"Hey, look," I said. "I appreciate what you tried to do, but it just didn't work the way you thought it would. Instead of easing my mind, it's done just the opposite. It's made me crazy."

Caskie's expression was as bleak as his voice.

"What do you want, Santos?"

"First off. I want to know why you said the killer was a 'she' the other day?"

"When did I say that? I never said that."

"Oh, yes, you did. As you drove off. And don't tell me I misunderstood you, because I didn't. You said, 'We'll see to it that *she* gets what's coming to *her*.' So how could Jessie's killer have been a woman if they're tracing the killer through DNA analysis of the semen they found in . . ." My stomach lurched.

Caskie's smile was grim and sour.

"You think the Bureau can't get a local coroner to change his report for matters of security? Wake up, Santos. That was put in there to make sure no one ever has the slightest doubt that they're looking for a male."

I wanted to kill him. Here I'd spent nearly a week believing Jessica had been raped before she was slashed up. And it had never happened. But I kept calm.

"I want her name."

"No way."

"Then I go to the *Times,* the *Post,* and the *News!* Right now!"

I turned and began walking up the alley. I'd gone about ten feet when he spoke.

"Ciullo. Regina Ciullo."

I turned.

"Who is she?"

"Bruno Papillardi's ex-girlfriend."

That rocked me. Bruno Papillardi. New York City's number-one crime boss. His racketeering trial had been in the papers for months.

"Is she that important to the case?"

"The way the judge is tossing out our evidence left and right, it looks like she's going to be the *whole* case. She may be a psycho, but she's not dumb. She made recordings while she and Bruno were in bed together. Seems that when all the grunting and groaning is done, Bruno tends to brag. There's one particularly juicy night where he talks about how he personally offed a Teamsters local boss who wouldn't play ball. With Regina Ciullo's testimony, we might be able to nail him for more than racketeering. We might get him for murder-one."

I didn't care about Papillardi. I cared about only one person.

"But Jessica . . . why?"

Caskie shook his head.

"I don't know. I'm not a shrink. But I know your daughter wasn't the first. Regina Ciullo's done at least two others over the past two years. The others were just never found."

"Then how do you—?"

"She told us. She gave us the slip on the Fourth. She returned the following morning around three. We found the knife in the backseat of the car. We made the connection, put the pressure on her, and she told us. We'd always known she was weird but . . ." He shuddered. "We never realized . . ."

I wanted to run from the alley, but I had to see this through.

"So you can see our dilemma," Caskie went on. "We can't turn her in. At least not yet. Papillardi's people are combing the whole Northeast for her. If she's arrested she won't survive her first night in jail. And if by some miracle she does, her lawyer will immediately enter an insanity plea, which will destroy the value of her testimony against Papillardi."

I swallowed. My throat was gritty.

"Where are you keeping her?"

"Are you kidding? I tell you so you can go out there and try to do a Rambo number on her? No way."

"I don't want to kill her."

"That's not what you said the other day at the cemetery."

I smiled. It must have been a hideous grimace because I saw Caskie flinch.

"I was upset then. A little crazy. I couldn't stick a knife in someone. Besides, I already have enough information now to kill her. If I want her dead, I can call Papillardi and tell him she's in Monroe. He'll do the rest. But I don't want that. I just want to know what she looks like. I want to see a picture of her. And I want to know where she lives so I can drive by every once in a while and make sure she's still there. If I can do that, I can survive the wait."

He was studying me. I hoped I'd been convincing. I prayed he'd buy it. But actually, I hadn't left him much choice.

"She's staying on Shore Drive in Monroe."

I couldn't restrain myself.

"In my hometown? You brought a child killer to my home town?"

"We didn't know about her then. But believe me, she won't get out of our sight again. She's hurt her last kid."

Damn right! I thought.

"I want to see her file."

"I can't get that—"

"You will," I said, turning. "And by tonight. Or I'll be on the phone. Bring it to my apartment."

I didn't give him my address. I was sure he already had it.

Back in my apartment, I took the magic marker and enhanced the drawing on Jessica's wall with a few details. I added a skirt. And long flowing hair styled in a flip. Then I picked up the knife and went to work with renewed vigor.

Caskie showed up around ten P.M., smelling like a leaky brewery, a buff folder under his arm. He brushed by me and tossed the folder onto the living-room table.

"I'm dead!" he said, pulling off his wilted suit jacket and hurling it across the room. "Two more years till my pension and now I might as well kiss it all good-bye!"

"What's the matter?"

"*That's* what's the matter!" he said, pointing at the folder. "When that turns up missing, the Bureau will trace it to me and put my ass in a sling! Nice guys really do finish fucking last!"

"Just a minute, now," I said, approaching him but staying out of reach. He looked *very* upset. "Hold it down. If you return it first thing tomorrow morning, who's going to know it was ever missing?"

He stared at me, a blank look on his face.

"I thought you wanted it."

"I want to *look* at it. That's all. Like I told you: just to know where she lives and what she looks like. If the killer's got a name and a place and a face, I can stay sane until the Papillardi trial is over."

As I was speaking, my body had been gravitating toward the folder. I wasn't aware of my legs moving, but by the time I'd finished, I was standing over it. I reached down and flipped the cover open. An eight-by-ten black-and-white closeup of a woman's face stared back at me.

"That's . . . that's her?"

"Yeah. That's Regina Ciullo."

"She's so ordinary."

Caskie snickered.

"You think someone with Bruno Papillardi's bucks and pull is gonna waste his time with someone 'ordinary'? No way. Good-looking babes are falling all over that guy. But Ciullo's weirdness is one of a kind. She's *anything* but ordinary. That's what attracted him.'' His voice turned serious. "You really mean that about not wanting to take the file?"

"Of course."

I picked up the photo and stared at it. Her irises were dark, the lashes long. Her hair was wavy and long, and very black. Despite strategic angling of the camera, her nose appeared somewhat on the large side. Her lips were full and pouty. She looked thirty-five or so.

Caskie peered over my shoulder.

"That picture's a few years old, when she was going under the stage name of Bloody Mary. Doesn't show any of her body, which is incredible."

" 'Stage name'?"

"Yeah. She used to be a dancer in a specialty club down in SoHo called The Manacle. She'd do a strip while letting a white rat crawl all over her body, and when she was down to the buff, she'd slice its throat and squeeze its blood down her front as she finished her dance." Caskie's expression was sour. "A real sicko, but she sure as hell got to Papillardi. One show and he was hot for her ass. Say, you got any beer?"

I pointed the way to the kitchen as I continued to stare at the photo.

"In the fridge."

This was the killer of dear Jessica. Regina Ciullo. When she tired of slashing rats she went out and found a child. I felt my pulse quicken, my palms become moist. The photo trembled in my grasp, as if she knew I'd be coming for her.

"Where on Shore Drive is she staying?"

Caskie popped the top on a can of Bud as he returned to the living room.

"The Jensen place."

"Jensen! How'd you get her in there?"

The beer can paused inches from his lips.

"You know them?"

"I just know they're rich."

He took a long gulp.

"They are. And they're hardly ever home—at least in this home—except in the spring. They're on a world cruise now. And since Mr. Jensen is a friend of the present administration, and a personal friend of the Bureau's director, he's allowed us to stash her in his mansion. It's a perfect cover. She's posing as Mr. Jensen's niece." He shook his head slowly. "What a place. That's the way to live, I tell you."

The woman who murdered my daughter was living in luxury out on Shore Drive, guarded by the FBI. I wanted to scream. But I didn't. I closed the file and handed it back to Caskie.

"I'll keep the picture," I said. "The rest is all yours."

He snatched the folder away from me.

"You mean it?

"Of course. You'll never hear from me again . . . *unless*, of course, Papillardi is convicted and she isn't indicted. *Then* you'll hear from me. Believe me, you'll hear from me."

I had put on a performance of Barrymore caliber. And Caskie bought it. He smiled like a death-row prisoner who'd just got a last-minute reprieve.

"Don't worry about that, Santos. As soon as Papillardi's case is through, we're on her. Don't you worry about that!" He turned at the door and gave me another of his thumbs-up gestures. "You can take that to the bank!"

And then he was gone.

For a while I stood there in the living room and stared at the picture of Regina Ciullo. Then I took it into Jessica's room and tacked it over the head of the latest outline on the wall. Then I stabbed the figure so hard, so fast, and so many times that there was a football-sized hole in the wall in less than a minute.

A week later the walls of Jessica's room were so swiss-cheesed with holes that there was no space left for new outlines.

Time for the real thing.

I'd been driving by the Jensen place regularly, sometimes three times a day. I always kept the photo on the seat beside me, for quick reference in case I saw someone who resembled Regina Ciullo. I was sure I'd know her anywhere, but it's good to be prepared.

The houses on Shore Drive all qualified as mansions—all huge, all waterfront, facing Connecticut across the Long Island Sound. Although there was always a car or two in the driveway behind the electric steel gate—a Bentley or a Jag or a Porsche Carrera—I never saw anybody.

Until Thursday. I was in the midst of cruising past when I saw the front gate begin to slide open. I almost slammed on the brakes, then had the presence of mind to keep moving. But slowly.

And who pulls out but the bitch herself, the slasher of my daughter, slayer of the last thing in my life that held any real meaning. She was driving the Mercedes. Speeding. She passed me doing at least fifty and still accelerating. On a residential street. The bitch didn't care. The top was down. No question about it. It was her. And she was alone.

Had she given the FBI guardians the slip again? Was she on her way to find another innocent, helpless, trusting child to slaughter?

Not if I could help it.

I followed her to the local Gristedes, trailed her as she dawdled along the cosmetics aisle, touching, feeling, sniffing. Probably looking for the means to whore herself up. As ordinary as the photo had been, it had done her a service. In the light of day she was extremely plain. She needed all the help she could get. And her body. Caskie had described it as "incredible." It was anything but that from what I could see. I guess there's no accounting for tastes.

I caught up to her in the housewares aisle. That was where they sold the knives. When I saw a stainless steel carving set displayed on a shelf I got dizzy. Visions of Jessica's mutilated body lying on that cold, steel gurney in the morgue flashed before me. A knife like that had ripped her up. I saw Martha's face, the expressions on her brothers' faces—*Your fault! Your fault!*

That did it.

I ripped the biggest knife from the set and spun her around.

"Remember Jessica Santos?" I screamed.

Shock on her face. Sure! No one was supposed to know.

I pretended she was one of the outlines on Jessica's wall. A deep thrust to the abdomen, feeling the knife point hesitate against the fabric of her dress, and then rip through cloth and skin, into the tender innards. She screamed but I didn't let that stop me. I tugged the blade free and plunged it in again and again, each time screaming. "This is for Jessica! This is for Jessica!"

Somebody pulled me free of her and I didn't resist. She'd been slashed like Jessica. The damage was irreparable. I knew my duty was done, knew I'd avenged my daughter.

But as I looked into her dying eyes, so hurt, so shocked, so bewildered, I had the first inkling that I had made a monstrous mistake.

I slammed my fist on the table.

"Call the FBI! Check it out with them!"

They'd had me in this interrogation room for hours. Against the advice of my lawyer—who wanted me to plead insanity—I'd given them a full statement. I wasn't going to hide anything. This was an open-and-shut case of a man taking justifiable revenge against his daughter's murderer. I wasn't going to be coy about it. I did it and that was that. Now they could do their damnedest to convict me. All I needed was the FBI file to prove that she was the killer.

"We *have* called the FBI," said Captain Hall, chief of the Monroe police department. He adjusted his belt around his ample gut for the hundredth time since he'd stuck me in here. "And there's no such agent as Caskie assigned anywhere in New York."

"It's a deep-cover thing! That woman posing as a Jensen is Regina Ciullo, a federal witness against Bruno Papillardi!"

"Who told you that?" Captain Hall said.

"Agent Caskie."

"The agent who doesn't exist. How convenient. When did you meet him?"

I described my encounters with Caskie, from the cemetery to my apartment.

"So you were never in his office—if he ever had one. Did anyone see you with him?"

I thought about that. The funeral had been over and everyone was gone when I'd met him in the cemetery. We'd stood side by side for less than a minute in the foyer of the FBI building, and then we'd been together in the alley and my apartment. A cold lump was growing in my gut.

"No. No one that I recall. But what about the picture? It's got to have Caskie's fingerprints on it!"

"We've searched your car three times now, Mr. Santos. No picture. Maybe you *should* plead insane. Maybe this FBI agent is all in your mind."

"I'm not crazy!"

Captain Hall's face got hard as he leaned toward me.

"Well, then, maybe you should be. I know you've had a terrible thing happen to your family, but I've known Marla Jensen since she was a girl, back when she was still Marla Wainwright. That was poor Marla you sliced up. And what's more, we think we've *found* the killer. The *real* killer."

He had to be wrong! Please God, he had to be! If I did that to the wrong woman—

"No! You got to listen to me!"

A disgusted growl rumbled from Captain Hall's throat.

"Enough of this bullshit. Get him out of here."

"No, wait! Please!"

"*Out!*"

Two uniformed cops yanked me out of the chair and dragged me into the hall. As they led me upstairs to a holding cell. I spotted Caskie walking in with two other cops.

"Thank God!" I shouted. "Where have you been?"

His face was drawn and haggard. He almost looked as if he had been crying. And he looked *different.* He looked trimmer and he held himself straighter. The rumpled suit was gone, replaced by white duck slacks, a white linen shirt, open at the collar, and a blue blazer with an emblem on the pocket. He looked like a wealthy yachtsman. He stared at me without the slightest hint of recognition.

One of the cops with him whispered in his ear and suddenly Caskie was bounding toward me, face white with rage, arms outstretched, fingers curved like an eagle's talons, ready to tear me to pieces. The cops managed to haul him back before he reached me.

"What's the matter with him?" I said to anyone who'd listen as my two cops hustled me up the stairs.

My attorney answered from behind me.

"That's Harold Jensen, the husband of the woman you cut up."

I felt my knees buckle.

"Her husband?"

"Yeah. I heard around the club that she started divorce proceedings against him, but I guess that's moot now. Her death leaves him sole heir to the entire Wainwright fortune."

With my sides tying themselves in a thousand tight little knots, I glanced back at the man I'd known as Caskie. He was being ushered through the door that led to the morgue. But on the threshold he turned and stole a look at me. As our eyes met, he winked and gave me a secret little thumbs-up.

This is the age of Lawrence Block. After more than thirty years of writing, Block is finally being recognized as one of our finest storytellers and craftsmen. The natural ease and grace of his style is matched by the rich observation of his stories, be they dark (as in the Matt Scudder novels), or light (as in the books about thief Bernie Rhodenbarr). He is a major voice in today's crime fiction.

Keller's Therapy
LAWRENCE BLOCK

"I had this dream," Keller said. "Matter of fact, I wrote it down, as you suggested."

"Good."

Before getting on the couch, Keller had removed his jacket and hung it on the back of a chair. He moved from the couch to retrieve his notebook from the jacket's inside breast pocket, then sat on the couch and found the page with the dream on it. He read through his notes rapidly, closed the book and sat there, uncertain of how to proceed.

"As you prefer," said Breen. "Sitting up or lying down, whichever is more comfortable."

"It doesn't matter?"

And which was more comfortable? A seated posture seemed natural for conversation, while lying down on the couch had the weight of tradition on its side. Keller, who felt driven to give this his best shot, decided to go with tradition. He stretched out, put his feet up.

He said, "I'm living in a house, except it's almost like a castle. Endless passageways and dozens of rooms."

"Is it your house?"

"No, I just live here. In fact, I'm a kind of servant for the family that owns the house. They're almost like royalty."

"And you are a servant."

37

"Except I have very little to do and I'm treated like an equal. I play tennis with members of the family. There's this tennis court in the back."

"And this is your job? To play tennis?"

"No, that's an example of how they treat me as an equal. I eat at the same table with them, instead of with the servants. My job is the mice."

"The mice?"

"The house is infested with mice. I'm having dinner with the family, I've got a plate piled high with good food, and a waiter in black tie comes in and presents a covered dish. I lift the cover and there's a note on it, and it says, 'Mice.' "

"Just the single word?"

"That's all. I get up from the table and follow the waiter down a long hallway, and I wind up in an unfinished room in the attic. There are tiny mice all over the room—there must be twenty or thirty of them—and I have to kill them."

"How?"

"By crushing them underfoot. That's the quickest and most humane way, but it bothers me and I don't want to do it. But the sooner I finish, the sooner I can get back to my dinner, and I'm hungry."

"So you kill the mice?"

"Yes," Keller said. "One almost gets away, but I stomp on it just as it's running out the door. And then I'm back at the dinner table and everybody's eating and drinking and laughing, and my plate's been cleared away. Then there's a big fuss, and finally they bring back my plate from the kitchen, but it's not the same food as before. It's—"

"Yes?"

"Mice," Keller said. "They're skinned and cooked, but it's a plateful of mice."

"And you eat them?"

"That's when I woke up," Keller said. "And not a moment too soon, I'd say."

"Ah," Breen said. He was a tall man, long-limbed and gawky, wearing chinos, a dark-green shirt and a brown corduroy jacket. He looked to Keller like someone who had been a nerd in high school and who now managed to look distinguished in an eccentric sort of way. He said "Ah" again, folded his hands and asked Keller what he thought the dream meant.

"You're the doctor," Keller said.

"You think it means I'm the doctor?"

"No, I think you're the one who can say what it means. Maybe it just means I shouldn't eat Rocky Road ice cream right before I go to bed."

"Tell me what you think the dream means."

"Maybe I see myself as a cat."

"Or as an exterminator?"

Keller didn't say anything.

"Let's work with this dream on a superficial level," Breen said. "You're employed as a corporate troubleshooter, except that you use another word for it."

"They tend to call us expediters," Keller said, "but troubleshooter is what it amounts to."

"Most of the time there is nothing for you to do. You have considerable opportunity for recreation, for living the good life. For tennis, as it were, and for nourishing yourself at the table of the rich and powerful. Then mice are discovered, and it is at once clear that you are a servant with a job to do."

"I get it," Keller said.

"Go on, then. Explain it to me."

"Well, it's obvious, isn't it? There's a problem and I'm called in and I have to drop what I'm doing and go and deal with it. I have to take abrupt, arbitrary action, and that can involve firing people and closing out entire departments. I have to do it, but it's like stepping on mice. And when I'm back at the table and I want my food—I suppose that's my salary?"

"Your compensation, yes."

"And I get a plate of mice," Keller made a face. "In other words, what? My compensation comes from the destruction of the people I have to cut adrift. My sustenance comes at their expense. So it's a guilt dream?"

"What do you think?"

"I think it's guilt. My profit derives from the misfortunes of others, from the grief I bring to others. That's it, isn't it?"

"On the surface, yes. When we go deeper, perhaps we will begin to discover other connections. With your having chosen this job in the first place, perhaps, and with some aspects of your childhood." He interlaced his fingers and sat back in his chair. "Everything is of a piece, you know. Nothing exists alone and nothing is accidental. Not even your name."

"My name?"

"Peter Stone. Think about it, why don't you, between now and our next session."

"Think about my name?"

"About your name and how it suits you. And"—a reflexive glance at his wristwatch—"I'm afraid that our hour is up."

Jerrold Breen's office was on Central Park West at 94th Street. Keller walked to Columbus Avenue, rode a bus five blocks, crossed the street and hailed a taxi. He had the driver go through Central Park, and by the time he got out of the cab at 50th Street, he was reasonably certain he hadn't been followed. He bought coffee in a deli and stood on the sidewalk, keeping an eye open while he drank it. Then he walked to the building where he lived, on First Avenue between 48th and 49th. It was a prewar high rise with an art deco lobby and an attended elevator. "Ah, Mr. Keller," the attendant said. "A beautiful day, yes?"

"Beautiful," Keller agreed.

Keller had a one-bedroom apartment on the 19th floor. He could look out his window and see the UN building, the East River, the borough of Queens. On the first Sunday in November he could watch the runners streaming across the Queensboro Bridge, just a couple of miles past the midpoint of the New York Marathon.

It was a spectacle Keller tried not to miss. He would sit at his window for hours while thousands of them passed through his field of vision, first the world-class runners, then the middle-of-the-pack plodders and finally the slowest of the slow, some walking, some hobbling. They started in Staten Island and finished in Central Park, and all he saw was a few hundred yards of their ordeal as they made their way over the bridge and into Manhattan. The sight always moved him to tears, though he could not have said why.

Maybe it was something to talk about with Breen.

It was a woman who had led him to the therapist's couch, an aerobics instructor named Donna. Keller had met her at the gym. They'd had a couple of dates and had been to bed a couple of times, enough to establish their sexual incompatibility. Keller still went to the same gym two or three times a week to raise and lower heavy metal objects, and when he ran into her, they were friendly.

One time, just back from a trip somewhere, he must have rattled on about what a nice town it was. "Keller," she said, "if there was ever a born New Yorker, you're it. You know that, don't you?"

"I suppose so."

"But you always have this fantasy of living the good life in Elephant, Montana. Every place you go, you dream up a whole life to go with it."

"Is that bad?"

"Who's saying it's bad? But I bet you could have fun with it in therapy."

"You think I need to be in therapy?"

"I think you'd get a lot out of therapy," she said. "Look, you come here, right? You climb the stair monster, you use the Nautilus."

"Mostly free weights."

"Whatever. You don't do this because you're a physical wreck."

"I do it to stay in shape. So?"

"So I see you as closed in and trying to reach out," she said. "Going all over the country, getting real estate agents to show you houses that you're not going to buy."

"That was only a couple of times. And what's so bad about it, anyway? It passes the time."

"You do these things and don't know why," she said. "You know what therapy is? It's an adventure, it's a voyage of discovery. And it's like going to the gym. Look, forget it. The whole thing's pointless unless you're interested.''

"Maybe I'm interested," he said.

Donna, not surprisingly, was in therapy herself. But her therapist was a woman, and they agreed that he'd be more comfortable working with a man. Her ex-husband had been very fond of his therapist, a West Side psychologist named Breen. Donna had never met the man, and she wasn't on the best of terms with her ex, but. . . .

"That's all right," Keller said. "I'll call him myself."

He'd called Breen, using Donna's ex-husband's name as a reference. "I doubt that he even knows me by name," Keller said. "We got to talking a while back at a party and I haven't seen him since. But something he said struck a chord with me and, well, I thought I ought to explore it."

"Intuition is always a powerful teacher," Breen said.

Keller made an appointment, giving his name as Peter Stone. In his first session he talked about his work for a large and unnamed conglomerate. "They're a little old-fashioned when it comes to psychotherapy." he told Breen. "So I'm not going to give you an address or telephone number, and I'll pay for each session in cash."

"Your life is filled with secrets," Breen said.

"I'm afraid it is. My work demands it."

"This is a place where you can be honest and open. The idea is to uncover the secrets you've been keeping from yourself. Here you are protected by the sanctity of the confessional, but it's not my task to grant you absolution. Ultimately, you absolve yourself."

"Well," Keller said.

"Meanwhile, you have secrets to keep. I respect that. I won't need your address or telephone number unless I'm forced to cancel an appointment. I suggest you call to confirm your sessions an hour or two ahead of time, or you can take the chance of an occasional wasted trip. If you have to cancel an appointment, be sure to give twenty-four hours' notice. Or I'll have to charge you for the missed session."

"That's fair," Keller said.

He went twice a week, Mondays and Thursdays at two in the afternoon. It was hard to tell what they were accomplishing. Sometimes Keller relaxed completely on the sofa, talking freely and honestly about his childhood. Other times he experienced the 50-minute session as a balancing act: He yearned to tell everything and was compelled to keep it all a secret.

No one knew he was doing this. Once, when he ran into Donna, she asked if he'd ever given the shrink a call, and he'd shrugged sheepishly and said he hadn't. "I thought about it," he said, "but then somebody told me about this massacre—she does a combination of Swedish and shiatsu—and I have to tell you. I think it does me more good than somebody poking and probing at the inside of my head.''

"Oh, Keller," she'd said, not without affection. "Don't ever change."

It was on Monday that he recounted the dream about the mice. Wednesday morning his phone rang, and it was Dot. "He wants to see you," she said.

"Be right out," he said.

He put on a tie and jacket and caught a cab to Grand Central and a train to White Plains. There he caught another cab and told the driver to head out Washington Boulevard and to let him off at the corner of Norwalk. After the cab drove off, he walked up Norwalk to Taunton Place and turned left. The second house on the right was an old Victorian with a wraparound porch. He rang the bell and Dot let him in.

"The upstairs den, Keller," she said. "He's expecting you."

He went upstairs, and 40 minutes later he came down again. A young man named Louis drove him back to the station, and on the way they chatted about a recent boxing match they'd both seen on ESPN. "What I wish," Louis said, "is that they had, like, a mute button on the remote, except what it would do is mute the announcers but you'd still hear the crowd noise and the punches landing. What you wouldn't have is the constant yammer-yammer-yammer in your ear." Keller wondered if they could do that. "I don't see why not," Louis said. "They can do everything else. If you can put a man on the moon, you ought to be able to shut up Al Bernstein."

Keller took a train back to New York and walked to his apartment. He made a couple of phone calls and packed a bag. At 3:30 he went downstairs, walked half a block, hailed a cab to JFK and picked up his boarding pass for American's 5:55 flight to Tucson.

In the departure lounge he remembered his appointment with Breen. He called to cancel the Thursday session. Since it was less than 24 hours away, Breen said, he'd have to charge him for the missed session, unless he was able to book someone else into the slot.

"Don't worry about it," Keller told him. "I hope I'll be back in time for my Monday appointment, but it's always hard to know how long these things are going to take. If I can't make it, I should at least be able to give you the twenty-four hours' notice."

He changed planes in Dallas and got to Tucson shortly before midnight. He had no luggage aside from the piece he was carrying, but he went to the baggage-claim area anyway. A rail-thin man with a broad-brimmed straw hat held a hand-lettered sign that read NOSCAASI. Keller watched the man for a few minutes and observed that no one else was watching him. He went up to him and said, "You know, I was figuring it out the whole way to Dallas. What I came up with, it's Isaacson spelled backward."

"That's it," the man said. "That's exactly it." He seemed impressed, as if

Keller had cracked the Japanese naval code. He said, "You didn't check a bag, did you? I didn't think so. The car's this way."

In the car the man showed Keller three photographs, all of the same man, heavyset, dark, with glossy black hair and a greedy pig face. Bushy mustache, bushy eyebrows and enlarged pores on his nose.

"That's Rollie Vasquez," the man said. "Son of a bitch wouldn't exactly win a beauty contest, would he?"

"I guess not."

"Let's go," the man said. "Show you where he lives, where he eats, where he gets his ashes hauled. Rollie Vasquez, this is your life."

Two hours later the man dropped Keller at a Ramada Inn and gave him a room key and a car key. "You're all checked in," he said. "Car's parked at the foot of the staircase closest to your room. She's a Mitsubishi Eclipse, pretty decent transportation. Color's supposed to be silver-blue, but she says gray on the papers. Registration's in the glove compartment."

"There was supposed to be something else."

"That's in the glove compartment, too. Locked, of course, but the one key fits the ignition and the glove compartment. And the doors and the trunk, too. And if you turn the key upside down, it'll still fit, because there's no up or down to it. You really got to hand it to those Japs."

"What'll they think of next?"

"Well, it may not seem like much," the man said, "but all the time you waste making sure you got the right key, then making sure you got it right side up—"

"It adds up."

"It does," the man said. "Now you have a full tank of gas. It takes regular, but what's in there's enough to take you upward of four hundred miles."

"How're the tires? Never mind. Just a joke."

"And a good one," the man said. " 'How're the tires?' I like that."

The car was where it was supposed to be, and the glove compartment held the Registration and a semiautomatic pistol, a .22-caliber Horstmann Sun Dog, loaded, with a spare clip lying alongside it. Keller slipped the gun and the spare clip into his carry-on, locked the car and went to his room without passing the front desk.

After a shower, he sat down and put his feet up on the coffee table. It was all arranged, and that made it simpler, but sometimes he liked it better the other way, when all he had was a name and address and no one to smooth the way for him. This was simple, all right, but who knew what traces were being left? Who knew what kind of history the gun had, or what the string bean with the NOSCAASI sign would say if the police picked him up and shook him?

All the more reason to do it quickly. He watched enough of an old movie on cable to ready him for sleep. When he woke up, he went out to the car and took his bag with him. He expected to return to the room, but if he didn't, he would be leaving nothing behind, not even a fingerprint.

He stopped at Denny's for breakfast. Around one he had lunch at a Mexican place on Figueroa. In the late afternoon he drove into the foothills north of the city, and he was still there when the sun went down. Then he drove back to the Ramada.

That was Thursday. Friday morning the phone rang while he was shaving. He let it ring. It rang again as he was showering. He let it ring. It rang again just as he was ready to leave. He didn't answer it this time, either, but went around wiping surfaces a second time with a hand towel. Then he went out to the car.

At two that afternoon he followed Rolando Vasquez into the men's room of the Saguaro Lanes bowling alley and shot him three times in the head. The little gun didn't make much noise, not even in the confines of the tiled lavatory. Earlier he had fashioned an improvised suppressor by wrapping the barrel of the gun with a space-age insulating material that muffled the gun's report without adding much weight or bulk. If you could do that, he thought, you ought to be able to shut up Al Bernstein.

He left Vasquez propped in a stall, left the gun in a storm drain half a mile away, left the car in the long-term lot at the airport. Flying home, he wondered why they had needed him in the first place. They'd supplied the car and the gun and the finger man. Why not do it themselves? Did they really need to bring him all the way from New York to step on the mouse?

"You said to think about my name," he told Breen. "The significance of it. But I don't see how it could have any significance. It's not as if I chose it."

"Let me suggest something," Breen said. "There is a metaphysical principle which holds that we choose everything about our lives, that we select the parents we are born to, that everything which happens in our lives is a manisfestation of our wills. Thus, there are no accidents, no coincidences."

"I don't know if I believe that."

"You don't have to. We'll just take it as a postulate. So assuming that you chose the name Peter Stone, what does your choice tell us?"

Keller, stretched full length upon the couch, was not enjoying this. "Well, a peter's a penis," he said reluctantly. "A stone peter would be an erection, wouldn't it?"

"Would it?"

"So I suppose a guy who decides to call himself Peter Stone would have something to prove. Anxiety about his virility. Is that what you want me to say?"

"I want you to say whatever you wish," Breen said. "Are you anxious about your virility?"

"I never thought I was," Keller said. "Of course, it's hard to say how much anxiety I might have had back before I was born, around the time I was picking my parents and deciding what name they should choose for me. At that age I probably had a certain amount of difficulty maintaining an erection, so I guess I had a lot to be anxious about.''

"And now?''

"I don't have a performance problem, if that's the question. I'm not the way I was in my teens, ready to go three or four times a night, but then, who in his right mind would want to? I can generally get the job done.''

"You get the job done.''

"Right.''

"You perform.''

"Is there something wrong with that?''

"What do you think?''

"Don't do that,'' Keller said. "Don't answer a question with a question. If I ask a question and you don't want to respond, just leave it alone. But don't turn it back on me. It's irritating.''

Breen said, "You perform, you get the job done. But what do you feel, Mr. Peter Stone?''

"Feel?''

"It is unquestionably true that peter is a colloquialism for the penis, but it has an earlier meaning. Do you recall Christ's words to Peter? 'Thou art Peter, and upon this rock I shall build my church.' Because Peter *means* rock. Our Lord was making a pun. So your first name means rock and your last name is Stone. What does that give us? Rock and stone. Hard, unyielding, obdurate. Insensitive, Unfeeling—''

"Stop,'' Keller said.

"In the dream, when you kill the mice, what do you feel?''

"Nothing. I just want to get the job done.''

"Do you feel their pain? Do you feel pride in your accomplishment, satisfaction in a job well done? Do you feel a thrill, a sexual pleasure, in their deaths?''

"Nothing,'' Keller said. "I feel nothing. Could we stop for a moment?''

"What do you feel right now?''

"I'm just a little sick to my stomach that's all.''

"Do you want to use the bathroom? Shall I get you a glass of water?''

"No, I'm all right. It's better when I sit up. It'll pass. It's passing already.''

Sitting at his window, watching not marathoners but cars streaming over the Queensboro Bridge, Keller thought about names. What was particularly annoying, he thought, was that he didn't need to be under the care of a board-certified metaphysician to acknowledge the implications of the name Peter Stone. He had chosen it, but not in the manner of a soul deciding what parents to be born to and planting names in their heads. He had picked the name when he called to make his initial appointment with Jerrold Breen. "Name?" Breen had demanded. "Stone," he had replied. "Peter Stone."

Thing is, he wasn't stupid. Cold, unyielding, insensitive, but not stupid. If you wanted to play the name game, you didn't have to limit yourself to the alias he had selected. You could have plenty of fun with the name he'd had all his life.

His full name was John Paul Keller, but no one called him anything but Keller, and few people even knew his first and middle names. His apartment lease and most of the cards in his wallet showed his name as J. P. Keller. Just Plain Keller was what people called him, men and women alike. ("The upstairs den, Keller. He's expecting you." "Oh, Keller, don't ever change." "I don't know how to say this, Keller, but I'm simply not getting my needs met in this relationship.")

Keller. In German it meant cellar, or tavern. But the hell with that. You didn't need to know what it meant in a foreign language. Change a vowel. Killer.

Clear enough, wasn't it?

On the couch, eyes closed, Keller said, "I guess the therapy's working."

"Why do you say that?"

"I met a girl last night, bought her a couple of drinks and went home with her. We went to bed and I couldn't do anything."

"You couldn't do anything?"

"Well, if you want to be technical, there were things I could have done. I could have typed a letter or sent out for a pizza. I could have sung *Melancholy Baby*. But I couldn't do what we'd both been hoping I would do, which was to have sex."

"You were impotent?"

"You know, you're very sharp. You never miss a trick."

"You blame me for your impotence," Breen said.

"Do I? I don't know about that. I'm not sure I even blame myself. To tell you the truth, I was more amused than devastated. And she wasn't upset, perhaps out of relief that I wasn't upset. But just so nothing like that happens again, I've decided to change my name to Dick Hardin."

"What was your father's name?"

"My father," Keller said. "Jesus, what a question. Where did that come from?"

Breen didn't say anything.

Neither, for several minutes, did Keller. Then, eyes closed, he said, "I never knew my father. He was a soldier. He was killed in action before I was born. Or he was shipped overseas before I was born and killed when I was a few months old. Or possibly he was home when I was born or came home on leave when I was small, and he held me on his knee and told me he was proud of me.''

"You have such a memory?''

"No,'' Keller said. "The only memory I have is of my mother telling me about him, and that's the source of the confusion, because she told me different things at different times. Either he was killed before I was born or shortly after, and either he died without seeing me or he saw me one time and sat me on his knee. She was a good woman, but she was vague about a lot of things. The one thing she was completely clear on was that he was a soldier. And he was killed over there.''

"And his name?''

Was Keller, he thought. "Same as mine,'' he said. "But forget the name, this is more important than the name. Listen to this. She had a picture of him, a head-and-shoulders shot, this good-looking young soldier in a uniform and wearing a cap, the kind that folds flat when you take it off. The picture was in a gold frame on her dresser when I was a little kid.

"And then one day the picture wasn't there anymore. 'It's gone,' she said. And that was all she would say on the subject. I was older then, I must have been seven or eight years old.

"Couple of years later I got a dog. I named him Soldier, after my father. Years after that, two things occurred to me. One, Soldier's a funny thing to call a dog. Two, whoever heard of naming a dog after his father? But at the time it didn't seem the least bit unusual to me.''

"What happened to the dog?''

"He became impotent. Shut up, will you? What I'm getting to is a lot more important than the dog. When I was fourteen, fifteen years old, I used to work after school helping out this guy who did odd jobs in the neighborhood. Cleaning out basements and attics, hauling trash, that sort of thing. One time this notions store went out of business, the owner must have died, and we were cleaning out the basement for the new tenant. Boxes of junk all over the place, and we had to go through everything, because part of how this guy made his money was selling off the stuff he got paid to haul. But you couldn't go through all this crap too thoroughly or you were wasting time.

"I was checking out this one box, and what do I pull out but a framed picture of my father. The very same picture that sat on my mother's dresser, him in his uniform and his military cap, the picture that disappeared, it's even in the same frame, and what's it doing here?''

Not a word from Breen.

"I can still remember how I felt. Stunned, like *Twilight Zone* time. Then I reach back into the box and pull out the first thing I touch, and it's the same picture in the same frame.

"The box is full of framed pictures. About half of them are the soldier, and the others are a fresh-faced blonde with her hair in a pageboy and a big smile on her face. It was a box of frames. They used to package inexpensive frames that way, with photos in them for display. For all I know they still do. My mother must have bought a frame in a five-and-dime and told me it was my father. Then when I got a little older, she got rid of it.

"I took one of the framed photos home with me. I didn't say anything to her, I didn't show it to her, but I kept it around for a while. I found out the photo dated from the World War Two. In other words, it couldn't have been a picture of my father, because he would have been wearing a different uniform.

"By this time I think I already knew that the story she told me about my father was, well, a story. I don't believe she knew who my father was. I think she got drunk and went with somebody, or maybe there were several different men. What difference does it make? She moved to another town, she told people she was married, that her husband was in the service or that he was dead, whatever she told them."

"How do you feel about it?"

"How do I feel about it?" Keller shook his head. "If I slammed my hand in a cab door, you'd ask me how I felt about it."

"And you'd be stuck for an answer," Breen said. "Here's a question for you: Who was your father?"

"I just told you."

"But *someone* fathered you. Whether or not you knew him, whether or not your mother knew who he was, there was a particular man who planted the seed that grew into you. Unless you believe yourself to be the second coming of Christ."

"No," Keller said. "That's one delusion I've been spared."

"So tell me who he was, this man who spawned you. Not on the basis of what you were told or what you've managed to figure out. I'm not asking the part of you that thinks and reasons. I'm asking the part of you that simply knows. Who was your father? What was your father?"

"He was a soldier," Keller said.

Keller, walking uptown on Second Avenue, found himself standing in front of a pet shop, watching a couple of puppies cavorting in the window.

He went inside. One wall was given over to stacked cages of puppies and kittens. Keller felt his spirits sink as he looked into the cages. Waves of sadness rocked him.

He turned away and looked at the other pets. Birds in cages, gerbils and snakes in dry aquariums, tanks of tropical fish. He felt all right about them; it was the puppies that he couldn't bear to look at.

He left the store. The next day he went to an animal shelter and walked past cages of dogs waiting to be adopted. This time the sadness was overwhelming, and he felt its physical pressure against his chest. Something must have shown on his face, because the young woman in charge asked him if he was all right.

"Just a dizzy spell," he said.

In the office she told him that they could probably accommodate him if he was especially interested in a particular breed. They could keep his name on file, and when a specimen of that breed became available. . . .

"I don't think I can have a pet," he said. "I travel too much. I can't handle the responsibility." The woman didn't respond, and Keller's words echoed in her silence. "But I want to make a donation," he said. "I want to support the work you do."

He got out his wallet, pulled bills from it, handed them to her without counting them. "An anonymous donation," he said. "I don't want a receipt. I'm sorry for taking your time. I'm sorry I can't adopt a dog. Thank you. Thank you very much."

She was saying something, but he didn't listen. He hurried out of there.

" 'I want to support the work you do.' That's what I told her, and then I rushed out of there because I didn't want her thanking me. Or asking questions."

"What would she ask?"

"I don't know," Keller said. He rolled over on the couch, facing away from Breen, facing the wall. " 'I want to support the work you do.' But I don't know what their work is. They find homes for some animals, and what do they do with the others? Put them to sleep?"

"Perhaps."

"What do I want to support? The placement or the killing?"

"You tell me."

"I tell you too much as it is," Keller said.

"Or not enough."

Keller didn't say anything.

"Why did it sadden you to see the dogs in their cages?"

"I felt their sadness."

"One feels only one's own sadness. Why is it sad to you, a dog in a cage? Are you in a cage?"

"No."

"Your dog. Soldier. Tell me about him."

"All right," Keller said. "I guess I could do that."

A session or two later, Breen said, "You have never been married?"

"No."

"I was married."

"Oh?"

"For eight years. She was my receptionist. She booked my appointments, showed clients to the waiting room. Now I have no receptionist. A machine answers the phone. I check the machine between appointments and take and return calls at that time. If I had had a machine in the first place, I'd have been spared a lot of agony.''

"It wasn't a good marriage?"

Breen didn't seem to have heard the question. "I wanted children. She had three abortions in eight years and never told me. Never said a word. Then one day she threw it in my face. I'd been to a doctor, I'd had tests and all indications were that I was fertile, with a high sperm count and extremely motile sperm. So I wanted her to see a doctor. 'You fool. I've killed three of your babies already, so why don't you leave me alone?' I told her I wanted a divorce. She said it would cost me.''

"And?"

"We've been divorced for nine years. Every month I write an alimony check and put it in the mail. If it were up to me, I'd burn the money.''

Breen fell silent. After a moment Keller said, "Why are you telling me all this?''

"No reason.''

"Is it supposed to relate to something in my psyche? Am I supposed to make a connection, clap my hand to my forehead and say, 'Of course, of course! I've been so blind!' ''

"You confide in me," Breen said. "It seems only fitting that I confide in you.''

Dot called a couple of days later. Keller took a train to White Plains, where Louis met him at the station and drove him to the house on Taunton Place. Later, Louis drove him back to the train station and he returned to the city. He timed his call to Breen so that he got the man's machine. "This is Peter Stone," he said. "I'm flying to San Diego on business. I'll have to miss my next appointment and possibly the one after that. I'll try to let you know.''

He hung up, packed a bag and rode the Amtrak to Philadelphia.

No one met his train. The man in White Plains had shown him a photograph and given him a slip of paper with a name and address on it. The man in question managed an adult bookstore a few blocks from Independence Hall. There was a tavern across the street, a perfect vantage point, but one look inside made it clear to Keller that he couldn't spend time there without calling attention to himself, not unless he first got rid of his tie and jacket and spent 20 minutes rolling around in the gutter.

Down the street Keller found a diner, and if he sat at the far end, he could keep an eye on the bookstore's mirrored front windows. He had a cup of coffee, then walked across the street to the bookstore, where two men were on duty. One was a sad-eyed youth from India or Pakistan, the other the jowly, slightly exophthalmic fellow in the photo Keller had seen in White Plains.

Keller walked past a wall of videocassettes and leafed through a display of magazines. He had been there for about 15 minutes when the kid said he was going for his dinner. The older man said, "Oh, it's that time already, huh? OK, but make sure you're back by seven for a change, will you?"

Keller looked at his watch. It was six o'clock. The only other customers were closeted in video booths in the back. Still, the kid had had a look at him, and what was the big hurry, anyway?

He grabbed a couple of magazines and paid for them. The jowly man bagged them and sealed the bag with a strip of tape. Keller stowed his purchase in his carry-on and went to find a hotel.

The next day he went to a museum and a movie and arrived at the bookstore at ten minutes after six. The young clerk was gone, presumably having a plate of curry somewhere. The jowly man was behind the counter and there were three customers in the store, two checking the video selections, one looking at the magazines.

Keller browsed, hoping they would clear out. At one point he was standing in front of a wall of videos and it turned into a wall of caged puppies. It was momentary, and he couldn't tell if it was a genuine hallucination or just some sort of flashback. Whatever it was, he didn't like it.

One customer left, but the other two lingered, and then someone new came in off the street. The Indian kid was due back in half an hour, and who knew if he would take his full hour, anyway?

Keller approached the counter, trying to look a little more nervous than he felt. Shifty eyes, furtive glances. Pitching his voice low, he said. "Talk to you in private?"

"About what?"

Eyes down, shoulders drawn in, he said, "Something special."

"If it's got to do with little kids," the man said, "no disrespect intended, but I don't know nothing about it. I don't want to know nothing about it and I wouldn't even know where to steer you."

"Nothing like that," Keller said.

They went into a room in back. The jowly man closed the door, and as he was turning around, Keller hit him with the edge of his hand at the juncture of his neck and shoulder. The man's knees buckled, and in an instant Keller had a loop of wire around his neck. In another minute he was out the door, and within the hour he was on the northbound Metroliner.

When he got home, he realized he still had the magazines in his bag. That was sloppy. He should have discarded them the previous night, but he'd simply forgotten them and never even unsealed the package.

Nor could he find a reason to unseal it now. He carried it down the hall and dropped it into the incinerator. Back in his apartment, he fixed himself a weak scotch and water and watched a documentary on the Discovery Channel. The vanishing rain forest, one more goddamned thing to worry about.

*   *   *

"Oedipus," Jerrold Breen said, holding his hands in front of his chest, his fingertips pressed together. "I presume you know the story. He killed his father and married his mother."

"Two pitfalls I've thus far managed to avoid."

"Indeed," Breen said. "But have you? When you fly off somewhere in your official capacity as corporate expediter, when you shoot trouble, as it were, what exactly are you doing? You fire people, you cashier divisions, close plants, rearrange lives. Is that a fair description?"

"I suppose so."

"There's an amplified violence. Firing a man, terminating his career, is the symbolic equivalent of killing him. And he's a stranger, and I shouldn't doubt that the more important of these men are more often than not older than you, isn't that so?"

"What's the point?"

"When you do what you do, it's as if you are seeking out and killing your unknown father."

"I don't know," Keller said. "Isn't that a little farfetched?"

"And your relationships with women," Breen went on, "have a strong Oedipal component. Your mother was a vague and unfocused woman, incompletely present in your life, incapable of connecting with others. Your own relationships with women are likewise out of focus. Your problems with impotence—"

"Once!"

"Are a natural consequence of this confusion. Your mother is dead now, isn't that so?"

"Yes."

"And your father is not to be found, and almost certainly deceased. What's called for, Peter, is an act specifically designed to reverse this pattern on a symbolic level."

"I don't follow you."

"It's a subtle point," Breen admitted. He crossed his legs, propped an elbow on a knee, extended his thumb and rested his bony chin on it. Keller thought, not for the first time, that Breen must have been a stork in a prior life. "If there were a male figure in your life," Breen went on, "preferably at least a few years your senior, someone playing a paternal role vis-à-vis yourself, someone to whom you turn for advice and direction."

Keller thought of the man in White Plains.

"Instead of killing this man," Breen said, "symbolically, I am speaking symbolically throughout, but instead of killing him as you have done with father figures in the past, you might do something to *nourish* this man."

Cook a meal for the man in White Plains? Buy him a hamburger? Toss him a salad?

"Perhaps you could think of a way to use your talents to this man's benefit instead of to his detriment," Breen went on. He drew a handkerchief from his pocket and mopped his forehead. "Perhaps there is a woman in his life—your mother, symbolically—and perhaps she is a source of great pain to your father. So instead of making love to her and slaying him, like Oedipus, you might reverse the usual course of things by, uh, showing love to him and slaying her."

"Oh," Keller said.

"Symbolically, this is to say."

"Symbolically," Keller said.

A week later Breen handed Keller a photograph. "This is called the thematic apperception test," Breen said. "You look at the photograph and make up a story about it."

"What kind of story?"

"Any kind at all," Breen said. "This is an exercise in imagination. You look at the subject of the photograph and imagine what sort of woman she is and what she is doing."

The photo was in color and showed a rather elegant brunette dressed in tailored clothing. She had a dog on a leash. The dog was medium-sized, with a chunky body and an alert expression. It was the color that dog people call blue and that everyone else calls gray.

"It's a woman and a dog," Keller said.

"Very good."

Keller took a breath. "The dog can talk," he said, "but he won't do it in front of other people. The woman made a fool of herself once when she tried to show him off. Now she knows better. When they're alone, he talks a blue streak, and the son of a bitch has an opinion on everything from the real cause of the Thirty Years' War to the best recipe for lasagna."

"He's quite a dog," Breen said.

"Yes, and now the woman doesn't want people to know he can talk, because she's afraid they might take him away from her. In this picture they're in a park. It looks like Central Park."

"Or perhaps Washington Square."

"It could be Washington Square," Keller agreed. "The woman is crazy about the dog. The dog's not so sure about the woman."

"And what do you think about the woman?"

"She's attractive," Keller said.

"On the surface," Breen said. "Underneath, it's another story, believe me. Where do you suppose she lives?"

Keller gave it some thought. "Cleveland," he said.

"Cleveland? Why Cleveland, for God's sake?"

"Everybody's got to be someplace."

"If I were taking this test," Breen said, "I'd probably imagine the woman living at the foot of Fifth Avenue, at Washington Square. I'd have her living at Number One Fifth Avenue, perhaps because I'm familiar with that building. You see, I once lived there."

"Oh?"

"In a spacious apartment on a high floor. And once a month," he continued, "I write an enormous check and mail it to that address, which used to be mine. So it's only natural that I would have this particular building in mind, especially when I look at this particular photo." His eyes met Keller's. "You have a question, don't you? Go ahead and ask it."

"What breed is the dog?"

"As it happens," Breen said, "it's an Australian cattle dog. Looks like a mongrel, doesn't it? Believe me, it doesn't talk. But why don't you hang on to that photograph?"

"All right."

"You're making really fine progress in therapy," Breen said. "I want to acknowledge you for the work you're doing. And I just know you'll do the right thing."

A few days later Keller was sitting on a park bench in Washington Square. He folded his newspaper and walked over to a dark-haired woman wearing a blazer and a beret. "Excuse me," he said, "but isn't that an Australian cattle dog?"

"That's right," she said.

"It's a handsome animal," he said. "You don't see many of them."

"Most people think he's a mutt. It's such an esoteric breed. Do you own one yourself?"

"I did. My ex-wife got custody."

"How sad for you."

"Sadder still for the dog. His name was Soldier. Is Soldier, unless she's changed it."

"This fellow's name is Nelson. That's his call name. Of course, the name on the papers is a real mouthful."

"Do you show him?"

"He's seen it all," she said. "You can't show him a thing."

"I went down to the Village last week," Keller said, "and the damnedest thing happened. I met a woman in the park."

"Is that the damnedest thing?"

"Well, it's unusual for me. I meet women at bars and parties, or someone introduces us. But we met and talked, and then I ran into her the following morning. I bought her a cappuccino."

"You just happened to run into her on two successive days."

"Yes."

"In the Village?"

"It's where I live."

Breen frowned. "You shouldn't be seen with her, should you?"

"Why not?"

"Don't you think it's dangerous?"

"All it's cost me so far," Keller said, "is the price of a cappuccino."

"I thought we had an understanding."

"An understanding?"

"You don't live in the Village," Breen said. "I know where you live. Don't look surprised. The first time you left here I watched you from the window. You behaved as though you were trying to avoid being followed. So I took my time, and when you stopped taking precautions, I followed you. It wasn't that difficult."

"Why follow me?"

"To find out who you are. Your name is Keller, you live at Eight-six-five First Avenue. I already knew what you were. Anybody might have known just from listening to your dreams. And paying in cash, and the sudden business trips. I still don't know who employs you, crime bosses or the government, but what difference does it make? Have you been to bed with my wife?"

"Your ex-wife."

"Answer the question."

"Yes, I have."

"Jesus Christ. And were you able to perform?"

"Yes."

"Why the smile?"

"I was just thinking," Keller said, "that it was quite a performance."

Breen was silent for a long moment, his eyes fixed on a spot above and to the right of Keller's shoulder. Then he said, "This is profoundly disappointing. I hoped you would find the strength to transcend the Oedipal myth, not merely reenact it. You've had fun, haven't you? What a naughty boy you've been. What a triumph you've scored over your symbolic father. You've taken this woman to bed. No doubt you have visions of getting her pregnant, so that she can give you what she cruelly denied him. Eh?"

"Never occurred to me."

"It would, sooner or later." Breen leaned forward, concern showing on his face. "I hate to see you sabotaging your therapeutic progress this way," he said. "You were doing so *well*."

From the bedroom window you could look down at Washington Square Park. There were plenty of dogs there now, but none were Australian cattle dogs.

"Some view," Keller said. "Some apartment."

"Believe me," she said. "I earned it. You're getting dressed. Are you going somewhere?"

"Just feeling a little restless. OK if I take Nelson for a walk?"

"You're spoiling him," she said. "You're spoiling both of us."

On a Wednesday morning, Keller took a cab to La Guardia and a plane to St. Louis. He had a cup of coffee with an associate of the man in White Plains and caught an evening flight back to New York. He took another cab directly to the apartment building at the foot of the Fifth Avenue.

"I'm Peter Stone," he said to the doorman. "Mrs. Breen is expecting me."

The doorman stared.

"Mrs. Breen," Keller said. "In Seventeen-J."

"Jesus."

"Is something the matter?"

"I guess you haven't heard," the doorman said. "I wish it wasn't me who had to tell you."

"You killed her," he said.

"That's ridiculous," Breen told Keller. "She killed herself. She threw herself out the window. If you want my professional opinion, she was suffering from depression."

"If you want *my* professional opinion," Keller said, "she had help."

"I wouldn't advance that argument if I were you," Breen said. "If the police were to look for a murderer, they might look long and hard at Mr. Stone-hyphen-Keller, the stone killer. And I might have to tell them how the usual process of transference went awry, how you became obsessed with me and my personal life, how I couldn't dissuade you from some insane plan to reverse the Oedipus complex. And then they might ask you why you employ an alias and just how you make your living. Do you see why it might be best to let sleeping dogs lie?"

As if on cue, Nelson stepped out from behind the desk. He caught sight of Keller and his tail began to wag.

"Sit," Breen said. "You see? He's well trained. You might take a seat yourself."

"I'll stand. You killed her and then you walked off with the dog."

Breen sighed. "The police found the dog in the apartment, whimpering in front of the open window. After I identified the body and told them about her previous suicide attempts, I volunteered to take the dog home with me. There was no one else to look after him."

"I would have taken him," Keller said.

"But that won't be necessary, will it? You won't be called upon to walk my dog or make love to my wife or bed down in my apartment. Your services are no longer required." Breen seemed to recoil at the harshness of his own words. His face softened. "You'll be able to get back to the far more important business of therapy. In fact," he indicated the couch, "why not stretch out right now?"

"That's not a bad idea. First, though, could you put the dog in the other room?"

"Not afraid he'll interrupt, are you? Just a little joke. He can wait in the outer office. There you go, Nelson. Good dog . . . oh, no. How *dare* you bring a gun. Put that down immediately."

"I don't think so."

"For God's sake, why kill me? I'm not your father, I'm your therapist. It makes no sense for you to kill me. You have nothing to gain and everything to lose. It's completely irrational. It's worse than that, it's neurotically self-destructive."

"I guess I'm not cured yet."

"What's that, gallows humor? It happens to be true. You're a long way from cured, my friend. As a matter of fact, I would say you're approaching a psychotherapeutic crisis. How will you get through it if you shoot me?"

Keller went to the window, flung it wide open. "I'm not going to shoot you," he said.

"I've never been the least bit suicidal," Breen said, pressing his back against a wall of bookshelves. "Never."

"You've grown despondent over the death of your ex-wife."

"That's sickening, just sickening. And who would believe it?"

"We'll see," Keller told him. "As far as the therapeutic crisis is concerned, well, we'll see about that, too. I'll think of something."

The woman at the animal shelter said, "Talk about coincidence. One day you come in and put your name down for an Australian cattle dog. You know, that's quite an uncommon breed in this country."

"You don't see many of them."

"And what came in this morning? A perfectly lovely Australian cattle dog. You could have knocked me over with a sledgehammer. Isn't he a beauty?"

"He certainly is."

"He's been whimpering ever since he got here. It's very sad. His owner died and there was nobody to keep him. My goodness, look how he went right to you. I think he likes you."

"I'd say we're made for each other."

"I believe it. His name is Nelson, but you can change it, of course."

"Nelson," he said. The dog's ears perked up. Keller reached to give him a scratch. "No, I don't think I'll have to change it. Who was Nelson, anyway? Some kind of English hero, wasn't he? A famous general or something?"

"I think an admiral."

"It rings a muted bell," he said. "Not a soldier but a sailor. Well, that's close enough, wouldn't you say? Now, I suppose there's an adoption fee and some papers to fill out.''

When they handled that part she said, "I still can't get over it. The coincidence and all.''

"I knew a man once," Keller said, "who insisted there was no such thing as a coincidence or an accident.''

"Well, I wonder how he would explain this.''

"I'd like to hear him try,'' Keller said. "Let's go, Nelson. Good boy.''

Ruth Rendell's novels and stories are all her own. You can usually tell a Rendell after a sentence or two because nobody else "sounds" quite like her. Her work is dark but not cynical; violent but not exploitative. In the same scene, she can break your heart and give you a long sad laugh. She is always a pleasure to read.

The Mouse in the Corner
RUTH RENDELL

"I think you know who killed your stepfather," said Wexford.

It was a throwaway line, uttered on parting and over his shoulder as he reached the door. A swift exit was, however, impossible. He had to bend almost double. The girl he spoke to was a small woman, the boyfriend she lived with no more than five foot six. Life in the caravan, he thought, would otherwise have been insupportable.

Stuck in the doorway, he said when she made no reply, "You won't mind if I come back in a day or two and we'll have another talk. All the same if I do, isn't it?

"You don't have to talk to me, Miss Heddon. It's open to you to say no." It would all have been more dignified if he could have stood up and faced her, but Wexford wasn't much concerned with dignity. He spoke rather gravely but with gentleness. "But if you've no objection we'll continue this conversation on Monday. I've a feeling you know a lot more than you've told me."

She said it, one of those phrases that invariably means its opposite. "I don't know what you're talking about."

"That's unworthy of someone of your intelligence," he said and he had meant it.

He opened the door and climbed out. She followed him and stood there, holding the door, a pretty young woman of twenty who looked even younger than her age because her blond hair was waist-length and her white blouse schoolgirlish.

"Monday, then," Wexford said. "Shall we say three-ish?"

"Suit yourself. " With one of her flashes of humour, she said, "You must feel like a Rottweiler in a rabbit hutch in here."

He smiled. "You may be right. It's true my bite is worse than my bark."

Possibly digesting this, she closed the door without another word. He picked his way back to the car, where Donaldson waited at the wheel. A path of cinders made a just usable track across the corner of a muddy field. In the cold haze the shape of a cottage converted from a railway carriage could just be seen against a grey tangle of wilderness. Two niches of rain had fallen in the week since Tom Peterlee's death and the sky of massive grey cumulus was loaded with more.

"Go by way of Feverel's, will you, Steve?" said Wexford. "I don't want to stop, just take a look."

The farm shop remained closed, though a wooden board offering for sale apples, pears, plums, and walnuts for pickling still stood by the gate. Wexford told Donaldson to stop the car and park for a few moments. Let Heather Peterlee see him. That sort of thing did no harm. He looked, for the dozenth time, at the shack that had been a shop, the huddle of wooden buildings, the house itself, and the inevitable caravan.

The house was a Victorian building, rendered in a pale stone colour that the rain had turned to khaki. The shallow roof was of dull grey slate. Some ten yards of bleak ground, part gravel and part scrubby grass, separated the house from the shop. In between and a little distance behind, the caravan stood on a concrete slab, and beyond it stretched the market gardens.

The shop, its double doors closed and padlocked, its windows boarded up, seemed a dilapidated hut. A sheet of the corrugated iron that roofed it had come loose and clanged up and down rhythmically in the increasing wind. It was a dreary place. No visitor would have difficulty in believing a man had been clubbed to death there.

As Donaldson started the engine a black spaniel came out from the back of the house and began barking inside the gate. Wexford had felt its teeth through his jacket sleeve, though blood had not been drawn.

"That the dog, is it, sir?"

They all knew the story, even those only remotely involved. Wexford confirmed that this indeed was the dog, this was Scamp.

Wexford spared a glance for the neighbours, Joseph Peterlee had a plant hire business and a customer was in the act of returning a mechanical digger. In conversation with her husband and the digger driver on the concrete entrance, an area much cracked, pitted, and now puddled, was Mrs. Monica Peterlee in her unvarying uniform of rubber boots and floral cross-over overall. And those are the characters in this drama, he thought, with the exception of one who (to paraphrase Kipling) has gone to the husband of her bosom the same as she ought to go, and one who has gone heaven only knows where.

Why was he so sure Arlene Heddon had the answer? Mike Burden, his second-in-command at Kingsmarkham CID, said with contempt that at any rate she was more attractive than the wife and the widow. With his usual distaste for those whose lives failed to approximate fairly closely to his own, he spoke scathingly of "the Peterlee girl" as if having no job and no proper roof over one's head directly conduced to homicide.

"Her name," Wexford said rather dourly, "is Heddon. It was her father's name. Heather Peterlee, if you remember, was a Mrs. Heddon before she remarried." He added, wondering as he did so why he bothered to indulge Burden's absurd prejudices, "A widow, incidentally."

Quick as a flash, Burden came back with, "What did her first husband die of?"

"Oh God, Mike, some bone disease. We went into all that. But back to Arlene Heddon, she's a very intelligent young woman, you know."

"No, I don't know. You must be joking. Intelligent girls don't live on benefit in caravans with unemployed welders."

"What a snob you are."

"*Married* welders. I'm not just a snob. I'm a moralist. Intelligent girls do well at school, go on to further education, get suitable well-paid jobs, and buy themselves homes on mortgages."

"Somehow and somewhere along the line Arlene Heddon missed out on that. In any case, I didn't say she was academically inclined. She's sharp, she's clever, she's got a good brain."

"And her mother, the two-times widow, is she the genius Arlene inherited her IQ from?"

This was neither the time nor the place to be discussing the murder, Wexford's house on a Saturday evening, but Burden had come round for a drink and whatever the topic of conversation, things had a way of coming back to the Peterlees. Wexford suggested they go over the sequence of events again. Dora, his wife, was present, but sitting on the window seat, reading tranquilly.

"You can set me right on the details," Wexford began, "but I think you'll agree it was broadly like this. On Thursday, October tenth, Heather Peterlee opened the farm shop at Feverel's as usual at nine in the morning. Heather had her sister-in-law Mrs. Monica Peterlee to help her, again as usual. Her husband, Tom, was working outside, and at lunchtime he brought up to the shop by tractor the vegetables he had lifted and picked during the morning.

"They ate their midday meal in the shop, keeping it open, and at three or thereabouts Joseph Peterlee arrived in his car to fetch his wife and take her shopping in Kingsmarkham. Tom and Heather served in the shop until closing time at five, when they returned to the house and Heather began preparing a meal. Tom had brought in the shop's takings with him, which he intended to put in the safe, but in the meantime he left the notes on the kitchen dresser that faces the outside door. The sum was about three hundred and sixty pounds.

He put the money on the dresser shelf and placed on top of it his camera in its case, presumably to stop it blowing about when the door was opened. He then went to the caravan to discuss raising the rent with Coral Fox, who had been living there since the summer.''

"Tom Peterlee was killed for three hundred and sixty pounds," said Burden.

"No, but various people would like us to think he was. It's a problem even guessing why he was killed. Everyone seems to have liked him. We have had . . ." Wexford hesitated, "golden opinions from all sorts of people. He was something of a paragon by all accounts, an ideal husband, good, kind, undeniably handsome. He was even handsome on the slab—forgive me, Dora.

"But I'll go on. They ate their meal at five-thirty. During the course of it, according to her statement, Tom said to his wife that they had fixed up the matter of the rent amicably. Carol wanted to stay on and understood the rent she was paying was inadequate . . ."

Dora interrupted him. "Is that the woman who'd left her husband and Heather Peterlee said she could have their caravan because she'd nowhere to live?"

"A friend of Heather's from way back, apparently. According to Heather, she told Tom she'd be round in an hour to accompany her on a dog walk. Heather always took the dog out after supper and Carol had got into the habit of going with her. Heather washed up their dishes and Tom dried. As I've said, he was an ideal husband. At some point he went out to the woodshed and fetched in a basket of logs to feed the wood-burning stoves, of which there was one in the kitchen and another in the living room.

"Carol knocked on the door and came into the kitchen at twenty past six. It wasn't raining but it looked like rain and Carol was wearing only a cardigan. Heather suggested she put on one of the rainproof jackets hanging behind the back door and Carol took a fawn-coloured one."

"Strange, wasn't it," Burden put in, "that she didn't fetch a coat of her own from the caravan? Especially a woman like that. Very conscious of her appearance, I'd say. But perhaps she wouldn't care, out on her own with another woman. It was a dull evening and they weren't likely to meet anyone."

Dora gave him a look, enigmatic, half-smile, but said nothing. Her husband went on, "If you remember, when the caravan was searched as the house was, the fact was remarked on that Carol Fox had no raincoat among her clothes. She has said, and Heather has confirmed it, that she always used one of Heather's. They took the dog and went for a walk through the Feverel's land, across the meadows by the public footpath, and down to the river. It was sometime between six-twenty and six-thirty that they left. It was still light and would be for another half-hour. What Tom did in their absence we don't know and probably never shall know, except that putting that money into the safe wasn't among his activities.

"At about ten to seven Arlene Heddon arrived at Feverel's, brought in her boyfriend's van.'' Wexford raised an eyebrow at Burden. ''The unemployed, married welder, Gary Wyatt. Arlene and Gary have no phone and Arlene got the message from grandma, on whose land she lives. She's not really her grandmother, of course, but she calls her grandma.''

''The old witch,'' said Dora. ''That's what people call her. She's well known.''

''I don't think she's as old as she looks and she's definitely not a witch, though she cultivates that appearance. To be the mother of Joseph and Tom she need be no more than sixty-five, and I daresay she's not. The message Arlene got from Mrs. Peterlee senior was that Mum had finished her jumper and if she wanted it for the Friday, could she come and pick it up? The time suggested was about eight. Grandma said she'd drive Arlene herself on account of she was going to her Conservative Association meeting in Kingsmarkham— I kid you not, Dora—but she said, no, Gary and she would still be eating their tea. Gary would take her in the van a bit later on.

''In fact, Gary wanted to go out at half-past six. He dropped her off at Feverel's, thus getting her there more than an hour earlier than her mother had suggested, and went on to have a drink with his pals in the Red Rose at Edenwick. Not that anyone has confirmed this. Neither the licensee nor the girl behind the bar remembers him being there. Which is in direct contrast to the evidence of the old witch's witnesses. Strange as her presence there might seem, every Tory in Kingsmarkham seems to remember her in the Seminar Room of the Olive and Dove Hotel that night. Not until seven-thirty, however, when the meeting started. Where had she been in that lost hour and a half?

''Gary promised to come back for Arlene in an hour. Arlene went round the back of the house and entered by the kitchen door, which was unlocked. As a daughter of the house, she didn't knock or call out, but walked straight in.

''There, in the kitchen, on the floor, she found the body of her stepfather, Tom Peterlee, lying face downwards, with a wound in the back of the head. She knelt down and touched his face. It was still faintly warm. She knew there was a phone in the sitting room but, fearing whoever had done this might still be in the house, she didn't go in there but ran back outside in the hope Gary had not yet gone. When she saw that he had, she ran the hundred yards or so to Mr. and Mrs. Joe Peterlee's, where she used their phone and dialed 999.

''Joe Peterlee was out, according to his wife. Arlene—all this is Arlene's evidence, partly confirmed by Monica Peterlee—Arlene asked her to come back with her and wait for the police but she said she was too frightened to do that, so Arlene went back alone. Within a very few minutes—it was now five past seven—her mother and Carol Fox returned from their walk with the dog. She was waiting outside the back door.

''She prepared them for what they would see and Heather cried out, pushed open the door, and rushed into the kitchen. She threw herself on the body, and when Arlene and Carol pulled her off and lifted her up, she began banging her head and face against the kitchen wall.''

Burden nodded. ''These two—what do we call them? Hysterical acts? Manifestations of grief?—account for the blood on the front of her jacket and the extensive bruising to her face. Or at least are possible explanations for them.''

''The police came and everyone was questioned on the spot. Of course no one had seen any suspicious characters hanging about Feverel's. No one ever has. Joe Peterlee has never been able to give a satisfactory account of his movements between six-twenty and six-fifty. Nor have Gary Wyatt and Grandma Peterlee.

''The money was gone. There was no weapon. No prints, other than those of Tom, Heather, Carol Fox, and Arlene, were found. The pathologist says Tom died between six-fifteen and seven-fifteen, a time which can be much narrowed down if Arlene is to be believed. Remember, she says he felt warm when she touched him at six-fifty.

''I think she's lying. I think she's lying all along the line, she's protecting someone, and that's why I'm going to keep on talking to her until I find out who. Grandma or her boyfriend or her Uncle Joe—or her mother.''

Dora wrinkled up her nose. ''Isn't it a bit distasteful, Reg, getting a girl to betray her own mother? It's like the KGB.''

''And we know what happened to them,'' said Burden.

Wexford smiled. ''I may only be getting her to betray her stepaunt by marriage, or isn't that allowed either?''

Burden left them at about ten to ten. He was on foot, for he and Wexford lived less than a mile apart. His route home was to take him past the big new shopping mall, the York Crest Centre. He deplored the name and the place, all a far cry from what Kingsmarkham had been when first he came.

Then there was life in the town at night, people entering or emerging from pubs and restaurants, cinema visitors, walkers strolling, in those days before the ubiquitous car. Television, the effects of recession, and the fear of street violence had all combined to keep the townsfolk indoors and the place was deserted. It was silent, empty but brightly lit, and therefore slightly uncanny.

His footfalls made a faint hollow echo; he saw his solitary figure reflected in gleaming shop windows. Not a soul passed him as he entered York Street, not a single being waited on a corner or at the bus stop. He turned into the alley that ran along the side of the York Crest Centre, to cut a furlong or so off his journey.

Into his silent speculation burst the raiders. It took him about thirty seconds to realise what this was. He had seen it on television but thought it confined to the north. A ram raid. That was what someone had named this kind of heist. The Land Rover first, turning on the paved court, reversing at the highest speed it could make into the huge glass double doors that shut off the centre by night. The noise of crashing glass was enormous, like a bomb.

It vanished inside, followed by two cars, a Volvo and a Volvo Estate, rattling over the broken glass, the wreckage of the doors. He didn't wait to see what happened. He had his cell-phone in his hand and switched on before the second car's taillights had disappeared. "No service" came up on its screen and "No service" when he shook it and pulled the aerial out. It had gone wrong. Never before had that happened, but it had to happen tonight when he was in the right place at the right time.

Burden raced down the alley to the phones on the post office wall, four of them under plastic hoods. The first he tried had been vandalised, the second worked. If he could get them there within five minutes, within ten even . . . He pounded back, remembered it would be advisable not to be heard, and crept the rest of the way. They were leaving, the Land Rover—stolen of course—with all its glass shattered, the two Volvos hard on its rear, and were gone God knew where by the time the Mid-Sussex Constabulary cars arrived.

The purpose of the raid had been to remove as much electronic equipment as the thieves could shift in five minutes from Nixon's in the Centre. It had been a tremendous haul and had probably taken twelve men to accomplish it.

The phone on the post office wall was repaired and on the following day vandalised again, along with all the others in the row. That was on a Monday, the date of Wexford's second conversation with Arlene Heddon. He went along to the caravan on old Mrs. Peterlee's land in the late afternoon. Arlene sometimes had a cleaning job but she was always in during the afternoons. He tapped on the door and she called out to him to come in.

The television was on and she was watching, lounging on the seat that ran the length of the opposite wall. She looked so relaxed even somnolent, that Wexford thought she would switch off by means of living/bedroom from kitchen, but she got up and pressed the switch. They faced each other, and this time she seemed anxious to talk. He began to take her through a series of new inquiries and all the old ones.

He noticed, then, that what she said differed very slightly from what she had said the first time, if in minor details. Her mother had not thrown herself on the body but knelt down and cradled the dead man's head in her arms. It was on one of the counters, not against the wall, that Heather had beaten her head.

The dog had howled at the sight of its dead master. The first time she said she thought she had heard a noise upstairs when first she arrived. This time she said she denied it, all had been silent. She had not noticed if the money was there or not when she first arrived. Now she said the money was there with the camera on top of the notes. When she came back from making her phone call she had not gone back into the house but had waited outside for her mother to return. That was what she said the first time. Now she said she had gone briefly into the kitchen once more. The camera was there but the money gone.

Wexford pointed out these discrepancies in a casual way. She made no comment. He asked, with apparent indifference, "Just as a matter of interest, how did you know your mother was out with the dog?"

"The dog wasn't there and she wasn't."

"You were afraid to use the phone in the house in case your stepfather's killer might still be there. You never considered the possibility that your mother might have been dead in some other part of the house? That Carol Fox might have taken the dog out on her own, as perhaps she sometimes did?"

"I didn't know Carol very well," said Arlene Heddon.

It was hardly an answer. "But she was a close friend of your mother's, an old friend, wasn't she? You might say your mother offered her sanctuary when she left her husband. That's the action of a close friend, isn't it?"

"I haven't lived at home since I was seventeen. I don't know all the friends my mother's got. I didn't know whether Carol took the dog out or what. Tom sometimes took him out and my mother did. I never heard of Carol going with my mother, but I wouldn't. I wasn't interested in Carol."

"Yet you waited for them both to come back from their walk, Miss Heddon?"

"I waited for my mother," she said.

Wexford left her, promising to come back for another talk on Thursday. Grandma was nowhere to be seen, but as he approached his car hers swept in, bumping over the rough ground, lurching through a trough or two, skidding with a scream of brakes on the ice, and, describing a swift half-circle round the railway carriage, juddering to a stop. Florrie Peterlee, getting on for seventy and looking eighty, drove like an eighteen-year-old madbrain at the wheel of his first jalopy.

She gave the impression of clawing her way out. Her white hair was as long and straight as Arlene's and she was always dressed in trailing black that sometimes had a curiously fashionable look. On a teenager it would have been trendy. She had a hooky nose and prominent chin, and bright black eyes. So far she had shown no grief whatever at the death of her son.

"You're too old for her," said the old witch.

"Too old for what?" said Wexford, refusing to be out-faced.

"Ooh, hard at him! That's a nice question to ask a senior citizen. Mind I don't put a spell on you. Why don't you leave her alone, poor lamb."

"She's going to tell me who killed your son Tom."

"Get away. She don't know. Maybe I did." She stared at him with a bold defiance. "I all but killed his dad once. I said, you've knocked me about once too often, Arthur Peterlee, and I picked up the kitchen knife and came at him with it. I won't say he never touched me again, human nature never worked that way, but he dropped dead with his heart soon after, poor old sod. I was so glad to see the back of him I danced on his grave. People say that, I know, it's just a way of talking, but me, I really did it. Went up the cemetery with a half-bottle of gin and danced on the bugger's grave.''

Wexford could see her, hair flying, black draperies blowing, the bottle in one hand, her wrinkled face dabbled with gin, dancing under the rugged ilexes and the yew tree's shade. He put up his eyebrows. Before she had more chances to shock him, or try to, he asked her if she had thought any more about telling him where she had been in that lost hour on the evening of her son's death.

"You'd be surprised."

She said it, not as a figure of speech, but as a genuine undertaking that she could astonish him. He had no doubt she could. She grinned, showing even white teeth, not dentures. The thought came to him that if she had a good bath, put her copious hair up, and dressed in something more appropriate for a rural matriarch, she might look rather wonderful. He wasn't too worried about her alibi or lack of one, for he doubted if she had the strength to wield the "blunt instrument" that had killed Tom Peterlee.

He was very certain he knew what that instrument was and what had become of it. Arriving at Feverel's within the hour, he had seen the wood splinters in Tom Peterlee's head wound before the pathologist arrived. With a sinking heart he had taken in the implications of a basket full of logs just inside the back door and the big wood-burning stove in an embrasure of the wall facing the door into the house. They would never find the weapon. Without being able to prove it, he knew from the first that it had been an iron-hard log of oak, maybe a foot long and three or four inches in diameter, a log used to strike again and again, then pushed in among the blazing embers in that stove.

He had even looked. The stove had been allowed to go out. Could you imagine anyone making up the fire at a time like that? A pale grey powdery dust glowed red still in one patch at the heart of it and as he watched, died. Later on, he had those ashes analysed. All the time he was up there the dog howled. Someone shut it up in a distant room, but its long-drawn-out cries pursued him up the road on his way to see Joseph and Monica Peterlee.

He remembered wondering, not relevantly, if she dressed like that to sit down at table, to watch television. At nine o'clock at night she was still in her cross-over overall, her black wellies. Her husband was a bigger and heavier version of his brother three or four years older, his hair iron-grey where Tom's had been brown, his belly fat and slack where Tom's had been flat. They alibied each other, uselessly, and Joe had no alibi for the relevant time. He had been out shooting rabbits, he said, producing his shotgun and shotgun licence.

"They done Tom in for the money," he told Wexford sagely. He spoke as if without his proffered information, such a solution would never have occurred to the police. "I told him. I said to him time and again, I said, you don't want to leave that laying about, not even for an hour, not even in daylight. What you got a safe for if you don't use it? I said that, didn't I, girl?''

His wife confirmed that he had indeed said it. Over and over. Wexford had the impression she would have confirmed anything he said. For peace, for a quiet life. It was two days later that, interviewing them again, he asked about the relationship between Tom and Heather Peterlee.

"They was a very happy couple," Joe said. "Never a cross word in all the ten years they was married."

Wexford, later, wondered what Dora would have said if he had made such a remark about relatives of his. Or Burden's wife Jenny if he had. Something dry, surely. There would have been some quick intervention, some, "Oh, come on, how would you know?" But Monica said nothing. She smiled nervously. Her husband looked at her and she stopped smiling.

The ram raiders were expected to have another go the following Saturday night. Instead they came on Friday, late shopping night at Stowerton Brook Buyers' Heaven, less than an hour after the shops closed. Another stolen Land Rover burst through the entrance doors, followed by a stolen Range Rover and a BMW. This time the haul was from Electronic World but was similar to that taken the previous time. The men in those three vehicles got away with an astonishing £35,000 worth of equipment.

This time Burden had not been nearby, on his way home. No one had, since the Stowerton Brook industrial site where Buyers' Heaven lay totally deserted by night, emptier by far than Kingsmarkham town centre. The two guard dogs that kept watch over the neighbouring builders' supplies yard had been destroyed a month before in the purge on dangerous breeds.

Burden had been five miles away talking to Carol Fox and her husband Raymond. To Burden, who never much noticed any woman's appearance but his wife's, she was simply rather above average good-looking. In her mid-thirties, ten years younger than Heather, she was brightly dressed and vivacious. It was Wexford who described her as one of that group or category that seems to have more natural colour than most women, with her pure red hair, glowing luminous skin, ivory and pink, and her eyes of gentian blue. He said nothing about the unnatural colour that decorated Mrs. Fox's lips, nails, and eyelids to excess. Burden assessed her as "just a cockney with an awful voice." Privately, he thought of her as common. She was loud and coarse, a strange friend for the quiet, reserved, and mousy Heather.

The husband she had returned to after a six-month separation was thin and toothy with hag-ridden eyes, some sort of salesman. He seemed proud of her and exaggeratedly pleased to have her back. On that particular evening, the case not much more than a week old, he was anxious to assure Burden and anyone else who would listen that his and his wife's parting had been no more than a "trial," an experimental living apart to refresh their relationship. They were together again now for good. Their separation hadn't been a success but a source of misery to both of them.

Carol said nothing. Asked by Burden to go over with him once more the events of 10 October, she reaffirmed six-twenty as the time she and Heather had gone out. Yes, there had been a basket of logs just inside the back door. She hadn't seen any money on the counter or the dresser. Tom had been drying dishes when she came in. He was alive and well when they left, putting the dishes away in the cupboard.

"I should be so lucky," said Carol, with a not very affectionate glance at her husband.

"Did you like Tom Peterlee, Mrs. Fox?"

Was it his imagination or had Raymond Fox's expression changed minutely? It would be too much to say that he had winced. Burden repeated his question.

"He was always pleasant," she said. "I never saw much of him."

The results came from the lab, disclosing that a piece of animal bone had been among the stove ashes. Burden had found out, that first evening, what the Peterlees had had for their evening meal: lamb chops with potatoes and cabbage Tom had grown himself. The remains were put into the bin for the compost heap, never into the stove. Bones, cooked or otherwise, the Peterlees weren't particular, were put on the back doorstep for the dog.

What had become of the missing money? They searched the house a second time, observing the empty safe, the absence of any jewellery, the absence of books, any kind of reading matter, or any sign of the generally accepted contributions to gracious living.

Heather Peterlee shut herself up in the house and when approached, said nothing. Questioned, she stared dumbly and remained dumb. Everyone explained her silence as due to her grief. Wexford, without much hope of anything coming of it, asked to remove the film from the camera that had weighted down the missing notes. She shrugged, muttered that he could have it, he was welcome, and turned her face to the wall. But when he came to look, he found no film in the camera.

Burden said Wexford's continued visits to Arlene Heddon were an obsession, the chief constable that they were a waste of time. Since his second visit she had given precisely the same answers to all the questions he asked—the same, that is, as on that second occasion. He wondered how she did it. Either it was the transparent truth or she had total recall. In that case, why did it differ from what she had said the first time he questioned her? Now all was perfect consistency.

If she made a personal comment there might be something new, but she rarely did. Every time he referred to Tom Peterlee as her stepfather she corrected him by saying, "I called him Tom," and if he spoke of Joseph and Monica as her uncle and aunt, she told him they weren't her uncle and aunt.

Carol Fox was her mother's great friend: Heather had known her for years, but she, Arlene, knew Carol scarcely at all.

"I never heard of Carol walking the dog with my mother, but I wouldn't. I wasn't interested in Carol."

Sometimes Gary Wyatt was there. When Wexford came he always left. He always had a muttered excuse about having to see someone about something and being late already. One Monday—it was usually Mondays and Thursdays that Wexford went to the caravan—he asked Gary to wait a moment. Had he thought any more about giving details of where he was between six forty-five and seven-thirty that evening? Gary hadn't. He had been in the pub, the Red Rose at Edenwick.

"No one remembers seeing you."

"That's their problem."

"It may become yours, Gary. You didn't like Tom Peterlee, did you? Isn't it a fact that Tom refused to let you and Arlene have the caravan Mrs. Fox lived in because you'd left your wife and children?"

"That was the pot calling the kettle," said Gary.

"And what does that mean?"

Nothing, they said. It meant nothing. He hadn't been referring to Tom. A small smile crossed Arlene's face and was gone. Gary went out to see someone about something, an appointment for which he was already late and Wexford began asking about Heather's behaviour when she came home after her walk.

"She didn't throw herself at him," Arlene said glibly, without, it seemed, a vestige of feeling. "She knelt down and sort of held his head and cuddled it. She got his blood on her. Carol and me, we made her get up and then she started banging her face on that counter."

It was the same as last time, always the same.

There had been no appeals to the public for witnesses to come forward. Witnesses to what? Heather Peterlee's alibi was supplied by Carol Fox and Wexford couldn't see why she should have lied or the two of them have been in cahoots. Friend she might be, but not such a friend as to perjure herself to save a woman who had motivelessly murdered an ideal husband.

He wondered about the bone fragment. But they had a dog. It was hardly too far-fetched to imagine a dog's bone getting in among the logs for the stove. Awkward, yes, but awkward inexplicable things do happen. It was still hard for him to accept that Arlene had simply taken it for granted her mother was out walking the dog with Carol Fox when she scarcely seemed to know that Carol lived there. And he had never really been able to swallow that business about Heather banging her face against the counter. Carol had only said, "Oh yes, she did," and Heather herself put her hands over her mouth and turned her face to the wall.

Then a curious thing happened that began to change everything. An elderly

man who had been a regular customer at the farm shop asked to speak to
Wexford. He was a widower who shopped and cooked for himself, living on
the state pension and a pension from the Mid-Sussex Water Authority.

Frank Waterton began by apologising, he was sure it was nothing, he
shouldn't really be troubling Wexford, but this was a matter which had haunted
him. He had always meant to do something about it, though he was never sure
what. That was why he had, in the event, done nothing.

"What is it, Mr. Waterton? Why not tell me and I'll decide if it's nothing."
The old man looked at him almost wistfully. "No one will blame you if it's
nothing. You still have been public-spirited and done your duty."

Wexford didn't even know then that it was connected with the Peterlee case.
Because he was due to pay one of his twice-weekly calls on Arlene Heddon,
he was impatient and did his best not to let his impatience show.

"It's to do with what I noticed once or twice when I went shopping for my
bits and pieces at Feverel's," he said and then Wexford ceased to feel exasper-
ated or to worry about getting to Arlene on time. "It must have been back in
June the first time, I know it was June on account of the strawberries were
in. I can see her now looking through the strawberries to get me a nice punnet
and when she lifted her face up—well, I was shocked. I was really shocked.
She was bruised like someone had been knocking her about. She'd a black
eye and a cut on her cheek. I said, you've been in the wars, Mrs. Peterlee,
and she said she'd had a fall and hit herself on the sink."

"You say that was the first time?"

"That's right. I sort of half-believed her when she said that but not the next
time. Not when I went in there again when the Cox's apples first came in—
must have been late September—and her face was black and blue all over
again. And she'd got her wrist strapped up—well, bandaged. I didn't comment,
not that time. I reckoned it wouldn't be—well, tactful.

"I just thought I ought to come and tell someone. It's been preying on my
mind ever since I heard about Tom Peterlee getting done in. I sort of hesitated
and hemmed and hawed. If it had been *her* found killed I'd have been in like
a shot, I can tell you."

He made it to Arlene's only a quarter of an hour late. Because it fascinated
him, hearing her give all those same answers, parrotlike, except that the voice
this parrot mimicked was her own, he asked her all the same things over again.
The question about her mother's bruised face he left till last, to have the effect
of a bombshell.

First of all, he got the same stuff. "She knelt down and took hold of his
head and sort of cuddled it. That's how she got his blood on her. Me and
Carol pulled her off him and lifted her up and she started banging her face
on the counter."

"Was she banging her face on the counter in June, Miss Heddon? Was she
doing the same thing in September? And how about her bandaged wrist?"

Arlene Heddon didn't know. She looked him straight in the eye, both her eyes into both his, and said she didn't know.

"I never saw her wrist bandaged."

He turned deliberately from her hypnotic gaze and looked around the caravan. They had acquired a microwave since he was last there. An electric jug kettle had replaced the old chrome one. Presents from Grandma? The old witch was reputed to be well-off. It was said that none of the money she had made from selling off acres of her land in building lots had found its way into her sons' pockets. He had noticed a new car parked outside the railway-carriage cottage and wouldn't have been surprised to learn that she replaced hers every couple of years.

"It'll be Tuesday next week, not Monday, Miss Heddon," he said as he left.

"Suit yourself."

"Gary found himself a job yet?"

"What job? You must be joking."

"Perhaps I am. Perhaps there's something hilarious in the idea of either of you working. I mean, have you ever given it a thought? Earning your living is what I'm talking about."

She shut the door hard between them.

After that, inquiries among the people who had known them elicited plenty of descriptions of Mrs. Peterlee's visible injuries. Regular customers at the farm shop remembered her bandaged arm. One spoke of a black eye so bad that it had closed up and on the following day Heather Peterlee had covered it with a shade. She explained a scab on her upper lip as a cold sore but the customer to whom she had told this story hadn't believed her.

The myth of the ideal husband was fading. Only the Peterlees themselves continued to support it and Monica Peterlee, when Burden asked her about it, seemed stricken dumb with fear. It was as if he had put his finger on the sorest part of a trauma and reawakened everything that caused the wound.

"I don't want to talk about it. You can't make me. I don't want to know."

Joseph treated the suggestion as a monstrous calumny on his dead brother. He blustered, "You want to be very careful what you're insinuating. Tom's dead and he can't defend himself, so you lot think you can say anything. The police aren't gods anymore, you want to remember that. There's not an evening goes by when you don't see it on the telly, another lot of coppers up in court for making things up they'd writ down and saying things what never happened."

His wife was looking at him the way a mouse in a corner looks at a cat that has temporarily mislaid it. Burden wasn't going to question Heather. They left her severely alone as they began to build up a case against her.

The day after the third ram raid—this time on the Kingsbrook Centre itself

in the middle of Kingsmarkham—Wexford was back in Arlene Heddon's caravan and Arlene was saying, "I never saw her wrist bandaged."

"Miss Heddon, you know your stepfather repeatedly assaulted your mother.
He knocked her about, gave her black eyes, cut her cheek. His brother Joseph
doubtless hands out the same treatment to his wife. What have you got to gain
by pretending you knew nothing about it?"

"She knelt on the floor and lifted up his head and sort of cuddled it. That's
how she got blood on her. Me and Carol sort of pulled her off him and then
she started banging—"

Wexford stopped her. "No. She got those bruises because Tom hit her in
the face. I don't know why. Do you know why? Maybe it was over money,
the shop takings he left on the dresser. Or maybe she'd protested about him
asking for more rent from Carol Fox. If your mother argued with him he
reacted by hitting her. That was his way."

"If you say so."

"No, Miss Heddon. It's not what I say, it's what you say."

He waited for her to rejoin with, "I never saw her wrist bandaged," but
she lifted her eyes and he could have sworn there was amusement in them, a
flash of it that came and went. She astounded him by what she said. It was
the last thing he expected. She fidgeted for a moment or two with the channel
changer on the divider between them, lifted her eyes, and said slowly, "Carol
Fox was Tom's girlfriend."

He digested this, saw fleetingly a host of possible implications, then said,
"What, precisely, do you mean by that term?"

She was almost contemptuous. "What everyone means. His girlfriend. His
lover. What me and Gary are."

"Not much point in denying it, is there?" said Carol Fox.

"I'm surprised you didn't give us this piece of information, Mr. Fox,"
Wexford said.

When her husband said nothing, Carol broke in impatiently. "Oh, he's
ashamed. Thinks it's a reflection on his manhood or whatever. I told him, you
can't keep a thing like that dark, so why bother?"

"You kept it dark from us deliberately for a month."

She shrugged, unrepentant. "I felt a bit bad about Heather, to be honest
with you. It was like Tom said I could live in this caravan on his land. He
never said it was right next door. Still, there was another girl he'd had four
or five years back he actually brought to live in the house. He called her the
au pair, as if those Peterlees weren't one generation from Gypsies when all's
said and done."

"Then I take it his visit to you that evening had nothing to do with raising
the rent?"

The husband got up and left the room. Wexford didn't try to stop him. His presence hadn't much inhibited his wife but his absence freed her further. She smiled just a little. "It's not what you're thinking. We had a drink."

"A bit odd, wasn't it, you going out for a walk with his wife? Or didn't she know? That's pretty hard to believe, Mrs. Fox."

"Of course she knew. She hated me. And I can't say I was too keen on her. That wasn't true about us often going out together. That walk, that night, I fixed it up because I wanted to talk to her. I wanted to tell her I was leaving, it was all over between me and Tom, and I was going back to Ray." She drew in a long breath. "I'll be honest with you, it was a physical thing. The way he looked—well, between you and me, I couldn't get enough of it. Maybe it's all worked out for the best. But the fact is, it'd have been different if Tom'd have said he'd leave her, but he wouldn't and I'd had it."

Wexford said, when he and Burden were out in the car, "I was beginning to see Heather's alibi going down the drain. Her best friend lying for her. Not now. I can't see Tom's girlfriend alibiing the wife she wanted out of the way."

"Well, no. Especially not alibiing the woman who'd killed the man she loved or once had loved. It looks as if we start again."

"Does anyone but Heather have a motive? What was in it for Arlene or Gary Wyatt? The man's own mother's capable of anything her strength allows her, but I don't think her strength would have allowed her this. Joseph had nothing to gain by Tom's death—the farm becomes Heather's—and it's evident all Monica wants is a quiet life. So we're left with the marauder who goes about the countryside murdering smallholders for three hundred and sixty quid."

Next morning an envelope arrived addressed to him. It contained nothing but a photographic film processor's chit which was also a receipt for one pound. The receipt was on paper headed with the name of a pharmacist in the York Crest Centre. Wexford guessed the origin of the film before he had Sergeant Martin collect the processed shots. Arlene, at home to him on Tuesday, was back at her parrot game.

"I haven't lived at home since I was seventeen. I don't know all the friends my mother's got. I didn't know whether Carol took the dog out or what. Tom sometimes took him out and my mother did. I never heard of Carol going with my mother, but I wouldn't. I wasn't interested in Carol."

"This is reaching the proportions of a psychosis, Miss Heddon."

She knew what that meant. He didn't have to explain. He could see comprehension in her eyes and her small satisfied smile. Others would have asked when all this was going to stop, when would he leave it alone. Not she. She would give all the same answers to his questions indefinitely, and every few weeks throw in a bombshell, as she had when she told him of Carol Fox's place in the Peterlees' lives. Always supposing, of course, that she had more bombshells to throw.

He knocked on the old witch's door. After rather a long time she came.

Wexford wasn't invited in and he could see she already had company. An elderly man with a white beard, but wearing jeans and red leather cowboy boots, was standing by the fireplace pouring wine from a half-empty bottle into two glasses.

She gave him the grin that cracked her face into a thousand wrinkles and showed her remarkable teeth.

"I had half an hour going spare, Mrs. Peterlee, so I thought I'd use it asking you where you were between six and seven-thirty on the evening your son was killed."

She put her head on one side. "I reckoned I'd keep you all guessing."

"And now you're going to tell me," he said patiently.

"Why not?" She turned and shouted over her shoulder at a pitch absurdly loud for the distance, "If that one's finished, Eric, you can go and open another. It's on the kitchen table." Wexford was favoured with a wink. "I was with my boyfriend. *Him.* At his place. I always drop in for a quick one before the meeting." She very nearly made him blush. "A quick *drink,*" she said. "You can ask him when he comes back. Rude bunch of buggers you cops are. It's written all over your face what you're thinking. Well, he'd marry me tomorrow if I said the word, but I'm shy, I've been bitten once. He may be nice as pie now and all lovey-dovey but it's another story when they've got the ring on your finger. Don't want another one knocking me to kingdom come when his tea's five minutes late on the table."

"Is that why Tom beat up Heather, because his meal was late?"

If she was taken aback she didn't show it. "Come on, they don't need a reason, not when the drink's in them. It's just you being there and not as strong as them and scared too, that's enough for them. You needn't look like that. I don't suppose you do like the sound of it. You want to've been on the receiving end. Okay, Eric, I'm coming."

Now that he no longer suspected her, after he had left her alone for a month, he went to Feverel's and saw Heather Peterlee. It was the night of the third ram raid and they knew it was coming when a Volvo Estate and a Land Rover were reported stolen during the day. But that was still three or four hours off.

Abused women have a look in common. Wexford castigated himself for not having seen it when he first came to the house. It had nothing to do with bruises and not much to do with a cowed beaten way of holding themselves. That washed-out, tired, drained appearance told it all, if you knew what you were looking for.

She was very thin but not with the young vigorous slimness of her daughter or the wiriness of her mother-in-law. Her leanness showed slack muscles in her arms and stringy tendons at her wrists. There were hollows under her cheekbones and her mouth was already sunken. The benefit of weeks without Tom had not yet begun to show. Heather Peterlee had neglected herself and her home, had perhaps spent her time of widowhood in silent brooding here in this ugly dark house with only the spaniel for company.

The dog barked and snarled when Wexford came. To silence it she struck it too brutally across the muzzle. Violence begets violence, he thought. You receive it and store it up and then you transmit it—onto whoever or whatever is feebler than you.

Even now she denied it. Sitting opposite him in a drab cotton dress with a thick knitted cardigan dragged shawl-like around her, she repudiated any suggestion that Tom had been less than good and gentle. As for Carol, yes, it was true Tom had offered her the caravan and not she. Tom had been told by a friend she wanted a place to live. What friend? She didn't know the name. And the "au pair"?

"You've been talking to my daughter."

Wexford admitted that this was indeed the case, though not to what weary extent it was true.

"Arlene imagines things. She's got too much imagination." A spark of vitality made a small change in her when she spoke of her daughter. Her voice became a fraction more animated. "She's brainy, is Arlene, she's a bright one. Wanted to go in for the police, you know."

"I'm sorry?"

"Get to be a policewoman or whatever they call them now."

"A police officer," said Wexford. "Did she really? What stopped that, then?"

"Took up with that Gary, didn't she?"

It was hardly an answer but Wexford didn't pursue it. He didn't ask about her husband's involvement with Carol Fox either. He had proof of that, not only in Carol's own admission but in the film from Tom Peterlee's camera. All the shots were of Carol, three nudes taken with a flash inside the Feverel's caravan. They were decorous enough, for Carol had been coy in her posing.

Wexford studied the three photographs again that evening. Their setting, not their voluptuous subject, made them pathetic. Sordidness of background, a window with a sagging net curtain, a coat hanging up, a glimpse of an encrusted pot on a hot plate, gave an air of attempts at creating pornography in some makeshift studio.

The identity of the sender of the processor's chit wasn't a problem. He had known that, if not from the moment he took it from its envelope, at least long before forensics matched with an existing set the fingerprints on the paper. He knew who had handed over the counter the film and the pound deposit. It was not even the subject of the shots that predominantly concerned him now. His slight depression vanished and he was suddenly alert. From those pictures he suddenly knew who had killed Tom Peterlee and why.

*   *   *

The police were waiting, virtually encircling the Kingsbrook Centre, when the ram raiders arrived. This time there were only four of them, all inside the stolen Land Rover. If others were following through the narrow streets of the town centre, some prior warning turned them back. The same warning perhaps, maybe no more than feeling or intuition, which halted the Land Rover on the big paved forecourt from which the centre's entrance doors opened.

At first the watchers thought only that the Land Rover was reversing, prior to performing its backwards ramming of the doors. It was a few seconds before it became clear that this was a three-point turn, forwards up to the fifteen-foot-high brick wall, reverse towards the doors, then, while they braced themselves for the crash of the doors going down and the Land Rover backing through, it shot forward again and was away through the alley into the High Street.

But it never entered the wider road. Its occupants left it to block the exit, flung all four doors open, and leapt out. The police, there in thirty seconds, found an empty vehicle, with no trace of any occupancy but its owner's and not a print to be found.

He said to Burden, before they made the arrest, "You see, she told us she didn't possess a raincoat and we didn't find one, but in this photo a raincoat is hanging up inside the caravan."

Burden took the magnifying lens from him and looked. "Bright emerald green and the buttons that sort of bone that is part white, part brown."

"She came into the kitchen when she said she did or maybe five minutes earlier. I think it was true she'd finished with Tom, but that she meant to go for a long walk with Heather in order to tell her so, that was a fiction. She wore the raincoat because it was already drizzling and maybe because she knew she looked nice in it. She came to tell Heather she'd be leaving and no doubt that Heather could have him and welcome.

"Did she know Tom beat his wife? Maybe and maybe not. No doubt, she thought that if Tom and she had ever got together permanently he wouldn't beat *her*. But that's by the way. She came into the kitchen and saw Heather crouched against the counter and Tom hitting her in the face.

"It's said that a woman can't really defend herself against a brutal man, but another woman can defend her. What happened to Carol Fox, Mike? Pure anger? Total disillusionment with Tom Peterlee? Some pull of the great sisterhood of women? Perhaps we shall find out. She snatched up a log out of that basket, a strong oak log, and struck him over the back of the head with it. And again and again. Once she'd started she went on in a frenzy—until he was dead."

"One of them," said Burden, "—and I'd say Carol, wouldn't you?—acted with great presence of mind then, organising what they must do. Carol took off the raincoat that was covered with blood and thrust it along with the weapon into the stove. In the hour or so before we got there everything was consumed but part of one of the buttons.''

"Carol washed her hands, put on one of Heather's jackets, they took the dog and went out down to the river. It was never, as we thought, Carol providing an alibi for Heather. It was Heather, alibiing Carol. They would stay out for three-quarters of an hour, come in the kitchen, pretend that Tom had gone away. What they didn't foresee was Arlene's arrival.''

"But Arlene came an hour early," Burden said.

"Arlene assumed that her mother had done it and she would think she knew why. The mouse in the corner attacked when the cat's attention was diverted. The worm turned, as grandma turned when her husband struck her once too often.''

He said much the same to Arlene Heddon next day after Carol Fox had been charged with murder. "You only told me she was Tom's girlfriend when you thought things were looking bad for your mother. You reasoned that if a man's mistress gave a man's wife an alibi it was bound to seem genuine. In case I didn't believe you and she denied it, you sent me the receipt when you took a film you'd removed from Tom Peterlee's camera along to the York Crest Centre to be processed. I suppose your mother told you the kind of pictures he took.''

She shrugged, said rather spitefully. "You weren't so clever. All that about me knowing who'd killed Tom. I didn't know, I thought it was my mother.''

He glanced round the caravan, took in the radio and tape player, microwave oven, video, and his eye fell on the small black rectangle he had in the past, without a closer look, taken for a remote control channel changer. Now he thought how lazy you would have to be, how incapacitated almost, to need to change channels by this means. Almost anywhere in here you were within an arm's length of the television set. He picked it up.

It was a tape recorder, five inches long, two inches wide, flat black. The end with the red "on" light was and always had been turned towards the kitchen area.

So confident had she been in her control of things and perhaps in her superior intelligence that she had not even stripped the tiny label on its underside. Nixon's, York Crest, £54.99—he was certain Arlene hadn't paid £55 for it.

"You can't have that!" She was no longer cool.

"I'll give you a receipt for it," he said, and then, "Gary, no doubt, was with his pals that evening planning the first ram raid. I don't know where, but I know it wasn't the Red Rose at Edenwick.''

She was quite silent, staring at him. He fancied she would have liked to snatch the recorder from him but did not quite dare. Serendipity or a long experience in reading faces and drawing conclusions made him say, "Let's hear what you've been taping on here, Miss Heddon.''

He heard his own voice, then hers. As clear as a phone conversation. It was a good tape recorder. He thought, yes, Gary Wyatt was involved in the first ram raid, the one that took place after the murder and after the first time I came here to talk to her. From then on, from the second time . . .

"I didn't know Carol very well."

"But she was a close friend of your mother's . . ." His voice tailed away into cracklings.

"I haven't lived at home since I was seventeen. I don't know all the friends my mother's got . . ."

"So that was how you did it," he said. "You recorded our conversations and learnt your replies off by heart. That was a way to guarantee your answers would never vary."

In a stiff wooden voice she said, "If you say so."

He got up. "I don't think Gary's going to be with you much longer, Miss Heddon. You'll be visiting him once a month, if you're so inclined. Some say there's a very thin line dividing the cop from the criminal, they've the same kind of intelligence. Your mother tells me you once had ambitions to be a police officer. You've got off to a bad start but maybe it's not too late."

With the recorder in his pocket, stopping as he made his way out of the caravan, he turned back and said, "If you like the idea, give me a ring."

He closed the door behind him and descended the steps onto the muddy field and the cinder path.

Margaret Maron is finally reaching the large audience her work deserves. In a time of in-your-face screamers, she is an elegant, even elegiac, writer; in a time of empty farceurs, she is an old-fashioned moralist. Here is a good example of her work at its best.

That Bells May Ring and Whistles Safely Blow
MARGARET MARON

"Deck the halls?" snarled Jane as she untied a rope of tinsel from a file cabinet and added it to the pile growing beside her reception desk. "I know one Hall I'd love to deck."

"And I know where I'd like to stick a few boughs of holly," Sheila agreed. She stood atop a step stool and unhooked the cluster of shiny stars that dangled from an overhead light.

I didn't speak. I believe actions speak louder than words and I was using all my breath to stuff our four-foot artificial fir tree into a huge plastic bag—lights, ornaments, icicles, and all.

'Twas two nights before Christmas, and we were three angry middle-aged mice as we stripped the office of every decoration. Santa Claus was a bully, Scrooge had triumphed, why continue the peace-on-earth-goodwill-to-men charade?

The annual Christmas party downstairs had put us in such a bleak mood that when we came back up for our coats, the jingle-bell festivity of our office repelled us. As one woman, we decided to bundle everything up and give it to someone deserving. The way our boss's bosses had reacted to Bridget's whistle-blowing, a shelter for battered women seemed the most appropriate.

Not that Sheila wasn't put out with Bridget herself.

"If she hadn't gone off half-cocked—" She tossed the stars atop Jane's pile of tinsel and paused to help me close the top of the tree bag.

"She's young," I said. "Things are more black and white when you're nineteen."

In truth, Bridget reminded me of myself at that age, which was more years ago than I like to contemplate: naive, idealistic, and full of youthful misconceptions.

Here in the Budget Department of the City Planning Commission, she'd soon learned that very few public officials actually serve the public. Clerical staff does most of the work while department heads hide incompetence, gross negligence, and outright dishonesty by playing the bureaucratic shell game: You cover my rear, I'll cover yours, and Santa will fill both of our stockings with sugarplums.

Our boss was one of Santa's best little helpers. Nicholas T. Hall exuded an air of confident ability. He spoke the jargon. He had an endless fund of risque stories that were clean enough to be told in mixed company, and he knew to the millisecond when to cut through the laughter with a "But seriously, guys, this problem we have here means we're gonna need to . . ."

As a result, he'd been promoted two notches above his level of competency. Nothing terribly unusual about that. We "girls" were used to covering our bosses' worst blunders. But then he began to muddle ineptitude with greed. Before his arrival, most contracts were still awarded to the lowest or most efficient bidder. Now reports had their figures padded or deflated depending on what was needed and what could be glossed over, and kickbacks ranged from bottles of scotch to God knew what.

Business as usual, right? It was only taxpayer dollars. Who gave a happy damn?

Well, as it turned out, Bridget did.

She'd seemed as militant as dandelion fluff when she first floated into our department right out of high school back in May. We soon learned that she'd fudged her application form and that she had no burning desire to work her way up from file clerk to senior administrative aide in the city's civil service system. She merely wanted to earn more than a student's usual summer job paid and she planned to quit at the end of August and go off to college.

Jane was a bit ticked because it would mean training someone else in the fall, but Bridget proved a quick learner and, though clearly not a dedicated worker, was at least willing to follow directions, so Jane kept her mouth shut to Mr. Hall.

Which was lucky because in mid-June, Bridget's parents and three perfect strangers were killed in a car crash that was clearly her father's fault. Funeral expenses and settling two messy civil lawsuits out of court took the house and most of her parents' modest estate. There were no relatives and Bridget's college plans had to be put on hold. She did manage to salvage some of her mother's furniture and a few family keepsakes from the sale of the house, and

Jane and Sheila helped her find a cozy little apartment near enough so she didn't need a car to get to work.

Bridget changed overnight. She'd been an adored only child and was very close to her parents. After their death, the lightness went out of her steps; and all through the fall, she threw herself into the job with a passion that gave a whole new meaning to the term workaholic. We knew her reaction wasn't completely healthy, but compulsive dedication was certainly easier to deal with than the crying jags that had gone before. Jane was pleased with her new thoroughness, Sheila was skeptical as to how long it could last, while I, keeping to the real agenda, was indifferent.

There were other, younger women in the department, but for some reason Bridget attached herself to the three of us even though we did little to encourage her. At coffee breaks she brought her hot chocolate to my cubicle, or she tagged along at lunch. Occasionally, she and I were even mistaken for mother and daughter. I'd seen pictures of Bridget's mother and knew there was a vague resemblance, but it wasn't something I wanted to promote. I had two perfectly satisfactory Siamese cats, thank you, and I certainly didn't want an emotional involvement with anyone's orphaned child. Nevertheless, there were times when something I said would remind her of happier times and tears would spill down her smooth cheeks. That's when it got hard to stay completely aloof.

Early in December, when Mr. Hall's Christmas booty began pouring in, Bridget started to notice. Soon she had matched the names on the gift cards with names on certain city contracts, and she came to us in outright indignation.

"Look at this!" she cried. "Davis Corporations's original bid. Here are their first figures and this is how Mr. Hall let them change it. And now they've sent him two bottles of scotch? They're going to get an extra four thousand a month from the city for two bottles of scotch?"

Sheila and Jane and I exchanged glances. We knew the scotch was but a socially acceptable token of Davis Corp's real appreciation, which was delivered every month in an unmarked envelope.

"And see what Mainline's done! They—"

"And just where did you get those contracts?" Jane asked sternly, snatching them out of her hands. "You have no business rummaging in those particular files."

Bridget's big blue eyes had opened even wider. "Don't you care that they're robbing the city blind?"

"Small potatoes," Sheila said heartlessly, "compared to what some others are doing."

I gave Sheila a cold glare and she shut up as I pulled on my boots against the snow falling outside. "I'm going to spend my lunch hour Christmas shopping," I announced, "Anyone interested?"

"I'll come," said Jane. She quickly refiled the contracts and closed those drawers with a crisp finality. "Rowan's has a sale on men's flannel shirts."

"Maybe I'll get one for Bill," said Sheila.

"How can you shop when—" Bridget's outraged protest broke off as the inner door swung open and our boss breezed through in his overcoat, heading out for his usual two-hour lunch.

He smiled at us in genial bonhomie. "Going Christmas shopping, girls?"

"Yes, Mr. Hall," I said.

If he ever remembered how long it took me to teach him his job here, and if he ever realized he still couldn't handle it without me, he never showed it. I could appreciate the irony, and unlike Sheila and Jane, I didn't resent the institutional unfairness of the situation. Might as well resent December for not being June. Makes as much sense. So what, if I still knew more about how the department functioned than he ever would? Clerical experience wasn't worth a reindeer's damn to the hierarchy. The job description for department head specified a college degree.

I didn't have one.

Nicholas T. Hall did.

That's why we called him Mr. Hall and he called us "girls."

"You got some Christmas presents," Bridget said, thrusting the beribboned boxes toward him. Unexpected acid etched her voice.

Mr. Hall held one up to his ear and beamed happily as he heard the expected liquid slosh from the bottle inside. "Good old Davis!" he chuckled. "Why don't you help me put these in my office, little lady?"

Davis Corp knew their man. He would probably take a quick nip before leaving and two or three more nips when he came back from his three-scotch lunch. Then he'd shove a few papers around his desk, sign the ones I'd left there, and about midafternoon ask us to hold his calls. At times like that, the rest of the staff thought he was concentrating on a project. Only Jane and Sheila and I knew that he sneaked long naps on the couch in his office, and he trusted us to cover for him. Four years of such indulgence had added an extra chin and puffed the bags beneath his eyes.

Indignation still burned in Bridget's eyes as Mr. Hall held the door for the three of us; and when we returned an hour later with our shopping bags crammed with gaily wrapped bundles, she spoke not a word but went straight on with her work on the far side of the office.

We let her sulk. December was hurtling past, the year was coming to an end, and we were so pressed for time on our own special project that we had none to spare for her. In fact, we used her sulks to rationalize our neglect. That was the guilt that gnawed at us and had sent us back up to the office to rip down the Christmas decorations that afternoon.

"If only we'd paid attention!" said Jane. "We could have headed her off."

"Who'd expect someone that young to get so uptight about morality?" asked Sheila.

"It's the young who do," I said slowly. "Once they get our age, most of them are too cynical to care anymore."

"They didn't have to fire her though," Sheila muttered.

Jane snorted and I gave Sheila a jaundiced look.

"Okay, okay," Sheila said. "You're right. But . . . I mean— Well, darn it all, it *is* Christmas."

"That's what *they* said," I reminded her.

As senior administrative aide in this department, I'd had to stand and listen that morning while Nicholas T. Hall and G. W. Parry, Hall's superior, fired Bridget.

When the flow of Christmas bottles reached its crest, that naive little bit of dandelion fluff had carefully listed all the donors and keyed their names to various contracts Hall had awarded. This morning, bright and early, she'd marched down to Parry's office, handed him the list, and stood there expecting to be told what a good little girl she was for blowing the whistle on crooked contractors.

Instead, she'd gotten a rude blast of reality and orders to clean out her desk before five o'clock.

"What else did you expect?" I'd asked her as we climbed the stairs back to our office. She was shaking in nervous reaction and trembling on the verge of tears, and I'd chosen stairs over the elevator so she'd have time to collect herself. "Okay, so city employees aren't supposed to take gifts. Nobody considers a few bottles of hooch a bribe. You're lucky they're satisfied just to fire you. You could have been sued for slander."

"Sued?" she whimpered. "Again?"

She'd endured agonies when everything her parents amassed had gone to settle the lawsuits over her father's car wreck. I hated to touch a hurt that had almost healed, but she needed to understand the consequences of going off half-cocked.

"Do you know what this is going to do for morale in our department?"

Tears did stream from her eyes then. "Oh, Glenna. I'm so sorry. I wasn't thinking."

I sighed and put my arms around her and let her cry. Inside, I burned with white-hot rage and impotence, but I kept my voice soothing as I patted her back and told her everything was going to be fine, just fine. She was such an emotionally fragile kid and here she was, being cut adrift at Christmas with no immediate job prospects and no shoulder to go home and cry on. Not even a cat.

When we reached our landing, the humiliation of having to clean out her desk while the whole department watched was more than she could take at the moment and she clutched at my hand.

"Don't make me go in there, Please, Glenna?"

I offered to do it for her, but she shook her head and began to edge down the stairs. "No, I'll come back this afternoon while everyone's at the Christmas party, okay?"

Reluctantly, I agreed but made her promise to wait while I got her coat. She seemed ready to bolt off into the snowy day with nothing on her arms but a thin pink sweater, and I didn't want her pneumonia on my conscience, too.

My return to the office coincided with Mr. Hall's. It was his year to play Santa Claus, to hand out the gag gifts and Christmas bonuses, and he had his red suit and wig in one hand and the white beard in the other.

"Damn shame," he said, fluffing out the beard. He'd decided to be noble and magnanimous, more sinned against than sinning, this hurts me more than it hurts her. "Such a pretty little thing. I thought Parry was a bit hard on her, but he seemed to think we had no choice."

What G.W. Parry had said, with more force than originality, was that when an apple (i.e., Bridget) turned rotten, it had to be plucked out before it spoiled the whole barrel (The Budget Department).

"And I agree," I told him with more sincerity than he realized.

"You do? Ah, Glenna, you girls always surprise me. Will you tell the others?"

"I thought I'd wait till just before the party, if that's all right with you?"

"Good thinking. The party will take their minds off it, and then with the whole Christmas weekend—You're right. By Tuesday morning they'll have forgotten this whole unpleasant situation."

On the whole, he probably hadn't underestimated his staff's compassion. In an announcement shortly before the party was due to start at two-thirty, I explained that Bridget had made certain unfounded accusations against Mr. Hall and that she'd been asked to resign in light of her poor team spirit. Rumors would fly, but except for Sheila, Jane, and me, Bridget had made no close friends among the other ten women in the department. Unless we discussed her actions in public, there'd be nothing to keep the rumors going.

Of course I'd told Jane and Sheila everything over lunch and by the time we'd had a few cups of the spiked punch down in Central Planning, the three of us had gone from rage to despair to a melancholy pity for poor Bridget. As the others drifted off early to their varied merry Christmases, we went back upstairs and found that Bridget had been and gone.

Her desktop was bare, the empty drawers stood ajar, but everything that had made the desk hers—nameplate, coffee mug, even a cloisonné brass pot full of pencils, pens, and scissors—had been dumped in the nearest trash can as if she'd suddenly changed her mind about taking anything with her.

That's when we got angry all over again and attacked the Christmas decorations. We were almost finished when Nicholas T. Hall staggered in, beard awry, reeking of scotch, and slurring his words. He made a half-hearted joke about mistletoe and pretty girls as he shucked off his red jacket, hat, and attached wig, and slung them toward the nearest coat rack.

We ignored him.

Wounded, he retreated to his office and a moment later we heard the tinkle of glass, then the whooshing sound that his leather couch always makes when he sprawls upon it full length. By the time we'd bagged all the decorations to take over to the women's shelter, muted snores were drifting through our boss's half-open door.

It was only a little past four, but the sky had darkened and a fifty-percent probability of fresh snow was predicted. The telephone rang just as we were putting on our coats.

"Glenna? Oh good. This is Louise Hall. Is my husband still there? He promised he'd be home early."

Automatically I spoke the sort of lies Mr. Hall had instructed me to speak in such circumstances. "I'm sorry, Mrs. Hall. He left about a half hour ago. I think he planned to do some Christmas shopping on the way home. I was just leaving myself."

As I opened my desk drawer for my purse, I found a small gaily wrapped package with my name on it.

"I thought we agreed no presents," I said. Then, across the room, I saw that Sheila and Jane had discovered similar boxes.

I looked again at the name tag and recognized the handwriting.

"From Bridget," I said.

"Oh, gee," said Jane, ripping the paper from hers. "With all her troubles, she went and did this for us?"

She lifted the lid from the box and gasped with delight. Inside was a beautiful snow dome, one of those glass balls filled with water and white flecks that create a swirling snowstorm when shaken. This one was old, almost an antique. I knew because I was there the day Bridget showed it to Jane, who collects snow domes. It held a miniature elf who trudged across the snowy field carrying a decorated tree on his shoulders. It had belonged to Bridget's grandmother.

My gift was a sterling silver bracelet I'd once admired. Her mother's.

Even Sheila was touched. "I can't take this," she said though she tenderly cradled the old-fashioned gold pocket watch in her hand and traced the intricate initials with the tip of her finger. "It was her great-grandfather's. Almost a hundred years old. She loves this watch."

Jane inverted the snow dome and watched the white flecks dance inside its polished glass. "This is one of her favorite things."

The thin silver bracelet suddenly felt like a sliver of ice on my wrist. "These *are* her favorite things. Why has she given them away?"

I looked into their faces and saw my own startled apprehension reflected.

* * *

My reserved parking space was nearest the back entrance and Sheila and Jane piled into the car with me. Bridget's apartment was only a few short blocks away and though we made it in minutes, we were at least a half hour too late.

She'd left the door unlocked.

She was still wearing the pink sweater, but now the front was drenched in blood. She must have come home and sat down in her mother's wingback chair then pressed a needlepoint cushion against her chest before pulling the trigger, as if the cushion would somehow soften the shot.

Nicholas T. Hall's gun.

Every once in a while he had to go out and inspect deserted job sites in the rougher sections of the city. Legally registered. We recognized the fancy bone handle. He kept it in his desk drawer and whenever he cleaned the damn thing, he'd leave his office door open so that we *girls* could catch a glimpse of the he-man in action, ready and willing to face all dangers, the city's very own rootin', tootin' gunslinger.

And now his gun had finally notched its first kill.

Bridget's blue eyes stared into eternity. With infinite tenderness, Jane leaned over and closed them; then, almost wordlessly, we did what had to be done.

Christmas arrived two days later and that morning, the police apologetically summoned the three of us back to the office. They had a search warrant.

Mr. Hall was there, too. He looked as if he'd discovered rats and spiders in his Christmas stocking.

"Tell them, girls," he said hoarsely. "Tell them how I fell asleep on the couch night before last and didn't wake up till after eight. Jane? Sheila? You were here when I came back from the party and—Glenna! You were still working when I woke up. Remember?"

We looked at him blankly.

"I'm sorry, Mr. Hall," I said. "You left the office immediately after the party. If you came back again, it must have been after we'd gone."

"Besides," added Jane, "why would Glenna work late that night? It was the beginning of our Christmas holiday."

"Fits with what Mrs. Hall said," one of the detectives muttered to another. "Let's get on with it."

They soon found the gun behind the couch where it'd dropped from Mr. Hall's comatose fingers. (Jane's idea, and a nice touch, I thought.)

They were equally pleased with the red jacket and white beard still dangling from the back of Mr. Hall's door. "The old lady across the hall said she saw a Santa ringing the girl's bell."

So many people had worn the company's Santa costume over the years, it wouldn't matter whose hairs they found on the cap and wig as long as one or two of them belonged to Mr. Hall.

The detectives were very good at their job. Within hours after the anonymous call late Christmas Eve, they'd also found the computer disks I'd hidden in Bridget's lingerie drawer as well as the papers I'd stashed in her flour canister.

Taken together, the papers and floppies documented four years of corruption that stretched from the Budget Department right up to the City Council itself. There were names and dates and bank account numbers and Xerox copies of dated deposit slips. Every allegation wasn't backed with solid proof, of course. Not as much as Sheila and Jane and I'd hoped to provide before Bridget so abruptly forced our hand, but more than enough to fuel the public investigation, we'd been planning for almost a year—especially when linked to the shooting of a pretty young city clerk.

Bridget's death, an apparently cold-blooded murder so she wouldn't go public with her tale of bureaucratic corruption, wasn't the sort of thing that could be glossed over like a few bottles of complimentary Christmas booze. Not if that television van parked downstairs meant what I hoped it did.

Scotch had fogged Mr. Hall's perceptions more than he realized. It was closer to nine than eight when he woke up and found me still stripping the electronic data of all links to the three of us and transferring it to the sort of floppies that Bridget's computer used. Sheila and Jane had families so they had washed the sulfites from Bridget's hands, taken away the cushion, and gone straight home. The rest was up to me; and if it'd taken longer than any of us expected, if Bridget's delicate young face kept coming between my tear-blurred eyes and the numbers on my computer screen, who would know? Siamese cats can't tell time. Can't testify.

Open and shut, said the detectives. "The kid let slip what she had on you; you got her fired. Then she threatened to blow an even bigger whistle and you got drunk and shot her."

"No!" whimpered Nicholas T. Hall.

"Drunkenness is no longer a defense against murder," warned the younger detective.

"Why won't you girls tell them?" Mr. Hall asked plaintively as they hauled him away like a defective Christmas present.

I pulled on my gloves and my own Christmas present gleamed against the soft leather, a slender shining hoop too delicate for everyday wear. Too easily crushed.

If Sheila and Jane and I had been younger, less cynical, perhaps we could have trusted her.

As soon as Cameron Jewelry begins its January clearance sale next week, I shall buy a tiny gold whistle to hang on Bridget's silver bracelet.

I shall blow it every Christmas.

Barb Collins' stories have been attracting attention for the sleek suburban truths they impart. She is a quintessentially American writer, her material alive with the neuroses and secret sorrows of "respectable" American lives. And she keeps getting better and better.

That Damn Cat
BARBARA COLLINS

The silver sorrel Somali walked in the gutter along Pennsylvania Avenue, its bushy red foxlike tail dragging in the dirt, a miniature streetsweeper.

Suddenly the cat stopped, and jumped up on the low wall separating the street from the sidewalk. To the cat, the three-foot-high reinforced concrete barrier was just another wall—that it was erected after 240 Marines died in Beirut when a dynamite-laden pickup truck smashed into their barracks was beyond its comprehension, highly intelligent though the Somali was. The obstacle was meant to protect the north end of the White House from a similarly explosive fate—not to keep out a cat.

The Somali crept along the wall, its graceful, elongated body moving lithely, then it jumped down and padded across the wide sidewalk, which was free from tourists and protesters in the early morning hour on this unseasonably cool summer's day.

Carefully, cautiously, the animal approached the black wrought-iron fence embedded into more concrete, and stuck its head through the spearlike rods. With almond-shaped eyes the cat gazed out across the expansive, immaculate White House lawn. Dew sparkled on the grass like millions of diamonds thrown carelessly out onto endless bolts of green velvet.

Quick as the rising deficit, the cat shot upward, over the concrete base and through the fence.

With powerful legs, summoning athletic ability accountable to its Abyssinian

89

ancestry, the Somali darted across the lawn, oblivious to any pressure sensors or motion detectors it might be setting off.

From around the northwest corner of the White House, two burly men in dark suits and sunglasses came running, machine guns in hand.

Immediately the cat saw them and froze, a lifelike lawn ornament.

The two men fanned out and approached the animal from opposite ends, their machine guns pointed at it.

The cat didn't move.

"Nice kitty kitty," one said. He was smiling, but the smile was nasty.

"Come to poppa," the other one said. He had an ugly scar on his cheek. Under his breath, he murmured, "Fifteen years with the Secret Service, and I wind up chasing a damn cat off the lawn. . . ."

As the two men dove to capture the animal, it shot out between them, and they cracked their heads together in a bone-crunching effect. With a Chaplinesque pratfall, the man with the scar keeled over, knocked out cold. But not before his machine gun went RAT-A-TAT-TAT, across the other man's foot.

The wounded agent howled and grabbed the foot and joined his partner on the grass, writhing in pain.

The cat seemed unaware of all this, however, continuing its forward assault on the White House.

Now another Secret Serviceman appeared—a bigger and even meaner-looking man. He had a snarling canine on a leash—the vicious dog, mouth peeled back showing sharp teeth, pulled the man along as it ran toward the cat.

Once more the animal stopped. Calmly the feline sat on its hindquarters, and waited for the dog to draw near.

When the yapping canine had almost reached it, the cat took off, circling around the man, one, two, three times. The dog followed, and in a matter of seconds the cursing Secret Serviceman found himself tied up in the dog's heavy chain.

The cat, a comet now leaving its orbit, blazed out again for the White House.

The dog, too stupid to know what had happened, tried to continue the chase, even though his master called out, "Heel!"

And the Secret Serviceman, legs bound by the leash, hit the lawn with a *whump*!

"Somebody get *that damn cat*!" the fallen man hollered.

But the silver sorrel Somali had already reached the north portico, and was triumphantly climbing the White House steps.

Up on the portico, the cat turned its head and looked back casually at the shambles it had left behind.

It almost seemed to smile.

"Cut!" yelled Christopher Hughes, a wide grin splitting his bushily bearded face. "Fan-tastic!" To himself he muttered, "If only every actor could hit his mark like that damn cat."

The slightly overweight director in gray sweats and baseball cap looked like he belonged at a Redskins game, not standing behind a movie camera.

Out on the lawn the actors began to pick themselves up, joking and laughing. A thin, thinning-haired young man wearing jeans and a navy windbreaker was ascending the White House steps where the cat sat waiting patiently. This rather anemic-looking man had a silver cat-carrier, into which the animal placidly allowed itself to be placed.

Christopher Hughes turned to the assistant director, a pretty, bespectacled dark-haired woman wearing a white silk blouse and short black skirt. She was holding a clipboard.

"That's a wrap," he said to her, pleased. "Tell everyone we'll see them back in L.A. on Monday."

"Right," she responded. Then hesitated. "For the Oval Office scene . . . ?"

"No, the state dinner scene," he answered, faintly irritated. "Keep up with the changes, Lisa, and for God's sake make sure all those pies are delivered and kept refrigerated. I want to do it in one take . . . otherwise, it's gonna be one hell of a mess to clean up for a retake."

"I thought the prop master recommended shaving-cream pies. . . ."

"I don't give a damn what he recommended. I told you three days ago I wanted *real* pies. We're in the business of selling *believable* lies—got it?"

"Got it," she said, nodding, making notes.

A Secret Service agent approached them—a real one. He looked no less mean than the actors had.

"Finished?" the agent asked the director.

Hughes nodded. "We're outa here," he smiled at the man. "And again, please convey our thanks and the studio's, to the president for allowing us to shoot here this morning."

The agent frowned. "Frankly, we advised him against it," he said, "but he's such a big fan of your movies . . ."

He'd said it like he couldn't for the life of him understand why.

"I bet he's screened *That Damn Cat Goes to Vegas* a dozen times," the agent continued. "We have a theater here, you know." He nodded toward the White House.

"Ah!" Hughes said. "Then, please, tell the president I'll send him his own personal print of *That Damn Cat Goes to Washington*, as soon as it's edited. Sixteen or thirty-five?"

The agent cocked his head, apparently confused. "Pardon?"

"Sixteen- or thirty-five millimeter? I'll need to know what kind of print to have made up."

"Uh, I'll have to find out, sir."

"Well, do it quickly, if you would, and tell that young woman over there."
He pointed to Lisa.

The agent nodded, and stepped closer. He took off his sunglasses; his eyes
were tiny black marbles.

"It's too bad someone didn't tell you," he said, lowering his voice.

"Tell us what?" Hughes raised his eyebrows.

"Secret Service doesn't carry machine guns. Unless we're in a presidential
motorcade, that is."

"Really?"

"Really. And," the agent continued in a hushed voice, "we don't patrol
the grounds. The Uniformed Division does. They're more like regular cops."
He paused, then added, "But we do use canines, you got that part right."

Hughes smiled at the man. "Well, thanks for the info," he said, "but we
knew all that. But seeing some poor cop get shot in the foot with a pistol
can't compare to some pompous jerk in shades and a suit getting his toes
blown off with an Uzi. Now *that* will make the kiddies laugh." Hughes reached
out and patted the taken-aback agent on the arm. "That's entertainment!"

Not far from Pennsylvania Avenue, north of the Capitol Building, Todd and
Julie sat on the white leather overstuffed couch in the deco-modern living
room of their charming little brick townhouse.

Outside, dusk had settled in.

Todd was a darkly handsome man in his early thirties, with slicked-back
Valentino hair, and sensuous eyes surrounded by long thick lashes. His lips
were pressed against the rim of a crystal goblet as he sipped red wine—
Château Latour. The jacket of his tan Armani suit lay neatly folded on the
back of the sofa, next to him.

Julie was a beautiful blonde so buxom she approached a parody of pulchri-
tude, though she by no means looked cheap in her red Kamali suit. A handsome
thirty, but looking it, she was slouched down on the couch, her shapely legs
up on a glass coffee table, where art books of Dali, Rousseau, and Parrish lay
carefully arranged. Her red-painted petticured toes showed through sheer nylons. Delicate fingers clutched her nearly empty wine glass, resting it on her
stomach as she stared into the fireplace, its flames dancing a hot little number.

Todd stared at the orange glow, too, knowing how badly they needed money,
knowing that—in the short-term—Julie was the one who could get it for them.
But bringing up the subject would be . . . difficult.

"What are we going to do about the car payment?" she asked.

He almost smiled, but repressed it; she'd opened the door. Good. Now he
had a chance. . . .

"Don't sweat the small stuff," he answered. "First priority, babe, is the
mortgage."

She frowned. "But I'll *die* if we lose the BMW!" she moaned, then brightened. "There's always plastic. . . ."

He shook his head. "Maxed out."

She sat up, dropping her feet off the table, and turned to him, looking at him with an expression that was part pout, part scowl. "You just *had* to have that Rolex!" she said sharply.

He said nothing. He was looking at the painting on the wall above the fireplace.

That would get her going, he thought.

"I suppose we could sell the Nagel," he sighed.

The strikingly beautiful nude blonde, hugging her long legs, stared accusingly back at them. The modern pinup in its sleek black and gray frame had bold lines, bold colors; a sophisticated symbol of the now distant '80s.

"No!" Julie said. "She looks too much like me. It would be like selling myself!"

He raised an eyebrow. "Sorry," he said. "I should have thought of that."

But, of course, he had.

She crossed her arms on generous breasts and huffed, "Besides, we'd never be able to afford another one."

They sat in brooding silence. Flames hissed on the fake logs in the fireplace. He waited for her to take the conversation another step. . . .

Then she lowered her voice, as if the place might be bugged. "I don't dare 'borrow' any more money from the inactive accounts. Those bank examiners could show up at any time. . . ."

"And," he added in a hushed tone, "I can't 'shift' any further funds at the brokerage. Not now, not again."

"Damn! Is there *anything* we can do?"

They fell silent again. Then he turned and gazed meaningfully into her eyes. They went wide. "Oh, no!" she said "Not *that*."

He leaned close to her, pressing his body against hers. "Just this one more time, to tide us over," he pleaded. "Until I can think of something *big*, to really get us back on our feet."

"But I *hate* it!"

"Nobody's asking you to sleep with anybody, babe. Just a little powder in a cocktail, some sexist letch takes a little nap, and you take his money." He said this casually, as if describing shopping for a specific flavored coffee.

"But you *promised* me I wouldn't ever have to do that again!"

He pulled away from her. "You're right," he said, shaking his head as if ashamed of himself. "I did. Tell you what . . . I ran into that senator's wife the other day . . . the one that couldn't keep her hands off me at the Crawford party? She made it perfectly clear she'd be willing to pay for my . . . company."

Julie glared at him; flames now danced in her eyes. "All right, all right!" she snapped. "I'll do it, damnit! But this is the last time! I mean it, Todd."

He put an arm around her. "Sure, babe," he said, nuzzling her soft, perfumed neck. "I just want you to have nice things."

And he kissed her, passionately enough, but when the kiss had ended Julie pulled away.

"Not now," she said, obviously punishing him. "I have to go get us some money, remember?"

She rose from the couch and picked up her red shoes and padded off across the white carpet toward the bedroom.

Todd smiled to himself and poured himself another drink, and sat back on the couch. That hadn't been so tough. . . .

After a few minutes, Julie came back, her blonde hair hidden beneath a lovely, flowing black wig. She was wearing a tight, low-cut black designer dress, dark nylons, and black patent-leather heels; a white fur wrap caressed her bare shoulders. With her white skin and full red lips, she looked like a twentieth-century vampire about to crash an inaugural ball.

Julie extended one hand and jingled her car keys.

"Drive me," she said. "I don't want to leave the car on the street."

He felt a little woozy; he didn't know if it was the wine, or this suddenly incredibly beautiful wife of his.

They went out into the cool summer evening, to the silver BMW convertible parked in the driveway. He opened the door for her.

"Got the powder?" he whispered.

She nodded, and slid inside.

He went around to the driver's side and got behind the wheel. "To the Watergate?" he asked.

"No," she answered, eyes focused straight ahead. "I can't go back there— not after the last one almost died on us. Make it One Washington Circle. And put the top down. I need some air."

He backed out into the street, then followed it to Pennsylvania Avenue, which was pulsing with traffic. They drove in silence. The scent of her Chanel No. 5, borne by the wind, teased his nostrils.

A few blocks from the posh hotel, Todd pulled into a loading zone. Julie started to get out.

"Be careful," he said, leaning over, grabbing her hand.

"I will," she whispered. "I'll call you when it's safe to pick me up."

"I love you," he said, as earnestly as he could.

She didn't answer for a moment. Then, sadly, said, "I love you, too."

He watched her for a few moments, as she walked toward the hotel. Then he pulled away from the curb and drove back to the townhouse.

Inside, he finished off the wine, then stretched out on the couch to wait for Julie to call.

He hoped she'd come through. Otherwise, he'd have to dump her.

The thought gave him no pleasure: it wasn't as if he'd be leaving her for a younger woman. To continue living in the fashion he craved and deserved, a wealthy widow would be his ticket. Unfortunately.

Feeling a chill, he rose to turn up the flame on the gas fire, sat near it, huddled there, waiting for the phone to ring.

At first, entering the hotel lounge, she thought she was out of luck: everywhere she looked, in the dimly lighted bar, were couples. Except for one man, sitting on a bar stool, and he looked like a bum! Bearded, in sweats and a baseball cap, he was hardly the sort of prospect she was after.

She decided to play a waiting game, taking a small round table for one against a mirrored wall. Somebody would wander in, looking for a little singles action. Some married man, perhaps. . . .

An attractive black waitress in a frilly white blouse and black skirt brought Julie the 7-Up with cherry she'd ordered. Julie had already had enough wine; she needed to keep a clear head.

"Letting the riffraff in?" Julie asked the waitress smirkily.

"Him? He's hardly riffraff, miss. That's Chris Hughes."

Julie sat up straight. "The movie director?"

"That's right."

The waitress smiled, shook her head and wandered off.

Julie carried her tall glass of soda with her when she took the stool next to Hughes. She didn't look at him. She could feel him looking at her. Crossing her legs, she began to wiggle her right foot, letting her high heel dangle on her toes.

She looked at her watch, sighed, shook her head.

She repeated this action, every thirty seconds or so, for five minutes.

Finally she smiled at Hughes, looking at him as if she realized for the first time that he was there, and said, "I guess I've been stood up."

A smile peeked out of the bushy beard. "Beautiful woman like you? Seems unlikely."

"Washington is full of surprises."

"You're not an actress, are you?"

"Actress? No, why?"

Hughes smiled again, swirled a glass of dark liquid that was probably bourbon. "Just wondering. I get . . . hit on by actresses a lot."

"Why's that?"

"I'm a movie director. Christopher Hughes?"

He extended his hand and she took it. "Sally Davis. I'm a secretary for a lobby group here in town. Would I have seen any of your films?"

"You might. *That Damn Cat*, perhaps?"

"That was yours? Well. I have to admit I may be the only person in the United States who *didn't* catch that one."

He laughed. "Believe it or not, that's a refreshing answer."

"But I did see the sequel . . . the one about Las Vegas? I loved it when that cat chased Siegfried and Roy's tiger off the stage! That animal is a wonder."

"I'd like a hundred actors like him. What sort of lobbying group do you represent?"

She thought fast. "The A.R.I.—Animal Rights Institute? We're trying to stop animal testing in cosmetics."

She hoped that would work: between Hollywood and *That Damn Cat*, maybe Hughes would be sympathetic to a cause like that.

"Admirable." He leaned in. "But isn't that a fox fur around your lovely shoulders?"

"Fake fur. Uh, that's our point . . . why should a woman bother with the real thing, when the imitation is cruelty-free? And less expensive."

"Good point. But you also seem to be wearing Chanel. I believe *they* use animal testing. . . ."

"It's an off-brand that smells exactly like the real thing. But absolutely *no* animal testing. I could send you a bottle for your wife, or your girl friend . . . ?"

"I don't have either. Have you had supper?"

"Why, no. That's what I was supposed to have, before I was stood up."

"You know," he said, grinning, "there's something you might like to see. Knowing your interest in animal rights."

Soon they were standing at a door on the seventh floor of the hotel. Room 714. The director was knocking.

"Stan? Are you in there?"

No answer.

"I have a key," Hughes said. He was just a little drunk. "Come on. . . ."

He opened the door and they were in a nice room—though not a suite—and on the bed was an unconscious man in his underwear. He was snoring loudly.

"Stan's the best trainer in the business," Hughes said, "but he's got a little problem with the bottle."

"Should we keep our voices down . . . ?"

"Don't bother. You set an atomic bomb off in here and Stan would saw logs right through it. Look at this!"

He was gesturing to a beautiful bushy-tailed foxlike cat, who had also been slumbering, but now raised its head to cast bored almond-shaped eyes upon these intruders.

"There's 'that damn cat,' " Hughes said.

She smiled. She bent over to have a better look; the cat cocked its head and purred lazily. "I never met a movie star before. It's amazing, in the one film I saw, the things this cat could do!"

"Amazing. Truly amazing. Now ... may I invite you to my room, for a late-night room-service supper?"

"You certainly may."

She talked him into letting her serve them a cocktail from the elaborate suite's wet bar before he could phone in a room-service order, and he was slipping an arm around her, risking a peck of a kiss, when the knockout powder kicked in.

He dropped to the floor like he was curtains and the rods had broken. She dug into his pocket and found the key to Room 714.

The shrill ring of the phone woke Todd. He looked at his Rolex. It was a little past midnight.

"Todd!" It was Julie, out of breath.

"Where are you?" he asked.

"In a hotel room at One Washington Circle." Her voice sounded strange.

"Did it go all right?" he asked.

"Yes!" she said, then. "No! I'll tell you when you get here ... take an elevator up to the seventh floor."

"What?"

"Just hurry up. I'll be waiting. I've found that 'something big' to get us back on our feet."

The phone clicked in his ear.

He put down the receiver, frowned at it, then smiled, and ran out to the car.

Todd walked casually through the lobby of the hotel—not too fast but not too slow. He didn't want to be noticed. Which was no trick, the lobby being relatively empty this time of night.

He stood at one of the large, bronze elevator doors and pushed the UP button. He patted his pockets, then fished around in them as if looking for his room key, in case anyone at the registration desk was watching, or some security guard in a back room somewhere had picked him up on a monitor.

The elevator door opened and he got on, and pressed the seventh-floor button. He faked a yawn—just a tired exec going back to his room after a boring evening with a client. The elevator door swished shut.

But on the seventh floor, when he got off, only long stretches of corridors greeted him. There was no Julie.

He stood there wondering what to do next, when a door opened about four rooms down, and Julie's black-wigged head popped out.

She beckoned to him animatedly with one hand.

Christ, he thought as he hurried along the plushly carpeted corridor, what the hell was this all about? Had she gone too far? Was he going to have to look at some dead guy's body?

Todd stepped inside the dimly lit room. Julie shut the door behind him.

She looked gleeful, and almost satanic, the way the shadows fell across her pretty face.

Todd shivered, then noticed the man sprawled across the bed. He was wearing ugly boxer shorts.

"Is he *dead*?" Todd whispered.

"Dead drunk's more like it," Julie smirked.

Todd moved toward the bed and looked more closely at the man.

"Jeez, babe," he whispered, "you're slipping . . . I can't imagine *this* geek's got much money."

"Never mind him," she said, "*there's* our ticket to paradise."

He followed her gaze to the head of the bed, where between two plump pillows lay a cat.

"What?" he asked, confused. "*That* damn cat?"

"Then you *do* know!"

"Know what?"

"About *That Damn Cat.*"

"What *about* that damn cat?" He raised his voice, irritated with her.

Suddenly the drunken, slumbering man on the bed gave out a quick snort. Todd and Julie froze. But the man returned to his labored breathing.

"Todd," Julie said in a hushed voice, "that damn cat is *That Damn Cat*!"

Somewhere in his head, a light bulb popped on. "The Washington *Post* did a feature on that cat," he said. "And how they were going to get to film at the White House. . . ." He paused and looked at the animal, which looked back at him as if understanding what he was saying. "But are you sure that's *the* cat?"

She told him about her encounter with the director.

He smiled, and started to reach for the cat, but quickly pulled back. "Isn't it dangerous?" he asked his wife. "Remember that scene from the second movie when it practically bit that guy's finger off?"

Julie just laughed and bent over to pick up the cat, which went limp in her hands. She held it against her bosom. It purred.

"I think it only responds to the trainer's commands," she said.

They both looked at the drunken, snoring man.

"Then let's get out of here," Todd said, "before he comes to and starts giving some."

Julie tucked the cat beneath her fur jacket.

At the door, Todd stopped. "You know," he told her, "that article said Lloyd's of London insured that cat for a million dollars!"

"Good," Julie said with a wicked little smile, "now we know how much money to ask for!"

Todd and Julie drove back down Pennsylvania Avenue in their convertible, with Todd behind the wheel and Julie next to him. The cat seemed content to be held in her arms, its face peeking out of her coat.

The street was nearly deserted now. Several limos streaked by, windows darkened, hiding some VIP no doubt, and a few cabbies were on the lookout for late-night customers. At a stoplight, Todd turned to Julie. "Maybe I should put the top up," he said.

She shook her head. "That might scare the cat," she replied.

He nodded, studying her; never had she looked so beautiful. Holding a million bucks' worth of cat did wonders for her.

"We're going to be so rich!" he grinned.

"We can trade the BMW for a Jaguar."

"And the townhouse for a mansion across the river."

"I love you," he said, meaning it.

"And I love you."

A car horn blared behind them.

"The light's turned green," Julie said.

"My favorite color. . . ."

Todd drove, the wind riffling his hair. He glanced over at Julie again. Her luscious lips were pursed in the sweetest smile . . . but Todd thought the cat looked strange.

Its head stuck farther out of her jacket, ears now pointing forward, eyes narrowed to tiny little slits.

Suddenly Julie shrieked as the cat clawed its way out of her coat, and leapt from her arms into the air, flying like some goddamn Super Cat, and disappeared over the side of the car.

Todd slammed on the brakes, tires squealing, and brought the car to a halt.

"There it is!" Julie shouted, pointing, looking back over her shoulder.

Todd could see the cat walking along in the gutter, then springing up on the reinforcement wall and running along it.

By the time Todd got out of the car, the cat had already jumped down from the barrier and was padding across the wide sidewalk, which was free from tourists and protesters in the early morning hour.

"Get it! Get it!" screamed Julie.

But Todd wasn't quick enough, and the cat disappeared through the White House fence.

"You *idiot*!" snapped Julie as she joined him on the sidewalk.

"Me?" he shouted. "If you'd let me put the top up on the car, this never would have happened!"

"Quit wasting time! Go over the fence and get it!"

"Are you *nuts*? I can't go in there!"

"Look!" she said, lowering her voice, pointing out onto the lawn. "It's just sitting there. . . ."

In the dark Todd could see the cat, not too far inside the fence.

"Go!" Julie said between clenched teeth. Then, almost spitting out the words, she said, "Do you want to lose a *million* bucks?"

Cursing, Todd grabbed the iron rods and began hauling himself up. The bars were cold and slippery. And at the top he had trouble getting over, and caught his Armani trousers on one of the sharp spear tips. *Rippppp*! went his expensive pants as he fell to the ground, cursing some more.

From a crouched position on the grass, Todd could see the cat, still sitting motionless. Good, he thought, he hadn't scared it. In the distance the White House looked dark and quiet.

"Hurry up!" Julie said from the other side of the fence.

Todd was rising to stand, when out of a bush stepped a uniformed cop. The officer had a mean, nasty look on his face, and a gun in one hand.

Startled, Todd jumped, then automatically threw his hands in the air.

"You're in a lot of trouble, pal," the cop said, and with his other hand threw the beam of a flashlight in Todd's face.

"Ah . . . look, officer," Todd stammered, squinting from the glare, "I was just trying to get my cat. . . ."

The cop flashed his light across the lawn, catching the animal in a circle of white. It sat almost bored.

"I don't care what your excuse is," the officer said gruffly, "this is restricted property, and you're under arrest."

Julie called out from the fence. "Oh, please!" she said. "Don't arrest him! It's all my fault . . . I made him go in there."

Now the cop shone his light on her.

She had hold of the fence, like a prisoner behind bars, pleading her innocence.

"The cat belongs to Senator Hartman," she explained convincingly. "We promised to take care of it for him. Please, officer, won't you help us? The senator will be so upset if anything happens to his pet."

Todd, hands still in the air, nodded sincerely. The cop seemed to vacillate. "Oh . . . all right," he finally said roughly, and lowered his gun.

"Thank you," Todd said gratefully, putting his hands down, "and I promise you, you'll never see us again."

The cop grunted, and put his gun away in his belt and motioned with his flashlight toward the cat, which still sat.

"Get it," he ordered.

"Can you help me?" Todd asked. "I'm afraid the cat doesn't know me very well."

The officer sighed irritably, but complied.

And the two men approached the animal from opposite sides.

The cat didn't move.

"Nice kitty kitty," the cop said. He was smiling, but the smile was nasty.

"Come to poppa," Todd said, arms outstretched.

As the two men dove to capture the animal, it shot out between them, and they cracked their heads together in a bone-crunching effect. With a Chaplinesque pratfall, the cop keeled over, knocked out cold. But not before the gun in his belt discharged, sending a bullet flying into Todd's foot.

He howled and grabbed that foot and joined the officer on the grass, writhing in pain.

The cat seemed unaware of all this, however, continuing its forward assault on the White House.

Now another uniformed policeman appeared. He had a snarling canine on a leash and the vicious dog, mouth peeled back showing sharp teeth, pulled the man along as it ran toward the car.

Once again, the feline stopped, and waited for the dog to draw near.

When the yapping canine had almost reached it, the cat took off, circling around the man, one, two, three times, and in a matter of seconds the cursing officer found himself tied up in the dog's heavy chain.

"Heel!" the cop hollered. But the dog tried to continue the chase, and the officer, legs bound by the leash, hit the lawn with a *whump*!

"Somebody get *that damn cat*!" the fallen man yelled.

But the silver sorrel Somali had already reached the north portico, and was triumphantly climbing the White House steps. At the top, it turned its head and looked back casually at the shambles it had left behind.

It almost seemed to smile.

Christopher Hughes sat on the edge of the bed in his hotel suite, still wearing the sweat suit he'd worn the preceding day. He held a cold washcloth to his forehead.

The director looked over with lidded eyes at the trainer, who sat on the couch nearby. The man, now in T-shirt and jeans, had an ice bag balanced on his head. The director wasn't sure who felt worse, on this morning after.

"I'm surprised at you," said the Secret Service agent who stood in front of Hughes, looking down his nose at him.

"A big Hollywood director like you," the guy continued with a smirk, "falling for a gag like that. I thought you were a city boy."

Hughes looked up at the agent—the one he had called a pompous jerk in shades—and opened his mouth to say something witty and cutting, but the thought never materialized in his still-doped brain, and the director closed his mouth again.

"You're lucky we recovered the cat," the agent said, gesturing to the animal that lay curled next to the trainer on the couch. "It was the president that recognized it . . . woke him up in all the commotion." The agent laughed. "I think that damn cat would have sat on the portico waiting for its next cue until hell froze over!"

Hughes just sighed.

"And," the Secret Service agent continued, "it didn't take much for that couple to turn on each other—and turn each other in . . . their kind always does."

The agent frowned and stepped closer to Hughes. "Well?" he said. "You don't seem very grateful your cat was recovered. The paper said that cat's worth a million dollars."

Hughes looked up at the agent and smiled slowly. "And here I thought *you* were a city boy. . . ."

"What do you mean?"

"I mean that's Hollywood hype."

"Hype?" the agent asked, confused.

Hughes grinned. "That cat's not insured for a million dollars. And there's not just *one* cat, there's a dozen of the damn things . . . maybe two." The director raised both hands and started checking off fingers. "One that does the cute closeup shots, one that climbs a ladder, another that high-dives into a pool . . . hell," he gestured to the slumbering cat on the sofa, its back rising and falling peacefully, "running berserk on a lawn is all *that* damn cat can do!"

Carole Nelson Douglas has written so well in so many genres and sub-genres that it's not exactly correct to call her a "mystery" writer, though mystery remains her first love. The Irene Adler books and the Midnight Louie books are making her a star in our field. But in addition to those, look up her two fine science fiction thrillers, *Probe* and *Counterprobe*. And then, of course, there are her very good high fantasies. And her romances . . .

Parris Green
CAROLE NELSON DOUGLAS
London: November 1886

I find no Sunday morning task more satisfying than that of rousing the slothful. Doubtless this is due to my upbringing as a parson's daughter, but it was aggravated by my days as a governess.

In this case the object of my dutiful disturbance had more reason than most to lie abed. Nonetheless, I crossed the threshold of her bedchamber with a certain smug rectitude. I, after all, had already been to church that morning, and she had not been to church in all of our acquaintance, unless it was to sing a solo.

The room lay beneath the drawn-curtain pall of half shadow that speaks of the sick chamber or the place of ill repute. A figure in the corner lurked motionless; luckily, I knew it for a dressmaker's form called "Jersey Lillie." I moved slowly to avoid stubbing a boot toe against the maze of trunks and hatboxes that lay scattered through the dim room. In due time I arrived safe and silent at the window, where I wrenched open the heavy brocade panels on their rods so swiftly that the curtain rings . . . well, rang.

"Agh!"

The bedclothes rose like a disturbed spirit as daylight scalded the coverlet,

103

then a head emerged from under the linens. My friend and chambermate Irene
Adler sat blinking in the sudden brightness.

"What on earth is it, Nell? Flood? Fire? The Apocalypse?"

"It is nearly noon on Sunday, Irene," I replied. "And that awful man has
called again."

She pushed tumbling locks of russet hair from her face, her eyes still wincing
at the light. Irene would never go to bed braided like a sensible woman.
"Awful man—oh, you mean that Norton creature who stormed our lodgings
a few weeks ago. Well, send him away!"

She swiftly grasped her coverlet—an oceanic expanse of emerald-green brocade that had begun as draperies—and coiled into an indiscernible lump under
the covers.

I went over to address this interesting cocoon.

"It is not that Norton creature. It is that odious self-appointed poet. He is
wearing brown velveteen breeches with yellow hose, an orange vest, and a
soft hat the color of rust. On the Sabbath," I finished with indignation, if
not relevancy.

"Oh." The buried form flailed to the surface again, finally flinging away a
tidal wave of green. "You mean Oscar Wilde. I believe that he has Roman
Catholic leanings. Perhaps that explains his gaudy Sunday attire. What does
he want?"

"You."

"He said nothing more than that?"

"He said a great deal more, but none of it made much sense."

"What time is it?" she asked with a frown.

I consulted the watch on my lapel. "Eleven."

"Eleven? How ghastly." Amid a froth of nightgown, Irene squirmed to the
bed's edge and swung a bare foot over the erratically carpeted floor. She
yawned. "He must have been at the theater last evening, too. What urgent
matter—imagined or real—could drag Oscar Wilde from his bed at such an
inopportune hour? Oh, very well. I'll come see for myself as soon as I'm
presentable. In the meantime, entertain him, Nell."

"How?"

"Make conversation."

"I cannot talk to the man! He is so full of elaborate nonsense that he quite
makes my head ache and my tongue tie."

"Of course you can talk to him. Oscar Wilde could make conversation with
a cockroach."

"Perhaps I should provide an audience of such, which will better appreciate
his company."

"The longer you dawdle here, the longer it shall be before I can emerge to
relieve you," Irene pointed out sweetly.

I sighed and returned to our parlor, where a very large and colorful spider awaited his sacrificial fly.

"Ah, the fair and faithful Penelope," he greeted me, presuming to employ my Christian name. "Four seductive syllables that end with o-p-e. Add the *H* from Huxleigh and you have all men's hope. Ope the door to my soul, my Psyche with a crochet hook."

I refused to rise to his ludicrous bait. Soon Mr. Wilde was safely discoursing on his favorite subject, himself, and quoting Mr. Whistler's cruel letter about him in *The World:* " 'He dines at our tables and picks from our platters the plums for the pudding he peddles in the provinces.' An outp-p-p-ouring of p-p-pathetically p-p-poor alliteration," Mr. Wilde stuttered mockingly in complaint. I never knew a man to thrive so on insult.

At last came the soft click of Irene's bedchamber door. This subtle sound was followed by the crackle of what I recognized as her crimson Oriental wrapper, hardly the proper garb in which to receive a gentleman caller on any day of the week, but the theatrical temperament will not be denied.

I saw our guest's long, slightly melancholy face brighten as if dashed with a dose of daylight, and turned to watch her arrival myself. At least she had put her hair up into a brunette satin arrangement of tendrils and chignon that glinted red and gold in the daylight.

"You must forgive me for calling at so inopportune a time, my dear Irene," the abominable Oscar began. "You have sung late at the theater and deserve to slumber undisturbed until twilight. I have given you scarce time to attire yourself, but one can never catch you *en déshabillé,* I suspect. You look splendid—like a savage empress from the court of Xanadu."

"Thank you," she said simply, sitting on the old armchair with its embroidered shawl hiding the wear. She crossed a leg over the other with a crackle of elderly silk sharper than paper rustling. A dainty foot just visible in its purple satin slipper swung in measured pendulum time. "Why am I so honored to have Oscar Wilde serving as my personal Chanticleer?"

"An ugly hour," he admitted with a sigh. "But an uglier event unfolds only miles away," he declaimed. That is another thing I have never liked about the man, his endless bent for self-dramatization. "A tragedy in the making, even as we speak."

Irene laughed. "My dear Oscar, at least half a million tragedies are in the making of a Sunday morning in London town. What is so special about yours?"

He sat on the fringed ottoman by the fireplace—an unfortunate choice, for the low seat jackknifed his long awkward legs like a stork's—and pushed the spaniel's ears of silky brown hair from his face. "It is perplexing. And scandalous."

"Ah." Irene's idle foot tapped the floor smartly. "You are consulting me about another . . . case." She had recently and successfully inquired into the whereabouts of a gold cross he had given to Florence Stoker when she was still Florence Balcombe.

He nodded soberly. "Have you heard of the artist Lysander Parris?" When Irene shook her head, he waved a languid hand. "No matter. He is not very successful—one of these dedicated souls who lived in Chelsea before it became fashionable, a neighbor of mine. He could earn more from selling his house than from his entire collection of works."

"An impecunious artist—a redundant description if I ever heard one. Are not all artists impecunious?" Irene asked ruefully. "What difficulty faces this Lysander Parris that makes him of any interest beyond a passing charitable instinct?"

"He has gone mad."

Irene waited. Mad artists, she might have pointed out, were no more notable than poor ones.

"Quite mad," Mr. Wilde repeated, rising to pace on the worn runner before the fireplace. When a man of more than six feet paces before two seated women, the effect commands their attention, if not their admiration. "He has barricaded himself in the attic studio with his latest model and will not cease painting her. He will answer no knock, take no food or drink, say nothing to his distraught wife and children. He will not even talk to me," Mr. Wilde added with utter disbelief.

"I cannot imagine that," Irene commented. "Can you, Nell?"

I murmured something indecipherable.

"Artists," she added loftily, "are given to such obsessive spates of work. No doubt he will emerge when his latest painting is done, or he is hungry and thirsty enough. Or when the exhausted model demands to leave."

"No." Oscar Wilde paused before our hearth, one hand thrust into the breast of his velveteen jacket. His momentary stillness and silence were ever so much more impressive than his chatter and clatter. "The exhausted model will not demand to leave. From all I can determine, she is dead."

Within the half hour, our mismatched trio was jolting along in a four-wheeler toward Chelsea. Irene had dressed in a striking bronze satin gown bordered with rose moiré, and she donned long, tan-colored gloves in the carriage.

"Tell me of the household," she instructed even as she thrust the final pins into her rose moiré bonnet. Its pink and white plumes trembled in protest of such treatment.

Mr. Wilde complied with far more grace than he had managed in whistling for the vehicle minutes before. He folded his hands atop his cane—his gloves at least were conventional, the color of spoiled clotted cream—and began with an odd smile.

"The household. What can one say of any painter's household? It is as irregular as his compositions may be symmetrical. I should begin with Parris himself. He is a man of late middle age, of no distinguishing social graces, who has achieved fame in only one arena: for the lovely, decadent, lush, languid, gorgeous, gilded, intricate greens that signal his work. He is a master of the color green. I cannot look at an acanthus leaf or meet the eye of a peacock's tail, or view the emerald on the forehead of the goddess Kali, but that I think of it as Parris green.''

"I presume that Mr. Parris is not Irish?" I asked somewhat tartly.

The poet's supercilious eye rested upon me with contempt. "I fear not, but you mistake my passion for green, dear Miss Huxleigh. I adore green not as a patriotic symbol but as the lost shadow of Eden in our world today; as the occult flame of jealousy; as the velvety unseen mosses that clothe and conquer the stone; as the ageless power in the very pinpoint of a cat's eye.''

I could not help shuddering. "I do not care for cats. Or green.''

"Of course not," Mr. Wilde said with something of pity in his voice. He turned to Irene. "Has my description been of assistance?''

"Of course not," she echoed him, "that is why your descriptions are always so enchanting. Mere usefulness would destroy their effect. Tell me, if you can, of the other inhabitants of the house, including the model who is now an apparent epitome of the still life.''

I shuddered again, but was not much noticed. Irene had an unfortunate talent for matching gloomy poetic maunderings macabre stroke for macabre stroke. No doubt it came of too long study of excessively mordant opera librettos— all blood and betrayal and death. In fact, her eyes sparkled with mischief behind the clouds of her veiling as she watched the poet struggle to report mere fact instead of fancy.

"As well compose a sonnet from a laundry list," he said sniffling. "Very well, the dramatis personae as recited by Bottom: We have the artist in question. We have his latest model, a pale and interesting girl employed as a housemaid, whom he has elevated from her knees on the kitchen stones to similar poses on a studio couch.''

"A kitchen maid? How long has Mr. Parris been so taken with her?''

"For months, say the gossips along Tite Street.''

"What of the artist's family?''

"His wife is an industrious little woman, much given to worrying, as any artist's spouse must.''

"Speaking of which," Irene injected, "I understand that I am to congratulate you upon the birth of a second son.''

Our fellow passenger sighed, a slight smile on his strong-bowed lips. "Vyvyan.''

"A lovely name," Irene said.

"Lovelier for a daughter, perhaps. I had hopes, but—''

"How commendable," I put in, "for a father to desire a daughter rather than an endless parade of sons."

"Praise, Miss Huxleigh?" Mr. Wilde's eyes were wickedly amused, as if he well understood how much he scandalized me. "I fear I had nothing to do with it. A higher power than mere hope determined the matter."

"And how is Constance?" Irene inquired.

"Well," he said of his wife, flicking a spot of lint from his velvet knee. "Better than Amelia Parris, poor woman. Her husband's mania for the new model has been the talk of Chelsea, but Mrs. Parris is a simple soul who cares more for the price of eggs than the bankruptcy of reputation."

"What other family members inhabit the house?"

"The usual parade of offspring, most young enough for the schoolroom, except for Lawrence."

"The eldest son?"

Mr. Wilde nodded, then leaned his slouch-hatted head out of the carriage window. For such gestures his unorthodox headgear was more suitable than the conventional top hat. "We near Cheyne Place. I will let you see young Lawrence for yourself."

Once the carriage had jolted to a stop, he stepped out to assist us. I hated to take the creature's hand, but there was no help for it. Nor could I forgo murmuring my thanks. I cannot say why I had taken such a dislike to Mr. Wilde; there was no more reason for it than for his taking such a mad fancy to me. Perhaps, like the clever puss, he made a point of loving those who hated him. I suppose that could be considered a kind of Christian charity, but in Mr. Wilde's case I felt that the impulse was far more perverse.

We stood for a moment on the cobblestones, surveying the house. Unlike many in fashionable Tite Street, where even I knew that such artists as Whistler and Sargent kept studios, this house had not been revived with fresh, stylish colors. A smoky patina fumed its dull brick facade, and the door was painted a sober but chipping black, as if in tawdry mourning.

Faded damask draped the windows, all in sinister shades of green.

"Why do you think Mr. Parris became so obsessed with his model?" Irene asked the poet.

"She was young and from outside this depressing house. He thought her beautiful, no doubt. Perhaps he had tired of failure and growing older, and painted a more appetizing future on his canvases."

"If you have been unable to enter the studio, why are you convinced that she is dead?"

"It is possible to view a section of the room through a ... er, keyhole. Yes, Miss Huxleigh, to such vulgar snooping even I was forced to stoop." Mr. Wilde eyed Irene again. "Parris had a strong lock put on the inside of the door years ago. He has always disliked being interrupted while painting. I can only attest to what little I saw with my own eyes: the lady in question not only is supernaturally motionless, but her pallor is beyond the ordinary pale of fashionable rice powder. Her lips have turned blue.''

I made an involuntary cry at this macabre detail, but Irene merely narrowed her eyes as if to better visualize the grisly scene. ''And what do you think has killed her? Or who?''

''That I am afraid to speculate upon,'' the poet admitted.

''Poor Parris must be made to forsake his studio so that the lady's body can be carried away before the neighbors and the police scent a scandal.''

''My dear Oscar, when the young woman's dead body is carried away, there is certain to be a scandal if her death was not natural.''

''No death is natural,'' he declared, launching another high-flown speech. ''A death should always be witnessed by a great poet, so that proper note may be taken of it.''

''I really do not see what you expect me to do in this instance,'' Irene said, ignoring his egocentric prescription for death scenes.

''Pry the madman loose from his easel! Although they do not know the depth of my suspicion, his wife and son cannot do it, despite all their beyond-the-door pleadings; that is why I was sent for. I know Parris well, and in fact had obtained him some meager employment for illustrations in the literary magazines,'' he added. ''Not my most eloquent words nor gilded syllables could wrest the man from his feverish painting. I count upon your woman's wit, my dear Irene. Besides, few men can resist you.''

She smiled ruefully. ''I encountered one of that rare breed only weeks ago.''

''No!'' Mr. Wilde drew back, clutching his breast. ''What manner of depraved creature is he?''

''A barrister,'' Irene answered dryly.

''Oh.'' The poet recovered his aplomb and dropped his theatrics. ''One cannot expect intelligence or sense from a barrister. My faith in your powers remains undiminished.''

''We shall see,'' Irene answered. ''Meanwhile—'' She gestured to the rather grimy stoop that awaited our footfalls.

The house was as I expected: dark and narrow, with a battered spine of stairway and that stale wet odor of domiciles built near the supposed advantage of a river.

A woman admitted us, a stern figure in black bombazine who might have been a widow. She identified herself as ''Mrs. McCorkle, the housekeeper'' in a voice like a hacksaw and regarded Mr. Wilde with visible skepticism. Mrs. Parris, we were told, lay prostrate in her bedchamber; the children visited the homes of assorted acquaintances, who had been told only that their father had fallen suddenly ill; Mr. Parris still kept to his studio.

''These ladies,'' said Mr. Wilde, gesturing to us both with one sweep of a plump hand, ''these lovely sibyls of Saffron Hill, will lend wisdom and succor to a sad situation. Miss Adler, Miss Huxleigh, and I will need no guidance to the upper stories.''

"As you wish, sir," the woman answered sourly. "No one is here to gainsay you." She eyed Irene and myself as if we were dingy laundry, then retreated into the dismal drawing room on our left.

We climbed the dark, uncarpeted stairs, a landing window offering a glimpse of neglected back garden gone to weed and wildness. Up we went, for what seemed endless turns of the ungracious stairs but was only four stories.

At last the stairs ended at a broad wooden door.

"Much of the top floor has been made into a studio," Mr. Wilde informed us in a whisper.

I saw why it had been so convenient to view the room. With the steps leading up to the door, one could stand two or three risers down, lean forward, and be eye level with the peephole.

Mr. Wilde demonstrated by backing down four steps and doing precisely that. Irene and I flattened ourselves against the yellowing walls, while I contemplated a larger and more intimate view of the poet's velvet breeches than I wished.

He finally unbent with an almost satisfied sigh. "Nothing has changed. Not the model, nor the sounds of paint slap-dashing on canvas. Parris works on quite assiduously."

"Allow me." Irene assumed the same undignified posture with much more grace and squinted through the brass keyhole. She straightened a moment later, looking less optimistic than the poet. "The long plait of hair that entwines her throat," she asked him, "was it there before?"

"It entwines her throat?" He blinked like a cogitating owl. "I confess I was more impressed by her pallor than the disposition of her tresses. I have never been partial to that unimaginative shade of chestnut. You believe that Parris strangled her with her own hair? A most artistic conceit. I would not have thought it of him."

"Or a most conceited artist, to think that a model would care to die for a painting. The question is how she was posed before she died. Mr. Parris may have planned another of these languishing ladies mimicking death so popular in the salons—Ophelia floating amid her waterlilies, or Desdemona adrift on her bed linens. The woman's pallor could be merely cosmetic; she could keep so still simply because she is an accomplished model."

I clasped my hands. "Oh, Irene, of course! This is all a silly misunderstanding. We need not have come here at all." I gave Mr. Wilde a pointed look.

She regarded me fondly. "However, I must confess in turn that she looks quite convincingly dead. Mr. Parris will not open the door?"

The poet shook his head until his doleful locks rippled.

Irene lifted a fist and knocked briskly.

"Go away!" a voice thundered promptly. "I told you meddling fools to go away. I am not finished yet."

"Mr. Parris, sir," she replied, "your family is most concerned, and no doubt your model is . . . exhausted."

"Go away, damn, impertinent disrupters! I must put it on canvas. I must capture that look—"

"And we all are impatient to see the results of your labors. Even Oscar Wilde is here, waiting to tell a wider world about your work."

"That fulminating fop! He tells no one about anything other than himself! I told him to leave my house, and you may go, too, madam, whoever the devil you are."

Irene drew back, then lowered her gloved fist.

"Well?" Mr. Wilde asked breathlessly.

"We retreat," she ordered. With great difficulty, and much unwelcome jostling, we turned in the cramped stairway and made our sorry progress below.

At the first landing Irene drew Mr. Wilde to a stop. "Are Mr. Parris's paintings kept anywhere besides the studio?"

"I saw a number of canvases in a second-floor room."

"Then I would like to see them."

"Why?" I asked. "Surely there is nothing we can do here. The man's door is bolted from within and he will not open it. It is a matter for the authorities."

"Perhaps," Irene conceded. "Ultimately. Until then, if the artist refuses to speak with me, I will make do with the next best thing: I will commune with his work."

Mr. Wilde lifted his eyebrows, but led us without comment to the room in question.

Within minutes Irene and Mr. Wilde had pulled the stacked canvases from the wall and had propped them against the furniture. Most of the canvases were narrow, and as tall as people.

Oscar Wilde made a face, which was not difficult for him to do under any circumstances. "Not to my taste."

"What is your taste?" Irene asked.

"*San Sebastian* by Guido Reni," he retorted with authority. "A sublime subject."

"Ah." Irene tilted her head with a Mona Lisa smile. "The swooning, half-naked young man pierced by arrows. How . . . interesting, Oscar."

"The martydom of St. Stephen!" I exclaimed, happy to have understood what they were talking about for once. "I know it. A most inspirational subject, though sad."

His smile was as mysterious as Irene's. "More inspiring than these modern, insipidly lethal belladonna madonnas cloaked in green, whose suffering is so much more commonplace."

I studied the array. We stood amid a company of the dead model's likeness in every guise, her long dark hair caught up in a jeweled snood while she strolled in classical garb with a peacock—"Jealous *Juno*," Irene pronounced; or she hung suspended in weed-swirled water clothed in mermaid's scales, a drowned sailor caught in the toils of her seaweed-dressed locks—*The Siren of the Rhine*, according to Irene; or she floated in diaphanous veils of lurid green from a bottle bearing a French label.

Irene nodded at the last work. "*La Fée Verte*—the seductive green fairy of absinthe, the liquor that entoils men and drives them mad. Does Mr. Parris drink it?"

Mr. Wilde shrugged. "Perhaps. All these . . . fancies feature the green pigments for which he is famous."

She nodded. "Parris green. Most effective. Most decadent. Is not arsenic a component of such green pigments?"

"Arsenic? I have heard—" Mr. Wilde's pasty complexion showed a more verdant cast. "You think that . . . ? I cannot see how."

"Nor can I. I merely comment on the fact that Mr. Parris's addiction to green has a deadly undertone. Of course, one would expect a pigment-based poison to affect the artist, not his model."

Irene strolled around the assembled pictures, contemplating their heavy-lidded subject face-to-face. "Mr. Parris's mania seems fixed upon the femme fatale, the kind of ruinous woman who preys upon men. One seldom sees the ruiners of women glamorized, perhaps because so few women paint, or are encouraged to. Yet the legions of ruined women must far outnumber the few men who stumble at the feet of a Delilah. At least my art—the opera—offers equal roles in villainy and heroics to men and women."

"Your art," the poet put in, "has an edge."

"So," said I, "does Irene. "And if she wishes a perfect model of an *homme fatale*, she need look no further than that Mephistopheles in miniature, the American artist, James Whistler."

Oscar Wilde laughed. "My neighbor, my mentor, my enemy, but then Jimmy is everybody's enemy, and his own most of all. A pity that he so seldom does self-portraits."

"Wicked women are too common these days to be intriguing," Irene put in. "It's Mr. Parris's heroines who intrigue me. Such unusual choices."

I studied the canvas she tilted into the light of the gasolier. Gone was the turgid hair; the figure's cropped head and rough masculine dress proclaimed Joan of Arc, if the copious fleurs-de-lis in the background had not already given away the subject.

Irene examined the brush marks. "From the looser strokes, a recent work, I would suggest. And this. What do you think, Nell?"

She indicated a female figure in long Renaissance robes, again the fleurs-de-lis figuring her gown, but a stern, almost fanatical expression on her gaunt, impassioned face.

"Can you guess, Oscar? No? Is this not a Daniel come to judgment? The female Torquemada of Mr. Shakespeare's plays?"

"Portia!" said I. "The artist marches to a grimmer tune of late."

"Indeed." Irene let the canvas lean back against the table and turned to a humble assembly near the window. "But what are these? They look intriguing."

"Hatboxes! Truly, Irene, you have a great quantity more than you need at home."

"But not so charmingly covered—with wallpaper—and some cut so the design of one lays against the pattern of another. Oh, I must have one—or several!"

"Easily done." Oscar Wilde exhibited the amused tolerance a man expends on a woman taken by something trivial. "Amelia's fancywork. She sells them to the ladies hereabout. I don't doubt that it shoes the children's feet. With Parris devoted to his mania for the servant girl model, he can't have sold much work of late."

"Well." Irene turned from the hatboxes. "To work. I must interview the vital members of the household. Mrs. Parris, her eldest son, and perhaps the so charming lady who answered the door. The children, I think, can be left to their ignorance. Bring me Mrs. Parris first. Tell her that I am interested in hatboxes."

The poet took no offense at being commissioned as a messenger. He withdrew to be replaced some few minutes later by a compact woman with fading brown hair. Her navy serge skirt's telltale box pleats and draped bustle indicated that it had been purchased several years before. Her face was as well worn as her gown, the eyes a wan blue set in dark circles of skin, but there was no sign of recent tears or hysterics.

"My dear Mrs. Parris!" Irene's voice warmed with welcome, as if she were the householder and Amelia Parris the visitor. "How good of you to meet with us. Oscar has hopes that I can persuade your husband to abandon his studio."

"Why should he listen to you?" Mrs. Parris inquired a trifle sharply. "I have never heard of an Irene Adler."

"Because Oscar has decided that he must. I am a singer you see, and poor Oscar is convinced that my voice can soothe the savage beast."

"Lysander is not particularly savage." Mrs. Parris sighed and tucked a dull lock of hair behind one ear. "Or at least he was not known to be. Before . . ."

"Before?"

"Before he developed a mania for one particular model."

"He has not had such a single-minded fancy previously?"

Mrs. Parris's features puckered listlessly. "There were models, of course, often the subjects of a series of paintings. That is why he put a lock on the inside of the studio door. He did not wish anyone to see his work in progress."

"When was the lock installed?"

She shrugged as listlessly as her face changed expressions. "Some years ago, perhaps six."

"Six," Irene repeated for no apparent reason, spinning away from the paintings. "What I am simply mad about are these enchanting hatboxes of yours, Mrs. Parris. You use—pardon the pun—Paris papers, do you not?"

A flush warmed the woman's drawn cheeks. "Why, yes. Thank you. However did you know?"

Irene dropped into a graceful crouch that only an actress could manage without seeming in imminent danger of toppling. She studied the piled round boxes with the intensity of a happy child.

"Why, by the patterns. None but the French show such whimsy, such joie de vivre—or use so many Napoleonic bees." Her gloved forefinger tapped an example of the latter. "But I do not see a single fleur-de-lis."

"I suppose not," Mrs. Parris admitted, "although I find the flower designs ... cheerful."

"And you appliqué one paper atop the ground of another, like lace," Irene went on admiringly. "How utterly clever."

Again the sullen cheeks burnished with pleasure at praise rubbed on so warmly. "I am not considered a clever person ordinarily," Mrs. Parris said, "but the ladies of Chelsea find my small efforts appealing."

Irene rose, her bronze silk skirts falling into folds around her, like a theatrical curtain descending after a performance. "I must have at least one—and one for my dear friend Miss Huxleigh."

"Oh, no—" I began to object.

"Nonsense, Nell." Irene's stage-trained voice drowned out my demurs without sounding rude. "You have been longing for the right hatbox; I am certain of it. Which one do you want?"

"I don't know," I began, meaning to say that I didn't even know the price of such a frivolity.

"Impossible to decide on just one." Irene turned again to the now openly pleased woman. "How do you choose which pattern to use? They are all so enchanting."

Mrs. Parris ducked her head in an odd combination of shyness and shame. "Many houses hereabouts are being redecorated in the new aesthetic manner. Some are old papers taken down; others remnants of the replacements. The ladies of the house see that I get them; I am awash in wallpapers."

"Wonderful," marveled Irene, adding in a kindly tone, "No doubt the sales of these lovely things come in handy in an artistic household."

The poor woman was so flushed by now that she could blush no more. Her answer flowed like paint from a brush. "Oh, yes. An artist's lot is hand to mouth, and so also for his family. Lawrence can only spare so much from his position."

"Your son. With a position. How proud you must be."

"He is only a clerk in the City. His father calls such employment 'tattooing with a goose quill for an association of geese,' but it brings in a regular salary."

Irene smiled. "I fear I share the artistic suspicion of matters mathematical, like accounting."

"You are utterly charming, Miss Adler," Mrs. Parris said suddenly, her face saddening again. "If anyone can coax Lysander from his ... mania, you can."

"Thank you," Irene said. "I will try, and try again, until I succeed. And then I will reward myself and Miss Huxleigh by purchasing two of your little masterpieces."

"No—a gift."

"We will debate that when I have earned the privilege," Irene insisted. "And now, I wonder, is your hardworking son at home?"

Mrs. Parris blinked at the sudden change in topic. "I believe he is below stairs. I will send him up, if you wish."

Irene beamed. "I do."

The moment the woman's skirts had hissed into the uncarpeted hall I broke my commendable silence with a stage whisper. "Irene! I do not require a hatbox."

"Are they not charming and original?"

"Yes! But my funds—our funds—are unoriginally meager."

She waved an airy hand. "Money can always be found for small necessities."

"Hatboxes?"

"Hush. I hear a firm tread on the stair."

In a moment a young man's form followed the sound of his approach into the room. He saw first us, then the array of propped-up paintings, and stopped at the threshold, frowning. "My mother said you wished to see me. Miss Adler, is it?"

"Mr. Wilde and I are concerned about your father," Irene said calmly.

He concealed sudden fists in his pants pockets, a graceless gesture that I should never have allowed in any charge of mine during my governess days.

"Father can go to hell, if he hasn't already," young Lawrence announced through his teeth.

I drew in my breath, but Irene remained unshaken. "You disapprove of your father's obsession with his model. Yet often such artistic obsessions produce many canvases and much money."

"Father's paintings are the fancy of a failing mind. That 'famous' Parris green you see there has eaten him away like some festering mental moss. An old fool has no right to be forcing himself on servant girls and elevating them to heights where they cannot keep their heads. Who does she think *she* is?" His broad gesture dismissed the model's many guises. "Who does he think *he* is—an old man whose fancy flies in the face of his family honor. Nobody. He should sign his damned puddles of putrid green 'Nobody.' "

"I take it that you do not approve of your father's calling when it becomes obsession."

"I do not approve of calling it art when it is something much more obvious. He has a mania for *her*, not for his paintings of her. He has painted her half to death, until she has exhausted herself into a shadow, and now he rushes to finish painting her before the sun sinks and even a shadow is too weak to be seen. May I go now? I do not like to see so many shadows spun through the poisonous web of his paintbrush."

He had turned on his heel before Irene could finish saying, "Leave if you must."

Again we were alone in the room, and I was mystified, "The young man disapproves of his father's mania, and rightly so. His mother is slighted by such obsessions, even if there's no harm in it."

"Oh, there's harm in it." Irene's face hardened to alabaster, as it often did when she confronted something dangerous. "Deep poison. Parris green poison."

"In the paints?" I asked, confused.

She turned to me. "In the paints, and in the persons who share the roof of this unhappy domicile."

"What poison is there beyond the arsenic pigment you mentioned?"

"Jealousy," she said obliquely. "And on that note, it is time to interview the key figure in this domestic tragedy."

She went to the door, where I was surprised to find that Oscar Wilde stood modest guard, and whispered something to our conductor into this den of death and deception. He vanished with a clatter of boots down the stairs. I found my stare passing numbly from the many paintings of a possibly murdered girl in shades of green to the gay towers of hatboxes awaiting owners. I saw all, but I saw nothing.

A more discreet set of steps announced a surprising person: the sour servant who had admitted us to the house.

Irene began without frills. "You are aware that your master has locked himself in the studio."

" 'Tis nothing new," the woman replied.

I had seen her sort before in the houses in which I was a governess: hardened by service into sullen semicooperation, slow to say anything yet quick to see all. She would give only what she had to, and that grudgingly.

"What is the situation here?" Irene asked.

"I thought you knew."

"I meant your own."

A rough shrug, one a world away from the timid gesture of Mrs. Parris. "I cook, clean if I have to, which I have to when the cleaning girl is lounging on a scarlet shawl under the eaves for the pleasure of the master's paintbrush.''

"Where do you sleep?"

Irene's question surprised the woman. "Under the eaves. Not all of the fourth story is given over to art. I have a room off the little landing just below there."

"And she?"

"She?"

"Your sister servant."

"Huh! She's no sister of mine, Phoebe Miller." The woman brushed the back of her hand across her nose. "She's got a cubbyhole, too, though she's not been in it lately."

"Some would suspect a man, a painter with a passion for depicting women, of harboring a passion for his model as well as his art. Do you?"

"Gossip is not my job, miss."

"I am not asking gossip. I am asking what you saw and heard."

"Saw and heard?" Mrs. McCorkle's face showed wary confusion.

"In your room. Under the eaves. Did the master ever visit the maid?"

The woman's feet shuffled uneasily on the floor, but Irene was implacable—a force that must be answered. A mistress interrogating a servant. Mrs. McCorkle finally spoke, her plain voice curdled with a thin scum of contempt.

"I heard noises. Footsteps. At night. The servant's stairs are narrow and dark. A light would slither along the crack under my door like a yellow snake. Footsteps from the bottom to the top. Sometimes they didn't go all the way up. Sometimes they stopped halfway." She frowned. "And sometimes they went all the way up, and came down soft so I couldn't hear, and went up halfway again. Did the master visit the maid, miss? Do snakes slither?"

Irene took a leisurely turn around the room, holding our attention as a strolling actor does. "What do you think of the young woman who models for Mr. Parris?"

"What I think doesn't matter."

"To me it does."

"Oh, you're nice, aren't you? Asking so sweet and sharp. Never wrinkling a brow or your petticoats. Well, I'll tell you, Miss Who Wants to Know! I'll tell you what it's like to be scrubbing the stoop and washing the stairs and the kettles and some so-called 'girl' is taking her ease behind locked doors and turning up with her face leering out for everyone to see—even his wife and son and little children."

Irene nodded, undisturbed. "What do you think of her?" she repeated softly.

"Isn't much to look at. Not really, especially now she's so thin and pale. Master must be losing more than his mind of late; eyesight more likely. Quiet, Phoebe is. Never looks at you straight—always cringing on the back stairs when we meet, like she expects me to hit her. I suppose she was steady enough at her work before the master brought her up to the studio.'' The woman frowned. "But she was always the favorite. There was the kitten, you see."

"Kitten?" Irene asked alertly.

"Starved wisp of a thing Phoebe found by the embankment. We're not allowed kittens in servants' quarters, though there be mice enough for 'em. This one was too young for mice—all fuzz and bone. Phoebe would feed it scraps from below. Not allowed, that. But no one took it from her."

"Perhaps no one knew," I put in, breaking the long silence I had kept as I watched Irene pull answers from this woman as a dental surgeon pulls rotten molars from diseased gums.

Mrs. McCorkle's harsh gaze turned on me. "Oh, someone knew, all right. The creature would mew something fierce when she left it alone all day. On and on. *He'd* have heard it, on the other side of the wall, working at his quiet painting. But he never said nothing; his favorite could have certain favors, you see."

"And Mrs. Parris was unaware of the kitten?"

"How would she know? Now there's a real lady, for all she has to hawk her hatboxes to her very own neighbors to pay for food on the table and the few pence servants cost. A sweet, honest soul. She didn't ignore me like I was a doormat to see only in coming and going. She even took some of them fancy papers she got from the likes of Mr. Whistler and Mrs. Wilde and put 'em up herself in my room—a real pretty pattern of these yellow birds and flowers, twining like. Brightened up the place. She even papered Phoebe's cubbyhole. I'll give that to Mrs. Parris. She's a charitable soul who sees past evil to do good."

"You mean that Mr. Parris's obsession with Phoebe was already evident when his wife papered the servants' quarters?"

"To all but the blind."

"Then Mrs. Parris must have seen the kitten," Irene suggested, "and said nothing."

Mrs. McCorkle shook her head. "No. It was dead by then."

"Dead!" I exclaimed weakly. I had been touched by the tale of a kitten that had found a home with the servants under the eaves.

Mrs. McCorkle nodded with weary callousness. "Too young, too ill-used. It stopped eating and retched its little insides out. They seldom survive when they're taken too young from the mother. Phoebe was a fool to try to save it."

"You may go," Irene said suddenly, as if disgusted.

Mrs. McCorkle caught her tone and flushed a bit, but turned without comment.

"You must be overrun with mice now," Irene added as suddenly.

"Mice?" Mrs. McCorkle stopped without turning. "No, don't hear them anymore. Maybe that silly kitten did some good before it died. I could use some quiet in the servants' quarters." She walked through the door. Shortly after we heard her discreet step on the stairs.

"The treads do creak in these old houses," Irene observed. "Imagine how they scream in the servants' stairway. What a story there is in a flight of stairs!"

Oscar Wilde's unwelcome face popped around the doorjamb like a puppet's at a Punch and Judy show. "I am aquiver with curiosity, dear Irene, and could barely remain away, save that I know an artist needs solitude to work. What have you learned, and how are we to release Parris from his lair and prevent a scandal?"

"I'm afraid that there is no way to prevent a scandal," Irene declared.

The poet fully entered the chamber. "That is the wonder you needed to work."

"I am not a wonder worker. As for Mr. Parris, I know of only one way to extract him."

"How?" Oscar Wilde demanded.

"Come and see." She swept from the room and I heard her firm, quick step on the front stairs as she ascended once again to the locked door.

We followed her mutely, the great lumbering poet and I, each drumming our own rhythm upon the stairs—his a heavy, regular tread as he took steps two at a time, mine a faint staccato as I followed him.

Irene was straightening from inspecting the keyhole when we arrived.

"Nothing has changed, and everything has changed," she announced.

"Then how are we to enter?"

She eyed him up and down. "*You* are to enter, dear Oscar. You are a brawny man. You and Bram Stoker make me wonder if blarney breeds giants, you are both such towering Irishmen. I understand that you excelled in sport as well as scholarship at Oxford." She stepped back against the wall, drawing her bronze silk skirts as close to her as forty yards of fabric would permit. "Break down the door at your leisure."

"Break it?" His homely face broke into an angelic smile. "I will be the talk of Chelsea. Of course. I must break down the door."

With this he clattered down a few steps, turned sideways, then went charging upward like a velveteen bull and hit the door shoulder first. There came a great groan of wood and wounded poet, but Mr. Wilde gamely drew back and hurled himself again at the barrier. Splinters flew as the door bowed inward. An enraged male voice thundered from within, then fell silent. Oscar and Irene braved the breach as one.

I was the last to broach that threshold, last to see the sight that had stilled and silenced my fellow intruders and even the man who had painted it.

She lay dead—of that there could be no question—her face a hollow death mask of palest ivory. Against her deathly pallor, the emerald silk of her gown lapped like a vast, poisonous sea. The uncompleted painting on the artist's easel shone wet, a ghastly reflection in an opaque mirror of green paint.

The artist himself had slumped onto a pigment-spattered stool. Light spilled from a skylight above, drawing in every cruel detail, including the lines in Lysander Parris's haggard features, the coarse, thick clots of white hair streaking his natural brown color, the shaking arm that loosely supported a predominantly green palette.

"My masterpiece," he said in a raw voice.

Irene approached the dead woman, drew the plait of long dark hair from across her throat. Mr. Wilde gasped at her gesture, but the braid merely rested there. No marks marred the slender neck.

Lysander Parris started up from his stool as if waking into a nightmare. "Do not disturb the pose! I am almost done."

The stairs creaked.

We turned.

Mother and son stood in the doorway, the wife's eyes upon her husband, the son's upon the dead model.

"We heard—" Mrs. Parris began, moving toward her husband, drawing the palette from his grasp to set it aside.

The son took two steps into the room, then stopped as if dumbfounded, staring sightlessly at the dead woman. "She's . . . not alive."

"No," Irene said gently. "She's gone. We should leave as well."

"But—" Young Lawrence looked up, his gaze afire with fury, then saw the wreck that was his father as his mother led him from the room like a sleep-walking child. "I don't understand. . . ."

Irene took his arm, then led him to me. Only an hour ago he had been storming in the room below; now he was the dead eye of the storm. I guided him down the stairs, my own adoptive child in tow, behind the artist and his wife.

I could hear the voices of Oscar Wilde and Irene Adler in consultation behind me.

Mrs. Parris bore her prize down to the drawing room, seating him on a settee covered in worn tapestry. At the door hovered Mrs. McCorkle.

"Tea," Mrs. Parris ordered as I guided her stunned son to a Morris chair crouching in a corner.

The men sat in common shock, while women bustled around them. I couldn't help thinking that Mrs. Parris was in her element—that her role and her rule came through mastering domestic crises; that the servant, Mrs. McCorkle, also took a certain pride in being of use; that some intimate mechanism had been rebalanced and a terrible tension eased.

Tea was steaming from four cups when Irene's figure darkened the doorway. I started.

"Nell, could you come with me for a moment?"

I murmured my excuses and left that dour drawing room with its silent population of victims and survivors.

"Where is Mr. Wilde?" I asked in the hall.

Irene was amused. "Surely you do not miss him."

"No, but—"

She took my arm in her most confiding, yet commanding way. "He has gone for the doctor, who will declare the poor girl dead and see to her removal. Nothing will be left of that macabre scene but the painting of it, and I wonder if that will survive."

"Why should it not? It is his 'masterpiece,' despite its price."

"What is its price, Nell?"

"Dishonor. Dishonesty. A family stricken."

She nodded, pleased. "You put it well. A family stricken, as virulently as if by poison. If they are fortunate, no one will suspect the murder."

"Murd—"

Irene's fingers clamped quite effectively over my mouth. "Hush, Nell! One can only invoke such words in ringing tones in a Shakespearian play, and this is merely a domestic tragedy by Webster."

She led me down the staircase to the kitchens below the ground floor. I sensed a cramped, dingy space and the shining bulk of a tea kettle on a hearth. Irene led me to a small door and opened it.

"What is this place?" I asked.

"The servants' stair."

"Oh. We're not going up there?"

"We most certainly are; otherwise I'll never know if my theory is correct."

"Theory?"

"Of how the murder was accomplished."

"Irene, I do not wish to climb any more stairs in this ghastly house. I do not wish to know how or why, or even if. Can we not go home to Saffron Hill and pretend that you slept undisturbed till curtain time and Mr. Wilde never came and—"

"And that you never enjoyed waking me up?"

"I did not! Enjoy, it, I mean. Not too much."

She was leading me inexorably up the narrow stairs. Each step moaned at our passage like a ghost trod upon.

"Not so much that I must pay penance," I added as the stair turned and grew darker. The walls felt damp as I brushed them, and were rough enough to snag Irene's silken skirts. I tried not to think how it must feel to mount such stairs every night, to be a forgotten housemaid, to be brought from such a place to a silk-draped sofa. Might not any poor wretch choose the studio over the garret no matter the price?

At a tiny landing, Irene paused, then half disappeared into the wall. I cried out despite myself.

"Mrs. McCorkle's bedchamber," Irene explained. A match struck, then smoke assaulted my nostrils. Light grew beyond Irene and she walked into it, out of my sight.

"Come in, Nell. There's nothing to fear here."

I followed to find her shadow thrown so large upon the room's cramped walls that it seemed all in shade. "Are you saying that Mrs. McCorkle is a murderer?"

Irene's hatted head shook on her shoulders and on her shadow. She seemed one of those monstrous pagan gods, horned and terrible. "Observe the wallpaper, Nell."

"There is too much shadow to see . . . yes, a print of yellow and ivory and blue. I see it in the corner. Wallpaper, Irene?"

Irene sighed, her shadow's shoulders heaving with her. "Few bother to paper servants' quarters, even such dreary holes as this."

"Mrs. Parris is indeed a thoughtful woman. I wonder that she can nurse her husband after what he has done."

Irene turned on me, her voice cold as steel. "What has he done?"

"Why—abandoned his family for a servant girl; pursued his art at the cost of every person around him. Look at the man! He is half mad and wholly deteriorated."

She brushed by me, a silhouette holding a burning coal of lamplight. I heard the stairs cry out as she mounted the last flight.

I did not want to go farther. I did not wish to know more. But I could not stop myself.

When I reached the very apex of the house, Irene blocked the last doorway. She crouched suddenly, in that graceful way she had, and I saw the miserable hole that served as home for the dead girl. It made me cringe, the barren meanness of it, the equation of cot and shelf and chamber pot. How hard to blame the one who lived here for anything. In the silence I thought I heard the faint scratch of kittenish paws, a phantom mewling added to the groans of the lost souls on the stairs below, and my eyes filled with tears.

"The wallpaper, Nell," Irene said in deep, sad, angry tones. "The wallpaper."

I could not see wallpaper. I could only see dark, and light, and more dark. But my eyes finally cleared and little figures danced into focus before me— blue butterflies on an ivory ground, gay, hovering creatures at the top of the house. Not butterflies, but fleurs-de-lis.

"Artists are not usually prone to puns," Irene's voice came ponderously. "Lysander Parris was an exception. That's why he called his trademark color 'Parris green.' "

"I don't understand, Irene."

"There is an actual, original 'Paris green,' named for that city of art and gaiety and fashion. That Paris green is a preparation used to keep certain colors—such as blue, paradoxically—from running in wallpapers. It is made from an arsenic compound and can never, ever lose its lethal properties. It will never die, Nell, and therefore it will deal death forever.''

"What are you saying?"

"The kitten, Nell. Remember the kitten."

"It died."

"Precisely."

"But if it was poisoned, surely the food from the kitchen, meant for Phoebe—"

"Not food. And the mice."

"There are no mice now."

"Precisely."

"Irene." I clutched her bronze silk sleeve. "Are we—"

"I would not linger," she said wryly, rising and lifting the lamp, so her silhouette blotted out the artful blue French wallpaper imbued with death and Paris green.

Four months later Oscar Wilde forwarded an invitation to a showing of Lysander Parris works at a small gallery near the British Museum.

"I am amazed the man still has a taste to paint," I said.

"He is an artist," Irene retorted. "The artistic temperament thrives on suffering. Look at me."

I did so. She was lounging on our sofa, sipping hot chocolate illegally brewed upon the fireplace fender, wrapped in another of her sunset-colored Oriental gowns.

"Indeed," I said dryly. "I do not care to see another Parris painting."

"The affair might be instructive. After all, no scandal resulted; no charges were brought. The word *murder* was heard only in the far reaches of the servants' quarters."

"If you are right, it was an unimaginably dreadful murder. That sweet woman so consumed with jealousy. And that poor girl, sleeping each night, her own chamber a death trap. No wonder she looked so properly pale and wan in those awful paintings—she was slowly dying."

"And the artist was in love with death, as artists so often are these days, whether it be with the green fairy of absinthe or some imagined temptress who may be only a housemaid at heart. But it is remarkable that Mr. Parris has lived to paint another day. *He* was being slowly poisoned as well. That is why he became so irrational and locked himself in with the dead woman. He never even noticed her condition."

"He was in jeopardy? How?"

"Need I point out the incident of the footsteps in the night?"

"Oh." I blushed for my innocence. "You mean that if he, when he . . . visited Phoebe, he also was exposed to the Paris green."

"Exactly. As he succumbed to the poison, he began putting the fleurs-de-lis—truly *fleurs de mal*, 'flowers of evil'—in his paintings. And the more often he visited, the more poison he absorbed through his very pores. An ingenious scheme—he would pay to the extent he abused his wife's honor. He would, in fact, dispense the dosage of his own death. If he was innocent of infidelity, only she would die."

"Irene, that's diabolical!"

"Is it any more diabolical than the propensity of artists to introduce the models with whom they are obsessed into the bosom of their families, expecting them to be accepted? And, in this case, the son *would* be foolish enough to rival the father."

"The son? He was involved in this folly as well?"

"Whose were the second footsteps that halted halfway up? Lawrence, too, had become enamoured of the girl. He knew what was going on and raged inwardly, but he was not as clever as his mother—who had been secretly seething over her husband's indiscretions for years, else why did Mr. Parris bar his studio door?—and Lawrence did not find a way to murder."

"Why was there no scandal, Irene? Did the authorities never question the death?"

"Never."

"Why not?"

"She was an artist's model, a poor servant. People of her sort and class die young all the time—of drink, of debauchery, of neglect. No one cared enough to note her passing."

"I have been very wrong."

"You certainly have not anticipated the turns of the case."

"Not that, Irene. I have judged that poor dead girl harshly. I have condemned her as a fallen woman, but the wronged wife in this case was willing to kill an innocent girl on mere suspicion. That poor Phoebe was not innocent does not lessen the wife's wrong."

Irene reached to the sidetable and selected one of her annoying cigarettes. I had to endure the perfume of sulfur before she would go on.

"She *was* innocent," Irene declared on a misty blue breath. "Perfectly innocent."

"How can you say that for certain?"

"Because I went to the morgue to identify the body."

"Irene! How could you do that?"

"Easily. I donned rusty black and a country accent and said I was the deceased girl's long-lost sister and, please, sir, could anyone say, did she die a ruined woman? And they talked and thought and hemmed and hawed and finally decided to relieve my sisterly mind and said no, she did not."

"How can they tell?"

"That is another bedtime story, Nell, and I am sick of telling this one."

"But the footsteps—"

"He went there often, but he did not succeed, despite all his pleadings. He captured her only in paint."

"So it was all for nothing."

"Murder usually is."

"And we will not go to the exhibition."

"We will see."

"We" did nothing of the sort. Irene decided to go, and I could not resist glimpsing the end of the story, even if it meant another encounter with Oscar Wilde.

The gallery was crowded, a long, narrow space glittering with gaslight and glasses of sherry and festively garbed people. Parris green leered from the walls. The gaslight gave Phoebe's plaintive features a sad beauty that even I could detect now.

Naturally, Oscar Wilde captured Irene the instant she swept in the door (at public events, Irene always swept).

"Parris says you are to have any one of his green period paintings you wish," he announced.

Her eyebrows arched at this generosity.

Oscar Wilde leaned down over the rim of his glass to speak in confidence. "His wife is confined in a remote establishment in Sussex. The room under the eaves has been walled off."

"Couldn't the paper have been stripped?" I demanded.

Irene shook her head. "The compound would have already seeped into the wood beneath. At least they will have no mice."

"Which will you choose?" Mr. Wilde wondered aloud, trailing us through the gallery. Irene passed Joan of Arc, Portia, the mermaid, and a dozen other representations of the woman we only knew secondhand.

Finally she stopped at a small, square frame of lacy gilt. "This one."

She had chosen no femme fatale in her green and lethal glory, only a sketch of Phoebe playing with the kitten condemned to succumb first to Paris green. If only someone had noticed! Tiger-striped, I saw with a lump in my throat. I was glad that Phoebe had found one friend in that house of horrors, even if only briefly.

Mr. Wilde shrugged. "None of them will ever be worth anything, but the ignorant would have been more impressed by the larger paintings."

"I am not interested in impressing the ignorant," Irene said blithely.

"Ah, but you shall, despite yourself!" Oscar Wilde trumpeted, pouncing. "Let me lead you, my dear Irene and my dear Miss Huxleigh, to an example of the radical new turn in Lysander Parris's work. It is a pity he did not feel up to being here tonight, for he has found a dazzling new model who has revolutionized his monomaniacal palette. But see for yourselves."

He led us through the crowd and around a corner.

A blazing full-length portrait greeted us like a sudden sunset. I recognized the subject matter instantly, though I suspect Irene was at a loss. Surely this gorgeously stern figure clothed in gossamer red-orange and holding a flaming sword against the green of forgotten forest represented the angel at the gates of Eden. The figure was the broad-shouldered, small-breasted one often done of heroic women, but the face floating above it in serene, haughty justice was unmistakably Irene's.

After a stunned moment, Irene laughed. She bent to read the bottom plaque bearing the title. *"Excalibur in Eden,"* she declaimed. "He has a flair for titles, if not for models."

Oscar Wilde smiled slyly. "I could better picture the indomitable Penelope as the angel with the flaming sword."

"I would not presume to portray an angel," I answered stoutly.

Irene laughed again. "I am no angel, either—nor do I ever care to be. Earth and the present tense is my medium—not the would-be of the promised Empyrean or the has-been of ancient Edens."

"And not, I trust," Oscar Wilde suggested limpidly, "Paris green."

Jan Grape's stories frequently concern the workingclass. Not the Archie Bunker workingclass of Hollywood sit-coms, but the old workingclass of James T. Farrell. Her stories are funny, sad, scary and bedazzling. She is finishing up a first-rate first novel and planning many more stories, all of which will doubtless be worth reading.

The Man in the Red-Flannel Suit
JAN GRAPE

Christmas was supposed to be a candy-making, turkey-baking time, I thought. With furtive trips to buy gifts to hide, special gifts for someone special. A time of joy and laughter, and singing carols about peace on earth and about the spirit of love.

"Merry Christmas, Zoe," someone called out as I walked out the back door of APD headquarters. I didn't recognize the voice.

"Merry Christmas," I said, but under my breath muttered, "bah, humbug." Christmas was meaningless when your police officer husband was in a coma in a nursing home with no hope of recovery, but there was no sense reminding people about Byron Barrow. Don't think I feel sorry for myself. Sure I did for awhile, but you have to go on. Put the past out of your mind and keep on trucking. It's just that I'd rather forget about Christmas, if no one minds.

It was sixty degrees in Austin, Texas, on the evening of December twenty-second and my ROP unit (Repeat Offenders Program), along with the other members of a special drug task force, had busted a crack house at midnight.

I had volunteered to work all week including the twenty-fourth and twenty-fifth to allow some of my fellow officers to be off with their families for Christmas. It was pointless to let myself think about Christmas two years ago, the last one Byron and I had shared. He was on duty when he was shot in the head and left in his present condition.

127

My unit was part of the back-up team and we'd hung back letting the other team members take care of their jobs. We arrested three suspects, but the house had been full of people. Four little children belonging to two of the suspects ran around crying, begging us not to take their mamma and daddy to jail.

The other people in the house weren't related to the children or didn't want to be responsible for four kids and we'd had to call Child Services. It was a heartbreaker right here at Christmastime.

After the bust, my unit returned to headquarters to take care of the paperwork. Everyone was still pumped—adrenaline highs—it always happens. You get up for the operation and when the bust goes well, you can stay up for hours.

"Hey, Zoe. Did you see that dude trying to get out the window? I was standing on the ground right beneath it and he nearly climbed out on top of me," said Corky. "Man, he was so surprised he almost wet his pants."

"Yeah, Corky. I saw." Corky was from narcotics and I'd known him for years. He's normally a quiet guy until after a big bust and then he'll talk your leg off.

"Zoe, check out this card," said Brad, one of the DEA agents. The card was a depiction of Santa and his sleigh sitting on top of an outhouse with Santa yelling curses at Rudolph and the other reindeer.

Brad opened the card and read the inside message aloud, "I said the Schmidt house, you fools!"

I'd probably seen the card six times already, but I laughed anyway.

It was after two in the morning when I finished my part of the necessary paperwork. Some of the team was going for breakfast at Denny's, but I begged off, saying I was tired and needed my beauty sleep. They pushed a little, but I reminded everyone I was due back on duty at ten A.M. and they gave up and left.

My adrenaline had already ebbed and, although I wasn't quite as tired as I'd made myself out to be, I was ready to get home.

I entered the parking garage of the old patrol building. It felt good to climb into the '92 Mustang I was driving this month. The ROP unit confiscates vehicles and we use them as undercover cars.

This time of year the ground can still be warm and when the air cools, fog forms, especially in the low-lying areas. A few tendrils of fog clutched at my car and I had to use the wipers to clear the wetness from the windshield. Fortunately the drive south on I-35 was short—exit on East Riverside Drive, cross the bridge, and head west.

The Texas-Colorado River, which meanders across central Texas, has been dammed in numerous places forming a chain of lakes. One of the smaller lakes, known as Town Lake, sits in the midst of downtown Austin. The major portion of the downtown area is on the north shore of the lake and my apartment complex is on the south shore a few blocks west of the Interstate.

Riverside Drive makes multiple curves following the lake's contours. With no traffic to speak of at that hour and because I knew the area like the inside of my mouth, I was driving at a good rate of speed. The moisture and fog in the air made it necessary to keep the headlight beams on low, otherwise I never would have seen the bundle of clothes in the right-hand lane.

I thought I saw the clothing move. My foot tapped the brakes automatically and I came to a complete halt a few feet past the bundle. Then I backed slowly until it was in front of my right fender. I backed up a little more and steered my car into the same lane as the clothes, my headlights bathing the scene in a surreal light.

"Oh shit. Tell me I'm not seeing this," I said, but there was no mistaking the fact that the clothing was a woman lying in an awkward position on the pavement, and a small girl hunkered down almost on top of the woman.

I got out and walked over. The little girl looked to be about three or four years old, her hair was long, curling slightly in the dampness. The woman's neck was in an unnatural position and I knew without even checking that she was dead.

The child was patting the woman's face, blood and all, and saying over and over, "Mommy, wake up. Get up, Mommy."

I did a quick visual check of the child, who didn't seem to have any noticeable injuries. The woman had cuts and abrasions on her face, nothing that looked terribly bad or even life threatening.

There wasn't any doubt in my mind about what had happened. A car had hit the woman, flinging her into the air and her neck had snapped when she hit.

I walked back to the Mustang, switched on the walkie-talkie and reported the accident to Dispatch. I took off my windbreaker and went back to the child. I wrapped it around her unprotesting shoulders and began talking to her. "Honey, I've called for some help for you and your mommy. Why don't you come with me to the car?"

The child kept begging her mother to get up. I don't think she even heard me.

I kept talking quietly to her, hoping to keep her from panicking. She became less agitated, but still didn't answer. The calls to her mother eventually stopped. Moments later, a squad car and EMS wagon pulled up and the medical attendants took over, one picking up the child to examine while the other began his futile attempt to revive the woman. There was nothing they could do, but by law they have to try.

I told them I was Zoe Barrow, showed my ID, and said I had no idea when the accident had happened. "It probably couldn't have been more than ten, fifteen minutes. Otherwise someone else would have found her. Called it in."

"Even if someone saw them, they might not want to get involved," said the EMS guy, who was holding the child.

"Well, it's not too easy to see along here, but how could they leave a child?"

"Go figure," he said.

There was nothing to identify the woman on her person and from the looks of both mother and daughter, they were probably homeless. Once the medical guy had completed his examination of the girl, I carried her to my car and put her inside. She didn't protest. She just looked back over to where her mother was, soundless.

"My name's Zoe. What's your name, honey?"

"April."

"That's a pretty name." She looked at me and her big brown eyes looked like a fawn's. "How old are you, April? Do you know how old you are?"

She held up four fingers, and said "Four" softly.

"Four. You're a big girl aren't you? What's your mommy's name?"

She looked puzzled and finally said, "Mommy."

"Okay. Do you know where you live?"

April shook her head.

"Where's your daddy?"

She didn't answer. She tucked her head down to her chest and began crying. But in a moment she stopped and looked at me and said, "Santa Claus."

Oh, Lord. For a minute I'd forgotten it was Christmas. "Well, yes. Santa Claus will come to see you soon." And vowed that I would make sure Santa brought April a toy or two.

But as I spoke, April began sobbing again. This time it was worse—not only heartrending. This time I thought I heard fear in her voice. I put my arm around her and tried to hold her, but she pulled back. Was she afraid of me?

Better to let her cry it out, I thought. Maybe she'd tire and go to sleep. Probably be the best thing for her.

Accident investigators (we call them "AIs"), a police photographer, patrol officers, and the medical examiner had all arrived while I was talking to April. I saw several patrol officers making a methodical search of the area, poking in the grassy weeds along the shoulder of the road. I knew they were hoping to find clues about the accident or something that would identify April's mother.

The AI in charge came over. I got out of my car and gave him an account of what I'd seen. Which didn't take long. He asked me to stop by headquarters later and make a formal statement. I assured him I would and started to get back into the car.

One of the patrol officers came over and handed me a teddy bear. "We carry these in the trunks of our units to give to kids. It usually helps if they have a pal."

"Great idea. Thanks."

I got back into the car and April grabbed the bear I held out as if she were drowning and I'd just thrown her a lifeline. Tears still glistened on her face and in a few minutes she started making that funny sub-sub noise kids make when they've cried a lot. I patted her shoulder and she leaned her head back, hugging the bear tightly. Her eyelids were getting heavy. I didn't try to talk to her or hold her. As long as she was quiet, it was probably best to leave her alone.

The mother's body was covered with a blanket. Measurements were taken of skid marks and the probable place of impact. I watched an officer pick up and bag some car headlight fragments.

The EMS attendant I'd talked to earlier came over and motioned for me to get out of the car. "The AI asked me to tell you, they called Child Services for the little girl, but it looks to be awhile. They've had a couple other emergencies."

"That's okay. I don't have any place I need to be and can stay here until they come."

"Uh, well, we still have a problem." He was short, redheaded, and had freckles across his nose. He looked around twenty-five, but his hair had receded back past his ears. "The ME said we could go ahead and transport the woman soon, but I think it's a bad idea to do it in front of the child."

"No problem. I'll drive April to headquarters and wait for Child Services there. We'll go now and you can take care of things."

"Good. I was hoping you'd say that."

I got back into the car and saw that April had indeed cried herself to sleep. I pulled the seat belt around her and fastened it. My car engine started with hardly a sound and I pulled slowly around the crime scene, heading west.

I intended to drive to headquarters with April. Honestly, I did. But my place was just down the road and when I reached the driveway of my apartment complex, I turned in almost automatically and pulled around to my parking space.

"Poor little kid doesn't need any more hassles tonight," I said as I turned off the ignition.

I picked up April. She was so frail, her little body couldn't have weighed more than thirty pounds. Her arms tightened around my neck and she mumbled something that sounded like, "Santa Claus."

"Okay, sweetie. Don't you worry. Santa is coming to see you."

She was dead asleep again and didn't even wake when I put her on my sofa and stripped off her soiled clothes. I got one of my T-shirts and pulled it over her head. I carried her to my bedroom and tucked her in bed. She roused enough to put her thumb in her mouth and then she zonked.

I sat for a few moments thinking it all over before I called downtown. I knew I'd get an argument, but I stuck to my guns and in the end got what I wanted. "I promise," I said. "She'll be there on the twenty-sixth."

I slept for about three hours and April didn't move or turn over. After I had showered, I called my mother because I desperately needed her help. There was no way I could take off work as we were down to a skeleton crew already.

My parents, Helene and Herbert Taylor, live in West Lake Hills, a section of Austin noted for canyons, hills, and homes with breathtaking views.

My parents aren't rich, but they could be considered comfortable. Dad has his own engineering firm and Mom retired from the University of Texas Chancellor's office last year. They built their home years ago when prices were still reasonable. It's worth a small fortune now.

I knew my mom would say she was busy with her final preparations for a big family dinner on Christmas Eve, but I also knew everything was already done.

My mom is the great goddess of organization and never procrastinates. She just likes to make us feel sorry for her by making us think she's harried at the last minute. She complained a bit, but agreed to come over about nine.

When Helene Taylor came in, she said exactly what was on her mind. "Zoe, I don't think this is a very good idea."

"It seemed like a great one at four o'clock this morning. Mom, it's just until after Christmas."

April woke up and started calling for her mommy and that was the end of the discussion.

When I got to work, I called the traffic division to see what the latest word was on the hit-and-run. I was glad to discover the investigator now in charge was Trey Gerrod. He had been one of my training officers and he was a first-rate officer. After we exchanged pleasantries, he clued me in on what they'd found.

"We've got paint samples and headlight fragments, Zoe. The car was identified as a 1991 Buick. Metallic blue."

"I suppose there are only ten thousand of those around."

"Yes, but we got lucky. It had been repainted recently and that means it was probably in an earlier accident. We'll be able to narrow it down soon."

He said they'd not identified April or her mother yet and I mentioned my plans about calling a news reporter friend to help. He said he'd been considering that idea, too, and for me to go ahead if I had a connection.

"Keep me posted, would you?" I asked.

"Okay. Hey, is it true the little girl is staying with you?"

"Well, just until after Christmas."

"Great. Is it okay if a few of the guys around here get her some Christmas presents?"

Tough cops? They're the biggest bunch of old softies when it comes to kids. "Sure. Y'all want to stop by tonight?"

"It's a deal," he said and we hung up.

My newspaper friend worked at *The Austin American Statesman*. Mildred Warner and I had been in some classes together at Austin Community College about a hundred years ago. She must be off for the holidays, I thought as I dialed, but she answered her phone. "Millie, Zoe Barrow. Merry Christmas."

"Zoe? Long time no hear from. Ho, ho, ho to you too."

When I explained the situation, she was more than willing to photograph April and run a "Do You Know This Child" article on her. We set up a late afternoon appointment at my house.

Paperwork kept me occupied for the next two hours and then it was time to hit some parties. Christmas is when each department at APD holds open house. Food, I never saw such good food: cookies, candies, spice and fruit cakes, banana nut and cranberry breads and muffins, huge trays of ham, turkey, shrimp, roast beef homemade tamales and cheeses, dips, chips, veggies, relish trays, no-nog eggnog, and punch. It was pig-out time—just for the holiday, you understand—I ate until I nearly got sick.

When I got home, Mom and April were getting along like old chums. April, brown hair brushed and curling a bit on top and with an occasional smile on her face was a totally different child. Although there was still a trace of a haunted look in her fawnlike eyes.

Mom had taken the child shopping and bought a whole wardrobe of clothes, shoes, underwear, and to top it off, a small Christmas tree. April spent five minutes telling me how much fun they had decorating.

"She's a sweetie," Helene said. "She's been brought up right." That was the highest praise my mother could bestow.

My mom is great with little ones. My brother, Chip, and his wife, Pat, have two—Kyle, three and Alicia, six. They stay with my folks on occasion and always have the greatest time.

Millie Warner came by and got the information for the article she planned to run on Christmas Day. Then her photographer showed up and we had a small crisis when April decided she didn't want her picture taken. Mom finally convinced April by showing her photos, in an album, of me at age four and five.

My younger brother and I always played pranks on each other. One picture showed me all dressed up in Easter finery and my brother sneaking up behind the chair and, just as the picture was snapped, Chip stuck his fingers up and it looked like I had horns on my head. Mom said it was entirely appropriate, because I often was a little devil, and April got so tickled she forgot she didn't want to sit still and pose.

Millie and the photographer left and my mom took off soon after, getting my promise that April and I would spend tomorrow night with her and my dad.

The doorbell rang a few minutes later and when I answered, Santa Claus stood on the front stoop with five uniformed police officers instead of elves, each holding a gaily wrapped present.

"April, look who's here. Someone special has come to see you."

I saw her out of the corner of my eye as she edged across the living room, but when she caught sight of the man in the red suit, April suddenly began screaming and ran down the hall to the bedroom.

"Why is she having such a fit? Is this kid strange or what?" I looked at the group, two women and three men, and said, "Sorry, guys. Come on in and sit. I'll go and see what I can do with her."

Santa, or rather Trey Gerrod dressed in the suit, said, "Take it easy, Zoe. Lots of little kids are afraid of Santa."

"Younger kids maybe, but a four-year-old?"

"Kids are all different. My five-year-old daughter still cries when she sees him—she doesn't scream, but she cries. My son, who is three, runs to him laughing, all excited to sit in Santa's lap."

"Okay, maybe I should just leave her alone a minute." I poured coffee and got some of my mom's fudge-and-divinity candy out for my guests. They put the presents they'd brought around the tree.

I told Trey about Millie's article and he said he hoped it worked. They sure didn't have anything on April's mother. All the while we talked, her screams grew louder. I finally gave up and walked down the hall to the bedroom.

"April, honey? This isn't a very nice way to act. Come to the living room with me, we'll have some candy and talk to Santa."

"I no want any canny," she said, between sobs. "I want my mommy. Where's my mommy?"

It wasn't going to be easy. My mom had told April this morning that her mommy had gone to live in heaven and that we couldn't go there right now. I tried to explain things again, but as she was too young to understand, I felt totally inadequate.

Since I'd never had children I knew much less about kids than most women my age. I couldn't help wondering if I'd made a big mistake by bringing this little girl home with me.

Finally, she stopped crying and stuck her thumb in her mouth. She still didn't want to go out to see Santa, so I left her on my bed, watching *Sesame Street*, and hugging the teddy bear she got last night.

When I returned to the living room, the little group had already left, all except Santa. Trey Gerrod made a great St. Nick, as he was on the roly-poly side, with round cheeks and blue eyes. He didn't have a beard though and had to wear the false whiskers.

He filled me in on the progress they'd made in identifying the hit-and-run vehicle. "We've narrowed it to three cars. All have been in the shop in the past eight to ten months for paint jobs. We've talked to the owners and each has a good alibi."

"What about the cars? What about damage?"

"No damage to two of them, but the third car has left town. Which sounds a little suspicious to me. The owner, a Mr. Randall Lack, says his son took

the Buick this morning to drive to Fort Worth to visit his mother. The parents
are divorced and the son lives with his father."

"And you think this could be the one?"

"It's only a guess. However, Lack does have the strongest alibi. He was at
a Christmas party and seen by about fifty people." Trey smiled. "He played
Santa and wore a suit and everything. Can you imagine a grown man acting
that way?"

I eyed Trey and realized his tongue was planted firmly in his cheek. "No,
I can't imagine it. So, Lack was there all evening?"

"He supposedly left around midnight to go home and we haven't proved
otherwise yet."

"So there's not . . ."

"We haven't given up, Zoe. I'm not called 'tenacious' for nothing." He
smiled and I'd have sworn his blue eyes twinkled. "I need to head on down
the avenue. We're taking our kids to my mom and dad's tonight. Tomorrow
we go to Sara's folks."

I walked with him to the door, "Thanks, Trey. Tell the others they were
sweet to come and I appreciate the presents. I'm sorry April didn't get into
the spirit."

"No problem. She's been through a lot and it's going to take a bunch of
love to get her back on track."

As I closed the door behind Trey, I thought about what he'd said. He was
right. April would need a lot of love. Someone to care for her unconditionally.
Someone to love her as much as their own. I knew her immediate fate was to
be sent to a foster home. Would they be capable of giving the love she needed?

I grilled a couple of chicken breasts, made a salad, cooked some rice, and
opened a package of brown gravy mix. My mind kept walking around the idea
of what it would be like to be a mother. It did have a certain appeal, I admitted,
but a kid with so many problems would be a handful. Even I could figure
that one.

Byron and I had talked about having kids. Sometime in the future, maybe,
we'd say, not yet. We'll get around to it. We hadn't known that his future
was limited. The doctors say he'll never wake up from the coma he's in and
I will never have the family we talked about. Now I'd never be a mother.

When I went to see if April was ready to eat, she'd gone to sleep. It didn't
surprise me. She'd worn herself out with her emotional outburst. She'd not
slept much last night and since she and my mother had run around half the
day shopping, sleep was inevitable. No wonder the little thing got the
screaming-meemies. She was worn to a frazzle.

After all the stuff I'd eaten earlier at the office, I realized I wasn't hungry
either, so I wrapped things up and put them in the refrigerator. I decided to
take a warm bubble bath and afterward, climb into bed to read. I'm not too
crazy about police and crime books—they're usually either too realistic or not

realistic enough—but I'd recently discovered a writer who writes about a female police chief in the fictional town of Maggody, Arkansas, who has the knack of tickling my funny bone. I'd just bought a recent paperback and was looking forward to it.

Around nine P.M., April woke up wanting something to eat. We raced to the kitchen, I let her win, and on the lower shelf of the pantry, I found a can of chicken noodle soup. Mom must have bought it because it wasn't anything I usually stocked. I heated the soup in the microwave and April got a spoon and some crackers out, even though it wasn't too easy, seeing as how she had a teddy bear in one arm. I dished up some of the salad I'd made earlier for myself.

"Are you feeling better now?" I asked as she began eating.

"Jey-es." She almost smiled and took a drink of milk, leaving a mustache of white above her lip.

"I'm glad. Did you and Mo . . ." I broke off. I knew what my brother's kids called Mom, but didn't know what she'd told April to call her. "Did you and Mamma Lene go to the grocery store today?"

"Jey-es."

"Good. Can you say yes?"

"Yes," and this time she did smile, lighting up her whole face.

"Very good, April." She was a cutie and would be even cuter with a little meat on her bones. "After you finish eating, we'll go turn on the Christmas tree lights. Would you like that?"

"Yes." She finished the soup and asked for more.

It was good to see her eating so well, even if it was an odd time for dinner. While April ate the additional soup, I looked in the refrigerator and pantry to see what extra goodies Mom had bought. I found a carton of Blue Bell Ice Cream—butter pecan—my favorite. April and I each had some.

We finished the ice cream, I washed her face and hands and then we walked to the living room where I turned on the tree lights. When the lights started blinking off and on, April clapped her hands in glee.

"You're a lucky little girl, April. Look at all these presents with your name on them. Look at what Santa Claus brought for you."

April started screaming again, but this time she ran to me and put her arms around my legs, almost toppling me. Not easy when you're five feet nine like I am. She's frightened, I thought. "Honey what's wrong? What are you afraid of?"

"That Santa Claus?"

"Jey-es."

Maybe if I was used to little kids I'd have snapped to it sooner. But now, at least, the light was beginning to dawn. "Why are you afraid of Santa? Did Santa hurt you?"

"No, he hurt Mommy."

"How did Santa hurt your mommy?"

"Mommy said, 'No, no.' He pushed her. Mommy fall out. Mommy cried."

"Santa pushed your mommy out of the car?" I needed to know if they had been inside the car. If they had it would open up the possibilities and help make the case.

"Jey-es. Mommy told me run. I run. Mommy run. Santa's big car hit Mommy." Tears welled up in her eyes.

I changed the subject. I didn't want her thinking about the bad part right now. "Santa took you for a ride in his car?"

"Je—yes. We go to Old McDonald's. And I got french fries."

"Do you like french fries?"

"Yes, with ketchup."

"I like french fries and ketchup too. Maybe we can go to McDonald's tomorrow and get french fries. I think it's time now for us to go to bed."

"Okay." She took my hand and led me down the hallway.

We held hands until she went to sleep. Maybe being a parent wasn't so difficult after all.

Thinking over my talk with April, I began to get a mental picture of what must have happened to her and her mom. The picture was still fuzzy, but it was a likely scenario that explained why April was afraid of anyone dressed as Santa.

A man dressed in a Santa suit had picked them up someplace. Trey Gerrod had mentioned that one of his metallic-blue car owners had dressed as Santa— that connected. Maybe he offered to buy them food and took them to McDonald's. Maybe he offered money for sex too, beforehand, and April's mom said okay, but feed us first. After eating maybe she wasn't so eager to go along with the sex part and refused to give him whatever he wanted.

That refusal made him angry and he shoved them out of his car. Maybe she taunted him or mouthed off at him. Whatever, his anger exploded and he ran the mother down. The idea was feasible and the best part, from the police point of view, was that April and her mom were in that vehicle. Some trace of hair or fiber could turn up in the car.

I'd thrown away the clothing April had worn—nothing had been worth salvaging. Tomorrow I'd dig them out of the garbage can and take them to the forensics lab for testing.

First thing the next morning, I called my sister-in-law to ask if I could bring April to her house while I was at work.

"No," said Pat. "Helene said for me to tell you to bring April to her house. She knew you'd hesitate to ask her help today."

"But she's got . . ."

"You know she's got everything done."

"I just thought April would enjoy playing with Alicia and Kyle."

"I'll be at your mom's most of the day and we can manage the three between us."

"Sound like you two have things all arranged."

Pat and Helene get along well since Pat is almost as good an organizer as my mom. They gave up on me a long time ago. I'm okay at work but in most everything else, I'm usually disorganized. Sometimes I envy Pat her relationship with Helene, but she will often side with me, keeping Mom off my back. Besides, I liked her.

"Okay," I said. "I'll take April over there and thanks for your help."

A Canadian cold front had moved down across the Texas plains and into central Texas overnight. Made it feel more like Christmas to be able to put on a jacket. Mom had bought a coat with a hood for April and she got so excited I wondered if the kid had ever had one before.

After I dropped April at Mom's, I dropped April's clothes at the lab at headquarters and headed to the East Station patrol building off East 7th to talk with Trey Gerrod. I found him in his lieutenant's office finishing up a telephone call. When I told him what April had said, he got a funny look on his face.

"I just talked to the ME," Trey said. "April's mother had had sex as recently as an hour before her death. I was getting ready to start looking for a boyfriend or a pimp."

"Or a customer?"

"That too. It had occurred to me she was killed by some weirdo or a disgruntled john." He leaned back in the chair and looked at me through narrowed eyes. "If she had sex with the guy, why did he get mad and run her down?"

"Who knows? Like you said, a weirdo with a weirdo reason."

"We do know Mr. Lack was dressed in a Santa suit."

"Right," I said.

He picked up the Austin telephone directory. "Do you want in on this?"

"You bet your buns."

Gerrod handed me the directory. "Look up the locations for all the McDonald's and we'll go talk to some civilians."

I contacted my boss, who gave me a green light to stay with the case. "Nothing except more parties going on around here," he said.

"Save some goodies for me."

He promised he would and when I'd hung up the phone, I flipped open the directory. "Good grief, Trey. There are seventeen McDonald's here. I had no idea there were so many."

"We only need the ones within two to three miles of East Riverside Drive."

I studied the addresses a moment. "That leaves four: East Ben White, East Oltorf, Barton Springs, and East Riverside Drive. But the Riverside one is probably too far east."

"Let's try the first three," he said. "We can move farther out if nothing turns up in one of those."

After a brief argument about who was going to drive, Trey and I left in my Mustang. It was his case, but I remembered riding patrol with him years ago. He drove like a little old country farmer and that made me crazy. We reached I-35 and headed south. "If you had to guess, Trey, where do you like best?"

"I like the Barton Springs location. He probably picked them up in the downtown area or near Zilker Park."

I had thought the Ben White location for the easy access to I-35, but Trey had made a good point. "Okay, let's go there first."

"You're driving," he said.

"Yeah, I remember Santa and the little girl," the young man said. "They pulled up to the window around twelve-thirty that night."

The hamburger emporium's night manager was working again this fine Christmas Eve morning. Guess McDonald's was on a skeleton crew, too. Trey and I ordered coffee and sat in the booth nearest the counter. The manager, Bob Cortez, was in his early thirties, short and thin, and had an Adam's apple that looked like he'd actually swallowed an apple. He sat beside me, keeping an eye on his three other workers.

"That's the same little girl in today's paper, isn't it?" he asked. "I was pretty sure it was her." One of the girls from the kitchen called for Cortez, sounding like it might be a major calamity and he said he'd be right back.

"April's in the paper today? I thought it was going to run tomorrow— Christmas Day." Trey shrugged and I said, "I didn't have time to even look at the newspaper this morning."

"Have a little trouble being a mother, did you?"

"It's not easy getting a kid and yourself bathed, dressed, fed, and out the door on time. Especially when you're not used to it." I could smile now, but this morning I wanted to tear out my hair. "April didn't want to wear the blue jeans I put on her. She wanted to wear the red corduroy pants today."

Trey laughed, "So, who won?"

"She looked cute in the red. It seemed too trivial to fuss about, but I had to take off the jeans and put on the corduroys because we were going to be late if I let her do it."

"You'll soon figure out how to work it."

"You're talking like she's going to stay with me. This is only temporary."

"I hear you. I just don't believe you." Trey pulled the front-page section of the paper out of his jacket pocket and handed it to me.

While I was reading the article Millie had done, Cortez came back, apologetic.

"No problem," said Trey. "Tell us what you remember."

Cortez remembered the car, the woman, and the child, but especially he recalled the man. "Someone dressed like Santa is hard to forget."

"Did he have on the full costume?" I asked.

"Everything except the whiskers."

"Did you get a good look at him?" asked Trey.

Cortez nodded. "Dark hair, young, maybe about twenty. That struck me as a little odd. I figured he was the woman's younger brother and had done this for the little girl."

When Cortez had nothing more to add, Trey and I walked out to the car.

"None of my blue Buick owners were young," said Trey.

"But one of them had a son old enough to drive."

"Mr. Lack," said Trey. "Let's go see old Randall Lack. Maybe he'll tell us why his son really drove up to Ft. Worth the next morning after a hit-and-run."

It was routine after that. Mr. Lack didn't want to cooperate until Trey Gerrod mentioned the Fort Worth police had Randall, Jr., in custody. A search warrant had been obtained for the car.

Lack finally admitted his son had told him he'd put on the Santa suit and had gone out to play a joke on his friends. Lack denied any knowledge about the hit-and-run.

I let Trey handle things from that point and drove over to my parents' house. Millie Warner called to say several people had called the *Statesman* saying they knew April and her mother. No one knew of any other family. April's last name was Collins and her mother's name was Reba. The newspaper was starting a fund for April and was also donating a funeral for Reba Collins.

My family, including aunts, uncles, and cousins, had all fallen for April and she was responding to their care and concern. Everyone kept asking me what was I going to do? Hell, I didn't know.

Later that evening, I slipped away from all the family festivities and drove to the nursing home to visit Byron. As I sat in the car outside the building housing my comatose husband, I was still unsure that what I wanted to do was the right thing for me or for April.

That night was clear and you could see millions of stars, bright and twinkling in the black sky. High wispy clouds were visible against the inky velvet, looking as if an artist had painted them there only a few minutes earlier.

Christmas is a time for giving and receiving love. Love was something a child could bring into my lonely life. I got out of the car and automatically looked upward to see if I could spot a miniature sleigh or Rudolph and eight tiny reindeer.

"Byron," I said aloud in the crisp night air, "guess what Santa brought me for Christmas?"

Susan Dunlap is another quiet writer who has never quite gotten her due for the well-turned phrase, the sudden and remarkable insight, the quirky (and frequently bemused) take on our present social mores. But one has the feeling, reading her books, that she will be around a lot longer than many of the shouters and screamers.

Checkout
SUSAN DUNLAP

There's probably not one of you who doesn't have some expectations of the afterlife. Some of you ponder it more than others, of course. But I'll bet most of you are like me: you think of eternity as little as possible, and never as a reality. And yet, even you, if pressed, would come up with some picture of it.

But few of you would have the right one. I sure didn't.

Let me backtrack here, so you know who you're dealing with. I had no particular religious attachments. I'd flirted with a number of theologies in an academic sort of way, so if indeed there were many mansions in Heaven, I could have described a lot of the rooms (like a postmortem version of one of those tacky vacation inns with the Beethoven Bath, the Schubert Suite, the Liberace Lounge). I wouldn't have been surprised to come across a newly painted white hallway with a bright light at the end and a helluva suction. A clutch of departed Tibetan monks ready to lead me on a side tour through the Bardo of the Book of the Dead for forty-nine days before dispatching me into my next incarnation would have given me little more than a moment's surprise. Finding nothing at all wouldn't have shocked me. (Well, really, how could it? What would it have shocked?)

I had considered and altogether dismissed any Final Judgment—sheep baaing smugly at disgruntled goats.

Even so, had I discovered myself eye-to-eye with Saint Peter, I would have been prepared to become wing-to-wing with the heavenly host, or fork-to-pitchfork with guys advertising ham spread. Cartoon heaven, I understood. But I never, ever expected this.

141

Dead. I was definitely dead. How did I know? Once a woman has shuffled off the mortal coil, she knows. Trust me. And where was I? No white hallway, no glowing saint, wizened monk, or prodding devil. I couldn't make out my surroundings at all. I didn't know where I was, but what I was doing was standing in line. Standing in line, of all miserable things. I could have done that alive. I *had* done that alive. It had driven me crazy, queuing up in the bank behind ten other people, squatting down, checkbook on knee, trying to fill out the deposit slip with each check number and amount. All the time I'd be watching for the line to move, and when it did I'd madly scoop up my half-done checks and duck-walk forward, trying to keep the checks from flying (not to say bouncing) all over the bank. I'd perform the whole thigh-killing gymnastic exercise to avoid standing blankly in the line for half an hour with two thoughts slapping at me: Not only was I wasting time here (one), but (two) I'd shot ten minutes before I got here writing out those checks.

But forewarned is not forearmed. If I had ten checks the line moved like lightning and I got to the window with every one unsigned and unnumbered and the teller silently berating me for holding up the line. (I never stopped to consider what the people behind me thought. I'll bet they could have killed me.)

Killed me? Had they dispatched me into the Brinks funeral cortege? I was, after all, dead. But you don't die because you delay the bank line. If you did, CitiCorp would put in a mortuary next to the vault.

In any case I didn't want to waste time pondering how I died. Dead was dead. And I had more pressing problems: these damned lines.

Lines! Lines everywhere! I really did hate waiting in line. And not only in the bank. But the airport. All flights east from California leave at 7:00 A.M., as if there were one big gust of air per day off the Pacific. How many sag-eyed 6:15 A.M.s have I spent behind thirty people accompanied by suitcases with wheels, pull straps, and sections expandable in all directions. They had backpacks, shoe racks, cloth sacks, kiddie strollers, bags of crullers, giant umbrellas. And three carryons apiece, each the size of a ram, unshorn. And every single item was without the name and address labels the agent insisted they spend five extra minutes filling out. They inched forward to the two ticket counters, herding their luggage like flocks of sheep that multiplied as they moved. Our communal 7:00 A.M. departures grew closer. Behind me travelers pressed in tighter as if at the moment of truth proximity to the counter would count. Ahead of me the Bo Peeps, tickets between their teeth, thrust their heads at the airline clerk, and when he'd pulled the sodden tickets free, insisted the entirety of their luggage would fit in the overhead compartments, demanded window seats and a list of the nightshades and crucifiers in the vegetarian meals. "Every seat lands at the same time," I told them, perhaps a mite more curtly than I intended. If they'd paid attention and moved along, they wouldn't have forced me to actual rudeness. But did they ever appreciate my good sense and concern about expediting everyone's wait? Hardly. I know some of them could have killed me; they told me so.

I paused again. I had tickets for New York in my purse right now. Had I died at the airport? But no—no matter how irrational the rest of those travelers were, they weren't likely to miss their planes just for the satisfaction of offing me. Even if it would have meant freeing up a window seat and a special fish plate lunch. No, much as they might have liked, they hadn't done me in and tossed me on the luggage conveyer to eternity.

Anyway, no point in worrying about that now. I didn't care how I died. What I wanted was to get out of this damned line. Lines, always lines; lines, life's penultimate example of stillness in motion.

The airport is bad, okay, but it's nothing to the true Purgatory: the California freeway. How many hours had I spent waiting in line just to get *on* the freeway, standing behind car after bus after truck waiting for that red light to turn green and admit the next vehicle to the slow lane? Enough people to populate Albania were driving on my freeway, and there was no need for them to be there! They weren't all going to work. Why couldn't those non-nine-to-fivers show a little consideration and stay home at rush hour? They had the whole rest of the day to dawdle on the road. It was bad enough to find the freeway jammed; I'd gotten used to that. I'd learned to force my way into traffic; it was a sport of sorts, eyeing the line of cars, "making" the drivers by how slowly they hit the gas, how far they lagged behind the car in front, how much wax and chrome adorned their own vehicle, and how desperate they were to protect it. Before a waivering wimp could blow his horns I'd spot cut in front with half an inch to spare and brakes squealing. And I'd heard enough hollers, seen enough clenched fists and digital birds flying to know what those wimps would like to have done to me.

Could I have been driving to the airport when I died? Rush hour starts before dawn on these freeways. Had I misjudged and cut in front of a truck without brakes or a lunatic with a rifle? But no. If there's one thing you can count on in rush hour, it's that no one's going fast enough to rear-end you into the hereafter. And freeway snipers don't snipe when they'll be stuck next to your corpse in traffic. No, indeed, my funeral cortege was not a first-gear-only affair in the diamond lane to Judgment.

Why was this question nagging me? It was like having a chatterer right behind you in line—one of those infuriatingly cheerful people who was sure everyone was doing his very best and there was a good reason why we were kept waiting. I dismissed the thought as summarily as I had them.

But neither the bank nor the freeway held the line I hated most. I took a breath and listened. The air was chilly. I wished I'd died wearing a sweater. My feet hurt. Why couldn't I have succumbed in running shoes, or even sandals? It was like I'd just rushed here on the spur of the moment and stumbled onto line. I hadn't expected it to turn out to be *this* line. I couldn't quite make out the surroundings. Undertakers don't bury you with your glasses on, so in the hereafter reality is a bit fuzzy. Music I couldn't quite place played in the distance. I strained to hear, but the melody was too bland to register. Then it stopped, and a voice said over the loudspeaker, "Attention, shoppers."

Oh no, I was in the most infuriating line of all, the nine-items-or-less in the supermarket! Nine items to eternity! The loudspeaker still slapped at my ears but I blocked out its words, a skill I'd mastered in life. Instead I focused on the mob in front of me. Clearly, this was not the Lucky Markets of eternity where they'd open a new line if more than four people were waiting. There were at least twelve people ahead of me, and some of them were not holding little plastic baskets, but leaning on full-sized grocery carts. Fuzzy-eyed or not, even I could tell there were more than nine items in those carts. I glared at the miscreants. Would there never be justice? How many times had I called for a bolt of lightning to crash down and strike gluttons just like these with ten different edibles in their carts! (Were we too high up for lightning now? Not yet. And I was not likely to be unless long suffering was the heavenly criteria.) The checkout clerks know when customers plunk ten items on the counter. You'd think they'd send them packing to the full-cart line. If those gluttons got tossed out a couple times they'd learn. Which was just what I told a few of them (the ones I couldn't shame out of line. A good, loud voice can pique humiliation in the most callous lout, and the rest of the cowards in line behind are willing enough to form a chorus once they know they're not in danger.) The routed louts sputtered; they glared; a couple have even waited for me outside—

Surely, I wasn't murdered there—not in the supermarket—and dispatched in a cortege of grocery carts. But no, the louts wouldn't have dared—not in public, not and take the chance of someone walking off with their groceries.

Dammit, why did my mind keep coming back to that useless question? My foot was tapping, my blood boiling as it had so many times in lines just like this. There was nothing to do but stand and fume. And glance through the magazines and stick them back in the wrong holders. It had always pleased me, I remembered, to page through those periodicals for free. And here, to my left, was a copy of Time (Is Up). It looked just like old Earth's Time. How many copies had I fingered through, glancing at the articles, checking the letters for well-known names, looking at the Milestones to see who had married, given birth, or died. Died!

I gave up. I sighed mightily and turned to the Milestone page and, skipping the happy occasions, moved right to the deaths.

I don't know what made me think I'd find my own passing there. I wasn't famous. But, in fact, there it was: DIED. ANN THOMPSON, 42. That was all! No mention of what I'd done in life to qualify for an obituary there. (Well, obituary was overstating it.) And more irritating yet, it didn't say how I died.

I slapped the *Time (Is Up)* back in the rack in front of a stack of *(Dead) People*. Well, dammit, how did I die?

I pulled free a copy of *Life (No More)* and turned to the index. Ignoring articles on "Pestilence, Familiar and Unexpected," "Plague, the Common Scourge," "War, Tried and True," and "Famine, the Familiar Favorite," I came upon one headed, "New Service at Final Checkout" on page 44.

When I turned to page 44 I almost stumbled back into the cart behind me. Pages 44 and 45, the centerfold, sported a picture of this store, this checkout counter, this very line I was in. And me in it! I turned to the next page. "Shoppers are no longer surprised to find new services available at the checkout," it proclaimed in big black letters. "They've long since become used to price scanners, check cashing, and charging their goods on credit. But never before have they been as eager to be rung up and handed their receipt! And why? Because it's not the receipt they're used to. It's a new, exciting game your grocery is offering just for you, the valued customer. A game so engrossing it's heartstopping! Just guess the answer at checkout and you walk away free and clear." "Free and clear" indeed. I understood what that meant, in the eternal sense.

And if I failed to answer the question? But of course, in true marketing fashion, they didn't spell that out.

They also didn't spell out what the question to be answered was. But I could guess.

I picked up a copy of *Condé Nast Traveler (Styx River Special)*. This time I didn't have to consult the index. The cover article was "How Did You Die? Win a Free Trip to Heaven." As quickly as possible I scanned the rules. (Why hadn't I worn contact lenses; the undertaker might have slipped up and buried me in those.) "Present your checkout clerk with one item and one item only," the rules insisted. "You have the whole market to choose from."

"What do they want—one carton of milk or one gallon of ice cream to signify how I died?" I demanded of the crowd in front of me. But the line that had been twelve somnolent slugs had suddenly dwindled to four beavers busily organizing their few items on the conveyor belt. They didn't have time to be bothered with me.

And I certainly didn't have time to waste on them. Frantically, I looked around for some clue. How had I died? What could possibly symbolize that? A knife from the cutlery department? A pack of cigarettes (even though I didn't smoke)? The aerosol hairspray from the display behind me? A can of cherry cola—that was as close to poison as I could think of.

How could I possibly choose if I didn't even know how I died? Dammit, this was like every contest I'd ever entered—astronomical odds and no way to beat them. Just like the lines—once you queue up, they've got you. Then they don't care how long you cool your heels.

Furiously, I looked around. My eyes lighted on a copy of *Country (No*

Longer) Living. I opened it to a picture of a road—a two-laner in the wine country. And on it was me. The page before was also me—three pictures of me. Me having had to wait for a table for brunch at the Tortoise Winery, me drumming my fingers while the waitress made her eleventh trip to the kitchen before she brought out my mimosa and eggs mercury, me slamming in my chair and stamping my foot till she finally brought the bill. The caption said: "Already half an hour late. Can make up the time on the way back to the city."

I stared at the picture of the country road—the two-lane road.

There were only three people ahead of me in the checkout line now. Had this still been life, my two predecessors would have had twenty-seven items each; they would have insisted on paying with out-of-state, third-party checks; they'd have scratched their heads, stroked their chins, and pondered the earth-shaking question: paper or plastic? The man in the business suit would have looked over his array of currency and finally settled on the hundred-dollar bill that would force the clerk to get change from the next aisle. The woman with the purse the size of a watermelon would have poured every last coin into her palms and begun sorting out pennies, counting them, trying to figure out how many she could get rid of here, all the time explaining to the clerk the curse of carrying around too many copper coins. Now, the one time I would have welcomed any of those maneuvers, the man in the business suit slid his credit card through the slot, grabbed his bagged food, and loped into the parking lot.

That left only two people ahead, and the picture of the country road in my mind. The two-lane road nearing the intersection. The intersection with the last four-way stop sign between me and the city.

Suddenly the minute of my death was clear. The intersection was a meeting with another two-laned road. As I neared it, I could see the cortege moving forward. I could see the beginning but not the end. The damned funeral line extended to eternity. And those corteges never let anyone through, as if their getting to the cemetery late would hold up the corpse. If I stopped I'd be here forever. But the stop was a *four-way* stop. I stepped on the gas. A four-way stop is a fool's stop. Four people stop; they sit; they wait. No sense in that, especially not when you're in a hurry. And with liveried drivers like the hearse driver, too many traffic tickets mean unemployment—they obey the laws. Some might have said I'd be cutting it close (some of my former passengers) but I knew there was plenty of time.

The woman with the watermelon purse smiled at the clerk and held out exact change. There was only one person between me and the final checkout. I didn't have time to reminisce about my demise. I had to choose the symbol.

I needed to think, but there was no time. Flinging the magazine down, I raced out of line—I could always cut back in—but I knew if my turn came and I missed it that was it for this line, and for me. There would be no chance to stare down the milk sops behind me and demand to take one of their places. And I certainly couldn't go to the end of the line—no such luck this time.

I raced past the aerosol display behind, ignoring the pictures of cheery green turtles with shiny, lacquered shells, past the deli counter where the egg salad had been laid out longer than I had, and skidded to a stop at the meat counter. There was a special on hamburger. People were lined up three deep for it, blocking access to every other item in the cooler. Was hamburger somehow the answer? Was that why they were all here?

I shoved forward, pushing past lamb chops, pork roasts, filet of flounder. Panic grabbed me; I began to sweat. This was a very ordinary supermarket. Maybe they wouldn't even have my item.

But no, there it was. I grabbed, shoved, raced, and plopped it on the counter just as the clerk was about to set my basket, my empty basket, aside.

"Fowl," the checkout machine read.

The clerk looked at me questioningly. "Are you sure? We've got a special on—"

I hesitated, seeing the rest of my penultimate moment of life. The two-lane road. The four-way stop. My foot moving toward the brake, then hitting the gas. I'd been in the intersection before I remembered that funeral corteges don't stop for red lights or stop signs. Before I realized how big a hearse was, I'd been spinning out of control. My car was splintering before I realized how flimsy it, and I, was.

She who hesitates is last. I stared down at my item on the counter. I'd made my choice—there was no time to second-guess now. "Sure."

I ran my credit card through the scanner.

The clerk punched in the code.

I looked down at my item. It was dead as me. It didn't even quack. After all, when that hearse hit I had been a dead duck.

The checkout buzzer blared.

The clerk shook his head. "I'm sorry, ma'am, your card has been rejected."

Panic filled me. "Rejected? What do you mean rejected? A dead duck—what's more appropriate than that?"

The clerk looked down at me with the scorn he might have shown a shoplifter. "A dead duck indeed. Rather banal, don't you think? You could have come up with the right answer—you could have won—if you just taken the time to look around, if you hadn't been in such a hurry."

From the customers behind me came a murmur of agreement.

Chiding is never pleasant, and decidedly less so at a time like this.

"Shall I show her the right answer?"

The murmur grew louder.

The clerk stepped around the register, took three steps behind me, and plucked from the display of smiling, shiny tortoises a cylindrical can with a plastic snap on lid. I looked at it in bewildered disgust. "Hairspray?"

The clerk shrugged, displaying his disbelief and disdain. "Hare spray—H-A-R-E."

"Hare spray!" I screamed. "Splattered like a dead rabbit, is that what you mean? The tortoise and the hare? I can't believe my whole eternity depends on a silly pun!"

Behind me, the glossy, grinning turtles stretched their glossy green necks and smelled the roses. The clerk nodded and smiled.

"Talk about banal!" I yelled. " 'Tortoise and the hair'! 'Stop and smell the roses'!" Furious, I grabbed for his throat, but the clerk and the counter disappeared and I found myself at the tail end of a long snaking line. I was ranting at, grabbing for the ghostly customer in front of me.

Exhausted, I let my hand drop. It was too hot for such histrionics. Better I should see what this line was for.

"Take a number, please," the loudspeaker demanded.

I reached up to the dispenser beside me and pulled loose a 100. I was an expert on lines; I knew how to handle this. Now that I had my number I could relax and see what we were waiting for in this line. I jutted by head forward (like the damned turtles), but the sign was so far away I could barely see. The whole place was steamy hot. Already my "100" slip was getting damp in my hand. I stretched as far forward as I could and squinted. Now I could make out the sign: 99 FANS FOR SALE.

Gillian Roberts quickly developed a following for her sleek and winning mystery stories. When you read the following, you'll see why. We're happy to welcome Gillian to the Year's Finest and hope to see her back again. When you finish this, you'll want to read her novels. Happily, they're all available in paperback.

Goodbye, Sue Ellen
GILLIAN ROBERTS

"I don't want a lifetime supply of chewing gum! I want *stock*!" Ellsworth Hummer looked around the conference table, pausing to glare at each of the other directors of Chatworth Chewing Gum, Incorporated.

Neither Peter Chatworth (Shipping), Jeffrey Chatworth (Advertising), Oliver Chatworth (Product Control), Agatha Chatworth (Accounting), nor Henry Chatworth (Human Resources) glared back. Instead, each adopted a rather sorrowful expression. Then they turned their collective attention to the chairperson of the board, Sue Ellen Chatworth Hummer.

Sue Ellen looked at her red-faced husband. "We've told you before, honey," she said in her sweetest voice, "Daddy didn't want it that way. This is the Chatworth *family* business."

"I'm family now, aren't I?"

His response was a mildly surprised widening of six pairs of disgustingly similar Chatworth eyes.

"You're my *husband* now, honey, but you're a Hummer, not a Chatworth," Sue Ellen said, purring. "Besides, you should be happy. After all, you're president of the company."

Ellsworth Hummer's blood percolated. She made it sound like playing house—You be the mommy and I'll be the daddy. Only Sue Ellen's game was, You play the president and I'll be the chairperson for real. His title was meaningless as long as Sue Ellen held the stock in her name only.

He'd received the position as an extra wedding gift from his bride, six

149

months earlier, but all it had yielded so far was a lot of free chewing gum. And now, for the sixth time in as many months, the board had voted him down, denied him any real control, any stock, any say.

Ellsworth stood up. The chair he'd been on toppled backwards and landed with a soft thunk on the thick Persian carpet. "I'm sick of Daddy and his rules!" he shouted. "Sick of Chatworths, one and all! Sick of chewing gum!"

"You can't truly mean that." Cousin Peter sounded horrified.

"I do!" Ellsworth shouted.

"But, honey," Sue Ellen said, "chewing gum has kept the Chatworth's alive. Chewing gum is our life! How can you possibly be sick of it?"

"What's more," Ellsworth said, "I am not interested in anything else you have to say, or in any of the business on the agenda today or in the future." And he left, slamming the heavy door behind him, cursing the fate that had brought him so far, and yet not far enough.

Once home, he settled into the lushly panelled room Sue Ellen had redecorated for him. She called it his "study," although she'd been unable to tell him what important documents he was supposed to study in there, so he used the room to study the effects of alcohol on the human nervous system. It was the most hospitable room in the rambling, semidecrepit mansion Sue Ellen had inherited. The place had gone to seed after Mrs. Chatworth's death and Sue Ellen had been too busy being his bride—she said—to begin renovations yet. So Ellsworth spent a great deal of time in his study. Now he poured himself a brandy and considered his options. Sue Ellen owned the house. Sue Ellen owned the company. And Sue Ellen owned him. That was not at all the way things were supposed to have worked out.

Divorce was not an option. He had signed a prenuptial agreement because, long ago, Sue Ellen's daddy had reminded her that she'd better not forget that husbands were outsiders, not family. All a split would get him was a one-way ticket back to his mother's shack, or, God help us all, to a nine-to-five job. Ellsworth shuddered at the thought of either possibility.

There was only one logical solution. Aside from what she made as chairperson of the present-day company, Sue Ellen was rich in trust funds and the fruits of earlier chewing gum sales, and he was Sue Ellen's legal heir. Ergo, Sue Ellen had to die.

He sighed, not with distaste for the idea itself, but for the work and effort involved in it. This was not how he'd envisioned the happily-ever-after part. He sighed again, and squared his shoulders. He was equal to the task and would do whatever was necessary to achieve his destiny.

All he'd been gifted with at birth was a well-designed set of features and a great deal of faith in himself. His mother, poor in every other way, was rich in hope. Her favorite phrase had always been. "You'll go far, Ellsworth."

And as soon as it was possible, he had.

He'd kept on going, farther and farther, until he finally found the perfect ladder on which to climb to success: Sue Ellen Chatworth, a plain and docile young woman who had spent her life trying to atone for having been born a female.

The elder Chatworths, including the much revered Daddy himself, had never paid attention to Sue Ellen. She was regarded as a bit of an error, a botched first try at producing a son. All their attention was focused on the point in the future when they would be blessed with their rightful heir.

After two heirless decades, during which time the daughter of the house attempted invisibility and was by and large raised by the servants, it finally dawned on the Chatworths that Sue Ellen and chewing gum were to be their only products.

Upon realizing this, Mrs. Chatworth quietly died of shame.

Given that Mr. Chatworth's entire existence was devoted to chewing gum, he was naturally made of more resilient material than his spouse had been. He came home from his wife's funeral and looked toward the horizons. As soon, he made it clear, as a decent period of mourning was over, he'd start afresh with a new brood mare.

But before he found a woman with the look of unborn sons in her, Ellsworth Hummer appeared and became the first human being to take Sue Ellen seriously. She was, understandably, dazzled. Her father took a dimmer view of the courtship.

He was not for a moment enchanted when Ellsworth appeared at his office door and formally asked for Sue Ellen's hand. "Blackguard!" he shouted. "Fortune hunter!"

Ellsworth merely grinned. "Now, now," he said. "You won't be losing a daughter. You'll be gaining a son at long last."

Mr. Chatworth was unused to either irony or defiance in even the most minute dosages. His veins expanded dangerously. His face became mauve, a color Ellsworth had never particularly cared for. Short of breath, he waved his fist at the young man on the other side of his desk. "You'll get *nothing*! I'll change my will!" he shouted. "If you and that daughter of mine, that—"

"Sue Ellen," Ellsworth prompted him. "Sue Ellen's her name, Pop."

Mr. Chatworth was now the color of a fully mature eggplant. "I'll see that you don't get what you want if it's the last thing I—"

"We were thinking of having the wedding in about two weeks," Ellsworth said mildly. "I'd like you to give your daughter away, of course."

"You'll marry over my dead body!" Mr. Chatworth shouted. And then he toppled, facedown, onto his desk and ceased this life thereby, as ever, proving himself correct and having the last word on the subject.

Grateful that the gods and high blood pressure had conspired to pave his way, Ellsworth sailed into marriage and a chewing gum empire. But a mere six months later, he recognized that his triumph was hollow. A sham. All he'd truly gotten was married. Very. And Sue Ellen thought that meant something, wanted to be close to him, seemed unable to comprehend that she was merely a means to an end, to the stock, to the money.

At each of the six monthly board meetings, Ellsworth wheedled, cajoled, charmed, argued, and pontificated about the necessity of his being given some real control. During six months' worth of non-board meeting days, Ellsworth suggested, hinted, insinuated, and said outright how much more of a man he'd feel if Sue Ellen would only treat him as an equal.

"Oh, honey," Sue Ellen would giggle from her pillow, "you're more than enough of a man for me already!"

Today's board meeting had been his last attempt. Now there was no remedy left except Sue Ellen's death.

But how?

Every eye in the impossibly tight-knit family would be on him. He needed a rock-solid alibi. No amateurish hacking or burying in the cellar would work. The cousins detested him as actively as he disliked them. He had to remain above suspicion.

"Hi, Ellsworth," Sue Ellen said brightly, interrupting his dark and private thoughts. "You working in here or something?"

"What work would I be doing?" he said. "What real work do I have to do?"

"Still sulking? Oh, my, honey, you don't want to be so glum about everything. After all, we've got each other and our health."

He was not cheered by being reminded of those truisms. "You and your cousins take care of all your business?" he asked tartly.

She nodded.

"Anything special?"

She lit a cigarette. "Oh, the company picnic plans and ... you know, this and that. Ellsworth, honey, you yourself said you weren't and never would be interested in the kind of stuff that concerns the board, and I respect that." She inhaled deeply.

"Those cigarettes will kill you," he muttered. But too slowly, he added to himself. Much too slowly.

"Aren't you the most considerate groom a girl could have?" she chirruped. "I know I have to stop, but maybe in a bit. Not right now. I'm a little too tense to think about it."

"Your family would make anybody tense," he said. "I hate them."

"Yes. I know that. But I like them." She had been leaning on the edge of his desk, but now she stood straight, then bent to stub out her cigarette in his otherwise unused ashtray. "I'm going to visit Cousin Tina this afternoon," she said. "She's been feeling poorly."

There was nothing newsworthy about either Tina's health or the weekly visit. Sue Ellen saw her crotchety cousin every Saturday afternoon. "Goodbye, Sue Ellen," he said.

"See you," she answered with a wave.

Studying the effects of more brandy, Ellsworth listened as his wife's car pulled out, beginning its way over the mountain pass to her cousin's. And he smiled, because Sue Ellen had just helped him decide the method of her death. She would meet her end in a tragic crash going down that mountain. A little tinkering with the brakes and the car would be too far gone after plummeting over the side for anyone to bother investigating.

Ellsworth had one week left before he became a widower. For seven days, he was almost polite to his wife, providing her with fond final memories of him. He kissed her goodbye on the morning of the last day.

"Good-bye, Sue Ellen," he said, and he repeated the words to himself several times during the day as he lay dreaming of how he'd spend the Chatworth fortune. He smiled as he dozed, waiting for the police to arrive and announce the accident.

"Ellsworth!" The voice was agitated, feminine and definitely Sue Ellen's. He opened one eye and saw her. The dull, drab, infinitely boring, and incredibly rich Sue Ellen was intact.

"You'll never believe what happened to me!"

"Try me," he said slowly.

"I was going over the pass and suddenly I didn't have any brakes! I just screamed and panicked and knew that I was going to die!"

Ellsworth sat up. So far, it was exactly as he'd planned it. Except for this part, with her standing here, very much alive. "What did you do, Sue Ellen?" For once, he was honestly interested in what she had to say.

"Don't laugh, but I lost my head and screamed for my daddy. 'Daddy! Daddy! Help me!' like a real idiot, I guess, or something. But then, like magic, suddenly I could *hear* him, clear as day, a voice from beyond shouting and impatient with me the way he always was. It was mystical almost, Ellsworth, like he was right there with me screaming, 'Don't be such an all-around idiot, girl, and don't *bother* me! Get a grip and leave me out of this!' It almost makes you believe, doesn't it?" She looked bedazzled.

"Well, what good is it to be told to get a grip?" Ellsworth asked.

"What good? Well, I always did what my Daddy said. So I got a grip—on the steering wheel. I stopped waving my arms and being crazy, that's what. And to tell you the truth, I think that's what my . . . my heavenly *vision* meant, because what else could I have gripped? That message from my dear daddy saved me, because I hung on, racing around those curves until finally I was on flat ground again, and then I just ran the car into Cousin Tina's barn to stop it." She finally drew a breath.

Ellsworth tilted his head back and glowered upward. He felt strongly that supernatural intervention—even of the bad-tempered kind—violated all the rules.

Sue Ellen's bright smile flashed and then faded almost immediately. "I pretty much wrecked it, though," she said.

"The barn?"

"That, too. I meant the car. I think they're both totaled. I have Cousin Tina's car right now."

Ellsworth mentally deducted the cost of a car and Tina's new barn from the inheritance he'd receive as soon as he came up with a second, more reliable plan for her disposal.

He was appalled by how few really good ways there were to safely murder anyone. He studied mystery magazines and books about criminals and was depressed and discouraged by the fact that the murderer was too often apprehended. It seemed to him that the most successful homicides were those semi-random drive-by shootings that seemed to happen in great uninvestigated clusters, but they were so urban, and Ellsworth and Sue Ellen lived nestled in rural rolling hills, not a street corner within shooting distance. Gang warfare would be too much of a stretch in the sticks.

The problem was, once the crime grew more deliberate and focused, there were horrifyingly accurate ways of identifying the culprit, right down to matching his DNA from the merest bit of him. It was Ellsworth's opinion that forensic science had gone entirely too far.

However, accidents in the home seemed more likely to pass muster. People clucked their tongues and shook their heads and moved on without undue attention or speculation. So one Monday morning, before he left for another day of sitting and staring at his office walls, Ellsworth carefully greased the bottom of the shower with Sue Ellen's night cream. Then he dropped the jar and left. Sue Ellen was fond of starting her day a bit later than he began his. She was "not a morning person" in her own clichéd words, and she required a steamy hot shower to "get the old motor turning over." This time, he hoped to get more than the old motor and the clichés twirling. He was confident she'd slip and either be scalded to death, die of head injuries, or cover the drain in her fall and drown. That sort of thing happened all the time and didn't even make headlines.

This plan had some latitude, and he liked it.

He was downstairs, drinking coffee and reading the morning paper, when the old pipes of the house signaled that Sue Ellen's shower was going full blast.

"Yes!" he said, raising his buttered toast like a flag. "Yes!" Soon he would call the police and explain how he'd found his wife's body in the shower, too late, alas, to save her.

And then he heard the scream. Yes, yes! He waited for the thud or the gurgle.

Instead, he heard a torrent of words.

Words were wrong. Words did not compute. Whole long strings of words were not what a slipping, sliding, fatally wounded woman would utter.

The words came closer, toward the top of the stairs. Two voices. Ellsworth tensed.

"I don't care if you're new!" Sue Ellen was behaving in a shrill and unladylike manner, to put it mildly. Her daddy would not have approved. "Somebody must have told you my routine. I *need* my morning shower!"

"But, miss, I wanted to make it nice. It was all greasy in there."

"That's ridiculous! It was cleaned yesterday afternoon. That's when it's always done. Well after I'm through."

"Messy. Greasy. But it's nice now."

And then the voices softened. Sue Ellen had a temper when crossed, but it was morning and she wasn't "up to speed" as she would undoubtedly say, so she made peace and retreated to her unslick, horribly safe shower.

Ellsworth refused to be discouraged. He decided to poison her instead, and he chose the family's Memorial Day gathering as the occasion. With forty relatives on his patio, there would be safety in numbers.

Cousin Lotta, according to Sue Ellen, was bringing her famous potato salad, just as she had every other year. Ellsworth had never tasted it, but he decided its recipe could nonetheless be slightly altered. He'd offer to help bring out the covered dishes. It wouldn't be difficult to make an addition in the kitchen.

The plan was brilliant. Many Chatworths would be sickened, but Sue Ellen, her portion hand-delivered by him and specially spiced, would be sickened unto death. And if anyone came under suspicion, it would be Lotta.

He sang all through the morning of the party. In his pocket were small vials of dangerous this and lethal that to be sprinkled over the potatoes, and a special bonus vial for his best beloved.

"I'll bring out the food," he told his wife later in the day.

"Oh, thank you." She spoke listlessly and looked pastier than ever. Her makeup barely clung to her skin. Unwholesome, he thought. Definitely unappetizing. "I'm feeling a bit woozy. I'd be glad to just sit a while longer. Thank you."

It was amazing how easy it was to doctor the salad with no one noticing.

Except that Sue Ellen didn't want to eat. "I'm not really feeling very well," she murmured.

Ah, but unfortunately, left to her own devices, she eventually *would* feel better, he thought. Or was she suspicious? He felt a moment's panic, then relaxed. She was merely being her usual uncooperative, dim self. "It's hunger," he insisted. "You know how you get when you forget to eat for too long. You need something in your stomach. Sit right there—I'll prepare a plate for you."

"Oh, no, I don't think . . . I really do feel quite odd."

"You're overexcited by this wonderful party, these wonderful people," he said. "Relax and let me take care of you."

He watched happily as she ate Gert's ribs and Mildred's pickled beans and

Lotta's quietly augmented potato salad. He had known that if pressed, Sue Ellen wouldn't dare hurt her cousins' feelings by refusing to eat their offerings. He could see the headlines in tomorrow's papers. "Tragedy Stalks Chatworth Barbecue: Chewing Gum Heiress Bites Potato Salad and the Dust."

Maybe he'd give the reporters Sue Ellen's wedding portrait. She looked almost good in it. "Good-bye, Sue Ellen," he whispered.

Suddenly, she stood up, horror and pain distorting her features, and she ran, clutching her mouth, toward the woodsy spot behind the house. He followed until he heard the sounds of her being violently ill. And then, slumping shouldered, he walked back to the party.

"Stomach virus," the doctor said later. "Comes on all of a sudden, just like that. Going around. Let her rest a few days. She's plumb cleaned out inside."

"I told you I felt awful," Sue Ellen murmured from her bed.

A few of the cousins also felt poorly. Too poorly to drive home, in fact, and Ellsworth spent the night in his study, trying to lock out the noises of people being sick all over the house.

He could not believe that of all the world, he alone was a failure at murder. He went upstairs and stared at Sue Ellen. She managed a faint wave of greeting.

"I'm so ashamed," she said. "Getting sick in front of everybody like that. Ruining the party. I could just die!"

Fat chance, he thought as he watched her drift back to sleep.

Finally, Sue Ellen regained her strength and began to visit her cousins again. They had a new source of conversation besides each other and chewing gum these days. Now they could review the Day the Chatworths Got the Stomach Flu. They also had a new project. While in residence, several of the cousins had noticed that the house could use some modernization and loving care. Sue Ellen had also become aware of needed work while she was on the mend. "Falling apart," she would now say.

"Not at all! It's a fortress! They built strong and sturdy places back then," Ellsworth insisted. The sort of remodeling she had in mind would cost a fortune—*his* fortune. Even talking about prospective expenses felt like being robbed, or having a favorite part of his body amputated.

Nonetheless, Ellsworth did not have any more of a vote in the future of his dwelling or his inheritance than he did in the chewing gum empire, which is to say he had none. The house was going to be thoroughly redone. Sue Ellen had developed a yen to "do it right," to use her unoriginal phrase. She wanted someday to be featured in *Architectural Digest*. The prospective tab was astronomical. Ellsworth suffered each planned purchase as a physical pain to his heart, and eventually he refused to listen.

"Let me tell you about what we're going to do up in the—" Sue Ellen would say.

"Not now. I don't understand house things, anyway. Besides, I'm busy," he'd answer.

And he was. He was constantly, frantically, obsessively busy with plans for shortening both the span of his wife's life and the duration of her spending spree. He had failed with the car, with the shower, and with the poison. His mother had always said that bad things come in threes. Perhaps that included bungled murder attempts.

People were dying all over the world. Was it asking too much for Sue Ellen to join them?

But their town had no subway for her to fall under. Their house had no large windows for her to crash through. Sue Ellen seldom drank or took even prescription drugs, and when she did, she was careful. A faked suicide was ridiculous, since she was so unrelenting cheerful—aside from a bit of a temper tantrum now and then, of course.

He thought he would go crazy formulating a new plan. He read accounts of perfect crimes, but couldn't find one that didn't hinge on intricate coincidences or isolation or strange habits of the deceased that had earned them a slew of enemies, all of whom could be suspects.

One evening, over dessert, Sue Ellen and Cousin Tina chattered away as Ellsworth mulled over murder and watched the women with disgust.

Sue Ellen lit a cigarette.

"You ought to stop smoking," Tina said. "It'll kill you."

"But not for *years*." Ellsworth had not meant to say it out loud.

Cousin Tina's spoon stopped midway to her mouth and she looked intently at Ellsworth.

"Sweet Ellsy," Sue Ellen said, "trying to keep me from worrying about my dreadful habit. But Tina's right. I should stop."

Ellsworth watched his wife's plain little face disappear behind a smoke screen and he suddenly smiled.

The next day Ellsworth carefully disconnected the positive battery contact in the upstairs smoke alarm. The change was nearly invisible. Nobody, even a fire marshal, would notice—and if he did, it would be chalked up to mischance. Ellsworth lit a match, held it up to the alarm, and smiled as nothing whatsoever happened. And then he waited until the time was right.

The time was perfect three nights later, when Sue Ellen stood in the living room in her stocking feet, contemplating her brandy snifter. They had just come back from an early dinner with Cousin Peter and his wife. They dined out frequently these days as half the house, including the kitchen, was pulled apart and chaotic. Besides, it was the housekeeper's evening off, and neither Sue Ellen nor Ellsworth was much good at figuring out what to do in a servantless pinch.

"I'm exhausted," Sue Ellen said. "Between the office and the remodeling, I feel like I'm spinning. Can't wait till we get past these practical things and to the fun stuff, like new furniture and wallpaper and things. I just hate even talking about the plumbing and the wiring and the replastering and—''

"Then don't," Ellsworth said. "Why don't you toddle up to bed instead, and get yourself some well-deserved rest?"

"You mean you're just as bored as I am about all that retrofitting and rewiring stuff?" Sue Ellen asked with a yawn. "I thought men liked that kind of hardware store thing. Why just today—''

"Tell me tomorrow," he said. "You must be completely exhausted."

Thirty minutes later, he tiptoed upstairs, Sue Ellen lay, snoring softly, in the pink and repulsively ruffled chamber she insisted on calling the master bedroom, although it made the theoretical master ill. It was symbolic of the many ways in which he was ignored and undervalued. Sue Ellen's pet husband. He looked down at his sleeping wife and felt not a single pang at what he was about to do. Her brandy snifter sat, drained, on her bedside table, next to an ashtray with one stubbed-out cigarette.

Ellsworth took a fresh cigarette from her pack and lit it, then placed it carefully on the pillow next to her. Then he tiptoed out, leaving the door open, the better to let the currents of air flow up the staircase and fan the fire.

He stretched out on his study's sofa and waited. When the smoke reached all the way to him, he would rush to save his bride but, tragically, it would be too late.

Just as everybody had told her—even her own relatives—smoking would be the death of her.

Ellsworth grinned to himself. "Goodbye, Sue Ellen," he said, and closed his eyes.

The howl hurled down the stairwell, directly into his skull. How had she awakened? Smoke wasn't supposed to do that to people—in fact, it was supposed to do just the opposite. The sounds from upstairs were loud and harsh and he closed his eyes again. In five minutes he'd go up far enough to burn his jacket. Then he'd call the fire department.

"Ellsworth! Ellsworth! Wake up!" The voice reached him from outside the study, but then, there she was. Without so much as a singed hair and in her nightgown.

The scream continued from upstairs.

"The house is on fire!" she said. "Upstairs. I already called the fire department." She helped him up. "You look so confused," she said. "You must have been sleeping very soundly." Then together they went and stood outside on the lawn.

"Sue Ellen," he said slowly, "somebody is still up there."

She shook her head. "There's only the two of us home tonight."

"But I heard screaming. In fact, I can still hear it."

"Screaming?" She looked puzzled for a moment, then she chuckled. "I tried to tell you! The contractor said our old alarm was unsafe. He made me light up directly under it and puff into it and he was right Ellsworth. It didn't even make a peep. That's incredibly dangerous! So he put in these new electronic ones, and now we have them all over the place.'' She looked back at the flaming roof. "Had," she said. "We had electronic ones."

They both sighed. But then Sue Ellen brightened. "We should look at the bright side, though. Maybe we lost some of the house and a lot of time and hard work, but we have our *lives*. Isn't it lucky that contractor was so sharp? And what a miracle—he put the new ones in today and they saved our lives tonight! It really makes you think, doesn't it?"

Ellsworth nodded dully. The thoughts it made him think were unbearable and endless, and only the whine of approaching fire engines finally distracted him.

"Oh, Ellsworth," Sue Ellen shrieked, "I'm a mess! The whole fire department will see me in my nightgown. I could just die!"

"Stop saying that!" he shouted.

He began to smoke himself shortly thereafter, needing to do something beside pace the floor through the long nights. He searched wildly for a solution to his problem. He considered hazardous sports, but they made him nervous and Sue Ellen was, by her own admission, rather a klutz.

He pondered whether a fish bone could be wedged down somebody else's throat.

He considered disguising himself as a robber and shooting Sue Ellen dead as he entered the house. But he couldn't figure out how to arrange a good alibi for the time since the only people he knew in town were her doting relatives.

He wept a great deal, lost weight, and bit at his bottom lip until he had a series of small sores there.

Then one fine Sunday, thirty-two days after Ellsworth had first decided that Sue Ellen must go, Sue Ellen herself provided him with the answer. "Oh," she gasped with excitement as she peered out of his study's window. They had been sleeping in the small room, living in much too close surrounds while the upstairs was repaired. "Look," she said. "We have a perfect day for it."

"For what?" he asked, although he had long since lost all interest in his wife's babble.

"For the board meeting!"

"What does the weather have to do with anything?" he asked. "Besides, it's Sunday."

"You left that last meeting, honey, so you didn't hear. We decided to have the next one on the river. Picnic lunch and all. Kind of combining business and pleasure."

"Well, then," he grumbled, "since I am finished with your kind of business, in that case, I'll see you tonight." The fact that it was time for another monthly meeting was incredibly depressing. *Tempus fugit* but Sue Ellen didn't. An entire month gone and nothing had changed. Nothing whatsoever. He was still

Ellsworth Hummer, possessor of nothing except a meaningless title, and the status quo might last forever.

"Nonsense!" Sue Ellen said. "We need you there. Oh, I know you had your little snit, but you are still the company president. Don't ruin everything. Besides, it'll be fun." She pursed her mouth and burst into an ancient and boring song, " 'Cruising down the river . . . on a Sunday afternoon—' I can't remember any more of the words," she said.

Wait a second, he thought. Rivers were good things. People drowned in them. And with a little help, so would Sue Ellen, this very day. "Goodie," he said. "A family picnic. What a treat."

He whistled as he drove. The river, he knew, turned and curved romantically between banks laden with trees. If he could get a head start and place their canoe beyond a curve, away from the relatives, he could push Sue Ellen into the water and hold her there long enough to finally do the job. A few minutes were all that were required—probably even less. A person could only hold her breath for so long. Then he'd release her, flounder around, and call for help. Her whole family would witness his desperate attempts to save her.

After a hearty lunch, Peter asked whether they wanted to hold the business meeting now or later.

"Later," Ellsworth said. "Always later and later."

"Ah," Peter said. "Are we then to take it you haven't had a change of heart toward chewing gum concerns or board matters? Is that how it still is?"

"I have the same heart I always had. Why change it?" Ellsworth said with a mean smile.

The seven board members headed for the river and climbed into canoes. Agatha said she'd rather paddle by herself, and the rest, including Ellsworth and Sue Ellen, divided up into pairs.

Ellsworth was younger and stronger than his fellow board members, so it was easy and fairly quick to get himself a wide lead and to station his canoe in the arc of a blind curve. He could hear the cousins laugh and call to one another just beyond the trees. This was good, because he'd be able to summon them quickly.

"Isn't this nice?" Sue Ellen said dreamily. "Wasn't this a great idea?"

He nodded and grinned.

"I'm so glad we had today together this way," she said. "For once you don't seem angry about the business or how we're running it."

"Well . . ." Ellsworth said, positioning himself. "Things change. People learn. Finally, I think I really understand what can be and what can't be and what must be. So goodbye, Sue Ellen."

Her Chatworth eyes opened wide. "Why, Ellsworth—" she began.

Quickly, he stood up in the canoe, but Sue Ellen instantly followed his lead, and her motions overturned the boat, throwing them both into the water.

The dive into the river was unplanned, but it didn't discourage Ellsworth. However, the hard clap on his head from Sue Ellen's oar definitely did.

As he sank, he heard her shouting. For help, he hoped. But then, he could hear nothing more as the pressure on his head grew heavier and heavier. Was little Sue Ellen really that strong? he wondered.

Then that and all other concerns left him forever.

Sue Ellen shivered as she climbed into Cousin Aggie's canoe.

Cousins Peter and Jeremy smiled at her from their boats and then Jeremy finally released his oar from Ellsworth's submerged head. "Went well, don't you think?" Jeremy said as he righted the overturned canoe and, with help from Henry, pulled the inert form into it.

"Exactly as planned," Peter said. "Ellsworth was wrong, you know."

"Dead wrong," Aggie said with a chuckle. "He should have stayed at that last meeting, don't you think?"

"He should have given chewing gum another chance," Henry said.

"He blew it," Aggie said. Her voice took on a chillingly Ellsworth-like quality as she mimicked him. " 'I have the same heart I always had. Why change it?' " She shook her head. "No turning back after that."

"We have a *good* board and we work well together. Look how smoothly this decision was implemented," Peter said. "Quite a pity that he never learned to appreciate our strengths or how the system works."

"Your daddy was right, Sue Ellen," Oliver of Product Control said. "The family can handle everything by itself, just like he always said."

"We'd best get back to report the unfortunate accident," Jeremy said.

"Yes," Sue Ellen agreed. "But first, I have to tell you one thing I surely can't tell the police. I'm positive that Ellsworth knew just what we were going to do and that he *approved*. He knew that he didn't fit in. He didn't belong. But in the end he understood. The last few weeks, he's been so kind to me, so concerned, so *serene*, you know? Why, it's almost like he knew the plan and accepted it. Especially today. Because just before I toppled us into the water, you know what he said, real sweetly? He said that he understood what must be—honest and truly, just like that, he said it. And then he said, 'Goodbye, Sue Ellen.' Makes you wonder, doesn't it?"

And with contented strokes she and her cousins and uncles and aunt paddled back to shore. Once she looked over at her late husband, nestled in his canoe.

"Goodbye," Sue Ellen whispered.

Doug Allyn is that rarest of writers, the one who can support himself by writing short stories. He writes a good number of them. But the important thing is how good each one is, how well-turned the phrases, how fresh and surprising the plots. The following is a good example.

The Ghost Show
DOUG ALLYN

"That guy onstage is the sorriest lookin' Elvis I've ever seen," Wardell grumbled as I eased down on the barstool next to him. "Elvis never wore no horn-rims."

"He's supposed to be Buddy Holly, chump." Doc sighed, giving me a what-do-kids-know look behind Wardell's back. "He may not look much like Buddy, but he moves like him. Like he's been dead a helluva long time. Wonder where they dug him up?"

"They held auditions in Chicago," I said. "Cohen ran an ad in *Variety,* hired a hall, the works. The black guy who's doing the Jimi Hendrix act is great. Overall, the show's pretty good."

"They're all just actors though," Wardell groused. "We're the only real band on the bill."

"So we are," Doc said. "Stoney and the Bones are the only real band in a dead-stars revue, and the actors are gettin' paid more than we are. That tell you anything, Wardell?"

"Yeah. We'll be makin' steady money for a change," Wardell said sourly.

I caught the bartender's eye. "Jack Black on the rocks," I said. "Do it twice."

"I thought you were on the wagon, Stoney," Wardell said.

"Singing's dusty work," I said. "Need a little lubrication for the pipes. How'd we sound, Doc?"

"Not bad for a first night, but Wardell's piano was a little loud and your guitar was thin. The bass and drums were solid. I'll tweak the sound setup tomorrow. How's your hand holdin' up?"

162

"Good as new," I lied. It hurt like hell, a painful reminder that motorcycles and trees are a bad mix. The bartender parked a double bourbon in front of me and I knocked back half of it at a single gulp. It cut a gully down my throat and exploded in the deep south. Velvet napalm. I sipped the rest of it slowly, scanning the room. Not a bad crowd for a show bar in Omaha. A mixed bag. Mostly stag flyboys from the airbase down the road, some cliques of yuppie singles and divorcees on the make. Doc wouldn't have any trouble finding temporary true love. His rugged puppy looks and shaggy blond mane would make him a trophy in a herd of half-smashed brush cuts.

The audience had applauded politely after our set, but I doubted that many of them knew who we were. Stoney and the Bones are strictly a golden oldies footnote now. People remember us as the band that introduced Bonnie McGee to the world. If they recall us at all. This crowd came for the beer and the rock-'n'-roll ghost show: Elvis, Buddy Holly, Jimi Hendrix, and a brand new act, the late, great Bonnie McGee.

"Anybody met the chick who's doin' Bonnie's act?" I asked.

Wardell shook his head.

"I stopped by her dressing room," Doc said. "You know, to say howdy, wish her luck."

"So?" I prompted. "Does she look much like Bonnie or not?"

"Not much." Doc shrugged. "Same size, I guess, but she ain't a redhead. She's got Bonnie's voice down pat though. I heard her singing in her room. Thought it was a record until I knocked."

"What's she like?"

"Neighborly. I said howdy, I'm Doc Feeny, road manager for the Bones. She told me to take a hike."

"Proves she's got taste, at least," I said.

"Maybe you shoulda worn a T-shirt without holes in it," Wardell said. "The grunge look's passé, Doc."

"The hippie look's comin' back," Doc said, "and so will the Bones. A hit song, a break or two, and we'll be big time again."

"Sure we will," Wardell said. "But while I'm waitin', think I'll crash back at the motel. We at the Holiday Inn?"

"Third floor," Doc said. "And don't smoke anything nasty in your room. They've got security."

"What? And blow my chance at stardom?" Wardell smirked. "See ya, Stoney." He sauntered off.

I waved goodbye with my glass.

"That punk needs a personality transplant," Doc said.

"He may not be Mr. Warmth but he can flat play a piano. And it's not like we're married to him. He'll move on. The Bones have always been a revolving-door group, players come and go."

"Everybody but you and me," Doc said.

"Which blows the theory that we get smarter with age."

"Amen." Doc smiled and we touched glasses in a toast to nothing in particular. The pseudo-Buddy Holly ended his set with a lame version of "Peggy Sue." The Bonnie McGee act was next. I killed my drink and ordered two more. Insurance. I'd seen dead-rocker shows before, but never a ghost act of anyone I'd actually known. Or cared about. I caught Doc's eyes and he slipped me a couple of Quaaludes under the table. I gulped 'em dry.

Len Cohen, the emcee/manager of the show, had worked with all the big acts at one time or another, including the Bones. He sprinted onstage, tall, dark, and geeky. His slicked, thinning hair and black tux made him look like an anorexic undertaker. "Ladies and gentlemen, here she is, the baddest biker mama of all time, back from her last tour in the land down under, and I mean *waayyy* down under! The one, the only, BONNIE McGEEEEE!!!"

The backup band kicked into the riff from "Ridin' the Iron," and Bonnie bopped into the spotlight. No problem. I felt nothing at all. For about five seconds. And then my heart stopped and my eyes were stinging, blurring my vision. I could barely see the stage. Which reinforced the jolt I'd felt that first instant. Time travel. It was Bonnie onstage. Sweet Jesus, it really was. Fiery red hair, black leather vest and spandex hotpants, tattoos on her arms and thighs, the way she moved . . .

I knocked back my second double without even tasting it.

She jumped into the first verse of the song. Doc was right, she sounded a lot like Bonnie. Exactly like her, in fact. I tried to pick out a flaw: tone, accent, anything. I couldn't find one. She was perfect. Perfect.

I closed my eyes, letting the music wash over me, and the memories. Feeling the buzz from the bourbon and the drugs kick in, letting Bonnie's voice take me higher than I'd been in years.

The ghost singer did Bonnie's set, song for song, note for note, exactly the way I remembered it. The way I'd heard it in my head a thousand times over the past ten years. And somewhere midway through the set, in the muddle of my mind, the germ of an idea took root and began to grow. A boozy fantasy that gradually solidified into a conviction.

I was hearing an encore. It really was Bonnie up there. Somehow she'd found a way to come back. She'd fought her way through the darkness or whatever was on the other side. And she'd returned to the place she was most alive. On a stage, in the spotlights, a band jamming behind her, amid the smoke and din of a rock-'n'-roll saloon. She'd come back to it. And to me.

I knew it was crazy, but between the booze and the Quaaludes and the pain of loss I'd been carrying all these years. . . . Each song intensified the idea, until I was almost sure it was true. Almost.

"Doc?" I said quietly. "Do you hear what I hear?"

"What do you mean?"

"Nobody's that good an imitator. Nobody could be. I think that's really Bonnie up there."

"You mean a tape? Nah, I helped Len's crew set up the PA system. It's not rigged for a lip sync. She's singing live."

"I know. That's what I mean. Check her out. Her voice, the way she moves, everything. I really think it's her, Doc. Somehow she . . . I don't know. She's come back."

Doc scanned my eyes, looking for a smile. We've got a history, Doc and me. He can read me. "What the hell?" he said slowly, "you're serious, aren't you?"

"Yeah," I said, swallowing. "I think I am."

Doc swiveled to face the stage, frowning. He seemed suddenly uneasy. "Well?" I said.

"I don't know, man," Doc said. "I admit it sounds a whole lot like her, but . . . Hell, Stoney, that's crazy. Dead people can't come back."

"Sure they can. Happens all the time. We call 'em ghosts," I said, standing up. Too fast. The room wobbled on its axis. "And this *is* a ghost show, right?"

"Yo, partner," Doc said, steadying my arm. "You okay?"

I pulled away from him and threaded my way through the crowd toward the stage. Slow going. The floor was pitching like a cruise ship in a rough sea. Tables kept blundering into my way. She saw me coming. She seemed to be singing to me, drawing me deep into her eyes. . . .

Her eyes. They seemed different. Darker than I remembered. Colder. I couldn't seem to focus on them. I needed to get closer. I vaulted up on the stage, stumbled to one knee, then stood up.

"Hey, boys and girls, look who's here," she said, grinning at me across the stage. "It's my old singing partner, the guy that gave me my big break, Mr. Keith Stone. Give him a hand, maybe we can do a few of our hits together."

One of the stage crew shoved a microphone in my hand. I eyed it stupidly for a moment, then dropped it. It hit the stage with a thump amplified into a thunderclap. Bonnie froze and the room fell silent. Up close her face seemed to be wavering, as though I was seeing her through a waterfall. I shook my head, trying to clear it.

"Bonnie?" I said.

"He's trashed," a stagehand said. "Get him the hell off." Somebody grabbed my arm. I tried to shake loose and couldn't quite manage.

"Bonnie?" I said again, squinting at her through the fog in my head. "It's you, isn't it?"

She hesitated a moment, glaring at me. And then she smiled. But with no warmth. "Yo, Keith, *maĺy bracie*. You didn't think you'd get rid of me that easy, did you?" Bonnie said. And in that instant I *knew*. Knew it to the core of my soul. It was Bonnie. But I couldn't seem to bring her into focus, or even stay on my feet. The stage was revolving like a wobbly turntable, picking up speed, spinning. And I was going down. . . .

My left eye wouldn't open. It was gummed shut, as if somebody'd licked it and tried to mail it to Seattle. The right one worked though. I could see my feet. Socks. Somebody'd taken my boots off and tossed a blanket over me. Doc, probably. Motel room. Right. Holiday Inn. Omaha. I risked a slow look around.

Len Cohen was hunched into a question mark, scowling over a newspaper at the dressing table. He'd traded in his tux for a rumpled sport coat, knit tie, cotton Dockers. Doc was sprawled across an armchair reading a *Mad* magazine. He was wearing faded jeans and a T-shirt. From last night? Hard to say. He seldom wears anything else. Sunlight glowed around the window blinds. Morning sun? Afternoon? Couldn't be sure.

"Good morning, butthole," Len growled.

I sat up, slowly, slowly. The room lurched. So did my stomach. I felt flat as a road-killed possum in a truck-stop driveway. I wanted to groan and die, but wouldn't give Len the satisfaction. Doc unfolded himself from the chair and poured me a cup of coffee from a carafe on the nightstand. It was lukewarm. Black, with triple sugar and laced with amphetamines. Doc Feeny's surefire cure for a morning after. I gulped half of it down and felt the amphetamines kick in. And decided I might just survive after all. And it'd serve me right.

"So," I croaked, "Doc said we sounded a little rusty last night."

"You sounded adequate," Len conceded. "It was the show you put on afterwards that's bothering me. When I offered you the gig you promised you'd stay straight, Stoney. What the hell happened?"

"It was tougher than I expected," I said slowly, remembering. "Hearing those songs again and especially . . . seeing Bonnie again."

"Yeah, that chick does a heckuva job, doesn't she? Her name's Carol Anspach. Best imitator I've ever seen, and I've seen 'em all."

"But that's the thing, Len. She seemed real to me. Not an act at all. It was like Bonnie'd come back somehow."

"Get real. That wasn't Bonnie onstage last night any more than it was Elvis or Hendrix. Or were you so wrecked you thought they were real too?"

"I know it sounds crazy but, look, you know me, Len. I may be a little wild, but I'm not nuts. I swear I thought it was her."

"Correction. I used to know you, Stoney, back when you were still somebody. But in case you've been smoking something extra heavy-duty, here's a reality check for you. Forget the tabloids that claim she's been spotted everyplace from Nome to Armpit, Idaho. Bonnie's long gone. She died of a drug overdose in Australia ten years ago. I even had the dubious honor of identifying her body afterwards. If you hadn't been in traction from cracking up your 'cycle you could have attended her funeral yourself.''

"I know, I don't mean it was *really* her, but . . . Dammit, Len, I'm telling you there was something uncanny about her voice, her moves, everything. Doc noticed it too. And when I got on stage she said something to me.''

"Like what?'' Len asked.

"I . . . can't remember. But it was definitely Bonnie's voice. Do you think I wouldn't know her voice?''

"Maybe she was possessed,'' Doc offered drily, winking at Len over the top of his magazine. "Maybe Bonnie took over whatsername somehow. You know, like Linda Blair in *The Exorcist*?''

"*The Exorcist,* right.'' Len echoed. "Very funny, Doc. Only I'm not laughing. Now listen up, you two burnouts. That wasn't Bonnie last night, and it wasn't her ghost or whatever. She's an actress from Chicago named Carol Anspach. She did a Janis Joplin act in Vegas for a while, and now she's doing Bonnie. She's damn good, audiences like her, and I think we've all got a shot at making some serious bucks here. But you'd better get this straight: Carol's the headliner for this show, not the Bones. I signed your group on because I figured the show'd be more realistic with you as an opening act, but my God, if you give me any more trouble I'll fire your sorry butts in a New York minute.''

"So why don't you?'' I said.

"Because believe it or not, that little episode last night actually got us some pretty good ink,'' he said, waving the paper at me. "The music critic of the *World-Herald* said Carol's so good she even fooled you. So if you want to rave at reporters about how Bonnie's really come back, be my guest. But don't try it as an excuse for getting wrecked again, Stoney. You stay straight from here on or you're gone. And just to show you I'm serious, Doc, you're fired.''

"No he's not,'' I said. "He's been with the Bones from the beginning and in the old days there were plenty of times you were damned glad Doc was along. How many shows did he get us through when we were in no shape to play?''

"You really don't get it, do you?'' Cohen sighed. "Maybe if your pal Dr. Feelgood isn't around to pick you up when you're too wrecked to play you won't get wrecked quite so often.''

"Don't blame that on Doc. We've all been legal grownups for a while now. And unless you'd like me to tell that music critic last night's little scene was your idea, Doc stays.''

"Fine, have it your way,'' Len said, unfolding himself from the chair. "But we'd better be clear on this, Stoney. The old days are gone. As dead as Joplin or Hendrix or Bonnie. It's all show biz now. You want to work, you stay straight.''

"I will. It won't happen again.''

"It better not," he said, pausing in the doorway. "You know, you could be right, though. Maybe Bonnie did come back for a minute last night. To remind you what happens when dopers get careless."

"Screw you, Len," I said.

His face darkened and for a moment I thought I'd pushed him too far. But he must've figured the Bones could still make him a few bucks. He slammed the door on his way out.

"Thanks," Doc said.

"*De nada,*" I said. "I mean it. You're the best roadie in the business and you've saved my tail more times than I can count."

"You want some pills?" Doc said, reading my eyes. "You look like you need 'em."

"Nah, I'd better pass, Doc. Len was serious and we definitely need the work."

"Whatever. Look, what you said before about Bonnie comin' back. Do you really believe that?"

"I don't know," I said slowly. "Len's right. I was blown away. That's probably all it was. A bad trip."

"Maybe," he said doubtfully. "I didn't wanna say anything with Len here. But I was straight, Keith, and she seemed so real she scared the hell out of me too."

"C'mon, Doc, after that monster Texas biker caught you with his mama I didn't figure anything'd ever scare you again."

"That dude was porky enough I figured I could outrun him," Doc said, smiling faintly. "How do you outrun a ghost?"

He was half serious. I know Doc's face as well as my own. I can't always tell when he's kidding. But I know when he definitely isn't.

"All right," I said slowly, "maybe we'd better settle this one way or the other. What did Len say that chick's name was?"

"Which one is she?" I asked, scanning the crowded restaurant.

"There, in the corner booth, readin' the book," Doc said, glancing at me curiously. "You saw her last night."

"Not very clearly," I said. "She looks different in daylight."

"Don't they all. Look, I gotta make a phone call," Doc said. "I'll catch up with you later."

"Whatever," I said absently as Doc faded into the crush. The girl in the corner didn't look anything like Bonnie. Same size maybe, same slender build, but her hair and eyes were dark, and her over-sized glasses and Cornhuskers sweatshirt made her look like a college coed. Pre-law. I worked through the crowd toward her table. She had a good face: wide-set eyes, aquiline nose, hair cropped close. Not punk, just short. She glanced up as I approached. If she was concerned, she hid it well. Good for her.

"Hi," I said. "I think I fell on my face before we were properly introduced last night. I'm Keith Stone."

"So I gathered," she said. "I've heard a lot about you. Mostly bad. And you certainly lived up to your reputation. What do you want?"

"For openers, to apologize," I said, sliding into the booth across from her. "I'm really sorry about what happened."

"Apologies don't cut much ice with me, Mr. Stone. Opening nights are tough enough without having a drunk crash my act."

"I know," I said, feeling myself flush. "I, ahm . . . I was upset. I guess I went a little heavy on the anesthetic."

"From your rep, I take it you get upset quite a lot. What was the problem last night?"

"I saw a ghost. Or thought I did. You must be really terrific at what you do, miss. You actually made me believe . . ." I swallowed, and looked away.

"Len told me what you said," she said, cocking her head, looking me over for the first time. "I thought he was joking. Maybe I should be flattered, but in the shape you were in, you would've seen Easter bunnies next."

"No," I said, "it wasn't just booze. It was your voice, the way you moved on stage, everything."

She shrugged. "I'm an actress. An interpretive artist. I used to do Joplin, now I do Bonnie. Maybe I'll never be as good as they were, but I try. I do research, I rehearse like a dog, and I take my work seriously. Which is more than you ever did."

"You don't like me, do you? And I get the feeling that it's about more than just last night. What's your problem?"

"Maybe I just resent what self-destructive jerks like you do to yourselves. And what you did to her."

"Did to *her*? Lady, you've got it exactly backwards. She was nobody when I met her. Joining the Bones was her big break. We had a few hits together, made some serious money. Then I cracked up a motorcycle and she quit us to go solo while I was still in the hospital. Didn't even say goodbye. Not that I hold that against her. It was the smart move and Bonnie was always smart. Still, if anybody owed anybody, she owed me."

"Did she? When you hired her, you hadn't written a hit in quite awhile and your band was on the skids. She helped put the Bones back on top again. And she was dead within a year."

"And you blame me for it? Figure I led her astray or something? Lady, why do you think her arms and legs were tattooed? Sure it gave her a terrific rock-'n'-roll image. But it also camouflaged needle tracks pretty well. I've got my flaws, but I've never turned anybody onto drugs in my life. She was a user when I met her, and I was ten thousand miles away when she overdosed."

"Methinks the gentleman protests too much."

"Bull. I just got steamrolled by some heavy memories last night. Maybe it was because I never got the chance to say goodbye, or even to go to her funeral, I don't know," I said, sliding out of the booth. "Look, I've apologized and that's the best I can do. And don't worry about it happening again. Up close, minus the red wig, you're nothing like her. Nothing at all."

"You're right, I'm not. I'm just good at what I do. And so are you, when you try. I caught your set last night. I was impressed. If you think you can stay sober long enough maybe we can work up a couple of the songs you and Bonnie did together. It could punch up the act."

"No thanks, lady. I may be a has-been working in a damned ghost show, but I'm not down to mooching off a dead girl's talent like a freaking graverobber."

She flinched, her face reddened as though I'd slapped her. She stared down at the table a moment, focusing on the pattern in the Formica. And when she looked up, she'd changed. Her eyes were burning, transformed, as though something was ablaze in her soul. "Yo, Keith, *maly bracie*. You think you'd get rid of me that easy? I'll be back."

It was Bonnie's voice. Unmistakably. My blood chilled, freezing my heart in place. And then her eyes seemed to melt. And she spoke again in her own voice. "You see, Mr. Stone," she said coldly, "it's not just wigs and makeup. It's art. And the only crime in art is to piss away your talent the way you have. Or to destroy someone else's. Now take a walk."

For a moment I couldn't speak. "What the hell is this?" I managed at last. "Who are you?" She ignored me, staring out the window as though I'd already gone. I turned, and bumped into Doc. I didn't know how long he'd been there, or what he'd heard, but his face was ashen. He looked as shaken as I felt.

The show finished the week in Omaha, then moved south for a weekend stand in Lincoln. Opening night was rough. My guitar amp shut down on me twice. The second time I kicked it halfway across the stage. The audience loved it. Len wasn't amused, but I felt a bit better. Temporarily.

The next night was a lot worse. As we finished our set and the curtain came down, the lights winked off for a moment. And Bonnie said, "You think you could get rid of me that easy? That easy?"

It was Bonnie again. I swear to God it was. Her voice was muffled, but it seemed to surround us. Then the backstage lights came on. The whole thing hadn't taken three seconds.

Len's crew was already shifting the equipment, getting ready for the Hendrix act. Doc stalked onstage from the wings and I tossed him my guitar. "Where's Anspach?" I snapped. "I've had enough of this garbage!"

"Forget it," Doc said grimly. "It wasn't her."

"What do you mean? Of course—"

"Stoney, she was standing five feet from me talkin' to Len when it happened. Besides, that was Bonnie's voice. And we both know it."

"But . . . Dammit, Doc, what are we gonna do?"

"Do?" he echoed. "Nothing. We do nothing, say nothing. Just keep on truckin' like it didn't happen. If somebody's runnin' a game on us, eventually they'll get bored. And if they're not ... Hell, if Bonnie really comes back we'll work her into our show, tell Len to cut Anspach loose and give the rest of us a raise."

He was grinning, but there was an edge to him, a wildness in his eyes I hadn't seen in years. He was definitely spooked, but there was no dog in him. He wouldn't run scared. And if he could handle it, so could I.

I sighed. "Right. Maybe we oughta set up an extra mike for Bonnie. She wasn't very loud."

"She was loud enough," he said, his smile fading. "I heard her just fine."

The show finished the run in Lincoln without any more incidents, then we packed up and rolled east into Iowa for a string of one-nighters. Des Moines, Sioux City, after the third or fourth town I lost track. A shakedown cruise, working out the glitches in low-rent saloons and concert halls, getting ready for bigger dates in Chicago and Vegas.

Usually the players on a tour coalesce into a kind of extended family, a kinship of the craftsmen, all the same bus chasing a neon rainbow. It's one of the pleasures of life on the road. It didn't happen with this show.

We were a house divided. I avoided Carol Anspach, and vice versa. We didn't talk, or catch each other's acts. The Bones opened every show but I'd split as soon as we finished. I told Len Cohen I was staying out of the bars to avoid temptation. But the truth was, I was ducking Anspach like a dog who'd been kicked. And the bars weren't the real danger anyway. It was the sense of déjà vu, as though touring with Bonnie's ghost had revived my own private demons. And brought the crazy days back. I found myself falling back on old standbys, booze and poppers. But I didn't have the constitution for it anymore. Often I was too high or too low to do the show. Without Doc and his stash I couldn't have made it.

Len knew what was going on, of course. But he didn't say anything. He wouldn't, as long as I could do my act. Hell, maybe he was hoping I'd OD too, so he could hire an actor to play me. Someone easier to control. Another square peg for his square new order.

He was right, times had changed. The people in the ghost show didn't drink or smoke. They read, or listened to self-improvement tapes on headsets. They did calisthenics at roadside rest stops. The guys in their road crew even wore matching coveralls with the show's logo on the back. Clones, the lot of 'em.

The Bones? We'd sit in the back of the bus and play high-stakes pinochle, or jam for hours on battered guitars, playing old songs or working up new ones. But mostly we played the old songs.

Doc was as edgy as I was. He hid it behind a wall of wisecracks, but I knew this thing was chewing at him. I'd catch him staring at odd moments, looking off to another place, some other time. We went back forever, Doc and me. We'd survived bar fights, bad dope, bum gigs, and crooked promoters. We were hardened rock-'n'-roll road warriors. But being part of a ghost show made us feel ancient, like dinosaurs blundering through a blizzard. Doc tried to kid me out of my funk. He said it was like *The Invasion of the Body Snatchers* had happened for real, and the Bones were the last people on earth who hadn't popped out of pods. The truth was, the Bones clung together like ragtag remnants of a defeated army. Surrounded. And outnumbered.

Until Doc evened the odds a little. He hired a new guy, an honest to God hippie throwback we picked up at a rest stop in Iowa. He called himself Gopher. I doubt he could remember his real name. His eyes were as empty as the bottom of a beer mug, but he was a free spirit, willing to work for food, a place to crash, and an occasional pop out of Doc's bag. He flatly refused to wear road-crew coveralls, called them fascist. So Doc quit wearing them too. Maybe the Bones weren't stars anymore, but by God we had our own road crew again, in torn denims and headbands and hair down to their waists. Scruffs defiant.

The one thing Doc wouldn't talk about was the ghost. I brought the subject up a couple of times but he blew me off. Said he didn't want to encourage my delusions. And he was right. Hell, I knew it was all a scam and Anspach was just an actress. I *knew* it. She'd learned to sing like Bonnie the way a parrot learns, by listening to records and mimicking the nuances. But what she'd said to me in the restaurant, and the voice we heard onstage in the dark . . . Remembering it raised the hair on the back of my neck.

Haunted or not, the ghost show's bad luck continued. The bus broke down on Highway 80 just west of Moline. We were stuck waiting for repairs most of the day and barely made it to Peoria in time to set up for the show. Len had booked a weekender in an American Legion hall, a barn of a place with hardwood floors and acoustics like the inside of an oil barrel. There were no dressing rooms, and the hall was jammed, standing room only by nine o'clock.

The Bones opened the show and got a pretty good response. It was an older crowd, definitely Geritol generation. They remembered us, or freaks like us, from their lost rock-'n'-roll youth.

The rest of the band split for the bus to play cards, but I stayed. I'd been stuck in the bus long enough for one day, and anyway, I was curious. I was ready to see how real Anspach's act would seem if I watched her from the wings, cold sober.

I didn't get the chance to find out. Len gave his usual spiel, the backup band kicked into the first song, and Bonnie/Carol came bopping out. I focused on her with every atom of concentration I could muster, trying to see past the wig, to remember the face of the woman I'd talked to in the restaurant. But I couldn't seem to separate them. Memories of Bonnie kept superimposing themselves on her imitator. If Anspach saw me standing there, she gave no sign. She spun to face the audience, grabbed the mike stand. And froze.

For a moment I thought it was stage fright—nobody ever truly loses it. But then I saw a faint wisp of steam from her fist where she was holding the stand. And realized she was burning.

"She's frying! Kill the power," I yelled at the roadies as I sprinted onstage, I slammed into Bonnie shoulder first in a flying tackle, spinning her away from the microphone, knocking her into a heap in the corner. Her eyes were glassy and her palm was seared from the electrical shock she'd received. She wasn't breathing. I tried to start mouth-to-mouth but one of Len's road crew thought I'd freaked and dragged me off. I took a swing at him, and then went down under a pile of clones in blue coveralls.

Len caught up with me at the motel desk, checking in.

"You oughta get that knot on your temple looked at," he said, eyeing me critically.

"I've been hurt worse falling off barstools. How's your star?"

"The emergency room treated her for shock, second-degree burns on her hand, and bruised ribs. Did you have to hit her so hard?"

"I didn't have to hit her at all. I could have let her toast to a golden brown. What the hell happened?"

"That burned-out roadie Doc hired back in Iowa, what's his name? Gopher?"

I nodded.

"He pinched a frayed power cord underneath the mike stand. Carol caught a hundred and twenty volts as soon as she touched it. She was lucky you were handy."

"If she was lucky it wouldn't have happened at all. And what makes you think it was Gopher's fault? It could have been one of your crew."

"Nah, it was Gopher. Doc admitted it and even apologized, which is a first. He's already cut him loose. But from now on if you want to hire the handicapped, clear it with me, understand?"

"Yassuh, Boss. Is Anspach still in the hospital?"

"Nope, they released her. She's up in her room, resting. She feels pretty rocky."

"Yeah," I said. "I'll bet she does."

It took her nearly ten minutes to answer my knock. She looked like a train wreck, but somehow no less attractive for it. Wearing an oversized bathrobe, her dark hair a tousled shambles, she could have passed for her own sickly sister. Her left hand was wrapped in greasy gauze and her eyes were dazed. Good.

"Hi," she said. "I guess I owe you a thank you. Thank you. And good night." She started to close the door, but I caught it.

"Sorry, but it ain't gonna be that simple. First let's get you back in bed where you belong,'' I said, pushing her gently into the room. "Then we have to talk. It's important."

"If it's about your friend being fired—"

"It's about him and a lot more. I need your help. Please." She let me lead her to the bed. She eased down on the edge of it, blinking, trying to collect herself.

"Are you okay?" I asked.

"I don't know," she said honestly. "My hand hurts and I'm half in the bag from the painkillers they gave me at the hospital. Which is an average day for you, right?"

"That's more like it," I said. "For a minute there I thought you were going to be civil."

"A lapse," she said, eyeing me warily. "It won't happen again. Now what do you want exactly?"

"I'm not sure. I guess I want you to break a mirror for me."

"Come again?"

"A mirror. Like in a fun house? I feel like I'm lost in a roomful of mirrors. People are getting hurt and I can't see what's happening or find my way out. But somehow I think you know the way out."

"Are you high or something? You're not making any sense."

"Look, I know you've got no use for me, but dammit, I saved your neck tonight. You owe me, lady. At least a mirror's worth."

"I see. And which mirror would that be?"

"Just explain one thing to me. That first night, I thought you sounded exactly like Bonnie. So much that I thought she'd—I don't know. Come back for one last encore or something. It was crazy, but I was stoned and that's what I thought. The next day though, I was straight, more or less, and you still sounded exactly like her. Even called me molly brochia, or something like that. Hell, I can't even pronounce it, but you could. Bonnie used to call me that sometimes. But only in private. You couldn't have gotten that off a record."

"No," she said. "I didn't. And before you ask, that bit back in Lincoln, when you heard the voice in the dark? I had one of the stagehands rig a cordless mike to play through one of your amps. Consider it a payback for messing up my opening night."

"You mean that was your voice?"

"No, it was Bonnie's. Look, explaining it would take more energy than I've got right now," she said, wincing as she tried to take a deep breath. "But I can show you. If you're sure you're up to it."

"Lady, at this point I'm ready for anything."

"There's a box in the closet. Get it for me."

"What's in it? A Ouija board?"

"No," she said, easing back against the pillows. "Something much better."

It was a portable VCR, and a few videocassettes. I glanced the question at her, but her eyes were closed.

"The tapes with numbers on them are bootleg videos of Bonnie when she was still with the Bones," she said without opening her eyes. "The third tape is the one you want. Len bought it from Bonnie's brother. *Maĺy bracie.*"

"What?"

"That's what it means. Little brother. In Polish."

"Bonnie was Irish."

"Her mother was Polish," she said. "An immigrant straight from the old country. Very uptight, which is why the family would never talk to the press about her. They were ashamed of the way she died." She sagged back into her pillow, pursing her lips against the pain in her hand. I hooked the VCR up to the TV set, turned the volume down, and inserted the cassette.

The tape was a pastiche, a collection of 8mm home movies transferred onto videotape. They weren't in any particular order and they'd been hacked up pretty badly to delete segments without Bonnie. It opened with her eighth-grade graduation, cut to Bonnie and another girl singing country music in a high-school gym, cut to a church picnic, Bonnie watching a mob of kids in plaid shirts and overalls play softball, cut to Bonnie singing in a local folkie bar, one of the songs she'd mailed to my record company. I'd liked the tune so much I asked her to come out to L.A. for an audition. . . . I stopped the tape, swallowing hard.

And realized Anspach was watching me. "Jesus," I said, "she was just . . . a hick. The tattoos, all that biker mama stuff, it was just a front. I don't understand."

"You might if you were a woman," Carol said. "She was coming out for a tryout with the Bones, right? A group with a reputation for being stone rock-'n'-roll crazies. She knew it was her big break and she'd have to fit in to make it. So she tried life in the fast lane. Your life. And it killed her."

"Look, I know it may look that way, but I swear she was already heavy into drugs when I met her. I didn't turn her on to anything. Hell, before she left she was stumbling around like a wino after every show."

"And did your pal Doc help her out?"

"She never hit on Doc for so much as a speeder that I knew of, and I would have known. Whatever happened to her, she did to herself."

"It doesn't matter now," she said, leaning back, closing her eyes again. "There's only a few minutes on the tape. You'd better see the rest of it."

I switched the VCR on. Bonnie finished the song. . . . Cut to the Bonnie I remembered, tattooed arms, hair cut short and spiky. She was sitting in a dressing room, holding a guitar. "Yo, Stoney, *maĺy bracie,*" she said, to the camera, and to me. "You think you can get rid of me that easy? I'll be back. But first I've got some thinking to do. And so have you. We've got a lot to talk about, you and me. Meanwhile, I've got half a song here. It needs a bridge and a final chorus. Give a listen.'' She played a brief introduction to the song, then sang two verses. ''That's as far as I've taken it. Give it your best shot and we'll polish it up together when I get back. And don't worry, I'll be back.'' She reached toward the screen to turn the camera off. . . .

Cut to Bonnie, age thirteen or so, walking hesitantly into a living room wearing a white confirmation dress. I stopped the tape and sat there a few minutes, getting my breathing under control. Then I turned and met Carol's eyes.

''You've had this all along?'' I said wonderingly. ''Knowing she made it for me? That's cold, lady. Damn, but that's cold.''

''Maybe it is. Actually, I intended to give it to you, but after that first night I changed my mind, decided to use it to run a game on you instead. Besides, it's obvious from the clip that she left the group to get away from the life you were in. Only she didn't make it. Whether you meant to or not, you destroyed her.''

''That's not true,'' I said.

''Perhaps you just don't want to believe it.''

''It's more than that. And anyway, there's something wrong with this film.''

''What do you mean, wrong?''

''I'm not sure, but . . . Something's missing. Or there's something I'm not seeing. Can I watch it again? I'll take it back to my room if you want to rest.''

''Watch it here,'' she said, closing her eyes. ''I'd rather not be alone and the tape won't bother me. I know it . . . by heart.''

Her voice faded. I think she was asleep before she finished speaking. I rewound the tape and watched it again, beginning to end. And then again. But it wasn't until the fourth or fifth time through that I realized what I'd missed earlier. Two things really. The twenty-year-old Bonnie singing in the little saloon didn't have any tattoos. But when we met a few months later, she looked like the biker mama she pretended to be. Tattoos on her arms and thighs to cover needle tracks. But even more important, in the last segment, of her confirmation day, if I looked past her carefully, I could see into a bedroom.

The room was out of focus, and I couldn't be sure it was hers. But I think it was. Because there was a kit on the nightstand beside the bed. A shooting kit. Cotton balls, a small bottle of alcohol, and a hypodermic syringe. And at the time, Bonnie couldn't have been more than thirteen years old.

Len opened the door in his pajamas, blinking. He looked at me with disbelief, then at his watch. ''What the hell, Stoney, it's five in the damn morning. What's wrong?''

''Everything. I need to talk to you.''

''About what?''

"About Bonnie," I said, pushing past him into the room. "I need to know what happened to her, Len. Exactly."

"Now? Can't it wait until morning?"

"No, it's waited too long already. Please, Len. It's important."

He hesitated, reading my eyes, and either figured I was dead serious or completely around the bend. "You know what happened," he said sourly, stepping back into the room. "Everybody does. She overdosed. Collapsed onstage. Ambulance took her to a hospital, but she died the next day without regaining consciousness."

"Died of what? Specifically, I mean? What was she on?"

"Hell, I don't know, some kind of heroin speedball mix."

"Where did she get it?"

"What do you mean?"

"The tour was just starting. You'd only been in the country a few days. Where did she get the stuff?"

"She walked it through customs. Damnedest thing I ever saw."

"Walked it through? How?"

"She had some official paperwork that said she was diabetic and had permission to bring some vials of insulin into the country. She had the harder stuff mixed in with it. The cops found it in the fridge in her dressing room. The hell of it was, the coroner who did the autopsy said she really was diabetic. Apparently had been all her life. She was the last person in the world who should have been using. Did you know?"

"No," I said, shaking my head slowly. "I guess there was a helluva lot I didn't know. Or was too buzzed to notice. Why didn't all this come out at the time?"

"The local law clamped a lid on it. Didn't want to publicize how easy it'd been to get drugs into the country. Which was okay by me. All I wanted was to get the hell out of there. Funny, I thought getting Bonnie away from you would be good for her. Thought you were a bad influence, that she'd be okay on her own. But I guess you weren't the problem after all. Or at least not the way I figured."

"Meaning what?"

"Nothing," Len said, glancing away. "Forget it."

"Jesus, don't jerk me around, Len. It's too late for games. Dammit, I have to know!"

"Fine, you want it all, sport? Here it is. Bonnie was pregnant!" he snapped. "Nearly three months along. They said she probably misjudged her fix because her body chemistry was changing."

"My God," someone said softly. Me, I guess. I sat down slowly on the edge of Len's rumpled bed.

"I'm sorry, I didn't mean to hit you like . . . Ah hell, we were all a little crazy back then. The mistakes we made, we just have to live with 'em. They're history, Stoney. It's over.''

"But that's just it. It's not over. I've got this awful feeling that it's all coming back, Len, and it's going to end just as ugly. Maybe it's bad karma or something, hell, I don't know. Bonnie getting hurt tonight helped me see it, but I think it's been there all along.''

"Stoney," Len said carefully, "Bonnie didn't get hurt tonight. Carol did.''

"Right," I said. "That's what I meant.''

I found myself walking along a side street. Wasn't sure where I was and it didn't matter. I've been in hundreds of towns that I've never seen in daylight. You roll in, do a show, move on. It's the life. After a while it seems normal. Almost. But I felt disconnected now. Like I was finally an honest to God member of the ghost show. My own ghost, drifting like smoke.

The videotape. It kept replaying in my head, frame by frame, superimposing itself on darkened shop windows and the sides of passing trucks. I glimpsed Bonnie's smile in gutters, the glow of her eyes in alley shadows. At times I heard the song. Two lonely verses repeating endlessly like an old 45 stuck in a groove. Or it'd just be a whisper of her voice on the wind. Her last message to me. Nothing profound, just a few sentences. But it troubled me. There was something unfinished about it, something . . . And after a while I realized what it was.

She hadn't said goodbye to me. Not in life, or on the tape. The last thing she said was: "I'll be back.''

"I'll be back.''

I could hear the drone of the television through the hotel door. I rapped twice, then again once, our signal for all clear. Doc peered cautiously out past the chain lock, then unhooked it and let me in.

"What's up?'' he said, blearily massaging his eyes. He was barefoot, wearing briefs and a T-shirt. I'd seen him this way before countless times. It seemed oddly intimate now. "Kinda early, isn't it?'' he said.

"I went to see Anspach," I said, glancing around the anonymous room, the rumpled bed. "We had a long talk.''

"Looks like you musta talked all night. Next show's not till nine. I can do you a couple downers if you wanna zone out.''

"You've got a stash here?'' I asked, surprised.

"With all the excitement I didn't have time to stow it proper. It's in the tank. You want some 'ludes?''

"Why not?'' I trailed him to the john, watched as he popped the toilet top and took out a flat, book-sized parcel sealed in a waterproof plastic Baggie. He expertly flicked the bag open with a fingernail and popped the box top. "Two enough?''

"For now," I said, cupping them in my palm. "Funny, whenever I need to get up or down you're always handy. Like the power company or something."

"The power company?"

"Sure. When you turn on the lights, you never think about where the juice comes from. You're like that. Doc Feeny, Dr. Feelgood. The power company."

"That's one way to look at it," Doc said warily, reading my eyes. "Somethin's up besides us, isn't it? What's wrong?"

"Not much," I said. "Just my whole damn life."

"That's a relief," Doc snorted. "For a minute there I thought it might be serious. Wanna narrow that down a little?"

"Sure. Let's start with Gopher. Len said you fired him."

"Had to. Hated to roll over on a buddy, but he was too far gone, man, a total screwup. He coulda killed that chick. I shoulda realized how blown he was. Never shoulda taken him on."

I stared at him a long time, reading his face. His very familiar face. "C'mon, Doc, all the time we've been together, I probably know you better'n your mama. Lie to her if you want, but not me. You knew exactly how blown away Gopher was. That's *why* you hired him. To take the fall for Anspach's accident. Hell, he's so burned out he probably thinks he really did it."

"But you don't?"

"I know he didn't. Because I know you. You're an ace roadie, one of the best in the biz. Much too good to make a mistake like that or let some screwup make it either. That was no accident. You set her up to get burned, maybe killed. I knew it from the first. I just couldn't figure why you'd do it. Ghost show or not, we're makin' more money than we've seen in years. It didn't make sense. Until I realized it wasn't her you were trying to get at. It was Bonnie. Wasn't it?"

"That's crazy! Bonnie's dead, dammit."

"But sometimes the dead come back. Hell, Doc, it's what we've both been thinking. That the ghost in our show is real."

He nodded, swallowing hard. "That day in the restaurant . . . We both saw it, heard it, in broad daylight. And then that night in the dark . . . That was Bonnie. No question. I haven't hardly slept since. Afraid to. Doin' speeders till I'm startin' to see the walls crawl. I hadda do somethin' about it or flip out altogether."

"Relax, Doc. It's over. There's no ghost. At least not the usual kind. Anspach got a videotape from Bonnie's family, a bunch of home movies cobbled together. That's how she made her act so perfect. That and pure talent. She's really good. Good enough to make us both believe in ghosts."

"You're sayin' she's been fakin' it? But that voice we heard in Lincoln couldn't have been her."

"She had a stagehand run a tape of Bonnie's voice through a cordless mike. Simple. If we'd had our heads on straight we'd have figured it out. But we haven't been straight. Either of us. It was easy for Anspach to mess with our minds. Or what's left of 'em.''

"Sweet Jesus Jenny on a bicycle," Doc said, slumping to the edge of the bed, burying his face in his hands, "I swear to God, Stoney. This thing's makin' me crazy. All I could think of was if I could run Anspach off, Bonnie'd go with her.''

"I figured it had to be something like that. Pretty risky, though. You might've killed her. And that bothered me. The idea that you were scared enough to risk killing somebody. Hell, Doc, you've got the guts of a burglar. Or a dope dealer. I could only come up with one reason you'd be afraid of Bonnie, dead or alive. Because you thought she'd come back for you. Didn't you?''

"You know, don't you?" he said slowly, looking up at me.

"Most of it," I said. "It's there on the video if you know what to look for. Tell me the rest.''

"Bonnie lit into me while you were in the hospital. Blamed me because you were stoned when you cracked up your bike. Called me a damn cancer. Like it's my fault you like to cop a buzz once in a while. And you know it's not true.''

"No," I agreed. "When I get trashed it's nobody's fault but mine. So what happened?''

"She got the offer for the solo tour. Said she was gonna get some bucks together and get you straightened out when she got back. And get rid of me. So I decided to run a little game on her. I found her stash. She had it hid in some medicine bottles in the fridge. Probably couple of 'em. Christ, I swear I never meant to really hurt her. I just figured she'd conk out or freak enough to get busted by the law. She'd draw a little slam time and forget about us. We'd go on like always.''

"An accidental overdose?" I said softly. "Is that it?''

"That's exactly what it was, man. I still can't figure out how it went wrong. I didn't boost 'em much.''

"It didn't take much. The medicine you found wasn't fake, she really was diabetic. I'm guessing she'd lost out on things all her life because of it, and didn't want to risk losing her chance to work with us. So she camouflaged it with tattoos. And fit right in. The boost you gave those bottles was probably the first fix she ever had. It killed her. And the baby she was carrying. My baby, Doc.''

"But sweet Jesus, Stoney, I didn't know. It wasn't my fault. You know me. Dr. Feelgood. I get people up or down sometimes, but nothin' heavy. I'd never hurt anybody on purpose, you know that.''

And he believed it. Bonnie was dead. And our child with her. And my life was a ghost show. Elvis and Jimi and me. We'd all died the same way. And Doc really believed that he hadn't hurt anyone. Dr. Feelgood. Dr. Death.

He was already spinning halfway across the room before I realized I'd hit him. He slammed into the wall and crumpled to the floor. I snatched up the chair from the dressing table. Doc looked up at me, dazed, cowering. He was crying and his nose was bleeding. And I couldn't hit him. Hell, he was right. In a way I was as guilty as he was. But I had to hit something.

I pitched the chair through the window, exploding the glass out on the street. And then I walked out. And I didn't look back.

I was packing. Len rapped once on my open door. "The cops busted Doc," he said, glancing around. "There was some trouble in his room and hotel security called the law. They caught him holding a couple grand worth of goodies." He paused, waiting for me to react. I zipped my shaving kit closed.

"Cop said his bail will be at least ten large. You got that kind of money?"

I shook my head.

"If you want an advance, maybe we can work a deal. Say a contract extension? At a slight pay cut?"

"No," I said. "I'm out."

"Out? You mean you're leaving? What about Doc?"

"He's on his own."

"Then what about the show? We've got contracts."

"Hire another ghost. Any street bum can play me in the shape I'm in now."

"What's wrong with you? What the hell's happened?"

I didn't answer. I couldn't.

"All right," Len said slowly. "Go on ahead. Maybe some time off the road will do you good. But remember, when you get ready to work again, you still owe me six months."

"I won't have to remember, Len," I said. "You will."

His beeper went off. "Duty calls. See ya, Stoney," he said, and trotted off to find a phone. I didn't even look up.

When I did, Carol was there, watching. She looked a little shaky, but better than she had earlier. She was pale, dressed in patterned jeans and a peasant blouse. Her left hand was wrapped in a clean gauze bandage. "Len says you're leaving," she said.

"I'm going home. To Indiana. Hang out at my granddaddy's farm awhile. He can use the help. So can I."

She smiled. "Sounds dull."

"I hope so," I said.

"Are you coming back?"

"Not to this show, no. I may have flushed my talent, I don't know. But I'm not a ghost yet. At least I hope I'm not."

"You look real enough to me. This farm you're talking about, does the house have a porch?"

"A porch?" I frowned, thinking. "It used to have. I haven't been there in a while. Why?"

"The show has a break scheduled in a few months. Maybe I can pop out to wherever it is. And we can sit on the porch, maybe sing a few songs. You've never heard me sing, you know. I mean, in my own voice. I'm pretty good."

"I'll bet you are," I said. "I'll let you know. I don't know if I'm into singing anymore."

"You will," she said positively. "Anybody who's survived the life you've been in can get through anything. Would you like a copy of that video? The one with the song on it?"

"No," I said. "I'm not likely to forget it. Thanks anyway."

"No charge," she said, straightening. "Well, have a safe trip."

"Hey, Anspach," I said. "There is one thing you can do for me, if you wouldn't mind."

"I guess I owe you one. What is it?"

"This may sound kind of odd to you, but . . . You see, we never had the chance to say goodbye. Bonnie and me. Could you . . . say goodbye to me? In her voice, I mean."

She stared at me for what seemed a very long time. Her dark eyes were a mystery. I thought she was going to run a game on me one last time. But she didn't.

"No," she said at last. "I guess not. I'll see you, Stoney. Good luck." And then she was gone.

I finished packing the last of my things, snapped the case shut, and carried it to the door. I glanced around to make sure I hadn't missed anything. The room was neat, anonymous. The bed was still made. Like no one had been there at all. Not even a ghost.

"Goodbye, Bonnie," I said.

Joseph Hansen has long been one of mystery fiction's leading stylists. In a field sometimes overloaded with bombast, he writes thoughtful, reflective stories and books that stay with his readers long after the cover has been closed and the book put away.

McIntyre's Donald
JOSEPH HANSEN

Around midnight, the sound of rain woke him, lashing the window glass, sluicing from the eaves. Wind bent the trees and made them creak. It interfered with his listening. For sounds from Margaret. He was going to lose her. It was only a matter of time—days, a week or two at most. So he slept lightly, though to lie awake in the dark was pointless. He could do nothing for her. Even the hospital, with all its glittering equipment, couldn't stop the inevitable. They plainly had given up when last Sunday the staff let her have her way and come home. She wanted to die at home.

She'd been through surgery twice, and chemotherapy, and feeble, fretful combat with the cheerful, no-nonsense experts sent around to help her tone up her muscles, get her to walking again, feeding herself, all that. Feeding herself? She scarcely ate anymore, a spoonful of soup, a sip of juice. To make him think she was trying. But the pain was worsening, and she wanted to die. She had not said so for fear of hurting him, careful as always of his feelings. But he knew.

He reached out, switched on the lamp, and with an old man's heavy slowness threw off the bedclothes, swung his feet to the floor, sat on the edge of the bed, sighing, putting on his glasses. He took his teeth from the bedside water tumbler, fitted them into his mouth. Ridiculous, like everything about growing old. He pushed his swollen feet into slippers, stood, took his bathrobe off the bedpost, flapped into it, and crossed the hall to look in at her.

There was a night-light. She was sleeping, breathing stertorously. That was the effect of the medication. So . . . all was as well as it would ever be. He

183

started to turn away, heard the drip of water, and turned back. He flicked the light switch. Rain was leaking through the ceiling. Not on the bed. Not yet. But he must stop it. He got a flashlight from a kitchen drawer, struggled into the stiff old raincoat that hung by the back door for emergencies, found a pail of patching tar and a putty knife in a wooden locker on the rear deck, and went down the steps.

An aluminum ladder lay beside the carport. He dragged it to the lowest segment of the roof, stood it up, settled its legs firmly, stuffed flashlight and putty knife into coat pockets, and, tar pail in hand, began to climb, squinting up into the dark, the rain in his face making his glasses useless.

He was too old for this. Stiff. Rheumatic. Every step was a struggle. He would have done better with both hands free, but not much better. It was slow going. His heart pounded with urgency, but he knew better than to try to hurry. At his age, when you tried to hurry you only made mistakes. And he mustn't fail. What would become of Margaret then?

His head came above the roofline. He was getting there. He drew a deep breath and took another step. Right leg. Left leg—the one that sometimes gave out on him without warning. The roof was at chest level. Another step. Now he could crawl onto the roof. He set the pail there. He brought his left leg up and pushed with the right, because it was the strongest.

But nothing happened. He'd grown too heavy, hadn't he? He'd have to climb higher on the ladder. And step out onto the roof. Grunting, he climbed higher on the ladder. How cold rain-wet metal felt to his hands! Now, then, he had to calculate how to get off the ladder onto the roof. To step off sounded fine when he said it to himself. But how to manage it? This side? That side? There was a pine branch to duck under. He leaned, put out one leg, thrust with the other, dropped onto the roof on hands and knees.

To get to his feet was a struggle, but he managed it. Picking up the tar pail, he climbed to the place where he knew the leak originated—a join in the roof that had given the same trouble before. He shone the flashlight on the place, knelt, pried open the pail, and smeared on the tar with the putty knife. He took out the flashlight again to inspect his work, added more tar, resealed the pail, and one small, cautious step at a time, made his way back down the wet slope to the ladder. He set the tar pail at the roof's edge, gripped again the cold metal of the ladder, and put out a leg, groping with his foot for a rung. He found the rung all right, but his leg wouldn't hold him. And he fell.

He was in his bed, It was still night, still raining. He should have been soaking, but he was dry, and in dry pajamas, and the bedclothes lay over him neatly. He switched on the lamp. His teeth leaned in the water glass. His bifocals lay folded beside the glass. What the hell had happened? He'd fallen off the roof. Crazy old fool. He tested fingers, arms, legs. All seemed in working order. His head ached. He touched his skull. Tender at the back.

Painful. But how had he got here? He started to struggle up. He was bruised, all right, bruised all over. With a groan he lay back down.

And the door opened. A young man in a black leather jacket looked in, then stepped inside, a strapping young man with a round face, thick dark eyebrows, and blue eyes. For a split second McIntyre thought he ought to know him. The young man said, "You're awake. Good. I was afraid you might be in a coma. I thought about calling an ambulance, but I couldn't find any broken bones. There could be internal injuries, though. You tell me."

"Just bruises." McIntyre peered. "I climbed up to patch the roof. It was leaking. Did I do it?"

A nod. "You did it. What's wrong?"

McIntyre was struggling to get up. "Across the hall. I want to see if the dripping's stopped. My wife—"

"I checked," the young man said. "It's stopped."

"Is she all right?"

"She's sleeping."

McIntyre felt lost. "Who are you? Where did you come from? It's the middle of the night."

"I was—just getting home," the young man said. "I heard you fall."

"I appreciate it," McIntyre said.

"Can I bring you anything? Aspirin? Hot milk?"

"No, thank you."

"You want me to phone Dr. Hesseltine?"

"I'm all right," McIntyre said. "You know me—a tough old bird."

The young man was watching him steadily. As if he expected something. Not like money. Not that. Something else. Did he want to be recognized? *You know me.* Now, why had McIntyre said that? To a stranger. Only he wasn't a stranger, was he? Inside McIntyre a beautiful light went on, and "Donald," he said, before he could stop himself.

"Yes?" The young man cocked his head, half smiling, half frowning.

"I'm sorry." McIntyre groped out for his glasses, put them on. His face grew hot with embarrassment. He felt preposterous. "I mistook you for someone else."

"I guess not," the young man said. "I'm Donald."

McIntyre shut his eyes. It was his head, wasn't it? He had struck it when he fell, and he was hallucinating. He squeezed his eyelids tight and breathed in and out deeply for a count of ten and opened his eyes again, and the young man was gone. He laughed shakily to himself. *Donald.* What had made him say that? Donald was not real. He was McIntyre's private dream. His imaginary son. He had no son. He had three daughters. Used to have. Now they lived in other corners of the country. They wrote, and sometimes phoned, but rarely visited. They had husbands, and children in high school, even in college. They were busy with their own lives. He had no son. He had lived his entire long life surrounded by women, as a boy with his widowed mother and her sister and his own three sisters, then as a man with Margaret and the three girls. He had never had a son.

But the old saying was not true—you *could* miss what you never had. He'd yearned for a son, and whimsically brought a son to life. In his mind, his daydreams. Whenever it pleased him, whenever he felt the need, alone at his insurance agency, when business was slow, or since retiring, walking on the beach, say, exploring the tide rocks for shellfish, chopping out poison oak from under the pines around the house, waiting long hours at the hospital. My son Donald. A tear-away runner and climber of trees, an artful looper of scuffed basketballs through rusty hoops, a hotdog rider of spiderbikes, a surfer in long, sun-faded trunks, a glum student slouched over homework at the kitchen table, can of soda in one hand, slice of pizza in the other, a boy. Sometimes younger, sometimes older. Donald, my son.

Smiling, McIntyre slept.

He skipped his early-morning walk today. He washed and fed Margaret. He changed the bed linens, while, wrapped in a blanket against the damp and chill, she huddled in a chair by the window, where she could look out. Ordinarily at these times, she was silent. In pain. This morning she spoke. "That's the second sheriff's car that's passed," she said. "I think they're coming from Gertrude Schumwald's." But that was all. Her eyes closed. Her head drooped. His bruises made it painful to lift her—out of the bed, into the bed. He groaned, but not aloud. Thrusting needles into her pathetically wasted flesh always made him flinch inside, but he smiled and spoke gently, doing it. She murmured, smiled for him, feebly squeezed his hand, and slept again.

Now he sat in the kitchen with coffee and the newspaper, and Henry Winston knocked on the back door and stepped inside. They'd been neighbors for years. Henry was retired, too. Used to own a drugstore in Morro Bay. Sold it to a chain outfit. It had lost all its character now. He hung up a Giants baseball cap and a windbreaker jacket. "You all right? Got a shopping list for me? Have to drive into San Luis today. Means a market with a lot more variety. Craving anything exotic?" He pulled out a chair and sat at the table. "How's Margaret?"

"No change." With a wince, McIntyre rose to get him a mug of coffee. When he set it down, he laid the list beside it. "Keeping her out of pain's about all I hope for."

"I see the ladder's up." Henry poked the list into his shirt pocket, and emptied a packet of sweetener into his coffee. "Roof leaking again, was it?"

"I patched it," McIntyre said.

"It needs to be replaced." Henry reached across for McIntyre's spoon, and rattled it in his coffee.

"Can't afford it." Henry had left the door ajar. McIntyre got up and closed it. "Hospitals, doctors."

"You've got insurance—you were in the business."

McIntyre snorted. "We'd be on the beach without it. Doesn't mean I've got thousands lying around for a new roof."

Henry shrugged. "Long as you can still climb up there."

McIntyre opened his mouth to tell Henry about his fall and what had happened afterward, but he didn't. In all his life, he had told no one about Donald. Not even Margaret. Especially not Margaret. She might have construed his daydream as a reproach to her for failing to give him a son. Were he to confide about Donald now, Henry would think he was out of his mind. Which, of course, at least last night, he had been. From concussion. But to explain away the many visitations of Donald in the past wouldn't be so easy. He could think of no excuse for those himself. "May I?" Henry picked up the newspaper and, squinting, turned over the pages noisily.

"What are you looking for?"

"Gertrude Schumwald had a break-in last night." Henry laid the paper down. "Guess it happened too late to get in here. They print this early so they can truck it up here from L.A."

A widow, Gertrude Schumwald lived in a two-story place up at the corner, surrounded by shaggy old pepper trees. Most of the trees in Settlers Cove were high-reaching spindly pines, shallow-rooted, likely to blow down in storms off the sea, but fast-growing, so the place remained a community in deep woods.

"A break-in?" McIntyre said. These had become common lately. Settlers Cove had once been free of crime. Now street people drove up from Los Angeles or down from San Francisco to mug elderly walkers of dogs in the woodsy lanes, to hold up the souvenir shops in Madrone, across the highway, to invade houses and take televisions, microwaves, jewelry—whatever they could sell to buy drugs.

"Gertrude heard a noise," Henry said, "got Ernie's old revolver out of the dresser drawer, walked to the stair head in her nightgown in the dark, and shot it off."

McIntyre laughed. "That's our Gertie."

Henry grinned. "He dropped the silverware chest, dived out the window, and ran like hell."

"On the other hand," McIntyre said, "it could have got her killed. Impulsive, foolhardy. She always was that way. Did she get a look at him?"

"A glimpse. There's the corner streetlight, you know, but it's dim, and the rain made it dimmer. He was young, that's all." Henry took a swallow of coffee, remembered, shook his head. "That's not all. He left footprints in the mud. Big fella—heavy, too, the way they sank in."

"Black, of course?" McIntyre said regretfully.

"Not this time. Deputies asked Gertrude more than once, but she stuck to her story—he was white."

McIntyre woke to heavy footsteps on the front deck. A stranger, then. Only strangers came to this house that way, up the long path and wooden stairs from the trail below. Friends came by the side trail to the back door. He lay on the couch, an afghan over him, the book he'd been reading splayed open on his big belly. His glasses? He pawed around for them, found them, laid the book aside, threw off the afghan, sat up. Pains jabbed at his lower back, his joints. His head still throbbed. He struggled to his feet. Someone knocked on the door. A firm, loud knocking.

"Coming," he said hoarsely and hobbled to open the door. The day was beautiful though chilly. The sky was washed a flawless blue. Splintered sunlight fell through the pines. The man who'd knocked wore neat khaki. He was a sheriff's deputy. He pushed back his hat. "Mr. McIntyre?"

"Yes. It's Lieutenant Gerard, isn't it?"

Gerard sketched a smile, and nodded. "How are you?"

"That's quite a question to ask an old man. I could keep you here for hours listening to a catalogue of my aches and pains. What's on your mind, deputy?"

"Mrs. Schumwald was robbed last night," Gerard said. "Around midnight."

"So Henry Winston told me."

"We're busy after the storm, so I'm on my own asking neighbors if they saw or heard anything. Mrs. Schumwald scared him off with a handgun. She says he hit the ground running. He didn't run past here, by any chance, did he?"

"If you mean down the road, I wouldn't have seen him. I was out back." He pointed with a thumb over his shoulder. "I doubt if I'd have heard him, either. Storm was making too much noise. My roof started leaking, I climbed up and put tar on the leak. Then I proceeded to fall off."

Gerard frowned concern. "Oh, no. Are you all right?"

McIntyre touched his skull, wincing. "Slight concussion—I think that's the worst of it. Wasn't much of a fall. It's a low roof back there. No bones broken."

"I can run you to the hospital. You should have X-rays. Best to be sure about these things."

"Thanks, I'm all right," McIntyre said.

"Well, you take it easy, now." Gerard went off across the damp deck that was strewn with pine needles and twigs the storm had brought down. "Sorry to bother you."

McIntyre said, "No bother," and closed the door.

"Aren't you going to tell him about me?" Donald said. There he was, big as life. He'd laid new logs on the fire and was poking up a blaze. He looked over his shoulder at McIntyre. What was his expression exactly? Those thick, dark eyebrows were raised. Was he smiling? The blue eyes seemed to twinkle, but McIntyre couldn't say whether they were mocking him or not.

"What are you doing here?" he said.

"You were asleep." The poker clanked against the fire basket. "I thought I'd better sit with Mother just in case. I read to her awhile. But I don't think she heard me."

"She's not your mother," McIntyre said sharply.

Donald straightened, set the poker back in place, and read his watch. "She'll need her medication in ten minutes." He left the room. "Don't forget." His voice came from the kitchen. A moment later, the back door closed.

McIntyre had never before in his life spoken a cross word to Donald. He felt a stab of remorse, and hurried to the kitchen. He snatched open the door. "Donald?" He stepped out onto the rear deck. "Please, I'm sorry." But Donald was gone. No one was in sight. Only a mule deer, a few yards off up the slope among the pines. It raised its antlered head, ears alert and twitching, looked at him for a second with large brown eyes, then bounded away, crashing through the undergrowth.

McIntyre stood on the deck, frowning to himself, wondering if the deer were real. Donald was certainly not real. Donald was a part of his mind—a maverick part, broken loose. Telling him it would soon be time for Margaret's injection. No stranger would know that. He, McIntyre, knew it, and had put the reminder to himself into Donald's mouth. *Aren't you going to tell him about me?* McIntyre had wondered for a moment there if he oughtn't to tell Gerard about Donald, and had tossed away the notion. And Donald had caught it. *Mother.* McIntyre shut the kitchen door. In Margaret's room, the book lay face down on the chair arm. *Pride and Prejudice.* He picked it up, peered at the page, but couldn't remember whether this was the place where he'd last left off reading to her himself or not.

Margaret spoke softly. She was very white against the pillows. He knew why: the morphine was wearing off.

"Something wrong?" she asked him.

"No, no. I fell asleep. Meant to come in and read to you. Would you—like me to read to you?"

She shook her head and turned it to see the small white bedside clock. "It's time for my injection."

"Of course." He laid the book down.

He was sweeping the front deck when the sound of a car in the driveway out back made him lift his head. A big, tough engine and, a moment later, the slam of a heavy door. A Cherokee. He knew those sounds, and wondered what had brought Belle Hesseltine. He leaned the broom by the door and went inside. By the time he reached the kitchen, Belle had let herself in.

A gaunt, upright old woman, in blue jeans, mackinaw, cowboy boots, she'd come to Settlers Cove years ago to retire, and had been busier doctoring here than she'd been in all her life before, or so she claimed. The fact seemed to be, she had no idea how to retire. Doctoring was what she'd always lived for. A love and compassion for people that she tried to hide behind a gruff manner wouldn't let her stop helping them. She hung up her Stetson. Her medical kit was in her hand.

"Sit down, Raymond. Sheriff Gerard is worried about you. He rang me to say you had a bad fall last night," She pulled out a chair at the table. "Concussion, he said, and you wouldn't let him take you to the hospital. Come on, sit down. Let me look at your head."

"What's wrong with my head," McIntyre said, "is inside. Nothing you can see. Forgetting names. Losing things."

"That's just old age." She pushed him down on the chair, set the kit on the table among the breakfast dishes he hadn't yet cleared away—he hadn't felt up to it earlier. She bent him forward, parted the hair at the back of his skull, gently touched the place he'd banged in his fall. She straightened him, removed his glasses, laid them with a click on the tabletop. She tilted up his chin, bent, and looked hard and closely into his eyes.

"How's your vision?" she asked. "Seeing double?"

He almost said he was seeing what wasn't there, but he bit that back. "No. Vision's about as good as usual—which isn't saying much."

"You've had these ten years." She handed him back the glasses. "Time you got fitted with new ones."

"Can you talk to Margaret a few minutes?" McIntyre put the glasses on. "You're one of her favorites. Not many people come anymore."

"A good many that would if they could," Belle said wryly, "are dead and gone."

"I know." McIntyre rose with a sigh. "But I can't say it to her anymore." He gathered up the dishes from the table and set them in the sink. "It sticks in my throat."

"I almost didn't make it myself." Belle took up her kit. "Big black-tailed buck cut across the road right in front of me. I didn't hit him. I braked, but the road's wet and slippery. I damn near piled up in the ditch."

"I saw him around noon," McIntyre said. "Out back here in the trees. Must be ten years since we had deer in Settlers Cove. Over across the highway, yes, but with all the building here—"

"There's been bears reported," Belle said, and headed for the hallway. "Haven't been bears on the central coast in a century. I wonder if our four-footed friends are trying to tell us something."

McIntyre laughed briefly, and began to run hot water into the sink. He poured detergent into the stream of the water. Fumbled for the dish mop. Began to wash the breakfast dishes. He rinsed each plate, mug, glass, under the running hot water and set it in a rubber-coated wire rack on the counter.

He moved slowly, and winced at the ache of his bruises. He must have groaned aloud. He did that sometimes in his weariness these days, more often than he should, because there was no one to hear. But at this moment there was. Belle had not left the kitchen. She'd stood watching him, and now she touched his arm.

"Raymond, where are those girls of yours? Why aren't they here, looking after their mother? You're not up to it. Seventy-six years old. All on your own."

"I manage," McIntyre said stiffly.

"Have you written them? Have you telephoned?"

"They've got husbands, children, jobs to look after. And they're none of them nurses. What could they do that I can't do? Besides"—annoyingly, tears came to his eyes, his voice wobbled, and he turned away—"it won't be much longer." He pulled a paper towel off the rack, dried his eyes, blew his nose. "For them to come all this way . . ."

"It's their mother who's dying, for God's sake," Belle said. "Aren't you even going to give them a chance to show they love their mother?"

McIntyre shook his head. "Emotional blackmail? That's not our style, Belle—not Margaret's, not mine."

Belle snorted again. "Raymond, what ails you is pride. You don't want anyone able to say you failed in your duty. You'll carry all the weight yourself if it kills you."

"Margaret will be waiting for you," McIntyre said. "She knows the sound of your car."

Belle sighed, studied him a moment, then with a grim shake of her head went off down the hall. By the time the dishes were dried and put away, the effort had drained him. He sat down heavily at the table to catch his breath. The table felt sticky. He looked at it—splotches, smears. And then at the floor, the counters, the stove. Everything was dingy, soiled, neglected. No wonder Belle felt he wasn't up to the task he'd assigned himself.

Well, it wasn't true. He'd been lazy, self-indulgent. Thrusting out his jaw, he pushed to his feet and shuffled out to get the plastic bucket, mop, sponges, scrub brush, soap, bleach. He'd make the place shine. He was coming in with his hands full when Belle entered the kitchen from the hall, carrying her kit. She studied him and his janitor's gear sardonically for a moment, and said, "I'd call a cleaning service, Raymond. Don't do this."

"Cleaning service, hell," he said. "Waste of good money. Nothing to mopping up a kitchen."

"Youth and strength," she said. "Raymond, no one keeps those forever." She took down her hat from the rack. "Growing old is nothing to be ashamed of." She went out into the sunlight of the deck and turned back. "One thing. Keep a written record when it comes to the morphine, will you? If I hadn't stopped by, Margaret would have been in a bad way. You were down to the last three cc's.''

He scowled. "No. Really? I was sure I had—"

"I replenished the supply from my kit," Belle said.

"Thank you," he said, bewildered. He seemed to see in his memory's eye three of the now all-too-familiar clear, bulbous vials lined up on the medicine chest shelf. But his memory's eyesight, it seemed, was no more to be trusted now than was his actual vision, blurred, mistaking what he thought he saw for what he saw. "I'll try to keep better track," he mumbled, and poured soap powder and bleach into the dusty bucket and ran hot water into it. The mop, which had hung in the locker on the deck, was dusty, and a spider ran out of it just as he was about to plunge it into the water. He stood watching the spider scurry under the cabinet doors beneath the sink. And Belle Hesseltine was back. She stepped inside and held something up in her thin fingers. It glinted in the sunlight.

"I think you ought to look at this," she said.

McIntyre leaned the mop against the counter and went to do as she asked. It was a silver spoon. Muddy, but until it had fallen into the mud, polished to a fine gleam. Sterling. Heavy. An ornate, old-fashioned pattern. He rinsed it under the tap, dried it, and stood turning it over in his fingers, examining it. He frowned.

"Where did you find it?"

"Lying at the foot of your ladder out here. Doesn't belong to you. Not with the initial S."

"Gertrude Schumwald?" McIntyre said.

Belle said, "I'm told she had a burglary last night."

"Well, how did it get here?" McIntyre asked.

But he knew, and the knowledge made him sick.

He blinked awake. The light outside was slanting from the west and turning ruddy. He had called the sheriff's substation in Madrone as soon as Belle Hesseltine had left. To report the spoon. He was too bruised to walk over to Schumwald's. Anyway, it was the correct thing to give the evidence to a law officer. But Gerard wasn't in. McIntyre left his name, then went back to the kitchen. He began mopping the floor, but grew tired before he'd finished, winded, achy, his heart pounding, and the back of his skull throbbing again. Henry Winston arrived with white plastic sacks from the supermarket in San Luis, and when McIntyre had written Henry a check, and put the groceries away, he went and lay down on the couch. And fell asleep. Now he wheezed to his feet and went to tackle the kitchen once more.

But he was too late. It gleamed in the red sunlight, every surface spotless, floor, stove, refrigerator shiny, cabinets as free of hand smears as if new.

Donald stood on the top of the little aluminum step stool, wiping down the last of the cupboards. He grinned at the gaping McIntyre.

"Pass muster?" he asked.

McIntyre said stupidly, "What are you doing here?"

"I live here," Donald said cheerfully, "don't I?" He climbed down the ladder, took the sponge to the sink, and rinsed it under the tap. "Haven't I always lived here?"

Far more quickly than usual these days, McIntyre's head cleared. Maybe anger cleared it. "Never," he said. The spoon was in the pocket of his shirt. He flung it on the table. "You're a thief. You robbed Mrs. Schumwald up at the corner last night. You were running away when you stumbled on me out here." He jerked his head to indicate the place of his fall. "You stopped to help me, and that dropped out of your pocket."

"I'll put these things away," Donald said, and began gathering up the cleaning stuff.

"I can do it, thanks," McIntyre said. "You've done enough."

"Youth and strength," Donald said with a smile, and went out with the mop, wrung dry and white, the bucket loaded with sponges, bleach, soap box, scrub brush.

McIntyre cried, "No, wait." He mustn't leave. He must be here when the sheriff came. McIntyre looked frantically down the hall, as if Gerard might have materialized in the front room. He took a step—he'd phone him again quickly. He stopped and shook his head in disgust. What good would that do? "Donald, wait." He hobbled across the kitchen and out onto the deck. But the locker doors were shut, and Donald was gone. "Donald?" he shouted. Into emptiness. There was only the wind in the pines, and from far off down the hill the crush of surf among the rocks.

Gerard touched his hat. "Sorry to have taken so long. Like I said before, the storm got us a lot of auto accidents, downed trees and power lines, runaway horses. Busy day. What's this about Mrs. Schumwald's spoon?"

"Yes. Come in. Sit down. Get you anything?"

Gerard stepped inside, took off his hat. "Thank you, that's all right. I'll head home soon for supper."

"This is the spoon." McIntyre gave it to him. "Belle Hesseltine found it this noon, out in back. At the foot of the ladder I put up last night to fix a leak in the roof. Around midnight."

"It's certainly clean," Gerard said.

"It was covered with mud. I washed it."

"Damn." Gerard rubbed a hand down over his face and blew out air. "That's no way to treat evidence, Mr. McIntyre. It could have had the thief's fingerprints on it."

McIntyre felt his face grow red. "Of course. You're right. I'm sorry."

"Belle shouldn't have picked it up in the first place." Gerard put the spoon into his pocket. "I must have told her twenty times to leave evidence alone." He sighed and looked past McIntyre, searching the sunset room with his eyes. "All right if I change my mind? I think I could use a drink."

"Good," McIntyre said. "Sit down. I'll fetch us some bourbon." He went to the kitchen, feeling strangely elated. It was a long time since he'd sat and had a drink with a man. Henry Winston never touched the stuff. And McIntyre didn't believe in drinking alone. He dropped ice cubes into glasses, poured generously from his dusty bottle of Old Grand-Dad, and carried the drinks back to the living room almost with a spring in his step.

"Thank you," Gerard said. "All right if I smoke?"

"Go right ahead," McIntyre said. "Belle won't let me use them anymore, but I still enjoy the smell."

Gerard lit up, tasted his drink, smiled appreciatively, and lifted the glass to McIntyre. "That's good whiskey." McIntyre nodded, smiled, tasted his own drink. It hit him like a blow in the chest. Another pleasure gone off limits? What was there to recommend old age? Nothing he could think of. Gerard said, "The spoon says he ran past out in back there, but you didn't see him, didn't hear him?"

"I did. I didn't understand you, earlier."

Gerard narrowed his eyes. "Didn't understand?"

"You said the thief ran down the road. The man I saw didn't. And I had no reason to think he was a thief. I fell off the roof, knocked myself cold. Next thing I knew I was safe and dry in my own bed. A young man was here. Said he'd heard me fall. Plainly he'd carried me in out of the rain, cleaned me up, put me to bed. If I hadn't regained consciousness, he was going to call the doctor."

Gerard stared. "A young man? What sort?"

McIntyre shifted in his chair. "White, six feet, late twenties, dark hair, blue eyes, hefty. Maybe he'd had some medical experience. He seemed to know I hadn't broken anything, that all that was wrong with me was a concussion."

Gerard said, "You should have told me this right off."

"I didn't connect him with the robbery," McIntyre said, shading the truth, wanting to believe in Donald, the Donald he'd created in his daydreams. There was no way his Donald could turn out to be a housebreaker. McIntyre refused to believe that. "After all, he was a good Samaritan. You don't think of someone like that as a criminal."

Gerard grunted and took another swallow of Old Grand-Dad. "You're sure you didn't come into the house on your own, get cleaned up, get into bed, without remembering it. A bad bump on the head can give people blackouts."

"You mean I imagined Donald?"

Gerard blinked. "Donald?"

"That's what he calls himself." This was like a dream. McIntyre heard himself say next, "He's been back twice today. Once, to read to my wife when I fell asleep. A second time, to clean up the kitchen for me—not an hour ago."

Gerard listened with a poker face. "Is that so?"

"Come look." McIntyre led him to the kitchen, switched on the light. "See how it shines? Well, I can tell you, it wasn't that way. It was very grubby. My wife's ill, you see, dying, and looking after her is about all I've got strength for." He grimaced. "Years do that to you."

"Looks nice." Gerard regarded the glistening surfaces thoughtfully. "And you say Donald did this for you?"

"I hate to think he was the one that stole Gertrude Schumwald's silverware," McIntyre said.

"You sure you didn't clean up the kitchen yourself?"

"Do you think I've lost my mind?" McIntyre said.

"I think you had a blow on the head." Gerard had brought along his drink and cigarette. He sat down at the table. "What did this Donald tell you about himself?"

McIntyre almost said, *He didn't have to tell me anything, I know everything about him. I invented him. Long ago. When I wanted a son for company, a son I could spend time with away from women, at ball games, hiking, sailing.* He didn't let himself say these things. Gerard was already half persuaded Raymond McIntyre was a loony. "He didn't tell me anything. Just asked how he could help."

"Why do you suppose he kept coming back?"

"He won't come back again. The second time, I knew about the spoon. I showed it to him, called him a thief."

Gerard frowned. "Risky. He could have hurt you."

"If he was that kind," McIntyre said, "why didn't he rob me? I'm old and slow. I don't keep a gun, like Gertrude Schumwald. My wife's helpless. He could have plundered this house—instead all he did was help me."

"Right." Gerard finished off his whiskey, put out his cigarette, rose. "Describe him again, will you?"

McIntyre obliged and added the black leather jacket.

"I'm going to send somebody here to take fingerprints." Gerard went to pick up his hat. As he started down the steps into the trees, McIntyre remembered how quickly Donald had vanished this noon, and called to the deputy: "Have you seen that blacktailed buck?"

"We've had reports," Gerard said. "Fish and Game will catch him, truck him back up in the canyons. Unless some trigger-happy householder around here shoots him first."

There were only two of them, but they seemed to fill the house. A tow-headed, simple-looking kid named Vern and a slender dark young woman whose badge said she was T. Hodges. She had slightly buck teeth, and beautiful brown eyes. They wore the same tan uniforms as Gerard, the same hats, and they were everywhere with their dusting powder, brushes, cellotape, blank white cards, ballpoint pens. They went over the kitchen inch by inch, the locker on the rear deck, mop, bucket, soap-powder box.

While they took his own fingerprints at the kitchen table, they asked him to recall for them just where Donald had been in the house, and so they checked the fireplace poker, too, didn't they? And quietly, courteously, the copy of *Pride and Prejudice,* and the chair beside sleeping Margaret's bed where Donald would have sat to read to her. They checked the bathroom, in case Donald had turned the taps there when he'd cleaned the mud off McIntyre after his fall.

They took photographs. They brought in a vacuum cleaner to run over all the places Donald had stepped and climbed and stood. They softly carried the chair out of Margaret's room and vacuumed that, and softly carried it back. When the door of their county car slammed below on the road and they drove off, the house seemed empty and lonely. McIntyre suddenly missed the girls. His daughters. Karen, the youngest, in particular—T. Hodges had reminded him of Karen. He closed the front door slowly, thoughtfully, and started toward the telephone. But Margaret called out to him, and he went to do what he could for her instead.

They were up in Sills Canyon, away back in the mountains. The trail they'd followed had finally just petered out. Driving in twisty ruts, McIntyre had grown doubtful, but Donald had kept urging him on. He was fifteen, now, and sure of himself. He knew this place. No, he wasn't mixed up. This was the way. And now they stood side by side at a pool shaded by old oaks draped with moss, a cool, hidden place, quiet except for the buzz of insects, the soft babble of Sills Creek as it washed down over boulders into the pool.

"Didn't I tell you?" Donald said. "A real trout pool."

"If you say so," McIntyre said.

"Give me the key," Donald said. "I'll get the rods."

He scrambled up the rocky, brushy slope. McIntyre gazed into the pool. And saw at its far side the clear, motionless, reflection of a mule deer, a buck, with antlers.

"Donald, come see," he called.

But right away the buck took fright and bounced off.

It was a cemetery, an old one, crowded with mossy headstones, statuary, even an occasional tomb. Where? He didn't know. He'd never been here. Out there was the ocean, slate-gray today, under a cold, gray sky. Gulls circled overhead, crying their creaking cries. A canvas awning on shiny poles sheltered a double row of metal folding chairs that faced a grave into which a casket had been lowered, a heap of hothouse flowers on its lid. The girls, their husbands, and five of their offspring whom McIntyre hardly recognized sat on the folding chairs, hands in their laps. They were dressed up, all of them. So was he, in a suit he hadn't worn in a long time. It was too tight. The white shirt he'd taken from a very old laundry wrapping strained its buttons over his belly. A bald clergyman, a folded umbrella hanging from his arm, read from a book so worn some of its leaves were loose. In the King James English McIntyre had requested. Margaret loved that language, and when she still had her vitality used to rail against the modernizing of the *Book of Common Prayer.* At "dust to dust," McIntyre stooped stiffly, picked up a handful of earth, dropped it onto the flowers below, and straightened, to find Donald beside him. He, too, was dressed up. He smiled, and said, "Don't worry. You won't be alone. I'll always be here." McIntyre awoke and, heart pounding, stumbled purblind and toothless across the hall. Margaret was there, drugged asleep, but there. He almost wept with relief.

When he came back from his sunrise walk, Donald was at the stove. His black leather jacket hung by the door. He'd tied on McIntyre's apron over a plaid shirt and jeans. The kitchen smelled of perking coffee and frying bacon. McIntyre stopped in the doorway. Disbelieving. Angry. Afraid. "What are you doing here?"

"Cooking your breakfast." Donald nodded toward the hall. "By the time you're finished with Mother, it will all be ready."

"The sheriff is after you," McIntyre said.

"She's been calling for you. Wait, here's her cereal."

Carrying the warm bowl of Cream of Wheat along the hall, McIntyre paused and put a hand on the telephone, but Margaret called out again, sounding panicky, and he went to her. He went through the gentle rituals. There was no need to change the sheets this morning, thank God, and that shortened the time a little. But impossibly he'd got mixed up about the morphine again. He couldn't imagine how or why, but there was only one vial in the medicine chest. His hand trembled as he gave Margaret the injection. He broke into a cold sweat as he hurried back to the kitchen with the cereal Margaret had barely touched, however much he'd coaxed her. Henry Winston looked at him from his place at the table.

"Where's Donald?" McIntyre set the bowl in the sink.

"You're white as a sheet," Henry said. "What's wrong?"

"How long ago did he leave?" McIntyre cried.

Alarmed, Henry stood up and pulled out a chair. "You'd better sit down. Nobody left. Nobody was here."

McIntyre looked wildly at the stove. A saucepan, two skillets. And through the oven's glass pane, he saw inside eggs, bacon, and toast on a plate. A mug of coffee steamed in front of Henry. One stood at McIntyre's place as well. He yanked open the door, stepped out on the deck. "Donald!" Henry called. "What the hell's the matter with you?"

"You sure you didn't see a young man?"

"I told you—there was no one to see."

"He was cooking breakfast"—McIntyre came inside again and closed the door—"when I got back from my walk." He took the warm plate from the oven. "See here? And where do you think your coffee came from?"

Henry tilted his head. "The pot—like every morning."

"No," McIntyre said. "I mean, yes, but Donald made it." He banged the plate down on the table. "Donald made my breakfast while I looked after Margaret."

Henry eyed him, worried, rubbing his white beard stubble. It was a privilege of retirement that a man didn't have to shave every morning of his life. Sometimes Henry indulged it for days running. "Donald?" he said.

"The one who rescued me when I fell off the roof," McIntyre said crossly. "The one who cleaned up this kitchen yesterday. I guess you didn't notice how it shines?"

"Fell off the roof? When was that? Look at you. You're shaking. Sit down here now, and eat."

McIntyre turned away. "I have to phone the sheriff."

"Will you make sense? The sheriff? What for?"

"It was Donald who stole Gertrude Schumwald's silver."

"Well, give Belle Hesseltine a call, while you're at it," Henry said. "Trying to do everything alone here, cook, housekeeper, nurse—the strain is affecting your mind. Raymond, nobody was in this kitchen. You made the coffee and cooked like always. You just forgot."

"Matter of fact," McIntyre said, "I'll call Belle first. You eat that breakfast. I'm not hungry." And he went to the phone and punched out the familiar number. Belle answered from her car. McIntyre could hear the engine. He asked, "About the morphine. You told me you'd replenished Margaret's supply. Are you sure?"

"I set them on the usual shelf in your bathroom cabinet. What's the matter?"

"How many?" McIntyre asked.

"Three," she said.

"There's only one this morning," McIntyre said.

"Call the sheriff," she said. "Don't waste any time."

"You call him," McIntyre said. "He'll believe you. He thinks that bump on the head scrambled my brains."

Gerard came to the back door this time. Henry was still present. McIntyre had hinted to him to leave, but his old neighbor was plainly worried about him and didn't think he ought to be alone. Left alone, McIntyre imagined things. Gerard sat with a mug of coffee at the kitchen table now and smoked a cigarette and listened without comment or even facial expression while McIntyre recited his story again. He followed McIntyre to the bathroom to look at the lone vial of morphine on the shelf there.

"So now we know why he keeps coming back," he said, and closed the mirrored cabinet door.

"Now we know," McIntyre said bleakly. "To get his hands on drugs."

"Urban scum." Henry had tagged along and stood in the hall. "They're all the same."

"Not exactly." Gerard left the bathroom. McIntyre and Henry followed him back to the kitchen. "His fingerprints tell us he used to be an orderly at the hospital in San Luis. He stole from the supplies there. They fired him without pressing charges." Gerard poured himself more coffee and sat down again at the table. "Everybody liked him and felt sorry for him." He lit a cigarette and made a face. "They ought to have had him arrested and charged, tried and locked up. He's been all over the area thieving to feed his habit." The deputy looked glumly at McIntyre. "You were the best break he ran into yet. No middle man."

McIntyre said, "The hospital. That's how he knew about Margaret's medication. That's where I'd seen him, isn't it? And he'd seen me. Funny thing— when I came to, after I fell off the roof, I thought I knew him. But not from where."

"Don't suppose he was wearing an orderly's outfit," Henry said, "was he? Clothes change a man."

"I thought he was—" McIntyre began, and stopped.

Gerard cocked an eyebrow. "Yes?"

"Nobody," McIntyre said, and added lamely, "someone I—used to know. As a—as a boy."

"He grew up in Seattle," Gerard said. "Alan Donald Abbott. Wanted to be a doctor. Flunked out."

"They say everybody has a look-alike," Henry said. "Someplace in the world. An identical twin."

"Is there any chance you'll catch him?" McIntyre asked.

"Unless he leaves the neighborhood," Gerard said. "Yes. When desperation drives people, they trip up." He snubbed out his cigarette and got to his feet. "Thanks for calling me. Appreciate your help." He opened the door, started out, and turned back. "I'm posting officers to watch this house, Mr. McIntyre. Abbott seems to regard it as home." Putting on his hat, he moved off across the deck. "All the same, I'd lock up at night, if I were you."

Supper and the hour after supper were the best times. He read to her by lamplight, or they watched television. Then she was tired. (He sensed often these days that she was tired well before she said so, and concealed it from him, aware of how he cherished their time together, and of how little time was left them in this life.) He set aside her extra pillows, gave her morphine, drew up the bedclothes, and she smiled and pressed his hand, and slept.

He tiptoed out, and went to lock the doors. Not possible. The lock on the front door was corroded in place, the spring lock on the kitchen door was clotted with coats of old enamel. How long had it been since they'd locked this house? Had they ever done so? He doubted it. There'd been no dangers to lock out in Settlers Cove. Not then.

He put on a jacket, took the flashlight, and went out. Across the front deck, down the steps to the trail. A patrol car sat there in the dark. It was dimly lit inside. Plainly, Gerard had meant Donald to see he'd posted guards to watch the house. Probably there was another car up the side trail. Vern, the towheaded boy, sat in this car. He blinked in the flashlight's beam.

"Mr. McIntyre?" He sat up quickly and squinted out. "Anything wrong?" He reached to open the car door.

"No, no," McIntyre said. "I just came out to tell you, my door locks don't work. Lieutenant Gerard asked me to lock up, but I can't. Haven't turned those locks in years."

"That right?" Vern said. "Well, it's okay. Don't worry. We'll keep an eye on things."

"I don't think he'll come back, anyway," McIntyre said.

"Best to be on the safe side," Vern said.

McIntyre looked into the darkness of the pines. "Is there another car?"

"Up at the rear," Vern said. "Lundquist."

McIntyre started off. "I'd better tell him."

"Save yourself a walk," Vern said. "I'll tell him on the walkie-talkie."

Now came the time of day he liked least of all, when he sat alone in the kitchen, waiting for his mind's weariness to catch up to the weariness of his body. He tried to concentrate on a book, or on *Newsweek* or *Natural History,* classical music from the college station faint from a small radio on the counter. He used to make himself cocoa to help summon sleep. But lately someone— had it been Gertrude Schumwald?—had told him chicken was the best of all nature's soporifics. So he'd had Henry Winston fetch him cans of chicken broth and, when he didn't forget, he heated up and drank chicken broth. He guessed it helped. He didn't dare sleep deeply, anyway—he had to keep an ear out for Margaret.

Now he was sipping at the soup, leafing over an article about Kodiak bears, looking at the pictures, when noises on the rear deck made him raise his head. There, at the window, stood the mule deer buck, peering in curiously, eyes wide, big ears poised. McIntyre was too startled to move, and he and the beautiful animal simply stared at each other for what seemed a long time.

Then there was a bang. Someone had fired a rifle. The deer shied. Its hoofs clattered away across the deck. McIntyre stumbled to his feet, flung himself toward the door, pulled it open. Darkness. He fumbled for the switch beside the door, and light fell across the deck. Splashes of blood. A trail of blood-stains. Someone came at a run into the light. A stocky deputy he hadn't seen before. He had drawn his pistol.

"Did you shoot?" he said.

"No. Someone out here." McIntyre's heart knocked in his chest. He couldn't get his breath. He caught the deck rail and leaned on it heavily. "Shot the blacktailed buck. Did you see the blacktailed buck?"

"No," Lundquist said. "Are you sure?"

"He was here, on the deck," McIntyre said, "looking in the window. What was the harm in that?"

"Don't look at me," Lundquist said. "I didn't do it."

Vern called out of the night, "What's going on?"

"Some son of a bitch shot that mule deer," Lundquist shouted. Someone, or maybe the deer, was crashing among the trees above the house. White-faced Vern appeared panting in the kitchen doorway. He carried a rifle. Lundquist said, "Come on. Let's get the bastard."

And the two of them charged up into the woods. McIntyre listened to them tramping around in the dark. He caught glimpses of their flashlight beams. Then he realized that now was the time for Donald to appear. No one was guarding the house. He went back indoors, took the half-empty vial from the bathroom shelf and dropped it into his pocket, got the poker from beside the fireplace, and went to sit by Margaret. He knew he wasn't worth much as a guardian. But he was the only one left.

Vern found him there, nodding in the chair. He cleared his throat. " 'Scuse me, Mr. McIntyre."

McIntyre looked up. "Did you catch him?"

"No. No sign of the deer, either." His smooth young face showed grief and anger. "But from the way he bled on your deck, I'd say he won't make it."

"You going to stay on guard now?" McIntyre was filled with a heavy sadness. He pushed up out of the chair. "If so, I'll go to bed. The young thrive on excitement." He managed a wan smile for Vern. "It wears old people out."

"We'll keep watching," Vern said.

He woke in the dark, and knew it was no use their being out there. Donald was in the room. He could hear him breathing. Panting, rather, and whimpering. He reached out and switched on the lamp. It shone on the glass with his teeth leaning in it, and glanced brightly off the lenses of his spectacles. He put these on, and turned. Donald sat on the floor, slumped back against the closet door. His right hand was over his heart. As if to salute the flag in a sixth-grade classroom. But the hand was bloody. Blood had run down the black jacket.

He was staring at McIntyre and trying to speak. McIntyre couldn't hear the words. He argued his heavy old bulk out of bed, and bent over Donald.

"I'm here," he said. "How did this happen?"

"Drugstore. In Morro Bay." The words came gasping. Donald caught McIntyre's sleeve. "Water?"

McIntyre brought water from the bathroom, knelt stiffly, and held the glass to Donald's mouth. But he was too weak to take more than a sip. He turned away his head.

"What were you doing at the drugstore?" McIntyre asked. "No, don't try to answer." He set the glass down. "I know."

"You know." Donald closed his eyes and nodded. "You always knew. Everything about me." He opened his eyes again and pleaded with his eyes. "I can't help it. You know that, too, don't you? I can't help it."

"There are police cars outside." McIntyre struggled to his feet. "They'll call an ambulance."

Donald whispered, "I didn't know that drugstore had a security guard, or I'd never have broken in." Blood leaked out of his mouth. "I'm dying. I don't want to die."

McIntyre looked down at him. "You told me I'd never be alone," he said bitterly. "At the funeral. You promised. You'd always be with me."

Donald didn't answer. His chin rested on his chest.

McIntyre went to find Vern. Vern called on the radio for Lieutenant Gerard and for an ambulance, then ran up the steps two at a time. When slow old McIntyre came in, the young officer was kneeling on the floor beside Donald. He climbed to his feet, shaking his head grimly.

"It's over. He didn't make it."

"He tried to rob a drug store in Morro Bay."

"I know. They radioed us. He was wounded. I figured they'd catch him. I didn't want to wake you up over it." He tilted his head. "Why did he come here, Mr. McIntyre? It's a long way, the shape he was in."

McIntyre shrugged numbly. "He'd helped me. I guess he thought I'd help him."

"We'll get him out of your way," Vern said, "just as soon as we can."

"Thank you."

McIntyre went to look at Margaret.

Julian Rathbone is one of Britain's bright lights, a pro among pros as it were, a man with a vivid style and a nice sense of the human angle. This story won Britain's prestigious "Golden Dagger" last year.

Some Sunny Day
JULIAN RATHBONE

On more than one occasion Baz has abused her great reputation as a criminal investigator for very dubious ends. The "murder" of Don Hicks was a case in point. On our return from Las Palomas we quarreled quite bitterly on the subject. Then, as she has also done on subsequent occasions, she produced a line of reasoning, which, were it not put into practice with remarkable results, I would find endearingly old-fashioned—a naïve amalgam of Hobbes and Nietzsche with a few other "philosophers" like de Sade filling in the harmonies.

Standing with her back to the forty-eight-inch TV screen which plays continuously but always silently in her living-room, and which serves the social purpose of an open fire, she rocked back and in her Tibetan snow leopard slippers came on like a pompous don.

"My dear Julia," she said, full of smug self-satisfaction because things had gone so well, in spite of my efforts to put them right, "there is only one personal morality that deserves more than a moment's consideration. Follow your own individual star, the promptings of your innermost soul—be true to that and nothing else—"

I interrupted as mockingly as I could: "Do it my way?"

Baz went on, unruffled.

"The morality you appeal to, the communally shared sense of what is right and wrong, is a fiction, a tissue of lies invented by man in his social aspect to allow society to function, to regulate the transactions we make one with another in our social lives." She sipped ice-cold Russian vodka—neat with a scatter of freshly ground black pepper. "My dear Julia, you are not ill-educated, and you are trained in the social sciences—you are therefore perfectly well aware that all societies hold their own moralities to be the only good ones, yet all societies swiftly and hypocritically change their moralities as soon as their survival is threatened if they do not . . .''

I attempted an interruption: ''I cannot recall a society which condoned or encouraged wholesale robbery on the scale perpetrated by your friend Hicks.''

She froze, then gave me that long cold stare which she knows I hate because of its element of Olympian scorn for the foolishness of a mere mortal.

''You forget Ruskin's truism that the wealth of Victorian England was built on the loot of empires.''

''And you forget,'' said I, pleased to find a rejoinder on the spot and not half-way down the stairs, ''that he also said you cannot put an unearned sovereign in your own pocket without taking it from someone else's.''

Well, enough of that, I leave the reader to judge between us.

I am well aware that Hicks's demise was well-aired in the media at the time, and that a couple of hacks have since cobbled together books about the whole affair, but I am also aware that such sensations are less than seven-day wonders and the more intelligent readers of these memoirs will have quite rightly by now forgotten all but a hazy outline of the sordid business. If however you have the sort of mind that does retain in detail the trivia of what passes for news, then I suggest you skip the next page.

In 1970 a gang of three evil hoodlums carried out the Grosswort and Spinks bullion robbery. In the process they killed a security guard but got clean away with thirty million pounds' worth of gold bars which were never recovered. Their getaway van had been stolen for them by a petty south London car thief called Don Hicks, who also drove it in the second stage of the robbery. He was arrested for the car theft and later accused of being an accessory—but the prosecution on the major charge was later dropped and he went down for only two years. The three hoodlums were arrested almost certainly on evidence supplied by Hicks, and they got twenty years each.

When Hicks came out he sold up his south London assets, a garage and a terrace house in Tooting Bec, and opened a small car workshop in Marbella, where he claimed to be providing an essential service a Spaniard could not supply—talking English to the English residents who needed their cars fixed.

Six months later he met and married María Pilar Ordoñéz, who was working as a hotel maid and cleaner. Two months after the wedding they moved into a luxury pad in Las Palomas, the smartest little bay between Marbella and Gibraltar. They had won the big one, the fat one the Spaniards call it, the Christmas lottery—six million in sterling at the then rate of exchange. No one believed them, nobody doubted that the money was the Grosswort and Spinks bullion, but no one could prove it, least of all Detective Inspector (as he was then) Stride, who had been in charge of the case. He was furious at this outcome—that Hicks should get off lightly for turning Queen's evidence was one thing, that he should end up seriously wealthy was quite another.

Sixteen years of well-heeled contentment followed, but then Hick's paradisaical life took two nasty knocks. First, his first wife, Sandra, went to Stride and said she was prepared to tell him all about Hicks's part in the Grosswort and Spinks robbery, including how he had masterminded the whole thing, but most important of all, where what was left of the bullion was, and so on. Second, the three hooligans he had shopped were let out. No one had any doubt at all they would head straight for Las Palomas—in the dock eighteen years before they had promised Hicks, in song, that don't know where, don't know when, we'll meet again some sunny day. The only question was: Would Stride get there first?

It turned out not to be a coincidence at all that Holmes and I were also on our way, club class BA Gatwick to Málaga. I passed her the plastic ham from my plastic tray and she gave me her orange.

I asked her, "Why?"

"Because," she said, smoothing her immaculately glossy, sleek black hair behind her small but perfect ear, "Don is a very old friend. A very good friend."

"You made a friend out of a robber?"

"He has wit, charm, and he is very, very clever."

"But I thought you occupied yourself with putting criminals behind bars."

"I occupy myself solving human problems whose ironic intricacies appeal to the intellectual side of my personality."

And she terminated the conversation by turning her head slightly away from me so the bony profile of her remarkable nose was silhouetted against the flawless empyrean of space at thirty thousand feet.

We were met at Málaga airport by an urchin in an acid house T-shirt which also carried the slogan Don't Worry, Be Happy. He wore jeans and trainers and looked every inch a Spanish street Arab until you saw his eyes which, beneath his mop of black hair worn fashionably stepped, were deepset and blue. He shook hands very politely with me, but to my surprise was awarded a kiss on both cheeks from Baz.

"*¡Madrina!*" he cried, "*¿Cómo estás?*"

"*Madrina?*" I asked, as he picked up our bags.

"Godmother," Baz replied.

I was stunned. I was even more stunned when Juan Hicks ("Heeks") Ordoñéz led us out to the car-park, threw our bags into the trunk of a large silver-grey, open-top Merc, and himself settled, with keys, into the driver's seat. I made rapid calculations.

"Baz," I said, "this lad cannot be more than sixteen."

"Sixteen next September."

"But he's driving. Isn't that illegal?"

"Yes. No doubt it would become an issue if he were involved in an accident. He bears this in mind and drives very well."

You could have fooled me. I was sitting directly behind him, with Baz on the other side. For most of the way Juan steered with his left hand, lay back into the corner between door and front seat with his right hand draped over the back of it. That way he was able to keep up a lengthy and animated conversation with Baz shouted over the roar of the horn-blasting diesel lorries he successively passed.

Baz's Spanish is fluent and perfect—she spent three years of her adolescence there studying guitar with Segovia amongst others—while mine hardly goes beyond the *"Un tubo de cerveza, por favor"* level, but I picked up some of it, and pieced together the rest from subsequent events—enough to offer the reader an approximate and much truncated transcription.

"How's Dad, Juan?"

"Not good. Very upset indeed. He's left the house and gone on the boat. He's there on his own, refuses to have anyone with him. He says the moment he sees either Stride or McClintock, Allison or Clough coming out after him, he'll start the engine and make for the open sea."

"What good will that do him?"

"None at all. But the boat's very fast. And very manoeuvrable too. He reckons he can get through the straits and out into the Atlantic before anyone catches him—unless they are prepared to rocket or shell him."

"What then?"

Juan shrugged, head forward on his neck, left hand twisted palm up.

"That's it. Adiós Papa."

Baz thought, then said, "A bad scene, Juan."

"Very bad."

"What does your mother think of it all? And the rest of the household?"

"The household shifts from catatonic trance to histrionic hysterics. Especially the girls, and all my cousins. The servants too. But Mama is doing the full dignified matriarch bit. Clytemnestra when she hears about Iphigenia, you know? But if he goes she'll probably throw herself off the quay. Anyway she'll try to but I shall be on hand to stop her."

"You won't be strong enough."

He shrugged. "Maybe your fat friend should be there too to help me."

After about twenty miles we swung off the *autovia* and into the hills between it and the sea. The hills were covered with urbanizations—small villas in lots of a hundred or more, all in each group exactly identical to its neighbours. They all had rosebushes and bougainvillea and tiny swimming pools, all were painted white, had red-tiled roofs which clashed with the bougainvillea, and heavy wrought-iron gates, multi-padlocked.

The radio phone bleeped and Juan picked up the handset without slowing down. Indeed after the briefest exchange he was accelerating with the thing still in his hand.

"Yes?" asked Baz.

"Stride's arrived. We have a friend in the Guardia Civil Cuartel and he says they're planning to move on the stroke of midday, in ten minutes' time. We might well be late."

The next five minutes were a hell of screeching tyres and a blaring klaxon. I was thrown from side to side, and when I held on to the fairing of the rear passenger door I lost the straw hat I had bought in Liberty the day before. It had a broad paisley-pattern silk band and streamers and cost thirty-nine ninety-nine, and that was the sale price.

Presently the view opened up and improved enormously. A small unspoilt fishing village huddled round a little harbour, set within a wider cove. There was a small marina beside the harbour, and about fifteen larger boats at anchor in the bay. The hillsides round the bay were dotted quite sparsely with large houses in varying styles of architecture, though 1970s Moorish predominated. The whole area was fenced but very discreetly; only as you approached the red and white striped barrier with its big notice proclaiming *Zona Particular y Privada* etc. did you see the ribbon of twelve-foot fencing snaking over the hillside amongst the olives. An armed security man heard us coming, he would have had to be deaf not to, and had the barrier up just in time. I have no doubt Juan would have crashed it if he had not.

Juan had to slow a bit—the streets were narrow and crowded, the car rumbled over cobbles and occasionally clanged against sharp corners. Then the bay opened up, we zipped along a short promenade of palm trees, oleanders and cafés, and out on to the mole that separated the harbour from the marina.

There was quite a crowd at the end. Three green Guardia Civil jeeps with the officers dressed in full fig for the occasion—black patent hats, yellow lanyards, black belts and gun holsters, the men in combat gear with automatic weapons. There was a black unmarked Renault 21 and Chief Inspector Stride was leaning against it. There were two television crews and about twenty journalists with cameras and cassette recorders. Above all there was the household. All the adults were dressed in black, but magnificently, especially three dolly-birds, no other word will do, in flouncy tops, fanny pelmets, and sheer black stockings. Eight children, uneasily aware of crisis but bored too, played listlessly while nannies and servants clucked over them if they went too near the water's edge. But above all was Mother—Señora María Pilar Ordoñéz, a veritable pillar of a woman indeed—tall, pale, handsome with an aquiline nose, heavy eyebrows beneath her fine black mantilla, it was impossible to believe she had ever been a chambermaid.

All eyes were fixed on a large but powerful-looking cabin cruiser at anchor in the roads between the headlands. One could discern the Spanish flag on the forearm, the Blue Peter at the yard, and the red duster of the British mercantile marine over the stern. A little putter of sound came across the nacreous water that just rose and fell with a small swell not strong enough to break the surface, and bluish-white smoke swirled behind the exhaust outlets. Hicks had the engine running, was ready to slip his anchor.

When Stride, a big man in a suit he'd grown too fat for, big pursy lips above turkey jowls, saw us, he lifted his hat and big, arched, bushy eyebrows. He's head of the City of London Police Serious Fraud Squad now and has often clashed with Baz, knows her well. He had been given the job of arresting Hicks, dead against all rules and precedents, solely because he was the last officer still operational who had actually worked on the Grosswort and Spinks bullion robbery back in 1970.

I expect he was about to say something too boringly obvious to be worth recording when the village church clock struck twelve, the notes bleeding across the air above the water. A Guardia Civil colonel, no less, touched his elbow and he and a party of Guardias began a slow descent down stone steps to a smart little cutter that was waiting for them. As they got to the bottom the village clock began to strike twelve again.

"In case you didn't count it the first time," Holmes murmured.

"Aren't you going to do anything for your fine friend?" I asked.

She shrugged with unusual stoicism, and sighed.

"I fear this time for once, my dear Watson, we are too late."

As the last note bled away into silence the cutter edged out from the quay and began to pick up speed. At the same time a figure appeared on the bow of the cabin cruiser and we saw him fling the anchor rope into the sea. He disappeared into the glassed-in cockpit, the cabin cruiser began to move, accelerated, began a wide turn throwing up a brilliant gash of bow-water against the black-blue of the sea and then . . . blew up. Blew up really well, into lots of little pieces that went soaring into the immaculate sky only to rain down again within a circle fifty metres across. The bang reverberated between the cliffs and sea-birds swooped up and away in a big soaring arc. It was not impossible to believe the soul of Don Hicks was amongst them.

Doña María Pilar at least thought so. With her hand to her throat she stifled back a cry of grief and moved with determination towards the unfenced edge of the quay. Her purpose was clear. I launched myself across the intervening space and grasped her round the waist at the last moment, causing her, and myself, to fall heavily on a cast-iron bollard and cobbles.

Naturally, she was the first to be helped to her feet. She looked down at me and said, in Spanish which Holmes was good enough to translate for me later:

"Who the fuck is this great fat scrotum, and what the fuck does he think he's doing?"

"We know," she said, two hours or so later, "who did it. What Señora

Basilia has to do is prove it. If," she waved a fork from which long strands of spaghetti still hung, "you can prove it so well that the police here will lock up McClintock, Clough, and Allison for ten years or more, then I shall pay you twenty million pesetas."

Well, at that time, just before the British economy went into what will probably turn out to be terminal decline, that was one hundred thousand pounds.

We were all, and I mean all, about fifteen of us, in the big dining-room in Casa Hicks. This was a splendid room, the central feature of which was a big, heavy, well-polished Castilian oak table with matching chairs, up to twenty could be found, for the Hicks family entertained often and lavishly, in the old style. The ceiling was coffered cedar. Three walls were done out with tiles to waist height, the patterns reproduced from the Alhambra. Above these were alcoves filled with arum and madonna lilies. Persian carpets hung between the niches, except on the wall opposite Doña María Pilar, at the far end of the long table, where the carpet space was filled with a full-length painting of Don Hicks done eight years earlier in the style of Patrick Proctor, possibly by Patrick himself. It portrayed him full length in a wet suit, with a harpoon gun in his right hand, while his left held a three-foot shark just above the tail so its nose rested on the floor. Hicks, done thus, was a striking figure, a very handsome, broad, tanned face set off a leonine mop of silver hair, the suit concealing the no doubt well-padded shoulders, the swelling tum, and the varicose veins.

The remaining wall was glass on to a verandah with a view of the harbour, but on this occasion rattan blinds were drawn on the outside and looped over the wrought-iron balcony, probably to cut out the mid-afternoon sun and heat while allowing air to circulate, possibly also because none of those assembled were prepared to look down on the spot of oily water, still with some debris floating, where their lord and master had suffered his demise.

"I have already determined to do so," said Baz, "and only required your permission before initiating my inquiries."

There was a murmur of appreciation from all those round the table who were silently or not so silently weeping. It was not a household in which one could readily grasp the relationships unless or until one accepted the unacceptably obvious. María Pilar ruled a harem, or more properly I should say a seraglio. There were her own three children—Juan who had driven us from the airport, his younger brother Luis and Luis's twin sister Encarnación. Then there were three, well, I'm sorry, but there's only one word for it, concubines: Dolores (or Lola), Carmen, and Purificación (or Puri). Lola and Puri were curvaceous and very, very feminine, Lola with deep red hair, Puri's black and gypsyish, both worn long. Carmen was tall, athletic, with natural dark-honey blonde hair worn short above green eyes. Between them all they had, I later gathered, six more children whose ages ranged from one to thirteen, though only the older three or four were with us for lunch.

What was even more scandalous was that Baz herself was apparently to some extent responsible for these arrangements. María Pilar had approached her fourteen years earlier with a problem: after the birth of her twins the doctors had told her more children would kill her. Since she was deeply Catholic this posed a problem: Don Hicks had not risked a lifetime in prison in order to end up a celibate on the outside. María Pilar's pride was such that she could not accept his having clandestine affairs, nor would she tolerate the gossip and innuendoes that would arise if he did. Baz proposed the solution: concubines. María would remain in control and in charge, the locals would have nothing to be sly about because it would all be in the open, and so on. It had been difficult to begin with but once Lola's first child arrived and Carmen moved in, it had worked beautifully—María Pilar finding great fulfilment in playing the role of super-mum to the whole household. As a sociologist I have to say I approve—since it works. As a strongly anti-Catholic feminist I'm not so sure. . . .

"As soon as the shops reopen," Baz continued, "I shall be grateful if Juan will be good enough to take me to the nearest reliable shop selling underwater equipment, I imagine the one his father used to use is reliable, and tomorrow, weather and the police permitting, I shall examine what is left of the wreck."

"You will charge the expenses to Don's account."

Baz inclined her head in acceptance of this offer.

"Meanwhile," she asked, "I need to know when McClintock, Clough, and Allison arrived here."

Luis, an attractive lad, fairer than Juan, chipped in. "They were first seen only yesterday morning. But they went straight to one of the smaller villas on the other side of the bay. It had been booked and prepared for them in advance, so it is likely they have confederates already working in the area."

"In any case," said Baz, "twenty-four hours would have been ample (she pronounces the word "ah-mpull," an irritating affectation) for them to have put a bomb in place, or more probably a mine. What very few people are aware of is that Brian McClintock is a member of the IRA and no doubt learnt the technology that blew up your father from those who did much the same to poor dear Louis."

The meal over, I declined a second opportunity to enjoy Juan's driving skills and pronounced myself eager, as eager as one appropriately could be in a house suddenly plunged into mourning, for a siesta. I was shown to a room at the back of the house, which yet had good views of the distant sierra above the olive and almond groves, and which shared a bathroom with the room on the other side, which had been allocated to Baz. My luggage was there ahead of me, and unpacked—a service I always find mildly impertinent on the rare occasions it happens to me.

However, sleep did not come easily, the excitements of the day had been too intense, and presently I pulled on my Bermuda shorts with the passion flowers and a plainer but comfortably loose orange top, and set off for a quiet and, I hoped, discreet exploration of the property. In truth I was hungry too. No doubt out of consideration for both the dead and bereaved, María Pilar had allowed lunch to consist only of the spaghetti, which normally would have been the first course merely, and fruit, and the so-called breakfast on the plane had been so relentlessly aimed at carnivores that I had not been able to take on board as much as I like to at the beginning of the day.

I padded down the corridors and stairs I had already climbed, into the spacious circular hall with a glass dome. For the most part the house was silent—the ghastly tragedy that had occurred may have stifled appetites for food, but not apparently for sleep. Though I was surprised at one point to hear two girls giggling behind a door, and then again *sevillanas* played quite loudly on Radio Málaga with castanets added in real. Servants, I supposed, less moved by their master's death than they appeared to be in front of his family.

In the hall, also tiled and with alcoves filled with roses this time, there was no mistaking the door to the kitchens and similar offices: it was slightly ajar, lined with green baize, and the stone steps led down. I now entered a quiet and blissfully cool world of larders and pantries lit only by small grills near the ceilings. It was all very clean and neat too—one could imagine that María Pilar's influence was as strong in these partially subterranean halls as every-where else. Presently I was in the kitchen—hung with whole sets of copper pans, with assorted knives in racks, and, precisely what I had hoped to find, a row of blackish-brown sheep cheeses, one of which had already been cut. The cheese was almost pure white, a sort of creamy marble, and crumbly—in short *à point,* or as the Spanish have it, *al punto.* It was with me the work of a moment to cut myself enough to fill a half *barra.* I wondered where the wine was kept. Such a good cheese deserved a fruity red.

At that moment I heard a totally indescribable noise. Nevertheless I shall do my best. It was a sort of rhythmical combination of squelching and slapping, each beat ending with a brisk noise somewhere between a squeak and the noise of torn cloth. It happened about twelve times, then stopped.

Of course I was petrified. Fat people, and I am very fat, live in constant dread of the ridicule which is provoked by the situation I was then in. Never-theless curiosity, and a loyal feeling too that Holmes should be aware of anything untoward that was going on in the house, prompted me presently to move in the direction from which the sounds had come. I passed through an open but bead-curtained doorway into a short narrow defile between white walls from which the sun's glare was instantly blinding. I waited until I could see—of course I had not brought my shades with me—and followed it into a wide sort of patio. It was clearly used by the gardener as a marshalling yard for potted plants—there were rows and rows of them, mostly perlagoniums in all their wonderful variety ranging from the brilliant simple vermilion people call geranium red, to wonderful concoctions in purples and mauves that to all but the most over-educated taste rival orchids for exotic beauty.

The floor was of polished terrazo chips. Pools of water lay round the bases of the flower pots, which, in spite of the adjustable rattan roofing which shielded the plants from direct sunlight, steamed gently in the heat. So too did the strangely shaped splodges of water which tracked, arrow-shaped, pointing away from the door of what was obviously a potting shed, across the yard, and out on to a gravel walk, and finally a steep slope of dried grasses and immortelles that dropped beneath olives to the sea—and I mean the sea, not the bay, for the house was set on the headland between the two. Unable to make anything of this, I returned to my room and ate my *bocadillo,* little mouthful. A little duty-free Scotch with water helped it down *faux du vin,* and soon I felt able after all to have a zizz.

"I hope, Julia, you have brought your long spoon with you."

"We are then, my dear Holmes, invited to sup with the Devil?"

"Precisely so. You know I do not readily indulge in hyperbole or other forms of linguistic excess: so you will heed me when I tell you the invitation came from one of the most evil men I have ever had to deal with."

Generally speaking, Baz's opinion of the male sex is low. We were then to dine with the lowest of the low. I was relieved, however, to learn that dining was at least on the agenda.

"The Devil has a name?"

"Brian McClintock. And I imagine Frank Allison and Malcolm Clough will be in attendance."

The bad news was that, Spanish style, dinner would not be served till ten. We were invited for drinks at half-nine.

I asked Baz if her shopping trip to Málaga had been successful.

"Indeed yes. And apart from the underwater equipment I bought one or two other odds and ends which will help us in our endeavours." From her silk and wool shoulder bag, woven in Samarkand, she pulled a small black plastic bag. It was sealed with black plastic tape.

"This," she said, "is a radio transmitter, part of an eavesdropping device of exceptional accuracy and power. While we are dining I shall attach the microphone and micro-transmitter to the underside of the dining-table. Later you will go to the ground-floor toilet which is in a vestibule off the main hall and close to the dining-room. I know all this, my dear Watson, because I also went to the agent who manages the villa our evil trio has rented. All I ask of you this evening is that you simply place this package in the cistern. The micro-transmitter will send its signal to the RT in the cistern, which will then relay whatever it picks up to the Guardia Civil Cuartel in Las Palomas."

"What if they frisk us on the way in?"

"I don't think they will. But if they offer to we shall plead our sex and go home. Not much will be lost, this is simply a back-up to my main strategy."

"I think they will. In their position I would."

"Ah, but what you do not understand is that they believe we are on their side. In fact they have already paid me a retainer."

"My dear Holmes, this is too much!"

"Isn't it just? But it will work out, you'll see."

The evil trio's villa, on the other side of the bay, was perhaps one of the nastiest buildings I have ever been to. Built some ten years earlier, probably on the cheap, it was already showing marked signs of wear. The outside wall by the front door was streaked with orange stains, and the stucco rendering was coming away off the corners to expose ill-laid cheap brick. The door itself was made of pine simulating oak, studded with nailheads and with a cast-iron grill simulating a convent gate. The varnish was lifting. Fortunately we could not see much of the garden as the dusk was already upon us, but there was the inevitable bougainvillea clashing with a profuse variety of nicotiana.

We were welcomed into a hall, where black mould grew up the outside wall, by Frank Allison, a tall dark man once handsome and strong, now a ruin of himself. He offered us what must once have been a conman's charm and was now the wheedling flattery of a conniving ex-con. The only good argument for the death penalty, and not one I would discount until the situation is reformed, is what long prison terms in our appalling prisons do to the inmates. I write as one who has been a Prison Visitor.

The interior he took us into had been furnished to appeal to the lowest common factor in taste and had sunk below even that. There were stained-glass lanterns over the lights, others were lacquered brass fittings from which the lacquer had peeled. The upholstered furniture was covered in grubby, ill-fitting loose covers of a wishy-washy design. The upright chairs were made from turned pine with stick-on mouldings, painted black. Cracked leatherette simulated leather. On a wall table a large bowl of opalescent glass in the shape of a stylized swan held English lilac which was no longer factory fresh. Worst of all was a painting of a gypsy girl pretending to sell sardines but really it was her boobs that were on offer, heavily framed in a bright, shiny gilt above a false fireplace that the occupants had been using as an ashtray.

"Lovely, isn't she?" said Brian McClintock, coming in behind us. He was a short, compact, tough-looking man, with a pale pock-marked face, and eyes the colour of year-old ice. He ran his fingers over the gypsy girl's boobs. "Original, see? You can feel the impasto. Glad you could make it, Holmes. And your friend. I don't think I've had the pleasure."

I took the grey claw he proffered and repressed a shudder at its chill. No shudder though for the chill of the strong g-and-t, well-iced, that came after it, accompanied by canapés of anchovy on Ritz biscuits, cream cheese with tiny pearl onions. Really, one might as well have been in Balham, though I doubt the drinks there would have been served so strong.

Incidentally all what he called "the doings" were handed round (and probably had been prepared) by the third of the evil trio—Malcolm Clough. He was fat and bald but with forearms and fists still solid and strong, the skin not gone loose, supported by muscle as well as fat. He affected a slightly camp style that went with the apron he was wearing. I got the impression that he supplied the muscle, Allison the mean, low cunning, but that McClintock was the leader—in terms of pure nastiness he had the edge on the others.

After the one drink, taken with the five of us standing and remarking on the continuing brightness of the weather and the possibility of thunder by the end of the week, Malcolm declared his paella would be sticking and would we be so kind as to go through. He showed us to places round an oval table with cracked veneer, dressed with plastic mats and Innox cutlery. Before he "dashed" he used a Zippo lighter on the single red candle set in a tiny tin chamber-pot bearing the legend "A Present from Bognor Regis." The place settings were already filled with bowls of gazpacho—which, I have to say, I found perfectly acceptable. Allison filled wine glasses with a semi-sweet, which was not. McClintock lifted his to Holmes.

"Cheers. Well, Baz. How's it going?"

"Early days yet, Bri, early days. I'm still not quite sure how it was done, but tomorrow I shall find out. Or the next day."

"We saw you was in Málaga," commented Allison "and bought the underwater gear. Have much trouble explaining why you wanted it?"

"None at all," replied Baz. "You will recall that the other side has retained me to fit you up as Hicks's assassins. In order to do that they expect me to recover faked evidence from the ocean floor. Little do they realize that I shall in fact use the opportunity to discover how Hicks got away from the boat in the second or so between when he was seen on the deck and the moment of the explosion. The evidence has to be there somewhere."

"But we retained you to locate the bastard. Not figure out how it was done."

"Of course, Bri. But since I am sure he has not returned to Casa Hicks, figuring out how it was done will provide essential clues as how far he has got. And in what direction. So it is important that I should work out just how he did get away. From that we should be able to deduce how far he was able to get in whatever he was using as a getaway vehicle. I already feel fairly sure that it was a heavily armoured midget submarine of Russian design. We know some of your bullion turned up on world markets via the Eastern bloc. If I am right, and there will be cleats on the hull of his cruiser and a hatch to link the two, and these are what I shall be looking for tomorrow, then I think we can safely say he got no further than Tangier, or the coast near by. In fact I already have people working for me there, scouring the souks and bazaars, the pubs and above all the male brothels. Did you know Hicks was that way inclined?''

"I'd believe any filth of a creepy cunt like Hicks," said Allison.

"Come, come," said Clough, returning to serve the paella, "nothing wrong with a bit of bum every now and then."

After the paella there was whiskey-soaked bought-in ice cream gâteau, and as it was served I felt the pressure of Baz's foot on my own. From that I understood that the microphone stroke micro-transmitter was in place, and that the ball was in my court as regards the more powerful transmitter. In fact this was a great relief since the cold of the ice-cream hitting the oily glutinous mass of rice mussels and prawns had provoked a reaction that booked no delay. It had become a problem—for if I went the once, how would I explain a second "visit" so soon after?

"Scuse I," I said, and pushed back my chair. Fortunately a glance at Baz's stony face brought me to my senses just in time, and I managed the obvious question I had been about to omit out of foreknowledge. "Where is it?"

"The ladies' room? Upstairs, second on the right," said Malcolm Clough.

I looked a question at Baz and received a tiny shrug which seemed to say go ahead anyway.

Up there, I popped the bag in the cistern—it was a high-level one but I was able to manage just by lifting the lid—unclipped my braces, negotiated the satin-edged cover on the seat, and then thought again. I did not fancy that the Civil Guard headquarters in Las Palomas should hear the first effects of tarta al whisky on paella. I rehoisted the nether garments and stood on the seat— necessary now because the bag had sunk to the bottom of the cistern. The seat, thin pink plastic, shattered. I retrieved the bag, pushed it outside the door, and contrived, with some haste now, and in spite of the shards of broken plastic, to answer one of Nature's more peremptory calls, perched on the cold porcelain pedestal. Then I retrieved the bag from the landing. But, I thought, when they discover the broken seat they may guess I stood on it and for why. I placed it instead in another pink plastic receptacle instructing ladies in terms so coy I cannot recall them to deposit tampons and sanitary towels in here and not down the loo. On my way back down I pondered some of what had happened, and had been said, and came to the conclusion that Baz was playing a pretty fishy game.

"Baz," I said, on the way home, "you're playing a pretty fishy game."

"So it may seem to you, dear Julia, so it may seem to you."

"And that bag you gave me, it's in the upstairs loo. Does that matter?"

"I think not."

We were wending our way down the short drive to the electronically controlled gate. The garden of the evil trio's rented villa was of course untended, and branches of hibiscus and plumbago brushed my face.

"It would be fairer for me, and render me more likely to play my part properly, if you told me the truth."

"Julia, so far you have performed magnificently—and as for the truth, remember, he who tells it is sure to be found out—but, as they say, hist!"

Her sudden movement banished from my lips my riposte to her second-hand epigram and she pulled from I know not where, for she was wearing a single-piece, pocketless garment cut like a boiler suit but made out of yellow wild silk, a small but powerful pencil torch. Its beam, as if laser-guided, fell instantly on the head of a woman standing pressed up against a cypress tree. As the light fell on her she flung up an arm to cover her face, but not before we had both recognized the tall, athletic and sullenly beautiful Carmen—the second of Hick's concubines.

"We shall ignore her," said Baz, extinguishing the torch, and taking my arm. "She has served her purpose. I imagine too she has the means of opening the gate we are approaching and hopefully has left it open for us."

This turned out to be the case.

Baz was never an early riser, her preferred hours of alertness and work being from midday until two, then from ten at night to five in the morning. She therefore engaged to be on the Hicks's second cruiser, with her underwater gear, no earlier than half-eleven—an arrangement which the Hicks family, being Spanish by birth or habit, found perfectly acceptable.

I, on the other hand, wake at seven and have to be up and doing by eight at the very latest, and that was the hour that found me next morning again padding about an almost perfectly silent house, bored and hungry. This time I felt no compunction about going straight to the kitchen: a hostess who cannot provide breakfast for her guests at a reasonable time must not be surprised if they fend for themselves. I found coffee in a filter jug, which I reheated, milk in a big fridge and a pack of four croissants in a cupboard. I found the means of heating them through, and I speedily got outside the lot. The moment then arrived which I dread—it is precisely as I pour my second cup of coffee that I most feel a dreadful urge to smoke again. I gave up five years ago, but still the only way to keep myself from a mad scramble for the nearest fag is to resort to displacement activity.

I recalled the extraordinarily handsome perlagoniums in the gardener's patio outside and resolved to pinch a few cuttings while no one was about. I supplied myself with several sheets of kitchen roll soaked in water and a pair of kitchen scissors, and stepped out into the already hot sunlight. I took my time selecting them, for I felt it would be impractical to take more than eight.

I had just snipped the fourth when I heard noises from the kitchen, much the same sort of noises as I had made a half hour earlier. What to do? Some people can be surprisingly shirty when they catch you taking cuttings, especially if they are of hybrids they have themselves created, as well might have been the case in this instance. I decided to hide in an alcove where there was a stone sink and a coiled hose, and wait until whoever was in the kitchen had gone. I gathered up my impedimenta, did just that, turned to face outwards and found I was looking across the patio at the man who had to be the gardener himself. He was tall but old, with short white hair and a big white moustache, and a big white beard, both stained with yellow. He was dressed in an orange mono splashed with mud and perhaps cement, wore heavy-duty gardening boots.

"*¡Hola!*" I offered. "*¡Buenas días!*"

He said nothing, which is unusual for a Spaniard when offered the time of day, but unbuttoned his breast pocket, took out a pack of Ducados, shook one out and lit it. The smell recalled painfully just why I had been caught so obviously *in flagrante delicto*. Then as he expelled the first puff, sandalled feet tick-tocked out of the kitchen and there was Lola, in a short and transparent nightie as well as gold sandals, carrying a tray with a bowl of coffee and a large chocolatina.

She didn't see me, but put the tray down on a large upturned flower-pot, perched up on to her toes and gave the gardener a big kiss.

"*¡Hola, Papa, croissantes, no quedan. No sé por qué ...!*"

So. The gardener was Lola's father—not an unlikely arrangement. I put down my stolen cuttings and sidled away muttering apologies in mixed Spanish and English which they ignored.

At midday then we were all out in the bay on the Hicks's second major craft, an elegant reproduction of a Victorian steam yacht, but with modern engines, radar and so on, and just over the spot where his more conventionally modern cruiser had been blown up. Presently Holmes and Juan appeared from below, clad in wet suits. On the deck they hoisted oxygen cylinders on to their backs, fixed masks, all that scene—one has seen it a thousand times on TV—and finally to the manner born toppled backwards over the taffrail.

When I say "all" I mean all—not only María Pilar and her children, the concubines including the strange and at the moment clearly agitated Carmen, and their older children, but also Stride, and the Colonel of the Civil Guards—again in full fig, black hat, black moustache, Sam Browne and the rest. Twenty minutes or so went by during which we all watched the rise and plop of bubbles through the oily water. After a time a brown scum crept by on which floated panty-pads and used contraceptives. I was amused that the efforts of the *ayuntamiento* de Las Palomas to cast a cordon sanitaire round their unspoilt haven were vitiated by the sea—the flotsam of the Costa del Sol, recently named Costa de Mierda, could not be so easily kept at bay. During all this Holmes apparently kept up a laconic conversation with the Colonel by phone.

Suddenly a big break of bubbles through the heaving scum heralded a shout of triumph. The Colonel stood up and explained, in Spanish of course but the gist was clear: "She's got it."

An underling in round, peaked cap strode across to the small funnel that rose in front of the staterooms, and yanked on a small lever. A shiny copper or brass horn near the top of the funnel emitted two short blasts and a long one that echoed across the bay. Our attention was drawn to the villa the evil trio had rented and its purlieus. It was nearer the water and nearer our boat than I had expected. What one saw was a platoon of Guardias, in full combat gear, snaking up over the terraces towards the house. A PA system boomed incomprehensibly, presumably calling upon the occupants to surrender. It was answered by the crackle of small arms, and tiny puffs of blue smoke drifted across the frontage. The Guardias replied and most of the villa's windows, shutters and all, disintegrated in the firestorm. Five seconds and a white flag was waved. Clough and Allison appeared on the terrace, their hands on their heads.

At this moment Carmen uttered a cry expressing horror and despair and jumped for the taffrail. Undeterred by my effort the previous day, I again launched myself at her, but she was too quick for me and I fell on my boobs and face on the spot where she had been standing. She was last seen doing a powerful crawl through the filth of the bay and out to sea. No one, apart from me, seemed bothered to try to stop her.

A familiar voice behind me: "Well, you could have got us up a bit smarter than that. We've missed all the fun." And Holmes, followed by Juan, both holding black plastic bags, squelched and smacked past me towards the companionway. I looked at the frog-footprints they left, arrow-shaped but pointing back to the rail they had climbed over, and all fell into place.

Lunch on board was, I have to say, magnificent though served as a finger buffet—a system that I normally find unsatisfactory: besides various hams and chicken and so on that I can't take there were giant prawns, calamares romana, Canary potatoes in hot cumin sauce, Russian salad, six other salads, and a huge cold sea bass. There was French champagne and the best in Spanish brandy. Oh yes, I almost forgot, there was cream Catalan, Pyjama ice-cream, water melon, peaches, loquats, and so on. And unlimited coffee.

When it was over we were all called into the main stateroom. A table had been set across one end beneath a second portrait of Hicks, this time one of him steering the boat we were on. Behind the table sat Holmes, Stride and the Colonel of the Civil Guards. The rest of us sat if we could, or stood in a crowd at the back. The Colonel opened the proceedings and Juan, whose English could be as good as his father's, whispered what he said in my ear.

The gist was simple. Condolences to the bereaved family delivered somewhat perfunctorily. Then congratulations to Holmes for so speedily sorting out and proving by whom and how the dreadful deed had been done. Three criminals with an unjustified grudge against Hicks had mined his boat and detonated their explosives by a remote control device, blowing him bite-size pieces. They had been assisted by Carmen, a close friend of Hicks, but who had also developed a grudge against him. She had been caught on the other side of the headland and confessed all. Meanwhile Holmes had recovered evidence of how the mine was detonated from the sea-bed, and the device used to transmit the signal would shortly be discovered in the villa. The Guardias under his command had attempted a peaceable arrest of the three murderers but they had resisted. One of them, Brian McClintock, had been shot dead.

Applause.

Stride took the floor. He was, he said, very grateful indeed to his colleague of the Spanish Guardia Civil, so long a force for law and order respected all over Europe and the world, for this magnificent achievement. Speaking on behalf of the English equivalents, his senior officers in Scotland Yard and in the Special Branch, he would like to say how pleased he was that these three nasties had been wrapped up for good, especially McClintock who was known to have had a hand in the assassination of Lord Mountbatten, even though he had been in prison at the time. No doubt the lefties back home would bleat as they usually did, as they had after the Gibraltar affair, at summary justice executed against known terrorists, but he was confident that Spain's handling of the whole business would be unequivocally endorsed by HMG.

He paused, sipped water, dropped his voice by an octave. He was, he said, saddened by the death of Don Hicks. He had always had a sneaking admiration for the man and had regretted quite deeply the duty that had brought him to these shores—namely to arrest him for a crime nearly twenty years old. So in a way it was a relief not to have to do this, and a great relief to be able to write once and for all finis to the Grosswort and Spinks bullion case. He had no reservations at all about adding his condolences to the Colonel's and offering them to the bereaved family.

Applause.

"Hang on," I said. My voice squeaked but I was determined. "This won't do, you know. Don Hicks is alive and well and living in his garden shed—"

"Julia!" Holmes's voice was like frozen prussic acid, but I ploughed on.

"Those three men were villains, I know, but this time they have been fitted up—"

"Watson!"

"I saw Hicks this morning. Lola, Dolores, over there, she brought him his breakfast. In the garden shed. Yesterday I saw his frogman-footprints—"

María Pilar intervened this time: "If no one else will silence that fat scrotum, I shall." And she came for me with a knife.

I don't know why she calls me that. I know I wear mannish clothes, but she can't really believe I'm a man. . . .

*　　*　　*

On the way back to the airport, Juan driving, my remonstrations with Holmes were again interrupted by a bleep on the radio phone. Juan passed the handset to Holmes.

"It's for you."

Holmes listened, then said, "I'll ask her."

She turned to me and her eyes, deep violet, dilated by the drugs she often uses at the successful outcome of a case, seemed to penetrate the inner recesses of my soul.

"Julia, the police cannot find the radio transmitter that detonated the bomb, and which you hid for me in the cistern of the upstairs toilet of the villa. Please tell me where it is."

Defeated, I told her.

A shadow of a smile crossed her lips though not her eyes.

"I imagine that being men they preferred not to look for it there."

One last footnote. When I got back home I found eight perlagoniums, fully grown, of real magnificence, delivered by a florist who is on the Designer Living Card list, of which more anon in a later tale. The card read "Gratefully yours, DH." They are very lovely and I cherish them. But plants bought ready grown never give the same pleasure as those one has reared from stolen cuttings—do they?

Marcia Muller is finally being recognized for A) launching the modern female private-eye and B) being the best practitioner of the form. While others were being wildly overpraised, Muller contented herself with getting better and better, stronger and stronger, as both novelist and social critic—to the point that today her books are among the richest, truest examples of serious popular fiction being published anywhere in the world. "The Wall" is a perfect example of what we're talking about.

THE WALL
MARCIA MULLER

I

I'd been on the Conway case for close to twenty-four hours before I started paying serious attention to Adrian's bedroom wall. A big oversight, considering it was dark purple and covered with a collage of clippings and photographs and junk that looked like it had been dug out of a garbage can. But then I've never been too quick on the uptake on Monday mornings, which was the only other time I'd seen it.

The wall, the missing girl's mother had explained, was a form of therapy, and even though its creation had more or less trashed the room, she—the mother, Donna Conway—considered it well worth the cost. After all, a sixteen-year-old whose father had run off a year and a half ago with a woman of twenty whom she—the daughter, Adrian Conway—insisted on calling "Dad's bimbo" needed *something,* didn't she? And it was cheaper than paying for a shrink.

Or for any more self-help books, I thought, *if* there are any left that you don't already have.

The Conway house made me damn twitchy, and not just because there wasn't a book in it that didn't have the words "relationship" or "self" in its title. It was in San Francisco's Diamond Heights district—a place that looks

221

like some alien hand has picked up an entire suburb and plunked it down on one of our southeastern hills. The streets are cutesily named—Jade, Topaz, Turquoise—and the Conways', Goldmine Drive, was no exception. The house, tucked behind its own garage and further hidden from the street by a high wall, was pretty much like all the other houses and condos and apartments around there: white walls and light carpeting and standard modern kitchen; skylights and picture windows and a balcony with a barbecue that could hardly ever be used because the wind would put icicles on your briquettes up there. The view was nice enough, but it couldn't make up for the worn spots on the carpet and the cracks that showed where the builder had cut corners. When Donna Conway told me—for God knows what reason—that the house was the sum total of her divorce settlement, I started feeling depressed for her. I didn't get much myself when I got divorced, but a VCR and half the gold silverware were at least hockable, and from the rust on the FOR SALE sign out front, I gathered that this house was not.

Anyway, Adrian Conway had been missing for two weeks by the time her mother turned for help to the firm where I work, All Souls Legal Cooperative. We're kind of a poor man's McKenzie, Brackman—a motley collection of crusaders and mainstream liberals and people like me who don't function too well in a structured environment, and one of the biggest legal-services plans in northern California. Donna Conway was a medical technician with a hospital that offered membership in the plan as part of their benefits package, so she went to her lawyer when she decided the police weren't doing all they could to find her daughter. Her lawyer handed the case to our chief investigator, Sharon McCone, who passed it on to me, Rae Kelleher.

So on a Monday morning in early November I was sitting in Donna Conway's drafty living room (God, didn't she know about weather stripping?), sipping weak instant coffee and wishing I didn't have to look at her sad, sad eyes. If it weren't for her sadness and the deep lines of discontentment that made parentheses around the corners of her mouth, she would have been a pretty woman—soft shoulder-length dark hair and a heart-shaped face, and a willowy body that about made me green with envy. Her daughter didn't look anything like her, at least not from the picture she gave me. Adrian had curly red-gold hair and a quirky little smile, and her eyes gleamed with mischief that I took to be evidence of an offbeat sense of humor.

Adrian, Donna Conway told me, had never come home two weeks ago Friday from her after-school job as a salesclerk at Left Coast Casuals at the huge Ocean Park Shopping Plaza out near the beach. Turned out she hadn't even shown up for work, and although several of her classmates at nearby McAteer High School had seen her waiting for the bus that would take her to the shopping center, nobody remembered her actually boarding it. Adrian hadn't taken anything with her except the backpack she usually took to school. She hadn't contacted her father; he and his new wife were living in Switzerland now, and the police there had checked them out carefully. She wasn't with friends, her boyfriend, or her favorite relative, Aunt June. And now the police had backburnered her file, labeled it just another of the teenage disappearances that happen thousands and thousands of times a year in big cities and suburbs and small towns. But Donna Conway wasn't about to let her daughter become just another statistic—no way! She would pay to have Adrian found, even if it took every cent of the equity she'd built up in the house.

I'd noticed two things about Donna while she was telling me all that: she seemed to harbor the usual amount of malice toward her ex's new wife, and an even larger amout toward Adrian's Aunt June.

On Monday I went by the book: talked with the officer in Missing Persons assigned to Adrian's case; talked with the classmates who had seen her leaving McAteer that Friday; talked with her supervisor at Left Coast Casuals and the head of security at Ocean Park Plaza. Then I checked out the boyfriend, a few girlfriends, and a couple of teachers at the high school, ran through the usual questions. Did Adrian use drugs or alcohol? Had she been having romantic problems? Could she be pregnant? Had she talked about trouble at home, other than the obvious? No to everything. Adrian Conway was apparently your all-American average, which worked out to a big zero as far as leads were concerned. By nightfall I'd decided that it was the old story: gone on purpose, for some reason all her own; a relative innocent who probably hadn't gotten far before becoming somebody's easy victim.

Sad old story, as sad as Donna Conway's eyes.

It was the memory of those eyes that made me go back to take a second look at Adrian's room on Tuesday afternoon—that, and the thought that nobody could be as average as she sounded. I had to find out just who Adrian Conway really was. Maybe then I could locate her.

I started with the collage wall. Dark purple paint that had stained the edges of the white ceiling and splotched on the cream carpet. Over that, pictures cut from glossy magazines—the usual trite stuff that thrills you when you're in your teens. Sunsets and sailboats. Men with chiseled profiles and windblown hair; women in gauzy dresses lazing in flower-strewn meadows. Generic romance with about as much relationship to reality as Mother Goose.

But over all that were the words. They leaped out in bold type: black, white, red and other primary colors. GO FOR IT! HOT. GONE FOREVER. STOLEN MOMENTS. FEAR. YES, NO, MAYBE. LOST. THE RIGHT STUFF. WHAT'S IN/WHAT'S OUT. FLASH, COLOR, CURVES, SPLASH. JUST DO IT! And many more . . .

Words as typical as the pictures, but interesting because they seemed important to a young woman who lived in a house where there wasn't a single book, unless you counted her school texts and her mother's stacks of mostly unread paperbacks on self-improvement.

Now, I'm no intellectual giant. I scraped through Berkeley by the skin of my teeth, and for years afterwards all I could make myself read were shop-and-fucks. I still don't read what passes for literature these days, but I do get mighty uncomfortable in a place where there aren't any old dust-catchers—as my grandmother used to call them—lying around. Apparently Adrian was fond of the written word, too.

Tacked, nailed, and glued to the words—but never completely covering them—was the junk. A false eyelash, like the hairy leg of a sci-fi spider. A lacy red bra, D-cup, with the nipples cut out. A plastic tag like the stores attach to clothing to prevent shoplifting. A lid from a McDonald's carry-out cup, Coke-stained straw still stuck through the opening. Broken gold neck chain, pair of fake plastic handcuffs, card with ink smudges on it that looked like fingerprints. Egret feather, dismembered doll's arm, syringe (unused). Lottery ticket with 7s rubbed off all in a row, $2.00 value unclaimed. And much, much more. . . .

Not your standard teenage memory wall. A therapy wall, as Adrian's mom had put it? Maybe. I didn't know anything about therapy walls. The grandmother who raised me would have treated me to two years of stony silence if I'd trashed my room that way.

Donna Conway was standing in the door behind me. She must have felt my disapproval, because she said, "That wall was Adrian's only outlet for her pain. She adored her father. After he left us, she needed a way to begin healing."

So why didn't she hire out to a demolition company? I thought. Then I scowled, annoyed with myself. Next thing you knew, I'd sound just like my boss, Sharon McCone. The generation gap wasn't something I needed to leap yet.

Donna was watching my face, looking confused. I wiped the scowl off and said, "Just thinking. If you don't mind, I'd like to spend some time alone with the wall." Then I started to blush, hearing how truly stupid that sounded.

She didn't seem to notice. Maybe because her daughter had put a private part of herself into the wall, it had become a sort of being to her. Maybe people who were "rediscovering and healing" themselves, as she'd said she was, were either too sensitive or too vulnerable to make fun of other people who expressed sudden desires to commune alone with inanimate objects. Whatever, she just nodded and left, closing the door so the wall and I could have complete privacy.

I sat down on Adrian's brass daybed, kicked off my shoes, and drew my legs up on the ruffly spread. Then I took a good look at the mess on the wall.

It had been a long-term project. Adrian started it, Donna had told me, the day the divorce papers were served. "We made an occasion of it," she said. "I had champagne and caviar, Adrian had Coke and a pizza. We painted. I guess it was the champagne that made me paint the edges of the rug and ceiling."

Now I replayed that. She hadn't painted the rug and ceiling because she was drinking champagne; the champagne had *made* her do it. So perfectly in tune with the philosophies of some of the books I'd glimpsed in passing. This was a household where little responsibility was ever assigned or acknowledged. Not healthy for an adult, and definitely bad for a teenager.

Back to the wall, Rae. You should be able to decipher it—after all, you were a psych major.

First the purple paint. Then the layer of pictures. Idealized, because she was trying to look beyond the bleak now to a better future. Next the layer of words. She was trying to talk about it, but she didn't really know how. So she used single words and phrases because maybe she wasn't ready for whole sentences. Hadn't worked through her feelings enough for whole thoughts.

Finally the layer of junk. Pretty ordinary stuff, very different from the pictures. Her feelings were more concrete, and she was trying to communicate them in concrete form. Unconsciously, of course, because doing it deliberately would be too sophisticated for a kid who'd never been in therapy. Too sophisticated for you, Rae—and you *have* been in therapy. Too bad they didn't encourage you to make a wall like this. Now, that would've given them something to eyeball at All Souls. . . .

Back to *this* wall. She's gone through a process of sorts. Has piled concrete things and real words on top of idealized pictures and vague words. And then one day she's through. She walks out of this room and goes . . . where? To do what? Maybe if I knew what the very last thing she added to the wall was . . .

I left the room and found Donna in the kitchen, warming her hands around a cup of tea. "What were the last things Adrian put up on her wall, do you know?" I asked.

For a moment she looked blank. Then she shook her head. "I never looked at the wall before she left. It was her own private thing."

"You never talked about it?"

"No."

"What *did* you talk about?"

"Oh . . ." She stared down into the teacup. "I don't know. About the healing process. About everyone's potential to be."

I waited for her to go on. Then I realized that was it. Great conversational diet for a kid to sink her teeth into: healing process, potential to be.

What happened when Adrian was worried about an exam? When she hurt because her favorite guy didn't ask her to the dance? When she was scared of any one of all the truly scary things kids had to face in this city, in this world? Where did she retreat to lick her wounds?

I was getting mad, and I knew why. Like Adrian, I'd grown up in a home where everything was talked about in abstractions. In my case, shoulds and shouldn'ts, what-will-people-thinks and nice-girls-don'ts. I knew where Adrian

Conway retreated: not to a nest of family affection and reassurance, but into a lonely lair within herself, where she could never be sure she was really safe.

I wasn't mad at Donna Conway for her arm's-length treatment of her daughter, though. I was mad at my dead grandmother, who raised me after my parents were killed in a car wreck. Donna Conway, even though she wasn't able to deal with emotion, had said she was willing to spend her last dollar to get Adrian back. Grandma wouldn't have given two cents for me.

I wanted to go back to All Souls and talk the case over with Sharon, but when I got to Bernal Heights, where the co-op has its offices, I made a sidetrip to our annex across the triangular park from our main building. Lillian Chu, one of the paralegals who worked our 800 line, lived in Diamond Heights, and I thought she had a kid at McAteer. Maybe there was something going on with Adrian Conway that the classmates the police and I had questioned couldn't or wouldn't tell.

Lillian was just going off shift. Yes, she said, her son Tom was in Adrian's class, and he was due to pick her up in about five minutes. "We're going shopping for new running shoes," she added. "The way he goes through them, I should have bought stock in Reebok."

"Could I talk with Tom for a few minutes?"

"Sure. I've got to run over to the main building and check about my payroll deductions. If you want, you can wait here and I'll send Tom in."

I sat in Lillian's cubicle, listening to phones ringing and voices murmuring on the 24-hour legal hotline. After a while a shaggy-haired young guy with a friendly face came into the cubicle. "You Rae? Mom says you want to talk to me."

"Yes, I want to ask you about Adrian Conway. Her mom's hired me to find her."

Tom Chu perched on the corner of the desk. His expression was still friendly, but a little guarded now. "What do you want to know?"

"Anything you can tell me."

"You mean like dirt."

"I mean anything that might help me locate her."

Tom looked uncertain.

"This isn't a game," I told him. "Or a case of a mother trying to find out more than her daughter wants her to know. Adrian's been missing for over two weeks now. She could be in serious trouble. She could even be dead."

"Yeah." He sighed heavily. "Okay, I don't really know anything. Not facts, you know? But . . . You talk with her boyfriend, Kirby Dalson?"

"Yes."

"What'd you think of him?"

"What do *you* think of him?"

"Bad news."

"Why?"

Tom drew one of his legs up on the desk and fiddled with the lace of his sneaker; from the looks of the shoe, Lillian *should* have invested in Reebok. "Okay," he said, "Kirby's . . . always into something. Always scamming. You know what I'm saying?"

"Drugs?"

"Maybe, but I don't think they're his main thing."

"What is?"

He shrugged. "Just . . . scams. Like a few times he got his hands on some test questions beforehand and sold them—for big bucks, too. And for a while he was selling term papers. Scalping sports and concert tickets that you knew had to be stolen. He's always got a lot of cash, drives a sportscar that everybody knows his folks didn't buy for him. He tells his parents he's got this parttime job in some garage, but all the time he's just scamming. The only job he ever had was cleaning up the food concession area at Ocean Park Plaza, but that didn't last long. Beneath him, I guess."

"What about Adrian—you think she was in on his scams?"

"She might've been. I mean, this past year she's changed."

"How?"

"Just . . . changed. She's not as friendly anymore. Seems down a lot of the time. And she's always with Kirby."

"Did this start around the time her father left?"

He shook his head. "After that. I mean, her old man left. Too bad, but it happens." His eyes moved to a photograph on Lillian's desk: the two of them and a younger girl, no father. "No," he added, "it was after that. Maybe six months ago."

"Do you remember anything that happened to Adrian around that time that might have caused this change?"

He thought. "No—sorry. I know Adrian okay, but she's not really a good friend or anything like that."

I thanked him and asked him to call me if he thought of anything else. Then I walked across the park to the freshly-painted Victorian where our main offices—and the attic nest where I live—are.

The set-up at All Souls is kind of strange for a law firm, but then even the location is strange. Bernal Heights, our hillside neighborhood in the southeastern part of the city, is ethnically mixed, architecturally confused, and unsure whether it wants to be urban or semi-rural. At All Souls we're also ethnically mixed; our main building is a combination of offices, communal living space, and employees' separate quarters; and most of us don't know if we're nineties progressives or throwbacks to the sixties. All in all, it adds up to an interesting place to work.

And Sharon McCone's an interesting person to work for. That afternoon I found her behind her desk in the window bay at the front of the second floor—

slumped spinelessly in her swivel chair, staring outside with that little frown that says she's giving some problem a workover. She's one of those slim women who seem taller than they are—the bane of my pudgy five-foot-three existence—and manages to look stylish even when she's wearing jeans and a sweater like she had on that day. When I first came to work for her, her dark good looks gave me attacks of inferiority because of my carrot top and freckles and thrift-shop clothes. Then one day I caught her having her own attack— mortified because she'd testified in court wearing a skirt whose hem was still pinned up waiting to be stitched. I told her she'd probably started a new fad and soon all the financial district power-dressers would be wearing straight pins around their hemlines. We had a good laugh over that, and I think that's when we started to be friends.

Anyway, I'd just about decided to stop back later when she turned, frowned some more, and snapped, "What?"

The McCone bark is generally worse than the bite, so I went in and sat in my usual place on her salmon-pink chaise longue and told her about the Conway case. "I don't know what I should do next," I finished. "I've already talked with this Kirby kid, and if I come back at him so soon—"

"Aunt June."

"What?" I'd only mentioned Adrian's favorite aunt and Donna's apparent dislike of her in passing, and Sharon hadn't even looked like she was listening very hard. She'd been filing her nails the whole time—snick, snick, snick. Someday I'm going to tell her that the sound drives me crazy.

"Go see Aunt June," she said. "She's Adrian's closest relative. Mom disapproves of her. Go see her."

If it didn't save me so much trouble, I'd hate the way she puts things together. I stood up and headed for the door. "Thanks, Shar!"

She waggled the nailfile at me and swiveled back toward the window.

II

Adrian's aunt's full name was June Simoom—no kidding—and she lived on Tomales Bay in western Marin County. The name alone should have tipped me off that Aunt June was going to be weird.

Tomales Bay is a thin finger of water that extends inland from the Pacific forty-some miles northwest of San Francisco. It's rimmed by small cottages, oyster farms, and salt marsh, and the largest town on its shores—Inverness—

has a population of only a few hundred. The bay also has the dubious distinction of being right smack on top of the San Andreas Fault. Most of the time the weather out there is pretty cold and gloomy—broody, I call it—and it's a hefty drive from the city—across the Golden Gate Bridge, then through the close-in suburbs and rolling farmland to the coast.

It was after seven when I found the mailbox that June Simoom had described to me over the phone—black with a silver bird in flight and the word WING-SPREAD stenciled on it, another tipoff—and bounced down an unpaved driveway through a eucalyptus grove to a small cottage and a couple of outbuildings slouching at the water's edge.

My car is a 1964 Rambler American. A couple of years ago when I met my current—well, on again, off again—boyfriend, Willie Whelan, he cracked up at his first sight of it. "You mean you actually *drive* that thing?" he asked. "On the *street?*" No matter. The Ramblin' Wreck and I have gone many miles together, and at the rate I'm saving money, we're going to have to go many more. Barring experiences like Aunt June's driveway, that is.

The cottage was as bad off as my car, but I know something about real-estate values (money is my biggest fascination, because I have too little of it), and this shoreline property, bad weather and all, would have brought opening offers of at least a quarter mil. They'd have to demolish the house and outbuildings, of course, but nature and neglect seemed to already be doing a fine job of that. Everything sagged, including the porch steps, which were propped up by a couple of cement blocks.

The porch light was pee-yellow and plastered with dead bugs. I groped my way to the door and knocked, setting it rattling in its frame. It took June Simoom a while to answer, and when she did . . . Well, Aunt June was something *else.*

Big hair and big boobs and a big voice. My, she was *big!* Dressed in flowing blue velvet robes that were thrift-shop fancy, not thrift-shop cheap (like my clothes used to be before I learned about credit and joined the millions of Americans who are in debt up to their nose hair). Makeup? Theatrical. Perfume? Gallons. If Marin ever passed the anti-scent ordinance they kept talking about, Aunt June would have to move away.

She swept—no, *tornadoed*—me into the cottage. It was one long room with a kitchen at the near end and a stone fireplace at the far end, all glass overlooking a half-collapsed deck. A fire was going, the only light. Outside I could see moonshine silvering the bay. June seated me—no, forced me down—onto a pile of silk cushions. Rammed a glass of wine into my hand. Flopped grunting on a second cushion pile nearer the hearth.

"You have news of Adrian?" she demanded.

I was struggling to remain upright in the soft nest without spilling the wine. "Umpfh," I said. "Mmmm-r!"

Aunt June regarded me curiously.

I got myself better situated and clung to the wineglass for ballast. "No news yet. Her mother has hired me to find her. I'm hoping you can—"

"Little Donna." She made a sound that might have been a laugh—*hinc, hinc, hinc.*

"You're Donna's sister?" I asked disbelievingly.

"In law. Sister-in-law. Once removed by divorce. Thank God Jeffrey saw the light and grabbed himself the bimbo. No more of those interminable holiday dinners—'Have some more veggies and dip, June. Don't mind if I do, Donna, and by the way, where's the gin?' " Now she really did laugh—a booming sound that threatened to tear the (probably) rotten roof off.

I liked Donna Conway because she was sensitive and gentle and sad, but I couldn't help liking June, too. I laughed a little and sipped some wine.

"You remained close to Adrian after the divorce, though?" I asked.

"Of course." June nodded self-importantly. "My own flesh and blood. A responsibility I take seriously. I tried to take her under my wing, advise her, help her to deal with . . . everything." She flapped her arms, velvet robe billowing, and I thought of the name of the cottage and the bird on her mailbox.

"When was the last time you saw her?"

Now June's expression grew uncertain. She bit her lip and reached for a half-full wineglass that sat on the raised hearth. "Well. It was . . . of course! At the autumnal equinox firing."

"Huh?"

"I am a potter, my dear. Well, more of a sculptor in clay. I teach classes in my studio." She motioned in the direction of the outbuildings I'd seen. "My students and I have ceremonial firings on the beach at the equinox and the solstice. Adrian came to the autumnal firing late in September."

"Did she come alone, or did Donna come, too?"

June shook her head, big hair bobbing. "Donna hasn't spoken to me since Jeffrey left. Blames me for taking his side—the side of joy and loving, the side of the bimbo. And she resents my closeness to Adrian. No, my niece brought her boyfriend, that Kirby." Her nose wrinkled.

"And?"

"And what? They attended the firing, ate, and left."

"Do you know Kirby well?"

"I only met him the one time."

"What did you think of him?"

June leaned toward the fireplace, reaching for the poker. When she stirred the logs, there was a small explosion, and sparks and bits of cinder flew out onto the raised stone. June stirred on, unconcerned.

"Like my name," she murmured.

"What?"

"My name—Simoom. Do you know what that is?"

"No."

"A fierce wind of Africa. Dry. Intensely hot. Relentless. It peppers its victims with grit that burns and pits the skin. That's why I took it—it fits my temperament."

"It's not your real name?"

She scowled impatiently. "One's real name is whatever one feels is right. June Conway was *not*. Simoom is fitting for a woman of the earth, who shelters those who are not as strong as she. You saw the name on my mailbox—Wingspread?"

"Yes."

"Then you understand. What's your last name again?"

"Kelleher."

"Well, what does that mean?"

"I don't know. It's just an Irish name."

"You see my point? You're alienated from who you are."

"I don't feel alienated. I mean, I don't think you have to proclaim who you are with a label. And Kelleher's a perfectly good name, even though I'm not crazy about the Irish."

June scowled again. "You sound just like Adrian used to. For God's sake, what's *wrong* with you young women?"

"What do you mean—about Adrian, that is?"

"Well, there she was, given a wonderful name at birth. A strong name. Adrian, of the Adriatic Sea. The only thing Donna did right by her. But did she appreciate it? No. She wanted to be called Melissa or Kelley or Amanda—just like everyone else of her generation. Honestly, sometimes I despaired."

"You speak of her in the past tense, as if she's dead."

She swung around, face crumpling in dismay. "Oh, no! I speak of her that way because that was before ... before she began to delight in her differences."

"When was that?"

"Well ... when she started to get past this terrible thing. As we gain strength, we accept who and what we are. In time we glory in it."

In her way, June was as much into psychobabble as her sister-in-law. I said, "To get back to when you last saw Adrian, tell me about this autumnal equinox firing."

"We dig pits on the beach, as kilns. By the time of the firing, they've been heating for days. Each student brings an offering, a special pot. The gathering is solemn but joyful—a celebration of all we've learned in the preceding season."

"It sounds almost religious."

June smiled wryly. "There's also a great deal of good food and drink. And, of course, when the pots emerge from the earth, we're able to sell them to tourists for very good money."

Now that I could relate to. "What about Adrian? Did she enjoy it?"

"Adrian's been coming to my firings for years. She knows a number of my long-term students well, and she always has a good time."

"And this time was no different?"

"Of course not."

"She didn't mention anything being wrong at home or at school?"

"... We spoke privately while preparing the food. I'm sure if there had been problems, she would have mentioned them."

"And what about Kirby? Did he enjoy the firing?"

Wariness touched her face again. "I suppose."

"What did you think of him?"

"He's an adolescent boy. What's to think?"

"I didn't care for him," I said.

"You know him?"

"I've spoken with him. I also spoke with a classmate of his and Adrian's. He said Kirby is always into one scam or another, and that Adrian might have been involved, too."

"That's preposterous!" But June's denial was a shade weak and unconvincing.

"Are you sure Adrian didn't hint at problems when you spoke privately with her at the firing?"

"She's a teenager. Things are never right with teenagers. Adrian took her father's defection very badly, even though he and I tried to explain about one's need for personal growth." June gave her funny laugh again—*hinc, hinc, hinc.* "Even if the growth involves a bimbo," she added.

"June," I said, "since you were so close to Adrian, what do you think happened to her?"

She sobered and her fingers tightened on the shaft of the poker. "I can't tell you. I honestly can't hazard a guess."

Her eyes slipped away from mine, but not before I saw something furtive in them. Suddenly she started stirring the fire, even though it was already roaring like crazy.

I said, "But you have suspicions."

She stirred harder. Aunt June wasn't telling it like it was, and she felt guilty.

"You've heard from her since she disappeared, haven't you?" Sharon taught me that little trick: no matter how wild your hunch is, play it. Chances are fifty-fifty you're right, and then their reactions will tell you plenty.

June stiffened. "Of course not! I would have persuaded her to go home. At the very least, I would have called Donna immediately."

"So you think Adrian's disappearance is voluntary?"

"I ... I didn't say that."

"Assuming it is, and she called you, would you really have let Donna know? You don't seem to like her at all."

"Still, I have a heart. A mother's anguish—"

"Come off it, June."

June Simoom heaved herself to her feet and faced me, the poker clutched in her hand, her velvet-draped bigness making me feel small and helpless. "I think," she said, "you'd better leave now."

When I got back to All Souls, it was well after midnight, but I saw a faint light in Sharon's office and went in there. She was curled up on her chaise longue, boots and socks lying muddy on the floor beside it. Her jeans, legs wet to the knees, were draped over a filing cabinet drawer. She'd wrapped herself in the blanket she keeps on the chaise, but it had ridden up, exposing her bare feet and calves, and I could see goosebumps on them. She was sound asleep.

Now what had she gotten herself into? More trouble, for sure. Was she resting between stakeouts? Waiting for a call from one of her many informants? Or just too tired to go home?

I went down the hall to the room of an attorney who was out of town and borrowed one of his blankets, then carried it back and tucked it around Sharon's legs and feet. She moaned a little and threw up one hand like you do to ward off a blow. I watched her until she settled down again, then turned off the Tiffany lamp—a gift long ago from a client, she'd once told me—and went upstairs to the attic nest that I call home.

Sometimes I'm afraid I'll turn out like Sharon: illusions peeled away, emotional scars turning white and hard, ideals pared to the bone.

Sometimes I'm afraid I won't turn out like her.

We're already alike in some ways. Deep down we know who we are, warts and all, and if we don't always like ourselves, at least we understand what we are and why we do certain things. We often try to fool ourselves, though, making out to be smarter or nobler or braver than we are, but in the end the truth always trips us up. And the truth . . .

We both have this crazy—no, crazy-*making*—need to get at the truth, no matter how bad it may be. I guess that's how we're most alike of all. The withheld fact, the out-and-out lie, the thing that we just plain can't understand—none of them stands a chance with us. For me, I think the need began when my grandmother wouldn't tell me the truth about the car wreck my parents were killed in (they were both drunk). With Sharon, I don't know how the need got started—she's never said.

I didn't used to feel so driven. At first this job was a lark, and I was just playing at being a detective. But things happen and you change—Sharon's living proof of that—and now I'm to the point where I'm afraid that someday I'll be the one who spends a lot of nights sleeping alone in her office because I'm between stakeouts or waiting for a phone call or just too tired to go home.

I'm terribly afraid of that happening. Or not happening. Hell, maybe I'm just afraid—period.

III

The next morning it was raining—big drops whacking off my skylights and waking me up. Hank Zahn, who pretty much holds the budgetary reins at All Souls, had let me install the skylights the spring before, after listening to some well orchestrated whining on my part. At the time they seemed like a good idea; there was only one small window in the part of the attic where my nest is, and I needed more light. But since then I'd realized that on a bad day all I could see was gray and wet and accumulated crud—nothing to lift my spirits. Besides, my brass bed had gotten crushed during the installation, and although the co-op's insurance covered its cost, I'd spent the money on a trip to Tahoe and was still sleeping on a mattress on the floor.

That morning I actually welcomed the bad weather because, my rainwear being the disguise it is, it actually furthered my current plan of action. For once the bathroom (one flight down and usually in high demand) was free when I needed it, and in half an hour I was wrapped in my old red slicker with the hood that hides nearly my whole head, my travel cup filled with coffee and ready to go. As I moved one of the tags on the mailboxes that tell Ted Smalley, our office manager, whether we're in or out, I glanced at Sharon's. Her tag was missing—she's always setting it down someplace it doesn't belong or wandering off and completely losing it—and Ted would have quite a few things to say to her about that. Ted is the most efficient person I know, and it puzzles him that Sharon can't get the hang of a simple procedure like keeping track of her tag.

The Ramblin' Wreck didn't want to start, and I had to coax it some. Then I headed for Teresita Boulevard, up on the hill above McAteer High School, where Kirby Dalson lived. I'd already phoned Tom Chu before he left for school and gotten a good description of Kirby's car—a red RX-7 with vanity plates saying KS KAR—and after school started I'd called the attendance office and was told that Kirby hadn't come in that morning. The car sat in the driveway of his parents' beige stucco house, so I u-turned and parked at the curb.

The rain kept whacking down and the windows of the Wreck kept steaming up. I wiped them with a rag I found under the seat and then fiddled with the radio. Static was all I got; the radio's as temperamental as the engine. Kirby's car stayed in the driveway. Maybe he had the flu and was bundled up in bed, where I wished I was. Maybe he just couldn't face the prospect of coming out in this storm.

Stakeouts. God. Nobody ever warned me how boring they are. I used to picture myself slouched in my car, wearing an exotic disguise, alert and primed for some great adventure. Sure. Stakeouts are so boring that I've fallen asleep on a couple and missed absolutely nothing. I finished my coffee, wished I'd brought along one of the stale-looking doughnuts that somebody had left on the chopping block in All Souls's kitchen. Then I started to think fondly of the McDonald's over on Ocean Avenue. I just love junk food.

About eleven o'clock the door of the Dalson house opened. Kirby came out wearing jeans and a down jacket and made for his car. After he'd backed down the driveway and headed toward Portola, the main street up there, I started the Wreck and followed.

Kirby went out Portola and west on Sloat Boulevard, toward the beach. By the time we'd passed the end of Stern Grove, I realized he was headed for Ocean Park Plaza. It's a big multi-story center, over a hundred stores, ranging from small specialty shops to big department stores, with a movie theater, health club, supermarket, and dozens of food concessions. It was built right before the recession hit by a consortium of developers who saw the success that the new Stonestown Galleria and the Serramonte Center in Daly City were enjoying. Trouble is, the area out there isn't big enough or affluent enough to support three such shopping malls, and from what the head of security at Ocean Park, Ben Waterson, had told me when I'd questioned him about Adrian the other day, the plaza was in serious trouble.

Kirby whipped the RX-7 into the eastern end of the parking lot and left it near the rear entrance to the Lucky Store. He ran through the rain while I parked the Wreck a few slots down and hurried after, pulling up the hood on my slicker. By the time I got inside, Kirby was cutting through the produce section. He went out into the mall, skirted the escalators, and halfway to the main entrance veered right toward Left Coast Casuals, where Adrian had worked before she disappeared.

I speeded up, then slowed to the inconspicuous, zombie-like pace of a window shopper, stopping in front of the cookware shop next door. Kirby hadn't gone all the way inside, was standing in the entrance talking with a man I recognized as Ben Waterson. They kept it up for a couple of minutes, and it didn't look like a pleasant conversation. The security man scowled and shook his head, while Kirby went red in the face and gestured angrily at the store. Finally he turned and rushed back my way, nearly bowling over a toddler whose mom wasn't watching her. I did an about-face and started walking toward Lucky.

Kirby brushed past me, his pace fast and jerky. People in the mall and the grocery store gave him a wide berth. By the time I got back to the Wreck, he was already burning rubber. The Wreck picked that minute to go temperamental on me, and I knew I'd lost him.

Well, hell. I decided to run by his house again. No RX-7. I checked the parking lot and streets around McAteer. Nothing. Then the only sensible thing to do was drive over to the McDonald's on Ocean and treat myself to a Quarter Pounder with cheese, large fries, and a Diet Coke. The Diet Coke gave me the illusion I was limiting calories.

I spent most of the afternoon parked on Teresita. I'd brought along one of those little hot apple pies they sell at McDonald's. By the time I finished it, I'd had enough excess for one day.

I'd had enough of stakeouts, too, but I stayed in place until Kirby's car finally pulled up at around quarter to five. I waited until he was inside the house, then went up and rang the bell.

While I was sitting there, I'd tried to figure out what was so off-putting about Kirby Dalson. When he answered the door, I hit on it. He was a good-looking kid—well built and tall, with nice dark hair, even when it was wind-blown and full of bits and pieces of eucalyptus leaves like now, but his facial features were a touch too pointy, his eyes a touch too small and close-set. In short, he looked rodenty—just the kind of shifty-eyed kid you'd expect to be into all kinds of scams. His mother wouldn't notice it, and young girls would adore him, but guys would catch on right away, and you could bet quite a few adults, including most of his teachers, had figured it out.

The shiftiness really shone through when he saw me. Something to hide there, all right, maybe something big. "What do you want?" he asked sullenly.

"Just to check a few things." I stepped through the door even though he hadn't invited me in. You can get away with that with kids, even the most self-assured. Kirby just stood there. Then he shut the door, folded his arms across his chest, and waited.

I said, "Let's sit down," and went into the living room. It was pretty standard—beige and brown with green accents—and had about as much character as a newborn's face. I don't understand how people can live like that, with nothing in their surroundings that says who or what they are. My nest may be cluttered and have no particular decor, but at least it's *me*.

I sat on a chair in a little grouping by the front window. Kirby perched across from me. He'd tracked in wet, sandy grit onto his mother's well-vacuumed carpet—another strike against him, even for a lousy housekeeper like me—and his fingers drummed on his denim-covered thighs.

"Kirby," I began, "why'd you go to see Ben Waterson today?"

"Who?"

"The security head at Ocean Park Plaza."

"Who says I did?"

"I saw you."

His little eyes widened a fraction. "You were following me? Why?"

I ignored the question. "Why'd you go see him?"

For a moment he glanced about the room, as if looking for a way out. "Okay," he finally said. "Money."

"Money? For what?"

"Adrian, you know, disappeared on payday. I thought maybe I could collect some of what she owed me from Left Coast."

"Owed you for what?"

He shook his head.

"For *what*, Kirby?"

"Just for stuff. She borrowed when she was short."

I watched him silently for a minute. He squirmed a little. I said, "You know, I've been hearing that you're into some things that aren't strictly legal."

"I don't get you."

"Scams, Kirby."

His puzzled look proved he'd never make an actor.

"Do I have to spell it out for you?" I asked. "The term-paper racket. Selling test questions when you can get your hands on them."

His fingers stopped their staccato drumming. Damned if the kid didn't seem relieved by what I'd just said.

"What else are you into, Kirby?"

"Where're you getting this stuff, anyway?"

"Answer the question."

Silence.

"What about Adrian? Did you bring her in on any of your scams?"

A car door slammed outside. Kirby wet his lips and glanced at the mantel clock. "Look," he said, "I don't want you talking about this in front of my mother."

"Then talk fast."

"All right, I sold some test questions and term papers. So what? I'm not the first ever who did that."

"What else? That wouldn't have brought in the kind of cash that bought you your fancy car."

"I've got a job—"

"Nobody believes that but your parents."

Footsteps on the front walk. Kirby said, "All right, so I sell a little dope here and there."

"Grass?"

"Uh-huh."

"Coke? Crack?"

"When I can get them."

"Adrian use drugs?"

"A little grass now and then."

"She sell drugs?"

"Never."

A key turned in the front-door lock. Kirby looked that way, panicky.

I asked, "What else are you into?"

"Nothing. I swear."

The door opened.

"What did you get Adrian involved in?"

"I didn't—" A woman in a raincoat stepped into the foyer, furling an umbrella. Kirby raised a hand to her in greeting, then said in a low voice, "I can't talk about it now."

"When?"

He raised his voice. "I have to work tonight. I'll be at the garage by seven."

"I'll bring my car in then. What's the address?"

He got a pad from a nearby telephone table and scribbled on it. I took the slip of paper he held out and glanced at it. The address was on Naples Street in the Outer Mission—mostly residential neighborhood, middle-class. Wherever Kirby wanted to meet, it wasn't a garage.

By seven the rain was really whacking down, looking like it would keep it up all night. It was so dark that I had trouble picking out the right address on Naples Street. Finally I pinpointed it—a shabby brown cottage wedged between two bigger Victorians. No light in the windows, no cars in the driveway. Had Kirby been putting me on? If he had, by God, I'd stomp right into his house and lay the whole thing out for his parents. That's one advantage to dealing with kids—you've got all kinds of leverage.

I got out of the Wreck and went up the cottage's front walk. Its steps were as bad off as the ones at June Simoom's place. I tripped on a loose board and grabbed the railing; its spindles shook. Where the bell should have been were a couple of exposed wires. I banged on the door, but nobody came. The newspapers and ad sheets that were piled in a sodden mass against the threshold told me that the door hadn't been used for quite a while.

After a minute I went back down the steps and followed the driveway alongside the house. There were a couple of aluminum storage sheds back there, both padlocked. Otherwise the yard was dark and choked with pepper trees. Ruts that looked like they'd been made by tires led under them, and way back in the shadows I saw a low-slung shape. A car. Kirby's, I thought.

I started over there, walking alongside the ruts, mud sucking at my sneakers. It was quiet here, much too quiet. Just the patter of rain in the trees overhead. And then a pinging noise from the car's engine.

It was Kirby's RX-7, all right. The driver's side door was open, but the dome light wasn't on. Now why would he leave the door open in a storm like this?

I moved slower, checking it out, afraid this was some kind of a set-up. Then

I saw Kirby sitting in the driver's seat. At least I saw someone's feet on the ground next to the car. And hands hanging loose next to them. . . .

I moved even slower now, calling out Kirby's name. No answer. I called again. The figure didn't move. The skin on my shoulders went prickly, and the feeling spread up the back of my neck and head. My other senses kicked into overdrive—hearing sharper, sight keener, smell . . . There was a sweet but metallic odor that some primitive instinct told me was blood.

This was Kirby, all right. As I came closer I identified his jeans and down jacket, caught a glimpse of his profile. He was leaning forward, looking down at his lap. And then I saw the back of his head. God. It was ruined, caved in, and the blood—

I heard somebody moan in protest. Me.

I made myself creep forward, hand out, and touched Kirby's slumped shoulders. Felt something wet that was thicker than rainwater. I pulled my hand back as he slumped all the way over, head touching his knees now. Then I spun around and ran, stumbling through the ruts and the mud. I got as far as the first storage shed and leaned against it, panting.

I'd never seen a dead person before, unless you counted my grandmother, dressed up and in her coffin. I'd never touched one before.

After I got my wind back, I looked at the car again. Maybe he *wasn't* dead. No, I knew he was. But I went back there anyway and made myself touch his neck. Flesh still warm, but nothing pulsing. Then I turned, wiping my hand on my jeans, and ran all the way down the driveway and straight across the street to a house with a bright porch light. I pounded on the door and shouted for them to call 911, somebody had been murdered.

Afterward the uniformed cops who responded would ask me how I knew it was a murder and not natural causes or an overdose. But that was before they saw Kirby's head.

IV

I sat at the oak table in All Souls's kitchen, my hands wrapped around a mug of Hank Zahn's super-strength Navy grog. I needed it more for the warmth than anything else. Hank sat next to me, and then there was Ted Smalley, and then Sharon. The men were acting like I was a delicate piece of china. Hank kept refilling my grog mug and trying to smooth down his unsmoothable wiry gray hair. Every now and then he'd take off his hornrimmed glasses and gnaw on the earpiece—something he does when he's upset. Ted, who likes to fuss, had wrapped me in an afghan that he fetched from his own room upstairs. Every few minutes he'd tuck the ends tighter around me, and in between he pulled on his little goatee. Men think women fiddle with our hair a lot, but really, they do more of it than we do.

Sharon wasn't saying much. She watched and listened, her fingers toying with the stem of her wineglass. The men kept glancing reproachfully at her. I guess they thought she was being unsympathetic. I knew differently. She was worried, damned worried, about me. And eventually she'd have something to say.

Finally she sighed and shifted in her chair. Hank and Ted looked expectant, but all she did was ask, "Adah Joslyn was the inspector who came out from Homicide?"

I nodded. "Her and her partner . . what's his name? Wallace." Joslyn was a friend of Sharon's—a half-black, half-Jewish woman whose appointment to the top-notch squad had put the department in good with any number of civil-rights groups.

"Then you were in good hands."

I waited. So did Ted and Hank, but all Sharon did was sip some wine and look pensive.

I started talking—retelling it once more. "He hadn't been dead very long when I got there. For all I know, whoever killed him was still on the scene. Nobody knows whose house it is—neighbors say people come and go but don't seem to live there. What I'm afraid of is that Adrian Conway had something to do with Kirby's murder. If she did, it'll about kill her mother. I guess I can keep looking for her, can't I? I mean, unless they tell me not to?"

Sharon only nodded.

"Then maybe I will. Maybe I ought to take a look at that bedroom wall of hers again. Maybe . . ." I realized I was babbling, so I shut up.

Sharon finished her wine, took the empty glass to the sink, and started for the door. Hank asked, "Where're you going?"

"Upstairs to collect my stuff, and then home. It's been a long day."

Both men frowned and exchanged looks that said they thought she was being callous. I watched her leave. Then I finished my grog and stood up, too.

"Going to bed?" Ted asked.

"Yes."

"If you need anything, just holler."

"I'm upset, not feeble," I snapped.

Ted nodded understandingly. Sometimes he's so goddamn serene I could hit him.

Sharon was still in her office, not collecting anything, just sitting behind her desk, where I knew she'd be. I went in there and sat on the end of the chaise longue. After a few seconds, I got up again and began to pace, following the pattern on the Oriental rug.

She said, "I can't tell you anything that'll help."

"I know."

"I'd hoped you'd never have to face this," she added. "Unrealistic of me, I suppose."

"Maybe."

"But maybe not. Most investigators don't, you know. Some of them never leave their computer terminals long enough to get out into the field."

"So what are we—unlucky?"

"I guess." She stood and started putting things into her briefcase. "You're going to keep looking for Adrian?"

"Yes."

"Good."

I stopped by the fireplace and picked up the gorilla mask she keeps on the mantel. It had a patch of hair missing right in the middle of its chin; I'd accidentally pulled it out one day during a fit over something that I couldn't even remember now, "Shar," I said, "it never gets any easier, does it?"

"No."

"But somehow you deal with it?"

"And go on." She put on her jacket, hefted the briefcase.

"Until the next time," I said bitterly.

"If there is one."

"Yeah." I suspected there would be. Look at what Sharon's life has been like. And yet, seeing her standing there—healthy and reasonably sane and looking forward to a good night's sleep—made me feel hopeful.

She came over to me and gave me a one-armed hug. Then she pointed at the gorilla mask and said, "You want to take him to bed with you tonight?"

"No. If I want to sleep with a gorilla, I'll just call Willie."

She grinned and went out, leaving me all alone.

After a while I put the gorilla back on the mantel and lay down on the chaise longue. I dragged the blanket over me and curled up on my side, cradling my head on my arm. The light from the Tiffany lamp was mellow and comforting. It became toasty under the blanket. In a few minutes, I actually felt sleepy.

I'd stay there tonight, I decided. In some weird way, it felt safer than my nest upstairs.

Donna Conway called me at eight-ten the next morning. I'd already gone down to my office—a closet under the stairs that some joker had passed off as a den when All Souls moved into the house years before—and was clutching a cup of the battery acid that Ted calls coffee and trying to get my life back together. When my intercom buzzed, I jerked and grabbed the phone receiver without first asking who it was.

Donna said dully, "The backpack I told you Adrian always took to school with her? They found it where poor Kirby was murdered."

I went to put my cup down, tipped it, and watched coffee soak into my copy of the morning paper. Bad day already. "They—you mean the police?"

"Yes. They just brought it over for me to identify."

"Where was it? In the yard?"

"Inside the house. It'd been there a long time because the yogurt—she always took a cup of yogurt to work to eat on her break—was spoiled."

Not good at all.

"Rae, you don't think it means *she* did that to Kirby, do you?"

"I doubt it." What I thought it meant was that Adrian was dead, maybe had been dead since shortly after she disappeared—but I wasn't going to raise *that* issue yet. "What else was in the pack besides the yogurt?"

A pause. "The usual stuff, I guess. I didn't ask. I was too upset."

I'd get Sharon to check that out with her friend Adah Joslyn.

Donna added, "The police said that Kirby was the one who rented the house, and that there was a girl with him when he first looked at it who matched Adrian's description."

"When?"

"Late last July. I guess ... well, with teenagers today, you just assume they're sexually active. Adrian and I had a talk about safe sex two years ago. But I don't understand why they thought they needed to rent a place to be together. I'm not home all that much, and neither are Kirby's parents. Besides, they couldn't have spent much time at that house; Adrian worked six days a week, after school and on Saturdays, and she was usually home by her curfew."

I thought about Kirby's "job" at the nonexistent garage. Maybe Adrian's had been a front, too. But, no, that didn't wash—the store's manager, Sue Hanford, and the plaza security man, Ben Waterson, had confirmed her employment both to me and the police.

"Rae?" Donna said. "Will you keep on looking for her?"

"Of course."

"Will you call me if you find out anything? I'll be here all day today. I can't face going to work."

I said I would, but I was afraid that what I'd have to tell her wouldn't be anything she'd want to hear.

"Yeah, the little weasel wanted to pick up her pay, in cash." Ben Waterson tipped back in the metal chair behind the front desk in the Ocean Park Plaza security office. Its legs groaned threateningly under his massive weight. On the walls around us were mounted about two dozen TV screens that monitored what was going on in various stores in the center, switching from one to another for spot checking. Waterson glanced at one, looked closer, then shook his head. "In cash, no less, the little weasel said, since he couldn't cash her check. Said she owed him money. Can you imagine?"

I leaned against the counter. There wasn't another chair in the room, and Waterson hadn't offered to find me one. "Why'd he ask you for it, rather than Ms. Hanford? Adrian was paid by Left Coast Casuals, not the plaza, wasn't she?"

"Sue was out and had left me in charge of the store." Waterson scratched at the beer belly that bulged over the waist of his khaki uniform pants. "Can you imagine?" he said again. "Kids today." He snorted.

Waterson was your basic low-level security guy, although he'd risen higher than most of them ever go. I know, because I worked among them until my then-boss took pity on me and recommended me to Sharon for the job at All Souls. It's a familiar type: not real bright, not too great to look at, and lacking in most of the social graces. About all you need to get in on the ground floor of the business is never to have been arrested or caught molesting the neighbors' dog on the front lawn at high noon. Ben Waterson—well, I doubted he'd been arrested because he didn't look like he had the ambition to commit a crime, but I wasn't too sure about his conduct toward the neighborhood pets.

"So you told Kirby to get lost?" I asked.

"I told him to fuck off, pardon my French. And he got pissed off, pardon it again, and left."

"He say why Adrian owned him money?"

"Nah. Who knows? Probably for a drug buy. Kids today."

"Did Adrian do drugs?"

"They all do."

"But did you ever know *her* to do them?"

"Didn't have to. They all do." He looked accusingly at me. From his fifty-something perspective, I probably was young enough to be classified as one of today's youthful degenerates.

I shifted to a more comfortable position, propping my hip against the counter. Waterson scanned the monitors again, then looked back at me.

"Let me ask you this," I said. "How well did you know Kirby Dalson?"

His eyes narrowed. "What the hell's that supposed to mean?"

I hadn't thought it was a particularly tricky question. "How well did you know him?" I repeated. "What kind of kid was he?"

"Oh. Just a kid. A weasel-faced punk. I had a daughter, I wouldn't let him near her."

"You mentioned drugs. Was Kirby dealing?"

"Probably."

"Why do you say that?"

He rolled his eyes. "I told you—kids today." Then, unself-consciously, he started picking his nose.

I didn't need any more of this, so I headed downstairs to Sue Hanford's office at Left Coast Casuals.

Hanford was a sleek blonde around my age, in her late twenties. One of those women who is moving up in the business world in spite of a limited education, relying on her toughness and brains. On Monday she'd told me she started in an after school job like Adrian's at the Redwood City branch of the clothing chain and had managed two of their other stores before being selected for the plum position at the then-new plaza. When she saw me standing in her office door, Hanford motioned for me to come in and sit down. She continued working at her computer for a minute. Then she swiveled toward me, face arranged in formally solemn lines.

"I read in the paper about the Conway girl's boyfriend," she said. "So awful. So young."

I told her about Adrian's backpack being found in the house, and she made perfunctorily horrified noises.

"This doesn't mean Adrian *killed* Kirby, does it?" she asked.

"Doubtful. It looked as if the pack's been there since right after she disappeared."

For a moment her features went very still. "Then Kirby might have killed . . ."

"Yes."

"But where is the . . . ?"

"Body? Well, not at the house. I'm sure the cops would have found it by now."

"Or else she . . ."

"She what?"

"I don't know. Maybe she ran away. Maybe he frightened her somehow."

Interesting assumption. "Are you saying Adrian was afraid of Kirby?"

Quickly she shook her head. "No. Well, maybe. It was more like . . . he dominated her. One look from him was all she needed, and she'd do whatever he wanted her to."

"Give me an example."

"Well, one time I saw them at a table near the food concessions in the middle of the mall. He had a burger, she was spooning up her yogurt. All of a sudden, Kirby pointed at his burger, then jerked his chin at the condiment counter. Adrian got up and scurried over there and brought him back some katsup."

"So he pretty much controlled her?"

"I'd say so."

"What else?"

She shrugged. "That's about the best example I can give you. I didn't really see that much of them together. We try to discourage our girls from having their friends come into the store during working hours.''

''When I spoke with you earlier this week, you said you doubted Adrian was a drug user. Are you sure of that?''

''Reasonably sure. I observe our girls very carefully. I can't have anything like that going on, especially not on store premises. It would reflect badly on my abilities as a manager.'' Her eyes lost focus suddenly. ''God, what if something has happened to Adrian? I mean, something like what happened to Kirby? That would reflect badly, too. The damage control I'd need to do . . .''

I said wryly, ''I don't think that as store manager you can be held responsible for what happens to your employees off-hours.''

''You don't understand. It would reflect badly on my abilities to size up a prospective employee.'' Her eyes refocused on my face. ''I can see you think I'm uncaring. Maybe to some degree I am, but I'm running a business here. I'm building a career, and I have to be strong. I have a small daughter to raise, and I'm fiercely protective of her chances to have a good life. I'm sorry Kirby Dalson's dead. If Adrian's also been killed, then I'm sorry about that, too. But, really, neither of them has anything to do with me, with my life.''

That's the trouble, I thought. The poet, whoever he was, said no man is an island, but nowadays *every* man and woman is one. A whole goddamn continent, the way some of them act. It's a wonder that they all don't sink to the bottom of the ocean, just like the lost continent of Atlantis is supposed to have done.

V

I wanted to dive by the house on Naples Street, just to see what it looked like in the daylight. The rain had stopped, but it was still a soppy, gray morning. The house looked shabby and sodden. There was a yellow plastic police line strip across the driveway, and a man in a tan raincoat stood on the front steps, hands in his pockets, staring at nothing in particular.

He didn't look like a cop. He was middle-aged, middle height, a little gray, a little bald. His glasses and the cut of his coat were the kind you used to associate with the movers and shakers of the 1980's financial world, but the coat was rumpled and had a grease stain near its hem, and as I got out of the Wreck and went closer, I saw that one hinge of the glasses frame was wired together. His face pulled down in disappointed lines that looked permanent. Welcome to the nineties, I thought.

The man's eyes focused dully on me. "If you're a reporter," he said, "you'd better speak with the officers in charge of the case." He spoke with a kind of diluted authority, his words turning up in a half-question, as if he wasn't quite sure who or what he was any longer.

"I'm not a reporter." I took out my i.d. and explained my connection to the case.

The man looked at the i.d., nodded, and shrugged. Then he sighed. "Hell of a thing, isn't it? I wish I'd never rented to them."

"This is your house?"

"My mother's. She's in a nursing home. I can't sell it—she still thinks she's coming back someday. That's all that's keeping her alive. I can't fix it up, either." He motioned at the peeling facade. "My business has been in a flat-out slump for a couple of years now, and the nursing home's expensive. I rented to the first couple who answered my ad. Bad judgment on my part. They were too young, and into God-knows-what." He laughed mirthlessly, then added, "Sorry, I didn't introduce myself. Ron Owens."

I'd inched up the steps toward the open front door until I was standing next to him. I shook his outstretched hand and repeated my name for him.

Owens sighed again and stared glumly at the wet street. "It's a hell of a world," he said. "A hell of a thing when a kid dies like that. Kids are supposed to grow up, have a life. At least outlive their parents." Then he looked at me. "You said the girl's mother hired you?"

"Yes. I haven't come up with any leads, and she's getting frantic. I thought maybe if I could see the house . . ." I motioned at the door.

For a moment Owens hesitated. "What the hell—they said they were done in there. Come on in, if you want."

I followed him into a narrow hallway that ran the length of the cottage. "Were you here when they found the girl's backpack?"

"Did that belong to her? Yeah. I came over and let them in as soon as they contacted me. First time I'd been here since the kids rented it. Place is a mess. I'm glad I stored most of my mother's things in the sheds and only left the basic furnishings. They didn't exactly trash it, but they didn't keep it up, either."

Mess was the word for it. Dust—both natural and from fingerprint powder—coated all the surfaces, and empty glasses and plates stood among empty bottles and cans and full ashtrays in the front room. Owens lead me back past a bathroom draped in crumpled and mildewy-smelling towels and a bedroom where the sheets and blankets were mostly on the floor, to a kitchen. It contained more dirty crockery and glassware. Wrappings from frozen entrees and fast food overflowed the trashcan. A half-full fifth of Jim Beam stood uncapped on the counter. The entire place reeked.

"The cops went through everything?" I asked.

"Yeah. They didn't think anybody had been here for a while. At least not last night. There weren't any muddy footprints inside, and the door was blocked by a few days' worth of newspapers."

"Where did they find the backpack?"

"Front room. I'll show you."

The table where the backpack had been was just inside the living room door. What was left there was junk mail and ad sheets—the sort of stuff you drag inside with you and dump someplace until you get around to throwing it out. "So," I said, "this was where she'd leave the pack when she arrived. But why not pick it up again when she left?"

Ron Owens made a funny choking sound, and I realized he'd jumped to the obvious conclusion. "No," I said quickly, "the cops would have found evidence if she was killed here. Did you see what was in the pack?"

He shook his head. "One of them said something about there being no money or i.d."

Adrian had been smart, carrying her cash and i.d. someplace else where it wouldn't be snatched if somebody grabbed the pack on the street or on the bus. Smart, too, because if she'd had to run out of this house suddenly—if Kirby had frightened or threatened her, as Sue Hanford had suggested—she'd at least have had the essentials on her.

I'd seen enough here, so I thanked Owens and gave him one of my cards in case he thought of anything else. I was halfway down the front walk when I remembered to ask him if I could see the sheds where he'd stored his mother's things.

For a moment he looked puzzled at the request, then he shrugged and fished a key ring from his pocket. "Actually, it wouldn't hurt to check them."

We ducked under the police line and went up the driveway. The trees dripped on the muddy ground where Kirby's car had been parked. There were deep gouges and tracks where the tow truck had hauled it out. Other than that, you would never have known that anything unusual had happened there. It was just an ordinary backyard that the weeds and blackberry vines were trying to reclaim.

Ron Owens fit a key into the padlock on the first shed. Unfastened it and then the hasp. The door grated as he opened it.

There was nothing inside. Nothing at all except for a little heap of wood scraps.

Owens's face went slack with surprise. Then bright red splotches blossomed on his cheeks. "They cleaned me out," he said.

"Check the other shed."

We hurried back there. Owens opened it. Nothing except for some trash drifted in the corners.

"But how did they . . . ?" He held up his key ring. "I had the only . . . There were no other keys."

I looked closely at the padlock. Cheap brand, more pickable than most. My boyfriend Willie would have had that off of there in five minutes, max—and he's out of practice. Willie's a respectable businessman now, but there are things in his past that are best not discussed.

"You better call the police," I told Owens.

He nodded, shoulders slumping. "I'm glad my mother will never have to find out about this," he said. "Her good china, Grandma's silver, the family pictures—all gone. For the first time I'm glad she's never coming home. There's no home left here anymore."

I watched Owens hurry down the drive to a car with a mobile phone antenna on its trunk. I knew how he felt. For me, the word "home" has a magical aura. Sometimes I can actually *see* it—velvety green like the plants in my nest at All Souls, gold and wine-red like the flames in a good fire. Silly, but that's the way it is for me. Probably for all of us people who've never had a real home of our own.

I turned away and looked back into the empty shed. Adrian had had a real home, but she'd left it. For this shabby little house? I doubted that. But she'd been here shortly after her schoolmates had last seen her, and then she'd probably fled in fear. For where? *Where?*

I decided to consult the therapy wall once more.

VI

The Conway house was warm for a change, and Donna had closed the drapes to hide the murky city view. Adrian's room, though, was frigid. Donna saving on the heating bill now that Adrian was gone? Or maybe the registers were closed because Adrian was one of those human reptiles who never need much warmth. My ex-husband, Doug, is like that: when other people are bundled in two layers of sweaters, he's apt to be running around in his shirtsleeves.

Before she left me alone, Donna said, "My sister-in-law called and said you'd gone to see her."

"Yes, Tuesday night."

"What'd you think of her?"

"Well, she's unconventional, but I kind of liked her. She seems to have a good heart, and she certainly cares about Adrian."

Donna pushed a lock of hair back from her forehead and sighed. She looked depressed and jumpy, dark smudges under her eyes. "I see she's fooled you, too.'' Then she seemed to relent a little. ''Oh, I suppose June's got a good heart, as you say. But she also has an unfortunate tendency to take over a situation and tell everyone what to do. She's the original earth mother and thinks we're all her children. The straw that broke it for me was when she actually advised Jeffrey to leave me. But . . . I don't know. She seems to want to patch it up now, and I suppose for Adrian's sake I should.''

The words ''for Adrian's sake'' hung hollowly in the cold room. Donna shivered and added, ''I'll leave you alone with the wall now.''

Honestly, the way she acted, you'd have thought the wall was my psychiatrist. In a sense that was what it *had* been to her daughter.

I sat on Adrian's bed like the time before and let the images on the wall speak to me. One, then the other, cried out for attention. Bright primary colors, bold black and white. Words, pictures, then more words. And things—incongrous things. All adding up to . . . what?

After a while I sat up straighter, seeing objects I hadn't noticed before, seeing others in a new light. What they communicated was a sense of entrapment, but not necessarily by the family situation. Material relating to her absent father—GONE FOREVER, THE YEAR OF THE BIMBO, a postcard from Switzerland where Jeffrey Conway now lived—was buried deep under more recent additions. So were the references to Adrian's and her mother's new life—JUST THE TWO OF US, A WOMAN ALONE, NEW DIRECTIONS. But on top of that . . .

Fake plastic handcuffs. Picture of a barred window. NO EXIT sign. SOLD INTO WHITE SLAVERY. Photo of San Quentin. Images of a young woman caught up in something she saw no easy way out of.

I got up and went over to the wall and took a good look at a plastic security tag I'd noticed before. There were similar ones on the higher-priced garments at Left Coast Casuals. Next to it, the word ''guilt'' was emblazoned in big letters; smaller repetitions of it tailed down like the funnel of a cyclone. My eyes followed them, then were caught hypnotically in the whorls of a thumbprint on a plain white index card.

On top of all these were Adrian's final offerings. Now that I'd discovered a pattern, I could tell which things had been added last. FREEDOM! Broken gold chain. A WAY OUT. Egret feather and silhouette of a soaring bird. She was about to break loose, fly away. I wasn't sure from what, not exactly. But guilt was a major component, and I thought I knew why.

I started searching the room. Nothing under the lingerie or sweaters or socks in the bureau drawers. Nothing pushed to the back of the closet or hidden in the suitcases. Nothing under the mattress or the bed. Nothing but school supplies in the desk.

Damn! I was sure I'd figured out that part of it. I had shameful personal experience to guide me.

The room was so cold that the joints of my fingers ached. I tucked my hands into my armpits to warm them. The heat register was one of those metal jobs set into the floor under a window, and its louvers were closed. I squatted next to it and tried to push the opener. Jammed.

The register lifted easily out of its hole. I peered through the opening in the floor and saw that the sheetmetal furnace duct was twisted and pushed aside. A nail had been hammered into the floor joist, and something hung down from it into the crawl space. I reached in and unhooked it—a big cloth laundry bag with a drawstring. I pulled the bag up through the hole and dumped its contents on the carpet.

Costume jewelry—rings, bracelets, earrings, necklaces—with the pricetags still attached. Silk scarves. Pantyhose. Gloves, bikini underpants, leather belts, hair ornaments. They were all from Left Coast Casuals.

Although the items were tagged, the tags were not the plastic kind that trip the sensors at the door. Left Coast Casuals reserved the plastic tags for big-ticket items. All of the merchandise was brand new, had never been worn. No individual item was expensive, but taken together, they added up to a hell of a lot of money.

This told me a lot about Adrian, but it didn't explain her disappearance. Or her boyfriend's murder. I replaced the things in the bag, and the bag beneath the flooring. Then I got out of there and went to bounce this one off Sharon.

Sharon was all dressed up today, probably either for a meeting with one of our tonier clients or a court appearance. The teal blue suit and silk blouse looked terrific on her, but I could tell she wasn't all that comfortable in them. Sharon's more at home in her jeans and sweaters and sneakers. The only time she really likes getting gussied up is for a fancy party, and then she goes at it with the excitement of a kid putting on her Halloween costume.

She said she had some time on her hands, so I suggested we stop down at the Remedy Lounge, our favorite bar-and-grill on Mission Street, for burgers. She hesitated. They serve a great burger at the Remedy, but for some reason Sharon—who's usually not fastidious when it comes to food—is convinced they're made of all sorts of disgusting animal parts. Finally she gave in, and we wandered down the hill.

The Remedy is a creaky local tavern, owned by the O'Flanagan family for longer than anybody can remember. Brian, the middle son and nighttime bartender, wasn't on yet, so we had to fetch our own food and drinks. Brian's my buddy, and when he's working, I get table service—something that drives everybody else from All Souls crazy because they can't figure out how I manage that. I just let them keep guessing. Truth is, I remind Brian of his favorite sister, who died back in '76. Would you refuse table service to a family member?

While we waited for the burgers, I laid out the Adrian Conway situation for Sharon. When I was done, she went and got our food, then looked critically at her burger, taking off the top half of the bun and poking suspiciously at the meat patty. Finally she shrugged, bit into it, and looked relieved at finding it tasted like burger instead of entrail of monkey—or whatever she thinks they make them from. She swallowed and asked, "All the stuff was lifted from Left Coast Casuals?"

"Uh-huh."

"Employee pilferage." She shook her head. "Do you know that over forty-three percent of shrinkage is due to insiders?"

I didn't, but Sharon's a former department-store security guard and she keeps up on statistics. I just nodded.

"A lot of it's the employers' fault," she added. "They don't treat their people well, so they don't have a real commitment to the company. The clerks see it as a way of getting even for low wages and skimpy benefits."

"Well, whatever Adrian's reasons were," I said, "she dealt with the loot in the usual way. Once she got it home, it wasn't any good to her. Her mother would notice if she wore a lot of new things and ask where she got the money to buy them. Plus she felt guilty. So she hid the loot away were Donna wouldn't find it and—more important—where she couldn't see it and be reminded of what she'd done. Out of sight, out of mind. Only it doesn't work that way. She was probably aware of that bag of stuff hanging between the floor joists every minute she was in that room. She probably even dreamed about it."

My voice had risen as I spoke, and I couldn't keep an emotional quaver out of it. When I finished, Sharon didn't say anything, just watched me with her little analytical frown. I ate some of my burger. It tasted like cardboard. I drank some Coke. My hand shook when I set the glass down.

"Anyway," I said, "Adrian being a shoplifter doesn't explain the important things. Did you ask Adah Joslyn what was in the backpack, like I asked you to?"

"I've got a call in to her."

She was still watching me. After a moment I gave it up. "All right," I said, "I used to shoplift."

"I suspected as much."

"Thanks a lot!"

"Well, you did get pretty worked up for a moment there. You want to tell me about it?"

"No! Well, maybe." I took a deep breath, wishing I'd ordered a beer instead of a Coke. "Okay, it started one day when I was trying to buy some nail polish. The clerk was off yapping with one of the other clerks and wouldn't stop long enough to notice me. So I got pissed, stuck the bottle in my purse, and walked out. Nobody even looked at me. I couldn't believe I'd gotten away with it. It was like . . . a high. The best high I'd ever felt. And I told myself the clerk had goaded me into it, that it was a oneshot thing and would never happen again.''

''But of course it did.''

''The second time it was a scarf, an expensive scarf. I had a job interview and I wanted to look nice, but I couldn't afford to because I didn't have a job—the old vicious circle. I felt deprived, really angry. So I took the scarf. But what I didn't count on was the guilt. By the day of the interview, I knew I couldn't wear the scarf—then or ever. I just tucked it away where I wouldn't have to see it and be reminded of what I'd done. And where my husband wouldn't find it.''

''But you kept stealing.''

''Yeah. I never deliberately set out to do it, never left the apartment thinking, today I'm going to rip some store off. But . . . the high. It was something else.'' Even now, years after the fact, I could feel aftershocks from it—my blood coursing faster, my heart pounding a little. ''I was careful, I only took little things, always went to different stores. And then, just when I thought I was untouchable, I got caught.''

Sharon nodded. She'd heard it all before, working in retail security.

I looked down at my half-eaten burger. Shame washed over me, negating the memory of the high. My cheeks went hot, just thinking about that day. ''God, it was awful! The security guy nabbed me on the sidewalk, made me go back inside to the store office. What I'd taken was another scarf. I'd stuffed it into a bag with some underpants I'd bought at K-Mart. He dragged it out of there. It was still tagged, and of course I didn't have any receipt.''

''So he threatened you.''

''Scared the hell out of me. I felt like . . . you know those old crime movies where they're sweating a confession out of some guy in a back room? Well, it wasn't like that at all, he was very careful not to do or say anything that might provoke a lawsuit. But I still felt like some sleazy criminal. Or maybe that was what I thought I deserved to feel like. Anyway, he threatened to call my employer.'' I laughed—a hollow sound. ''That would really have torn it. My employer was another security firm!''

''So what'd you do—sign a confession?''

''Yes, and promised never to set foot in their store again. And I've never stolen so much as a stick of gum since. Hell, I can't even bring myself to take the free matchbooks from restaurants!''

Sharon grinned. ''I bet one of the most embarrassing things about that whole period in your life is that you were such a textbook case.''

I nodded. ''Woman's crime. Nonsensical theft. Doesn't stem from a real need, but from anger or the idea you're somehow entitled to things you can't afford. You get addicted to the high, but you're also overcome by the guilt, so you can't get any benefit from what you've stolen. Pretty stupid, huh?''

"We're all pretty stupid at times—shoplifters haven't cornered the market on that."

"Yeah. You know what scared me the most, though? Even more than the security guy calling my employer? That Doug would find out. For a perpetual student who leaned on me for everything from financial support to typing his papers, he could be miserably self-righteous and superior. He'd never even have tried to understand that I was stealing to make up for everything that was missing in our marriage. And he'd *never* have let me forget what I did."

"Well, both the stealing and Doug are history now." Sharon patted my hand. "Don't look so hangdog."

"Can't help it. I feel like such a . . . I bet you've never done anything like that in your life."

Sharon's eyes clouded and her mouth pulled down. All she said was, "Don't count on it." Then she scrubbed her fingers briskly on her napkin and pushed her empty plate away. "Finish your lunch," she ordered. "And let's get back to your case. What you're telling me is that Adrian was shoplifting and saw a way to break free of it?"

"A way to break free of something, but I'm not convinced it was the shoplifting. It may have been related, but then again, it may not." My head was starting to ache. There was too damn big a gap between the bag of loot under the floor of Adrian's room in Diamond Heights and the abandoned backpack in the living room of the house on Naples Street. I'd hoped Sharon would provide a connection, but all she'd done was listen to me confess to the absolutely worst sin of my life.

She looked at her watch. "Well, I'll try to find out what you need to know from Adah later this afternoon, but right now I've got to go. I'm giving a deposition at an upscale Montgomery Street law firm at three." Her nose wrinkled when she said "upscale."

I waved away the money she held out and told her I'd pick up the tab. It was the least I could do. Even though she hadn't helped me with the case, she'd helped me with my life. Again.

I've always felt like something of a fraud—pretending to be this nice little person when inside I'm seething with all sorts of resentments and peculiarities and secrets. But since I've been with All Souls, where people are mostly open and nonjudgmental, I've realized I'm not that unusual. Lately the two me's— the outside nice one and the inside nasty one—are coming closer together. Today's conversation with Sharon was just one more step in the right direction.

VII

I'd come up with a plan, an experiment I wanted to try out, and while it probably wouldn't work, I had a lot of time on my hands and nothing to lose. So after I finished my burger, I went back up the hill to our annex and got Lillian Chu to call her son Tom at McAteer and command his presence at my office as soon as school let out. When Tom arrived, he'd traded his friendly smile for a pout. To make up for my highhandedness, I took him to the kitchen and treated him to a Coke.

Tom perched on one of the countertops and stared around at the ancient sink and wheezy appliances. "Man," he said, "this is really retro. I mean, how can you people *live* like this?"

"We're products of a more primitive era. You're probably wondering why I—"

"Pulled this authority shit. Yeah. You didn't have to get my mom to order me to come here."

"I wasn't sure you would, otherwise. Besides, the people at McAteer wouldn't have called you to the phone for me. I'm sorry, but I really need your help. You heard about Kirby, of course."

The anger in his eyes melted. He shook his head, bit his lip. "Oh, man. What an awful ... You know, I didn't like the dude, but for him to be *murdered* ..."

"Did you hear that Adrian's backpack was found in the house whose back-yard he was killed in?"

"No." For a few seconds it didn't seem to compute. Then he said, "Wait, you don't think *Adrian* ...?"

"Of course not, but I'm afraid for her. If she's alive, it's possible Kirby's killer is after her, too. I need to find her before anyone else does."

Tom sat up straighter. "I get you. Okay, what can I do to help?"

"You have a group of friends you hang out with, right? People you can trust, who aren't into anything—"

"Like Kirby was."

"Right."

"Well, sure I do."

"Can you get some of them together this afternoon? Bring them here?"

He frowned, thinking. "Today's Thursday, right?"

"Uh-huh."

"Okay, football practice'll be over in about an hour, so I can get hold of Harry. Cat and Jenny don't work today, so they should be around. Del—he's just hanging out these days. The others . . . probably. But it'll be getting close to suppertime before I can round them all up."

"I'll spring for some pizzas."

Tom grinned. "That'll help. At least it'll get Del and Harry here."

I realized why when I met Del and Harry—they each weighed around two hundred pounds. Harry's were all football player's muscle, but Del's were pure flab. Both waded into Mama Mia's Special like they hadn't eaten in a week. Even the girls—Anna, Cat, Jenny, and Lee—had appetites that would put a linebacker to shame.

They perched around the kitchen on top of the counters and table and chopping block, making me wonder why teenagers always feel more at home on surfaces where they have no right to plant their fannies. Each had some comment on the vintage of the appliances, ranging from "really raunchy" to "awesome." The staff couldn't resist poking their noses through the door to check out my young guests, but when Tom Chu, who knew full well who Hank Zahn was, pointed to him and called, "Hey, Rae, who's the geezer?" I put a stop to that and got the meeting underway. After shutting the swinging door and shouting for them to get serious, I perched on the counter next to Tom. Seven tomato sauce-smudged faces turned toward me.

I asked, "Do all of you know what brainstorming is?"

Seven heads nodded.

"What we're going to do," I went on, "is to share information about Kirby and Adrian. I'll ask questions, throw out some ideas, you say whatever comes into your heads. Anything, no matter how trivial it may seem to you, because you never know what might be important in an investigation."

The kids exchanged excited glances. I supposed they thought this was just like *Pros and Cons*.

"Okay," I began, "here's one idea—shoplifting."

Total silence. A couple of furtive looks.

"No takers? Come on, I'm not talking about any of you. I could care less. But think of Adrian and Kirby."

The angelic-looking blonde—Cat—said, "Well, Adrian took stuff from the place where she worked sometimes. We all suspected that."

"*I* didn't," Harry protested.

"Well, she *did*. At first she thought it was a giggle, but then . . ." Cat shrugged. "She just stopped talking about it. She'd get real snotty if you mentioned it."

"When was this?" I asked.

"Sometime last spring. Right about the time things started getting very heavy between her and Kirby."

"When she started sleeping with him," Del added.

"Okay," I said, "tell me about Kirby's scams."

Beside me, Tom muttered, "Dope."

"Test questions." Anna, a pretty Filipina, nodded knowingly.

Cat said, "He sold stuff."

"Like L.L. Bean without the catalog." The one sitting crosslegged on the chopping block was Jenny.

I waited, letting them go with it.

Harry said, "Kirby'd get you stuff wholesale. He sold me the new Guns 'n Roses CD for half price."

"You wanted something," Anna added, "You'd give him an order. Kirby filled it."

"A real en-tree-preneur," Del said, and the others laughed. All of them, that is, except Lee, a tiny girl who looked Eurasian. She sat on the far side of the oak table and had said nothing. When I looked at her, she avoided my eyes.

Jenny said, "It's not funny, Del. Kirby was *so* into money. It was like if he got enough of it, he'd really be somebody. Only he wouldn't't've been because there was no one there. You know what I mean? He had nothing inside of him—"

"Except money hunger," Tom finished.

"Yeah, but don't forget about his power trip," Cat said. She looked at me and added, "Kirb had a real thing about power. He liked pushing people around, and I think he figured having money would mean he could push all he wanted. He really was a control freak, and the person he controlled best was Adrian."

"Jump, Adrian," Harry said. "How high, Kirby?"

Anna shook her head. "She was getting out from under that, though. Around a week before she disappeared, we were talking and she said she'd about had it with Kirby, she was going to blow the whistle and the game would be over. And I said something like, 'Sure you are, Adrian,' and she goes, 'No, I've worked it all out and I've got somebody to take my side.' And I go, 'You mean you got another guy on the line who's going to stand up to Kirb?' And she goes, 'Yes, I've got somebody to protect me, somebody strong and fierce, who isn't going to take any shit off of anybody.' "

"Did you tell the cops about that when they came around?" Del asked.

Anna tossed her long hair. "Why should I? If Adrian took off with some guy, it's her business."

I caught a movement to one side, and turned in time to see Lee, the silent one, slip off the table and through the swinging door to the hall. "Lee?" I called.

There was no answer but her footsteps running toward the front of the house. I was off the countertop and out the door in seconds. "Help yourself to more Cokes," I called over my shoulder.

By the time I spotted her, Lee was on the sidewalk heading downhill toward Mission. As I ran after her I realized what truly lousy shape I'd let myself get into these past few months, what with the caseload I'd been carrying and spending too much time with Willie. There's only one kind of exercise that Willie likes, and while it's totally diverting, it doesn't do the same thing for you as aerobics.

Lee heard my feet slapping on the pavement, looked back, and then cut to the left and started running back uphill through the little wedge-shaped park that divides the street in front of All Souls. I groaned and reversed, panting.

At the tip of the park two streets came together, and two cars were also about to come together in a great blast of horns and a shout from one of the drivers that laid a blue streak on the air. Lee had to stop, I put on some speed, and next thing I knew I had hold of her arm. Thank God she didn't struggle— I had absolutely no wind left.

Lee's short black hair was damp with sweat, plastered close to her finely fashioned skull, and her almond-shaped eyes had gone flat and shiny with fear. She looked around desperately, then hung her head and whispered, "Please leave me alone."

I got my breathing under control. "Can't. You know something, and we have to talk. Come on back to the house."

"I don't want to face the rest of them. I don't want any of them to know what I've done."

"Then we'll talk out here." There was a makeshift bench a few yards away—a resting place one of the retired neighborhood handymen had thrown together for the old ladies who had to tote parcels uphill from the stores on Mission. Hell, I thought as I led Lee over there, he'd probably watched me trying to jog around the park before I totally lost it in the fitness department, and built the thing figuring I'd need it one of these days. Eventually I'd keel over during one of my workouts and then they'd put a plaque on the seat: *Rae Kelleher Memorial Bench—Let This Be a Warning to All Other Sloths.*

I gave Lee a moment to compose herself—and me a moment to catch my breath—and looked around at the commuters trudging up from the bus stop. The day had stayed gray and misty until about three, then cleared some, but new storm clouds threatened out by the coast. Lee fumbled through her pockets and came up with a crumpled Kleenex, blew her nose and sighed.

I said, "It can't be all that bad."

"You don't know. It's the worst thing I've ever done. When my father finds out, he'll *kill* me."

I tried not to smile, thinking of all the kids down through the ages who had been positively convinced that they would be killed on the spot if they were ever caught doing something wrong. I myself was in college before it occurred to me that parents—normal, sane parents, that is—don't kill their offspring because kids are too damned expensive and troublesome to acquire and raise. Why waste all that money and effort, plus deprive yourself of the pleasure of becoming a burden to them in your old age?

"Maybe," I said to Lee, "he won't have to find out."

She shook her head. "No way, not this."

"Tell me about it, and then we'll see."

Another tremulous sigh. "I guess I better tell somebody, now that Kirby's been murdered and Adrian . . . but I'm afraid I'll go to jail."

Big stuff, then. "In that case, it's better to come forward, rather than be found out later."

Lee bit her lip. "Okay," she said after a moment. "Okay. I don't know Kirby very well, just to say hi when I'd see him around, you know? But then one day last August he came to my house with these pictures while my parents were at work."

"What pictures?"

"Of me taking stuff from where I work. You know that stationery and gift shop at Ocean Park Plaza—Paper Fantasy? Well, I worked there fulltime last summer and now I go in three days a week after school. I kind of got into taking things—pen-and-pencil sets, jewelry, other gift items. I didn't even want them very much. I mean, the stuff they sell is expensive but pretty tacky. But it made me not feel so bad about having this crummy job . . . Anyway, that's what Kirby's pictures showed, me taking jewelry from the case and stuffing it under my sweater." Lee's words were spilling out fast now; I was probably the only person she'd ever told about this.

"There was no way you could mistake what I was doing," she went on. "The pictures showed it clear as could be. Kirby said he was going to go to my boss unless I did what he wanted. At first I thought he meant, you know, sex, and I could have died, but it turned out what he wanted was for me to steal stuff and give it to him. I said I would. I would have done *anything* to keep from being found out. And that's what I've been doing."

"So Kirby got the merchandise he was selling by blackmailing people into shoplifting for him. I wonder if that's the hold he had over Adrian?"

"It might have been. When they were first going together, they were, you know, like a normal couple. But then she changed, dropped all her friends and other activities, and started spending every minute with Kirby. I guess he used her shoplifting to get control of her."

"What about the other kids? Do you know anybody else who was stealing for Kirby?"

"Nobody who'll talk about it. But there's a rumor about a couple of the guys, that they take orders and just go out and rip off stuff. And a lot of the things he has for sale come from stores where I know other kids from school work."

Kirby had had quite a scam going—a full-blown racket, actually. And Lee was right: There was no way this could be kept from her father. She might even go to juvenile hall.

"The pictures," I said, "did Kirby say how he took them?"

"No, but he had to've been inside the store. They were kind of fuzzy, like he might've used a telephoto."

"From where?"

"Well, they were face on, a little bit above and to the left of the jewelry counter."

"Did you ever see Kirby in the store with a camera?"

"No, but I wouldn't've noticed him if we were busy."

"Would you have taken something while the store was busy?"

"Sure. That's the best time." Lee seemed to hear her own words, because she hung her head, cheeks coloring. "God, those pictures! I looked like a *criminal!*"

Which, of course, she was. I thought about Kirby and his corps of teenaged thieves. What if he'd tried to hit on the wrong person? Homicides committed by teenagers, like all other categories—were on the upswing. . . .

"Lee," I said, "you're going to have to tell the cops investigating Kirby's murder about this."

She nodded numbly, hands clenching.

The phrase "shit hitting the fan" isn't a favorite of mine, but that was exactly what was about to happen, and a lot of perfectly nice parents were going to be splattered, to say nothing of their foolish but otherwise nice children. Parents like Donna Conway. Children like Adrian.

I pictured the pretty redhead in the photo Donna had given me—her quirky smile and the gleam in her eyes that told of a zest for living and an offbeat sense of humor. I pictured her quiet, concerned, sad mother— a lonely woman clinging to her stacks of self-help books for cold comfort. Maybe I could still find Adrian, reunite the two so they could lean on each other in the tough times ahead. If Adrian was still alive, there had to be a way.

And if she was dead? I didn't want to think about that.

VIII

Lee and I went back to All Souls, where the rest of the kids were standing around the foyer wondering what to do next, and while she escaped to my office to call her father, I thanked them and showed them out. Tom Chu hung back, looking worried and throwing glances at my office door. Since he was the one who had put this together for me, I filled him in on some of what Lee had told me, after first swearing him to secrecy.

Tom didn't look too surprised. "I kind of suspected Lee was in trouble," he said. "And you know what? I think Del might've been mixed up with Kirby, too. He got real quiet when Lee ran out on us, and he left in a hurry right afterwards."

"Those're pretty shaky grounds to accuse him on."

"Maybe, but Del . . . I told you he's basically just hanging out this fall? Well, where he's hanging out is Ocean Park Plaza."

Ocean Park Plaza—the focus of the whole case. I thanked Tom and gently eased him out the door so Lee wouldn't have to deal with him when she finished calling her dad.

Her father arrived some fifteen minutes later, all upset but full of comforting words, and agreed to take Lee down to the Hall of Justice to talk to Adah Joslyn. I called Joslyn to let her know a witness was on her way. "Adah," I added, "did Sharon ask you what was in Adrian Conway's backpack?"

"Yeah. I've got the property list right here." There was a rustling noise. "Some raunchy-smelling yogurt, makeup, a Golden Gate Transit schedule, couple of paperbacks—romance variety—and an envelope with the phone number of the Ocean Park Plaza's security office scribbled on it."

"Security office? You check with them?"

"Talked to a man named Waterson. He said she'd lost her i.d. badge the week before she disappeared and called in about getting it replaced. What is this—you trying to work my homicide, Kelleher?"

"Just trying to find a missing girl. I'll turn over anything relevant."

When I got off the phone, Lee and her father were sitting on the lumpy old couch in the front room, his arm protectively around her narrow shoulders. He didn't look like much of a teenager-killer to me; in fact, his main concern was that she hadn't come to him and admitted about the shoplifting as soon as "that little bastard"—meaning Kirby—had started hassling her. "I'd've put his ass in a sling,'' he kept saying. I offered to go down to the Hall with them, but he said he thought it would be better if they went alone. As soon as they left, I decided to head over to Ocean Park Plaza, check out a couple of things, then talk with Ben Waterson again.

The mall wasn't very crowded that night, but it was only Thursday, and the merchants were still gearing up for a big weekend sales push designed to lure in all those consumers who weren't suffering too much from the recession—getting started early on the Christmas season by urging everybody to spend, spend, spend in order to stimulate the economy. The sale banners were red, white, and blue and, really, they were making it sound like it was our patriotic duty to blow every last dime on frivolous things that—by God!—had better be American-made if Americans made them at all. Even I, much as I love to max out my credit cards, am getting totally sick of the misguided economists' notion that excess is not only good for the individual but for the nation. Anyway, the appeals from the politicians and the business community probably wouldn't meet with any more success with patrons of the Ocean Park Plaza this coming weekend than they had with downtown shoppers the previous one, and tonight they were having no affect at all.

When I got to Paper Fantasy I found I was the only browser—a decided disadvantage for checking out the possible angles from which Kirby might have taken the photographs of Lee. I checked anyway, under the suspicious eyes of the lone clerk. Over there was the counter where Lee had been standing when she'd five-fingered the pen set, and from the way she'd described the pictures, Kirby would have had to be standing not only in front of it, but some three feet in the air. Impossible, unless . . .

Ahah! There it was—a surveillance camera mounted on the wall above and to the left of the counter. One look at that and I recalled the banks of screens in the security office upstairs, closed-circuit TV that allowed you to videotape and photograph.

I hurried out of Paper Fantasy—possibly provoking a call to security by the clerk—and headed for Left Coast Casuals.

Only two salesclerks manned the store, and there were no customers. I wandered up and down the aisles, scanning for the cameras. There were four, with a range that covered the entire sales floor. While stealing the jewelry, Adrian would have had to stand around here, in plain sight of that one. For the lingerie, camera number two would have done the observing.

Stupid. How could the kids *be* so stupid?

Of course I knew the answer to that—anybody who's ever shoplifted does. The cameras are there, sure, but you just assume they're not recording your particular store at the time, or being monitored. And you're certain that you're being oh-so-subtle when actually you're about as discreet as a moose picking its way through a bed of pansies. And then there's that urge that just washes

over you—ooh, that irresistible impulse, that heady pulse-quickening temptation to commit the act that will bring on that delicious soaring high.

Yeah, the kids were stupid. Like I'd been stupid. Like a drug addict, an
alcoholic, a binge-eater is stupid.

"Ms. Kelleher?" The voice was Sue Hanford's. "Can I help you?"

I swung around. She'd come out of the stock room and stood a few feet
away from me, near the fake angora sweaters. "I was just looking the store
over once more, before going up to see Ben Waterson."

Her face became pinched, two white spots appearing at the corners of her
mouth. "You won't find him in the office. I know, because I just called up
there. I'll tell you, I've about had it with him not being available when I
need him."

"This happens a lot?"

"Well, yesterday morning around eleven-thirty. He said he'd come and talk
about the problem I've been having with a gang of girls who are creating
disturbances outside and intimidating my customers, but then he never showed
up. I called and called, but he'd taken off without saying why. He didn't come
back until six."

But yesterday morning at around eleven-thirty I'd seen him just outside the
store, arguing with Kirby Dalson. Waterson had claimed Sue Hanford was the
one who was away, leaving him in charge. "Were you in the store all day
yesterday?" I asked.

She nodded. "I worked a fourteen-hour shift."

"And today?" I asked. "Waterson wasn't available again?"

"Yes. He took off about half an hour ago, when he's supposed to be on
shift till nine-thirty."

"I see."

"Ms. Kelleher? If you do go up there and find Ben has come back, will
you ask him to come down here?"

"Sure," I said distractedly. Then I left the store.

A taco, I thought. There was a taco stand down in the food concession area.
Maybe a taco and a Coke would help me think this one through.

Okay, I thought, reaching for Gordito's Beef Supreme taco—piled high with
extra salsa, guacamole, and sour cream—somebody in the security office here
has been getting the goods on the kids who are shoplifting and turning the
evidence over to Kirby so he could blackmail them into working for him. If
I wasn't trained not to jump to conclusions I'd say Ben Waterson, because his
behavior has been anything but on the up-and-up lately. Okay, I'll say it
anyway—Ben Waterson. Kirby was a good contact man for Waterson—he
knew the kids, knew their weak spots, and after they ripped off the stuff he
could wholesale some of it at school, keeping Waterson out of the transaction.

Kind of a penny-ante scheme, though, if you think about it. Would hardly have brought in enough to keep Kirby, much less Waterson, in ready cash. And there had to be something in it for Waterson. But then there were the other kids—like Del—who didn't work here but ripped things off for Kirby, maybe big-ticket items, here and at other malls as well. And there was the rented house on Naples Street.

Those storage sheds in the backyard—sheds full of Ron Owens's mother's things, that Owens claims were worth quite a bit—I'll bet all of that got fenced, and then they filled up the sheds with new merchandise while they tried to find a buyer for it. Not hard to find one, too, not in this town. Neighbors said a lot of people came and went at Naples Street, so it could have been a pretty substantial fencing operation.

I know a fair amount about fencing, courtesy of Willie Whelan, who in recent years, thank God, has "gone legit," as he puts it. So far the scenario made sense to me.

The taco was all gone. Funny—I'd barely tasted it. I looked longingly at Gordito's, then balled up the wrappings and turned my attention back to the case.

Where does Adrian fit into all this? Last spring she starts to change, according to her school friends. She's been taking her five-finger employee discount for a while, oblivious to what Kirby and Waterson are up to. Then Kirby comes to her with pictures, and suddenly he's got the upper hand in the relationship. Adrian's still pretty demoralized—the father leaving, the mother who's always spouting phrases like "potential to be"—so she lets Kirby control her. Did she steal for him? Help him with the fencing? Had to have, given that she was familiar enough with the Naples Street house to walk in and plunk her backpack down in the living room. I'm pretty sure she slept with him—even the other kids know that.

Okay, suppose Adrian does all of that. Maybe she even glamorizes the situation as young women will do in order to face themselves in the morning. But fetching the condiments for the hamburgers of a young man who can damned well get them himself grows real old real fast, and after a while she starts to chafe at what her therapy wall calls "white slavery." So, as she tells her friend Anna, she's decided to "blow the whistle and the game will stop." How? By going to the cops? Or by going to the head of mall security, Ben Waterson?

I got up, tossed my cup and the taco wrappings in a trashbin, and headed for the security office.

Waterson wasn't there. Had left around six after a phone call, destination unknown, the woman on the desk told me. I persuaded her to check their log to see if Adrian Conway had reported losing her i.d. badge about a week before she disappeared, as Waterson had told Adah Joslyn. No record of it, and there would have been had it really happened.

Caught you in another lie, Ben!

Back down to the concession area. This time I settled for coffee and a Mrs. Fields cookie.

So Adrian probably went to Waterson, since she had the phone number of the security office scribbled on an envelope in her backpack. And he . . . what? Lured her away from the mall and killed her? Hid her body? Then why was her backpack at Naples Street? Waterson would have left it with the body or gotten rid of it. And would Waterson have gone to such lengths, anyway?

Well, Kirby was murdered, wasn't he?

But would Kirby have kept quiet if he thought Waterson had murdered his girlfriend? The kid was a cold one, but . . . Maybe I just didn't want to believe that anybody that young could be that cold. And that was poor reasoning—if you don't believe me, just check out the morning paper most days.

Another thing—who was this person Adrian had talked about, who would take her side and not take any shit off of anybody? Maybe Waterson had played it subtle with her, pretended to be her protector, then spirited her off somewhere and—

The prospects for her survival weren't any better with that scenario.

I was so distracted that I bit clear through the cookie into my tongue. Swore loud enough to earn glares from two old ladies at the next table.

Back to Ben Waterson. Kirby came to the mall the other day and argued with him—not about getting hold of Adrian's back pay, as they both claimed, because Waterson lied about Sue Hanford leaving him in charge at Left Coast Casuals. And right after the argument, Kirby stormed out of the mall and drove off burning rubber. Waterson took off around that time, too. And tonight Waterson left again, after a phone call around six—about the time the kids, Del preceeding them, left All Souls. Did Del or another of them warn him that everything was about to unravel? Is Waterson running, or did he leave for purposes of what Sue Hanford calls damage control?

Damage control. I suppose you could call Kirby's murder damage control. . . .

I got up, threw my trash in the bin, and began walking the mall—burning off excess energy, trying to work it out. If only I knew what Kirby and Waterson had argued about. And where they'd each gone Wednesday afternoon. And why Kirby had asked me to meet him at the Naples Street house. Had Waterson found out about the meeting, gotten there early? Killed Kirby before he could talk with me? And what about Adrian? If she was dead, where was her body? And if she was alive—

And then I saw something. It wasn't related to my case at all, was just one of those little nudges you get when you have all the information you need and are primed for something to come along and help you put it all together. I'm sure I'd have figured it out eventually, even if it hadn't been for the poster of the African veldt in the window of a travel agency—a poster that made the land look so parched and windswept and basically unpleasant that you wondered why they thought it would sell tours. But as it was, it happened then, and I was damned glad of it.

IX

The Wreck and I sped through the night, under a black sky that quickly started leaking rain, then just plain let go in a deluge. The windshield wipers scraped and screeched, smearing the glass instead of clearing it. Dammit, I thought, why can't I get it together to buy a new car—or at least some new wiper blades? No, a whole car's in order, because this defroster isn't worth the powder to blow it to hell, and I'm so sick of being at the mercy of third-rate transportation.

Then I started wondering about the tread on the Wreck's tires. When was the last time I'd checked it? It had looked bad, whenever, and I'd promised myself new tires in a few hundred more miles, but that had to be several thousand ago. What if I got a flat, was stranded, and didn't reach Adrian in time? She was probably safe; I didn't know for sure that Waterson had figured it out. Hell, *I'd* barely done that. Could anybody manage, without knowing Adrian the way I did from her therapy wall?

The rain whacked down harder and the wind blew the Wreck all over the road. My shoulders got tense, and my hands actually hurt from clinging to the wheel. Lights ahead now—the little town of Olema where this road met the shoreline highway. Right turn, slow a little, then put the accelerator to the floor on the home stretch to Aunt June's.

She lied to me—that much was obvious at the time—but I hadn't suspected it was such a big lie. How could I guess that Adrian was with her—right there on the premises, probably in June's studio—and had been with her since shortly after her disappearance? Maybe I should have picked up on the fact that June didn't seem all that worried about her niece, but otherwise I'd had no clues. Not then.

Now I did, though. The Golden Gate Transit schedule in Adrian's backpack, for one. Golden Gate was one bus line that ran from the city to Marin County, and she would only have needed it if she planned a trip north. There had been no one with a Marin address other than June Simoom on the list of people who were close to Adrian that the police had checked out. And then there was the graphic evidence on the therapy wall—the soaring bird so like the symbol of June's place, Wingspread, next to one broken gold chain and the word

FREEDOM. But most of all it was Adrian's own words that had finally tipped me: "somebody to protect me, somebody strong and fierce." That was June's way of describing herself, and Adrian had probably heard it enough to believe it. After all, her aunt had taken the name of a fierce, relentless African wind; she had called her home Wingspread, a place of refuge.

But there was another side to June—the possessive, controlling side that Donna Conway had described. Frying pan to fire, that's where Adrian had gone. From one controlling person to another—and in this case, a control freak who probably delighted in keeping the niece from the hated sister-in-law. June hadn't called Donna after my visit to make peace; she'd probably been fishing to find out if I'd relayed any suspicions to her.

I slowed to a crawl, peering through the smears on the windshield and the rainsoaked blackness for the mailbox with the soaring bird. That stand of eucalyptus looked about right, and the deeper shadows beyond it must hide Tomales Bay. Hadn't the road curved like this just before the turnoff to the rutted driveway? Wasn't it right about here . . . ?

Yes! I wrenched the wheel to the left, and the Wreck skidded onto the gravel shoulder.

What I could see of the driveway looked impassable. Deep tire gouges cut into the ground, but they were filling with muck and water. Better not chance it. I turned off the engine—it coughed and heaved several times, not a good sign, Willie had recently told me—and then I got out and started for the cottage on foot.

The wind blew even stronger now, whipping the branches of the trees and sending big curls of brittle bark spiraling through the air. The rain pelted me, stinging as it hit my face, and the hood of my slicker blew off my head. I grabbed at it, but I couldn't make it stay up, and soon my hair was a sodden mess plastered to my skull.

Adrian, I thought, you'd better be worth all this.

I couldn't see any lights in the cottage, although there was a truck pulled in under the trees. That didn't mean anything—the other night June had relied on the fire for both heat and light, and there was no reason she would have turned on the porch lamp unless she was expecting company. But what kind of a life was this for Adrian, spending her entire evenings in darkness in that crumbling shack? And what about her days—how could she fill the long hours when she should have been in school or working or doing things with her friends? If her mother hadn't hired me and I hadn't figured out where she was, how long would she have hidden here until reality set in and she began to want to have a life again?

My slicker was an ancient one, left over from my college days, and its waterproofing must have given out, because I was soaked to my skin now. Freezing, too. Please have a fire going, June, because I'm already very annoyed with you, and the lack of a fire will make me truly pissed off—

Movement up ahead, the door of the cottage opening. A dark figure coming out, big and barrel-shaped, bigger than June and certainly bigger than Adrian. . . . Ben Waterson.

He came down the steps, hesitated, then angled off toward the right, through the trees. Going where? To the studio or the other outbuilding?

I began creeping closer to the cottage, testing the ground ahead of me before I took each step. Foot-grabber of a hole there, ankle-turner of a tree root here. At least the wind's shrieking like a scalded cat so he can't possibly hear me.

The cottage loomed ahead. I tripped on the bottom step, went up the rest of them on my hands and knees, and pushed the door open. Keeping low, I slithered inside on a splintery plank floor. There was some light at the far end of the room, but not much; the fire was burning low, just embers mainly.

What's that smell?

A gun had been fired in there, and not too long ago. I opened my mouth, tried to call to June, but a croak came out instead. The room was quiet, the wind howling outside. I crept toward the glowing embers. . . .

There June was, reclining on her pile of pillows, glass of wine beside her on the raised hearth. So like the other night, but something was wrong here, something to do with the way she was lying, as if she'd been thrown there, and why was the fireplace poker in her hand—

Oh God June no!

I reeled around, smashing my fist into the wall beside me. My eyes were shut but I could still see her crumpled there on the gaudy silk pillows, velvet robes disarrayed, hand clutching the poker. Why was she still holding it? Something to do with going into spasm at the moment of death.

Disconnected sounds roared in my ears, blocking the wind. Then I heard my voice saying bitterly to Sharon, "Until the next time," meaning until the next death. And Sharon saying to me, "If there is one."

Well, Shar, this is the next time, and I wish you were here to tell me what to do because what I'm about to do is go to pieces and there's a killer somewhere outside and a helpless young woman who I promised to bring back to her mother—

Go to the phone, Rae, and call the sheriff.

It wasn't Sharon's voice, of course, but my own—a cool, professional voice that I'd never known I had. It interrupted the hysterical thoughts that were whirling and tumbling in my brain, calmed me and restored my balance. I dredged up memories of the other night, pictured an old-fashioned rotary-dial phone sitting on the kitchen counter. I felt my way until I touched it, and picked up the receiver.

No dial tone.

Maybe the storm, maybe something Waterson had done. Whatever, there wasn't going to be any car full of Marin County Sheriff's deputies riding to my rescue.

You'll just have to save yourself—and Adrian.

With what? He's armed. I don't even have a flashlight.

Kitchen drawer. I felt along the edge of the warped linoleum counter, then down to a knob. Pulled on it. Nothing in there but cloth, dishtowels, maybe. Another knob, another drawer. Knives. I took one out, tested its sharpness. Another drawer, and there was a flashlight, plus some long, pointed barbecue skewers. I stuck them and the knife in the slash pocket of my slicker.

And then I went outside to face a man with a gun.

The wind was really whipping around now, and it tore the cottage's door from my grip and slammed it back against the wall. I yanked it closed, went down the slick, rickety steps, and made for the eucalyptus trees. As I ran I felt the flashlight fall from my slash pocket, but I didn't stop to find it. Silly to have taken it, anyway—if I turned it on, I'd be a target for Waterson.

Under the trees I stopped and leaned against a ragged trunk, panting and feeling in my pocket for the knife and the skewers. They were still there— not that they were much of a match against a gun. But there was no point in stewing over the odds now. I had to pinpoint those outbuildings. If I remembered correctly, they were closer to the shore and to the left of this grove.

I slipped through the trees, peering into the surrounding blackness. Now I could make out the shoreline, the water wind-tossed and frothy, and then I picked out the shapes of the buildings—two of them, the larger one probably the studio. Roofs as swaybacked as the cottage's, no lights in either. Windows? I couldn't tell. They sat across a clearing from me, a bad way to approach if there were windows facing this way and if Waterson was inside and looking out. A bad way if he was outside and looking in this direction.

How else to get over there, then? Along the shore? Maybe. June had said something about a beach. . . .

I went back through the trees, their branches swaying overhead, ran for the cottage again, then slipped along its side and ducked under the half-collapsed deck. The ground took a sudden slope, and I went down on my butt and slid toward the water. Waves sloshed over my tennis shoes—icy waves.

Dammit! I thought. What the hell am I doing out here risking pneumonia— to say nothing of my life—for a thieving teenager I've never even set eyes on?

I pulled myself up on one of the rotten deck supports—nearly pulling it down on my head—and started moving again. Then I stopped, realizing there was no beach here now, just jumbled and jagged rocks before the spot where the sand should begin. The beach was completely submerged by the high storm-tide.

Stupid, Rae. Very stupid. You should have realized it would be this way and not wasted precious time. You should have gotten back into the Wreck as soon as you found June's body and driven to the nearest phone, called the sheriff's department and let them handle it.

No time for recriminations now. Besides, the nearest phone was miles away, and even if I had driven there immediately, the deputies wouldn't have gotten here fast enough to save Adrian. I wasn't sure *I'd* gotten here fast enough to save her.

I crawled back up the incline and looked around, trying to measure the distance I'd have to run exposed to get to the shelter of the outbuildings. From here it was twenty, maybe twenty-five yards. Not that far—I'd go for it.

I hunched over, made myself as small as I could, and started running—not much of a run, but still the longest, scariest of *my* life. I kept expecting the whine of a bullet—that's what you hear, Sharon's told me, before you hear the actual report, and she ought to know. You hear the whine, that is, if the bullet doesn't kill you first.

But all I heard was the howl of the wind and the banging of a door some-place and the roaring of my own blood in my ears. Then I was at the first outbuilding, crouching against its rough wood wall and panting hard.

The banging was louder here. When my breathing had calmed, I crept around the building's corner and looked. Door, half off its hinges, and no sound or light coming from inside. I crept a little closer. Empty shed, falling down, certainly not June's studio.

I moved along until I could see the larger building. The space between the two was narrow, dark. I ran again, to a windowless wall and flattened against it, putting my ear to the boards and trying to hear if anyone was inside.

A banging noise, then a crash—something breaking. Then an angry voice—male, Waterson's. "Where the hell is it?"

Sobbing now, and a young woman saying, "I *told* you I don't know what you're talking about. Where's Aunt June? I want—"

"Shut up!" It sounded like he hit her. She screamed, and my hand went into my pocket, grasping the knife.

More sobbing. Waterson said, "I want those pictures and the negatives, Adrian."

"*What* pictures? What negatives? I don't know anything about them!"

"Don't give me that. Kirby said you were holding them for him. Just tell me where they are and I'll let you go."

Sure he would. He'd shoot her just like he had June, and hope that this would go down as a couple of those random killings that happen a lot in remote rural areas where weirdos break into what look like empty houses for stuff to steal and sell for drug money.

"I wouldn't hold *anything* for Kirby!" Adrian said through her sobs. "I'm scared of him!"

"Then why did he come out here yesterday after he tried to hit me up for money? Coming to get his evidence to prove to me that I'd better pay up, that's why. And don't lie to me about it—I followed him."

"No! I didn't even see him! He figured out where I was and wanted to talk me into going back to the city. I hid from him, and Aunt June ran him off."

So this was where Kirby had gone when I'd lost him. I remembered the eucalyptus leaves in his hair, the sand on his shoes when I'd talked with him at his parents' house—probably picked up while he was skulking around outside here, looking for Adrian after June had told him he couldn't see her. Waterson had not only followed Kirby here, but later to the Naples Street house, where he'd killed him.

There was a silence inside the studio, then Adrian screamed and cried some more. He'd hit her again, I guessed. Then he said, "I'm not going to ask you again, Adrian. Where're the pictures?"

"There *aren't* any! Look, Kirby's always bullshitting. He had *me* fooled. I was going to go to you about what he was doing at the plaza, until I saw you at the house with him, making a deal with that fence."

That was what had made her run out of the Naples Street place so fast she'd left her backpack—made her run straight to Aunt June, the only person she'd told about the trouble she was in, the person who'd offered to take her side and shelter her. Well, June had tried. Now it was up to me.

I started moving around the building, duck-walking like my high-school phys ed teacher had made us do when we goofed off in gym. Inside, I heard Waterson say, "You never knew about a hidden camera at that place in the Outer Mission?"

"No."

"Kirby never asked you to take pictures of me doing deals with the fences?"

"Neither of us took any pictures. This story is just more of Kirby's bullshit."

Waterson laughed—an ugly sound. "Well," he said, "it was Kirby's last shovelful of bullshit. He's dead."

"What . . . ?" Adrian's question rose up into a shriek.

I stopped listening, concentrated on getting to the corner of the building. Then I peeked around it. On this side—the one facing the water—there was a window and a door. I duckwalked on, thanking God that I still had some muscles left in my thighs. At the window I poked my head up a little, but all I saw were shadows—a big barrel-shaped one that had to be Waterson, and some warped, twisted ones that were downright weird. The light shivered and flickered—probably from a candle or oil lamp.

The door was closed, but the wind was rattling it in its loose frame. It made me think of how the wind had torn the cottage door from my grasp. I stopped, pressed against the wall, and studied this door. From the placement of its hinges, I could tell it opened out. I scuttled around to the hinged side, paused and listened. Adrian was screaming and sobbing again. Christ, what was he *doing* to her?

Well, the sound would hide what I was about to do.

I stood, pressed flat as could be against the wall, then reached across the door to its knob and gave it a quick twist. The door opened, then slammed shut again.

"What the hell?" Waterson said.

Heavy footsteps came toward the door. I tensed, knife out and ready.

Don't think about how it'll be when you use it, Rae. Just do it—two lives are at stake here, and one's your own.

The door opened. All I could see was a wide path of wavery light. Waterson said, "Fuckin' wind," and shut the door again.

Well, hell.

I waited a few seconds until his footsteps went away, reached for the knob again, and really yanked on it this time. The wind caught the door, slammed it back, and it smashed into me, smacking my nose. I bit my lip to keep from yelling, felt tears spring to my eyes. I wiped them away with my left hand, gripped the knife till my right hand hurt.

The footsteps came back again, quicker now, and I grasped the knife with both hands—ready, not thinking about it, just ready to do it because I had to. When he stepped outside, I shoved the door as hard as I could with my whole body, slamming him against the frame. He shouted, staggered, reeled back inside.

I went after him, saw him stumbling among a bunch of weird, twisted shapes that were some sort of pottery sculptures—the things that had made the strange shadows I'd glimpsed through the window. Some were as tall as he was, others were shorter or stood on pedestals. He grabbed at one and brought it down as he tried to keep his balance and raise his gun.

The gun went off. The roar was deafening, but I hadn't heard any whine, so his shot must have gone wide of me. Waterson stumbled back into a pedestal, flailing. I lunged at him, knife out in front of me. We both went down together. I heard the gun drop on the floor as I slashed out with the knife.

Waterson had hold of my arm now, slammed it against the floor. Pain shot up to my shoulder, my fingers went all prickly, and I dropped the knife. He pushed me away and started scrambling for the gun. I got up on my knees, grabbed at the base of the nearest sculpture, pushed. It hit his back and knocked him flat.

Waterson howled. I saw the gun about a foot from his hand and kicked out, sending it sliding across the floor. Then I stood all the way up, grabbed a strange many-spouted vase from a pedestal. And slammed it down on his head.

Waterson grunted and lay still.

I slumped against the pedestal, but only for a moment before I went to pick up the gun. The room was very quiet all of a sudden, except for sobbing coming from one corner. Adrian was trussed up there, dangling like a marionette from one of the support beams, her feet barely touching the plank floor. She had the beginnings of a black eye and tears sheened her face, and she was jerking at her ropes like she was having some kind of attack. I located the knife, made what I hoped were reassuring noises as I went over there, and cut her down. She stumbled toward a mattress that lay under the window and curled up fetus-like, pulling the heavy blanket around her. I went over to Waterson and used the longer pieces of the rope to truss *him* up.

Then I went back to Adrian. She was shivering violently, eyes unfocused, fingers gripping the edge of the blanket. I sat down on the mattress beside her, gently loosened her fingers, and cradled her like a baby.

"Sssh," I said. "It's over now, all over."

X

I was lolling around All Souls' living room on Friday night, waiting for Willie and planning how I'd relate my triumph in solving the Conway-Dalson case to him, when the call came from Inspector Adah Joslyn.

"I just got back from Marin County," she told me. "Waterson's finally confessed to the Simoom murder, but he denies killing Kirby Dalson."

"Well, of course he would. Dalson was obviously premeditated, while the poker in Simoom's hand could be taken to mean self-defense."

"He'll have to hire one hell of a lawyer to mount a defense like that, given what he did to the niece. But that's not my problem. What is is that he's got a verifiable alibi for the time of Dalson's death."

"*What?*"

"Uh-huh. Dalson didn't leave his parents' house until six-twenty that night. Six to seven, Waterson was in a meeting with several of the Ocean Park Plaza merchants, including Adrian Conway's former boss."

I remembered Sue Hanford saying Waterson had taken off the morning before Kirby was killed and hadn't come back until six. I hadn't thought to ask her how she knew that or if he'd stayed around afterwards. Damn! Maybe I wasn't the hotshot I thought I was.

Adah asked, "You got any ideas on this?"

Unwilling to admit I didn't, I said, "Maybe. Let me get back to you." I hung up the phone on Ted's desk, then took the stairs two at a time and went to Sharon's office.

She wasn't there. Most of the time the woman practically lived in her office, but now when I needed her, she was gone. I went back downstairs and looked for her mailbox tag. Missing. There was one resting on the corner of the desk, like she might have been talking with Ted and absentmindedly set it down there. I hurried along the hall to the kitchen, where five people hadn't yet given up on the Friday happy hour, but Sharon wasn't one of them. Our resident health freak, who was mixing up a batch of cranberry-juice-and-cider cocktails, said she'd gone home an hour ago.

I said, "If Willie shows up before I get back, will you ask him to wait for me?" and trotted out the door.

Sharon doesn't live far from All Souls—in Glen Park, a district that's been undergoing what they call gentrification. I suppose you could say her brown-shingled cottage—one of a few thousand built as temporary housing after the '06 quake that have survived far better than most of the grand mansions of that era—has been gentrified, since she's remodeled it and added a room and a deck, but to me it's just nice and homey, not fancy at all. Besides, things are always going wrong with it—tonight it was the porch light, shorting out from rain that had dripped into it because the gutters were overflowing. I rang the bell, hoping it wouldn't also short out and electrocute me.

Sharon answered wearing her long white terry robe and furlined slippers and looking like she was coming down with a cold—probably from the soaking she'd gotten Tuesday night, which meant I would be the next one in line to get sick, from the soaking I'd gotten last night. She looked concerned when she saw me on the steps.

Last night, after I'd dealt with the Marin authorities and driven home feeling rocky and ready to fly apart at the slightest sound or movement, she'd come over to the co-op—Ted had called her at home, I guess—and we'd sat quietly in my nest for a while. Neither of us had said much—there was nothing *to* say, and we didn't need to, anyway. This second horror in a week of unpleasantness had changed me somehow, maybe forced me to grow up. I wasn't looking to Sharon for wisdom or even comfort, just for understanding and fellowship. And fellows we were—members of a select group to which election was neither an honor nor a pleasure.

Tonight I could tell that she was afraid I was suffering delayed repercussions from the violent events of the week, so quickly I said, "I need to run some facts by you. Got a few minutes?"

She nodded, looking relieved, and waved me inside. We went to the sitting room off her kitchen, where she had a fire going, and she offered me some mulled wine. While she was getting it, her yellow cat, Ralph, jumped into my lap. Ralph is okay as cats go, but really, I'm more of a dog person. He knows that, too—it's why he always makes a beeline for me when I come over. The little sadist looked at me with knowing eyes, then curled into a ball on my lap. His calico sister Alice, who was grooming herself in the middle of the floor, looked up, and damned if she didn't wink!

Sharon came back with the wine, wrapped herself in her afghan on the couch, and said, "So run it by me."

I did, concluding, "Adrian couldn't have killed Kirby. Her hysterics when Waterson told her he was dead were genuine."

"Mmmm." Sharon seemed to be evaluating that. Then she said, "Maybe one of the other kids Kirby was blackmailing?"

"I thought of that, too, but it doesn't wash. Adrian talked a little while we were driving to Point Reyes to call the sheriff. She said none of the kids knew about the house on Naples—Kirby insisted it be kept a secret."

"What about one of the fences he dealt with? Maybe he'd crossed one of them."

"I tend to doubt it. Fences don't operate that way."

"Well, you should know. Willie . . ."

"Yeah." I sipped wine, feeling gloomy and frustrated.

Sharon asked, "Who else besides Adrian knew about that house?"

"Well, Waterson, but his alibi is firm. And Aunt June. Adrian called her from a pay phone at a store on the corner the day she walked in on Kirby and Waterson making a deal with a fence, and June drove over to the city and picked her up. Adrian had told June about the trouble she was in when she and Kirby went to Tomales for the autumnal equinox firing in late September, and June'd offered to take her in after she went to security about what was going on. I don't know how June thought Adrian could escape prosecution for her part in the scam, but then, she didn't strike me as a terribly realistic person."

"Caring, though," Sharon said. "Caring and controlling."

I nodded. "June, the fierce protectress. Who died with a fireplace poker in her hand. Waterson had a gun, and she still tried to go up against him."

"And Kirby had come out to her place. Had scared Adrian."

"Yes," I said.

Sharon got up, took our glasses, and went to the kitchen for refills. I stared moodily into the fire. When I'd taken this job, I'd assumed I'd be running skiptraces and interviewing witnesses for lawsuits. Now I'd found two dead bodies, almost killed a man, almost gotten killed myself—all in the course of a few days. Add to that an ethical dilemma . . .

When Sharon came back I said, "If I suggest this to the police, and June really was innocent, I'll be smearing the memory of a basically good woman."

She was silent, framing her reply. "If June was innocent, the police won't find any evidence. If she was guilty, they may find a weapon with blood and hair samples that match Kirby's somewhere on the premises at Tomales, and be able to close the file."

"But what will that do to Adrian?"

"From what you tell me, she's a survivor. And you've got to think of Kirby's parents. You've got to think of justice."

Leave it to Sharon to bring up the J-word. She thinks about things like that all the time, but to me they're just abstractions.

"And you've got to think about the truth," she added.

Not fair—she knows how I feel about the truth. "All right," I finally said, "I'll call Adah back later."

"Good. By the way, how are Adrian and her mother doing?"

"Well, all of this has been rough on them, will be rough for a while. But they'll make it. Adrian is a survivor, and Donna—maybe this will help her realize her 'potential to be.' "

We both smiled wryly. Sharon said, "Here's to our potential to be," and we toasted.

After a while I went into her home office and called Adah. Then I called All Souls and spoke with Willie, who was regaling the folks in the kitchen with stories about the days when he was on the wrong side of the law, and told him I'd be there soon.

"So," Sharon said as I was putting on my slicker. "How're *you* holding up?"

"I'm still rocky, but that'll pass."

"Nightmares?"

"Yeah. But tonight they won't bother me. I plan to scare them off by sleeping with my favorite gorilla."

Sharon grinned and toasted me again, but damned if she didn't look a little melancholy.

Maybe she *still* knew something that I didn't.

Mat Coward is a new British writer who manages to do something fresh with every story he writes. There's a deceptively impish quality to some of his stories—but don't be misled. There's a Swiftian eye and heart at work here, one that is amused and amusing but also quite serious. This is the year's final Golden Dagger nominee.

History Repeats Itself, and It Doesn't Even Say Pardon

MAT COWARD

Before becoming a north London copper, Colin Mann had been a south London villain.

Not many people knew this. Indeed, until yesterday Colin would have said that nobody else knew it. Now, however, he knew that at least one other person did know, and that, of course, was a problem which needed to be sorted.

At the end of roll-call, at the start of the shift, Colin caught PC Dunne as he was leaving the room. "You're in the area car, Nigel."

"Yes, Skip."

"I'll come with you. I want a word."

"Right, Skip. Great."

They walked out to the vehicle bay. Nigel Dunne kept looking at his sergeant, then looking away again. Colin said nothing, just kept thinking. He'd been a policeman for eleven years; he liked it. He thought he was quite good at it. He liked the pay, he liked the work. He didn't like coppers much, but you couldn't have everything. If it was possible, he wanted to stay in the job, stay and get his pension. He liked the way that, in the job, if you had a problem you sorted it. That's what you were good at, if you were any good at all.

Once they were in the car, belted up, ready to go, Colin said, "Drive to the Shaw Estate. We'll have a chat."

"Yes, Sarge." The boy didn't look worried, Colin thought, he looked—what? Excited. As if the sergeant were about to stand him a treat.

"Pull up over here. We'll sit here for a while."

They sat for a while, Colin just watching Dunne out of the corner of his eye, not surreptitiously, but not obviously. Dunne didn't even glance at Colin. He stared straight ahead, through the windscreen, and played his fingers back and forth along the steering wheel, like a pianist doing exercises. He looked very young, and very happy.

"So, how old are you, Nigel?"

Nigel spun his head round to face Colin, eager and fresh, his face shining in the urban twilight. "Twenty-one, Sarge." He made it sound like a boast, or a promise. "I've only been in two years, I was at college before that. College boy!"

"What were you studying?" He was genuinely curious. He couldn't see PC Dunne as graduate-entry.

"No, you know, just GCSEs, A-Levels. I got French. Good that, handy for holidays."

"So you're a bright lad. You're not just another plonk, like the rest of us."

"Nothing like that, Skip, honest. I wish I'd joined earlier, tell you the truth. I just never thought of it until the recruitment staff came round, at college."

Colin brought out a packet of cigarettes, lit one, then offered them to Dunne. Dunne didn't smoke, but he took one anyway, accepted a light, then held his head at an angle so the smoke wouldn't get in his eyes.

"What you said to me yesterday, Nigel. In the canteen."

"What was that, Skip?" He wanted to hear the exact words, from his sergeant's mouth. He'd taken ages working them out just right, and now he wanted to hear them, hear how good they sounded. How well he'd done.

"You said you knew where I grew up. You knew what I did before I joined the force."

"That's right, Sarge. I do."

Colin blew smoke in the young cop's face, blew it right into his eyes, in a fine, hard stream, and said, "I worked for my sister's husband, delivering motor parts. We had a van."

"No, no you didn't." Nigel shook his head, kept on shaking it, not in denial, but in complicity. Little foams of spit gathered at the corners of his mouth. "I know you were a driver, but you didn't drive a van. Not delivering parts, you didn't. No you never." Grinning like a dog.

Colin ground his cigarette out on the side window, thoroughly and violently, trying to make it look like he wasn't really content to be doing such violence to a fag end, but a fag end'd do, for now, until something better came along. "That's what it says on my record."

"I know what it was like back then, Sarge. Early eighties, it wasn't like now, it was dead easy to get in the job then. They were desperate. Dead easy for a man like you. A clever, hard man like you. No sweat. ''

"You married, Nigel?"

"No, Sarge. Sort of . . ." He stopped.

"You've got a girl?"

"I wouldn't want the job to know. I mean, not you, Skip, you're different, I don't mind you knowing. She's older than me. You've met her, actually. In the Fat Duck, when Mr. Johnson retired. She was with me then. You said hello."

"We can't leave it like this, Nigel. You understand?" He wasn't going to say *What do you want from me?* He wasn't going to say *What's your price*? You couldn't start paying people, not after eleven years.

"Sure, Sarge. What are we going to do?"

"I'm going to do this," said Colin. He reached across to take the keys out of the ignition, got out of the patrol car, walked off into the darkness and disappeared. These are my skills, he thought, this is what I can do: arresting people, hurting people, and disappearing. It had always proved enough, so far.

He walked around the rest of the night, ignoring the shouts from his radio, just walking. He called in once, to say he was going off air for a bit, and he knew what they'd think in the CAD room—he'd got a bird. That was all right, he never gave them any trouble, they'd cover for him just this once.

It wasn't what Nigel Dunne wanted from him—whatever that might turn out to be—that worried him. He didn't care what the price was, didn't have to care, because he wasn't going to pay it. It was Dunne knowing—simple as that. He couldn't have anyone knowing. It would have to be sorted, obviously.

He'd only ever killed one person. That man, too, had been a blackmailer of sorts, and if he had told what he knew, the people Colin ran with then would have killed Colin. So Colin had killed him. And then disappeared.

That was all right. He didn't like it, he wasn't a nutter, but it was all right. If it was justified.

Around midnight, he found a park bench and sat on it, lit his last cigarette. He liked being a copper. He'd never much liked being a villain; he could do either, certainly, do one as well as the other, probably, but he knew which he preferred. And this problem . . . it did have to be sorted. Now way round that.

But first he needed to know how Nigel had found out. That was important. The boy was too young to have recognized him, had never lived in south London, anyway. Colin had checked. Which meant—*Oh, Christ!*—which meant there had to be more than one person who knew about him.

Just how many fucking problems were there? And was he up to sorting them all?

*   *   *

He should have brought a book, he thought. One of those magazines with all puzzles in them, crosswords, anagrams. Usually, on an observation, you could chat with the others, pass the time telling old jokes. But today, in his own car on his Saturday off, parked across the street from PC Dunne's house, he was bored out of his mind. And then he saw her.

Coming out of the house. Stopping to put the milk in, then walking on down the street, towards the tube station. Going shopping, perhaps, or to the hairdresser's. Going to visit her mum, maybe.

No, not visiting her mum, definitely not; her mum was long dead. Because he knew her now, now that he had some idea what he was looking for, knew where he knew her from. Remembered her history, and realized how she might have remembered his, across eleven years, not put off by the grey hair, the new name, the uniform.

Nigel opened the door to his second ring of the bell. "Skip! Great, great to see you, come in. You've just missed Sam." In his dressing-gown and pyjamas, Dunne looked like any other young man having a weekend lie-in. Not like a policeman who'd forgotten to put his helmet on, the way the older coppers always looked off duty.

"Yeah, I know. I saw her go."

"Right," said Nigel, leading his guest through to the kitchen at the back. "Right, so you recognized her now. You never recognized her the other time, at Mr. Johnson's retirement do. She remembered you straight off, though. She was full of it on the way home—all about what a lad you used to be, all the things you and her brother got up to, in the good old days. You want coffee?"

"Thanks." Colin sat down at the pine table, while Nigel hooked two big red mugs from a pine mug-tree on top of the fridge. He looked around: nice place, clean, tidy, but homely. She kept a good house, Sam did. Always had done. Nigel moved around it with cautious pride, as if he couldn't quite believe his luck.

"How do you come to know her, then?"

"I know!" said Nigel, laughing, hovering over the boiling kettle. "The odd couple, eh? When I was at college, she worked in a pub there."

"Where?"

"Islington way. She did what you did, see—got out. Came north. She speaks very highly of you, you know, big fan of yours. More bottle than any man she's ever met, she reckons. You and her must have been pretty close, I suppose, in the old days."

"Mind if I smoke?" Nigel almost pulled a muscle in his haste to put a clean ashtray in front of Sergeant Mann. "Not that close. We saw each other around, got on all right." He lit up. "How d'you get on last night, then?"

"After you nicked my keys? Ah-ha! I know a few tricks, Skip. I don't know them all, like, not like you, not yet. But I know a few."

"Spare keys."

"I got a spare to just about every key in that station. Including the super's drinks cabinet. I have, honest!"

He wouldn't have to kill both of them, would he? Christ, yes, of course he would. He couldn't just kill the boy and leave the woman, a grieving not-quite-widow, with no pension and a big mouth. What a mess. He drank his coffee—nice coffee—smoked his cigarette, and thought "Christ, what a mess."

"I want to come in with you, Sarge. Please!"

"What?" Nigel was kneeling, actually fucking *kneeling*, on the lino by Colin's feet. "Get up, for God's sake."

"Sam reckons, the three of us, we could do real magic. Maybe I could get a job in the collator's office, maybe even at Area. It'd be great. Go on, Skip. It'd be like old times, only better."

The boy thought he was at it! The kid and the woman, they thought he was playing both sides. The hard man, the glamour boy, more bottle than anyone she'd ever met. They didn't know about his talent for disappearing, they thought it was all a great scam.

And Nigel wanted in. That was the blackmailer's price.

"They weren't your old days, Nigel. You don't know what you're talking about."

"Yeah, I know, Skip, but—"

Colin got up, walked towards the door. "Meet me in the Fat Duck, Monday night. Half-six. We'll go for a ride."

"Thanks, Sarge! We going to do some business?"

"Yeah. That's fine."

"Thanks, Skip. Wait till Sam hears! I'll be ready, you'll see." His dressing-gown swung open as he danced down the hall to get the door open before Colin could reach it and have to open it himself. "I'll be well ready, Skip, I promise you!"

Before leaving his flat on Monday evening, Colin stood in front of his hall mirror and gave himself a briefing: this is how it'll go.

Eighteen-thirty hours, meet PC Dunne at the Fat Duck. Give him a good few drinks, let all the other coppers in the place remember how drunk he was when they left. "I'd better give him a lift home, he's well gone."

Nineteen-thirty hours, leave the pub, drive to Nigel's place. Twenty-hundred hours, arrive at Nigel's. Do her first—she looked stronger than the boy—then him. Twenty-twenty to twenty-thirty-five hours, arrange the scene of crime. Twenty-forty hours, phone it in.

"When we got home, it was obvious she'd had a man there. She must have thought we'd be out all evening, we were planning to go on to a snooker club, but PC Dunne had too much to drink, so I had to take him home early. We arrived unexpectedly. Her attire was in disarray, she was dressed for bed, there was an empty wine bottle on the living-room table. PC Dunne flew into a rage, shouting, 'Oh no, not again, not again, you filthy slut, oh no, not again.' He ran upstairs to the bedroom, then came down again, shouting, 'In my bed, my own bloody bed, how could you, you slut, how could you.' I attempted to reason with him, but he was beyond it. 'I'll swing for you, you whoring cow,' he shouted, and before I was able to intervene, he picked up a knife from the kitchen side, and drove it repeatedly into her chest and face. I wrestled with him, and managed to get him into an arm lock. Suddenly he went limp, and to my horror I realized that he was dead. I attempted emergency resuscitation on both victims, but without success. They were both dead. I can only surmise that the fatal injury to PC Dunne's neck occurred during my struggle with him. This is a nightmare which I will carry with me for the rest of my days. I do not require compassionate sick-leave, as I believe that the best therapy for me would be to return to active duties as soon as possible.''

It wasn't perfect, even for short notice. A lot of it would depend on Colin being a police officer, on Sergeant Colin Mann's own fine but not flashy record working in his favour, on his version being accepted, without too much investigation.

But it was better than paying, especially when you don't even have the price that's being demanded.

No, it wasn't perfect, but it would have to do. He put on his leather bomber, checked the pockets for fags, lighter, keys, wallet. Right then: better get it sorted.

The reluctant hero entered the pub at a minute before six o'clock, but saw no sign of the acolyte. Instead he saw, in his usual seat by the door, a sergeant from one of the other reliefs, sitting there puffing on that stupid, poncy pipe of his. Sherlock Holmes with a salt-and-pepper crew cut.

Colin approached Bob Miller with an affability that rarely exists, except between two men whose hatred is mutual, irrational and strong.

"Evening, Bob,"

Miller reacted to Colin Mann's arrival with deep and reptilian pleasure, even more so than a shared antipathy would normally demand. "You looking for your mate Dunne?"

"Yeah," said Colin, bunching his fists in his pockets. "You seen him?"

Miller shook his head from side to side, slowly, with his lips stretched wide and his teeth together, clenching his poncy pipe, spreading the smoke in little bursts like a lawn-sprinkler spreads water.

"No," he said. "Won't be seeing him either, not for a while. He's in custody."

"He's on duty? I thought he was—"

"No, he's not in the custody area, Colin," all drawled and sarky, so that it sounded like *custardy air-ear, Cor-lynne.* "He's *een custardy.* He's *beeen* arrested. All right, mate?'' Sergeant Miller turned back to his pint and his poncy pipe, pretending he thought the conversation was over.

"Right, fine,'' said Colin. For a moment he couldn't remember where he was. Or rather, he knew where he *was* of course, in the Fat Duck, but just for a second, no more than that, he couldn't quite think what was going on. "So what's he done then, Bob, he smacked someone, has he?'' He tried to add a matey laugh, but it came out like a nasal problem.

"Who, young Nigel?'' Miller said, as if he'd forgotten who they were talking about. "No, nothing like that. Seems he's got some friends, wrong sort of friends, you know. They've been supplementing his private pension plan for him. For information received.''

Fine, thought Colin. Fine.

"You want a drink?'' said Miller.

"No, you're all right, Bob.''

"Hope you haven't been getting too friendly with your little friend, Colin. Word is he's coughing his guts out in there. They start young these days, eh? Well, they've got the best teachers, haven't they?''

"Fine,'' said Colin. "That's fine, fine,'' and he began to walk out of the pub, unconsciously bumping a table here, jogging a drinker's elbow there, thinking to himself, "That's all right. That's fine. I done it once, I can do it again. Fine, that's fine.''

And as he got into the car (home first, grab some stuff? No, best not: straight for the motorway, that's favourite), as he drove away from the Fat Duck, and from north London, and from being a copper (Bristol? Yeah, Bristol's good, big city, plenty of opportunities for a man who'd been a crook and been a cop and knew which he preferred, but could do either), as he left one life behind, and left behind the life behind that one, he was thinking, in some small department of his head, how glad he was that he hadn't, after all, had to kill anyone.

Not today, anyway.

Birmingham's bigger, of course. More people. No: rains all the time, can't stand the accent. Got a cousin lives in Birmingham.

Bristol it is.

Kristine Kathryn Rusch writes science fiction, fantasy and mystery, and edits one of the world's most distinguished periodicals, *The Magazine of Fantasy and Science Fiction.* Her crime stories, as here, are exceptional, both in plot and in style. There are several major suspense novels taking shape in her head and we're eager to read each and every one of them. Our field will be hearing a lot more from her.

Strays
KRISTINE KATHRYN RUSCH

It happened during Clinton's first hundred days. D.C. was a changed town. Arkania was in. So were strong women. Wife No. 3 had left me just after the inauguration, and Secretary No. 45 quit, vowing to file a sexual harassment suit. She was a great girl, with legs that wouldn't quit, and I was sorry to see her go. The secretary, that is. Not the wife.

My fancy-schmancy office was cold and empty without her. I no longer needed the front room with its oak desk, cool blue walls, and indoor-outdoor carpet. The phone system was too complicated for me to use, so one afternoon I pulled it from the wall, and reverted to my black rotary. The commissions I got from the Bush people for staking out Democrat parties vanished on November 4, and since Wife No. 3 cleared out half the savings, I couldn't hire Secretary No. 46. I spent January looking for new digs, and February advertising in the *Post*'s classifieds because I couldn't break the lease I had. The cases were few and far between. The money even scarcer. I followed a Democratic senator's wife for three days before he found out I used to work for the Bush people. The commission wasn't bad, but it didn't make the rent. I scoped out a bunch of women for Senator Packwood, but that job ended when the press got wind of it.

I was reduced to insurance claims investigation when the call came in. Woman's voice, very concerned. Address fell in the middle of an upscale brownstone neighborhood in McLean. Lots of money, well hidden. Real money that didn't need the parade of wealth to prove it was rich. Bush country. Home.

I drove my silver Thunderbird on the George Washington Parkway, glad the car at least was paid off. Can't be a dick without wheels. Still, they don't make T-birds like they used to. No pickup in the new models, and the design looks like Sports Cars for Suburbia. The baby had speed though once it got going. Sometimes I needed speed. Along the way I passed lots of nondescript blue sedans, most with vanity plates. I stared at one, DAN 1996, all the way into McLean. Some folks never gave up.

The brownstone was in a tree-lined neighborhood that had a hush so deep it seemed like all the occupants had died. I knew they hadn't though. Curtains moved all over the block when the T-bird parked in front of 1256 (lettering neogothic, no name beneath the script). I felt like a cop in a whorehouse: couldn't see a thing, but knew lots of folks were seeing him.

The door chime was three soft tones designed to echo through the house without disturbing the occupants. The dame herself answered the door. Surprised me. I expected a genteel male butler with a voice as soft-spoken as the chimes.

She had been a looker once. Still was, if truth be told. Mass of silver hair, expertly styled to curl and fall in a dignified way around her face. Her figure was trim, her undergarments firm so that her breasts poked out like an eighteen-year-old's. Her legs put No. 45's to shame. Her skin had that papery look brought on by age and good nutrition. She didn't look so much old as softened.

A white cat wound its way around her legs, peeking through at me like a flirtatious child. "Mr. Ransom?" the woman said. "I'm Beverly Conner."

I took the offered hand, felt the knobby knuckles that indicated arthritis, and did not squeeze. I stepped inside. The entry was done in browns, a deacon's bench by the door, a hand-carved mirror near the coatless coatrack, and a Rembrandt sketch—original, judging by the framing—near the closet. The faint odor of cat piss seemed out of place.

She led me through the hall to a kitchen that was made of windows. Sunlight dappled in from the garden, and the warmth enveloped me. The oak table was clean except for the German tea service waiting on the tabletop.

"Please sit," she said.

I sat.

Her obvious wealth didn't impress me as much as the cats. They watched like small sentries from the most unlikely of posts. A calico sat on top of the refrigerator. A black one slept on the chair opposite me. I had noticed another curled on the back of the couch as we passed the living room. She must have kept housekeepers employed full time just mopping up the cat hair.

I thought only poor old ladies kept a zillion cats. Guess I was wrong.

"What do you need, ma'am?"

She plopped a newspaper clipping in front of me. I recognized it. It had run in the *Post* just the day before, and I had read all the way to the end, even though it gagged me. The *Post*, bastion of the Washington elite, had run an obituary on page one.

Of a cat.

Granted, it was a famous cat, even by D.C. standards. Bob, the Weather Cat, who had paraded in his cute little weather outfits—yellow rain slicker for rain, sunglasses and Hawaiian print shorts for heatwaves—on Fox 5 every night during the five o'clock news. Bob put up with it with an amazing dignity—he was a cat after all—but folks watched to see if this week Bob would rebel. He hated the snow parka, and bit it off during a two-day storm that dumped five feet on downtown last winter, and he destroyed the rain slicker after a particularly bad stretch of showers by, you guessed it, peeing on it.

Bob, D.C.'s favorite contrary character, had been brutally murdered. His obit, on the front page of a paper that put the deaths of first-term congressmen in the Metro section, read with a seriousness usually reserved for presidents. Memorials were to go to the D.C. Chapter of the Humane Society. Seems our pal Bob had started life as a stray. Something else he shared with most of Washington's power elite.

Murdered. And I was sitting in a houseful of cats.

I had a bad feeling about this.

I shoved the paper back to her. "Yeah. I seen this."

"Bob lived next door," she said. "He isn't the first cat to die in this neighborhood."

"Cats get murdered all the time," I said. "Poisoned meat, hit and runs, steel traps. No one thinks it's any kind of conspiracy."

She blanched. "Perhaps you're not the man for the job, Mr. Ransom," she said primly.

A tabby wound her way between my legs, motor running. A white cat jumped on my lap in a flurry of fur. A black kitten meowed from the top of the microwave. They looked like the guard for a South American *junta*—charming on the surface with a bit too much animal underneath. "I usually do political jobs," I said.

"Well," she said, crossing her arms and turning her back on me, "this job is just humoring an old lady."

She walked over to the window and petted a graying black tom. He chirruped with pleasure and rolled onto his back, nearly dislodging the plastic screen covering a wealth of African violets.

Something in her movement suggested a loneliness that she couldn't completely hide. I had noticed no pictures of children when I walked in, no too-small wedding ring embedded into her left hand. This lady lived for her cats, and they seemed to love her.

My lack of employment was making me too sentimental.

"Okay," I said. "I'll humor you."

She turned. Her smile was radiant, transforming her elderly face into the face of a girl.

"For a five-hundred-buck retainer and a hundred bucks a day expenses," I said.

She didn't even flinch. Should have charged her my political rates in which everything got multiplied by ten—and even that was cheap by government standards.

She reached for her billfold which sat by the grocery-list pad on the counter. She picked it up, took a gold Cross pen out of the Sigma Delta Chi mug next to the pad, and came over to the table. As I watched, she wrote a thousand-dollar check in perfect cursive then handed it to me.

"You undercharge, Mr. Ransom."

Didn't I know it. It never was more clear than at that moment.

"Okay," I said. "I know about Bob. Give me the poop on the other murders."

She pushed her billfold aside and folded her hands on the oak tabletop. "I beg your pardon, Mr. Ransom," she said. "But I don't think you do know the—poop—on Bob. The papers didn't report it all. It was too horrible."

She shuddered, a dainty movement that made me think of romance novels and debutante balls. (The things a man sees in my profession . . .) She grabbed the teapot for support.

"Tea?" she asked, her voice shaking.

I nodded. She poured into two small, wafer-thin cups, then set the pot down and opened the sugar jar. "One lump or two?"

"None," I said, taking my cup. My thumb nearly dwarfed it. I took a sip and drained it. I barely had a chance to taste it. "Bob?"

She nodded, flung the tea back like a strong brandy and poured herself another cup. "He was tied between four bushes in my garden like vets do when they spay, gutted from stem to stern, and his heart was removed. He was shaved before they strung him up, and the police say he was alive when he was gutted."

Vets. Vets. For a moment, I thought she meant Vietnam vets. Then I realized. Veterinarian.

She belted the second cup back, and poured a third. I stuck my teacup under the pouring spout wishing for something strong. No wonder she was upset.

"The other cats, were they killed the same way?"

She shook her head. "Baggins was a victim of a hit and run. Seemed like an unfortunate accident, but he was shaved too. Then there was Sophie, whose throat was slit; Ridicio, who was hanged; and Rin Tin Tin, who was nailed to a tiny cross." She sighed and buried her head behind a wrinkled, ring-studded hand. "The police think some crazy is on the loose, but they don't have time to look for him. They just want me to keep my babies indoors."

She dropped her hand. Her mouth was a thin line, her blue eyes flashed. "I want him caught. No one should be allowed to menace innocents."

I had my doubts about whether cats were innocents—I'd seen more than one torture a mouse—but I wasn't about to let my opinion tamper with a much-needed commission. I had almost made that mistake once today. "Who's the on-site officer?" I asked, and the case officially began.

II

The precinct smelled like old, wet tennis shoes. The concrete walls had a layer of grime over them from poor heating systems and summer dampness. I sat on an ancient green office chair with springs missing in the middle, sipping lukewarm watery coffee, and waiting for Lieutenant Thornton to get off the phone so that he could talk to me. He had been gesturing and swearing into the receiver for the last fifteen minutes. From what I could tell, he was dealing with a call from home.

Three transvestites in black fishnet were cuffed together and being dragged through by a female police officer. An elderly woman clutched her right arm and looked down as she spoke to a burly man at the desk beside me. She had been mugged and lost her Social Security check, all her identification, and the fifteen dollars that was going to carry her through the month. The officer was polite, but bored. He had seen it all before.

So had I.

I made it a practice to look away.

Thornton slammed the receiver down. "Stupid bitch," he muttered. I had been right. Wife. He leaned forward. "Long time no see, Ransom. I thought they were sending you home with Ronnie's boys."

"We'll be back in four more years," I chanted.

"Yeah, right." He leaned back and lit a cigarette with the filter broken off of it. "At the rate our friend Bill is screwing up, probably. What can I do for you?"

I set my paper coffee cup on the only bare spot on Thornton's desk. "Bob, the weather cat."

He laughed and leaned back, smoke coming out of his mouth and nostrils. "Lord, how the mighty have fallen."

I grinned. "Hey, I'm not a big city cop who is handling a case outside his jurisdiction. The McLean homeboys sent me over to you. How come D.C. gets to handle a Virginia case?"

Thornton rolled his eyes. "McLean's department is small. We usually take the famous as a favor to them. I guess that includes famous animals. So who hired you? The station or that crazy old bat next door?"

"The old bat."

He nodded. "She calls every day. I don't have the heart to tell her that the case is way down on our priority list—like below the subbasement."

"She knows. That's why she hired me."

Thornton took another long drag off the cigarette, then stamped it out in the full ashtray near the phone. "She just needs to keep her precious babies inside. Then they won't get gutted by the neighborhood Satanists."

"You know that, and I know that. But if I can pin a face and a name to Bob's murder, then I get a $5,000 bonus."

Thornton gave me a half smile. "Seems to me that was a starting fee once upon a time."

"Yeah, well, the gravy train has retired to Kennebunkport."

Thornton stood up and stretched, his beefy arms straining against his regulation tee. "You should work for the district, man. Same old shit at the same old pay, but you don't have to worry when the rubes come to town."

"Maybe I like holding the hands of little old ladies."

"You just weren't smart enough to rig the election when you had the chance."

I ran a hand through my thinning hair. "I thought Gennifer Flowers was a good move."

"Maybe, if you were trying to trap a Kennedy. People expect a man with a wife like Hillary to get some on the side." Thornton took out another cigarette and pounded it against the desk top. "I'll get you the files on our friend Bob."

"Thanks."

He disappeared into the back. The old lady next to me burst into tears, her voice finally rising above the general din. "But how will I *live* for the next month?"

The cop was shaking his head. "You have to talk with the Social Security people."

"But I don't even have enough for dinner tonight!"

I stuck a hand in my pocket and fingered the crisp twenty I always carried there for emergencies. The woman stood and wiped her eyes with a crumpled handkerchief. Then she stuck the handkerchief back in her sleeve. "That's not your problem, is it?" she said to the officer. "I'm sorry."

I stood too, and blocked her way. She was tiny, about four feet nine, and weighed less than a hundred pounds. The kind of woman I would expect to have a cat-filled house that smelled of piss. "Lady," I said, "I overheard. Can't do much about the mugging, but I can help with tonight."

I shoved the twenty at her. She stared at it for a moment. "I don't take charity, young man," she said. She handed it back to me, and walked around the desk, hunched and clutching her arm.

"It's not charity," I said, but she didn't turn. It *was* charity—we both knew it—but she didn't want it. So much for trickle-down economics.

Thornton came back with the file. It was thick, filled with publicity stills of Bob in life and ugly shots of Bob in death. The cat's limbs had been stretched out of their sockets. The cat must have put up a hell of a racket while he was being killed. Someone had to have heard something.

But who paid attention to a howling cat?

Other than the details of the death, the file was useless. I took a sip of my now-cold coffee. It tasted like colored swamp water. "Hey, Thornton! What about the other deaths?"

Thornton frowned. He was lighting one cigarette from another. I noticed a white band of skin on his left finger—where his wedding ring used to be. "What other deaths?"

"The shaved hit and run, the cat nailed to a cross, all those?"

He shrugged. "No one called us on 'em. We only heard about them after the Weather Kitty bit it. Of course we're going to watch any other deaths, but the old ones just don't factor."

"Did you interview any neighbors? "

"For chrissakes, Ransom. It was only a cat—a famous cat, mind you, but still a cat."

He had a point. In a city with the highest murder rate per capita, where little old ladies got mugged at bus stops, where mayors thought nothing of sticking candy up their noses, one cat didn't matter a hell of a lot.

To anyone except a rich woman with too much time on her hands.

And me, because she was paying me.

I photocopied the report on the station's in-house copier. Black streaks marred the paper, but at least I could still read it. I thanked Thornton and left.

Two blocks away from the station, I saw the little old lady, walking as if her feet hurt, head bent, hand clutching that useless arm. I pressed the window button and the passenger window rolled down. I leaned across the leather upholstery. "At least let me drive you to a hospital."

She looked up. A bruise had started to form on her left cheek. "What are you so worried about me for?"

I couldn't answer that, not even to me. Maybe I saw myself in her shoes not too many years away. Maybe I had a soft spot. Maybe I wanted to focus on something else beside dead cats. Maybe I wanted to believe that in her youth she had great tits. I shrugged. "I was a bad man in a previous life. The angel Gabriel met me at the pearly gates and told me they would be locked forever unless I did one good deed. You're it. Now get in."

She smiled, revealing a mouthful of bad teeth. "'You don't expect me to believe that, do you?"

"Do I look like the kind of guy who would be kind for the hell of it?"

"No." She pulled the car door open with her good hand. "When I saw you upstairs, I pegged you for a Republican."

III

I dropped her at Washington General, helped her with the admittance forms, and promised to talk with the Social Security people. I also got the details of the mugging—in broad daylight near the Jefferson Memorial (and the lovely tourists stood around and *snapped pictures*)—and promised to keep an eye out for the creep. Muggers had a pattern, and if Dolores fit into that pattern, well then maybe I might clean one speck of dirt off the city streets.

Damn. Dems in office and everyone becomes a bleeding heart.

I was back in McLean by midafternoon. Fortunately for me, feminism is a token word there. Women of Beverly Conner's status did not work. They stayed home and baked cookies, in Hillary parlance. Of course, that would change by '96, but we were still feeling the effects of Reaganism.

Thank god. Otherwise no one would have been home.

I parked on a side street and canvassed the neighborhood on foot. I learned early in my career that to say I'm a private dick in D.C. was tantamount to getting a door slammed in my face. In this town, everyone had a secret. Even people who didn't have secrets liked to pretend they had one. The more secrets a person had, the more powerful. And the more they hated investigators.

They didn't mind the police though. Cops kept the neighborhood safe and were notoriously poor at closing cases.

I had some pretty good fake ID. Had to. The folks in this town were also paranoid.

In each house, I got coffee and a sob story about poor Bob. The first three houses had an empty dog run in back and a kitten playing on the floor. The things people did to be trendy. Socks had made D.C. into a cat-person's heaven. Dogs were suddenly pets *non grata*. I didn't learn anything until house No. 5.

The woman who answered the door was considerably younger than her neighbors. An adult Siamese perched on her shoulder. She was slight and near the end of a pregnancy. Her T-shirt, which read BABY with a large red arrow pointing toward her stomach, was too tight.

I told her my spiel. She introduced herself as Suzanna Blackwell, and let me inside a house filled with children's toys, family photographs, and warm brown tones. A house she had decorated herself, obviously, but the first one I had walked into that actually felt lived-in.

She sat me at the kitchen table (formica that looked like faked marble) and wiped it off. Then she gave me a plate of cookies and offered coffee or milk. When I discovered that all she had was instant, I took the milk.

"I heard it, you know," she said. She had to push her chair away so that her distended stomach wouldn't brush the edge of the table. "About six in the morning, some cat was yowling. But it sounded like it was in pain, not in heat." She reached up and petted the cat on her shoulder. Its slanted eyes watched me with a cool appraisal. "I looked out the window and saw nothing. Then the yowling stopped and a man ran through my bushes, covered with blood. That's when I called the police."

"You called?"

She nodded. "I used to let Whiskers here go out, but not anymore. Too many deaths in the neighborhood. We got him for the kids, but he's really closer to me."

Obviously. I had never seen a cat content to ride on someone's shoulders before. Especially shoulders as small as hers.

"Can you describe the man?"

She nodded. "He was wearing dark clothing, and he was white. He had a regulation haircut—looked almost military—and he was about ... taller than six feet because his head brushed that tree limb out there."

"The investigating officer didn't talk to you?"

Suzanna smiled and pulled the cat off her shoulder. She rubbed her chin against the top of its head. "He didn't think it all that important."

"You did tell him you saw a man, not a boy?"

"Oh, yeah," she said. "But he was so convinced that it's some gang that he wouldn't even listen to me. Now Whiskers doesn't go outside at all, and I don't even let the kids play in the yard after school. I hope you catch this guy because my husband is talking about finding a place outside the beltway. I don't want him to make the commute from the White House. The drive is long enough now as it is."

Suddenly all my meters started ticking. "Your husband's a political appointee?"

She shook her head. "He's actually detailed from State. He's been at the White House since '86. He's not an appointee so Clinton's people don't want to mess with him. They can't even fill the seats they're supposed to fill. No sense adding a few more—at least for a while."

"Does everyone here work with the government?" I meant the comment as sarcasm, but she seemed to take me seriously.

"Sure. Except Mrs. Conner, and it seems to me her husband used to work for CIA."

"Her husband?" I had seen no evidence of a man's presence in that house. "Oh, he's been dead for years. They say he died doing some work in Vietnam in the late sixties, but my husband says that Mr. Conner was actually in Red China when he died. All very hush-hush, even now." But clearly something she enjoyed gossiping about.

"But everyone else works for the government."

"Oh, yes." She bit the head off a gingerbread man and talked around the food. "Willis, next door, is Treasury. The Sanderses just moved in. He's with HHS. I could go on."

"What about Bob's owner?"

"Oh, Julie! I forgot about her!" Suzanna bit off the gingerbread man's torso. "She just moved in a few months ago. She trains animals for local stunts and stuff. The house used to belong to Senator Symms from Idaho. He sold it to a new woman appointee from Washington State, but she didn't like the neighborhood—too chichi, she said—so Julie got it."

I frowned. Old habits died hard. "How many Clinton people in the neighborhood?"

She laughed. "Too many, according to my husband. I think three-quarters of the houses turned over at the turn of the year."

That explained the dog runs and the cat-filled households. Not political chauvinism but new owners reflecting the president's bias. Cat people, all of them.

"And no one is upset about the cat deaths?"

Suzanna shook her head. "Willis spoke to us all about gangs the other day, saying that they're not neighborhood oriented any more, that they go where the money is." She sighed. "You just have to put up with things living in the big city. I can't wait until my husband retires and we can get away from all this. Of course, by then, I probably won't think anything of living in fear. I hate it now though." She patted her stomach. "Doesn't seem right somehow."

"No, it doesn't," I said. I stood, having had my fill of gingerbread and milk. "Thanks again, Mrs. Blackwell."

She trailed me to the door, which didn't give me time to study the photographs. Some of them, I noted, were of a skinny man in a suit posed with Bush, or Reagan, or several better-known congressmen. The rest were snapshots of two towheaded boys, going from smiling babies to gaptoothed children. Twins, it looked like, and at her size, she could be carrying two more.

Amazing the things pictures told about a family and its values. I said my goodbyes and was walking to the next house before I remembered.

Snapshots.

How could I have been so dumb?

IV

The rest of the neighborhood proved a wash. Cool reception and even cooler interaction. Bob's owner, Julie, wasn't home, so I made a mental note to contact her later.

I had to clear my mind from the cat garbage. I went to my local information sources and left messages for any tourists with pictures of that day's mugging at the Jefferson Memorial, promising to pay top dollar for a clear shot. That kept me from spending cash on the development charge, and also gave me a way out so that I wouldn't have to spend money on the naïfs who would photograph a crime instead of stop it.

I stopped at Washington General on my way home to see Dolores. She was asleep when I got there, her skin a faint china blue against the crisp white sheets. Her bones looked brittle. Her right arm was in a cast and an IV was feeding into her left. I went and found the duty nurse who told me that Dolores would have to remain for a few days because her malnourishment made her injury more serious than a broken arm and a few cracked ribs would normally be.

"We see lots of this," the duty nurse said. "They can't afford to pay all their bills on Social Security, so they only eat a meal a day and even skip that at the end of the month."

I frowned. "I thought the government was supposed to cover her expenses."

The nurse laughed, a bitter sound. "The government probably won't even cover her hospital bill, since she waited a few hours before coming in. I think we're the only medical workers in the city who support Clinton's health-care reform ideas. Maybe then we'll actually get paid for the work we do."

She trudged off, her well-worn heels squeaking against the linoleum. Her legs were on a par with No. 45's but the shoes did her no good. Didn't matter though. She kept trim by working crowded hospital corridors. Number 45 used an overpriced exercise bike.

I found the nurse's legs much more appealing.

V

The phone woke me up at 6:00 A.M. Beverly Conner sobbing into the line, "Please come, right away!"

As I turned on the light and rolled out of my waterbed, sliding on the black satin sheets, I wondered which one bit it: the little kitten mewing on top of the microwave? The big tom by the window? The white cat that twined its way around my ankles? I kicked aside piles of unwashed clothing, slid on a pair of jeans, a sweatshirt and stuffed my wallet in my back pocket. I hurried through the living room, narrowly avoiding all the electronics equipment which I too rarely used, and grabbed my raincoat off the credenza Wife No. 3 did not want. Then I hurried out the door.

I had forgotten that the GW Parkway was full this time of the morning. Commuters in their Beamers, car phones pasted to their ears, trying to be the earliest person in the office. That would change in the middle years of the administration, when everything became routine, and change back just before the election in case Clinton managed to squeeze a second term out of the voters. Fortunately, I was heading *to* McLean. My side of the GW Parkway was nearly empty.

I pulled up behind the Virginia police. They had two squads sitting in the middle of the road, lights flashing. Faces peered through curtained windows as they had done on my first visit. I strode up the stone steps to Beverly's house and knocked.

Her face was puffy and her eyes bloodshot. "Mr. Ransom," she said with such relief that I was tempted to put my arms around her. She stood aside to let me in.

The faint odor of vomit covered the scent of cat piss. But the house looked tidy as ever. Half a dozen cats watched warily from the hallway. Another four sat in the picture window, tails twitching.

"What happened?" I asked.

"I found another one, tossed in my rose bushes, shaved. Lieutenant Thornton thinks it is some kind of gang—"

"Let me go talk to him," I said.

I slipped out the back door and joined the three policemen huddled around the rose bushes on Beverly's well-manicured lawn. Clumps of black and white hair covered the dew-coated grass as if the shaving had occurred right there.

The cat's body looked naked and pathetic on its bed of thorns. "Anyone know who the cat belongs to?" I asked.

"The Reeds down the street," Thornton said, his hands stuck in his back pocket, the cigarette in his mouth unlit. "They've had the cat for two years. They're pretty broken up about it. I think they're even going to let their little girl stay home from school."

"Reed?" I said. "That a name I should know?"

"Doubt it," Thornton said. "They're old Friends of Bill. He was going to give Mrs. Reed a political appointment, but had to settle for a Schedule-C. That nanny thing again."

"How old's the girl?"

"Chelsea's age. Goes to Sidwell Friends, the same school."

I frowned. "You know, Mrs. Blackwell next door saw a man go through her bushes after the last murder."

"Murder?" Thornton said. "You're beginning to sound like the bat."

"Shhh." I glanced over my shoulder at the window. Six cats had crowded onto the sill, but there was no sign of Beverly. Thank god. "She said, the man looked military. He sounded more Secret Service to me."

Thornton nodded. "I'll check it out."

I left the site. Something about that cat, discarded and pathetic in death, made me think of Dolores, lying in the hospital bed and pasted to an IV she couldn't pay for.

I went back inside. Beverly was sitting at her polished dining-room table, looking lost. I couldn't tell if she had overheard Thornton's burst of sensitivity or not. "How'd you get all these cats?"

She smiled, then. It was a sad smile that accompanied a glance out the window. "Most of them were strays," she said. "Dumped by former owners, or lost, or abandoned kittens. Funny thing about cats. They don't beg, no matter how hungry or injured they are." She swallowed hard. "I keep thinking about that. I didn't hear the little guy cry out. I didn't hear anything. I just imagine him trying to maintain his dignity while they were removing it. . . ."

Her voice trailed off. I sat down across from her, trying to imagine how she had lived over the years. Husband with the CIA, always gone, always focused on work. No children. The cats were her life. They were her babies. A cat's death was the same to her as a child's.

Then it all went rocket clear. "Let me see that picture of Bob again."

She frowned, but stood, obviously relieved to have something to do. She went into the study and came back clutching the newspaper clipping. I studied the photograph for a moment.

"How many children are on this block?"

"I don't know. Quite a few. They all play together."

"Young children?"

She shook her head. "Young teenagers. Mostly girls. One of them got invited up to the White House last week. It was quite a big deal.'' She pushed an orange cat off her chair and sat down. "What do you want with the picture of Bob?"

I showed it to her. "Does he look like anyone to you?"

She took it, then pulled a pair of half glasses out of her breast pocket and stared at it. "There are an awful lot of cats that look like Bob," she said. She glanced outside. The latest victim had shared Bob's coloring and general body shape. She glanced back at the photo. "Oh, my god," she whispered. "He looks just like Socks!"

VI

The pound had a small herd of black and white cats. I took the friendliest one, who reached out at me through the little triangular holes in his cage each time I passed. The pound let me have him for free. Fortunately, he'd already had his nuts chopped off, or I would have had to wait a few days. I didn't have a few days. I was afraid Mrs. Conner would change her mind by the time I got back.

She hadn't. She had a room specially designed as a cat isolation ward. I guess she used it when a cat was pregnant or seriously ill. Socks II: The Sequel went into that room for the night, and I bunked down on the floor with my watch alarm set for 4:00 A.M. At that time, Sequel and I would hit the streets.

Mrs. Conner went to bed at nine. I watched the end of the third Indiana Jones movie on Channel 20, then joined Sequel in his little room, watch alarm set. I woke up at midnight with the cat sitting on my back, nuzzling its nose in the hair at the nape of my neck, purring like a souped-up V-8 engine. I pushed him off and got him to settle, only to wake up an hour later as a scratchy tongue rubbed a hole in my chin. Finally I grabbed him, wrapped an arm around him (as much to hold him down as to give him comfort) and tried to sleep again. When the alarm went off at four, Sequel had one paw across my chest like a lover.

What was it Thornton had said? Some cliché about how the mighty had fallen?

He had no clue.

I had fixed a little homing device to Sequel's collar just in case. Then I picked him up and carried him to the back door. Together we went out. He prowled and I followed.

The sky was faintly pink at the horizon. The air had an early-morning chill and dew had already formed on the grass. By the time Sequel had done his personal business, my tennis shoes were soaked.

I had never trailed a cat before. He didn't have a care for sidewalks, streets or the other amenities of civilization. He crawled under bushes and leapt over fences, ran around houses and hid behind drain pipes. I followed as quietly as I could. Once I lost him when he hid for forty minutes under a rose bush tracking a mouse. I scraped my finger on barbed wire, and stubbed my toe on a hidden brick. By midmorning, Sequel was camped out on Mrs. Conner's backyard, snoozing in the sun. I was crouched in the bushes, trying to stay out of sight while dislodging the thorns I had picked up from the neighbor's rose bush.

The only thing I had learned all morning was that my fingernails were too short to act as tweezers. That, and the fact that cats led dull little lives enhanced by their overactive imaginations. If people had that much fun doing mundane tasks, factory workers would be whistlin' while they worked.

Fat chance.

I was no better. I had gone from trailing Ted Kennedy in the predawn hours to following a black and white cat who looked like Socks. Of course, if Sequel still had his nuts, the job wouldn't be all that much different.

VII

It took three days, two pairs of tennis shoes and fifteen cuts to the right hand alone before I hit pay dirt. Sequel and I headed out at our customary 4:00 A.M., and I marveled at the neighborhood. I had been prowling through bushes and climbing over fences for days now, and not a soul had called the cops. No wonder the upper class needed security systems. Anyone with a different social standing was beneath their notice—whether that anyone looked like a thief or not.

The morning was foggy, and the only way I could tell dawn was approaching was because the mist took on a Stephen King/end-of-the-world pink glow. I had discovered a hole in a trellis big enough to hide me but with enough view through the leaves to allow me to keep Sequel in sight most of the time.

Sequel had chased a squirrel under his favorite rose bush when I heard a car door slam a few blocks away. A chill ran down my back. Leather shoes clicked against the asphalt bike path. The wearer either belonged to the neighborhood or had learned what I did about the so-called Neighborhood Watch program.

He came out of the fog like a movie commando bursting through a haze of smoke. He looked just the way Suzanna Blackwell had described him: Over six feet, broad shoulders held with military precision, haircut so perfect it looked glued on. His clothing was invisible Washington blue and his tie was knotted so tight I wondered how he could breathe. He clutched a tape recorder in one hand and a dish in the other. With a flick of his thumb, he turned the tape recorder on. It made a funny whirring sound that I could almost identify.

Sequel perked up his ears, squirrel forgotten.

"Here, kitty, kitty," the man said, voice soft.

Sequel ran toward him like the man was God himself. The man shut off the tape recorder and crouched, putting the dish on the ground. Half a beat too late, I realized what the sound was.

A can opener.

The man had recorded the sound of a can opener opening a can. Sequel approached, friendlier than I had seen him with anyone but me. Tail twitching in anticipation, yowling like he was about to get a great treat.

The food was probably drugged.

I burst out of the bushes, twigs scraping my thinning hair, trellis tottering, and launched myself at the man. Sequel screamed and darted for his rosebush as I caught the man in the middle. The dish went flying and landed with a crash that echoed in the fog-shrouded street.

The man was all muscle and as solid as the Lincoln Memorial. He landed on his back and grunted as the wind left his body. Lucky for me I had the element of surprise or I never would have taken him. I shoved a knee to his groin and put my whole weight on it as I yanked my cuffs off my belt.

"Stupid son of a bitch," I said, "what are you doing picking on cats?"

Then I looked down at him and knew. One of Quayle's men. They had all gone their own way when Danny returned to Indiana—loose cannons without a brain cell among them. It had been charming in their boss, scary in men with bodies like Arnold Schwarzenegger. With a grunt, the man shoved me off him. I rolled away in time to push Sequel from the plate of overturned food.

"Beverly!" I cried. "Call 911! Beverly!"

I tucked Sequel under one arm and deposited him near the house as I ran after Mr. Macho. My tennis shoes gave me the advantage of silence, but his training gave him speed. He made it to the nondescript black sedan parked half a block away, slipped in and drove off.

But not before I saw the license plate.

DAN 1996

Dream on, asshole. With folks like him working on Quayle's re-election campaign, Bill and friends would have to be real incompetents to lose.

I stood in the middle of the street wheezing like an eighty-year-old with one lung. Sequel twined himself around my legs, licking the remains of canned food off his whiskers.

"Great, buddy," I said, picking him up. "Now we got to get you to a vet and pump your stomach."

At that moment I knew it was too late. I had become a cat-loving bleeding heart with conservative aspirations.

Another Clinton Democrat.

I guess it had only been a matter of time.

VIII

Thornton tracked our man and brought him in. They don't know what they'll charge him with yet, but they'll make it a felony so the guy will have to spend some time behind bars.

Turns out Mr. Macho had worked for Quayle (my memory was as good as I thought it was) but had been fired for being too stupid—and acting on those harebrained ideas during the 1992 Bush reelection campaign. Too stupid to work for Uncle Danny. I had been in Washington too long. I had finally seen everything.

This harebrained scheme was right up there with Dan's speech about canals on Mars. Mr. Macho decided to terrorize the little friends of Chelsea Clinton, killing the Socks look-alikes in hopes that the word would get to Chelsea, and she would think Washington a horrible place. The pressure would wear on Bill and he would decide not to run in '96. Or something like that. The ultimate goals of the plan were as foggy as that last morning. Apparently Mr. Macho was not too good at future planning.

What a surprise.

I had more good news. My little messages left at strategic places had turned up several good prints of Dolores's mugging. The cops even knew the guy, a former informer for the DEA, cut loose after the Marion Barry deal. He was behind bars now. Dolores didn't get her purse back, but Justice Was Served.

Me, I go over to Beverly's house twice a week for tea and conversation. My apartment has the faint odor of cat piss, thanks to Sequel, and my secretary's legs are for shit. But Dolores needed work and before her marriage in the early forties she used to be LBJ's personal secretary, back when he was an unknown congressman from the Great State of Texas. She's a ball-busting, no-holds-barred Democrat with a long memory that has served me well on at least two occasions. Amazing how many sons in positions of power will work hard to keep their fathers' memories from being unscathed. Amazing how many senator fathers have senator sons. And then some.

I work for the Dems now. Scoping out H. Ross Perot isn't as much fun as going after the Kennedys—the little man with big ears doesn't have quite the appetite for parties that Ted has—but it is work that pays well. Lord knows I'll need the money if Hillary's VAT tax goes through.

But I shouldn't complain. I'm an official FOB now, with a photograph behind my desk to prove it. But it's not the picture of me and Clinton that is my prize possession. It's the gift from Beverly—a political cartoon clipped from the Washington *Post*. It's a picture of Socks walking down the street surrounded by cats in suits, obviously Secret Service. The cutline reads: "Socks Goes to Washington." Beverly stuck a photo of my face over one of the security cats with "My Hero!" scrawled on the side. Sappy sure. But someone has to make this city safe—even if it is for a small subset of the population.

Besides, compassion is in these days. Compassion for cats is even better. Ever since the news broke, my phone has been ringing off the hook. I'm the only D.C. detective to get his photo in *People* magazine—right next to a picture of Bob, the Weather Cat, of course. But who's complaining? The cat's the one wearing the ugly yellow rain slicker.

Billie Sue Mosiman's Edgar nomination a few years ago finally brought her a modicum of the recognition she deserves. She is a genuine original, both in voice and spirit. The following story is a good introduction to Billie Sue's world, quietly unsettling and profoundly human.

The Lesson
BILLIE SUE MOSIMAN

Jodie was a boy who knew the stakes and how to win the game. He thought himself invincible, that nothing could ever stop him.

He knew the house and the old couple well before he ever approached the rusty screen door. He knew their routines, their meal and bed times. He knew the old man favored Red Man tobacco and the old woman Brewton snuff. He knew the endearments they used in place of each other's names. He knew they missed their grandchildren who had moved to California.

He knew enough to manipulate them the way he wished.

He tapped on the frame of the door and waited with the appropriate waifish, lost look on his small grubby face.

It was the old woman who came to answer the knock. He stepped back to allow her room to push open the screen. "Now who do we have here?" she asked pleasantly.

He did not like the bitter, snuffy smell of her, but that did not show on his face. He grinned winningly and glanced down at his feet as if in embarrassment. "I'm Jodie Weavers," he said.

"Well, hello, Jodie Weavers. Are you lost?"

He knew she would ask that. He shook his head so that his long sandy bangs flipped around his high forehead. "Just traveling through, ma'am. I was wondering if I could do some chores for you, maybe spend the night . . ."

"Traveling through!" The old woman turned in the shadowy doorway and called to her husband. " 'Miah! There's a boy here."

Jodie waited. Shuffled his feet in a way that indicated he was somewhat

301

afraid of coming harsh judgment. The old woman pulled him to her side, and he found his right cheek smothered against her big, floppy old woman's breast. He fought the urge to jerk away. He held his breath and counted to ten.

Jeremiah Davis came through the cool interior shadows of the hallway. "What's this?" he asked.

"This boy says he's traveling through. Wants to stay the night. Doesn't that beat all? It's children on the roads this year."

This year was 1930. Surely they had seen children come by the old farmhouse before, Jodie thought. The old woman was pretending to be shocked for his benefit.

"Then bring him inside," Jeremiah said. "Here, boy, let me take your bag." He reached for Jodie's dirty torn-sheet baggage, but Jodie pulled it back before the old man's gnarled hand could touch it.

"No, that's okay, it's not heavy. Just a couple changes of clothes I got."

The old woman ushered him indoors and guided him down the hall behind Jeremiah to a back room that Jodie knew would be the big open aromatic kitchen. His mouth salivated so much he had to swallow twice. He hadn't eaten for hours and hours.

"It's a shame about children put out on their own. You can't be . . . more'n ten!" The old woman scrutinized his thin arms and legs. She brushed the unkempt bangs from his forehead.

Motherly. He let her touch him though he wondered briefly if he was going to be able to stand all this pawing. Well, he'd just have to. To get what he wanted, he always had to play the silly games. Pretend he was a little innocent boy beset by hunger (he was), a poor child in need of care (he was not).

"I'm nearly eleven," he said quietly. And shuffled his feet again, licked his lips while glancing at the plate of biscuits on the wide bleached oak table.

"Here, sit down, let me feed you. Bet you haven't had a square meal in days."

"No, ma'am, I ain't eaten regular in some time."

Jeremiah took a chair and offered one to the boy. "Where you hail from? I don't recognize you from 'round here."

"I'm from Kentucky." Jodie pulled the tin plate the old woman set before him closer to his chest. He watched her pour a stream of golden maple sugar syrup into it. Syrup! He hadn't had sweets in ever so long. It might be all right here for more than a day or two. If only *she* didn't smell like old spit and *he* didn't ask too many questions.

"Why look at him eat, 'Miah. Makes my heart squeeze shut to see children hungry in this country. It just ain't right, going to bed without a bite to eat."

"Kentucky?" Jeremiah asked. "That's a far piece for a boy your age to come from. Where's your folks? They still up there?"

"Dead. Died."

The old woman clutched the material of her flour-sack dress at the neckline.

"Oh, that's just awful," she said, " 'Miah, ain't that just awful? An orphan he is, poor little thing."

"Terrible," Jeremiah agreed. "How'd it happen?"

Questions. Couldn't even let him eat, so many questions. Damn ole rednecks. "Milk fever," he mumbled, mouth full. He swallowed noisily. "I don't drink milk. I didn't get sick."

The old couple exchanged sad looks. "You poor thing," the old woman said. "All alone in the cold world."

Jodie endured the rest of the afternoon during which the old woman prattled her pity and the old man went to work filling a galvanized tub with water heated on the wood cook stove for his bath.

That night bathed, fed, dressed in a pair of Jeremiah's overly large cotton longjohns, Jodie sat at the window of the bedroom he had been given and looked out at the rising moon. He hated Louisiana. It was the end of the earth in his opinion. Too flat down here and too swampy and too Suffering Jesus sultry hot even at night.

He'd have to finish off the old couple in a few days. He needed to leave this state and head west to Texas. He had heard East Texas was a lot like Kentucky. Hilly, forested, cool. And there he'd find more old people, that's for sure. In this day of families breaking apart, moving on to find work, the elderly were left behind to hold down the homesteads. Easy pickings. Unsuspecting, eager to help out a young boy on his own. In the cold world . . . the cold, cold, world.

They thought they were adopting him. He let them think it and played to their lonely passions. He even wangled a new set of overalls from the country store ten miles distant and the old woman took a scissors to his hair.

While Jodie made himself useful—hauling water, fetching wood, rising early to start the stove fire—he found time to scout the old couple's bedroom when they were otherwise occupied. He found a real gold pocket watch Jeremiah had received on retirement from the railroad. He found an opal and pearl brooch the old lady told him she wore on her wedding day oh so long ago. He also found the hoard. They always hoarded, these backwoods types. It was never a fortune, but plenty enough to get him to where he wanted to go. Six silver dollars and assorted change. Plenty.

Full as a hound tick, rested from his travels, Jodie prepared to move on. He had the stolen treasures securely tied in his sheet and satchel. The old woman had cooked a yard turkey and made a pile of cornbread dressing. This ensured he would have food for the trip.

He had used a butcher knife on his parents. But he liked variety. He thought he needed practice with different weapons in order to be ready for anything. Some of the old folks he'd run up against were tough as rawhide. The last old geezer, a widower and a mean, hateful, suspicious viper at that, took the shotgun right out of his hands, and him with a hole big enough to wade through gaping and dripping from his belly. You just couldn't depend on things going right. If Jodie had learned anything, that was it. Things could mess up in a hurry and you had to think quick to save your skin. He'd had to club the widower across the head with a stick of pine kindling. Messy business.

"My, but you're looking better," the old woman crooned the morning of her death. She tousled his hair. He winced and drew back.

"What's wrong?" she asked. "Didn't you sleep good?"

Dumb old biddy. What did sleeping well have to do with disliking her touch? Oh, the old could be so stupid. Jumped to conclusions. But if they didn't, he'd never have been able to cross the country and be sure of safe havens and traveling money along the way. Yet he was losing patience with all these unexpected caresses. It put the chill on his back and made him shiver down near the bone. Just because he was small, did that give them permission to constantly maul him? What would they do if he grabbed them and hugged them in a bear hug, wouldn't let them go? Bet they wouldn't like it. Nosirree.

"It's nothing," he said. "Can I have eggs for breakfast?" She usually served up gummy oatmeal. Their chickens had not been producing much since they had to cut back on buying laying mash.

"Sure you can," she said. "You want them fried or scrambled?"

"Scrambled," he said. When her back was turned he pulled the scythe he'd hidden behind the kitchen wood pile and struck her a killing blow.

Jodie knew how to put power behind his skinny arms. One day he figured he'd have muscles, he thought, standing over the prone woman. Huge, rippling forearms strong enough to wield a bale of hay on his own. Or a wood axe. One or the other.

She sighed where she lay upon the cracked linoleum floor. Her eyelids fluttered at him. Her wrinkled lips tried to form words, but all that came from them was a brown Brewton snuff spittle to mix with the pooling blood. What a disgusting sight she was. How he wanted to stomp in her face right there, wipe that look off forever.

Jodie watched the life fade from her watery blue eyes before he went to the stove and removed the black iron skillet from the burner. Didn't want to start a fire. Not just yet.

He ate a biscuit stuffed with sausage on the way to the barn where Jeremiah sat upon a turned over bucket milking the cow.

"Hey there," Jeremiah called. "Come to learn how to milk? I can teach you if you want. Only take a few minutes."

A chaw of Red Man bulged his cheek and made his speech slurred.

"I just come to watch," Jodie said.

"Had your breakfast?"

"Have now." Jodie raised what was left of the sausage biscuit to show the old man.

He checked the milk bucket and saw the milking was almost done, the foamy white liquid more than halfway filling the container. The cow snorted, flicked her snake-like tail at flies.

Through the open barn doors buttery yellow morning light spilled onto the hay-strewn earth. Soon it would be so hot outdoors the ground would crack like peanut brittle and the cow, let out to graze, would instead slump down in the shade of a chinaberry tree and chew her cud. Hades couldn't hope for worse temperatures come summer noon in Louisiana.

"How do you like it here?" Jeremiah asked, squinting back over his shoulder at the quietly-standing boy. "You happy with us?"

He senses something wrong, Jodie concluded. He's asking his questions again. Nosy bastard. Be glad to be rid of *him*.

"Aw, I like it all right." He moved toward the stacked hay in the corner in an aimless, just-messing-around way. The pitchfork was speared into a bale, its blond handle worn smooth and dark from a thousand sweaty palmings.

He jerked the pitchfork free and hefted it in his hand like someone ready to throw it a few yards to see if it would stick in the dry ground. Just aimless play. That's what the old geezer would think he was doing. Boys fooled around. You couldn't stop boys from being boys, all the old people knew that.

"Say your folks died of the milk fever?"

"Uh huh. Got real sick. Doctor couldn't help."

"And you didn't have any brothers or sisters, huh?" Jeremiah paused and flexed his fingers before tackling the heifer's teats again. He had paid no attention to the boy's play with the pitchfork.

"Nope. Was just me."

"And you never liked to drink milk, did you?"

The pinging of streams of milk hitting the side of the bucket was the only sound in the barn.

"Never did like milk." Jodie moved across the barn floor silent as a wraith. He now stood near enough Jeremiah to stab him in the back, but he hesitated bringing the pitchfork up into the air above his shoulder. He wanted to hear these particular questions. Something about the direction they were taking intrigued him ungodly. Just what was it the old man was getting at?

"Must have changed your mind. About milk, that is," Jeremiah said, rising from his sitting position, wiping his hands on his denims. He turned to stare sternly at Jodie, his gaze taking in the pitchfork before going back to the boy's sturdy, emotionless face.

"Why's that?"

" 'Cause I been noticing the milk jug's always half empty every morning. Now that must mean you been snitching a couple glasses every night unless we got rats and they've taken a liking to milk I ain't never heard of before."

Jeremiah stepped closer to the boy. He was scowling. He spit tobacco juice to the side, but his stony gaze never left Jodie.

"I don't reckon you hate milk all that much. I don't reckon you *ever* hated milk, by my lights. I don't even reckon your folks up and died of the milk fever like you said."

"Did too." Damn him to hell! He knew he should have stayed out of the kitchen at nights, but days on the road made him take risks when it came to food. He never seemed to get enough. And he couldn't drink milk in front of them, not after the lies he'd told.

Jeremiah shook his great gray shaggy head. "I don't think so, boy. I think maybe there's another story you got to tell, now ain't that right? One that might not be good to hear. Ain't that right?" He spit again and moved even closer.

Jodie could not throw the pitchfork now. He hadn't the room to maneuver. It was all going bad, going sour and deadly as pork on a blistering day.

Suddenly Jeremiah clamped his big hand around the handle of the pitchfork and took it from Jodie. "Let's go inside and let's talk about where you come from, Jodie Weavers. And where you're going."

As Jodie walked ahead of the sharp tines of the pitchfork poking him in his bony young back, he wondered how in the world it had all come tumbling down this way. He wondered why he'd thought this old farmer stupid. He wondered if he'd never make it to East Texas.

Somehow he thought not, at least in the foreseeable future. Unlike the widower, Jeremiah, upon seeing his dead wife, would not be disposed to let her killer make even the slightest move.

Sweet suffering Jesus. Going to prison down south in Louisiana had to be just about the worst fate Jodie might ever have envisioned.

It was so hot here. Swampy. Flat.

Some of the people were too smart to die when the time came. He never should have hesitated in the barn. He'd let his curiosity get the best of his good sense.

He ever got free, he'd remember that. Next time—and there'd be one since he was just a little kid. They couldn't keep him locked up forever. And next time . . . next time he'd take them out first opportunity presented itself. He had learned his lesson.

No hesitation. No mercy.

By the time the sheriff arrived Jodie was calm and wearing his most contrite face. He was almost looking forward to the coming punishment.

At the door when the law had him by the neck collar to lead him to the car, Jodie turned and grabbed Jeremiah's old shaking hand. "Thank you, sir. Thank you so much for your hospitality."

The last thing he saw was the old man rubbing the palm of his hand along his overalls as if he'd just stuck his hand into a pile of horse manure.

The sheriff said, "Don't you be laughing, boy. You in a peck of trouble."

Jodie held in the laughter until it felt like a balloon was blowing up his chest. When he let it out as weeping and the sheriff turned in his seat to look over at him, he thought he saw a ghost of sympathy cross the swarthy country face.

The balloon deflated, the tears stopped, and all the way to town Jodie ingratiated himself to his captor.

Every day he was learning more of the fine points of winning the game. Nothing was ever going to stop him.

Jeremiah Healy has put his own stamp on the private-eye sub-genre, no easy task given the number of private-eye books that have been published in the last fifteen years. He writes in an easy-going, laconic style that conceals all the hard work that goes into stories this polished and true.

Spin-a-rama
JEREMIAH HEALY

The campaign headquarters for Riley Concannon was a storefront on the main street of the district's largest town. There were catchy posters taped in the windows and pleated buntings draped over them, the buntings flapping a little in the October breeze. I parked my old Honda Prelude at the curb and walked toward the door.

Inside the storefront, the colors red, white, and blue figured heavily in the decor. Volunteers staffed telephones that seemed hastily installed, the cables tied in bunches with those toothy plastic things that come with garbage bags. There were maps on the wall and coffee stains on the floor and card tables buckling under the weight of issue flyers that just had to be printed on recycled paper. The volunteers tended toward the young, with a sprinkling of cheery retired folks, mostly females.

A spry woman in her seventies bounded up from behind a counter where she'd been stuffing envelopes. The nametag over her left breast read "Doris" in curly, Palmer-style handwriting.

She said, "Can I help you?"

"I'm here to see Riley Concannon."

"Can I tell him your name?"

"Better not."

Doris looked at me, then decided against asking her next question. "One minute, please."

She walked toward the back of the space, touching the cardigan sleeve of a burly old gent in a Boston Bruins cap who was using a sponge to wet and seal envelopes. Doris leaned down and probably whispered something to him, because he nodded grimly and stopped with the envelopes and watched me until she reappeared.

The woman with Doris was about forty, five five and a medium build under a gray suit. She had sharp features and a wary smile. Her reddish hair was thick and ripply, pulled back behind her head with the sides bowing a little as they went past her ears.

The smile stayed wary as she thanked Doris and came up to me alone. In a low voice, she said, "Can I help you?"

"Riley Concannon called and asked me to come here."

The smile widened, but the voice stayed low. "John Francis Cuddy?"

I nodded.

Her hand came up to shake mine brusquely. "Nona Shapiro. I'm Riley's campaign manager. We appreciate your discretion."

"We won't look discreet much longer out here in the boiler room."

Her turn to nod.

As we moved toward the back of the building, I could feel the eyes of Doris and her burly friend on me, but there wasn't much I could do about it. Shapiro took me down a corridor and pulled open an old six-paneled door that led to an office best described as cluttered. A broad-shouldered man about my age rose from behind a desk cramped into the corner. He had a buy-you-a-drink? grin and a nose to go with it, the cartilage broken honestly, the capillaries probably a little less so. His hair was sandy and professionally styled, the tie tugged down and the shirtsleeves rolled up eight inches before the elbow. He stayed behind the desk, so I can't say much about his trousers.

The hand extended itself on its own before he said, "Riley Concannon."

The firm shake of a man who wishes he could spend more time with you. "Mr. Concannon, John Cuddy."

"I don't know much about how the private investigator business works, but we really appreciate your coming up on such short notice."

I felt twice as appreciated as I had before. "Only a twenty mile drive, and you sounded pretty urgent on the phone."

Concannon tilted his head, gauging something. "So why don't we cut short the preliminaries?"

"Since I'm on an hourly basis, it might make sense."

The bar grin again. "I like a man who gets down to business. Have a seat. Nona?"

Concannon resettled into his desk chair. Shapiro tapping a visitor's chair for me while taking one to my right.

She said, "What do you know about Riley, Mr. Cuddy?"

I said, "If we're going to call him Riley, you can call me John."

Shapiro didn't move her head to gauge me the way Concannon had. She just bored in with her eyes. "Meaning?"

"Meaning if it's his problem, why doesn't he tell me about it?"

Concannon said, "Nona's just looking out for the candidate, John."

I glanced from her to him. "I don't know anything."

Concannon's face clouded a little. "What?"

"I'm answering her original question. I don't know anything about you."

Shapiro said, "Riley was the best Democratic selectman the town of Beacon Harbor ever had. When the Republican incumbent for the state senate seat from this district decided to step aside to accept a judgeship, our party nominated Riley in a heartbeat to run against the Republican challenger, Thomas Whiting."

Her last sentence sounded practiced, like she'd polished it for a press release. "Isn't Whiting a state rep now?"

Concannon said, "That's right, John. I know him pretty well. Hell, we both live in Beacon Harbor, our kids even go to the same school. He's represented this area for almost six years at the statehouse."

"Sounds like he's got a head start on you."

Shapiro said, "In more ways than one. This district's heavily suburban with some really old money, including Whiting's. It's voted Republican since Lincoln was inaugurated."

"So far your kind of problem doesn't sound like my kind of problem."

Concannon sighed and used a key to open a drawer in his desk. He rummaged under something, then came out with an envelope that was too short to be from a business and too narrow to hold a greeting card.

Shapiro said, "We have to be sure that what we're about to show you goes no farther than this room."

"There's a confidentiality statute in Massachusetts that prevents me from revealing anything to anybody except a judge under the right compulsion. I'm not a lawyer, so I'm not sure what 'the right compulsion' would have to be, but as far as I know, there've been no cases interpreting that."

Concannon fanned himself absently with the envelope. "Thought you said you weren't a lawyer?"

I shifted in my chair. "Look, you want a private investigator, you could have your pick. I happen to know who referred you to me, because that lawyer called me about two minutes before you did this morning. You asked him whether he could recommend me, he told you he could because I kept my mouth shut after a very bad case went sour for him. You can rely on me, or you can rely on the confidentiality statute and somebody else. Your choice."

Concannon said, "Nona?"

She looked at him.

He said, "I'm persuaded."

Shapiro looked back to me. "I am, too. Show it to him."

Concannon flipped the envelope toward my side of the desk as though he were dealing poker. "Read it to yourself, okay? I'm pretty sick of it."

The return address was embossed in brown raised ink. Just three initials, "E.O.P.," with periods after them, but an address of "Olde Marsh Lane," no street number, in Beacon Harbor. I opened the flap and took out a parchment piece of notepaper embossed in the same ink with the full name "Evelyn Otis Poole" at the top. It didn't take long to read the note:

Dear Mr. Concannon,

You may recall our meeting at the Friends of the Library breakfast last month. While I was pleased to be introduced to your son, I am afraid I bear rather disturbing news about him.

Last Wednesday, while shopping in Boston, I was shocked to see your son in the company of a disreputable boy. I observed them for only a few moments, but it was evident that the second boy was what I believe is called a "street hustler," and they entered an alley together off Boylston Street.

Obviously, I did not remain to see them emerge. However, I do feel it my duty to alert you to this appalling situation and provide you the opportunity to correct it, if possible.

Very truly yours,
Evelyn Otis Poole

I reread the letter. The handwriting was crabbed but had a few flourishes that compared to Doris's nametag. Then I folded the notepaper, put it back in the envelope, and returned the package to Concannon. "Well, you have a problem."

He locked the thing in his drawer. "Kevin's the one with the problem."

"Is that your son's name?"

"Yes."

I said, "Being gay isn't the problem. If Kevin's hanging out with the sparrows on lower Boylston, though, he's running one hell of a health risk."

Concannon started to say something, then bit back and shook his head.

Shapiro filled in for him. "You see, John, Tom Whiting is an upstanding, family-values kind of candidate."

Concannon said, "And I'm not?"

She looked at him. "Riley, please?"

He shook his head some more but shut up.

Shapiro came back to me. "If this Poole woman ever approaches Whiting or one of his people with her story, there's no way I can run it through the spin-a-rama."

"The what?"

"The spin-a-rama. You know, put a spin on the story that would sell through to the voters."

I said, "Any chance this is a setup by the other camp?"

"I don't think so. That Friends of the Library event was on the level."

Concannon said, "Family thing, everybody gets to meet the candidates and the spouses and all."

Shapiro seemed to hold her breath, as though she were relieved that's all he had to say on the subject. "After we got her letter, I called Poole on the phone."

I said, "Something like this, you didn't see her personally?"

Shapiro said, "I remembered her from the breakfast. One of the staunch types, the kind who'd send back her eggs if they were a little runny. Besides, I—we weren't sure how seriously to take this."

"And?"

"And Miss Poole—she made a real point of that, by the way, 'Miss,' not 'Miz'—was sure she wasn't mistaken."

I turned to Concannon. "Have you asked your son about it?"

He swallowed hard. "It's not the kind of thing I usually bring up with him, no."

"I meant, maybe there's a reasonable explanation."

Shapiro said, "We've gone through and over this, Riley and I. What we'd like you to do is try to find a reasonable explanation."

"I don't get you."

Concannon said, "We want you to follow Kevin. Not for a week, like spying on him or anything. Just try to figure out whether what Poole says is true."

"And if it is?"

Shapiro cut in. "Then we want a couple of photographs, enough evidence so Riley knows he'd be quitting a lost race instead of dropping out of just a tough one too early."

"Photos? Why not simply take my word for it?"

Concannon's voice cracked with emotion. "Because I want to have something in my pocket if I have to talk to my son about this, John. I want him to know that we—his mother and I—are concerned about his health, both medical and mental. If you find out Poole's right, and Kevin denies it, I want to be able to confront him with some proof without your having to be there. I want to force him to seek help."

"I don't think that's the way to do it."

"It'd be my way, and I'm his father."

Shapiro said, "Will you help us?"

I thought about it. If I passed on the job, somebody else would still do it, maybe somebody who'd try to sell the results both ways. Or somebody who'd tell Concannon, "Hey, no problem," then shake down the kid for as many years as it took him to get out of the house.

I said, "What do you have in mind?"

She glanced to Concannon. "Riley, check me on this. I think all you need to do, John, is follow Kevin this Wednesday."

Concannon said, "Kevin gets out of school at one on Wednesdays."

"Following somebody by car isn't as easy as it looks on TV."

Shapiro shook her head. "No, no. Kevin doesn't drive yet. If he did go to Boston, it would be by train."

I said, "Not many commuters that time of day. I could probably just meet the train at North Station in Boston, pick him out as he left the platform."

Concannon said, "That makes sense."

"You have a picture of him?"

The candidate didn't have to dip into the drawer. He spun a photo toward me. It showed a dozen teenagers posed standing and kneeling under a banner that said "Civics Club." Two of the boys had sandy hair and a hint of Concannon's shoulders, but there was no caption. "Which one is he?"

Concannon said, "Kevin's on the far right. I thought this shot would show you how he looks in relation to other boys his age."

I studied the photo. The boy had an anxious smile, like he was afraid the flash would go off before he was ready. "Can I take this?"

"I'd rather you didn't. I had to borrow it from a teacher at Kevin's school."

Okay. I returned it to him. "When do you want to hear back from me?"

Shapiro said, "Yesterday."

"Hey, John Cuddy! I thought you'd be coming up last summer."

"For the beach, you mean?"

"Yeah, I told you, Beacon Harbor's got the nicest sand on the north shore, and the parking's still just five bucks, even—"

"On the weekends. I remember, sergeant."

"You remember that, you also got to remember that I don't like the 'sergeant' stuff. I'm outa uniforms to stay. Sit down."

I took the chair next to Joe Patrizzi's desk on the second floor of the police station. There was a nice view of an autumn-dotted hillside out the window. A benny you tended not to get in the city.

Patrizzi slurped some coffee from a mug with DAD IS THE GREATEST baked into the side of it, "So, what can I do you for?"

"Nothing this trip. Just a courtesy call, let you know I'm poking around a little up here."

He ran his tongue around the inside of his mouth. "The killing we had last spring?"

"No, I'm finished with that, far as I know."

"This poking you're doing, you figure it'll draw some blood?"

"Not the way it looks right now."

Patrizzi nodded judiciously. "You do me a favor, huh? Its looks start to change any, you pick up the phone, let me know."

"If I can."

"If. That don't sound too courteous to me, Cuddy."

The narrow macadam skirted the harbor and a rocky bluff before straightening out into a country lane. I finally saw a converted cottage overlooking about five acres of salt marsh. If you can call a sprawling twelve or fifteen rooms a "cottage." That's what the sign on Olde Marsh Lane called it, though. "The Poole Cottage." The only building in sight on Olde Marsh Lane, too. Probably the way Miss Poole wanted it.

I walked up the flagstone path to the weathered-shingle porch and forest-green door, crickets chirping from the meadow grass. Riley Concannon wouldn't be too keen on my seeing his pen pal, but I wanted to get a look at her from a credibility standpoint before I cooled my heels in a train station for an hour or so on Wednesday.

The woman who answered my knock was pushing sixty and dressed rustically, like an advertisement from L. L. Bean before it got fashionable. Her brown and gray hair was short all around, barely touching her collar in the back. "Yes?"

"Miss Poole?"

"Yes."

"My name's John Francis. I'm investigating the situation you described in a letter to Mr. Concannon."

"Investigating? Oh my word, do come in."

You have money long enough, maybe other people stop trying to take it from you and you grow to trust them. She led me into a comfortable living room with antique furniture so good it probably never would look old. She asked if I'd like tea, and I declined because it was obvious that the woman really wanted to talk with me.

After we sat down, she said, "I was hoping someone would take my note seriously."

"We do, ma'am. But because of the delicacy of the matter, I have to ask you to promise not to reveal anything we discuss to anyone."

"Oh, of course."

"I wonder, can you elaborate on what you said in the letter?"

"Well, yes, at least a bit. I'd taken the ten oh-four into Boston to do some shopping. I cabbed from North Station to Copley Place, but it's just so tourist-oriented, I tend never to stay for very long."

"I agree completely."

"I visited Lord & Taylor's as well, and then had an exquisite lunch at DuBarry's on Newbury. There are so few good French restaurants left to us, given all that yuppie nonsense."

"Do you recall when you finished lunch?"

"Oh, I had no need to look at my watch, but I went from there to Shreve,

Crump & Low on Boylston. One must always stop at Shreve's, even with the financial . . . embarrassments of their recent past.''

"When did you see Mr. Concannon's son?"

"Coming out of Shreve's. I distinctly remember looking at my watch, because I wanted to be sure to make the two forty-two from North Station. Any later than that, and it becomes nearly impossible to obtain a decent seat for reading.''

"And what time was it?"

"What . . .? Oh, when I looked at my watch? Two twenty-three exactly. I saw the Concannon boy halfway up the block. He approached this . . . urchin, I suppose would be the polite phrase, though I was a bit more direct in my note. I didn't see any money change hands, but from the way the other boy was dressed, it was quite obvious what the purpose of the transaction was.''

"You're sure it was Kevin?"

"Kevin? Is that his name? I met him only the once at the Friend's breakfast, but I'm certain it was he.''

"Miss Poole, you said you were half a block away.''

"Yes, but he is quite distinctive, you know.''

"Distinctive?"

"Yes. His . . . tic I suppose you might call it. Or perhaps it's more like a . . . flinch?''

Poole flicked her head to the right, mimicking a punch-drunk boxer. I thought about Kevin Concannon's anxious smile for the photographer, the boy maybe concerned about moving involuntarily at the wrong moment.

I said, "Anything else?"

"Well, I watched them walk toward me and around the block to an alley. One might say a 'convenient' alley. Obviously, I did not remain any longer than that.''

"Well, I appreciate your time, Miss Poole.''

"I just do hope your Mr. Concannon does the responsible thing.''

"I'm sorry?"

"Withdraw from the race before a scandal like this smears him forever.''

The view from her hillside isn't like the ones Patrizzi and Poole enjoy. There's only the green of the lawn gone brownish from night frosts and the engine noises from commercial boats coming into Boston Harbor. The roses I laid diagonally to her headstone riffled in the breeze off the water.

Roses. What's the occasion?

"A case, Beth. One I feel a little guilty taking.''

Why?

I explained it to her.

Sad that the father can't talk outright to his son.

Beth and I had never had any kids. Never wanted them, really, but I know what she meant. "Well, maybe this'll be a step in the right direction."

I hope so, but don't let it get you down if it's not.

As I nodded, the wind came up a tad stronger, forcing me to realign the flowers so the blooms wouldn't be blown off the stems.

North Station is a quirky kind of place. It's located in the rear end of Boston Garden, where Orr used to skate and Bird used to shoot. On a game night, it's a zoo, fourteen thousand people jamming up the ramps to find their seats. But on a Wednesday afternoon in October, the station is a quiet place of suburban shoppers waiting for irregular trains, homeless people waiting to be rousted, and tourists from countries where train travel is a more accepted way of sight-seeing.

Sitting on a scarred wooden bench, I checked the schedule in my right hand. The train that left Boston Harbor half an hour after Kevin Concannon got out of school would be arriving in about ten minutes. I was decked out in a ski sweater, khaki slacks, and running shoes as walking shoes. I also had a 35-millimeter camera, an unfolded map of Boston, and the stupidest hat I could find. The hat was a baseball cap, the crown over its bill sporting a cartoon lobster wearing a bib. Since I'd have to have a camera around my neck, I decided the cap would help me blend in as a tourist because nobody in Boston has ever seen anyone from Boston with a lobster-anything on them.

The Beacon Harbor train arrived, and I spotted Kevin Concannon right away. He had a gangly, rolling gait, and the head flicked to the right erratically just the way Miss Poole had demonstrated. He wore pressed wool trousers and a lamb's wool sweater himself, no hat stupid or otherwise.

Concannon passed my bench. I waited ten strides, then rose and started after him. Outside the station, he crossed Causeway Street and hopped a Green Line trolley like he'd done it all his life.

I got on the next car and edged my way to the front of it, watching Kevin through the windshield as both trolleys jounced up and down on the rails. He stayed on past Park Street station, not getting off until Arlington. I followed him up the stairs to the first block of Boylston Street.

It didn't take long.

Concannon made eye contact with a scraggly kid who might have been twenty trying very hard to look sixteen. He wore a bandanna around his neck and tight hiking shorts on a day way too cold for them. The kid smiled at Kevin, talked and joshed a little with him, then inclined his head toward the corner. I snapped off three shots of the boys before they turned and began walking. I got to the head of the alley just as they were choosing a dumpster to go behind. I took two more shots and kept walking past the alley.

Twenty minutes later the kid with the bandanna came out, Concannon trailing him by a minute. Kevin walked back to Boylston, then crossed it, taking an outside table at Au Bon Pain and having a pastry and a Styrofoam cup of something that steamed into the fall air.

After about fifteen minutes, a boy walking past the tables lingered a little. This one wore a turquoise body shirt and studded black jeans over cowboy boots, doing his lingering to hitch up one of the boots. Concannon left his table and joined him, the two of them making their way to the same alley. I took basically the same establishing shots again.

This time it was twenty-five minutes, but Kevin came out first, checking his watch and starting to hoof it a little. He flagged a cab, and the taxi took off down Boylston, making the turn at Charles toward North Station and, I guessed, home.

On Thursday morning, Riley Concannon and Nona Shapiro gave me the impression I was their first priority conference of the day. I hoped so.

I laid the manila envelope on the cluttered desk. Concannon's hands twitched, like they didn't really want to open it.

Shapiro said, "Bad?"

"About what Miss Poole described. Two different hustlers within the span of an hour."

Concannon said, "Jesus, Mary, and Joseph."

Shapiro's eyes bored into me. "You can trust the place that developed these?"

"Completely."

She nodded. "Look, John, I know this hasn't been easy for you, either. I thank you for making it a little easier for us."

"Can I see you outside for a minute?"

Shapiro glanced over at Concannon, who was still just staring at the manila envelope. "Okay, but just a minute."

The corridor beyond the six-paneled door was empty, the volunteers, even Doris, not yet on the job. Shapiro closed the door gently behind her. "If it's the money—"

"What we agreed to is fine. And will be fine. This isn't a shakedown, just a suggestion."

"What is it?"

"Before Riley pulls the plug on the campaign, be sure he talks to Kevin first."

"That's kind of his business as the boy's parent, don't you think?"

"I think that if Kevin hears the plug got pulled before he and Riley work things out, a lot more'll be lost than a seat in the Massachusetts senate."

Shapiro pursed her lips. "Thank you, John. Thank you for caring."

I'm not particularly political, but I found myself scanning the Metro section of the *Globe* each day, watching to see what would happen to Concannon's campaign. It took almost a week till the following Monday, but the story made the front page. I felt my stomach turning as I read the headline.

It said, "CANDIDATE WITHDRAWS IN SHOCK OVER DEATH OF SON." The article reported that the boy fell from a rocky promontory near Olde Marsh Lane in Beacon Harbor. I pictured it from my visit to Miss Poole's cottage. The last paragraph told me that the candidate was withdrawing from the race to mourn the loss, the family expected to be in seclusion for several days.

That much was understandable. The part that wasn't included the photographs and the captions underneath them.

One photo showed a stern-looking man with cotton balls of gray gracing his temples. The caption read, "Thomas Whiting." The other shot showed the boy I'd followed and photographed. It wasn't the yearbook club display, but there was no mistaking the anxious smile.

The caption under him read, "David Whiting."

I tried out my voice to make sure it was working, then picked up the telephone.

"Police, Patrizzi."

"This is John Cuddy calling."

"Cuddy! Look, ordinarily I'd be happy to kibitz a while, but we had kind of a tragedy here yesterday, you know what I'm saying?"

"I read about it. The politician's son?"

"Yeah."

"Tough thing."

"Maybe tougher than you think."

"How do you mean?"

"Well, I don't know if it's ever gonna come out, but it does, you didn't hear it from me first, right?"

"Right."

"Okay." Patrizzi lowered his voice a little. "We got a maybe eyewitness."

"A 'maybe' eyewitness?"

"Yeah. Woman driving her kid to the sitter's, using that part of the harbor road that winds around the bluff. She says she only got a little glimpse like of the Whiting boy, but she's pretty sure he didn't fall."

"No?"

"God's truth. She says he jumped."

"Miss Poole?"

"Yes?"

"Miss Poole, this is John Francis calling. We spoke last week at your cottage."

"Oh my word, yes. I must say, I feel just terrible about this."

"We all do."

"I just hope my confusing which boy was which at the Friends breakfast didn't have anything to do with . . . well, to do with what happened."

"I'm sure it didn't, Miss Poole."

"Well, I'm certainly relieved to hear that."

"I do have a question I forgot to ask you, though."

"Another question?"

"Yes. Just to round out my report."

"What is it?"

I told her, and she told me.

I hung back at campaign headquarters, catching the tail end of the press conference with a couple of dozen rubberneckers packed just inside the door. The television kliegs made everything seem hot and close, Riley Concannon in what I took to be his trademark tie-tugged-down, sleeves-rolled-up posture behind the impromptu podium, Nona Shapiro just out of camera range on the right, surveying the crowd, not noticing me. Doris and her burly friend stood respectfully in a klatch of volunteers on the other side of the podium. The candidate managed to twist the last question into seeming to fit the perfect, sound-bite answer he gave that had everybody in the room nodding.

After Concannon and Shapiro repaired to the rear corridor, I waited until the camera crews had broken down and the print reporters had rewound and listened to their audio-tapes. Then I sidled through the waning crowd without Doris or her friend's seeing me.

When I got to the six-paneled door, I didn't bother knocking. Shapiro and Concannon were just breaking a hug in front of his desk. Not passionate, just the sort of spontaneity you jump to when the home team comes from behind to score the winning touchdown.

I said, "A little early to be celebrating, don't you think?"

Shapiro recovered while Concannon's mouth was still open. "John. I was hoping you'd be by."

"I doubt it, Nona, I really do."

Concannon started to say something, but Shapiro put her palm on his chest, and he stopped.

I said, "Good advice, Nona. Hear what I've got first, right?"

Shapiro said, "Would you like to sit down?"

"Thanks, no. I'm not sure I trust even the furniture in this room."

Concannon said, "Now just a—"

"Can it, you sanctimonious son of a bitch. You get me up here, show me Miss Poole's letter and that club photo—"

Shapiro rode over me. "We realized what happened there, John. You see, as you were looking at it, Riley said Kevin was the boy on the far right, but he was thinking *his*—Riley's—right, not yours."

"Nice try, but I'm afraid it just doesn't wash."

Concannon said, "It was an understandable mistake. I was upset, concerned about Kevin."

"When you first got Poole's letter, sure. But after Nona here made her ever-so-obtuse phone call to the woman, you realized exactly what had fallen into your lap."

Shapiro said, "I don't know what you're—"

"On the telephone, Nona. Miss Poole tells me that she mentioned to you about 'Kevin's' tic or flinch or whatever, the poor Whiting boy had."

Concannon said, "You weren't supposed to see Poole. We told you—"

"So after that call, Riley, you and Nona knew it was Whiting's son Miss Poole saw in Boston, and you had to figure just what to do with it. Only it had to be obtuse, like Nona's phone call. A setup that preserved deniability, which is what you're doing now. That's where I came in. Right, Nona?"

Shapiro crossed her arms and rested her rump on the desk. "It's your pipedream, John. You tell it."

"More than a pipedream, Nona. You got me to acknowledge the confidentiality statute to you, keeping me from going to anybody after you or Riley or more likely some go-between gave Thomas Whiting those photos I took. How did you phrase it, a 'kindness'? Did your message read something like, 'Tom, despite our respective positions on the issues, the enclosed is something I think any parent deserves to know'?"

Concannon began to speak again, but Shapiro said, "He can't do anything with this, Riley. Don't you see it? That's why he's here ragging us. Cuddy tells anybody about this, about what he even thinks we did, and he loses his license for violating a client's confidence."

I said, "Did you even think about what a candidate who's as four-square on 'family values' as Whiting would do? How he'd broach it to his son? What the kid might do after that?"

Concannon got resolute. "I think we've said all we're going to say, Cuddy."

"Not quite, Riley."

He stared at me, but I addressed Shapiro. "Here's the new program, Nona. I'm so overcome by grief that I can't sleep. I go to Whiting, apologize to him and—"

Shapiro said, "We'd have your license in an—"

"Interrupt me again, and I'll belt you." It seemed to sink in. "I'm guessing the board that registers me would understand. Guilt and grief are strong emotions, Nona. They make you do impulsive things. Like withdraw from the race."

Neither said anything.

I held up my hand, index finger and middle fingers extended. "Your choices are two. Number one, you can withdraw now, I don't talk to anybody, and nobody goes after my license. You don't get sued by Whiting's family and so tarred from the litigation you never run for anything again. Number two, you can stonewall it, have me go to Whiting while you come after my license. His lawyers will hound you, and Whiting or any warm, breathing body the Republicans put up will blow you away at the polls. Number one or number two, but either way, you're out of this race.''

Concannon said, "Time. You have to give us—''

"Tomorrow morning, boyo.''

Shapiro said, "Tomor—''

"Tomorrow morning, Nona. I don't hear a bulletin about Riley pulling out by then, my grief and guilt will compel me to follow number two.''

Concannon said, "But that doesn't give us a chance to—''

"What? Put my new program through the old 'spin-a-rama'? You're right, folks, it doesn't.''

I managed not to slam the six-panel, but I found the optimism in the boiler room so thick I nearly gagged walking to my car.

"The Mood Cuckoo" shows off several of Jonathan Gash's bright and sassy narrative gifts. While he used to be known only in England, his novels have developed a considerable following in America. This is also a Golden Dagger nominee.

The Mood Cuckoo
JONATHAN GASH

Hong King slammed at her, just like the old days. The man next to her on the economy flight had been a pest. All through that interminable Cathay Pacific CX 260 he'd been "amusing" with the garrulous impertinence of the unwelcome. What hotel was she at, why Hong Kong, and not Bangkok. He resorted to whining, he'd been surcharged £54 a day at the Mandarin, some late-booking thing. Helen thought, what was Morris's dictum, Great Britain exports her best menfolk, her worst women?

The slam was the assault of the subtropics. The colony hadn't lost the knack. So many changes! The heat was the same, the traffic, verve, the gain-driven pandemonium the norm. She looked for similarities with the Hong Kong she had known over twenty years before, but that first day she was defeated.

Kai Tak's size! The cleaning amahs appearing from holes in runways to crouch endearingly in the aeroplane's shade. A quarter of a century back, the aerodrome had been a stone strip in the harbour. She didn't recognise a thing. The beautiful travel courier fizzed with energy. Hong Kong girls still had perfect bottoms, first-class honours degrees in sociology, meagre breasts, and were fervent about money. Use the Hang Seng Bank, no commission and a good exchange rate; street money-changers charged over 10 per cent, do avoid them. Helen listened dutifully to the girl's prattle on the coach, managed not to smile when the girl said to the driver in Cantonese, "This lot will be broke by Monday."

322

Quite the worst of it was that Helen had no bearings. It was ridiculous. She wandered from the hotel, sun-blinded. What was Kellet Island doing among traffic? St John's Cathedral once dominated the skyline; she finally found it huddled below impossible flyovers and filled with Filipinos. She had picked a hotel right on the Star Ferry; except she no longer recognised the pier. And goodness, if anybody knew Wanchai, she did, had. But now you *drove underneath* the harbour, a choice of tunnels. You didn't need to catch the bus for Sham Shui Po; you got the Tube.

Everything was gone, altered. Even the Kowloon-Canton Railway clock tower had been moved; it stood forlornly on the waterfront, a posh ectopic wart.

So she almost wept with joy when, walking south from those impossible waterfront high-rises, she heard a familiar whirring. She ran, unmanageable heels and in that heat, blundering among crowds, apologising reflexly in regenerating Cantonese—and beheld a real live tram! Calamitously discoloured instead of sap green and shamefully covered in adverts, but there it undoubtedly was: old, noisy, exasperating, and not altered in the slightest. Deliriously happy, she fumbled in her handbag, buffeted by pedestrians. The hotel's transport pass worked for the tram, she discovered. You still got on at the rear, alighted from the front.

To orientate, she decided to go the dear tram's whole journey, Shau Ki Wan (maddeningly spelled six different ways) to Kennedy Town. She had always loved Hong Kong's trams. This moved as ever like a great indifferent whale among shoals of fish. Standing was still allowed on the top deck, compulsory even. The impossible standing hurled you about, yes, but the tram gave her points of reference and proved she was right to come. Hong Kong was the place.

To a stranger, she thought, getting a seat at Pedder Street, these points might not seem much. To Helen, they were a lifeline. She scored yet more successes on the clamorous swaying run out of Sheung Wan: a wicker tray of fish sun-drying on top of a tram stop; traffic signs obscured by dangles of flattened ducks craped to desiccate. She began to list them, for there might be no time when she confronted Evadne. Of *course* there were differences, bound to be. The absence of junks in the harbour; you simply couldn't lose 20,000, each one galleon-size with families, goats, chickens, garden boxes. And the harbour was clean; where was the floating dross? (She remembered bad oranges bobbing in an oily slick of planks and plastic.) Then she spotted a familiar doorway god by an offal shop, with his red light glowing on his tribute of four piled oranges, so the colony had not altered altogether beneath its tumult.

Irritation, her hallmark of well-being, returned. She became quite optimistic, sure now that she was right to fight here. She concentrated on letting herself be annoyed. It was patently absurd for the tram route to make that absurd loop. Western Market was simply no excuse. And why did the terminus skulk in a side street near a tatty godown? Twenty-five years ago she had written sternly to the Tramways Authority, still nothing done!

She cooled on the return journey, confidently noting more unchanges. Murder was a stupid, pretentious word, so, quickly, make memory use its DEL key with its reverse arrow. Only foreigners resorted to such exaggerations. She thought of her decision, six months old now, instead as "that M word." Teutons, psychotics all, would say "murder" outright; and gormless Gauls; and carping Celts awash in self-pity pretending to love their slithery P and Q languages none of them could speak. Plus Americans, to whom life was code for death as merriment. No, she thought, proudly riding the crowded tram, we English are above it all. Helen knew her attitude was not nationalism; no, it was there like Royal Doulton, to be brought out on the right occasion. English murderers like Jack the Ripper were probably throwbacks, Levantines cloned from an Armada wreck, who knew?

For two days Helen excavated *her* Hong Kong Statue Square, such as it was; the Supreme Court building, minute and chasmed; the old temple in Hollywood Road above Cat Street. It was duty, something she never shirked. The cuckoo survives by conviction; host fledglings die for lack of it. Mood was everything, morale to a warrior. She had trained herself for half a year to be a cuckoo of mood. The intolerable alternative was to suffer yet more defeat at Evadne's hands.

To her astonishment, her language came back with thrilling slickness. She barred for sandals with aplomb. Only occasionally did she falter, stricken, as when explaining her circumstances to a Des Voeux Road shopkeeper, *My husband, who passed away a few months since* ... remembering in the nick of time God there's no relative pronoun in Cantonese. A narrow squeak. Helen resorted to terse unconvolutions and took the stand-up comedian's oath: *Stick to one-liners!*

By the third day her points of reference formed a veritable library. It included surprising minutiae like, the Hakka women road-diggers wore jeans now instead of black cotton trousers; and, my goodness, *thousand* dollar notes? The cadres of exhausted suited youths on the *Shining Star* now dozed clutching portable phones. And so on.

Her mood just right, she rang Evadne.

"No, Evadne, I wouldn't have dreamt of coming a second sooner." Helen was firm. "Jet-lag conversation? I endured enough of those when we lived here, thank you very much!"

"I began to worry!" Evadne told Helen. "Flying tomorrow and everything!" Evadne gave one of her troubled falsetto laughs, supervising supper. Helen wondered how on earth George had managed to stand those inane giggles, seeing the middle-aged bitch on sly holidays year after year, but gave an approving smile of innocence. "I wouldn't have been able to introduce Rol, show you the flat!"

Helen's apologetic smile included Rol Groombridge, Evadne's nearly famous writer. Out of his depth, poor man, what with two women and vexed his tame typist was leaving for a month. "You forget I know these flats, Evadne. Cape Mansions are the only place Hong Kong hasn't obliterated."

Evadne was determined to spot possible gloom, her prophylactic proving her irreplaceable qualities. "Jenny has her foibles, Helen!"

Evadne's Filipino live-out amah (but now you said maid) was bickering in the kitchen with Rol's Hong Kong Cantonese live-in amah Ah Fung (you still said amah). Helen's spirits rose.

"Oh, I'll manage." She bided her time. Then, when Evadne simply had to go and see what was delaying the blueberry tart, Helen started her campaign with quiet humour. "It's the oldest things I *do* manage."

"What things?" Rol said, with the politeness that just avoids silence.

"It sounds silly. I'd quite forgotten it's proper to join others' conversations. I had a high old time on the tram, two old *fokis* about water bills."

Rol showed a flicker of interest. "You speak Cantonese?"

"I did," with a trace of rue. "It's coming back."

It better had be. The revision course at London's School of Oriental Studies cost the earth and was riddled with neurotic linguists. It was the first of her weapons, honed over five hard months. She laughed shyly, better than Evadne's mad cackle any day. "Hong Kong's street puppeteers had the oddest speech mannerisms. Do they still perform near Cleverly Street, sort of Punch and Judy? Such wondrous stories! I loved *The White-Haired Girl.* No wonder that legend dominated all China throughout the sixties. And every *shroff* used the abacus, not now. And *cheong-saams* were everywhere. I haven't seen a one . . . But I'm sorry, you'll know all that. Am I talking too much?"

"No—"

She coursed on, preventing his excuses. Of course he didn't know. You had to have lived in the colony through that murderous Red Guard mayhem, the curfews, bombs, and droughts, the lunatic ideologies of those days. And hadn't Evadne's friendly letters to her explained how her beloved nearly famous writer wanted to create the last great colonial novel—and failed, and failed, and failed?

Helen spoke urbanely of the festivals. Cantonese jokes. "Don't they simply love puns . . . ?" and so on, until it was, "Oh, here comes Evadne!"

Evadne was followed by the two sulky servants. The blueberry thing was fine. Their row was all about cream, Jenny battling to add sugar, Manila style, Ah Fung ginger. Helen mad a timely postponement of using weapon two. She ascertained, by canny eavesdropping, that Jenny, Catholic sureness translated to ethnic disdain, had virtually no Cantonese; Ah Fung's muttered blame proved it. The minute Helen got the chance—Jenny triumphant in the kitchen,

Ah Fung siding away, Evadne doling out her last drop of Macau Portuguese red—she managed with quiet amiability to tell the amah to make less noise. Ah Fung was so astonished hearing correct tonal Cantonese that she almost dropped the plates with a delighted *"Waaaiiii."* Helen instantly knew she had an ally: tenacious, opinionated, and utterly reliable.

Helen decided not to mention her word-processing proficiency until Rol escorted her to the bus. It was a short walk down Mount Davis Road, past his house at Felix Villas. He showed the colonist's relief at not having to drive a guest to some hotel. Helen insisted, no, the bus was fine. Gracious, she'd lived here years!

She could tell Rol was glad the evening was over, meeting Evadne's middle-aged friend. The only reason he'd agreed to come was that he would need access to his manuscripts. Evadne stored them, her air-conditioned flat saving his papers from Hong Kong's corrosive summer moulds. Impossible to air-condition his antique four-storeyed house; those great flappy fans always had been a waste of time, Helen agreed. She bade Evadne a teary goodbye, which was really marvellous of her, seeing the bitch was only leaving to rake in the profits—holiday home at Scratby-on-Sea, time shares in Tuscany, Spain, some trust fund—from two decades of illicit consorting with Helen's George, deceased. Poor George, hoarding Evadne's explicit letters. Thank God it was she, Helen, and not one of the children who had found Evadne's field letters ("Tax: Valued-Added"; "Private: Confidential"). She had brooded a fortnight, then decided to rid herself of Evadne. The traitorous cow had earned sanctions, along with real estate. Fair's fair.

Strolling in the hot humid night with Evadne's nearly-made-it writer, Helen used weapon two.

"I miss the bauhinias, Rol," she said after the have-a-nice-flight goodbyes. "Their roots practically held the mountainside up! And the Wall-Building Ghost—it lived along this stretch—never lifted a finger to prevent landslides." She was speaking humorously.

Rol coughed, hesitant. "You know the colony well."

"Nothing of the kind! I *knew* it *almost* well. Now I'm quite lost. If they rebuild the Gloucester Tea Rooms I might just get my bearings!" She let his unamused chuckle go. "The colony's ladies used to congregate in such splendour! I called them The Ladies Who Tea! Not so ritzy as these Samsonite executives in the five-stars in Central, but immeasurably grander!"

They waited to let a car go by, dragged by its cone of headlights.

"I'm interested in the colony as it was," Rol said. "I've only been here five years."

"Oh, then I'm the one for you!" She masked her elation with a little sadness. "Hardly a commendation, is it, to be valued for reminiscence!" He said nothing. There was enough light to walk by, gateway lamps and the sky glowing with momentary heat. "The apple lady used to come up here. Cantonese, looked a Hakka but was a true Punti, people said. Such a chatterbox! Not at all like these young salesmen you suffer now. They really aren't up to scratch, not even in word-processing."

"You do word-processing?"

Helen knew he wrote longhand, revising on Evadne's laboured typescripts, three months each draft. Evadne's letters to Helen had explained that Rol held strong views against composing on electronics.

"Mhhh? Oh, yes. I do my brother's manuscripts." She didn't, of course. She gave a light non-Evadne laugh, to reassure Rol that her brother was no threat to a nearly-famous writer like himself. "Every Friday, a hundred thousand words, clockwork."

"A week?"

"Edited script, the rate Bernard goes. Four weeks from autograph; takes longer, you see. He's in administration," she invented, safely deleting her non-writing gardener sibling. "Bores for England—was that Muggeridge's phrase?"

"Autograph manuscript typed in a month, edited in a week?"

"Fortnight and four days respectively, *if* you please! Unless I have something else on." She made herself sound dismissive, for an instrument is innocent. She asked with a hint of awe, "Do you compose on a PC?"

"No."

"Oh. Well, if there *is* anything I can do . . ." She tutted as they reached the main road to Kennedy Town. "What a pity they've built that terrible wall! I used to run to this very spot to see the typhoon signal on Green Island. It was quite an occasion, the amahs relaying my shout up to the squatter shacks, scores of thousands of refugees in lean-to shelters up the hillside *nullahs*."

The 5B bus was predictably but annoyingly punctual. She hurriedly squeezed in shy envy at Evadne's superb luck at helping a "real writer." She also got in one or two last zingers: "Oh, do please tell your amah—Ah Fung, isn't it?—that cobra is $63 a catty in Causeway Bay. Scandalous! And deer tails are cheapest in Wanchai. Do you let her cook Cantonese? How rare street opium smokers are now along Hollywood Road! And I've hardly seen a single one in Tsim Sha Tsui; the influence of the Tube, do you suppose . . . ?" Et babblingly cetera.

Then she was on the bus, making the driver grin by betting him a dollar he couldn't take the bus via the Wanchai Star Ferry, making sure Rol heard her oven-ready speech.

Her goodbye smile was as casual as she could make it.

She felt she had got it right, at least made a start on Evadne's downfall. A writer wanting to break the colonial perception barrier needed the local language, indigenous folklore, and docile non-creativity among all others. Hitherto, Rol Groombridge had enjoyed only the last, in Evadne. Helen convincingly offered him all three.

After which Evadne could resume her suicidal gestures, in her cramped little nest in Cape Mansions. Cyclical depressions had been Evadne's specialty until three years ago when she had "found"—her execrable term—Rol, whose literary demands cured her of "all that nonsense". Helen had analysed this before coming to flat-sit for Evadne. The bitch's depressions had possibly been worsened by George's inability to cut free from Helen and marry the cow. George could never have done it; too orthodox, too addicted to his surreptitious holidays, with his breathy plump Chanel-scented mare. The cache of letters had formed a decisional matrix. (Helen had heard the term at night school: computers, Intensive Unit Three-C. She had excelled.)

The 5B dropped her off in Central District, which cartographers still tried to con everybody into calling Victoria. She told the concierge she would be leaving in the morning.

She took up residence in Evadne's flat in Cape Mansions as arranged.

Evadne flew on time, thank goodness, leaving the colony ethnically cleansed. Helen began war instantly. Jenny seemed willing to put up with the situation. A month was not long.

Three days of Helen's vigorous sweetness put paid to the Filipino. It was easy. Evadne's letters to Helen—all camouflage, year after year, cloaking the real correspondence with Hoarder George—had detailed Evadne's perennial bribes that kept the invaluable Jenny from leaving her. Helen picked at Jenny, found fault with everything. She was joyously matter of fact, seeing her off when the crunch came then, satisfying alone, got down to business.

She surveyed the flat, wasting no time gloating. Those Third World Catholics learned guilt well, par for the course, but could never come to grips with hate. That required true English constancy. Another word for propriety, perhaps, once so evident in the Gloucester Tea Rooms? Helen smiled, enjoying the increased elbow room.

Rol's manuscripts were heaped in boxes, neatly labelled and stacked on two shelves in the spare bedroom Helen was to use. So as not to be taken by surprise, she immediately perused several, and was disappointed. Did Rol Groombridge really have the makings of a latter-day Somerset Maugham? Firmly she laid the question aside. Rol's literary excellence was irrelevant. She had to be about her task, which was to keep her image clear in Rol's nearly-famous mind. Humble Mrs. Blake type helper, language fluency, super manuscript; he would summon her before long, as if slavery was an unearned knighthood for which one ought to be grovellingly grateful. The call would come.

Making breakfast, Helen found she was actually enjoying herself. She admired the lovely view over the Lamma Channel almost as much as she admired herself. As reward, she rearranged all the furniture, and got rid of two of Evadne's pictures. (One drained all possible color from the walls, the other looked a nasty spillage.) The curtains were eminently swappable. One pair had to go.

For two days more she made satisfying judgments of this kind. Then she went across to ask Ah Fung's help in making a Chiu Chow dish. She reduced the amah to helpless laughter at her ineptitude, Swatow fried chicken with cheunjew sauce. With humility, she deferred to the amah's bullying instruction and left a large deposit of gossip about Visit-Missie's culinary mistakes and exploration of the island. She knew Ah Fung would recount them to Rol in her limited English. He would—should—be impressed by Helen's search for old villages and departed people. She had included remembered disasters—mudslides, droughts, riots, famous financial collapses, typhoons, scandals, folklore. Of course, back home she had sweated blood over her old diaries, phoned half-forgotten acquaintances on the thinnest pretexts, really slogged.

Watching the sun set—you could just see it going down over the Pearl River if you stretched—she felt gratified. If she had Rol's ambitions right, he would find her irresistible. Just across the road, for God's sake, the "research" a writer craved. She would seem a window on the colony's past, his chance. He *must* take it.

He reviewed books, examined local school Eng. Lit., taught part-time in a couple of drossy academies. She had delved, was confident nothing about him would take her by surprise. The two newspapers—*South China Morning Post*, the old *Standard*—advertised jobs she could have walked into. If nothing came of this before Evadne got back from cashing in on George's death, well it might be necessary to think again.

The phone rang. It was Rol inviting her to supper: would tomorrow be all right? nothing special, seeing she was on her own.

Helen said diffidently, "Why, how kind! Are you sure? I don't want to interrupt . . ." Effortless, in how many days?

From there, she found it surprisingly hard going. Ah Fung was as valuable as Helen had predicted. Rol himself proved the problem. She wondered if she had overdone it, that first supper, inserting her gems to quite good effect, she thought. It came to her that she had not fathomed the creative writer's paranoia.

She changed her tactic when, on guard, Rol said the language was beyond him. He had tried.

"I don't know anyone who hasn't tried and given up." It was said in self-defence. "Those tones finish you."

"I was just lucky," Helen apologised quickly, shaking her hair, done that very day at the New Scholar hairdresser in Bonham Road, still there, like Government House. "Some quirk in me caught the Cantonese tonality. Two hard years. Then it became a hobby. I'm so uncreative," she said, paper-trailing for him like mad. God, what a *dawdler*. "Little oddities, like one syllable having several meanings, according to the pitch. And the use of opposite meanings! Yesterday I used the original word for tongue instead of a mutated verb!" She laughed, fanning herself in mock relief.

He watched her warily, impressed but not following. She hoped her altered course didn't show and went on, "I've kept it up, bits at a time. But you'd think I'd have found some way to use it, over two decades. Except it's going to be obsolete in what, three years and China takes Hong Kong back? Everybody'll have to speak Mandarin, all that *shirbu-shir* business. Ugh!" She shivered, smiled. "Then I *shall* be an anachronism."

"There will be a resurgence of interest. As now for the fifties."

"Will there?" she asked, being bovine.

"Literature goes in cycles," he pronounced. Ah Fung flopped in with the sweet millet soup, finish of her grand little meal. Any moment now she'd bring out an orange in a brown paper bag for Missie to take home, the traditional one for the road.

"Does it?" Helen asked, round of eye.

"It seems to." He nodded pontifically, shadows whipping across his face in synchrony with the beating fan. "There are various theories, none successful."

"Really?" She was humble, intent.

He began to expound, very much as she supposed he must to students in his seminars along Caine Road, Wednesdays. She listened, very adoration of the magus. As she left that evening (bagged orange at the door, Ah Fung laughing making the presentation) Rol cleared his throat and made the concession she needed.

"Look, Helen. If you really are at a loose end, you could do me a couple of pages . . ."

Helen gasped in awe, delight, amazement, sheer grovelling exultation at being so favoured. She cried out that her luck was in and that she hoped she was up to his standards . . .

That night she did not sleep. Her excitement at landing him was less than she'd expected, for Rol the nearly-made-it creative writer was a dud. He would never make it in a million years. The pieces she'd read were derivatively mundane. She made tea about three o'clock and looked out at the sheen of the South China Sea, and the ugly coal-fired power station some lunatic planners had built near Yung Shue Wan to mar paradise.

Rol could write for ever, he'd be ninth-rate. As somebody famous once said, "Writing? That's *typing*." Rol had the academic's disease of yardage and replication. Helen had assembled a file of writers' Ten Commandments, Robert McKee to Mario Puzo, and believed not a single line.

By dawn, she realised Evadne would now be Home and taking possession of the Scratby pavilion, the time share properties, milking George's probate. She seethed, deliberately broke one of Evadne's best cups, saying "Whoops!" as she flung the saucer after it. She swept up and binned the fragments with relish.

She reported for duty on time, collected Rol's two chapters, not mere pages, and whacked them off on her PC, working through the next day. It was a brilliant job, a tabulated list of spellings, flagged stickers to show where she queried his accuracy—the colony's folklore, speech idioms. She was exhausted, but chattering brightly with Ah Fung about weird Fukienese sauces when Rol returned home. She made a breathlessly deferential exit.

He rang, casual, about eight o'clock, donated airy thanks and asked her over for a drink. She did her giddy are-you-sure act, and sprinted across before he changed his mind. Seen as human endeavour, of course, she was throwing good time after bad. But seen as part of the Destroy-Evadne campaign it was loading the guns.

The evening was dire. Rol started worriedly over his story word by weary word. Had Helen been a man she'd have called Rol's masterpiece utter crap, but convent schooling had been convent schooling in her day and she had to live with it. His balderdash concerned a prim Hong Kong Cantonese girl dragged into a Customs fraud and heading for perdition possibly by Chapter Seven. Helen pretended to be enthralled by Rol's imagination, ecstatic at his grasp of "Hong Kong's inner self." His book, she guessed tiredly as ten o'clock chimed from his copy-Swiss hall clock (Haiphong Road, $40 HK), would be some recycled metaphor for the demise of colonial life in a changing new world order, if you please.

"Tremendous!" she exclaimed when Rol modestly outlined exactly that about half-eleven. "I want to know what happens! Does she survive . . . ?"

Released at one a.m., she went back to Evadne's flat and to bed, knowing that soon she would be indispensable, and Evadne superfluous. Tit for tat, really, was her goodnight thought, for hadn't that sow displeased me, George's wife? The fact is, you can *not* be a half-hearted cuckoo. You had not merely to supplant but throw out the enemy fledgling to certain death. Evadne's long history of teetering on the edge of depression, from which entering Rol's service had clearly rescued her, would provide the final topple. It was eminently satisfying. Half-measures were repellent. She slept, and awoke refreshed and singing.

The month passed with intolerable swiftness. Rol's creation progressed apace. Helen settled his romanisation problems, finally going for a miserable concoction of the ugly Meyer-Wempe system without those grotesque accents. He of course worried what academic linguists might say. She cheerily got on with his novel, saying to herself what did Yale University know anyway. Unless some easy-touch publisher had a rush of blood to the head Rol's tripe would never see the light of printed day anyhow.

Two cards had come from Evadne, claptrap about relatives cluttering up the Cotswolds, hasn't Home changed and all that. Helen used them to line the kitchen waste bin. Two others, filled with worship, arrived at Rol's. Helen read them before Rol arrived home—she mostly worked at Felix Villas now, having bought a compatible laptop. This had the benefits of conscripting Ah Fung, who was dismayed by the prospect of losing her Cantonese-speaking Missie, and of reducing the pile of typescripts in Evadne's flat. Helen presented Rol with the first disc, containing a dozen old review articles. "You see, Rol," she lied gravely, "discs last for ever, and are a permanent record for posterity." He saw the wisdom of that, and wrote and wrote.

His story got worse. The man had very little imagination; his mundanities and fourth-form metaphors were driving her to screaming pitch. But war is war, and she'd come too far, with Evadne's third card promising she'd return on time. Meanwhile Rol's heroine was involved in a shoot-out near Stonecutter's Island between two Pearl River Junks while a Royal Navy minesweeper, Christ, stood off helplessly in deeper water symbolising Western inadequacy. Helen was too sickened to correct that particular chapter. Rol was clearly a moron.

Later, she was to wonder if it was her growing contempt for the man that led to his taking her into his bed in that last week. She was utterly astonished. She had of course vaguely wondered if he and Evadne had ever "taken steps," as she mentally classified sexual activities. Wholly unprepared, she went through the carnalities with a sort of anxious preoccupation rather than anything approaching passion, though he entered into it with the male's usual efficient abandon. There was very little manoeuvre, no gradual seduction. It was almost matter of fact. Rol seemed gratified—she had always checked with George immediately after, at least in the first few years, after which it had fallen off as an event.

She urgently wanted to know if dear Evadne had brought Rol to this pitch of activity, but wisely forbore asking. It was the night Ah Fung slept out— she had a child in Hung Hom, bus from Robinson Road then the ferry direct from Wanchai, dollar-twenty—so presumably Rol had decided on his move well beforehand. It took some moments to plot her response. She finally opted, more from doubt than conviction, to be mistily gratified. It worked well. To her further surprise she found herself making love a second time, not without positional difficulty and a few bruises that might need Max Factor pancake. Eventually when he was quiet she dozed, wondering if Whiteway's Store was still on the harbourside; they always stocked that invaluable Leichner heavy-duty make-up in the old days. But even such worries were superfluous, for who was to accuse her? George was gone. Rol seemed replete, and men, in her limited experiences, always declined responsibility for damage. Except, a bruise and an air of repletion might prove a telling opportunistic weapon when Evadne arrived, displayed with a welcome-home-guess-what innocence.

With two days to go—Helen evasively humble, Rol not mentioning That Night—he asked what she was going to do when Evadne returned. Helen showed quite good sadness and said she would go Home, just as the really interesting Chinese festivals were approaching and—she did a really sincere blush—she had more reasons than ever for wanting to stay.

Rol said she could always lodge in Felix Villas, he had plenty of room, and his book was reaching a critical juncture.

Helen hesitated. "Won't Evadne mind, Rol? I'd hate to seem, well, *pushy* . . ."

When Evadne's flight declined at that strange angle behind the MOTOROLA sign on Kowloon side into Kai Tak, Helen wasn't there to meet her, and she made certain the phone was unanswered. She strolled in an hour after Evadne reached the flat, and made minimal fuss. Evadne, tired, was taken aback by the disposition of the furniture.

Helen assumed an abstracted air, several times saying, "Mmmmh?" as if thinking of something else. She explained Jenny's departure: some Filipino tantrum she couldn't quite understand, no forwarding address but it was probably all to the good. Then, with Evadne still reeling, Helen sweetly said she was staying with Rol, because his writing must come first. She asked absently after Evadne's friends at Home, but was unable to resist getting their names wrong.

She left Evadne to her own devices after thirty minutes. As she left, she called instructions over her shoulder about milk in the fridge, the small air-conditioner being on the blink, and so forth.

Pleased, she told Rol that Evadne was too tired to call; the flight had aged her. She thought she'd been quite superb.

The loneliness of Hong Kong, Helen knew, is not the enervating Middle East kind. It does one of two things. It prods the expatriate into being an entrepreneur of breathtaking flair, or it dooms. Mix in sports, zoom into the Hong Kong Singers' next *Iolanthe*, or stay alone and rot. The suicide rate is prodigious among certain segments.

As time went by, Evadne's withdrawal into the predictable depression became increasingly evident. Helen grew impatient. The woman was clearly superfluous, so what on earth was the delay, for heaven's sake? She should leave Planet Earth without more ado. The round of coffee mornings, a narrow circuit, quickly dried up for the stupid mare, and her desperate forays into social events only exposed her as a lonely woman craving company in a confined place that, rushing from hour to dollar-driven hour, showed no compassion. Helen made sure she saw her once or twice, simply to remind Evadne of her inadequacies.

Incredibly it took an amazing four months for Evadne to do the necessary. Helen wondered if she should persuade Rol to incorporate Evadne's tumble from her Cape Mansions balcony into his manuscript, but his brain was too set in its ways. She had to face it, when at last Ah Fung flapped in, horrified, just as Helen arrived back, the amah calling that a Missie had fallen from a flat across the road and ambulances and the police were already . . . The terrible truth was that Rol was simply not up to it. His novel was rubbish—who'd believe the worn symbolism of a train entering a tunnel to conclude *three* chapters? His characters were wooden. She had slaved to make him see sense about prostitution—it was no shame to Hong Kong, never had been. The stupid man simply couldn't leave Edwardian Hampstead. She sent flowers for Evadne: the colonial cemetery in Happy Valley, a race day.

She slept with Rol regularly now. They made love. She became Missie at Number Four, Felix Villas. Ah Fung was delighted with her as long as she made regular mistakes in buying or ordering, that the amah could laugh about with other Chinese amahs on the terraces. She did his word-processing, translated his Cantonese, explained festival ceremonies, told how the colony really was a quarter of a century before.

Hopeless, all terrifyingly hopeless. In short, a complete waste of time.

The book was rejected eight months later, naturally. Rol was almost suicidal, a spin-off she disliked. He faced her over supper, haggard. "What's wrong, Helen? Nine publishers! I did everything right. All the ingredients: history, social details, language!"

Darling, she should have said, *your themes are undergraduate, like Cambridge Fringe on telly; Campus Capers, in Dickie Henderson's damning phrase.*

Instead, "There's nothing wrong, darling!" she cried loyally. "It's wonderful, the great colonial novel. Booker material!"

"I'm lost, Helen!"

"I have an idea, darling." She found the right words after rather fetching supportive smiles across the tureen of black-faced carp congee. "Could it be that you are . . . well, stale? Look how you've positively *slogged*, ever since whatsername, Evadne Thing, proved so useless."

"I can't stop now!"

She said firmly, "Of course you can't. But you deserve a rest. Recharge your batteries!" She winced at that, but the idiot's brow cleared.

"And not rewrite?"

She smiled at the sacrilege. "Not you, darling. *Me!*"

"You?" His paranoia resurfaced, but she was as disarming as ever.

"Of course, darling! Who else? Then you could come back to the redraft refreshed!"

"You think so?"

She smiled endearingly through the candle flames at his anxious face. "Solved! I promise I'll have it organised in a month's time." Which was how they left it that night.

The trouble was, Helen thought, in her—well, in Rol's so far—elegant old house, looking out over the quiet waters to Lamma Island, that she had fallen for Hong Kong all over again. Just as when she was young, the children at Glenealey School, George in his Government accounts job. Hong Kong had recaptured her heart. Yet she'd accomplished her task; shouldn't she simply go?

The whole colony seemed silent tonight. Rol was late, revision classes at Sai Ying Pun. Traffic had dwindled. The buses to Aberdeen on the lower road ran muted, hardly a gear change. The ships glided in the sunset, the huge black butterflies and the birds stuporous, hardly making it to the next hibiscus.

There was something else, though. She had not touched Rol's manuscript lately. There was no need. Her own colonial novel, offered under her maiden name, was already accepted. The question was whether Rol was superfluous. He suspected nothing about Evadne's death, of course. Helen could share her success with him, just as creatures shared a living space in the wild, got along, made the best of things. She could tell the publishers it was a joint authorship.

But the more she thought the more Rol seemed impedimenta, not needed on voyage. Or was he? This, after all, might actually *be* her destined voyage. He was acceptable, served. If she decided on partnership, they might wed. He was already dependent on her. Think of Ah Fung's excitement at a marriage feast, the "face" the amah would gain! It would be worth it for that. But how would Rol view a wife/lover who was a successful creative writer? Somebody threatening his space, in the modern phrase?

Or she could convince Rol that her book was simply a rehash of his . . . Hong Kong was destined to vanish off the map in three years; worth batting out time, surely?

In the twilight she looked down the steep hillside, down among the bauhinia trees with their gentle pastel flowers, the hibiscus, the bougainvillaeas, and the unceasing loyal lantanas. Hong Kong's picturesque heights were paradise. So beautiful, so serene, but such a long way for somebody to fall.

George Alec Effinger is a fine science fiction writer who has always worked on the edges of crime fiction—frequently by using suspense techniques in his sf and fantasy. Here's a very good example of how well sf and suspense fiction can be fused. The italicized section below was given Effinger by Mike Resnick, the editor of the anthology in which the story appeared. Resnick gave out the premise and Effinger built a story around it.

The Ugly Earthling Murder Case
GEORGE ALEC EFFINGER

The inhabitants of Proxima Centauri II come in four genders, and all four are capable of teleportation.

A drunken human tourist accidentally kills a member of a four-alien sexual grouping (tantamount in their society to marriage). He is apprehended and tried, and found innocent of murder. Instead he is convicted of accidental homicide and given a suspended sentence.

While he is gathering his belongings prior to his release, he is murdered with a blunt instrument. Lest this cause yet another interstellar incident, a detective (alien or human, take your choice) is assigned to find out who killed him. The three most obvious suspects are the three remaining members of the sexual grouping; all are incensed that he got off scot free, but all deny killing him.

The only clues at the scene of the crime are a pocket mirror, a handkerchief with a blue stain that the police lab has not been able to identify, and an alien tool that was probably the murder weapon.

Solve it.

No one had liked Fredrick Tolliver. No one on earth, his own home world; no one on Proxima Centauri II; no one in the known universe, as far as I could tell. My name is Ferencz Ipolyi-Toth. I'm what used to be called a detective, or a private investigator, or quite a few less neutral and more unflattering things. Nowadays, we in the trade don't call ourselves anything at all. We just open offices with only our name painted on the door, yet our clients find us easily enough. I was located in the ancient town of Buda, the half of the Hungarian capital on the right bank of the Danube.

My current client was Waters Plasmonics Corporation, a large, wealthy, and impenetrable high-tech operation based in Rochester, New York, and Geneva, Switzerland. I knew they were impenetrable because I'd once been hired by someone else to find out what Dr. Bertram Waters was up to these days. After six weeks I gave up, admitted defeat, and returned my client's retainer.

It was kind of interesting to have WP Corporation hire me. Maybe along the way I might accidentally pick up some information about Waters and his associates, not that it would do me any good now. But I like to pick up loose information whenever I have the chance. You never know when it might come in handy, and I had plenty of computer storage space.

Of course, Fredrick Tolliver had been one of WP Corporation's top dreamers. That's pretty much all he'd done for them. He sat around all day in his office and wrote down everything that came into his mind that began with the words "say, what if . . . ?" It wasn't a bad job, as jobs go, except he'd had to put up with Rochester winters. Even in Budapest, we've heard about Rochester winters, and we're not unused to harsh winters ourselves. The mitigating factor was that he'd earned more in one year than I make in ten, enough to make even the Frozen North of the U.S.A. seem attractive.

Sitting in the comfortable black leather armchair beside my desk was Gerhardt Schnellenbogl, a group leader out of WP Corporation's Geneva branch. "The police in Chivakatopran City, on Proxima Centauri II, have ruled Tolliver's death an accident. Must've been some bizarre accident, the way the back of his skull was crushed in. We believe he was murdered, and the Ukolsti— that's their name for themselves—are trying to stave off an interstellar incident. Commendable sentiment, we suppose, but we'd also like to learn the truth."

I nodded. "I get a thousand EC dollars a day plus expenses. Minimum of ten days, payable now."

Schnellenbogl didn't even blink. "Cash or check?" he asked.

"Gold," I said.

He just opened his very thin briefcase and clinked together a stack of twenty EC $500 coins.

I stood up from behind my desk and came forward to shake his hand. "Thank you, sir," I said, "and you'll have my report within a few days."

I know. I probably sounded pretty damn self-confident. Nevertheless, this wasn't like investigating Waters Plasmonics. This was simply a murder. I didn't think the inhabitants of Ukol could've come up with something I'd never seen before. Of course, as I've admitted, I've been wrong before.

Even after a century of use, the interstellar tunnels were still expensive. WP

Corporation was picking up my travel costs, of course, so I was on the next day's shuttle to the Proxima Centauri system. My destination, the second planet, was very Earthlike in such matters as size, atmosphere, and amount and nature of the radiant energy it received from its sun. You'd expect that to be true for any world on which intelligent creatures in any guise had developed. There were also some primitive life-forms in the cold oceans of Proxima Centauri III. Right now, they didn't interest me. The Ukolsti, however, certainly did.

The dominant race on their planet, the Ukolsti came in four genders, although to my inexpert eyes half of them looked like moderately alien men and the other half like moderately alien women. I'm not sure now if four genders made them tetrasexual or quadrisexual. Following the pattern of uni- and bisexual (versus mono- and di-), I will go along with quadrisexual. If I have committed a linguistic blunder here out of ignorance, I will tell you a small secret: I couldn't care less, and, I'm sure, neither could the Ukolsti.

I was met at the shuttle terminal in Chivakatopran City by a member of one of the two Ukolsti male sexes. The Ukolsti were on the average shorter and heavier than humans, and their skin colors ranged from a pale ice-blue through a dark red-violet. My new companion was the azure of a hazy summer's morning sky in the countryside beside the Danube. He was perhaps considered tall on his world, but he was still several inches shorter than me. However, he looked broader and stronger, and I made a mental note that I didn't really want to put the comparison to any sort of scientific evaluation, such as an arm-wrestling contest in a Ukolsti tavern some night. If the Ukolsti had taverns, that is. That's how little I knew about these people whose hospitality I'd depend upon during my stay.

I knew that I'd also have to rely on the expertise of my guide, a Ukolsti physicist who had for some time been a corresponding alien expert for Waters Plasmonics. His name was Asparatimundic egli don Sagragaratil.

We introduced ourselves when he met me at the gate in the tunnel terminal. "As we will be working rather closely together," he said, "I think it best if we leap directly to the informal terms of address and forms of behavior. We'll have other things to occupy our minds. In that spirit, please call me Mundic."

I learned later that such an invitation to dispense with the rigorous and taxing Ukolsti formalities was something of an honor. I suspected as much, because the same thing is the case in many cultures, Earth-derived or otherwise. "And you may call me Ferencz," I said. He dipped his head in a slight bow of acknowledgment. From then on, we concentrated on the death of this unpopular Earthling, a death that bound together for a time the destinies of two planets.

Mundic took one of my two suitcases and led me from the tunnel terminal. "I think we should begin," he said, "with Mr. Tolliver's trial."

"Excuse me?" I said, baffled. "What trial?" Wily Gerhardt Schnellenbogl hadn't mentioned anything about Tolliver standing trial on Ukol.

My warning senses began screaming that I'd walked blithely into something much worse than I'd been led to believe. I'd been set up, in other words. Well, it's happened before, it goes with the business; but then at least I'd been on Earth, where I was comfortable about the local rules. Now here I was, several light-years from Earth, alone among aliens with an entire set of new rules I had only begun to learn.

We left the terminal building. I paused for a moment, set my suitcase on the sidewalk, and looked around at Chivakatopran City. The older-looking buildings were very baroque stone towers, heavily decorated with architectural details whose names I could look up if I felt like it. Lots of small statues in niches and reliefs and structures that stuck up and out.

The newer buildings were higher, but they were transparent enclosures. If more land had been available downtown, they might have been domes. Domes take up a lot of space. These newer buildings were stacks of floors, none of which extended to the outer walls. Each floor was environmentally connected to the others. Light, heat, and air circulated unhindered among them. The structures were like tall, rectangular domes beneath the pink sky.

"My vehicle," murmured Mundic. I grabbed my suitcase and got into his automobile. He leaned forward and gave directions to his driver, then sat back and relaxed.

"As I asked before, what trial?"

Mundic frowned. "I am unhappy that you don't already have this information. It means that I need to do quite a bit of explaining."

"We may blame WP Corporation for that," I said.

"Possibly. Or possibly some individual did not want you to have this information. Perhaps that individual has even prevented WP Corporation from having it."

I gave that a moment's thought. "Some individual, you say. You mean the murderer."

"Possibly," said Mundic. I couldn't read his expression. It was always carefully neutral. I'd soon learn that that was common among the Ukolsti.

Fredrick Tolliver had arrived in Chivakatopran City about an Earth month ago. He had been met by Mundic, who had taken him to dinner and showed him around the city. Tolliver had acted the complete boor throughout. Whatever wonder he saw, he was unimpressed. Whatever beautiful or astonishing thing Mundic showed him, Tolliver shrugged and explained how the same thing was done better on Earth. In a few hours, Mundic had had enough and left Tolliver at a hotel where WP Corporation had reserved a suite.

That's when things began to deteriorate at an amazing rate. Tolliver behaved like the worst sort of intolerable visitor from Earth. Before the era of interstellar travel, tourists from one nation would invade another, dumbly insensitive to their hosts' culture. Where there was once, for example, the "ugly American," today, we have the "ugly Earthling." That seems to have summed up Fredrick Tolliver rather neatly.

After Mundic left him at the hotel, Tolliver made himself comfortable in his suite for an hour, and then went out to see what kind of entertainment he could find on this deceptively Earthlike world. This was taken from testimony of the Ukolsti desk clerk from Tolliver's hotel.

Evidently there were indeed taverns in Chivakatopran City, because the next witness who testified against the Earthling was a bartender. Tolliver walked about three-quarters of a mile to the east, and found himself in an area of restaurants and bars. These catered to the local Ukolsti residents rather than off-worlders, who tended to remain near the downtown hotels and the entertainment district immediately to the west.

Tolliver entered a bar called Nightclub #2655. He sat alone at the bar, at the end nearest the entrance. He might have felt hesitant about coming in any farther, into the dimness that even he must have realized covered an alien way of life he did not comprehend. The bartender said he'd been surprised to see a human in his establishment; it had happened before, perhaps once or twice in the preceding twelve Ukolsti years. Nevertheless, Ukolsti courtesy demanded that the bartender mask his emotions and serve the human.

Tolliver was wholly ignorant of Ukolsti liquors and did not know what to order. The bartender testified that he made a suggestion, advising Tolliver to drink only a locally manufactured fermented beverage that was equivalent to a strong beer. At first Tolliver took the bartender's recommendation, but then quickly and loudly announced that the beer had a repulsive taste that wasn't worth the small kick he was getting from it. He wanted to try some of the stronger stuff.

The bartender said that he tried to talk Tolliver out of it, saying that he couldn't be responsible for the unknown effects the powerful distilled liquors might have on the human. Tolliver insisted. The bartender admitted that by this time, he'd quite grown to dislike the Earthling, and his attitude was to let Tolliver suffer the consequences of his own bad judgment. The bartender further admitted that after he learned what Tolliver had done later, he'd experienced great guilt and swore that he'd never serve another human again.

The bartender set a small glass of light yellow-green liquor beside Tolliver, along with a glass of water. All this time, the human had been rudely forcing himself into a conversation among a four-member sexual grouping—the Ukolsti counterpart of a marital union, which was out celebrating the promotion of one of the females in her corporate clan.

Tolliver swallowed the liquor, gagged, and drank about half the glass of water. He immediately ordered another. "I've tasted worse around the Mediterranean," he said. The bartender obliged. He quoted the following bit of conversation which he could not help but overhearing, even if he hadn't been listening closely in the first place.

"So," said Tolliver, drunkenly, "I understand you Ukolsti got four sexes. What I want to know—what the people of Earth are speculating about—is how that works? I mean, we only got two sexes, and sometimes even that seems too many."

One of the males turned to Tolliver and said, with carefully restrained outrage, "The Ukolsti sexual relationship among the four partners is very different from that of humans."

"I know, I know," said Tolliver petulantly. "But exactly how? I mean, does one of you—"

"We are somewhat uncomfortable discussing these matters in public with a human," said the male. His words seem diplomatic enough on the page, but the bartender said the male was close to striking Tolliver then and there. In fact, according to the bartender's testimony, all four of the Ukolsti were visibly upset, and the bartender himself had to fight down the desire to reach across the bar and grab the Earthling by the throat.

"Aw, c'mon, you blue sons of bitches, what's the big deal? On Earth—"

One of the males growled something in the Ukolsti language. A female vigorously shook her head no. The other male said something. Again the female shook her head. She leaned forward and addressed Tolliver. "If it will satisfy you and put an end to your unacceptable behavior, I will tell you briefly. The first male, the sperm father, has intercourse with the first female, the egg mother. Then the egg mother has intercourse with the second male, the egg father."

Tolliver frowned, his brows drawing together. "Uh huh," he said. "But there's got to be another step. There are four of you, and I imagine you got to make another transfer."

The four Ukolsti got to their feet. One of the males dropped some money on the bar. The female said in a very tight voice. "You are correct. The egg mother and the sperm mother must have intercourse."

"I don't see—" began Tolliver, but by that time the quadrisexual unit had walked stiffly from Nightclub #2655. The human turned to the bartender. "What's she mean?" he asked.

The bartender drew himself up to his full height and spoke slowly and precisely. "That matter is never spoken of, even among ourselves."

"Aw, bloody hell," said Tolliver. He staggered out into the darkness. It was the bartender's opinion that he was going in search of the four-member unit.

The next important testimony came from one of the males of the unit, the egg father. Evidently, Tolliver succeeded in following the family back to their living quarters. The Ukolsti do not believe in locked doors, and this marital unit lived in one of the open-floored buildings. It was a simple matter for Tolliver to enter quietly and hide himself.

"We did not know of his presence until after we'd begun an intimate and joyous sexual celebration of Shelandariva's promotion," said the egg father.

"I heard some noises from a curtained closet area and grew suspicious. I left our bed and went to the closet, where I discovered the Earthling, who'd been spying on us using a pocket mirror.

"My rage overcame my social restraint, and I began to wrestle with the human. The others came to see what the disturbance was about. The human struggled and kicked out, and my other family members tried to separate the two of us. In the chaos that followed, he kicked Shelandariva in the chest. She immediately began to choke and gasp for breath, falling to the floor. Her ribs had been broken, and the fractured bones punctured both her heart and lungs. She was dead before the emergency medical squad arrived.

"We immobilized the Earthling, and he was duly arrested and taken away to jail. He was charged with murder. Various forces I will not name have worked long and hard behind the scenes to ensure that he is not convicted. I do not anticipate that justice will be done."

The egg father's prediction at the trial was absolutely correct: Fredrick Tolliver was found innocent of the murder of Shelandariva, found guilty of an accidental slaying, given a suspended sentence, and released. Justice may not have been done, but in the larger picture it helped to avoid a serious interstellar incident.

I was appalled. "I wish I could somehow present the sincere apologies of my race and my home world," I said. I wondered if WP Corporation had enough influence by itself to get one of its employees off the hook, even on a distant planet. Or did the company have help, perhaps from various human governments that benefited from the company's deliberations and advice? It was impossible for me to say.

"It is not necessary," said Mundic in a wooden voice. "We understand that Fredrick Tolliver was not a typical representative of the human race. We have such individuals among the Ukolsti, as well."

"Then how," I asked, "did Tolliver die?"

Mundic explained, his face as expressionless as always. "Later that day, as he was gathering his belongings prior to release, he was murdered with a blunt instrument. Ukolsti officials, fearing that this, too, might cause an interstellar incident, ruled his death an accident, although it was absolutely clear to everyone that such a thing was impossible.

"All that was found at the scene of the covered-up crime was a pocket mirror—perhaps the same mirror referred to by the egg father in his testimony—a handkerchief with a blue stain that our police labs cannot identify, and a Ukolsti tool that was probably the murder weapon. But, as I've said, as of this moment there is no murder. It was just an accident. Lately there have been a few too many accidents . . ." he said, letting his voice trail off.

Just then we arrived at the hotel. Mundic helped me carry my bag inside. "Is this the same hotel where Tolliver stayed?" I asked.

"Yes, it is. There are floors with rooms for off-worlders. Those rooms all have four walls, unlike the rooms reserved for Ukolsti visitors. We have learned that many off-worlders prefer it this way. They tend to be squeamish about unrailed floors that overlook drops of a couple dozen stories. Therefore we provide enclosed rooms for our guests who are, shall we say, altitudinally challenged."

"Thank you," I said, suppressing a shudder. He accompanied me to my suite, which was very comfortable and fitted out accurately with everything a human traveler might expect to find in a fine hotel on Earth.

Mundic consulted a clock in the suite's sitting room. "I would be pleased if you'd be my guest for dinner," he said. "Afterward, it will still be early enough for you to begin interviewing the witnesses. Or, if you'd prefer, we can put that off until tomorrow morning."

I was a little weary from the traveling. "Let's see how I feel after dinner," I said.

"Excellent. There is a very good dining room just downstairs, if you're agreeable?"

I spread my hands. "I'm completely open to your suggestions," I said. As if I were going to go out wandering about an alien city like Fredrick Tolliver, looking for a place to get something to eat.

We rode the elevator back down to the lobby area, and went into the dining room. We were seated quickly because it was still before the dinner rush. We were also seated in separate booths which were closed off completely by heavy, cream-colored cloth hangings. I was given a menu by a waiter, and when I opened it up I found an excellent selection of human dishes chosen from several different cultures on Earth itself, and three or four from human colony worlds. I decided to reserve judgment until I saw how the Ukolsti chefs handled what were to them alien cuisines.

"I'll have the Chinese potstickers for an appetizer," I said. "Then the Poulet Rochambeau, fresh cauliflower in a cream and pecorino cheese sauce, and boiled pierogies stuffed with sweetened sauerkraut."

"Yes, sir," said the waiter. "Would you care for a beverage?"

"A Coke, now, please. I'll choose a wine to go with the dinner."

"Yes, sir."

As the waiter turned to leave, I asked a question. "Pardon me," I said, "but this is my first day on Ukol. Do you take all your meals in privacy?"

The waiter looked uncomfortable. "It is something we hesitate to talk about," he said. "But yes, most Ukolsti prefer to dine alone or in the presence of their immediate family members only."

"Thank you very much." I watched the waiter leave with my order.

It seemed that the Ukolsti came supplied with a full complement of cultural taboos. I wondered what others there were, and quietly hoped that I wouldn't cause offense through ignorance. Tolliver had, and now Tolliver was dead; of course, Tolliver had not merely transgressed a subtle social pattern. He'd worked long and hard at it.

Despite my doubts about the culinary expertise of the Ukolsti, when the meal arrived every bit of it was excellent. It was an extremely pleasant surprise, but I reminded myself that I was in the dining room of a large hotel that customarily housed off-worlders from many planets. I might not enjoy the food anywhere else in Chivakatopran City. I saw no urgent reason to learn the truth.

When I asked for my check from the waiter, he smiled and told me that my dinner companion had insisted on paying for both of us. That was fine by me. "May I have a receipt, then?" I asked. No point in letting a few EC dollars sleep in Gerhardt Schnellenbogl's pocket when they could be in mine.

I met Mundic again in the hotel lobby. "Mundic," I said, "I owe you my thanks."

"I hope it was pleasant to you," he said.

"More than I'd expected."

"Good." That's all we were going to say about the meal. "Now, Ferencz, do you feel up to speaking to the witnesses?"

Did I? Well, not particularly, but that's what I was getting paid for. "All right," I said.

Mundic nodded. "The most likely suspects are the three remaining members of the marital unit. The bartender in Nightclub #2655 is a suspect also, to a lesser degree. It depends on how offended he was by Tolliver's behavior. You must understand that among the Ukolsti, death is the common punishment for gross negligence in observing the social taboos. And anyone outraged enough is permitted to inflict that penalty. We try to make allowances for alien visitors who don't know our culture, but Fredrick Tolliver was, how shall I say—"

"He was Fredrick Tolliver, and that explains everything." We left the hotel and got into Mundic's waiting car.

"I've arranged this meeting with Shelandariva's mourning wife and husbands," he said. "They've already been questioned many times by the police investigators of both Ukol and Earth, as well as certain other officials. Please remember that they are under no obligation to answer your questions. We have no genuine authority. I had to exert a certain amount of influence."

"I'm sure WP Corporation is grateful," I said, staring out the window as the car moved swiftly through the clean, broad streets of Chivakatopran City. "If I were one of Shelandariva's family, I wouldn't want to have to go through these events all over again."

"They expressed the hope that this will bring the matter to a close. They want to be left alone in their grief. Please remember that when you speak with them."

"Of course," I said.

Shelandariva's family unit lived in one of the tall, enclosed residential blocks east of the downtown area. Mundic had been here before, so I let him lead me up in the elevator to their apartment. It was cool and dimly lighted within, and even though I'd prepared myself, I couldn't suppress a strong feeling of vertigo whenever I glanced at the edge of the floor, where open air tumbled straight down a shaft a hundred feet to ground level. I didn't want to go tumbling down after it, so I tended to stand nervously in the very middle of the parlor while Mundic spoke quietly with the three distressed Ukolsti in their own language.

Finally, Mundic turned to me. In English he said, "Everything is well, but remember what I've told you."

"Yes, thank you," I said. I turned to the surviving female and the two males. "I want to express my personal condolences to you, and the regrets of my employers on Earth. This was a tragedy that need not have happened. I also want to thank you for allowing me to intrude on your privacy."

"Yes, yes," said one of the males impatiently. His attitude was also markedly belligerent. Perhaps he thought all Earthlings were like Fredrick Tolliver, and he was prepared to penalty-kick me down the airshaft at the first opportunity.

"Kalikun," said the female, "remember your courtesy. We have guests in our home."

The male looked abashed. "I apologize," he said. He would not go farther than that.

"Welcome," said the other male, "and think of this as your home while you are with us. We have Mundic's assurances that you respect our culture enough to want to avoid any unpleasantness. That is all we ask."

"What Mundic has told you is true," I said. "I have a few questions for each of you. I will need to speak individually with all of you, in turn. I will make the process as brief as possible. Is there some etiquette involved with whom I speak to first?"

"No, none," said Kalikun, "but I volunteer."

"You have my gratitude. Is there somewhere we can speak in private?"

"This way," said Kalikun, leading me to their kitchen. We sat down at a large, gleaming aluminum table.

"I know you've answered these questions for the other authorities, but no one provided me with that material. Fredrick Tolliver was killed in the early afternoon on the twenty-first day of Mmach. Where were you at that time?"

Kalikun glared when I mentioned Fredrick Tolliver. When he spoke next, it was with barely-concealed fury. "I am a teacher of young, mentally handicapped children. At that hour, I have a physical training period with them. On the day in question, I was at the school. I believe I organized my class into two teams for sunig. It would take too long to explain the game to you."

I raised a hand. "It's not relevant in any event," I said. I smiled. I felt I had to. The resistance and dislike poured from Kalikun in almost visible waves of energy. If he felt that way about me, I could only begin to imagine how much hatred he'd felt for Tolliver. Here was a man who could have killed, given the unusual Ukolsti social arrangements and their ideas about society's vengeance against the breaker of taboos. "Then there would be others at your school who could substantiate your alibi?" I asked.

"All this is already a matter of record," he said with a growl.

"No one has given me the record."

"Then, yes, there are many who could and who have vouched for my presence at the school at the time of the killing."

"You did not leave at any time during the early afternoon?"

"No."

I thought for a moment. "Are you the member of the family who spoke so vehemently at the trial about justice not being done?"

"Yes, that was me. And wasn't I correct?"

I felt my shoulders slump a little. "Yes," I said sadly, "you were correct. Thank you for your time."

Kalikun said nothing, but got up and left the kitchen. A moment later, the female entered. She sat in the chair Kalikun had vacated.

"May I ask your name, madame?" I said.

"Venaahelocenai," she said.

"I must ask you the same question I asked Kalikun—"

"Did he give you permission to call him by his familiar name?" she asked.

"No," I said, "I just heard you speak it before. I did not ask him his full name."

She frowned. "That was an error on your part."

I closed my eyes for a moment, then opened them again. I felt too warm. "In any dealings between alien races, there will be errors, even with the best of intentions on both sides. I assure you that I do, indeed, have the best of intentions."

She nodded. "I can tell that you are nothing like that Earthling Tolliver. I am glad of it."

"Then may I ask, where were you in the early afternoon of the twenty-first day of Mmach?"

"I was at my desk at my job. I am a data shunt for a large banking and suicide-control firm. My desk is at the right rear of a large room, and there are scores of people sitting around me who have already attested to my presence there throughout the workday."

"Thank you, madame," I said. "I'm very sorry about what happened, and I'm very glad for your generous cooperation."

"Let this be the end of it. Please, let this be the end of it." She didn't even look at me as she rose and went back to the parlor.

The other male took her place at the table. I asked him the same questions, and he told me that he was a musician who'd spent the afternoon rehearsing for a recital with three others. They had already made sworn statements to back up his alibi.

We walked together back into the parlor. "It was very important for me to conduct these interviews," I said. "I have to ask this, however: I may need to return to ask a further question or two after I've spoken with some other witnesses, merely to clarify small details I may not understand. Is it presuming too much upon your hospitality and forbearance to ask permission to return, if the situation demands it? I emphasize that this may not be the case, but I feel obliged to warn you in advance of the possibility."

"Yes, come," said the female. "You've caused no offense."

Mundic stepped toward me and grasped me by the elbow. "Then we will leave you in peace." He spoke a few words in their language, then steered me to the door. In a few seconds, we were riding the elevator back to the ground.

"Very good, very fine," he said approvingly. "You behaved admirably. I'm sure your conduct reassured them about humans, perhaps just a little."

"I'm glad," I said. As an investigator, I've become hardened to tragedy over the years, but I felt a strong emotional response to this case.

Once more in Mundic's automobile, he asked, "Where would you like to go next?"

"I'd like to see the holding area where Tolliver was killed. And I'd like to see the tool that was used to crack his stupid head open."

Mundic nodded agreement. "Both are in the same building—the local police have been slow about releasing Tolliver's personal effects, because he had no family or friends on Ukol, and the authorities are not sure to whom to give the items. I've applied, as a correspondent employee of WP Corporation, but no decision's been made yet."

I glanced at my watch, which was still set on Budapest time. The information it gave me bore no relation to where I was now. Glancing out the window, I saw that Proxima Centauri was hanging low above the horizon. It would be night soon.

I told Mundic what the three members of the marital unit had said. He shook his head. "I would've sworn the killer was one of them," he said. "But they all have perfect alibis."

I laughed gruffly. "No such thing as a 'perfect alibi,' Mundi. People in my profession used to be called detectives, because we detected things ordinary people never noticed. Even an airtight alibi may have disguised holes in it. For instance, even though a person claims that he was on a carnival float in full sight of half a million people, as well as being televised to places on five continents, there is still a chance he could've snatched just enough time to get off the float, commit murder, and return unnoticed. Ordinary people tend to forget about routine breaks in a daily schedule—a teacher's open period between classes, for instance, or lunch breaks, or what have you. I've shaken many an unshakable alibi in my time. I haven't crossed any of those three off my list as yet."

"Ah, I see. Well, of course, you're the expert. That's why WP Corporation sent you here."

Our stop at the police holding area—I hesitate to call it a jail—was brief. Mundic and I were taken to the place of confinement, which was a huge room furnished with benches, where the prisoners milled around and held conversations or sat forlornly by themselves. The Ukolsti police didn't use jail cells to segregate their prisoners. They relied on Ukolsti social dynamics to keep order, and for the most part it seemed to work.

"Tolliver was kept here," Mundic said. "After he received his suspended sentence, he was brought to the properties room to collect his belongings. He was killed shortly thereafter."

I looked around. "Where was his body found?" I asked.

"In the elevator to the ground floor."

I nodded. "Now I want to see the weapon itself."

"This way," said Mundic. I followed him through a maze of corridors to a small window with a metal grate over it. Mundic went to the window and conversed for a while with a uniformed woman on the other side. Evidently he'd arranged in advance for me to view the weapon, just as he'd arranged for me to interview the three aliens, because in a few minutes the woman returned from the depths of her domain, carrying a long metal pipe fitted into a circular metal disk. The woman slid open the window and pushed the murder weapon through. Mundic gave it to me.

I hefted it. It was extremely heavy. It made a first-rate blunt object. "What is it?" I asked.

"It's a Ukolsti calibrating device, used with certain types of high-temperature furnaces."

"Uh-huh," I said, giving the thing back to him. He returned it to the officer in charge of evidence. We left the police building.

"Was that of any use to you?" Mundic asked.

"As much as anything else has been so far," I said.

"I suppose investigation is a long, slow process of gathering bits of information. It must demand a particular way of thinking, a certain frame of mind."

"Sometimes," I said. "And sometimes not. On rare occasions, solutions present themselves gift-wrapped like birthday gifts."

"Has that happened in this case?"

I laughed. "Let you know when it does."

"Where would you like to go next?" he asked.

"I'd like to speak to the bartender at Nightclub #2655."

"Yes, of course," said Mundic. He leaned forward and murmured his directions to the driver. We headed back in the direction of my hotel.

When we arrived, it was obvious that Mundic was somewhat uncomfortable about accompanying me into the bar, despite the usual lack of expression on his face. Mundic was not a party type of guy. That was all right. We weren't going to be there long.

The bartender was displeased to see another human in his establishment, but Mundic spoke with him, and then he cooperated with me freely. I learned that he'd been hugely angered by Tolliver's behavior, but who hadn't been? The interesting thing was that the bartender had a very weak alibi for the time of Tolliver's killing. "I work nights here," he said. "When that off-worlder was punished, I was at home, in bed and asleep. You can ask my wife."

I took his name and address, and then I said, "Give me one of the drinks Tolliver ordered that night."

"That's a very bad idea," said Mundic, severe disapproval in his voice.

"I'm not going to drink it," I said. "I just want to see it, smell it, it maybe taste it."

"If you say so," said the bartender. He poured the yellow-green liquor into a glass and set it before me. Mundic paid for it because I had no local currency. I lifted it to the lights and looked through the sickly-looking fluid. I sniffed it, and it made me gag. I cautiously raised the glass to my mouth and took a small sip. It was the most horrible tasting stuff I'd ever experienced. Even thinking about it now makes my palms sweat and my belly sick. I'm not going to compare the taste of the liquor to anything else; imagine it for yourself.

I thanked the bartender for his help, and Mundic and I left the nightclub. We got back into his car. "Could he have killed Tolliver, do you think? His alibi is the thinnest yet."

"He could've killed Tolliver, depending upon how ferociously outraged he'd become. Anyone could've had access to the elevator in the police building, and the bartender had the day free."

"And the testimony at the trial described how angry the bartender got that evening. Almost as angry as the egg father."

"The case is much less opaque now than when I first arrived," I said. "It won't take much longer to solve. I'm very confident about that."

"Next?" asked Mundic.

"I'm not sure," I said.

"I have a list of minor suspects—waiters, desk clerks, officers and prisoners he came into contact with in the police building. Some of them were rather fierce in their denunciation of Tolliver, but I don't think any of them had as much motivation to kill him as those people you've interviewed this evening."

"I—" I broke off, aware that I was about to become violently sick in the back of Mundic's automobile. I motioned meaninglessly with one hand, at the same time desperately fighting down nausea. I did heave once, but contained it, except for a slight dribble that escaped my lips. I took out a handkerchief and wiped my mouth. I was astonished to see the cotton material stained blue.

"The same thing must've happened to Tolliver," I said weakly. "Except he had a beer and two complete drinks. He must've been monstrously sick, and yet he managed to follow the marital unit to their apartment building.''

"And the experience of his horrible reaction to the liquor taught him nothing," said Mundic thoughtfully. "I suppose that to the moment of his death, he never truly understood that he was on another world, among another race, and not back on his familiar home world where he could behave as he'd always behaved."

There was no doubt a lot of truth in that. "In some ways, he was brilliant," I said. "Otherwise, he couldn't have been hired for his job at WP Corporation. In many other ways, Tolliver was among the stupidest people I've ever heard about."

Mundic nodded. "Now, as to these minor suspects. Do you feel well enough to see them tonight? Or should we put them off until tomorrow?"

I waved a hand. "There's no need," I said. "I'm rather sure I know who killed—let's not dance around the euphemism, the word is murdered—Fredrick Tolliver."

Mundic stared at me curiously. "Who was it, do you think?" he said.

I smiled. "Why, it was you, Mundic. When you heard that Tolliver had killed a Ukolsti citizen, it was enough for you to seek revenge. You met him at the interstellar tunnel terminal, just as you met me. You took him to dinner, just as you took me. You spent more time with him than anyone. I'm willing to bet that he had plenty of opportunities to heighten first your displeasure, then your disgust, and finally your righteous wrath. Even though he was an off-worlder, and you wished to show him every courtesy, when you heard that he'd actually killed one of your fellows, poor Shelandariva, you decided that your socially dictated need for revenge had to be satisfied."

"You are quite right," he said in a composed voice. "You know, he spied on me at dinner with that pocket mirror, just as he spied on Shelandariva and the rest of her family in their most private of moments. Tolliver was spotted by a waiter and asked to leave. Tolliver made such a disturbance that it attracted my attention from within my booth, and I learned what he'd done. I was willing to swallow my anger at that point, but he insisted on aggravating the situation. At last it became too much to bear."

"I suppose I agree," I said.

"How did you know it was me?"

"The weapon was another giveaway. I spent some time investigating WP Corporation. I recognized the device as something used only by plasmonics engineers. 'High-temperature furnaces,' indeed."

Mundic's carefully masked expression began to waver. "I suppose now you intend to hand me over to the police?"

I shrugged. "Not at all. I was paid to find the identity of Tolliver's killer, not to 'bring him to justice,' in Kalikun's words. I'll make a report to Gerhardt Schnellenbogl. I'm pretty certain that will be the end of it. You're too valuable to the corporation to prosecute. In any event, no one on Earth liked Tolliver in the first place. I doubt if there will be any unpleasantness as a result of my investigation, either here or on Earth. I think they just wanted to know.''

"Thank you," murmured Mundic. In a couple of minutes, the automobile stopped outside my hotel. "I will come by tomorrow morning to take you back to the shuttle terminal.''

"That is most kind of you, Mundic. I hope you realize that I think of you as a friend.''

Ukolsti social conventions that I knew nothing of prevented him from replying. I got out of the car and headed into the hotel. I discovered that I couldn't wait to leave this world of pink skies and blue people, and return home to blues skies and pink, Hungarian people.

The following story is one of those gems that really speaks for itself. All we know about Mark Timlin is that his story appeared in Maxim Jakubowski's *Constable New Crimes 2* and that he's British and that this story was a Golden Dagger nominee.

Sweetheart of the Rodeo
MARK TIMLIN

The ring on my flat doorbell came at about eight o'clock on a hot and sticky Wednesday night in June.

I wasn't working. Just kicking back with a can of cold beer and what passed for entertainment on the terrestrial channels of my TV.

I was dressed in an old cotton shirt, blue jeans that had seen better days a long time previous, and a pair of scuffed Timberland loafers with no socks.

I took the beer downstairs to the front door with me for company.

The woman who stood outside was tall in a pair of high-heeled, two-tone, green-suede-on-green-ostrich-skin cowboy boots, and she was fanning her face with a black straw Stetson that would have added another three or four inches to her height with no problem.

The rest of her outfit consisted of a mid-grey cowgirl outfit that perfectly matched the colour of her eyes. It had all sorts of tassels and stuff hanging down from the shoulders and sleeves. It was a little wrinkled and travel-stained around the edges. But then, as I'm sure I've remarked before, no one's perfect. But she was pretty good.

Her skirt was very short and exposed legs that went on for ever, sheathed in charcoal nylon. Her dark brown, almost waist-length hair was backcombed out *real* big, like the woman in *Dallas*. I was intrigued to say the least. I looked her in the eye and said, "Yes?"

"Is your name Nick Sharman?" she asked.

She had an accent straight out of the deep south of America.

"Yes," I replied.

"Do you know a guy called Skinner?"

"Who?"

"Skinner. He's a musician. Plays lead guitar."

Skinner. Sure. I knew him. To call him a musician was something of an overstatement now. Maybe once upon a time. In the disco days of the seventies, perhaps. But now he was too old. And too short. And too fat. So fat that his trousers didn't fit right. Too fat to be a teenage idol. Mind you, Elton John hadn't done too badly. And he was bald too. But Skinner was no Elton John, and that was a fact.

These days Skinner was up to all sorts. Mostly semi-legal. And that was an understatement. He hung out in east London. Well away from my manor, thank God. I'd met him years ago in a pub in Soho, but I'd seen him around before that. One Saturday afternoon session we'd both been in the boozer, and whoever he was with had bought a drink for the company I was in, or vice versa, and as we'd all combined to form one large group, Skinner and I had ended up next to each other and said hello, as you do. Much later. After chucking-out time, I'd bumped into him again at a hot-dog stand in Charing Cross Road where we were both paying good money to risk salmonella or worse. He was staying in Brixton at the time, and thankfully was without wheels as he was as pissed as a pudding, and we'd shared a cab home. On the way, we decided that a late drink at the Fridge, where he knew one of the doormen, was in order, and I'd woken up the next afternoon in the bath in some stranger's flat, where Skinner was dossing down, and we'd been more or less mates ever since.

Mostly less. And certainly not mates enough for what followed.

"Sure," I said. "What about him?"

"I was supposed to be staying at his house. I've just arrived from the States. He said he'd meet me at Heathrow, but he didn't show up."

I wasn't surprised.

"I went to his place, and got this note he left," she said.

She took a crumpled piece of paper from a huge handbag that swung from one shoulder and looked like it didn't contain much more than all I owned in the world.

I straightened the paper. It read:

Sweetheart,

I've had to go away on a gig.

It came up suddenly, and I couldn't get in touch. Your phone's always engaged.

Go and see a bloke called Nick Sharman. He'll look after you.

I'll be in touch as soon as I can.

Love,

Skinner

My home address was scribbled at the bottom of the page.

"And you are?" I asked.

"Sweetheart," she said. "That's my name, right there. Pleased to make your acquaintance." If she was, she wasn't exactly showing it.

I looked at her. "Sorry," I said. "I don't know a thing about this." As far as I was concerned, she was just another of Skinner's women. Fat and unattractive as he might be, he seemed to pull pretty well. Maybe it was the lemon-yellow Stratocaster slung between his legs.

Her grey eyes changed color and flashed a dangerous shade of blue. "Jesus," she said. "Where's your British hospitality? I've flown over three thousand miles today. Aren't you even going to invite me in?"

I looked at her and made my choice. I should have shut the door straight in her face. "Sure," I said, and stepped back in the doorway. You would have done the same.

"My things are in that cab," she said. "Suitcases and stuff." And pointed to a black Metrocab parked opposite with its engine running. "You'll have to pay him. I haven't got any English money."

I shook my head. This had to be a piss-take. But I decided to go along with the gag, and said, "Go on up. All the way to the top. The door's open. I'll get your bags. There's a beer in the fridge."

"Thanks," she said and brushed past me. I went over to the taxi.

"How much?" I asked.

"Hundred and fifty-two quid," said the cabbie, dead straight-faced.

"*How much?*" I said.

He repeated the sum. "And the meter's still running," he added.

"From Heathrow?" I said. "Did you go the pretty way, through Huddersfield, or what?"

The cabbie looked at me disgustedly. "Listen, mate," he said. "I picked her up at the airport about four hours ago. First of all we have to go to Harrods so she can do some shopping. Then it's off to Edmonton, where she has a long chat with a couple of dikes at the house where she's gone. Then she decides she wants a drink, but the first three boozers don't suit. Eventually we find one she likes, and she's in there for half an hour. Then it's over the river here. I mean, what do you want from me?"

"Nothing," I replied shortly. "Wait here . . . And turn the sodding meter off." And I went upstairs and got my chequebook.

"Do you know how much the fare is?" I demanded when I got back into my flat and found Sweetheart sitting demurely on the sofa sipping at a Heineken and watching the end of *Coronation Street*.

"No," she replied, "I never look at cab meters."

How convenient, I thought, and found my chequebook and card in the chest of drawers where I keep them, and went back downstairs.

I had to do three cheques. Fifty pounds each, and two quid cash.

When I'd paid him, the driver got Sweetheart's luggage out of the cab. It consisted of four Harrods carrier bags and three huge suitcases made from lizard- or snakeskin. Jesus, I thought, I'd hate to be around her if I was an endangered species.

Little did I know.

When all her stuff was on the pavement, the cabbie said, "What about my tip?"

"Your tip," I said. "Here's your tip. Don't pick up American women with big hair from the airport. That's the only tip you're getting out of me."

He wasn't best pleased by that. "I know something you don't," he said.

"What?"

He rubbed the thumb and forefinger of his right hand together in the age-old gesture.

"Tell me," I said. "Don't fuck about."

He shook his head.

I was tired, and getting fed up with playing games. "A fiver," I said. "And it had better be good."

"Get away."

All right, I was interested, and he knew it. When Skinner's involved, you'd better get all the information you can. I'd learnt that long ago. "A tenner," I said.

"Ten per cent," he said.

"Fifteen quid?" I said back. "Are you kidding?"

"It's the recognized amount for a gratuity."

"It's the recognized amount for daylight bloody robbery if you ask me."

He shrugged.

"And for what?"

"Pay up and find out."

I took three fivers out of my back pocket and he reached out his hand.

I pulled the money back and shook my head. "Don't be soft," I said.

"How do I know you'll pay?"

"You don't. Just trust me."

He thought about it for ten seconds or so, then shrugged again. "We were followed."

"What?"

"We were followed," he repeated. "Two geezers in a motor."

"From where?"

"Edmonton. The house where she spoke to them two dikes."

He had a real way with words.

"Are they still with you?" I asked.

He grinned spitefully. "Sure. They came to the pubs after us and waited, and if you look down the road there," his eyes moved in a downhill direction, "you can see them for yourself."

"What car?" I said.

"Grey Granada."

I let my eyes follow his. Parked about fifty yards down the street was a gun-metal-grey Ford Granada. The latest model.

"Are you sure?" I asked.

He pulled a face. "What do you think?" he asked.

I pulled a face back.

"What about my money?" he said.

"One minute," I said, and picked up two of the suitcases and the carrier bags and walked them across the road and into the doorway of the house.

I walked back, but instead of going to fetch the last case I turned and sprinted in the direction of the Granada.

I heard the starter grind and the car took off with a faint screech from the tyres. I was in the middle of the road, maybe twenty yards from it, and whoever was driving spun the wheel and the car lurched towards me, forcing a serious change of direction on my part and making me almost lose my balance and end up in the gutter. As it was, I felt my bad foot react to the effort with a sharp stab of pain.

The car sped away in the direction of Streatham with a puff of smoke from its twin exhausts.

I limped back to the cab.

"Told you," said the cabbie, with rather more satisfaction than I appreciated, and held out his hand.

I put the three fivers into it, picked up the other case and went across the road into my house. I collected the rest of her baggage and took it all upstairs.

Sweetheart was still sitting where I'd left her, but she'd discovered *Brookside*, and she was on her third beer.

I put the bags down on the carpet, and she looked up from between her can of lager and the TV set.

"Thanks," she said. "I appreciate what you did. Up until then, if today had been a fish, I'd've thrown it back."

Country style. How quaint, I thought. "We've got to talk," I said.

"About?"

"You were followed from Edmonton."

"Tell me something I don't know."

"What?"

"I saw those guys. That's why I stopped off at a load of bars. Just to see if they stuck with me."

"You *knew*."

"Sure. I come from Texas. They grow them smart down there."

"*Smart*. You pick up a tail and bring it to my house. And you call that smart."

"Are they still around?"

"No," I said.

"You chased them off."

"You might say that."

"And I've got a place to stay?"

"Yes."

"Then I would call that smart. What would you call it?"

The actions of a stupid bitch, I thought. And she knew exactly what I was thinking, and her eyes changed color again, to emerald green, and her skirt slid another inch or two up her thigh, and I just knew that I was being manipulated in the worst way.

I looked down at her and said, "Forget it. It's done now."

She smiled a smile like a cat with cream and said, "Looks like Skinner sent me to the right guy."

"Sure."

"So what do you do then, Sharman?"

"I'm a private detective. When I work."

"A private eye. No shit." She laughed like a drain, and snorted like a pig at the thought.

I stood there straight-faced throughout.

"And what exactly do you do?" I asked.

"I'm in the rock and roll business."

"*No shit*," I said.

"What exactly does that mean?"

I shrugged. "I never would have guessed," I said. "I thought you might be a Jehovah's Witness when you arrived at the door."

"Fuck right off," she said, and her eyes were suddenly that dangerous shade of blue that I'd seen before.

I kicked the Harrods bag that was nearest to me. "And if you've got no dough, how the hell could you do a load of shopping on your way here?"

She reached into her handbag that was sitting on the sofa next to her and took out a wallet made from yet more skin of some poor little beast that had never done anything to her personally. She extracted two plastic cards and flicked them dangerously close to my head.

"Credit, pal," she said. "Never heard of it?"

The cards hit the wall and fell on to the carpet. One was white. The other, olive green. Harrods store cards. I smiled tightly back. "OK. Now tell me why persons unknown followed you here."

She shrugged. "I don't know."

"Why were you meeting Skinner?"

She shrugged again.

"Don't fuck with me, Sweetheart, or whatever your name is," I said. "Tell the truth and shame the devil."

"Sweetheart it is," she replied. "Sweetheart of the Rodeo. Like the song."

"I'm impressed," I said. "Now tell me, why were you meeting Skinner?"

"We had a business deal going."

"Oh really. I've come across his business deals before. What he means is, you give him a bunch of money, and at some unspecified future date you'll get it back plus a whole load of interest. Trouble is it never happens."

"It happens this time. He promised."

"Is that why he wasn't at the airport to meet you? And why I just paid for your cab fare? And almost got run over by a car load of people who followed you here?"

Her eyes went grey again and she said, "Did they hurt you?"

"Would you care?"

She nodded. "Sure I would. What do you think I am? I'm here in your house, drinking your beer. Where I come from that means we're friends."

"Where I come from it means you're probably going to ask to borrow more money."

"Very funny."

And then she started to cry. Just like that. Great big tears squeezing out of the corner of her eyes and rolling down her cheeks, where she let them drip on to the material of her outfit, where they soaked into big blobs of darker grey on her breasts.

Shit, I thought. I might have guessed. Hard as nails on top. The kind of woman who lights matches on the skin of her thighs. And underneath all soft and mushy. Just my luck. Right then, if Skinner had walked into the room I'd've kicked him right in the nuts.

I stood there awkwardly. "What's the matter?" I asked.

She looked up at me through mascara-smudged eyes, which I must admit were kind of appealing, even though deep down I knew I was being manipulated again. "It's just that I feel so lousy, what with the journey and all. Could I get some sleep?"

"Sure," I said.

"Your bed feels kind of comfortable. I just tried it."

"It is. Guests usually sleep on the sofa bed, though," I said, choosing not to preface "guests" with "uninvited." And tugged off the cushions and pulled out the bedsprings and mattress. It was made up with two sheets and a blanket, for emergencies.

"Looks kinda short to me," she said.

"Could be."

"I'm tall. You know."

"I know," I replied. "So am I."

She gave me another of her appealing looks, and I knew there was no point in arguing, so instead I said, "Tell you what. You have the bed for tonight. I'll sleep on the sofa."

The tears stopped miraculously and she said, "You're cute."

"How kind."

"Now will you . . ."

"What?"

"Let me get my night things out and get changed."

"I'm not stopping you."

She looked round. "This is a nice place," she said. "Much better than that dump Skinner lives in, and I'm not complaining. But it's kinda cramped in here."

Cramped. I ask you. It's a one-room studio conversion with kitchen attached, and separate shower and toilet. What the hell did she expect? Longleat Manor?

"It's perfect for one," I said.

"But there's two of us here now."

So I'd noticed, I thought. "If I'd known you were coming I'd've made alternative arrangements," I said as sarcastically as possible. But Yanks never get sarcasm.

"There's no need for that."

"What do you want me to do, then?"

"Could you leave for a few minutes?"

"Can't you use the bathroom?"

"I used it already. There's not room to turn round in there. And I need some space."

"OK," I said. "I'll take a walk. But I'll be back in twenty minutes."

"That's plenty of time," and she smiled again, showing a mouthful of perfect teeth.

I went down the pub and didn't get back until almost eleven. When I opened the door to the flat, all the lights were off, except for the small lamp that stood on top of the dead TV. It was still lit, and she'd draped a scarf over the shade so that the light was diffused. There was just enough illumination to see that the place was all messed up. It looked like as she'd unpacked, she'd simply dropped her stuff on to the carpet where it still lay. The three suitcases and the carrier bags were scattered across the room, and dresses, underwear, papers, tapes, books, and all sorts of other junk were everywhere. And from somewhere had appeared another three pairs of cowboy boots, that now stood with the ones she'd been wearing when she arrived, in a line next to my bed as if guarding her as she slept. I looked at them. One leopard-skin pair, one zebra-skin pair and one black-and-red-leather pair, next to the green ones I'd already seen.

Sweetheart was curled up in bed asleep, snoring softly with a light tick-tick sound like a baby. She'd washed her face clean of make-up, and she frowned slightly as she slept.

I left the place as it was, went to the bathroom, waded back through her stuff, took the pillow from next to the one that her head was resting on, and went to bed. Of course I couldn't sleep. The sofa bed was too short. And she wouldn't stop snoring.

The next morning I was up first. I went into the bathroom and shaved and showered. When I came back she was sitting up in bed yawning. She gave me a glimpse of all her teeth again. "Good *morning*," she said. "And how are you today?"

"Lousy," I replied.

"*Oh*. A grouch in the morning. That won't do."

"Could you keep the volume down until I've had at least one cup of tea?" I asked. Not impolitely, I thought, under the circumstances.

"Of course, *mate*," she said with what was possibly one of the worst attempts at a cockney accent I think I'd ever heard. "Whatever you say."

I put the kettle on, and as it boiled I found a pair of mugs in the cupboard. "Tea? Coffee?" I said.

"Coffee. Milk. No sugar."

I started to prepare the drinks.

"I'm going to get up and get dressed," she said.

"If you think I'm going out again, you're right out of luck. And listen. Get this place tidied up. It's like a tip."

"What's that?"

"A dump. A garbage dump."

"I think you might have been living alone too long, Mr. Sharman."

"Maybe."

Not that it was any of her damn business.

She snorted a laugh and pulled the covers back. She jumped out of bed and made a run for the bathroom. The nightie she was wearing was long, but not long enough to hide the fact that she was wearing a pair of grey woollen socks on her feet.

"Socks," I said. "How can you wear socks in bed? It's summer for God's sake."

"Summer! Call this summer? It's like winter in this goddamned town all year round," and she slammed the bathroom door behind her.

When she returned, her coffee was ready, and we sat opposite each other at the breakfast bar and drank our drinks. By the time I had finished mine I was feeling a bit more human. I lit a cigarette.

"No more messing," I said. "Tell me. What was the deal with Skinner?"

She sighed. "He called me at home last week and told me that if I sent him five thousand pounds sterling, I could quadruple it by yesterday."

"And you believed him?"

She shrugged. "Why not? It seemed like a good deal. I wired him my last ten thousand bucks and bought the first cheap ticket to London I could get."

"And he was going to meet you?"

She nodded.

"But of course he didn't."

"He'll have a good reason."

"Christ. You have more faith in him than I do."

"By the way you act, I have more faith in *anyone* than you do."

"That's not hard."

"So I gathered. What are we going to do?"

"We're going to Skinner's this morning. Try and find out where he is."

"I've already tried. I told you."

"I'm a detective. I might have more luck."

She looked towards the heavens as if to say, "Fat chance."

Somehow we both managed to get ready to go, without any more hassle. Sweetheart ended up in some kind of dude ranch ensemble in mostly black and gold. I went for clean Levis and a Wrangler shirt. Roy Rogers and Dale Evans, or what?

We went downstairs together and got into my E-Type—which as far as I could gather was my first possession that Sweetheart approved of, although she would persist in calling it an XKE—and arrived at Edmonton at about eleven. We weren't followed. She gave me Skinner's address and I found the street in the A-Z.

"What's with these women you talked to then?" I asked *en route*. "Are they lesbians, or what?"

"Skinner's fan club," said Sweetheart. "They're dikes all right. Chuck and Bo. Skinner named them after his favourite guitarists. The big one's the one to watch. Chuck."

Chuck and Bo, I thought. Outstanding.

I left Sweetheart leaning on the wing of my car and knocked on the door. A massive woman in dungarees with a short haircut answered. It was one of those times when I just knew that whatever boyish charm I'd managed to hang on to was going to be totally wasted. "Hi," I said.

The woman chewed on the side of her mouth and didn't answer.

"You must be Chuck," I said.

"S'right."

"I'm looking for Skinner."

"You and a million others. Including your girlfriend out there."

As she spoke, another woman appeared behind her. Mousy and frightened looking. But pretty in a beaten-down way. I smiled past Chuck and the other woman smiled nervously back. "And you're Bo," I said.

"So you know our names," said the first woman. "Is that supposed to fill us with confidence? The poll-tax inspector knows them too."

I smiled, but I could have kicked her.

"Skinner's away," I said. "On tour, I believe."

Chuck didn't bat an eyelid.

"Look, I'm a friend of his. So is she." I glanced round at the car. "It's urgent that we speak to him. Really urgent."

"I told her last night I didn't know where he was. I gave her the note he left. That's all I'm prepared to do. Now go away, will you. We're busy." And she slammed the door in my face. The last thing I saw was Bo's frightened look before the wood filled the hole with a bang.

I went back to the car. "Told you," said Sweetheart.

Don't you just hate people who are always right?

"Lunch," I said.

She nodded.

Before we drove off, I dropped one of my business cards with my home number on the back through the letterbox of the house. I didn't expect a response, but you never know.

We ate at some overpriced bistro in the West End, and I got a ticket on the car. Terrific.

So that looked like that. There had been no sign of a tail all day. Maybe we were off the hook, maybe we weren't. Whichever it was, only time would tell.

On the way home I stocked up on booze at the office and picked up twenty quid's worth of rocky from a pal of mine who runs a second-hand furniture shop in Herne Hill, and we went back to the flat. Sweetheart had two packets of leopard-skin-patterned rolling papers that matched her boots, and we spent the rest of Thursday and Friday hanging out in my place getting righteously wrecked.

She played me some of the tapes she'd brought with her. All country. I particularly liked a couple by a geezer called Guy Clark, and made her keep playing them as I got more and more wasted. Every time I hear those songs now, I think of us together in that little flat on those two, long, hot summer days when the air smelled of her perfume and dope and booze.

Thursday night she had my bed again, and I slept on the sofa. Big surprise.

The call came Friday night. Late. I answered the phone and heard a small, nervous voice on the other end of the line. "Is that Nick Sharman?"

"Yes," I replied.

"You're a friend of Skinner's. You came round to our house yesterday. You left your card."

"That's right."

"I'm Bo. I saw you at the door."

Somehow, I hadn't thought it was Chuck. "I remember," I said. "What can I do for you?"

"Some men came round looking for Skinner. They were here before. Horrible men. They said horrible things."

Horrible men often do, I thought, but said nothing.

"They threatened us. Chuck's terribly upset. I thought I should call you."

I couldn't get my head round the idea of Chuck with an attack of the vapours, so I let it go. "Yes, Bo," I said.

"She told them about you and that American girl."

"Not a good idea."

"It was the only way we could get rid of them."

"How long ago?"

"Just a few minutes. I thought I should warn you."

"Thank you, Bo."

"And there's something else."

"What?"

"Skinner's going to be at the Holiday Inn in Dortmund tonight."

"Dortmund?"

"In Germany."

Thanks, Bo, I thought, but I did get my O-Level geography.

"I've got the number if you want it," she said. "I don't know what room he's in or anything. But he did say he'd be there tonight, before he went away. If we needed to get in touch or anything. He's with a band called Satan's Spawn."

"Satan's Spawn," I repeated. "Great. That's a big help. Really."

She reeled off the number, and I jotted it down on the back of an envelope.

"I hope we haven't got you into any trouble," she said.

"No more than usual," I replied. "Thanks for calling." And I hung up.

I told Sweetheart what had happened as I dialled the number that Bo had given me. She came and stood close to me as I did it.

The phone rang twice. A foreign-sounding ring, strange to my ears. Then a male voice said, "Holiday Inn, Dortm . . ."

I cut in before he could say more. "Do you speak English?" I asked.

"I certainly should, sir," replied the voice. "I come from East Grinstead."

"Great," I said. "Do you have any bands in tonight?"

His voice grew cooler. "Four, sir. You may choose from Heavy Metal, Grunge, Retro-Punk or Psychobilly."

"Is one of them called Satan's Spawn?"

"They are staying in the annexe, sir," said the voice.

"Is it cheaper?"

"No, sir. It's just not so many floors up, when they start throwing television sets out of the windows."

"That sounds like my man's style. Is there a Skinner checked in with them?"

I heard the sound of a computer keyboard being punched up.

"Is he there?" Sweetheart asked.

As she spoke her hair brushed against my cheek, and I felt her breath tickle my ear.

"Yes, sir," said the voice after a moment. "We do have someone of that name registered. Shall I try to locate the gentleman?"

"If you wouldn't mind."

"He's there," I said to Sweetheart.

When the receptionist returned, he said, "There's no answer from the bar. Shall I try his room?"

"Please. And make it quick. I'm calling from London. You know, England. The poor man of Europe."

"I'm well aware, sir," said the voice. "I'll try the room."

There was another dead silence. Then a voice said "Yeah?" It wasn't the receptionist.

"Skinner?"

"Who's this?"

"Nick Sharman."

"And Sweetheart," shouted Sweetheart.

"Christ. How did you find me?"

"Bo told me."

"Jesus! I was going to call."

"Course you were. It's just taken you a few days to get it together."

"It's the fucking band. They're bloody mental. They're only a bunch of kids. They never sleep. Thank God we've got tonight off so's I can get some rest."

"How come you've got a gig with them?" I asked.

"I haven't really. The lead guitarist can't play a note. He's always too stoned. I stand behind the speaker stacks and play his lead lines, and he mimes."

"Jesus Christ, Skinner. When will you ever learn?"

"It's a living. At least for the next six weeks. Till this tour's over."

"And a good way to get out of the country," I said. "Do you know we're being followed?"

"I thought it might be possible."

"Cheers, Skinner. You're a pal. And what about Sweetheart and this money?"

"It's a long story."

"Tell it. And make it the seven-inch version. I'm paying for this call all by myself."

"I met a geezer in a pub."

"No."

"Yeah. He was the stoppo for a three-handed firm of blaggers."

"Are they re-running *The Sweeney* where you are?" I asked. "Big in Dortmund, is it?"

"No. but you understand what I'm saying?"

"Yeah, of course. The driver for a gang of armed robbers."

"Quite right. They'd done a big job in Oxford and stashed the money away.

The driver wanted out, and told me that for a certain sum he'd sell me the location where the dough was hidden.''

"And you believed him? He didn't have a machine with him that changed fivers into twenties by any chance?''

"I thought you were worried about the price of the call?'' Skinner said dryly. "Carry on.''

"I had some dough. I called Sweetheart. She supplied the rest. It was all on the up and up.''

I shook my head in wonderment. Just what were this man's parameters on what wasn't on the up and up then?

"How much was involved?''

"On our side? Fifteen K.''

"And the money from the blag?''

"A hundred thousand.''

"A pretty good deal.''

"I thought so.''

"So what happened? Did he do a runner with the dough you were going to pay him?''

"No. I wish he had. Everything was fine. I went where he'd said the money would be. And it was there. I left a mate of mine. A roadie. Chalky. Remember him? With this bloke and the cash for the deal.''

"If the driver needed cash so bad, why didn't he just go and pick up the blag money himself?''

"You know I never thought of that till after.''

"Till after what?''

"Till after they pulled his body out of a skip in Hoxton. Near the Bass Clef, with his knees nailed together.''

"Christ! Was that him? I remember reading about that.''

"That was him all right.''

"Do you know who might have done it?'' I hardly liked to ask.

"I know all right,'' said Skinner. "Why do you think I'm here? I hate fucking Germans. When I heard what had happened to the driver, I made a few enquiries about who the other two blaggers were.''

"And?''

"It was the Beverley Sisters.''

I almost dropped the phone. "The Beverleys,'' I said. "Christ, Skinner, do you know what you've got yourself involved with? Sweetheart involved with? Me involved with? And you'd better not let them hear you call them the Beverley Sisters. Even for a joke. They don't take to it at all.''

Now, for anyone not familiar with the Beverley Sisters, they were a female British singing trio, very popular in the late fifties and early sixties. There were, and still are, three of them. A pair of twins and an elder sister. All blonde. Now the Beverley *Brothers* are a pair of right nutty villains with black hair. I mean *really* nutty. Crazy. Couldn't give a fuck for anything or anyone. People call them the Beverley Sisters for a laugh. But only in close company, out of earshot of strangers. Like I said, they don't take to it at all. In fact, an extended stay in hospital for the comedian often follows. You might wonder, apart from the play on the name, why there isn't another Beverley to make the joke perfect. Well, there is in a way. The younger of the two brothers, Derek, claims that the embryo of his unborn twin brother lives in the space between his brain and the inside of his skull. Swimming in the gunk there, and sleeping in a tiny space inside the bone over Derek's right eye that he, the twin brother that is, has nibbled over the years with his little embryonic gums. Derek refers to his twin as Kevin.

In short, a right nutter.

But a right nutter or not, Derek is the brains behind the operation. I remember once speaking to someone who went to school with the Beverleys. He told me that the only way to beat them in a fight was to put Derek away early. Then Raymond, the eldest one, would go to pieces, and that was that. Not that many people managed to put Derek away even in those days. Now, no one even tries.

"You've done it now, Skinner," I said into the hum of the line. "Right and proper."

"I know. What can we do?"

"We, is it?"

He didn't reply.

"Tell me where the money is," I said.

"What?"

"You heard."

"So that you can get it?"

"No. So that I can give it back to them. I've had dealings with them in the past. Years ago."

Nothing much. Nothing that could possibly have earned me more than the amputation of one or two fingers at the first knuckle. Nothing at all really. They'd probably forgotten all about me. Fat chance.

"Why should you do that for me?" asked Skinner.

"I'm not. It's for Sweetheart."

"Oh yeah."

"Yeah."

"Why would that be?"

I looked at her. "None of your fucking business," I said.

"Like that, is it?"

"No. As a matter of fact it isn't."

He was silent.

"So tell me," I said.

"We'll lose all our money."

"Better than losing all our lives." I let the words hang.

"OK. But don't ..." he said after a moment.

"Skinner," I interrupted. "Don't fuck about. This call is costing me a fortune. Just tell me where the dough is. I'll take care of it after that. And if the Beverley boys don't take to me, I want Guy Clark played at my funeral."

"Who?"

"Never mind. You'll find the tape in my stereo."

So he told me. He was very exact. I like that in a person. It gives me confidence. I didn't write it down. It took a while. When he'd finished, he said, "There's just one other thing."

"What?" I replied.

I heard him draw breath down the international line and he said, "When you find the money, there's ..."

And the door of my flat burst open and two bodies hurled themselves into the room.

Sweetheart screamed as one of the bodies grabbed her by the hair, forced her down on to the sofa, and stuck an extremely large handgun into the side of her head. The other body placed the barrels of a sawn-off shotgun under my chin. I noticed that both triggers had been messily tied together with silver wire. Twin barrels. One squeeze, and two cartridges loaded with God knows what gauge shot would take my head off. Not a pretty thought, especially as his finger was trembling inside the trigger guard.

The body with the shotgun, who as it happened was Derek Beverley, grabbed the phone and said, "Hello. Hello," into the mouthpiece, but got nothing but the click of a receiver being replaced at the other end for his trouble.

"Nick Sharman," he said. "I might have known you're webbed up in all this."

I looked down the length of the gun at him. His head *was* a weird shape. Like he'd been dropped on it a few days after birth, before the bone had set properly. And there was a lump over one eye. He was wearing a light mac over a purple-and-blue shellsuit. Fashion terrorist.

I looked over at the other body. Brother Raymond, naturally, who was holding Sweetheart by her hair and grinding his gun into her ear. "Tell the neanderthal to ease up, will you," I said to Derek. "She won't hurt him."

Derek glanced around quickly, but never let the gun he was holding on me move a centimetre. "Ray," he ordered. "Cool it."

Raymond looked up through eyes fogged with generations of interbreeding and abuse, loosened the grip he had on Sweetheart's hair and pulled the gun back a fraction. "Are you sure?" he asked with his nasty wet little mouth.

"I'm sure," replied Derek. "Nick here's not going to give us no trouble. Are you, Nick?"

I held my hands up in surrender. "Not me, mate," I said.

"Don't call me mate, you cunt. You're not my mate," spat Derek.

"Sorry," I said.

"Who were you talking to on the dog?" he demanded.

"No one special."

Derek saw the number written on the envelope and picked it up. "It was that fucking Skinner, wasn't it?" he said. "Where the fuck is he?"

Under the circumstances I thought there was no point in denying it. "Germany," I said.

"Bastard! He had it away with our dough. That little shit who was driving for us stitched us right up. Where is it?"

"I don't know what you're talking about," I said, and he hit me round the side of the head with the shotgun. Hard enough for me to see fireworks and have to grab the back of the sofa bed to stop me falling over.

"Don't lie," he roared. "We know you know."

"How do you know?"

"Skinner got drunk the other night. Just before he split. And blabbed it around Soho that some cowgirl was going to make him rich. With our dough as it happens. Then we caught up with the geezer who drove for us on the job and we got the whole story out of him. When we found out where Skinner lived and that he was gone, we waited around in case she showed up. Simple."

Elementary, in fact.

"Now where is it?" he demanded.

"Why didn't you call by the other night. When you tried to run me down?" I asked conversationally. Although I was feeling anything but conversational. Scared shitless in fact. This had all the ingredients of a night to forget in a hurry.

"Didn't recognize you straight away. It's been a long time. You've let your hair grow. If we'd known it was you, we would have done."

I put my hand up and ran it through my barnet. "Yeah," I said.

Sweetheart, who was now sitting up on the sofa, said, "Old home week, guys?"

Raymond gave her a backhander and she cried out with pain. "Shut up, cunt," he said.

"Don't do that again, Raymond," I said. "It's not nice."

"What you going to do about it?" he demanded.

I said nothing. There was nothing to say. Everyone in the room knew that I was going to do nothing about it at all. I just shook my head at Sweetheart, and hoped she took the hint.

"You went round Skinner's house yesterday and left your card," continued Derek. "And the two cunts there showed it to us."

Thanks, Chuck. Thanks, Bo.

"The fat bitch said you said it was urgent. A hundred grand urgent, we reckoned." He shoved the gun further into my face, it seemed. "Tell us,

Sharman, or I swear I'll get Raymond to stripe the Yank so bad that her own mother won't know her."

I saw Raymond smile in anticipation.

After that I thought there was no point in screwing around any further. "I was going to give it back to you," I said.

Derek seemed amused at the concept.

"But you'll never see a penny of it, if Raymond touches her again," I said.

"Big talk."

It was all I had.

"Where is it?" asked Derek, after a moment. Seemingly a little more self-controlled.

"Out of town," I said. "Skinner told me where," and I tapped my head. "It's all up here."

"Take us."

"And if I say no?"

He grabbed me, and spun me round and pushed me in the direction of Sweetheart, and came up close behind me and whispered into my ear. "Then I'll shoot the tart's arm off," he said. "Anyway, what's the problem? You were going to give it back to us, weren't you?"

"On my terms," I replied.

"Now it's on our terms. So let's go."

I hesitated, but only for a second. "It's buried," I said. "You'll need a shovel."

"You got one?" interrupted Raymond.

"I live on the top floor," I said. "What do I need a shovel for? My window box?"

Derek dug the barrel of the shotgun into my kidneys. Hard.

They had handcuffs with them, the new, one-piece plastic ones, and they trussed our wrists up tightly. Then took us down to the grey Granada that was parked outside. They pushed us into the back, and Derek climbed into the front passenger seat, looked over the back of it, and said, "Sit quiet, and say nothing or I'll kill her. Don't think I won't." Then he said something to Raymond through the window, who vanished, to reappear a few minutes later with a spade that he threw into the boot, and got in behind the steering wheel.

A little spot of petty larceny in the night.

Raymond started the car, put the gear shift into drive, and headed up the hill. "Where to?" asked Derek.

"Make for Oxford," I said. "The scene of the crime. Where we want is off the M40."

Derek seemed satisfied, and didn't say more, just sat so that he could look into the back of the car, with the shotgun poking over the centre console, just to remind us it was there.

I moved my leg so that it touched Sweetheart's and pressed it gently up against hers. She pressed back, and turned and gave me a weak-looking smile. I was proud of her.

We took the South Circular as far as Clapham, then headed over the river and up to Shepherd's Bush, and picked up the A40 and eventually the motorway. I told Raymond to come off at junction 7, then I directed him to turn off the A329 on to the B4011. I counted three more turnings, saw the pub on the corner that Skinner had told me about, took the next road to the right, over a bridge over a river, then I made Raymond slow right down until we came to a lane that disappeared off into the darkness.

"Up there," I said. "And keep the speed down."

He did as he was told, and we came to a five-barred gate, then the lane widened enough for us to pull the car over without blocking the way. "This is us," I said.

The Beverleys helped Sweetheart and me out of the car, and Raymond got the shovel out of the boot, and we walked back to the gate, which wasn't padlocked, and opened it. By the light of torches that Derek and Raymond had brought with them, we followed a faint path that ran along the edge of a copse of trees.

Sweetheart and I, still both cuffed up, stumbled along but the boys refused to untie our wrists.

We walked for maybe a quarter of a mile before I saw what I was looking for. It was the red light on top of a telecommunication mast that stood on a hill about five miles away.

"We're almost there," I said for something to say.

I kept my eye on the light, until it stood exactly midway between the arches of the railway bridge over the river that gleamed in the moonlight in the valley below us. From where we were standing there wasn't a house light in sight. Skinner had picked the perfect place.

I turned and looked up at the dark mass of trees that loomed over the path where we were standing. "Straight up there," I said.

We cut across the rough grassland and keeping the red light behind me I found the lightning-scarred tree that Skinner had described. "It's on the other side," I said.

We walked round the tree and found ourselves in a tiny clearing. In the centre, the earth was bare, and surrounding it was dry-looking undergrowth. Derek uncuffed me, and I massaged some life back into my hands. Raymond tossed me the spade. "Get digging," he ordered.

"Aren't you going to untie her?" I asked.

In the wash of light from their torches, Derek shook his head.

"Then dig it your fucking self," I said. The chances were that I was only digging our own graves anyway. Why make it easy for them?

Derek shrugged, and unfastened Sweetheart's wrists too, and pushed her in the direction of Raymond. "Keep an eye on her," he said. "Now you dig, Sharman, or she'll suffer."

"Throw us a torch down here," I said.

Derek did as I asked. I stuck it in the fork in a branch and let the light shine on the ground in front of me.

I pushed the spade into the dirt and it seemed loose, like it had recently been turned over, which made me think that Skinner had been telling me the truth. It didn't matter if he had or not. We were well fucked either way.

I looked at the three of them standing in front and slightly above me. Derek was on my left, shotgun in both hands. Raymond was next to him, torch in one hand, gun in the other, pointing nowhere in particular. Sweetheart was on his left, and to my right.

I started digging. It was a warm night, but I didn't have a coat, so I didn't start to build up a sweat for a few minutes. When I did, I felt better. Never better in fact. Strange, when I knew that I could be dead at any moment.

I dug a pretty big hole. Big round, I mean. I wasn't in any hurry and none of the others said a word as I worked.

After about fifteen minutes' digging, with the earth piling up around me, the blade of the shovel clunked on something hard, sending a shock up both my arms.

"What's that?" demanded Derek.

"Hold on," I said. "Give us a chance."

I went back to my digging, but I was more careful, and in the light of the torch I saw the edge of a black box emerge from the earth that surrounded it.

"It's a box," I said.

"Get it out," ordered Derek.

"All right," I said. "Don't be so impatient."

I dug the earth from around the box with the edge of the spade, then got down on my knees and used my hands.

The box was big, with rope handles, and I dragged it out from the earth where it was anchored and dumped it on the edge of the hole.

"Open it," ordered Derek.

I did as I was told and flipped back the lid. It only went half-way back, the top being attached to the edges by rope hinges. Lucky for me that Derek and Raymond couldn't see inside, because on top of the piles of neatly banded cash was a revolver. I looked at it and decided that Skinner wasn't as dumb as he pretended. It was a Smith & Wesson Model 27 .357 magnum. A right tasty weapon.

I hoped that it was loaded.

There was only one way to find out. I hunkered down on my heels in front of the open box, looked at the gun, then up at the three of them standing over me. "Come on, don't fuck us about. Is the money there?" said Derek, grinding the words out between his teeth.

"It's here," I replied, and I saw him grin and he started towards me. It was now or never, but I just needed him off balance a little. "How is Kevin by the way?" I asked. "Doing all right in there, is he?"

Derek's eyes widened, and I thought for a moment they were going to pop out of their sockets, and he moved closer still, the shotgun barrel pointing up into the air. I grabbed at the gun, brought it up, and pulled the trigger. The first bullet hit Derek just above the right eye and blew half his head, his brain and presumably the embryo of little Kevin, if it existed, all to hell and gone. At the moment of impact, as his body crumpled to the ground, Derek pulled the triggers of the shotgun. The noise was deafening and the shot ripped through the tree above us, bringing down a load of leaves. The blast lit up the clearing we were in, just as I fired at Raymond. I shot him three times in the chest, and he fell backwards into the bracken, kicked his heels and was still.

I sat down on the edge of the box, dropped the gun into the dirt and sat for a moment trembling and making funny little noises with my mouth. Sweetheart moved away from the bodies, and leant against a tree making little noises of her own.

She pulled herself together first, and came over and looked down at me. "Come on, Sharman," she said. "Get a grip."

I looked up at her. "Jesus," I said through dry lips. "Oh, Jesus."

"Come on," she repeated. "We've got to get this mess tidied up."

"You go back to the car and wait," I said. "I'll do it."

"Be the little woman?" she said. "Fuck off. My great-great-grandmother took Apache scalps in the Indian wars, and was her own midwife eighteen times."

"Yeah, I know," I said. "They grow 'em tough in Texas."

"Cor-rect. Anyhow, it'll take two of us to get that box back. It looks heavy. Now let's do it. This place is beginning to give me the creeps."

Beginning? It had been giving me the creeps ever since we'd arrived.

"Come on," she said again. "Let's do it."

So we did it.

We pulled the box away from the hole, then enlarged it, and together we rolled Derek and Raymond's bodies into it, and covered them with earth, then pieces of bracken and leaves. In the light from the torches it looked OK, and with the place being as remote as it was, I doubted that anyone would ever bother even to visit it, let alone be interested enough to dig there. Before I buried Raymond, I went through his pockets and found the car keys.

Sweetheart was great. A tower of strength. There were a couple of times I'd've called it a day if she hadn't been there, I'm sure. But she kept me at it, until she was satisfied that no one would ever know what happened in that clearing in that wood near Oxford.

She was wearing her zebra-skin boots, and she took them off in case they got covered in dirt, and worked in stockinged feet.

You don't argue with a woman like that.

As we lugged the box of money and the guns and the spade back to where the car was parked, dawn was breaking on the horizon.

All the time we were there, we never saw or heard another soul, and as far as I can make out no one saw or heard us.

I drove sedately back to London, keeping to the speed limit all the way. Sweetheart didn't say anything until we'd crossed the river and picked up the South Circular again. Eventually she asked, "What are we going to do with the money?"

"Keep it," I said.

"Won't someone be looking for it?"

"Without a doubt. Too bad. We've earned it. We'll split it three ways. One third for you, one third for me, and one third for Skinner. That'll keep him quiet. He was prepared to lose every penny last night. I'm sure he'll be happy with over thirty grand."

"What about those two women at his house?"

"What about them? They don't know the Beverleys actually came to see us, do they? And I think they've been scared enough already for them to be happy that they never have to see the rover boys again. Anyway Skinner'll sweet talk them when he comes back. They'll be OK."

She nodded and was silent for a moment, and then said, "I didn't know you guys in Britain went in for gun-play."

"You'd be amazed," I replied.

"I was. It was like Saturday night in downtown Dallas there, for a while."

"It must have made you feel right at home," I said as drily as possible.

"It did." She was silent again, and then she turned in her seat to face me. "Do you think they *were* going to kill us?"

"Well I don't think our well-being was their major priority, exactly," I replied.

"But if they did," she said, "they'd've had to go back and get Skinner, and maybe even Chuck and Bo."

"People like that don't think that far into the future," I said. "They were nuts. Crazy men. We crossed them and they didn't like that one bit. It was a chance I couldn't afford to take. I had to make a call, and I made it."

"But won't someone be looking for them?"

"I doubt it. They weren't the most popular pair in London."

"Won't they be missed?"

"Who's going to miss them? They had no families. Just each other. They were totally self-sufficient. Old Bill ... that's the police," I said as a look of puzzlement crossed her face, "might wonder what's become of them. But even they won't care. They'll just be grateful that the crime rate's fallen. No, doll. I doubt that many tears'll be shed about the Beverley Brothers. People'll think

they've scarpered to Spain or somewhere. They'll be forgotten in twelve
months. Good riddance."

"I'll never forget them."

"Nor me."

She was silent again, and then with a look of utter bewilderment on her
face she said, "And who the hell is Kevin?"

"Don't ask," I said.

For all my brave talk, I had to stop twice on the way back because I started
to shake so hard I couldn't drive. Both times Sweetheart leaned over and held
me tight, and I could smell her perfume, and her sweat, and her fear, and a
faint tang of earth on her. Each time, after a few minutes or so, I was all right.

It was about five when I reversed the Granada up on to the open space in
front of my house. To tell you the truth, I was a bit worried about letting it
be seen, but I had to take that chance. I went upstairs and got an old blanket
and wrapped the guns and the shovel in it, before taking them into the house.
After they were safely inside, Sweetheart and I took the box of cash up to my
flat and emptied the money on to the carpet in the middle of the room.

"You sort out the money while I dump the motor," I said.

"What about the box?"

"I'll find a skip and drop it in." I don't know if they have skips in America,
but I imagine she got the concept.

"OK. Don't be long."

"Just as long as it takes, babe," I said.

She smiled tiredly at me and started putting the banded stacks of bank notes
into three piles.

I left the Granada in Victoria, doors and windows open, key in the ignition.
The only other thing I could have done was leave a note under the windscreen
saying "Steal me." But I thought that was a trifle excessive. I wore gloves
and wiped all the places I remembered touching, just in case. I hopped an
early morning bus to Tulse Hill and got back to Sweetheart around seven.

Her stuff was all packed away in her unecological suitcases. I was going to
miss her shit everywhere. The money had been neatly divided into three, and
put into plastic shopping bags she'd found in the kitchen drawer.

"When are you going back?" I asked, when I'd got a cup of tea.

"On Tuesday."

"So you've still got a few days."

She nodded.

"But now you've got enough cash to stay five-star."

She nodded again.

"Anywhere in mind?" I asked.

She nodded yet again.

"Hilton? Intercontinental? Brown's? The Connaught? The Savoy? What?"
She shrugged.
"Well, at least I'll get my bed back."
Nod number three.
"Want a lift anywhere?"
Shrug number two. Then she said, "Can I ask you something?"
"What?"
"How come you've never hit on me since I've been here? Aren't I sexy enough for you?" Her eyes were that perfect shade of grey as she spoke.
"Give it a rest," I said. "No. I just assumed that you and Skinner had something going together."
"Is that what he says?"
"No. He's never mentioned you. I just assumed it. Don't you?"
She smiled. "You might call it that. Once."
"Once what?" I asked. "Once, one time only. Or once upon a time."
"Once, once," she said. "In Burnley, on some godforsaken tour."
"Why?" I asked. Thinking about it, Skinner would probably just about come up to her left tit. Still, not a bad job, I suppose.
"What else do you do on a wet afternoon in Burnley? It was a mistake. One of those things. Nothing happened anyway. I didn't even get my skirt creased. Christ. Just look at the guy, will you? Whoopee-fucking-do. You don't give me much credit for taste, do you, Sharman?'"
"Sorry. So where's it to be?" I asked. "What ivory tower of luxury shall I transport you to?"
She went and sat on my bed. "I want to stay here," she said.
"That sofa's breaking my back. And I deserve a good night's sleep," I said.
"Who said you'd be sleeping on the sofa?"
"You want to swap?"
This time she shook her head.
I looked at her, and she patted the bed again. "Christ, Sharman," she said. "Do I have to draw you a map?"
As a matter of fact, she didn't.

Tim Heald won a Golden Dagger nomination for the following story. You will immediately see why. You'll also remember this story long after you've finished reading it.

A Vacance en Campagne
TIM HEALD

1 August

I can't think what possessed Jill to agree to a holiday with Brian and Lulu. They're perfectly OK in Putney in small doses but the idea of being holed up with them in a barn in Brittany for two whole weeks is frankly unspeakable. The ferry was bloody and not made any easier by Brian's attitude. It doesn't help to bang on and on about it being "a Frog boat." We're all in the EC now so we might as well muck in and even though the fellows on the car deck were absolute swine the food is a sight better than on those ghastly British boats. Entrecote and frites. Crème brûlée. Very decent little Nuits-Saint-Georges. Café filtre and a large Armagnac. But Lulu just had to send her steak back because it was pas bien cuit. Brian put away an alarming quantity of Armagnac because, he said, it stopped him getting seasick. As the Channel was flat as a mill pond this seemed a pretty feeble excuse.

Mercifully the boys were absent. we gave them enough cash to get a self-serve supper in the cafeteria along with the back-packers and the train passengers and the rest of the great unwashed. I think they spent most of it on the fruit machines. Richard came in at some unearthly hour and snored till I threw a shoe at him.

1 August

This is going to be a bloody nightmare unless Mum and Dad sort it. Gary's parents are pigs too. Actually his mum's not too bad but his dad's like weird. And if anything he's even more of a fascist than Dad. The way he was talking to the French was really embarrassing.

Mum and Dad had their usual map-reading row getting to the ferryport and then Dad stalled on the car deck and this big French bloke in overalls started shouting and it was well funny only Dad didn't think so and his ears went all pink like they do when he knows he's done something pathetic.

After we'd found the cabins they all wanted to go off to the posh restaurant only they didn't want us around which I don't mind because the food's all muck in there and Mum and Dad always get in a great thing about table manners and not eating with your fingers and chugga-lugging and that so Gary and I played the machines which were well wicked. Then we had a frankfurter and some fries and met these French girls who'd been hitching round Angleterre and we had some drinks with them. Gary bought me some stuff called Pernod which is sort of like water only when you mix it with lemonade it goes all cloudy and tastes like Liquorice Allsorts. Terrific kick. I got quite a high. In fact I didn't think I'd be able to find the cabin only Véronique didn't think my idea of sharing her sleeping bag on deck was a very good one, so she helped me find the cabin. Then just when I got to sleep Dad started shouting and throwing things. Still Gary and I have got our own room at this "jeet" thing. Gary's dad Brian keeps going on about the "jeet" but I don't think he knows what it is any more than anyone else. Gary says it's all been fixed up with some bloke they met in Putney whose dad is a French Count.

2 August

Some bloody gîte! Why in God's name we couldn't have fixed it through Chris at Vacances en Campagne like we usually do I cannot think. I mean what can one expect of someone at a party in Putney who claims to be some sort of French aristo? He was pure Maurice Chevalier atte Bowe. Probably born under the family barrow in the Old Kent Road! It's not as if it's cheap either—in fact it's outrageously expensive. And everything's extra. You get charged for the electricity—what there is of it—and the Calor gas—and the wood for the "open" fires (actually they're more like "closed" fires because it's quite obvious that the chimneys haven't been swept since the Revolution). There's no phone so he can't charge for that. Even the water's on a meter and the bedlinen is ten francs a pillowcase and twenty a sheet. Brian and Lulu, naturally, are putting a brave face on it. No more talk about "bloody Frogs" just endless, "Oh isn't it charming?" and "It's too enchantingly typical" and—worst of all—"Not like home, eh Gordon?" I could have belted him when he said that. I could have done him a serious mischief. Still, even though she is a silly cow you can't help fancying Lulu. For a woman of her age she's got terrific legs.

Oh Jesus, where to begin?!

First of all the house is in the middle of absolutely nothing and miles from nowhere. The nearest village is a place called Tréguerpoul-le-Grand. I'd like to know what Tréguerpoul-le-Petit is like. Le Grand has a "Bar des Sports" with a pool table and a handful of chaps in blue overalls puffing away on filthy unfiltered cigarettes and drinking cider out of mugs. Then there's a village shop which is run by an old bag with one tooth. It sells gumboots, chocolate biscuits and gallon containers of vin ordinaire. There was a "crêperie," but that's closed for summer. The church has a steeple with holes in it. Apparently this is to stop it being blown over by the prevailing gale—though at the moment there is no wind at all, just a light drizzle and a thin blanket of fog.

T. le Grand is about a kilometre away if you walk over the artichoke fields but by car it's about five. The "gîte" as Brian and Lulu will keep calling it is entirely surrounded by artichokes. "Well, we won't starve," said Brian. "Ho, ho, ho." I had never noticed before how Brian signals his jokes with this thigh-slapping. "Ho, ho, ho" as if he were one of the seven dwarfs.

Anyway, Brian's "gîte." Barn is putting it kindly. Yes it's true there are three double bedrooms in the sense that there are three bedrooms into which it is possible to insert two average-size human beings. And if you don't mind sleeping on horsehair there is not a lot wrong with the beds. Provided you get on all right with your partner and go easy on the garlic. The bathroom has a bidet but no bath—only a shower which has two temperatures: scalding or freezing.

The living-room is at least big but it leaks and there are draughts everywhere. Some musty old prints on the walls, exposed beams, threadbare rugs on the floor. There are mice too. The armchairs are uncomfortable and the dining table wobbles even when you stick folded newspaper under the legs. The kitchen has a fridge with mould in the ice compartment—which doesn't freeze—and a stove with a one-speed oven. There is one frying pan, two saucepans and a job lot of spoons, knives and forks and the whole thing smells of gas.

Thank God we stocked up on duty-free. At least a few stiff Scotches keep out the worst of the damp and cold. Sally and Lulu cooked spaghetti with a tinned Bolognese sauce which we'd brought with us. There were, naturally, no shops open apart from the one in T.-le-grand which is effectively useless unless you want roast gumboot. Christ, Gary's table manners are dreadful— even worse than Richard's. He seems completely unable to keep his mouth shut while eating. He and Richard went out after supper while we played bridge. God knows what they got up to. They didn't get back till after we'd gone to bed. We should have left them at home or sent them to some kind of summer camp. Borstal, preferably. I never realised what a constant provocation teenage boys could be.

2 August

I hate old people. If anything Gary's old people are worse than my old people but there's not much to choose between them. Luckily we were able to escape after supper. Mum and Gary's mum did a spag bol which was like well revolting only none of them seemed to notice. They'd bought some massive bottles of booze on the boat so they were all too pissed to taste anything. They're horrible when they're drunk. All laughing at each other's feeble jokes all the time. I think Dad fancies Gary's mum. He's always eyeing her up.

Gary and me played pool in the village. Gary has a torch so we made it through the fields. I think I like Pernod. Also we bought some Gauloise cigarettes which are well smoky.

When we got back they were all snoring and the walls are so thin the whole jeet shakes.

3 August

To the seaside at Perros-Guirec. A sort of Bognor-sur-mer. They have scrabble tournaments every Monday and when we arrived there were a whole lot of people in track suits prancing about on exercise mats under the leadership of a rather fanciable gamine brunette. Brian and I swam briefly before the fog rolled in; the girls found a café and drank kirs; and bloody Gary and Richard buggered off and did God knows what in the casino. I slipped Richard a 50-franc note, which was worth it just to get them out of our hair. Lunched on langoustes and Muscadet then a supermarché shop, back to base, slurped some duty-free, supper, bridge and bed. Could be worse, I suppose. The boys sloped off after the evening meal griping about not having anything to do, not having enough cash etc. etc. I told them they were extremely privileged to be enjoying the sort of holiday most of their friends would give their eye teeth for. They didn't seem convinced.

3 August

Christ, another twelve days of this. We went to the seaside which was just like the seaside in England except there were all these French people hitting balls at each other on the beach. Sort of ping-pong without a table or a net. Dad and Gary's dad ogled some middle-aged women wobbling about in time to continental house music—not very heavy metal. Mum and Lulu went off to start getting pissed—which is all the oldies seem to think about—and Dad and Brian went swimming which was pretty pathetic. They've both got dreadful beer bellies but they strutted down the beach sucking their breath in and sticking their chests out and trying to look like they were well smart but they just looked white and pathetic and English and old. I hope I never look like that.

The evenings are really dreadful. The jeet is cold and miserable and they just sit about talking crap and then they have supper and then they play cards and the only time they like notice us is to complain about what we're wearing or what we're doing or not doing. Like, "Why don't you read a good book?" or, "Why don't you go for a walk?"

Tomorrow night Gary and me are going to cook supper. We might slip in some really poisonous berries. One of the old blokes in the bar tried chatting us up, which was a bit spooky. Good pool table though and I do like Pernod. When we got back they'd left one of the burners on in the kitchen. Dad had made Breton coffee—Nescafé and calvados which is some sort of apple brandy. Also they'd left some money lying around on the sideboard. Not much but we nicked it anyway. Hope they won't notice.

4 August

Rained again. Sally and Brian both said they were feeling a bit hung over so they stayed home while Lulu and I drove in to do a shop in Tréguier. We took the boys and dumped them outside the cathedral. For once they didn't ask us for money. After the shopping we adjourned to the bar at the Hôtel Estuaire and sank a couple of beers. I must say Lulu *has* got bloody good legs and actually once she's away from Brian she's not nearly as insular and stupid as I'd thought.

Brian and Sally seemed a bit peeved that we were so late getting back. Actually we weren't that late and anyhow I blamed it on the boys. At least they have *some* uses.

We've practically finished the duty-free but we bought some calvados (excellent) and some Breton whisky (doubtful) at the supermarché. Richard and Gary cooked supper, which, I have to admit, wasn't too bad. They did a spaghetti carbonara which was really bacon and scrambled egg with pasta, but it was properly cooked which you can't always say about the girls' offerings. Afterwards, however, we tried teaching them how to play bridge. Not a success. Gary swore, unforgivably, at his father. Actually I was inclined to side with the boy. Brian had taken far too much of the Breton whisky and it's just not practical to order a sixteen-year-old to go to his room. The pair of them buggered off out and didn't come in till the small hours. God knows where they'd been but for once I'm not sticking my head above the parapet.

Incidentally, I made some Breton coffee with some of the whisky when we'd finished the bridge but everybody dozed off before I'd finished. So I'm afraid I slurped the lot—and then nodded off myself. I only woke when the boys came in, by which time the others seemed to have gone to bed. Maddening. Naturally I pretended I'd stay up late reading, had a long day, just nodded off for a second or two but I could see the little beasts smirking. I shall have to talk to the others about their coming in so late. We really can't have them lager-louting round the French countryside at all hours of the night.

4 August

I hadn't realised old people were so like, well, pathetic really. All they want to do is play cards and get pissed and take it out on us. We found a wicked pool table in Tréguier in the morning. Then in the evening after Gary and I cooked this brill carbonara they decided they'd teach us to play cards. Honestly, it was *so* boring and then Gary did something he shouldn't have done with his ace of clubs—I think—and his dad got well mad and started having a right go at him and told him to go to his room as if he was a baby so Gary was well gutted and told his dad to get stuffed and his dad went an amazing colour and his eyes all sort of shrunk and piggy and Gary's mum looked as if she was going to start blubbing and Mum and Dad just looked at their cards and pretended nothing was happening.

So we went out and instead of going to the village we went to the end of the road and managed to hitch a lift into Tréguier and went and played pool in this bar and hung around and there were some French kids who spoke a bit of English and it was quite nice really and one of them had this really beaten up sort of van and he gave us a lift almost all the way home and when we got in there was this terrible smell of gas because they'd forgotten to turn the stove off and Dad was asleep on the sofa and snoring, so we woke him up only he was really too smashed to know what was going on.

5 August

Richard asked for money again. I don't know what to do about him and his bloody money. He spends it like water and seems to think it grows on trees.

We compromised in the end and I gave him half what he'd asked for. It's not as if he does anything to earn it. Neither of them even make their beds and their room's like a pigsty. More rain and fog. An interesting tête-à-tête with Lulu when Sally and Brian went to investigate the architectural pleasures of the local château. I get the distinct impression that all is not as well as it might be between her and Brian. The boys disappeared around lunch and didn't get back till about midnight. Brian and I agree that we must have serious words with them both. We should never have brought them.

5 August

I don't know why Gary and I have parents as naff and disgusting as ours. You'd think they'd be glad to pay us to keep out of their way so they can get drunk and have it off with each other—there's definitely something funny going on between Dad and Gary's mum and if you ask me Mum and Gary's dad have sussed it and are going to pay them back by getting up to something themselves. If it wasn't so pathetic it would be well disgusting. Gary says it's like something out of *Eldorado*. Anyway we both asked for money and you'd think we'd asked for cocaine or snuff movies or something. Both dads were the same, like really really angry and lots of stuff about how all we ever did was complain about not having anything to do and going out and money money money. I mean if we were home I could get a job even if only a paper round but I can't see us getting a paper round in Tréguerpoul-le-Grand. Gary says we could try and get work in the supermarché at Tréguier but I don't think our French is up to it even if we were just humping boxes around. We certainly couldn't do the checkout. So I don't know what Dad's problem is. I didn't ask to come to Brittany with them, I'd much rather stay home, but now he's blaming me for everything—even the freezing fog.

Still we got another lift into Tréguier and met Philippe and he's lent us like serious money—well 200 francs. We'll have to try and nick some from one of the old people's wallets. They always leave them lying around.

6 August

Sun. Absolute bliss. We went to the beach at Tregastel and lay in the sun and swam and had a heavenly assiette de fruits de mer in a bar overlooking the sea. Considering her age, Lulu looked bloody marvellous in her swimsuit— plain black, one-piece. The boys scarpered but who knows where or what they did. The main thing is they weren't in our hair. We even bought a pair of those curious oversized ping-pong bats and balls. There doesn't seem to be any scoring system but I have to say I'm a great deal better at it than Brian.

Picked up some tuna steaks in a pêcherie plus stacks of Muscadet. The boys failed to make our rendezvous by the Grand Hotel so after a while we went home. They're old enough to fend for themselves and they know where the gîte is. If they want to be independent then let them be independent.

6 August

God, parents are like well shitty! They were all in a terrific mood in the morning because the fog had gone and you could actually see the sky. Hello sky! Hello sun! Hello birds! Hello flowers! So we all went off to the beach again. You'd think we were in a tropical heat wave the way the oldies were all carrying on but actually it was still pretty freezing.

No way were we going to join in being silly like them so we went off and tried to find where it was like at and actually it wasn't that bad. We met these English kids and had a great time with them playing the machines in the casino and eating frites and glacés and complaining about parents. They all have the same problem. What *is* it with old people?

We got to our meeting place outside the Grand Hotel and they didn't show. We waited and waited but eventually we decided they'd given us up. Quelle horreur! comme on dit en France. So we went back to hanging out and having a good time, then like hitched back and walked the last mile or so through the artichokes. Got in at about 1 A.M. and they're all snoring fit to bust.

Horrible smell of gas. Hardly dared have a fag in case we blew the whole place sky high. So smoked in the garden.

7 August

Brian and I have had serious words with the boys. I explained very patiently in my view that going on holiday together was a team effort and that therefore everyone bloody well had to pull together and if we, for example, made a rendezvous then the rendezvous had to be kept otherwise the whole shooting-match collapses, no one knows where anyone is, the gendarmes have to be alerted and it's all utter confusion.

Richard said, "But you didn't call the gendarmes, Dad. You didn't give a fuck!" which caused Brian to lose his temper and shout, "Don't get smart with your father, sunshine. If you were my son I'd lay you across my knee and give you a right thrashing." Which was understandable but not altogether sensible. So I said, "I think perhaps you'd better leave this to me, Brian." Which seemed to make him even madder, though he didn't say anything coherent, just spluttered, but there was an almost understandable sentence which sounded suspiciously like, "If you spent less time chasing other men's wives and more time disciplining your offspring . . ."

I ignored this, of course.

"I wish you wouldn't swear," I said to Richard, and I did think he looked embarrassed. He's not a bad boy, really. Just absolutely maddening. But maybe it's his age.

And that was about it really. Reading it through I can see it looks rather weedy and wimpish but what was I supposed to do? I told the boys that they weren't helping, that, like it or not, we had another whole bloody week in Brittany and if they went on behaving in this ridiculous selfish way they would make life an absolute misery and even if they didn't care about us they owed it to their mothers to behave in a less mean-spirited way and attempt to be a little more grown up. Gary, I'm sorry to say, said something to the effect that if being grown up was what we were doing then he didn't ever want to grow up thank you very much, which made his father even more apoplectic. I thought he was going to have a cardiac arrest then.

Anyway, Richard said he had a proposal, which was that if we gave them enough money they would, as he put it, "stay out of our hair" until the end of the holiday. Brian said that was blackmail and Richard said that it wasn't blackmail it was a business proposition and I'm afraid I said, "How much?" And in the end I agreed. So did Brian, sort of, though he wasn't really capable of speech. It was more than we could really afford, but it seemed worth it and off they went to God knows where.

Brian said I shouldn't have given in and he'd get even with the little bastards. I said something flippant about the one thing they weren't was little bastards. That didn't go down very well, and Oh shit, I'm going to have a drink. I don't like writing this down. It's demeaning.

7 August

Well, we finally had the big bust up. Gary's dad is a complete jerk and real bully or he would be if he had the guts. He's like well violent except now we're big enough to smack him back he daren't do it. Gary says he used to hit him well hard with a leather belt and with hairbrushes. Anything he could get his hands on. He says he used to beat his mum sometimes too, especially when he'd had a few.

Dad on the other hand is just pathetic, a real wimp. I knew the one thing he didn't want was serious trouble, like he's frightened of a bad argument and scared of getting hurt and especially of upsetting Mum. Mum's much stronger than he is. In fact she completely dominates him. She's just sort of the one who wears the trousers and tells him to shut up when he says something stupid or pig-ignorant which is most of the time.

Anyway I screwed some money out of him by being like dead reasonable. Gary was going to make a big fight out of it because he's like his dad, sort of well violent. He can do a vicious head-butt.

So after we got the money we went down Tréguier and met Philippe and some English kids in the "Irish Bar" which is this mean place with a pool table and a whole lot of Irish stuff like Irish flags and Pogue tapes and Guinness and Paddy whiskey. It's all because they're like Celts or something and talk the same language. Don't ask me what it's all about but it's a great place to hang out and there were some kids from Cork who said there'd been this wicked accident on their camp-site. This caravan like just blew up because there was something wrong with the gas cylinder. Apparently this bloke just went to make himself a mug of Nescafé and he lit a match and the whole place went Poof! They said you could hear the explosion all over the camp-site and there was a helicopter to take the bloke and his wife to the hospital in St. Brieuc. All the windows got blown out. Gary said it sounded like the sort of gas gear we have back at the jeet and he gave me a funny look and said, "Makes you think dunnit?"

8 August

Sun shone. To the beach. Dropped the boys who said they'd be back around midnight. Swam. Muscadet and langoustines for lunch. Sunbathed. Played bridge. Cooked some magret de canard which I picked up at the market in Lannion. Peaches. Some gungy Livarot also from a farmer's stall in the marché.

If I say it myself I think we've sorted out our domestic troubles quite successfully. The boys didn't say much. In fact they didn't say anything at all. But at least they weren't rude or particularly hostile. Lulu was impressed with the way I handled things. She says Brian is so violent. She likes quiet, civilised people.

8 August

Well hot day. Hung out. Philippe was impressed by the dosh. He wanted to know whether our parents were rich which Gary and I didn't really know how to deal with. I mean there's always enough. We're not exactly skint but if we were really rich we'd be down the south of France in a smart hotel not freezing to death in a crummy jeet in Brittany. Even though it is hot today.

He is a funny bloke, Philippe. He wants to come and have a look at the jeet when the old people are out. Says it might be embarrassing if they were there. Which is right. I mean they wouldn't like Philippe on account of they're not into pigtails and tattoos. He's got one on his bum of this naked woman and a snake. It's dead rude.

9 August

This is more like it. Another fine day weatherwise. Food, drink, sea, sand though alas no sex. Just as well there isn't much more of the holiday because I think both Lulu and I . . . well let's just say that we've agreed to meet for a little lunch soon after we get back. I don't think Brian and Sally suspect anything. In fact they seem quite engrossed in each other, which is a relief. The boys slept here last night but that's about it. They go their way and we go ours.

9 August

We showed Philippe the jeet. He couldn't believe the rent we were paying. He thought it was a real rip-off. He said no self-respecting Frog would think of living in a place like it, especially not in the middle of an artichoke field.

This is really weird coming from him because the place he lives in is just a shed—all corrugated iron and an outside bog. He says his parents kicked him out when he was fifteen. Gary thought this was well cool. At least that's what he said later. Only he did say that even though he'd rather not have to live with his boring parents he wouldn't like to live in a dump like Philippe's. There's not even a TV.

Gary really hates his mum and dad. I mean I like think mine are dead boring, and embarrassing and irritating but Gary really hates his. I mean hates. He thinks we should do something clever with the gas cylinder to teach them a lesson for being so shitty. I thought he was joking and he said yes he was joking because it wouldn't be like the explosion in the caravan because the jeet's so big and draughty. It would just be a little joke. Nothing serious. He really meant it. No one would ever know we had anything to do with it, it would look like an accident. All we had to do was make sure the gas was leaking well good, then go down the bar and leave them to light up later.

10 August

Quelle drame! Another quiet day with the boys out of our hair. I thought as they were behaving so relatively well etc. etc that it might be an opportunity to extend the proverbial olive branch. To my surprise Gary suggested we all have a drink together. So we piled off to Tréguier and for once there were no rows. To my relief Brian and Gary didn't come to blows for once. Afterwards the boys went off to do whatever it is they do while we went home to cook supper.

Then lo and behold we were just driving back down the drive all feeling rather jolly when there was a bloody great explosion from the gîte. Well of course we charged off and arrived to find the kitchen completely wrecked and a bloke in jeans and a pigtail lying face down on the floor. Dead, I'm afraid. A burglar I suppose. Presumably he struck a light so he could see and the gas must have been left on—and Poof! Quelle palaver! Had to summon the gendarmes and God knows what. Oddly enough when the boys came home, Richard seemed much more upset than the rest of us. More sensitive than we thought, perhaps. The girls were pretty devastated and I have to say I was a bit shaken. Gary and Brian, however, appeared completely unmoved. They both took the attitude that the burglar got what he deserved. Maybe Gary has more in common with his father than he'd like to think.

10 August

Oh God I can't wait to get out of this place. I mean suddenly Gary gives me the creeps. There's something really sinister about him. He seems to think it's all some sort of joke. He says it was nothing to do with him but I don't believe him. He says I've gone soft and I daren't say I think he's gone mad because he frightens me, he really does. He even laughed about it. Actually laughed out loud only it wasn't the sort of laugh you get when someone tells a funny story it was sort of, well, different. All his dad thinks about is the insurance. And the mums and Dad are all being wet about it but only in a sort of sentimental selfish way. Like, "How could such a horrible thing happen to *us*. On *our* holiday." They don't seem to think of Philippe being a human being. When I saw him lying all dead on the kitchen floor I just thought of how we'd had some good times together. I mean he wasn't what you'd call normal but he was sort of a friend even if he was Frog and I don't understand how Gary can just say "he blew it" and then do that horrible laugh of his.

Mind you, if Philippe hadn't blown himself up then . . .

Robert Bloch's *Psycho* is arguably the most influential suspense novel of this century—it marks the beginning of the modern era in crime fiction. But Norman Bates is hardly Bob Bloch's only major contribution to our genre. In literally dozens of short stories, and at least half a dozen novels, Bloch shows us work of the very first-rank. Look up his recent novel *Psycho House*. Whatever type of mystery fiction you like, you'll agree that this is an unqualified masterpiece.

It Takes One to Know One
ROBERT BLOCH

Kevin Ames took the elevator to the thirty-fifth floor, thinking about earthquakes all the way. When he arrived his involuntary sigh of relief echoed along the carpeted corridor as Ames made his way to the double doors at the far end. Here he halted to read the gold-lettered legend identifying the offices of *Tischler, Tischler, Phelps, Obendorrf & Associates*.

This time his sigh was voluntary. It was easy for him to understand why attorneys band together; obviously there's safety in numbers. But why did they list so many names? Wouldn't it be simpler to assume a group identity, like *Ali Baba and the Forty Thieves?*

Kevin Ames shrugged, then squared his shoulders, forced a smile and opened the right-hand half of the door guarding a reception area beyond.

Its decorous decor did little to put him at ease as he entered, and the matching receptionist behind a glass partition added no comfort to the occasion. Her prim lips parted in a smile of greeting usually reserved to welcome child-molesters at Disneyland.

"Good afternoon," he said. Apparently it wasn't, not for her anyway, because her smile went blank.

There was no change of expression in her unlifted face as he gave his name and received the *whom-did-you-wish-to-see?* routine in return. But when he answered that question her reaction was unmistakably evident.

"Mr. Tischler *senior?*" Her voice italicized her incredulity.

Ames nodded. "I have an appointment. For four-thirty."

"One moment, please." There was a flicker of disbelief in her eyes—the kind of look you'd give someone who brings a doggie-bag to the Last Supper.

Concealing his impatience, he stood waiting as she turned to address the intercom. "Grace? Did he come in this afternoon? No, they didn't say anything to me. Do you have something down about a four-thirty appointment? There's a Mr.—"

"Ames, Kevin Ames." His answer filled her pause, but he wasn't really listening. He'd started taking inventory of her desk.

Not much to see, really. No papers, no pads: it all goes on tape or into computers nowadays. But there was still the bud vase with the single rose, always a single rose in a pricey office like this, and a single receptionist who wouldn't be caught dead at a singles bar. At a certain age she still might or might not manage a face-tuck just to keep up appearances, but in any case or any age you could bet that her bra would always be a white one.

His speculation ceased abruptly as she switched off the intercom and addressed him. "Mr. Tischler will see you now, Mr. Ames."

Did he imagine it or was there a new note of respect in her voice, a warmer current flowing under the ice? If so, the thaw was generated by Tischler's name, not his.

Somewhere inside his skull, soundless queries emerged from cerebral silence. *Kevin? Kevin who? Never heard of him. What does he do?*

Practices anonymity, he responded, his answer as unvoiced as the question. That's the nice thing about talking to yourself, you never have to worry about being heard. And you always get the last word. Come to think about it, writing was also a way of getting the last word. Perhaps that was one of the reasons he'd been attracted to such a career. Or, more accurately, a profession. People who remain anonymous after a lifetime of effort can hardly claim their futile efforts towards recognition actually constitute a career.

"Good God! Has it really been that long?"

This voice he actually heard, and it wasn't coming from inside his head but from here, inside the private office. The paneled, polished claustrophobic quarters of Danton Tischler, Sr., attorney-at-law to the great, the near-great and the ingrates of Greater Los Angeles.

The voice didn't sound in the least as he remembered it. A once-hearty baritone was now a cracked, almost falsetto whisper—*probably through falsetto teeth*, Ames reflected—which one might expect from an elderly man. But then, this was an elderly man speaking; the young Danny Tischler he'd once known wasn't an occupant of Century City, because Century City didn't even exist in those days. The young Danny lived in memory as the sole resident of a bungalow-courtyard law office somewhere out along the wilds of Ventura Boulevard, where Edgar Rice Burroughs still ruled Tarzana.

Just how long ago *had* that been? Ames didn't need to ask, for the old man was already providing the answer.

"Forty years," he murmured.

Impossible. But there it was, in black and white, on the upper left-hand corner tab of the file folder which Tischler tapped as he spoke. His fingers, Ames noted, were like breadsticks.

"That's right," Ames said. "Time flies when you're having fun."

Tischler glanced down at his breadstick fingers. "You call old age fun?"

Ames shrugged. "Perhaps it's all a matter of viewpoint. If you look at it another way, life is an ongoing obituary."

The elderly attorney managed a dry chuckle. "You should have been a philosopher instead of a writer."

"No percentage in it," Ames told him. "And I'm not just talking about money. Have you ever heard a pretty little girl say, 'When I grow up, I want to marry a philosopher'?"

"So you went in for writing instead?"

"One of the reasons, I suppose. When you're young you think that way."

"Then how come you never married?"

"Because I grew up and stopped thinking that way."

"Any regrets?"

"I'm grateful just for having survived," Ames said. "Regrets are for the others who didn't make it."

"You stayed friends over the years?"

Ames frowned. "I wish I could say that. Remember, we used to meet for lunch at that Chinese place in Sherman Oaks every week and talk shop? But then we started moving around, job to job. Before you know it you've lost touch. When I think of how close we were when all of us started out doing horror for the magazines—"

"Right." Tischler's glance strayed again to the folder before him. "That name you fellows picked—*The Skull Club.* Maybe you thought it was a gag back then, but it's sure appropriate today." He looked up abruptly. "Know something? I never expected you'd be the one."

"I'm a little surprised myself," Ames told him. "Maybe 'shocked' is a better word. At least that's how I felt last week when I read about Jesse."

"Hadn't seen him lately?"

"No reason to. And you?"

"The same." Tischler nodded. "I did send him an invite when we had the party to open the new offices here, but he didn't show up. For that matter, neither did you."

"Sorry, I was out of town."

The breadstick fingers flicked in a gesture of dismissal. "No sweat. There was such a mob scene here that night I probably wouldn't have spotted you. Everybody who wasn't out of town came running for the free Dom Perignon."

Tischler paused. "Which reminds me. Better get down to business." He opened the folder and squinted at its contents. "Guess there's no point reading this again. Nobody's touched it in all these years." He reached down to pull out an oblong manila envelope, raised its flap, and extracted a small sheaf of papers. "Besides, I have these."

"What are they?"

"Copies of the death certificates. Care for a look?"

Ames shook his head quickly. "Not necessary. I know they're dead."

"Never hurts to be sure." Tischler slid the sheaf back into the envelope.

"Once a lawyer, always a lawyer," Ames said. "Do you want me to take a medical examination to prove I'm still alive?"

"A notary's statement will do." This time the attorney actually smiled. Rising, he crossed the room and pulled out the bottom drawer of an oaken filing cabinet. Ames watched him as he stooped, scrabbled, and straightened up again, gripping the straw-covered bottle.

"Here's your wine," Tischler said.

He returned to his seat behind the desk, depositing the rounded broad-based bottle in Ames' outstretched hands as he moved past.

Ames blinked. "I thought you kept this in your safe."

"I did, at first, but you're talking forty years ago." Tischler's chuckle was still dehydrated. "Every time the firm expanded we moved, but we kept running out of room. By the time we came here last fall, even a walk-in vault wouldn't hold all the sensitive material. When I ran across the wine I just stuck it in here where there was room, and I knew it'd be safe. Not that anybody would want to steal a bottle of cheap Chianti."

Ames glanced at what he was holding. "Cost us ninety-eight cents plus tax. All we could afford back then." His glance rose. "Brings up a point. What do I owe you?"

"No charge." Tischler nodded. "My pleasure."

"But you're entitled to something for storage and keeping your eye on it," Ames said. "If you hadn't volunteered, the five of us would have been stuck with safety-deposit box rental for forty years—"

"—and I would have missed the chance to tell my learned colleagues about the tontine." Again Tischler was smiling as he broke in. "Gave me something different to talk about. There aren't many lawyers around today who even know Lorenzo Tontine's name." He added a few wrinkles to his forehead. "Come to think about it, I don't believe I did until you told me. Getting a bottle of wine for the last survivor of the bunch was your idea, wasn't it?"

"I guess so. Though it was Everly who brought up a tontine to begin with. At first he was thinking along the regular line—everybody putting some money into a special account, letting the interest accumulate." Ames shrugged. "In the end, we had to settle for a fifth of Dago Red. That's what they used to call it in the old days."

"It's the sentiment that counts." Tischler nodded. "Do you plan to drink it?"

"Of course. As you say, it's the sentiment that counts."

Kevin Ames thought about sentiment as he drove home through the darkened downpour on drenched streets. It didn't rain very often in what TV weather forecasters refer to as the Southland, but who cared? Rain or shine, he had the wine. And should it prove sour, the taste would still be sweet.

Revenge is sweet.

Now there's a sentiment for you. Sentiment enough to compensate for sediment, if forty years had produced any in this bottle, this priceless bottle, more precious than the finest champagne.

Out of the corner of his left eye he caught the flicker of neon from a restaurant window, and his stomach responded with a warning growl. Perhaps he ought to stop for dinner.

He slowed down just long enough to note that in spite of rain the small parking area to one side was full, and there were no openings at the curbside nearby. All right, the lot was full and he was empty, but there'd be plenty of time to eat later. Waiting a few hours for a meal was nothing, not to a man who'd waited forty years for a drink. First things first.

Or was it last things last?

Ames was the last, Last of the Mohicans, last of his tribe—all those ignoble redskins who'd once whooped around the campfire fed by pages they'd produced for the pulps at a penny a word. When it went out they went on, following fresh trails to fresh fires sparked by the scattered sheets of paperback novels or the multicolored revisions of television scripts. The flames were fitful, but enough to keep the young braves warm.

In time more seasoned warriors could fuel their fires with hot properties, but even the blaze of glory hadn't warded off the chill forever. They were cold now, all of them, and only he knew warmth.

Warm car to heated garage, heated garage to comfortable kitchen, comfortable kitchen to dark den. Or was it a rec room?

Names kept changing. At the time Ames managed to put a down-payment on the place it was just a cheap tract-house in the boonies. Now it was a desirable residential property on a choice view lot.

Too bad he couldn't boast of equal improvement in forty years! Entering the room Ames switched on the light and its reflection bounced off the picture-window, transforming the surface into a mirror. For a moment he caught a glimpse of his reflection, and winced at the gargoyle in the glass. He drew the drapes hastily, trying to avoid looking at the backs of his hand as he did so. He hated the sight of blue veins, corded and crisscrossing like the routes on a freeway map. Next would come the liver spots.

Or would they? Nothing wrong with his liver; he'd never been much of a drinker. Until now, that is.

Now was a matter of putting the bottle down on the counter, shucking his jacket, opening the cupboard to search out a wine-glass from the bottom shelf.

Wonder of wonders, he actually found one, and after circling its inner surface his forefinger came away dust-free. He located the corkscrew next, a fancy-looking gadget at the back of the top shelf, still nestled in a gift-box and still unused. Corkscrews were metal mysteries to him.

Actually, employing it wasn't as much of a challenge as he'd anticipated. Once he fitted the twisted tip into the top of the cork and clamped the hood over the bottle's neck, he tightened the levers at both sides, pulling the cork out as they retracted. Simple as brain-surgery.

The wine poured easily, no specks of sediment surfacing as it rose to fill the glass. There was nothing you could call a bouquet—what the hell do you expect for ninety-eight cents?—but he thought he did detect a slight musky smell. Or was it merely the usual musty smell emanating from those moldering paperbacks and ancient pulp magazines lining the bookshelves row upon row?

If he'd had any sense he'd have dumped the lot years ago. They had no value to dealers or collectors, and no value to readers, either. But these tattered, battered specimens with their garish covers wrinkled like the faces of old whores held value to him. They represented the sum total of his lifework. No matter how they smelled, this was all he had to show for forty-odd years of effort.

On the lower shelves were the hardbacks—not his, but those of contemporaries and colleagues. If he was starting out again he wouldn't waste his time and talent on penny-a-word short stories and cheap paperback originals. Hardcovers were solid and substantial, made to last; the pages and their contents didn't smell. No doubt about it, this was the route he'd go.

But you can't turn back the odometer. And maybe it wouldn't matter even if he could. Let's face it, he *had* aimed for respectable publishing markets when starting out, just like his friends were doing. The difference was that they made it and he didn't.

There'd been no way of knowing where any of them would end up, no sure road-map to success. Forty years ago, high school kids didn't study genetics; they read the Declaration of Independence and graduated believing that all men are created equal. So if a half-dozen of those kids from roughly-similar backgrounds decided on a writing career, why shouldn't their chances of success be just about equal too?

Luck was a factor, of course, but at first luck seemed to be everybody's good buddy. Luck brought them together—Everly, Jesse and himself in class, the other two through mutual acquaintances. Hanging out together but working separately, they made their first sales to the same few remaining pulp magazines, their first breakthroughs into the expanding paperback markets.

Come to think of it, there'd been a sixth candidate for the Nobel Prize in Literature back then whose name he had trouble recalling today. Frank Osric, that was it. For a beginner, Frank was a pretty good candidate for a full-time career. But he'd also been a sexual athlete, world-class, who married a bimbo whose father owned a factory. So with a baby on the way, he ended up punching a time-clock instead of a typewriter.

The Skull Club members were the five who stuck together. Funny how they'd all written pretty much the same sort of stuff back then; a little science fiction, and a lot of fantasy before it split up into dark, light, or shocking pink with polka-dot stripes.

It was only later that they branched out individually into the mystery markets, spy-thrillers, police procedure product. It was after television moved from New York to Hollywood that they really broke up, as their lives split up into deals, deadlines, and rewrites over the weekends.

Kevin cupped his glass, wondering as he did so why nobody ever spoke of glassing their cups. English is a strange language, and writers are strange people.

Or maybe he was the strange one, the way he'd tried to keep in touch with his friends during the early years of their rise to fame and fortune. And he had tried, dammit. Phoned for lunch-dates and got excuses. Then, as their success soared, he got secretaries. And finally, thanks to the miracle of modern technology, he got answering machines.

After the others scattered, leaving the Valley for more trendy territory, contact with them dwindled to Christmas cards. Eventually even the cards stopped Hallmarking the passage of years, and that's when he got the message.

It was about time because the message had been awaiting his attention for ages, delivered by a diversity of sources. It had come from New York agents who couldn't sell his books to the right publishers, it came from agents out here who couldn't peddle his spec-written scripts to television or films. And while his work continued to appear in the lesser genre zines or paperbacks, the message came from critics loud and clear, in the form of silence.

Kevin ignored it for a long time, telling himself to hang in there, do the job, have patience. So he hung, and he jobbed, and eventually the patience ran out.

Reading was what scared it away; reading articles, essays and books about the work of his colleagues. He was shocked to see the first references, perhaps a dozen years ago; shocked not so much by their content as by the realization that so much time had passed since the days they'd all started out together. His mirror had already begun to tell him the same story, and he was tempted to try shutting his eyes while shaving. But he couldn't close his eyes to the facts. Pimply punks, who didn't even exist when the Skull Club was alive and flourishing, had been born, grown up, and become critics. Critics who knew genre fiction and its writers, who even mentioned the Skull Club in passing when discussing the work of the others.

The others. That's who the critics wrote about, the others. Jesse and Everly, Rondbeck and Fargo. Everybody except Kevin Ames.

Turning away from the bookshelves, he grimaced in rueful recollection. To be fair about it, his name actually had been mentioned, several times in several places, but only in passing, one of a long list of lesser or at least less-known talents. And one creep had managed to misspell it. *Kevan Aims.* So much for critical perception.

But none of the others suffered such careless treatment. No critic had a problem identifying Roy Fargo.

Kevin paused to confront the wall beyond the shelves. That's where the pictures were, the photographs from newspapers and magazines he'd clipped and pinned to a corkboard during the past decade, just for old times' sake.

Or so he'd told himself at the start. Now, of course, he knew the truth. It had never been for old times' sake, not even at the beginning.

Roy was the beginning, the first to go up, and that in itself had been hard to take. Not that Roy Fargo was much more of a success than Kevin himself. True, he lived in Beverly Hills, but his apartment was on the very tip of the south-of-Wilshire area, and this was before the real-estate boom. Roy never made it into the megabuck neighborhood: all he wanted was a chance to move from paperback to hardcover markets. By then the major publishers were concentrating on clones of Stephen King, but small specialty houses sprang up to feed the nostalgia craze for Golden Oldies from the Golden Age. They sold mainly through mail-order, putting out signed and limited editions, including genuine leather bindings for the true collector and/or greedy speculator.

At first, established writers shied away from small advances and small printings, so specialty publishers took what they could get. One of the first they got was Roy Fargo, who soon became a familiar name amongst the literary leather-freaks. His timing was right, because pop art was becoming popular with those who took credit for turning obscurity into celebrity.

That's when critics started paying him serious attention, cannibalizing each other's articles and reviews, pumping up a new audience for an old name.

And that's when some genre-oriented zine published the photo of Fargo which, haloed by a fringe of other newsclippings, occupied the left-hand side of Kevin's corkboard display. Below it was the story headline—*ROY FARGO, MASTER OF MYSTERY, WINS WIZARD AWARD.*

Kevin squinted at the picture in the dim light. A good photo, yes, but not a good likeness. Maybe because the Fargo he'd been familiar with was a younger man.

The passage of those subsequent decades had fattened the face, thinned the hairline, wrought wrinkles and wattles. Only the set of the fish-mouth remained unchanged; Roy Fargo was the kind of man who only smiled at funerals.

Even so, that headline should have made him laugh out loud, because he'd never written a real mystery in his life. To Kevin the only mystery was why editors accepted such dated whodunit fare, such hardboiled potboilers with their dumb-dick antihero and his gat, rod, heater, equalizer or piece aimed to put a notch in somebody's crotch.

Kevin thought of what he himself had written over the same period of time, genuine mysteries with authentic backgrounds, not just updated slang and the same old phallic fallacisms.

What right did Fargo have to steal Kevin's blood-and-thunder? If there was any justice, that should have been his prize. Both Fargo and himself had been nominated for the Best Paperback Novel award that year; it had been Kevin's first and only time. When he heard about it he'd felt a surge of encouraging excitement. The Wizard Award was prestigious; it meant something to editors who paid winners more attention, and higher advances. Ten years ago it would have given Kevin Ames a chance to snuggle under hardcovers with a major publisher.

If there were any justice.

But there was no justice, and Fargo was the one who accepted his trophy at the annual banquet, Fargo who signed a three-book hardcover contract, Fargo who was photographed.

Kevin stared at the photo and the photo stared back. That's the way they'd stared at each other ten years ago, just two months after Roy accepted his prize.

The phone rang and Kevin started at the sound, then realized there was no ring, merely an echo. An echo sounding down the corridors of time; an echo of the phone's sudden and surprising ring on that evening a decade ago. Actually the surprise had not been in the ringing but in the voice which responded when Kevin answered the call.

"Kevin, old buddy—how are you? This is Roy."

"Fargo?"

"As in North Dakota."

"Well I'll be damned!"

"Your prediction, not mine." A sort of chuckle sounded over the wire, a muffled sound which might issue from a fish-mouth. Or the mouth of someone who'd been drinking like a fish, as they used to say long years ago.

Only they didn't say it about Fargo, since he drank very little in the old days. Couldn't afford to, for one thing. But times and fortunes change, because he'd obviously had a few and he was calling from the bar at some steak-house off Melrose that Kevin never heard of before.

"What're you doing down there?" he asked.

"Tell you about it when I see you," Fargo said.

"See me?"

"That's right. They've got great steaks here. I'm inviting you to dinner."

"Now—you mean tonight?" Kevin hesitated. "But—look, I have plans for the evening—"

"Change them."

He did, and they met.

When Kevin arrived at the crowded side-street restaurant his host was already seated in a booth just off the noisy upfront bar. Recognizing Fargo came as a shock, for his photo had scarcely hinted at the ravaged reality, the flab of flesh, the face with its mottled veins broken like pledges to Alcoholics Anonymous. But the greatest change was in the fish-mouth, now set in a permanent smirk of smug satisfaction.

Coming here on impulse had been a mistake, but Kevin realized it too late for retreat; he could only sit down and lighten up.

Tonight, a decade later, he couldn't pretend to recall any of their preliminary greetings or small-talk. Drinks before and during dinner helped ease his tension, and Roy had already achieved an alcohol level which would intoxicate any vampire who drank his blood.

But the steaks were every bit as good as promised, and it was over dessert that their conversation really began. Instead of coffee, Fargo opted for a double Turkey-and-rocks. Kevin, conscious of his own limited ability to handle liquor, settled for a small cognac. Now he felt a trifle more relaxed, but it was still hard to equate this bloated and aging stranger with the Roy he'd once known, or thought he'd known, so well. *I wish I hadn't come*, he told himself.

"I'm glad you came," Fargo told him. "Been wanting to get hold of you for a long time."

"I should have called you," Kevin said. "When I heard the news—"

"About the prize?" Fargo shrugged. "No problem. Charlie Rondbeck was at the awards banquet so we talked there, but I haven't heard word one from old Jesse or Everly either. And I didn't expect to hear from you, considering."

"Considering what?"

"Considering you're the guy who should have gotten the award in the first place." Fargo raised his glass with a flourish that ruffled the Turkey's feathers. "Cheers!"

Kevin downed his drink, feeling its warmth mingle with the glow kindled by Roy's words. It was difficult to resent a man who admitted the truth. Fargo wasn't just flattering him; he must be feeling guilty about what happened, or else why would he bother inviting him to dinner?

"Thinking about you when I was at the bar earlier," Fargo said. "How we lost touch all this time, and then the award business coming up. So I called."

Kevin found himself smiling. "You still haven't told me what you're doing down here."

"Oh, that." Fargo set his glass down, rattling the rocks. "Got myself a Volvo last week. Runs like a dream."

"Good for you," Kevin said.

"Not so good." Fargo captured his glass again in a pudgy grip. "Yesterday some bastard put a dent in the left rear fender while I parked at the market. This afternoon I took it over to the dealer's body-shop around the corner from here. Figured straightening out the fender would be a ten-minute job, which just goes to show you how long it's been since I owned a new car. Turns out that now they replace the whole damn thing on these models. Costs you an arm and a leg because it's not covered by the warranty, but what can you do? So I told them go ahead, and wandered over here.''

Kevin's inner glow had faded during Fargo's wordy account, replaced now by a rising resentment.

"So that's why you got hold of me," he said. "You need a lift home, right? Been cheaper for you just to call a cab."

Fargo shook his head. "You got it all wrong, old buddy. Shop stays open 'til nine, so the car'll be ready by now. I was just killing time."

"And wanted me to kill it with you," Kevin broke in.

"Knock it off." Fargo groped for his glass, eyed its emptiness, and signaled to the passing waiter. "Want a refill?"

"No. I'd better be going." Not only had Kevin's glow faded; what he felt now was an icy numbness, and he made no effort to keep the chill from his voice. "Seeing as you don't need me—"

"But I do need you! That's why I called." Fargo leaned forward as the waiter returned to switch the empty glass with a full one. "Told you I got to thinking. That's how I came up with the idea."

"Get to the point."

"Remember I said you should have won that award?" Fargo reduced his double to a single as he spoke. "Just knowing it was enough to put me on a guilt-trip, but I'm getting off at the next station."

"Talk sense."

"I'm talking dollars and sense, for both of us. I'm talking collaboration."

Kevin opened his mouth but Fargo gestured with his glass, intercepting interruption. "Heard about my new deal, right? Three-book contract, no options. Upfront advance is—they don't want me to say, but take my word it's a good chunk of cash. And this idea of mine will fix things so you'll get your share."

"You want me to write those books with you?" Kevin said.

Fargo lowered his gaze and his voice. "I want you to write those books *for* me."

"You're drunk."

"Damn right I am. I've been working at it ever since I signed that contract."

Unprepared for such an admission, Kevin scarcely knew how to respond. "Does your agent know about this?" he faltered.

"Yeah." Fargo nodded. "He says he's seen it before. Guy's used to being kicked around all his life, then something like this happens and he goes into shock, can't cope. Every time I think about doing these books for that kind of money, I freeze. You don't jump from the Little League into the majors, not at my age."

"Writer's block," Kevin said. "Get some help to dry out, find yourself a good shrink—"

Roy gestured with his glass again. "A shrink can't write those books for me. You can."

"But there are plenty of full-time ghost writers around. Ask your agent."

"No way! I don't want this to get out. Got to have somebody I can trust to keep their mouth shut. Somebody who'll work in my style, only better. That's you."

Sharp flattery or blunt truth? Kevin realized it didn't matter. Another question did, and he asked it.

"Okay, perhaps I could do the job. But why should I?"

"For old times' sake. Because we're friends. Because you need the money."

"I'm doing all right."

Fargo shook his head. "Cost of living's rising, but your sales aren't going up with it."

The little ball of anger that had formed in the pit of Kevin's stomach was starting to roll. He tried to halt it as he spoke. "Who told you that?"

"Never mind, I checked it out. You're hurting, old buddy." Fargo set his empty glass down. "But not to worry, help is on the way." The fish-mouth fissured in a grin. "Money talks, and all you got to do is listen. My proposition is we make a work-for-hire deal, no royalties, just a flat fee, half up front, half on delivery. And seeing as it's you, I'm willing to go ten thousand per book."

Kevin couldn't control the roll of rage so he concentrated on controlling his voice. "You've got to be getting a lot more for those books, just in advances alone. Plus the royalties to come, paperback and foreign rights, maybe even film or TV sales somewhere down the line."

Roy Fargo was having his own vocal problems. "Who knows?" He wagged a fat finger. "All you gotta know is there's thirty grand in it for you, guar'nteed. Way you grind stuff out, shouldn't take more'n two months apiece. How long's it been since anybody paid you thirty thou for six months' work?"

"Never got that much," Kevin said. "But if I ever do, it won't be for something that has your name on it."

"Think you're too good to ghost for me?" Fargo's forefinger jabbed air. "Well, let me tell you somethin', old buddy. I don't think you're good enough! On'y reason I called is I felt sorry for you, wanna give you a break. So what thanks do I get—"

"That's enough," Kevin said. He was amazed that he could speak so calmly while feeling the ball rolling deep inside him. "Get out of my face."

"I'm gone." Roy Fargo slid out of the booth and rose askew but upright as he spoke. "I got no time to waste on you, old buddy. You're jus' a hack, always will be. Jus' a hack—"

Kevin watched him weave down the aisle; not until after his host departed did he realize Fargo had left without paying the tab.

Adding insult to injury came to a total of seventy-eight bucks for drinks, dinner, tax and tip. A sizable bite, ten years ago.

But at the time Kevin scarcely felt it. What he felt was the ball in his gut, grinding as it grew, *way you grind stuff out, just a hack, always will be.*

Somehow he paid and made his way to the exit, the ball rolling, the rage swelling, the rain falling.

Kevin blinked. There hadn't been any sign of rain when he arrived. But then there hadn't been any sign of Fargo's pretended pity or that insulting suggestion to sell out, betray his talent for thirty pieces of silver. All right, so it was thirty thousand pieces. Probably came to about ten percent of what Fargo was getting as an advance alone. He'd still end up with most of the money, and all of the glory.

Hell with it. Hell with him. Hell with this goddam rain, coming down in buckets, turning the damn potholes into swimming pools. Dark as pitch, too; no light except the one way down at the corner. Where was his car parked? Oh yeah, down here. Next question—where're the keys? Got 'em. Final question—how'd you get so loaded?

And loaded he was. Load in his gut. Stop rolling. Put key in ignition and start rolling. Now.

Windshield wipers working. Back and forth, to and fro. Don't look at them, dummy—look past them. Keep your eye on the road. Potholes. Water. Splashing.

There, that's better. Car revving up, stomach settling down. Forget Fargo. Forget the bastard playing him for a sucker, laughing up his sleeve all the way to the bank.

It didn't matter, didn't matter a damn. Into each life some rain must fall and that's what mattered now, rain on the windshield, headlight beams blurring across puddles in the street, flashing over the figure that staggered out from the crosswalk and slipped on the wet pavement.

Fargo fell, in what seemed like slow-motion.

Everything happened in slow-motion, except the sudden resurgence of rage. It was still there after all, but it wasn't still, it was rolling, the car was rolling, hands whirling the wheel, foot flooring the gas-pedal.

A crunch, a bump, a shriek of brakes. And then he was around the corner, gunning the motor, *don't look now, they may be gaining on you.*

But they didn't gain.

Kevin could grin because they'd never gained on him, not in ten years. If they had, of course, he'd have explained it was an accident.

At the time, in his drunken and panic-induced flight, he'd really believed this, or wanted to. Not until long afterward did he admit it was murder.

In a way it was actually premeditated murder, because he'd killed Fargo many times before, in his dreams. Of course nobody knew about the dreams, let alone the reality.

Nobody knew he and Fargo were meeting. And when they did, neither had been recognized in the crowded restaurant. They weren't seen arriving or leaving together. And there were no witnesses on the rainy street when a drunken pedestrian was struck down in the dark by some hit-and-run driver.

Kevin had committed what mystery-writers strive to achieve—the perfect crime.

How about a Wizard Award for *that*? Or at the very least, perhaps a Sorcerer's Apprentice?

He lifted his glass to the fat face framed on the wall before him, then drank deeply. Cheap wine, and bitter; not at all comparable to the cognac he'd enjoyed during that last meeting with Fargo a decade ago. And yet bitter was better, infinitely better, because it quenched his thirst. Years and years of thirst for just this moment, the moment of triumph.

Kevin gripped the lumpy neck of the straw-wrapped bottle and refilled his glass before moving on past Fargo's wall-eyed stare. Carrying the Chianti with him for convenience's sake, for old times' sake, he scanned the corkboard for a faded Polaroid print of Arthur Rondbeck in out-of-focus closeup.

This face was thin and drawn, just as he remembered it, the face of a diabetic asthmatic cancer-riddled and heart-damaged hypochondriac.

Even as a young man Rondbeck had never enjoyed good health when he could revel in illness. Here was someone who purchased pills for extra energy but lacked the strength to swallow them: a man who was too tired to lie down. And yet, Kevin noted, he was probably the most prolific member of the Skull Club group. The only problem being it seemed hard to tell if his work was the product of a word-processor or an enema.

Where had he found time to turn out a book of critical essays on his fellow writers, and why would a publisher accept him as an authority? But a publisher *did* accept him, and his manuscript too.

Kevin squinted up at the Polaroid, trying to bring Rondbeck's bleached-out features into focus. What had that sallow face looked like seven years ago?

For the life of him he couldn't recall; apparently he lacked a photographic memory. But he did remember the letter Rondbeck sent him with a copy of the chapter on Kevin's work, a labor of love entitled *Blood Brothers*. And seven years later he still remembered that enclosure, every vicious word of it. Words like *derivative, stock characterization, predictability, over-obvious plots*. The labor of love was actually a labor of hate.

But Rondbeck hadn't sent the chapter to ask for an opinion; what he wanted was verification of biographical data dealing with Kevin's career which preceded the pages that demolished it.

His letter had arrived on a bad day. Kevin's immediate impulse was to pick up the phone and, for the first time in many years, communicate with his old friend—communicate his anger at this unprovoked and unwarranted attack. But as luck would have it, the phone was disconnected and would remain so until he paid his long-overdue bill. And that wasn't about to happen until Kevin finished the novelization, also overdue, of the sleazo film-script he'd been stuck with.

His second impulse, to write Rondbeck a letter of rebuttal concerning his errors of judgment as well as fact, was equally impractical, because that very morning his typewriter had conked out. Another three days and God knows how many dollars shot to hell, no wonder he had one of those pounding headaches, now on top of everything else this letter arriving to make his day—

There was only one thing to do; drive out to West LA and confront Rondbeck face to face. Tell him that under no circumstances would he allow such an attack to be published. With this kind of garbage spread around, pretty soon Kevin wouldn't even get assignments to novelize bad movies, let alone contracts for books of his own.

Driving west, Kevin's anger mounted as the sun sank, its slanted rays blinding him as he crawled through the homeward-bound traffic.

Blinding. But he could see Rondbeck plainly enough, standing in the abandoned hallway after he opened the front door of the old two-story house just north of Pico.

See but not hear, because of the pounding in his head. *Pounding headache.* Didn't have to hear, because just the sight of that stupid face and sickly grin told him all he needed to know, more than he needed to know about Rondbeck's motives, about his deliberate attempt to smear his name, his reputation, his whole damned life-work. Kevin told himself not to listen, and he didn't listen, but all the while Rondbeck kept on talking, talking as he led the way up the stairs and into his workroom. Here was the printer fed by the word-processor, here was the word-processor fed by the stupid, grinning character-assassin who couldn't stop talking because he was afraid.

Yes, that was it, Kevin could see it now; the fear behind the grin, the apprehension in the eyes, the alarm. There must have been something in his own face, his own silence, which triggered the alarm to go off and sent Rondbeck into a flurry of excuses, explanations, apologies.

And without needing or heeding the actual words, Kevin knew what Arthur Rondbeck was saying and why. He'd turned off deliberately because he didn't want to get the message, there was only one way to deal with the headache, get rid of it, stop the pounding, and now that his mind was made up there was no point getting confused by apologies.

There'd been enough confusion anyway, and Kevin had to make a deliberate effort to keep calm. Cool, calm and collected. Don't do whatever you did with your face to scare Rondbeck that way, keep your voice down, just tell the man it was all a mistake, your turn to apologize, let bygones be bygones, we'll both forget it ever happened, sorry but I've a pounding headache, got to go now.

Go to the hall. Go to the landing. Let Rondbeck lead the way. And over the pounding, when push comes to shove—

The crash.

The crash as the railing gave way, the sudden gasp, the rush of air, the thud.

Sprawled at the foot of the stairs far below, neck twisted to an impossible angle, lay the figure. The body. The corpse.

That's all it was now, just a cold, contorted thing, its head stamped with a bloody caricature of Arthur Rondbeck's face. The grin was gone. And so was the grinner.

Kevin was gone too, as soon as he'd run his handkerchief over the inner and outer doorknobs and made sure the front door itself was locked behind him.

He looked around for his car and couldn't see it. For a moment he froze, then relaxed, realizing he'd parked around the corner.

It wasn't until he was almost home that he realized something else. There'd been no reason for him to park where he did. No conscious reason, because he'd been hiding it behind the headache. Behind the headache was the rage and behind the rage was the reality. He'd gone to Rondbeck intending to kill him from the very first.

Another premeditated murder? But how could that be? He hadn't planned anything in detail, any more than he'd planned the death of Roy Fargo. Murder involved a risk that should only be taken when fully warranted, when utterly necessary to eliminate a threat or an enemy.

Or a rival?

Kevin saluted Rondbeck's photo-face with a full glass, then remedied its emptiness before moving on.

Seven years ago he'd confronted the *rationale* of his behavior. Or misbehavior; it didn't matter which. What mattered was that Fargo and Rondbeck were dead. Just as he wanted them to be, just as he wanted all of them to be, because they were the ones who drank the wine of life and left him the dregs, but he'd have the last laugh, the last laugh after they'd drawn their last breaths.

And they would, all of them. Once he'd made that resolve he was willing to wait. And wait he did, without fear of suspicion; two of his four rivals were in their graves and neither had risen to point a bony finger at him.

Rondbeck's death, recorded as accidental, was scarcely incidental, and merited only brief mention in fine print. But both Lloyd Everly and Jesse Cross had been the subjects of occasional interviews. In recalling their early careers, each made a passing reference to the Skull Club. Just a few words of nostalgia, yet one never knew; if a third and a fourth member met accidental death in the near future, somebody checking old news articles for an obit could note the tie-in, perhaps even get curious about the survivors.

So best to wait, Kevin had decided. There was no personal reason to resent those two as he had the others; it was only their success he hated.

Only their success, and his failure. Neither had been deserved, but then everything's a matter of luck, and if you want justice you have to go after it yourself. Even if it means waiting five more years.

That's how long Kevin waited before he paid his visit to Lloyd Everly. Five long years of reading and hearing about Everly's latest novels and movie sales, with no consolation for Kevin except the knowledge that time was on his side. Everly's appearances on television talk-shows revealed a steadily-receding hairline and a steadily-advancing network of wrinkles. If Kevin's tentative plans worked out, death from natural causes would be a logical verdict. And he'd no longer have to put up with the sight of that aging have-a-good-day face on the TV screen. It was bad enough seeing the autographed photo on the corkboard with a *printed* signature if you please, or even if you don't please.

Kevin hadn't requested anything at all; the glossy 8 × 10 showed up unannounced and uninvited in the day's mail. That's what did it—the photo and the accompanying message.

Compadre:
  Long time no, sí?
  Thought you might like this. Why don't we get together one of these days and compare swimming-pools?
                                                                    —*Lloyd.*

Yes, that's what did it, all right. Only a jerk like Everly would come up with a smart-ass way to point out he had a pool and Kevin didn't, never would. But unwittingly he'd pointed out something else: the method for murder.

Discarding his earlier plan, Kevin made his move. This time he prepared in advance. Three days beforehand he cased the dead-end street in the pricey neighborhood abutting Bel Air. A block away from the house was an ideal place to park without being seen by traffic, because there wasn't any. His next move required immobility, sitting in the car for two full days to learn the comings and goings of local residents, their gardeners or other hired help. He noted no nannies or other live-ins; Everly himself was a widower who'd lived alone here since his wife died, so that didn't complicate matters. Some of his neighbors employed maids or cleaning-ladies, but they all cut out sometime between four and five, when the wives came home from Rodeo Drive. It wasn't until six or later that the husbands drove in from Century City and the Cedars-Sinai Medical Complex.

Obviously the safest interval would be from five to six. He mustn't call about stopping by until just before driving up; that way left less chance of Everly mentioning his impending visit to anyone else. The rest was obvious. Wear washable jeans and jacket, and don't forget the rubber gloves.

Kevin chuckled as he thought back on it now. Old Haji never wore rubber gloves, but that's what he was doing—playing Haji. Just the way Otis Skinner and Ronald Colman played him in those ancient movies, just the way Alfred Drake did in the old musical they'd made out of *Kismet*.

Funny that he'd remembered their big scene, and now he got the chance to do it himself. Grabbing the villain and silently submerging his head in the pool until he drowned, then pushing the body in. So simple, once Everly let him in and they had a quiet poolside drink together. Whisky straight, that's what Lloyd Everly wanted, but he ended up with water for a chaser. Lots and lots of water.

Remembering it, Kevin almost choked on his drink. The way Everly had choked, but it wasn't all that funny to him. *Kismet* means fate in Arabic, doesn't it? Well he met his fate all right. And it was all right, no problems except to carry away the second glass so as to leave no evidence of a visitor when the pool-man came by two days later and found his employer drowned.

So Everly had been liquidated. Clever phrase, clever method, clever man; Kevin felt a surge of self-appreciation, or was it just the wine?

But no, he wouldn't be here drinking the wine if he hadn't been the cleverest of the lot. Fargo, Rondbeck, Everly—all so-called mystery writers, but none of them could come up with complex plots and simple solutions. All they'd done in their careers was to go with the flow—the flow of blood, the rising red tide of—

Why the lecture? This was supposed to be a celebration. "God bless," Kevin said, gesturing toward Everly's photo with his empty glass and refilling it from the half-empty bottle. Half-empty? No wonder he had this warm feeling, felt good all over.

That's how he'd felt after Everly was deep-sixed two years ago, because it was almost all over. Only one other survivor to deal with, down and dirty, just slip him the Ace of Spades.

Kevin had waited so long with the others, so patiently, but these past two years had been real torture. Or imaginary torture, because he was always thinking about what he'd do when he finally got his shot at Jesse George.

It wouldn't be an actual shot, of course; nothing that obvious. Or that quick. Timing was everything. Perhaps he could use a variation of the method he'd worked out for Everly before the pool idea came to him. But whatever he decided on, he'd have to cool it before he cooled Jesse. And there were problems.

One of the problems was a young wife Jesse had recently acquired, some little bimbo with naturally-stringy hair and the usual wifely problem of her own—there wasn't any room in her clothes-closet and she didn't have a thing to wear. Kevin picked up these fascinating tidbits from gossip columns in literary journals sold at supermarket checkout counters.

True or false, the setup made for complications, but Kevin knew simplicity was still his best bet. Only it couldn't be a bet, couldn't be a gamble; he needed a sure thing. Which was why waiting became torment as he tried figuring how to mark the cards, load the dice, rig the game.

Up to now Jesse looked like the winner. He'd always been the biggest winner of the whole gang, and during the past two years his success seemed incredible as he made the complete career-leap, from the Skull Club to the Book-of-the-Month Club. The novel following stayed on the chart for nineteen weeks, then sold to films on a deal that included a percentage of the gross.

Halting before the fourth picture, Kevin peered at it with narrowed eyes. Hard to make out because it wasn't even a photograph, just a caricature from some article in a magazine he'd stolen from his dentist's reception-room. Over the years Kevin hadn't found any photos; old Jesse was either camera-shy or just plain cautious. It might be both, because he didn't do TV or book-signings or any personal appearance shots. His success had come without any Wizard Awards, critical acclaim or paid publicity. In spite of the news items about his career, he shunned the spotlight.

Maybe it was smart to play it that way, living somewhere in the mountains up near Santa Barbara and avoiding the Hollywood scene. Safer too, because Kevin had all this trouble finding a way to kill him.

And when he finally did—or thought he did—old Jesse outfoxed him again. Just like that, no warning, he dropped dead. Keeled over from a heart attack right there in his own home, only a week ago.

"Party-pooper!"

Kevin lifted his glass with a frown of annoyance. He'd really been looking forward to taking care of Jesse himself, closing the books on his Book-of-the-Month, out-grossing that gross-out film.

He hadn't read the book or seen the movie, but it didn't matter. What mattered was that others did, thousands of readers, millions of filmgoers. Jesse George got fame and acclaim, and though he never sought celebrity, hundreds of mourners were at his graveside.

If Kevin ever had a funeral, it would be attended by a crowd estimated at nearly twelve people. Which wasn't fair, seeing as how the others, except for Jesse, wouldn't even have had funerals if it weren't for his efforts. Efforts which were, as usual, unappreciated and anonymous. Story of his life.

Kevin squinted at the caricature on the corkboard and the caricature squinted back. Ugly artwork. Now that all four of the other Skull Club members were gone he could take their pictures down, tear them up. Too bad he never got a chance to tear up the real Jesse. It would have been great, seeing him die, feeling the surge of adrenaline, the taste of triumph on the tongue.

That was the secret, wasn't it? All these years, this lifetime, writing about psychopaths and never knowing why they did what they did or what they actually got out of their efforts. But he knew now.

He knew the greatest moment was when the anger or envy that drove you to the deed disappeared in the doing. All those inhibiting emotions vanished;

there was no fear, no shame, no guilt, no empathy for anyone or any thing. To inflict rather than endure—that was the real victory. Which was more than Roy Fargo, Arthur Rondbeck, Lloyd Everly and Jesse George would ever learn. They'd lost, he'd won. Let them keep their fame, he had the game.

Damn betcha, he'd won. That's why he was here now. And here he'd stay. Maybe get rid of Tischler next, just in case that legal mind of his started working overtime. No law said he had to stop with the lawyer, either. He could go on to anyone he liked. Or disliked. Truth is, each time had been easier, kept getting better and better, and—admit it—now he *wanted* to go on.

In vino veritas. Damn betcha.

Nodding, Kevin raised his hand again and the wine sloshed in the glass. "Easy does it," he said, suppressing a belch. Little too much of that *vino veritas.* But who had a better right? Not this imitation Rogues' Gallery on the wall, these phonies pretending they understood what they wrote about. All they ever did was write. He was the only one who *lived* it.

"So this time, here's to me," he told himself. And gulped.

The drink really hit him. Sledgehammer wrapped in cottonwool. Better lay off, too much booze.

Kevin tightened his grip on the bottle in its straw wrapper, its straw cradle. Like Jesus. Little Lord Jesus in the cradle on Holy Night, when the Wise Men came.

But he was the wisest, not those fools on the wall. Hot in here. And hard to hang on to the wine. Why did they always wrap Chianti in straw? And why was the straw creased on one side?

Wait a minute. There was something stuck underneath there, wedged down, only the edge of the corner showing. See if you can grab hold and pull it out. Careful, don't tear it.

Kevin tugged and freed a sheet of blue paper; it was folded over, just thick enough to make a slight bulge under the straw. Did somebody put it there on purpose, to be found?

A letter, that's what it was. Goddam handwritten letter. Hard to see in this light, hard to make out the words. But the salutation, whatever they call it, was his name.

Dear Kevin:

Just a line to congratulate you. Because it is you, right?

When Fargo died I wondered a little, but accidents happen. And when Rondbeck fell victim to another accident I began to wonder more. Nothing to go on, just a hunch, but if there was anything at all to my crazy idea, the logical suspect was Lloyd Everly.

Then Everly became the third accidental death, and I knew. Knew what you were doing, knew what you were after.

Kevin blinked, trying to clear his vision, clear his thoughts. Jesse was the letter-writer. But what was he trying to do, prove how smart he was? Much good it did—he was dead like the others, and dead is dumb.

Kevin peered down again, peered at squiggly lines on crumpled paper.

I knew I'd be next, so I'm getting out of town, going where you won't be likely to find me. But if something goes wrong, chances are you'll be reading this and gloating over winning. I can understand, because the two of us are basically very much alike. And as they say, it takes one to know one.

Again, heartiest congratulations,

Jesse

Yes, it really said that. *Heartiest congratulations!* Kevin had to laugh, laughed so hard he couldn't stop, laughed until his sides hurt. Sides and stomach and chest. The room started to spin and he slid down the side of the wall, clenching his fists. Through blurring eyes he saw that he'd dropped the letter as he fell, turning the page over to expose what was written on the other side. Through shimmering waves of pain he read the final words.

P.S.:

Sorry you missed old Tischler's party. I went, but he didn't notice me in that mob-scene. It was easy to sneak into his private office without being seen. After all, it only took a few minutes—just long enough to find the bottle, pull the cork, and poison the wine.

Bill Pronzini's Nameless series will survive our time for a simple reason—it is the only series that attempts, in the course of many novels, to be a serious spiritual autobiography. And Pronzini gives us reportage, as well—in addition to being excellent stories and the fever-chart of a most passionate man, Pronzini notes many of the culture changes that have both pleased and confounded us as a society. Here is a very good Pronzini to read between Nameless stories.

Shade Work
BILL PRONZINI

Johnny Shade blew into San Francisco on the first day of summer. He went there every year, when he had the finances; it was a good place to find action on account of the heavy convention business. Usually he went a little later in the summer, around mid-July, when there were fifteen or twenty thousand conventioneers wandering around, a high percentage of them with money in their pockets and a willingness to lay some of it down on a poker table. You could take your time then, weed out the deadheads and the short-money scratchers. Pick your vic.

But this year was different. This year he couldn't afford to wait around or take his time. He had three thousand in his kick that he'd scored in Denver, and he needed to parlay that into ten grand—fast. Ten grand would buy him into a big con Elk Tracy and some other boys were setting up in Louisville. A classic big-store con, even more elaborate than the one Newman and Redford had pulled off in *The Sting*, Johnny's favorite flick. Elk needed a string of twenty and a nut of two hundred thousand to set it up right; that was the reason for the ten-grand buy-in. The guaranteed net was two million. Ten grand buys you a hundred, minimum. Johnny Shade had been a card mechanic and cheat for nearly two decades and he'd never held that much cash in his hands at one time. Not even close to that much.

He was a small-time grifter and he knew it. A single-o, traveling around the country on his own because he preferred it that way, looking for action wherever he could find it. But it was never heavy action, never the big score. Stud and draw games in hotel rooms with marks who never seemed to want to lose more than a few hundred at a sitting. He wasn't a good enough mechanic to play in even a medium-stakes game and hope to get away with crimps or hops or overhand runups or Greek-deals or hand-mucks or any of the other shuffling or dealing cheats. He just didn't have the fingers for it. So mostly he relied on his specialty, shade work, which was how he'd come to be called Johnny Shade. He even signed hotel registers as Johnny Shade nowadays, instead of the name he'd been born with. A kind of private joke.

Shade work was fine in small games. Most amateurs never thought to examine or riffle-test a deck when he ran a fresh one in, because it was always in its cellophane wrapper with the manufacturer's seal unbroken. The few who did check the cards didn't spot the gaff on account of they were looking for blisters, shaved edges, blockout or cutout work—the most common methods of marking a deck. They didn't know about the more sophisticated methods like flash or shade work. In Johnny's case, they probably wouldn't have spotted the shade gaff if they had known, not the way he did it.

He had it down to a science. He diluted blue and red aniline dye with alcohol until he had the lightest possible tint, then used a camel's hair brush to wash over a small section of the back pattern of each card in a Bee or Bicycle deck. The dye wouldn't show on the red or blue portion of the card back, but it tinted the white part just lightly enough so you could see it if you knew what to look for. And he had eyesight almost as good as Clark Kent's. He could spot his shade work on a vic's cards across the table in poor light without even squinting.

But the high-rollers knew about shade work, just as they knew about every other scam a professional hustler could come up with. You couldn't fool them, so you couldn't steal their money. If you were Johnny Shade, you had to content yourself with low-rollers and deadheads, with pocket and traveling cash instead of the big score.

He was tired of the game, that was the thing. He'd been at it too long, lived on the far edge of riches too long, been a single-o grifter too long. He wanted a slice of the good life. Ten grand buys a hundred. With a hundred thousand he could travel first-class, wine and dine and bed first-class women, take his time finding new action—maybe even set up a big con of his own. Or find a partner and work some of the fancier short cons. Lots of options, as long as a guy had real money in his kick.

First, though, he had to parlay his Denver three K into ten K. Then he could hop a plane for Louisville and look up Elk Tracy. Ten days . . . That was all the time he had before Elk closed out his string. Ten days to pick the right vics, set up two or three or however many games it took him to net the seven thousand.

He found his first set of marks his first night in Frisco. That was a good omen. His luck was going to change; he could feel it.

Most weeks in the summer there was a convention going on at the Hotel Nob Hill, off Union Square. He walked in there on this night, and the first thing he saw was a banner that said WELCOME FIDDLERS in great big letters. Hick musicians, or maybe some kind of organization for people who were into cornball music. Just his type of crowd. Just his type of mark.

He hung out in the bar, nursing a beer, circulating, keeping his ears open. There were certain words he listened for and "poker" was one of them. One of four guys in a booth used it, and when he sidled closer he saw that they were all wearing badges with FIDDLER on them and their names and the cities they were from written underneath. They were talking the right talk: stud poker, bragging about how good they were at it, getting ready for a game. Ripe meat. All he had to do was finagle his way among them, get himself invited to join the play if the set-up and the stakes were right.

He was good at finagling. He had the gift of gab, and a face like a Baptist preacher's, and a winning smile. First he sat himself down at a table near their booth. Then he contrived to jostle a waitress and spill a fresh round of beers she was bringing to them. He offered to pay for the drinks, flashed his wallet so they could see that he was flush. Chatted them up a little, taking it slow, feeling his way.

One of the fiddlers bought him a beer, then he bought them all another round. That got him the invitation to join them. Right away he laid on the oil about being in town for a convention himself, the old birds of a feather routine. They shook hands all around. Dave from Cleveland, Mitch from Los Angeles, Verne from Cedar Rapids, Harry from Bayonne. And Johnny from Denver. He didn't even have to maneuver the talk back to cards. They weren't interested in his convention or their own, or San Francisco, or any other kind of small talk; they were interested in poker. He played some himself, he said. Nothing he liked better than five-stud or draw. No wild-card games, none of that crap; he was a purist. So were they.

"We're thinking about getting up a game," Harry from Bayonne said. "You feel ike sitting in, Johnny?"

"I guess I wouldn't mind," he said. "Depending on the stakes. Nothing too rich for my blood." He showed them his best smile. "Then again, nothing too small, either. Poker's no good unless you make it interesting, right?"

If they'd insisted on penny-ante or buck-limit, he'd have backed out and gone looking elsewhere. But they were sports: table stakes, ten-buck limit per bet, no limit on raises. They looked like they could afford that kind of action. Fiddle-music jerks, maybe, but well-dressed and reasonably well-heeled. He caught a glimpse of a full wallet when Mitch from L.A. bought another round. Might be as much as four or five grand among the four of them.

Verne from Cedar Rapids said he had a deck of cards in his room; they could play there. Johnny said, "Sounds good. How about if we go buy a couple more decks in the gift shop. Nothing like the feel of a new deck after a while."

They all thought that was a good idea. Everybody drank up and they went together to the gift shop. All Johnny had to do was make sure the cards they bought were Bicycle, one of the two most common brands; he had four shaded Bicycle decks in his pocket, two blue-backs and two red-backs. Then they all rode upstairs to Verne from Cedar Rapids's room and shed their coats and jackets and got down to business.

Johnny played it straight for a while, card-counting, making conservative bets, getting a feel for the way the four marks played. Only one of them was reckless: Mitch from L.A., the one with the fattest wallet. He'd have liked two or three of that type, but one was better than none. One was all he needed.

After an hour and a half he was ahead about a hundred and Mitch from L.A. was the big winner, betting hard, bluffing at least part of the time. Better and better. Time to bring in one of his shaded decks. That was easy, too. They'd let him hold the decks they'd bought downstairs; simple for him to bring out one of his own instead.

He didn't open it himself. You always let one of the marks do that, so the mark could look it over and see that it was still sealed in cellophane with the manufacturer's stamp on top intact. The stamp was the main thing to the mark, the one thing you never touched when you were fixing a deck. What they didn't figure on was what you'd done: You carefully opened the cellophane wrapper along the bottom and slid out the card box. Then you opened the box along one side, prying the glued flaps apart with a razor blade. Once you'd shaded the cards, you resealed the box with rubber cement, slipped it back into the cellophane sleeve, refolded the sleeve ends along the original creases, and resealed them with a drop of glue. When you did the job right—and Johnny Shade was a master—nobody could tell that the package had been tampered with. Sure as hell not a fiddler named Dave from Cleveland, the one who opened the gimmicked deck.

The light was pretty good in there; Johnny could read his shade work with no more than a casual glance at the hands as they were dealt out. He took a couple of medium-sized pots, worked his winnings up to around five hundred, biding his time until both he and Mitch from L.A. drew big hands on the same deal. It finally happened about 10:30, on a hand of jacks-or-better. Harry from Bayonne was dealing; Johnny was on his left. Mitch from L.A. drew a pat full house, aces over fives. Johnny scored trip deuces. When he glanced over at the rest of the deck, he saw that the top card—his card on the draw— was the fourth deuce. Beautiful. A set-up like this was always better when you weren't the dealer, didn't have to deal seconds or anything like that to win the pot. Just read the shade and it was yours.

Mitch from L.A. bet ten and Johnny raised him and Mitch raised back.

Verne from Cedar Rapids stayed while the other two dropped, which made Johnny smile inside. Verne owned four high spades in sequence and was gambling on a one-card draw to fill a royal or a straight flush. But there was no way he was going to get it because Mitch had his spade ace and Johnny had his spade nine. The best he could do was a loser flush. Johnny raised again, and Mitch raised back, and Verne hung in stubborn. There was nearly a grand in the pot when Mitch finally called.

Johnny took just the one card on the draw, to make the others think he was betting two pair. Mitch would think that even if Johnny caught a full house, his would be higher because he had aces up; so Mitch would bet hot and heavy. Which he did. Verne from Cedar Rapids had caught his spade flush and hung in there for a while, driving the pot even higher, until he finally realized his flush wasn't going to beat what Johnny and Mitch were betting; then he dropped. Mitch kept right on working his full boat, raising each time Johnny raised, until he was forced to call when his cash pile ran down to a lone tenspot. That last ten lifted the total in the pot to twenty-two hundred bucks.

Johnny grinned and said, "Read 'em and weep, gentlemen," and fanned out his four deuces face up. Mitch from L.A. didn't say a word; he just dropped his cards and looked around at the others. None of them had anything to say, either. Johnny grinned again and said, "My lucky night," and reached for the pot.

Reaching for it was as far as he got.

Harry from Bayonne closed a big paw over his right wrist; Dave from Cleveland did the same with his left wrist. They held him like that, his hands imprisoned flat on the table.

"What the hell's the idea?" Johnny said.

Nobody answered him. Mitch from L.A. swept the cards together and then began to examine them one at a time, holding each card up close to his eyes.

Harry from Bayonne said, "What is it, shade work?"

"Right. Real professional job."

"Thought so. I'm pretty good at spotting blockout and cutout work. And I didn't feel any blisters or edge or sand work."

"At first I figured he might be one of the white-on-white boys," Verne from Cedar Rapids said. "You know, used without fluid on the white borders. Then I tumbled to the shading."

"Nice resealing on that card box, Johnny," Dave from Cleveland said. "If I hadn't known it was a gimmicked deck, I wouldn't have spotted it."

Johnny gawped. "You knew?" he said. "You all *knew*?"

"Oh sure," Mitch from L.A. said. "As soon as you moved in on us down in the bar."

"But—but—why did you . . .?"

"We wanted to see what kind of hustler you were, how you worked your scam. You might call it professional curiosity."

"Christ. Who are you guys?"

They told him. And Johnny Shade groaned and put his head in his hands. He knew then that his luck had changed, all right—all for the bad. That he was never going to make the big score, in Louisville or anywhere else. That he might not even be much good as a small-time grifter any more. Once word of this got out, he'd be a laughingstock from coast to coast. And word *would* get out. These four would see to that.

They didn't belong to some hick music group. They weren't fiddlers; they were FIDDLERs, part of a newly formed nationwide professional organization. Fraud Identification Detectives, Domestic Law Enforcement Ranks.

Vice cops. He'd tried to run a gambling scam at a convention of vice cops. . . .

Tony Hillerman created an entirely new sub-genre of suspense fiction with his tales of Navajo life. If one had to bet on which body of work will survive our era, one would certainly bet on Hillerman's because of its poise and grace and originality.

First Lead Gasser
TONY HILLERMAN

John Hardin walked into the bureau, glanced at the wall clock (which told him it was 12:22 A.M.), laid his overcoat over a chair, flicked the switch on the teletype to "ON," tapped on the button marked "BELL," and then punched on the keys with a stiff forefinger ...
A L B U Q U E R Q U E ...
YOU TURNED ON? ...
S A N T A F E
He leaned heavily on the casing of the machine, waiting, feeling the coolness under his palms, noticing the glass panel was dusty and hearing the words again and that high, soft voice. Then the teletype bumped tentatively and said:
S A N T A F E ...
AYE AYE GO WITH IT ...
A L B U Q U E R Q U E
And John Hardin punched:
A L B U Q U E R Q U E ... WILL FILE LEAD SUBBING OUT GASSER ITEM IN MINUTE. PLEASE SEND SCHEDULE FOR 300 WORDS TO DENVER ... S A N T A F E ...
The teletype was silent as Hardin removed the cover from the typewriter (dropping it to the floor). Then the teletype carriage bumped twice and said:
S A N T A F E ... NO RUSH DENVER UNTHINKS GASSER WORTH FILING ON NATIONAL TRUNK DIXIE TORNADOES JAMMING WIRE AND HAVE DANDY HOTEL FIRE AT CHICAGO FOLKS OUTJUMPING WINDOWS ETC HOWEVER STATE OVERNIGHT FILE LUKS LIKE

418

HOTBED OF TRANQUILITY CAN USE LOTS OF GORY DETAILS THERE. . . . A L B U Q U E R Q U E

Their footsteps had echoed down the long concrete tube, passed the dark barred mouths of cell blocks, and Thompson had said, "Is it always this goddam quiet?" and the warden said, "The cons are always quiet on one of these nights."

Hardin sighed and said something under his breath and punched . . .

A L B U Q U E R Q U E . . . REMIND DENVER NITESIDE THAT DENVER DAYSIDE HAS REQUEST FOR 300 WORDS TO BE FILED FOR OHIO PM POINTS . . . S F

He turned his back on the machine, put a carbon book in the typewriter, hit the carriage return twice, and stared at the clock, which now reported the time to be 12:26. While he stared, the second hand made the laborious climb toward 12 and something clicked and the clock said it was 12:27.

Hardin started typing, rapidly . . .

First Lead Gasser

Santa Fe, N.M., March 28—(UPI)—George Tobias Small, 38, slayer of a young Ohio couple who sought to befriend him, died a minute after midnight today in the gas chamber at the New Mexico State Penitentiary.

He examined the paragraph, pulled the paper from the typewriter and dropped it. It slid from the top of the desk and planed to the floor, spilling its carbon insert. On a fresh carbon book Hardin typed . . .

First Lead Gasser

Santa Fe, N.M., March 28—(UPI)—George Tobias Small, 38, who clubbed to death two young Ohio newlyweds last July 4, paid for his crime with his life early today in the New Mexico State Penitentiary gas chamber.

The hulking killer smiled nervously at execution witnesses as three guards pushed three unmarked buttons, one of which dropped cyanide pills into a container of acid under the chair in which he was strapped.

Hulking? Maybe tall, stooped killer; maybe gangling. Not really nervously. Better timidly; smiled timidly. But actually it was an embarrassed smile. Shy. Stepping from the elevator into that too-bright basement room, Small had blinked against the glare and squinted at them lined by the railing—the press corp and the official creeps in the role of "official witnesses." He looked surprised and then embarrassed and looked away, then down at his feet, and the warden had one hand on his arm. The two of them walking fast toward the front of the chamber, hurrying, while a guard held the steel door open. Above their heads cell block eight was utterly silent. Hardin hit the carriage return.

The end came quickly for Small. He appeared to hold his breath for a moment and then breathed deeply of the deadly fumes. His head fell forward and his body slumped in death.

The room had been hot. Stuffy. Smelling of cleaning fluid. But under his hand, the steel railing was cold. "Looks like a big incinerator," Thompson said. "Or like one of those old wood stoves with the chimney out the top." And the man from the *Albuquerque Journal* said, "The cons call it the space capsule. Wonder why they put windows in it. There's not much to see." And Thompson said, with a sort of laugh, that it was the world's longest view. Then it was quiet. Father McKibbon had looked at them a long time when they came in, unsmiling, studying them. Then he had stood stiffly by the open hatch, looking at the floor.

Small, who said he had come to New Mexico from Colorado in search of work, was sentenced to death last November after a district court jury at Raton found him guilty of murder in the deaths of Mr. and Mrs. Robert M. Martin of Cleveland. The couple had been married only two days earlier and was en route to California on a honeymoon trip.

You could see Father McKibbon saying something to Small—talking rapidly—and Small nodded and then nodded again, and then the warden said something and Small looked up and licked his lips. Then he stepped through the hatch. He tripped on the sill, but McKibbon caught his arm and helped him sit in the little chair, and Small looked up at the priest. And smiled. How would you describe it? Shy, maybe, or grateful. Or maybe sick. Then the guard was reaching in, doing something out of sight. Buckling the straps probably, buckling leather around a warm ankle and a warm forearm which had MOTHER tattooed on it, inside a heart.

Small has served two previous prison terms. He had compiled a police record beginning with a Utah car theft when he was fifteen. Arresting officers testified that he confessed to killing the two with a jack handle after Martin resisted Small's attempt at robbery. They said Small admitted flagging down the couple's car after raising the hood on his old-model truck to give the impression he was having trouble.

Should it be flagging down or just flagging? The wall clock inhaled electricity above Hardin's head with a brief buzzing sigh and said 12:32. How long had Small been dead now? Thirty minutes, probably, if cyanide worked as fast as they said. And how long had it been since yesterday, when he had stood outside Small's cell in death row? It was late afternoon, then. You could see the sunlight far down the corridor, slanting in and striped by the bars. Small had said, "How much time have I got left?" and Thompson looked at his watch and said, "Four-fifteen from midnight leaves seven hours and forty-five minutes," and Small's bony hands clenched and unclenched on the bars. Then he said, "Seven hours and forty-five minutes now," and Thompson said, "Well, my watch might be off a little."

Behind Hardin the teletype said ding, ding, ding dingding.
S A N T A F E . . . DENVER NOW SEZ WILL CALL IN 300 FOR OHIO PM WIRE SHORTLY. HOW BOUT LEADING SAD SLAYER SAMMY

SMALL TODAY GRIMLY GULPED GAS. OR SOME SUCH???? . . .
A L B U Q U E R Q U E

The teletype lapsed into expectant silence, its electric motor purring. Outside a car drove by with a rush of sound.

Hardin typed:

Small refuted the confession at his trial. He claimed that after Martin stopped to assist him the two men argued and that Martin struck him. He said he then "blacked out" and could remember nothing more of the incident. Small was arrested when two state policemen who happened by stopped to investigate the parked vehicles.

"The warden told me you was the two that work for the outfits that put things in the papers all over and I thought maybe you could put something in about finding . . . about maybe . . . something about needing to know where my mother is. You know, so they can get the word to her." He walked back to his bunk, back into the darkness, and sat down and then got up again and walked back to the barred door, three steps. "It's about getting buried. I need someplace for that." And Thompson said, "What's her name?" and Small looked down at the floor. "That's part of the trouble. You see, this man she was living with when we were there in Salt Lake, well, she and him . . ."

Arresting officers and other witnesses testified there was nothing mechanically wrong with Small's truck, that there was no mark on Small to indicate he had been struck by Martin, and that Martin had been slain by repeated blows on the back of his head.

Small was standing by the bars now, gripping them so that the stub showed where the end of his ring finger had been cut off. Flexing his hands, talking fast. "The warden, well, he told me they'd send me wherever I said after it's over, back home, he said. They'd pay for it. But I won't know where to tell them unless somebody can find Mama. There was a place we stayed for a long time before we went to San Diego, and I went to school there some but I don't remember the name of it, and then we moved someplace up the coast where they grow figs and like that, and then I think it was Oregon next, and then I believe it was we moved on out to Salt Lake." Small stopped talking then, and let his hands rest while he looked at them, at Thompson and him, and said, "But I bet Mama would remember where I'm supposed to go."

Mrs. Martin's body was found in a field about forty yards from the highway. Officers said the pretty bride had apparently attempted to flee, had tripped and injured an ankle, and had then been beaten to death by Small.

Subject: George Tobias Small, alias Toby Small, alias G. T. Small. White male, about 38 (birth date, place unknown); weight, 188, height, 6'4"; eyes, brown; complexion, ruddy; distinguishing characteristics: noticeable stoop, carries right shoulder higher than left. Last two joints missing from left ring finger, deep scar on left upper lip, tattoo of heart with word MOTHER on inner right forearm.

Charge—Violation Section 12-2 (3) Criminal Code.

Disposition—Guilty of Murder, Colfax County District Court.

Sentence—Death.

Previous Record: July 28, 1941, sentenced Utah State Reformatory, car theft. April 7, 1943, returned Utah State Reformatory, B&E and parole violation. February 14, 1945, B&E, Resisting Arrest. Classified juvenile incorrigible. August 3, 1949, armed robbery, 5–7 years at . . .

Small had been in trouble with the law since boyhood, starting his career with a car theft at twelve, and then violating reformatory parole with a burglary. Before his twenty-first birthday he was serving the first of three prison terms.

Small had rested his hands on the brace between the bars but they wouldn't rest. The fingers twisted tirelessly among themselves. Blind snakes, even the stub of the missing finger moving restlessly. "Rock fell on it when I was little. Think it was that. The warden said he sent the word around about Mama but I guess nobody found her yet. Put it down that she might be living in Los Angeles. That man with us there in Salt Lake, he wanted to go out to the coast and maybe that's where they went."

It was then Thompson stopped him. "Wait a minute," Thompson said. "Where was she from, your mother? Why not . . ."

"I don't remember that," Small said. He was looking down at the floor.

And Thompson asked, "Didn't she tell you?" and Small said, still not looking at us, "Sure, but I was little."

"You don't remember the town, or anything? How little were you?" And Small sort of laughed and said, "Just exactly twelve," and laughed again, and said, "That's why I thought maybe I could come home, it was my birthday. We was living in a house trailer then, and Mama's man had been drinking. Her too. When he did that, he'd whip me and run me off. So I'd been staying with a boy I knew there at school, in the garage, but his folks said I couldn't stay anymore and it was my birthday, so I thought I'd go by, maybe it would be all right."

Small had taken his hands off the bars then. He walked back to the bunk and sat down. And when he started talking again it was almost too low to hear it all.

"They was gone. The trailer was gone. The man at the office said they'd just took off in the night. Owed him rent, I guess," Small said. He was quiet again.

Thompson said, "Well," and then he cleared his throat, said, "Leave you a note or anything?"

And Small said, "No, sir. No note."

"That's when you stole the car, I guess," Thompson said. "The car theft you went to the reformatory for."

"Yes, sir," Small said. "I thought I'd go to California and find her. I thought she was going to Los Angeles, but I never knowed no place to write. You could write all the letters you wanted there at the reformatory, but I never knowed the place to send it to."

Thompson said, "Oh," and Small got up and came up to the bars and grabbed them.

"How much time have I got now?"

Small stepped through the oval hatch in the front of the gas chamber at two minutes before midnight and the steel door was sealed behind him to prevent seepage of the deadly gas. The prison doctor said the first whiff of the cyanide fumes would render a human unconscious almost instantly.

"We believe Mr. Small's death will be almost painless," he said.

"The warden said they can keep my body a couple days but then they'll just have to go on ahead and bury me here at the pen unless somebody claims it. They don't have no place cold to keep it from spoiling on 'em. Anyway, I think a man oughta be put down around his kin if he has any. That's the way I feel about it."

And Thompson started to say something and cleared his throat and said, "How does it feel to, I mean, about tonight?" and Small's hands tightened on the bars. "Oh, I won't say I'm not scared. I never said that but they say it don't hurt but I been hurt before, cut and all, and I never been scared of that so much."

Small's words stopped coming and then they came loud, and the guard reading at the door in the corridor looked around and then back at his book. "It's the not knowing," he said, and his hands disappeared from the bars and he walked back to the dark end of the cell and sat on the bunk and got up again and walked and said, "Oh God, it's not knowing."

Small cooperated with his executioners. While the eight witnesses required by law watched, the slayer appeared to be helping a guard attach the straps which held his legs in place in the gas chamber. He leaned back while his forearms were strapped to the chair.

The clock clicked and sighed and the minute hand pointed at the eight partly hidden behind a tear-shaped dribble of paint on the glass, and the teletype, stirred by this, said ding, ding, ding.

S A N T A F E ... DENVER WILL INCALL GASSER AFTER SPORTS ROUNDUP NOW MOVING. YOU BOUT GOT SMALL WRAPPED UP? ... A L B U Q U E R Q U E

Hardin pulled the carbon book from the typewriter and marked out "down" after the verb "flagging." He penciled a line through "give the impression he was" and wrote in "simulate." He clipped the copy to the holder above the teletype keyboard, folding it to prevent obscuring the glass panel, and switched the key from "KEYBOARD" to "TAPE" and began punching. The thin yellow strip, lacy with perforations, looped downward toward the floor and built rapidly there into a loopy pile.

He had seen Small wiping the back of his hand across his face. When he came back to the bars he had looked away.

"The padre's been talking to me about it every morning," Small had said. "That's Father McKibbon. He told me a lot I never knew before, mostly about Jesus, and I'd heard about that of course. It was back when I was in that place at Logan, that chaplain there, he talked about Jesus some, and I remembered some of it. But that one there at Logan, he talked mostly about sin and about hell and things like that and this McKibbon, the padre here, well, he talked different." And Small's hands had been busy on the bars again and then Small had looked directly at him, directly into his face, and then at Thompson. He remembered the tense heavy face, sweaty, and the words and the voice too soft and high for the size of the man.

"I wanted to ask you to do what you could about finding my mama. I looked for her all the time. When they'd turn me loose, I'd hunt for her. But maybe you could find her. With the newspapers and all. And I want to hear what you think about it all," Small said. "About what happens to me after they take me out of that gas chamber. I wanted to see what you say about that." And then Small said into the long silence: "Well, whatever it's going to be, it won't be any worse than it's been." And he paused again, and looked back into the cell as if he expected to see someone there, and then back at us.

"But when I walk around in here and my foot hits the floor I feel it, you know, and I think that's Toby Small I'm feeling there with his foot on the cement. It's Me. And I guess that don't sound like much, but after tonight I guess there won't be that for one thing. And I hope there's somebody there waiting for me. I hope there's not just me." And he sat down on the bunk.

"I was wondering what you thought about this Jesus and what McKibbon has been telling me." He had his head between his hands now, looking at the floor, and it made his voice muffled. "You reckon he was lying about it? I don't see any cause for it, but how can a man know all that and be sure about it?"

The clatter of the transmission box joined the chatter of the perforator. Hardin marked his place in the copy and leaned over to fish a cigarette out of his overcoat. He lit it, took it out of his mouth, and turned back to the keyboard. Above him, above the duet chatter of tape and keyboard, he heard the clock strike again, and click, and when he looked up it was 12:46.

McKibbon had his hand on Small's elbow, crushing the pressed prison jacket, talking to him, his face fierce and intent. And Small was listening, intent. Then he nodded and nodded again and when he stepped through the hatch he bumped his head on the steel hard enough so you could hear it back at the railing, and then Hardin could see his face through the round glass and it looked numb and pained.

McKibbon had stepped back, and while the guard was working with the straps, he began reading from a book. Loud, wanting Small to hear. Maybe wanting all of them to hear.

"Have mercy on me, O Lord; for unto Thee have I cried all the day, for Thou, O Lord, art sweet and mild: and plenteous in mercy unto all that call upon Thee. Incline thine ear, O Lord, and hear me: for I am needy and poor. Preserve my soul, for I am holy: O my God, save Thy servant that trusteth in Thee."

The pile of tape on the floor diminished and the final single loop climbed toward the stop bar and the machine was silent. Hardin looked through the dusty glass, reading the last paragraph for errors.

There was his face, there through the round window, and his brown eyes unnaturally wide, looking at something or looking for something. And then the pump made a sucking noise and the warden came over and said, "Well, I guess we can all go home now."

He switched the machine back from "TAPE" to "KEYBOARD" and punched . . .

SMALL'S BODY WILL BE HELD UNTIL THURSDAY, THE WARDEN SAID, IN THE EVENT THE SLAYER'S MOTHER CAN BE LOCATED TO CLAIM IT. IF NOT, IT WILL BE BURIED IN THE PRISON LOT. . . .

He switched off the machine. and in the room the only sound was the clock, which was buzzing again, and saying it was 12:49.

AUTHOR'S NOTE: Whatever the merits of "First Lead Gasser" as a short story, it is important to me. The incident it concerns happened (with "only the names changed to protect the innocent") and it caused me to think seriously for the first time about writing fiction. The Thompson of the short story was the late John Curtis of the Associated Press. I was Hardin, then New Mexico manager of the now defunct United Press. Toby Small, under another name but guilty of the same crime, did in fact inhale cyanide fumes at midnight in the basement gas chamber of the New Mexico State Prison. Thus "First Lead Gasser" is more or less autobiographical. That alone is scant reason to present it to a magazine whose readers have come to expect mystery short stories.

What makes it important to me, and perhaps of some interest to you, are two facts. First, my inability to deal with the "truth" of the Toby Small tragedy in the three hundred words allotted me by journalism stuck in my mind. How could one report the true meaning of that execution while sticking to objective facts? I played with it, and a sort of nonfiction short story evolved. Second, Toby Small's hands on the bars, Toby Small's shy smile through the gas chamber window, and the story Toby Small told Curtis and me became part of those memories a reporter can't shake.

Those of you who have read *People of Darkness* met Toby Small under the name of Colton Wolf, reincarnated as he might have evolved if fate had allowed him to live a few murders longer. The plot required a professional hit man. Since it seems incredible to me that anyone would kill for hire, I was finding it hard to conceive the character. Then the old memory of Small's yearning for his mother came to my rescue. I think I did a better job of communicating the tragedy of Small in the book than in the short story. A quarter century of additional practice should teach one something. But I'm still not skilled enough to do justice to that sad afternoon listening to a damaged man wondering what he would find when he came out of the gas chamber.

Bruce Holland Rogers is a name new to most readers. He sold his first story less than two years ago, but has already developed a very genuine audience of readers and editors. His story here was nominated for an Edgar Award from the Mystery Writers of America.

Enduring as Dust
BRUCE HOLLAND ROGERS

I drive past the Department of Agriculture every morning on my way to work, and every morning I slow to a crawl so that I can absorb the safe and solid feel of that building as I go by. The north side of Agriculture stretches for two uninterrupted city blocks. The massive walls look as thick as any castle's. Inside, the place is a warren of offices and suboffices, a cozy organizational hierarchy set in stone. I've often thought to myself that if an H-bomb went off right over the Mall, then the White House, the Capitol, the memorials and the reflecting pools would all be blown to ash and steam, but in the midst of the wreckage and the settling dust, there would stand the Department of Agriculture, and the world inside its walls would go securely on.

I don't have that kind of security. The building that houses the Coordinating Administration for Productivity is smaller than our agency's name. The roof leaks. The walls are thin and haven't been painted since the Great Depression.

That I am here is my own fault. Twenty years ago, when I worked for the Bureau of Reclamation, I realized that the glory days of public dam building were over. I imagined that a big RIF wave was coming to the bureau, and I was afraid that I'd be one of those drowned in the Reduction In Force. So I went looking for another agency.

When I found the Coordinating Administration for Productivity, I thought I had found the safest place in Washington to park my career. I'd ask CAP staffers what their agency did.

"We advise other agencies," they would say.

"We coordinate private and public concerns."

"We review productivity."

"We revise strategies."

"We provide oversight."

"But clearly, clearly, we could always do more."

In other words, nobody knew. From the top down, no one could tell me precisely what the administrative mission was. And I thought to myself, I want to be a part of this. No one will ever be able to suggest that we are no longer needed, that it's time for all of us to clear out our desks, that our job is done, because no one knows what our job is.

But I was wrong about the Bureau of Reclamation. It hasn't had a major project for two decades, doesn't have any planned, and yet endures, and will continue to endure, through fiscal year after fiscal year, time without end. It is too big to die.

The Coordinating Administration for Productivity, on the other hand, employs just thirty civil servants. We're always on the bubble. With a stroke of the pen, we could vanish from next year's budget. All it would take is for someone to notice us long enough to erase us. And so, as I soon learned, there was an administrative mission statement after all: Don't Get Noticed.

That's why we never complained to GSA about the condition of our building, why we turned the other cheek when FDA employees started parking in our lot and eventually took it over. That's also why no one ever confronted the secretaries about the cats named Dust. And above all, that is why I was so nervous on the morning that our chief administrator called an "urgent meeting."

I sat waiting outside of the administrator's office with Susana de Vega, the assistant administrator, and Tom Willis, Susana's deputy. "I don't like this," Tom said. "I don't like this one damn bit."

Susana hissed at him and looked at the administrator's secretary. But Roxie wasn't listening to us. She was talking, through an open window, to the cat on the fire escape. The cat was a gray tom with the tattered ears of a street-fighter. He backed up warily as Roxie put the food bowl down. "Relax, Dust," she said. "I'm not going to hurt you."

It was January, a few days before the presidential inauguration, and the air coming in through the window was cold, but nobody asked Roxie to close it.

"When has Cooper ever called an *urgent* meeting?" Tom continued in a lower voice. "Hell, how many times has he called a meeting of any damn kind? He's up to something. He's got to throw his goddam Schedule-C weight around while he still has it to throw."

Throwing his weight around didn't sound like Bill Cooper, but I didn't bother to say so. After all, Cooper was a political appointee on his way out, so whether he threw his weight around or not, Tom's underlying point was correct: Cooper was a loose cannon. He had nothing to lose. Intentionally or not, he might blow us up.

Roxie waited to see if the cat would consent to having his chin scratched, but Dust held his ground until the window was closed. Even then, he approached the food warily, as if checking for booby traps.

Susana told Tom to relax. "Two weeks," she reminded him. "Three at the outside."

"And then god only knows what we'll be getting," Tom said, pulling at his chin. "I hate politics."

Roxie's intercom buzzed, and without turning away from the cat she told us, "You can go in now."

I followed Susana and Tom in, and found Cooper nestled deeply in his executive chair, looking as friendly and harmless as he ever had. His slightly drooping eyelids made him seem, as always, half asleep. He waved us into our seats, and as I sat down, I realized how little he had done to personalize his office in the twelve years of his tenure. Everything in the room was government issue. There weren't any family pictures or the usual paperweights made by children or grandchildren. In fact, there wasn't anything on the surface of his desk at all. It was as if Cooper had been anticipating, from the day he moved in, the day when he would have to move out.

There was *some* decoration in the room, a pen and ink drawing on the wall behind Cooper, but that had been there for as long as I had been with the CAP. It showed an Oriental-looking wooden building next to a plot of empty ground, and I knew from having looked once, maybe fifteen years ago, that the drawing wasn't just hung on the wall. The frame had been nailed into the paneling, making it a permanent installation.

"People," Cooper said from deep inside his chair, "we have a problem." He let that last word hang in the air as he searched for what to say next.

Susana, Tom and I leaned forward in our chairs.

"An impropriety," he went on.

We leaned a little more.

"A mystery."

We watched expectantly as Cooper opened his desk drawer and took out a sheet of paper. He studied it for a long time, and then said, "You people know my management style. I've been hands-off. I've always let you people handle the details," by which he meant that he didn't know what we did all day and didn't care, so long as we told him that everything was running smoothly. He tapped the sheet of paper and said, "But here is something that demands my attention, and I want it cleared up while I'm still in charge."

And then he read from the letter in his hand. The writer represented something called the Five-State Cotton Consortium, and he had come to Washington to get advice on federal funding for his organization. He had taken an employee of the Coordinating Administration for Productivity to lunch, picking her brain about the special appropriations process as well as various grant sources. The woman had been very helpful, and the letter writer just wanted Cooper to know that at least one member of his staff was really on the ball. The helpful staffer's name was Kim Semper.

At the sound of that name, I felt ice form in the pit of my stomach. I stared straight ahead, keeping my expression as plain as I could manage. I knew some of what Cooper was going to say next, but I tried to look genuinely surprised when he told us what had happened after he received the letter.

"I wanted to touch base with Ms. Semper and make sure that the citizen hadn't actually paid for her lunch. You people know as well as I do that we don't want any conflict of interest cases."

"Of course not," said Susana. "But I don't see how there could be any such conflict. We don't actually make funding decisions."

"We don't?" Cooper said, and then he recovered to say, "No, of course not. But you people will agree that we wouldn't want even the *appearance* of impropriety. And anyway, that doesn't matter. What matters is that in my search for Kim Semper, I came up empty. We don't have an employee by that name."

Trying to sound more convincing than I felt, I said, "Maybe it's a mistake, Bill. Maybe the letter writer had the name wrong, or sent the letter to the wrong agency."

"Hell, yes!" Tom said with too much enthusiasm. "It's just some damn case of mistaken identity!"

But Cooper wasn't going to be turned easily. "I called the citizen," he told us. "No mistake. Someone is posing as an officer of our agency, a criminal offense."

I said, "Doesn't there have to be intent to defraud for this to be a crime?"

Cooper frowned. "The citizen did buy lunch for this Kim Semper. She benefitted materially." He shook the letter at me. "This is a serious matter."

"And one we'll get to the bottom of," Susana promised.

"I want it done before my departure," Cooper said. "I don't want to saddle my successor with any difficulties," by which he meant that he didn't want to leave behind any dirty laundry that might embarrass him when he was no longer in a position to have it covered up.

Susana said again, "We'll get to the bottom of it."

Cooper nodded at Tom. "I want a single point of responsibility on this, so the personnel director will head up the investigation."

With Cooper still looking at him, Tom looked at me expectantly, and I felt compelled to speak up. "That would be me," I said. "Tom's your deputy assistant."

"Of course," Cooper said, covering. He turned to me. "And you'll report to him." Then he added, "You aren't too busy to take care of this matter, I assume."

"It'll be tight," I said, thinking of the Russian novel I'd been wading through for the last week, "but I'll squeeze it in."

Outside of Cooper's office, Susana patted Tom's shoulder, then mine, and said with complete ambiguity, "You know what to do." Then she disappeared down the hall, into her own office.

Roxie's cat was gone, but Roxie had something else to distract her now. She was reading a GPO publication called, *Small Business Administration Seed Projects: Program Announcement and Guidelines*. She didn't even look up when Tom hissed at me, "Sit on it!"

"What?"

"You know damn well what I mean," Tom said through his teeth. "I don't know what this Kim Semper thing is all about, and I don't want to know! This is just the kind of problem that could blow us out of the goddam water!"

I said, "Are you telling me to ignore an assignment from the chief administrator?"

I could see in Tom's eyes the recognition that he had already been too specific. "Not at all," he said in a normal voice, loud enough for Roxie to overhear if she were listening. "I'm telling you to handle this in the most appropriate fashion." Then he, too, bailed out, heading for his own office.

I found my secretary, Vera, trying to type with a calico cat in her lap. The cat was purring and affectionately digging its claws into Vera's knee.

"Damn it, Vera," I said, surprising myself, "the memo specifies feeding only. Everybody knows that. You are not supposed to have the cat inside the building!"

"You hear that, Dust?" Vera said as she rubbed behind the cat's ears. "It's back out into the cold with you." But she made no move to get up.

"Hold my calls," I growled. I went into my office and closed the door, wishing that I had a copy of the legendary memo so that I could read chapter and verse to Vera. It was bad enough that the secretaries had distorted the wording of the memo, issued well over twenty years ago, that had allowed them to feed a stray cat named Dust, "and only a cat named Dust." It seemed like every so often, they had to push beyond even the most liberal limits of that allowance, and no manager was willing to make an issue of it, lest it turn into a civil service grievance that would bring an OPM investigation crashing down around our ears.

I didn't stew about the cat for long. I still had Kim Semper on my mind. It took me a few minutes to find the key to my file cabinet, but once I had the drawer open, there weren't many folders to search through before I found what I wanted. I untaped the file folder marked PRIVATE and pulled out the letter. It was addressed to me and sported an eleven-year-old date. "After failing to determine just who her supervisor is," the text began, "I have decided to write to you, the Director of Personnel, to commend one of your administrators, Miss Kim Semper." The story from there was pretty much the same: a citizen had come to Washington looking for information, had stumbled across the Coordinating Administration for Productivity, and had ended up buying Semper's lunch in exchange for her insights on the intricacies of doing business in the Beltway. Though he had been unable to contact her subsequently, her advice had been a big help to him.

After checking the personnel files, I had called the letter writer to tell him that he'd been mistaken, that there was no Kim Semper here at the CAP. Maybe, I suggested, he had gone to some other agency and confused the names? But he was sure that it was the CAP that he had consulted, and he described our building right down to the tiny, nearly unreadable gray lettering that announced the agency's name on the front door.

In a government agency, a mystery, any mystery, is a potential bomb. If you're not sure of what something is, then you assume that it's going to blow up in your face if you mess with it. At the CAP, where everything was uncertain and shaky to begin with, the unknown seemed even more dangerous. So I had buried the letter.

Now maybe it was coming back to haunt me. I wondered if I should cover my tail by Xeroxing my letter and bringing Cooper a copy right now. "Hey, Bill. I had to check my files on this, to make sure, but would you believe . . ." Maybe that would be good damage control.

But maybe not. After all, Cooper seemed to think this was an urgent matter. I had known about it for eleven years and done nothing. And my letter was so old that I probably didn't have to worry about it hurting me if I didn't bring up its existence. By now, the writer himself might not even remember sending it to me. Perhaps the man was even dead. If I kept my mouth shut, it was just possible that no one would ever know about my Kim Semper letter. And if that was what I wanted, then it would help my cause to do just what Tom had urged: To sit on the investigation, to ignore Kim Semper until the executive branch resignations worked their way down, layer by layer, from the new president's cabinet to our agency, and Cooper was on his way.

Either option, hiding the letter or revealing it, had its dangers. No matter how I played it out in my mind, I couldn't see the safe bet. I returned to what I'd been doing before the meeting with Cooper, and I should have been able to concentrate on it. Napoleon was watching this Polish general, who wanted to impress him, trying to swim some cavalry across a Russian river, but the horses were drowning and everything was a mess. It was exciting, but it didn't hold my attention. I read the same page over and over, distracted with worry.

At the end of the day, there was no cat in Vera's lap, but there was a skinny little tabby begging on the fire escape. At her desk, Vera was pouring some cat food into a bowl labeled, "Dust."

"Sorry I snapped earlier," I said.

"Bad day?" Vera said, opening the window.

"The worst," I told her, noticing the stack of outgoing mail on her desk. "Is that something I asked you to do?"

"Oh, I'm just getting some information for the staff library," she said.

I nodded, trying to think of something managerial to say. "You're self-directed, Vera. I like to see that."

"Oh, I've always been that way," she told me. "I can't stand to be idle." She opened the window to feed the cat and said, "Here you go, Dust."

Cooper called another meeting for Thursday of the next week. It was the day after the inauguration, and he must have felt the ticking clock. Before the meeting, Tom called me.

"How's your investigation coming?" he said.

"Slowly."

"Good. That's damn good. See you in the old man's office."

For once there wasn't a cat on Roxie's fire escape. Cooper's door was open, and I walked right in. Susana and Tom were already there, and Cooper motioned me to a seat. Cooper didn't waste any time.

"What have you got?"

I opened my notebook. "First, I double-checked the personnel files, not just the current ones, but going back twenty-five years." I looked at Cooper grimly. "No one by the name of Kim Semper has *ever* worked for the Coordinating Administration for Productivity."

"Yes, yes," Cooper said, "What else?"

"I called over to the Office of Personnel Management. There is not now, nor has there ever been, anywhere in the civil service system, an employee named Kim Semper." I closed the notebook and put on the face of a man who has done his job well.

Cooper stared at me. I pretended to look back at him earnestly, but my focus was actually on the framed pen and ink behind him. If I had to give it a title, I decided, it would be, "Japanese Shed With Empty Lot."

At last Cooper said, "Is that all?"

"Well, Bill, I haven't been able to give this my full attention."

"It's been a week, a *week* since I brought this up to you people."

"And a hellish week it's been," I said, looking to Tom for help.

"That's true," Tom jumped in. "The inauguration has stirred things up. We've had an unusually, ah, unusually heavy run of requests." Cooper frowned, and I could see Tom's hands tighten on the side of his chair. He was hoping, I knew, that Cooper wouldn't say, "Requests for what? From whom?"

Susana saved us both by saying, "I'm ashamed of the two of you! Don't you have any sense of priorities? And, Tom, you're supposed to be supervising this investigation. That means staying on top of it, making sure it's progressing." She turned to Cooper. "We'll have something substantial next week, Bill."

"I don't know, people," Cooper said. "Realistically, something like this is out of your purview. Maybe it calls for an outside investigator."

Cooper was almost certainly bluffing. Any dirt at the bottom of this would cling to him like tar if we brought in the consul general's office. He wanted to keep this internal as much as we did.

Even so, Susana paled. She played it cool, but it was a strain on her. "Why don't you see what we come up with in seven working days? Then you can decide."

Minutes later, in the hallway, Tom said, "So what now?"

"Don't look at me," Susana told him without breaking stride. "I pulled your bacon out of the fire, boys. Don't ask me to think for you, too." Then over her shoulder, she added, "You'd just better appear to be making progress by our next little get-together."

Before he left me standing alone in the hallway, Tom said, "You heard the lady, Ace. Let's see some goddam action."

In my office, with the door closed behind me, I finished another chapter of the Russian novel and then got right on the case. I cleared space on the floor and laid out the personnel files for the last eleven years. It made sense to assume that "Kim Semper" was an insider, or had an inside confederate who could arrange her lunchtime meetings. And I knew that Ms. Semper had been working this free-lunch scam since at least the date of my letter. I figured that I could at least narrow down my suspect pool by weeding out anyone who hadn't been with the CAP for that long.

Unfortunately, this didn't narrow things much. Even Cooper, by virtue of three straight presidential victories for his party, had been with the CAP for longer than that.

So what did I really have to go on? Just two letters of praise for Kim Semper, dated eleven years apart. The letter writers themselves had met Kim Semper, but there were good reasons for not calling them for more information. After all, I wanted to keep my letter buried to preserve my plausible deniability. And Cooper's letter writer had already been contacted once about Kim Semper. If I called again and grilled him, he might resent it, and I could use up his good will before I even knew what questions to ask. Also, he might get the impression that the Coordinating Administration for Productivity didn't have its act together, and who knew where that could lead? I didn't want a citizen complaining to his congressional rep.

What I needed was another source, but there wasn't one.

Or was there?

I arranged the personnel files on the floor to look like an organizational hierarchy. If someone were to send a letter praising an employee of the CAP, where might that letter go?

To the top, of course. That was Cooper.

And to the Director of Personnel. That was me.

But what about the space between these two? What about the Assistant Administrator and her Deputy? That is, what about Susana and Tom?

Outside of Susana's office, her administrative assistant, Peter, was preparing to feed a black cat on the fire escape. Almost as soon as he opened the window, Peter sneezed.

"Susana in?"

"Yes," Peter said, "but she's unavailable." he set the cat bowl down and closed the window. Then he sneezed again.

"If you're so allergic," I said, "how come you're feeding the kitty?"

"Oh, I like cats, even if they do make my eyes swell shut." He laughed. "Anyway, feeding Dust is the corporate culture around here, right? When in Rome . . ."

From the other side of Susana's door, I could hear the steady beat of music.

I watched the stray cat as it ate. "I'm surprised, with all the cats on our fire escapes, that it isn't just one continuous cat fight out there."

"They're smart animals," Peter said. "Once they have a routine, they stay out of each other's way."

I nodded, but I wasn't really paying attention. Over the beat of the music, I could hear a female voice that wasn't Susana's counting *one-and-two-and-three-and*—

I went to her door and put my hand on the knob.

"I told you," Peter said. "Susana's unavailable. If you want to make an appointment . . ."

"This can't wait," I said. I opened the door.

Susana was in a leotard, and I caught her in the middle of a leg lift. She froze while the three women on the workout tape kept on exercising and counting without her.

"I told Peter I wasn't to be disturbed," she said, still holding her leg up like some varicolored flamingo.

"This won't take but a minute," I said. "In fact, you can go right on with your important government business while we talk."

She stopped the tape and glared at me. "What do you want?"

"To get to the bottom of this Kim Semper thing. And if that's what you really want too, then you can't be throwing me curve balls."

"What are you talking about?" She pushed the audiovisual cart between two file cabinets and threw a dust cover over it.

"I'm talking, Susana, about sitting on information. Or call it withholding evidence. I want your correspondence file on Kim Semper."

Susana circled behind her desk and sat down. Ordinarily, that would have been a good gesture, a way of reminding me that she was, after all, the assistant admin, and this was her turf I had invaded. But it was a hard move to pull off in a leotard. "Just what makes you think I even have a such a file?"

That was practically a confession. I fought down a smile. "I'm on your side," I reminded her. "But we've got to show some progress on this. Cooper is on his last official breath. Dying men are unpredictable. But if we hold all the cards, how dangerous can he be?"

She stared over my head, no doubt thinking the same thoughts I had about my own Kim Semper letter. How would Cooper react to knowing that she'd had these letters in her files all along?

"You've got the file where, Susana? In your desk? In one of those cabinets? If I close my eyes," I said, closing them, "then I'll be able to honestly tell Cooper that I don't know *exactly* where my information came from. It was just sort of dropped into my lap."

It took her a minute of rummaging, and then a folder fell into my hands. I opened my eyes. The three letters ranged from two to ten years old.

"Read them in your own office," she said. "And next time, knock."

On my way out, I noticed that Peter was reading something called *America's Industrial Future: A Report of the Presidential Colloquium on U.S. Manufacturing Productivity for the Year 2020 and Beyond.* A thing like that wouldn't ordinarily stick in my mind, except that Tom's secretary, Janet, was reading the same report. She was also holding a mottled white and tan cat in her lap. I didn't bother to confront her about it—that was Tom's fight, if he wanted to fight it. I just knocked on Tom's door and stepped into his office.

He swept a magazine from his desk and into a drawer, but he wasn't fast enough to keep me from noting the cover feature: THE GIRLS OF THE PAC TEN. "What the hell do you want?" he growled.

"A hell of a lot more than I'm getting," I barked back. "Damn little you've done to help this investigation along, Willis. Enough bullshit. I'm up to here with bullshit. I want your goddam Kim Semper correspondence file."

"Like hell." Tom glowered, but a little quiver of uncertainty ran across his lowered eyebrows. He wasn't used to being on the receiving end of such bluster.

"Cut the crap, Tom. This goddam Semper bullshit will toss us all on our asses if we don't give Cooper something to chew on. So give."

A little timidly, he said, "I don't know what you're . . ."

"Like hell," I said, waving de Vega's letters. "Susana came across, and I'd sure as hell hate to tell Cooper that you're the one stalling his goddam investigation."

He bit his lip and took a file cabinet key from his desk drawer. "Jesus," he said. "I've never seen you like this."

"You better hope like hell you never see it again," I said, which was probably overdoing things, but I was on a roll.

As I read it in my office, the first of Tom's letters cheered me considerably. One was twenty years old, which altered my suspect list quite a bit. From my array of files on the floor, I removed anyone who hadn't been with the CAP for the last two decades. That left just myself, Tom Willis, and Tom's secretary Janet. I picked up Janet's file and smiled. Kim Semper, I thought, you have met your match.

And then I read Tom's other letter, the most recent one of all, excepting Cooper's. It praised Mr. Kim Semper, for *his* dedication to public service.

No, I thought. This can't be right.

Unless there was more than one Kim Semper.

I sat down behind my desk. Hard. And I thought about the cat named Dust, who came in a dozen variations, but who, by long tradition, was always Dust, was always considered to be the same cat, because the ancient memo had allowed for the feeding of a cat named Dust, "and only a cat named Dust."

I picked up the phone and dialed the number of the man who had written to praise Mr. Semper. "Mr. Davis," I said when I had him on the line, "one of our employees is in line for a service award, and I just want to make sure it's going to the right person. You wrote a letter to us about a Mr. Kim Semper. Now, we've got a Kim Semce on our staff, and a Tim Kemper, but no Kim Semper. Could you do me the favor of describing the man who was so helpful?"

As lame stories go, this one worked pretty well. It sounded plausible, and it didn't make the CAP look bad. And it brought results. Davis was only happy to make sure Semper or Semce or Kemper got his due. The description fit Peter to a T.

I tried the next most recent letter, but the number had been disconnected. The next one back from that—I changed Tim Kemper to Lynn—brought me a good description of Roxie. The third call, the one that cinched it, paid off with a description that could only be my own Vera.

That's when I buzzed Vera into my office.

"I want a copy of the cat memo," I told her.

"The cat memo?"

"Don't fence with me. If you don't have a copy of it yourself, you know how to get one. I want it within the hour." Then I lowered my voice conspiratorially. "Vera, I don't have anything against cats. Trust me on that."

She had a copy in my hands in five minutes. When I looked at the date, I whistled. Dust the cat had been on this officially sanctioned meal ticket for more than forty years, much longer than I had supposed. The memo also named the secretary who had first started feeding Dust. After a phone call to OPM, I was on my way to Silver Spring, Maryland.

The house I stopped in front of was modest, but nonetheless stood out from all the other clapboard houses on that street. There were abstract, Oriental-looking sculptures in the garden. The white stones around the plum trees had been raked into tidy rows, and there was a fountain bubbling near the walkway to the front door.

A white-haired woman holding a gravel rake came around the side of the house, moving with a grace that belied her eighty years.

"Mrs. Taida?" I said. She looked up and waved me impatiently into the garden. As I opened the gate, I said, "I'm the one who called you, Mrs. Taida. From the Coordinating Administration for Productivity."

"Yes, of course," she said. As I approached, she riveted me with her gaze. Her eyes were blue as arctic ice.

"You are Janet Taida, yes?"

"You expected me to look more Japanese," she said. "Taida was my husband's name Sakutaro Taida. The artist." She waved at the sculptures.

"I see," I said, then reached into my pocket for the photocopied memo. "Mrs. Taida, I want to talk to you about the cat named Dust."

"Of course you do," she said. "Come inside and I'll make some tea."

The house was furnished in the traditional Japanese style, with furniture that was close to the floor. While Mrs. Taida started the water boiling in the kitchen, I looked at the artwork hanging on the walls. There were paintings and drawings that seemed vaguely familiar, somehow, but it wasn't until I saw the big pen and ink on the far wall that I knew what I was looking at.

"There's a drawing like this in the administrator's office," I said when Mrs. Taida came into the room with the teapot.

"A drawing *almost* like that one," Mrs. Taida said. She waved toward a cushion. "Won't you sit down?" she commanded. She poured the tea. "That's a Shinto temple. It has two parts, two buildings. But only one stands at a time. Every twenty years, one is torn down and the other is rebuilt. They are both present, always. But the manifestation changes."

"The drawing at work shows the other phase," I said, "when the other building is standing and this one has been torn down."

Mrs. Taida nodded. A white long-haired cat padded into the room.

"Dust?" I said.

Taking up her teacup, Mrs. Taida shook her head. "No, there's only one Dust."

I laughed. "But like the temple, many manifestations." I unfolded the memo. "This memo, the Dust memo, mentions you by name, Mrs. Taida. You started it, didn't you? You were the administrator's secretary when the secretaries received their sanction to keep caring for, as it says here, 'a cat named Dust.' "

"Once we began to feed one, it was very hard to turn the others away. So I read the memo very carefully."

"Mrs. Taida, cats are one thing, but . . ."

"I know. Cats are one thing, but Kim Semper is far more serious, right?" She lowered her teacup. "Let me explain something to you," she said. "The Coordinating Administration for Productivity was commissioned over fifty years ago. They had a clear wartime purpose, which they completed, and then the agency began to drift. Your tea is getting cold."

She waited until I had picked it up and taken a sip.

"A government agency develops a culture, and it attracts people who are comfortable with that culture. After its wartime years the CAP attracted ostriches.''

I opened my mouth, but she held up her hand.

"You can't deny it," she said. "For forty years, the CAP has been managed by men and women who wanted to rule over a quiet little fiefdom where nothing much happened."

She sipped her own tea.

"Do you have any idea what it's like to be a secretary under conditions like that?" She shook her head. "Nothing happens. There's too little to do, and the day just crawls by. You can't have any idea how hard it was, at the end of the war and with a Japanese husband, to get a government job. And then to have to sit on my hands all day, doing nothing. . . .''

"Mrs. Taida . . .''

"I am not finished speaking," she said with authority, and I felt my face flush. "As I was saying, working at the CAP was like being a sailor on a rudderless ship. Have some more tea."

I held out my cup, as commanded.

"What endures in a government agency?" she asked as she poured again. "The management? The support staff? Job titles shift. Duties change. But the culture remains. It's like the tradition of a secretary feeding a stray cat at ten in the morning. The secretary may retire, but another will come, and if there's a tradition of feeding the stray cat at ten, then the person who takes the job will likely be someone who likes cats anyway. The cat may die or move on, but another will appear before long. The feeding goes on, even if who is fed and by whom changes over time."

She put the teapot down. "Administrators come and go, but the culture endures. And Kim Semper endures. When a citizen calls the agency for help, he isn't referred to management. No one at that level knows anything. No, the citizen is referred to Kim Semper. And for the pleasure of the work itself, of knowing things and being helpful, the secretaries do the job of the Coordinating Administration for Productivity. And they do a very good job. How many of those people who are helped by Kim Semper bother to write letters, do you suppose? And how many of the letters that are written actually end up in the hands of CAP administrators? Kim Semper provides good answers to hard questions about productivity and legislative action. I gave the CAP a rudder, you see. It operates from the galley, not the bridge."

"There's the question of ethics," I said. "There's the matter of lunches paid for by citizens, of benefit derived by fraud."

She looked at me long and hard. It was a look that said everything there was to say about collecting a GS-13 salary working for an agency where the managers were fuzzy about how they should fill their days. She didn't have to say a word.

"Well, what am I supposed to do then?" I said. "Now that I know the truth, what do I say when the administrator asks for my report?"

"You didn't get to where you are today without knowing how to stall," Mrs. Taida said. "You do what you do best, and let the secretaries do what *they* do best."

"What about *after* Cooper is gone." I said. "This is a bomb just waiting to go off. This is the kind of thing that can sink a little agency like ours."

"The Coordinating Administration for Productivity is a fifty-year-old bureaucracy," Mrs. Taida said, "with a little secret that no one has discovered for forty years. You're the only one who threatens the status quo." She picked up our teacups and the pot. "If you don't rock the boat, I'm sure the CAP, along with Dust and Kim Semper, will endure for time without end. And now, if you don't mind, I have things to do."

I drove back to the office slowly. I knew what I had to do, but I didn't know exactly how to get it done. At least, not until I got as far as the Department of Agriculture. There, I pulled into the right lane and slowed to a crawl.

Size, I thought. The thing that comforts me about the Department of Agriculture is its size. It is big and white and easy to get lost in. That's what safety is.

I drove back and got right to work. It was a big job. I enlisted Vera and Roxie, along with Janet, Peter, and some of the secretaries from downstairs. I didn't explain in great detail what we were doing or why it was important. They understood. In a week, we had generated the very thing that Bill Cooper had called for.

"Results," I announced, shouldering between Susana and Tom to drop my report onto Cooper's desk. It landed with a thud. Cooper blinked slowly, then opened the heavy white binding to the first page. *A Report on Personnel and Operational Dislocation at the Coordinating Administration for Productivity*, it read. "Everything you need to know about Kim Semper is in there."

Cooper nodded. "It's, ah, impressive. You people really knocked yourselves out."

"Yes, sir," I said. "I can't take all the credit. Susana and Tom were instrumental, really."

Neither of them looked up. They were still staring at the report.

Cooper began to scan the executive summary, but his eyes began to glaze when he got to the paragraph about operational location as a time- and institution-based function not contingent upon the identity of the individual operator. "So can you summarize the contents for me?"

"Well," I said, "it's a bit involved. But you can get the gist of it in the summary that you're reading."

Cooper kept thumbing through the summary. It went on for ninety-three pages.

"To really get a complete sense of the situation," I said, "you'll need to read the complete report. Right, Susana?"

She nodded. "Of course."

"Tom?"

"You bet your ass. It's all there, though. Every damn bit of it." He said it with pride, as though he really had made some contribution.

"It took a thousand pages to get it said, Bill. And it really takes a thousand to make sense of it all. So, you see, I can't just give it to you in a sentence."

"I see," Cooper said, nodding, and he was still nodding, still looking at the four-inch volume, when Susana and Tom and I left the room.

"You're a goddam genius is what you are," Tom said. And Susana told me, "Good work."

And when Cooper cleared out for good, he left the report behind. It's there still, taking up space on his successor's desk. Sometimes when I see it sitting there, I think to myself that a bomb could go off in that room, and everything would be blown to hell but that plastic-bound, metal-spined, ten-pound volume of unreadable prose. It wouldn't suffer so much as a singed page.

It gives me a safe and solid feeling.